100
CROOKED LITTLE
CRIME STORIES

100
CROOKED LITTLE
CRIME STORIES

EDITED BY

ROBERT WEINBERG,

STEFAN R. DZIEMIANOWICZ,

& MARTIN H. GREENBERG

Sterling Publishing Co., Inc.
New York

Library of Congress Cataloging-in-Publication Data
Available

2 4 6 8 10 9 7 5 3 1

Published by Sterling Publishing Co., Inc.
387 Park Avenue South, New York, NY 10016
Originally published by Barnes & Noble, Inc.,
by arrangement with Martin H. Greenberg
Copyright © 1994 by Robert Weinberg,
Stefan Dziemianowicz, and Martin H. Greenberg
Distributed in Canada by Sterling Publishing
c/o Canadian Manda Group, One Atlantic Avenue, Suite 105
Toronto, Ontario, Canada M6K 3E7
Distributed in Great Britain by Chrysalis Books
64 Brewery Road, London N7 9NT, England
Distributed in Australia by Capricorn Link (Australia) Pty.
Ltd.
P.O. Box 704, Windsor, NSW 2756, Australia

Book design by Mario A. Moreno

Fingerprint art by Andrius Balukas

Manufactured in the United States of America

Sterling ISBN 1-4027-1100-X

ACKNOWLEDGMENTS

Grateful acknowledgment is made to the following for permission to reprint their copyright materials:

"Good Night, Sweet Alibi" by Rufus Bakalor; "A Helping Hand" by Rufus Bakalor. Copyright © 1951 by Popular Publications for *Detective Fiction*. Reprinted by permission of Argosy Communications, Inc.

"All Sewed Up!" by Curt Hamlin; "Beyond Reasonable Doubt" by Robert C. Dennis; "Brand of Cain" by Dan Gordon; "Dead Man's Drop" by R. Van Taylor; "Eight Dollar Murder" by Robert Sidney Bowen; "Graveyard Race" by Andrew Fell; "The Guy Who Heard Murder" by Francis K. Allan; "How to Show a Corpse" by Johanas L. Bouma; "Jackie Won't Be Home" by Dane Gregory; "Let Nature Take Its Corpse" by C. William Harrison; "Strictly Accidental" by Morgan Talbot.

All of the above are copyright © 1939–1949 by Popular Publications for *Detective Tales*. Reprinted by permission of Argosy Communications, Inc.

"Ferry Slip" by Don James; "The Grave Joker" by Morris Cooper; "If the Shoe Fits" by Ken Lewis; "Imperfect Alibi" by D. L. Champion.

All of the above are copyright © 1942–1950 by Popular Publications for *Dime Detective*. Reprinted by permission of Argosy Communications, Inc.

"Blind Date" by J. Lane Linklater; "Death's Old Sweet Song" by George William Rae; "Each Night She Dies . . ." by William Brandon; "Easy Kill" by William Hellman; "I Hope They're Worried" by Don James; "It's Your Neck" by George William Rae; "Last Laugh" by Lix Agrabee; "A Matter of Proof" by Grover Brinkman; "Mine Host—The Ghost" by Costa Carousso; "One Man's Poison" by Curt Hamlin; "Side Door to Hell" by Cyril Plunkett; "Till Death Do Us Part" by Dana McQuire; "The Time Is Now!" by Dorothy Dunn; "The White Square" by Everett M. Webber; "The Witch's Way" by Joseph Shallit.

CONTENTS

xvi

INTRODUCTION

How long does it take to plot and commit a serious crime? According to the stories collected in *100 Crooked Little Crime Stories*, no more than ten minutes. Celebrating the fascination with a subject that has grown into one of the most popular genres in contemporary fiction, we present the reader with 100 tales of crime and suspense in the short-short-story form, the type of tale conducive to clever crimes and cleverer solutions.

The selections span more than 200 years and encompass virtually every story type known in the genre: the puzzle tale in Alexandre Dumas's "The Man of the Knife," the classic detective story in Headon Hill's "The Sapient Monkey," the modern hard-boiled story in Joe R. Lansdale's "The Job," the police procedural in Gerald Tollesfrud's "Switch," and the *noir* thriller in Ernest Leong's "Incense Sticks." The police blotter of crimes investigated includes fratricide in Allen Beck's "Always Together," embezzlement in Ferenc Molnár's "The Best Policy," serial murder in Gary Lovisi's "New Blood," swindling in Michael A. Black's "The Pigeon Drop," kidnapping in Edgar Wallace's "The Slave-Maker," bigamy in Joyce Kilmer's "Whitemail," drive-by shootings in Dane Gregory's "Jackie Won't Be Home," the ever-reliable homicide in Chet Williamson's "First Kill," and a crime so bizarre in Geoffrey Vace's "The Hard-Luck Kid" that it hasn't yet got a name by which it can be described.

Readers who enjoy their crimes "straight" will find that the lion's share of these stories take a hard-nosed approach to their subjects. For those who enjoy a respite from the often-grim chore of seeing criminals brought to bay, several stories offer laughter as the only possible solution to their predicaments. In all, the contents of *100 Crooked Little Crime Stories* show that petty crooks are not the only criminals dealt with in the short-short crime story.

—*Stefan Dziemianowicz*
New York, 1994

ALL SEWED UP!

CURT HAMLIN

The cat lay stretched on the window sill, dozing motionless except for its twitching tail. Beyond was the narrow air-well, filled with the night's darkness, fainter than the room's close black, making the cat a grotesque silhouette.

Mamie sat in the rocker, hands in her lap, thin fingers laced. She was staring at the cat without seeing it. All she could see was Joe. Clear as if he was in the room with her. Joe—and the gun.

It didn't begin with the gun. It began with Mamie working as a hasher in a Second Avenue joint, and Joe hanging over the counter, kidding her. Big, flashy, good-looking Joe. Mamie swallowed his line the way a kid swallows a lump of stolen candy, all in one gulp.

That was the beginning, like the first reel of a picture. The second reel was Mamie and Joe getting married. That was Mamie's idea. Joe argued a lot, but Mamie knew what she wanted.

It took a month, or maybe two months, for Mamie to find out she'd made a mistake. In a way, she'd suspected it from the first. Joe didn't work, but he always had money. Not a lot of money, but enough. Enough for rent on the cheap three-room walk-up, enough for groceries. Enough to buy Mamie a new dress once in a while and keep himself in flashy clothes. Sometimes the money ran out. Joe went out and got more. He went out nights. When he came back he had money. He didn't make explanations.

At first, Mamie only suspected. After she found the gun, she knew.

She saw it first one Tuesday morning, shoved into the back corner of Joe's shirt drawer, a cheap, nickel-plated revolver. Her fingers groped for it, drew it out. She was standing there, the thing balanced horribly in her hand, when Joe came up behind her. The face

1

she saw in the clouded glass of the dresser mirror, his face, was no longer good-looking. It was ugly and dangerous.

He said, "You shouldn't have done that, Baby." There was ugliness in his voice, too. He reached over her shoulder, lifted away the gun, and cradled it in his hand, the snout pointed carelessly at the middle of Mamie's back. "Guns is dangerous. Especially loaded ones. This one's loaded, Baby."

Mamie licked feverishly at her lips. Dryness made her tongue clumsy.

"Joe."

His fingers stiffened. The carelessness was gone. There was a sharp edge to his tone, rough as ragged glass. "Don't say it."

For a long moment neither of them moved. Then Joe pushed Mamie to one side, replaced the gun and covered it with shirts. He closed the drawer and went back to the other room. They didn't talk about it again.

They didn't have to talk about it again, Mamie thought. She began to rock a little, turning the thing over in her mind. They didn't talk about it but it hung between them. After that, whenever Joe went out at night, Mamie knew he took the gun. He had taken it tonight.

Far off, below her, a door slammed. She stopped rocking to listen. The steps were quiet, light and furtive. She knew it was Joe.

He opened the door, came inside, and shut it. Standing there, just inside the room, he whispered hoarsely for her. "Mamie?"

She moved wearily in the rocker. "I'm here, Joe."

She heard his fingers fumbling for the electric switch. "How come you've got the place dark?"

Mamie didn't answer. He found the switch and flipped it.

"Hiya, Baby."

He stood for a moment by the door, grinning at her. There was something feverish and unnatural in the grin. His Hollywood-type blazer was thrown over his arm. It was loud and flashily cut, red and yellow and brown, with dull red buttons. Joe came away from the door and dropped the blazer on the table.

"Cat got your tongue?"

Mamie didn't answer. Joe lit a cigarette, flipped the dead match toward the air-well. Casually, too casually, he drifted into the bedroom. The dresser drawer opened and closed.

From the bedroom Joe said, "Let's put on the glad rags and do the town. We're in the money."

"What money, Joe?"

"Never mind. You put on that new red dress you got and we'll go have a drink."

"It's a green dress, Joe."

"Red—green, it's all the same to me." He came out of the bedroom and stood in front of her. "One looks just like the other. Anyway, how about it?"

Mamie shook her head. "I don't feel so good, Joe. My eyes hurt. Besides, it's late. It's after one o'clock."

"You must be crazy." He got the clock from the bedroom and returned with it. "See? Only five to twelve."

Mamie didn't look at Joe and she didn't look at the clock. "I looked at it an hour ago. It was after twelve then."

"You made a mistake." He didn't touch her, but his words did. The menace was as real as fingers curling at her throat. "Like I told you. It's five to twelve. And don't forget it."

"What difference does it make, Joe?"

"Don't get nosy. Just remember. I came in before twelve."

"Yes, Joe."

"Don't forget it."

"No, Joe."

"Okay." He went into the bedroom, still carrying the clock. She heard the bed creak under his weight. "I'm turning in," he said. "You better come, too."

"Yes, Joe."

She pushed herself out of the rocker and moved toward the light switch. The cat woke, yawned, stretched, jumped off the window sill and curled up on its bed under the table. Mamie flipped off the switch.

She got up at six. She hadn't slept. Her eyes were parched and burning. She moved slowly about her dressing, the weight of sleeplessness and fear heavy on her shoulders. At six-thirty she went down to the corner newsstand and bought an early edition of the morning paper. Walking back, she read the story.

There wasn't much to it. A man had been robbed and killed, shot three times. Police placed the time of the crime at a little after midnight. There was no clue except a dull red button found clutched in the fingers of the corpse. Mamie stuffed the paper into a city trash can. When she got back to the apartment Joe was still asleep. She sat in the rocker and stared dully at the brick wall of the air-well.

It was nearly eleven before Joe began to move about the bedroom. He didn't come out right away. Mamie opened the door and looked in at him. He was seated on the bed, cleaning the nickel-plated revolver.

"I'm busy, Baby."

Mamie didn't move out of the doorway.

"I said I was busy. Beat it."

"Where'd you get the money, Joe?"

"What money?"

"You know what money. You didn't have any when you went out last night."

Joe squinted carefully through the gun barrel. "I won it. I gambled with a guy. He lost—plenty."

"You don't lie good, Joe."

"It's what I'm telling you. That's my story and you're stuck with it."

"I'm your wife, Joe. I got a right to know the truth."

Joe polished the revolver with a rag, tried the action twice. The double *click* of the hammer was loud in the little room. Very deliberately he pushed six cartridges into the cylinder, spun it, snapped it shut. The gun lay in his hand, pointing at Mamie. "Look, Baby. All you got to remember is that no wife can go into court and rat on her ever-loving."

"I might leave you, Joe. I might divorce you."

"Yeah?" Joe looked at the gun. Then he looked at Mamie and back at the gun. His grin was unpleasant. "I wouldn't like that, Baby. I wouldn't like that at all. It might make me mad. You can't tell what I might do if I got mad."

Mamie closed the door and went back to the rocker.

When Joe came out of the bedroom he was smoking a cigarette. He stood by the window, blowing smoke out into the air-well. "You get a paper this morning?"

"No, Joe."

"I'll go get one." He blew more smoke out the window. "And maybe a beer. Only first you got to fix my blazer. One of the buttons came off last night."

It was a little time before Mamie could force words through the tightness of her throat. "Where's the button, Joe?"

"How should I know? I lost it. You put another one on just like it." He swung from the window to face her. "Get that? Just like it."

"Yes, Joe."

She dragged herself out of the rocker, carried the blazer into the bedroom and spread it out on the bed. There were places for five red buttons. The middle one was missing. It took her awhile, pawing through the sewing basket, to find the button she wanted. She selected a spool of thread and began to sew, slowly. Joe came in as she was finishing.

"Is it the same as the others, Baby?"

She held it up to him. "Can you tell the difference?"

He squinted at it carefully. "Looks the same to me." He shrugged at it.

"I'll be back in an hour."

It was fairly warm out. He unbuttoned the blazer and let it hang free under his swinging arms. At the corner he bought a paper and read as he walked. Once his fingers stole down to twirl the button Mamie had sewed on for him. It was still there. He shoved the paper into a pocket and began to whistle. In the middle of the second block he turned into a tavern.

Mike, the barkeep, had a beer on the counter before Joe's foot was settled on the rail. Joe drank greedily. He pulled the paper out and spread it in front of him on the bar. "Some guy got bumped last night."

Mike said, "Yeah."

"Too bad."

"Yeah."

"Must've flashed a roll some place."

"Yeah. He must've."

"Gimme another brew."

When the beer came he gulped of it.

Mike said, "That dick's back again."

Joe turned to look. The door of the tavern opened and closed. The man who came in was tall and thin. He walked bent over, like the weight of his overcoat dragged on his shoulders. Mike took him a beer and came back to Joe. He leaned over the bar and whispered. "He's looking for a guy with a missing red button."

"It ain't me," said Joe. "I got my buttons."

Mike's eyes travelled casually down the front of the blazer—and froze! Sudden panic crawled like ants across Joe's shoulders.

"What ya looking at?"

"Nothing, Joe."

"Got my buttons, ain't I?"

"Yeah. Sure, Joe."

"What ya looking at, then?"

"Nothing," said Mike. "Nothing."

He began to drift away. The detective forgot his beer. He was inching toward Joe, eyes fixed on the middle of the blazer. A grin curled along the corners of his mouth.

Sweat gathered on Joe's forehead. "What ya looking at?" He backed into a corner. "What is it?"

The detective's hand dipped out from his coat. "Easy," he said. He was pointing a gun at Joe.

"I got my buttons."

"Yeah." The detective clicked cuffs around Joe's wrists. "Color blind, ain't you?"

"So what? I got my buttons."

He chuckled. With one finger he jiggled the center button on the blazer, the one Mamie had put there. With all the rest of them, red, he said, he wondered why that one was bright green.

Joe began to swear, but it didn't help him at all.

# ALWAYS TOGETHER

ALLEN BECK

That isn't how you're supposed to *do* that, you know!"

Minerva Bembridge peered over her sister's shoulder at what Jillian was stirring on the stove. "If I've told you once, I've told you a thousand times. You're to *brown* the meat first in the frying pan."

"Oh, shut up!"

"What? What did you say to me?"

"I said shut up," Jillian muttered without turning her head.

"Don't you dare talk to me that way, Jillian Bembridge!"

"Then leave me alone."

"I will not leave you alone. When it's your turn to cook, you're to take the time to cook properly. *I* do when it's my turn, as you very well know. Now you just take this frying pan and use it the way you're supposed to."

Bending, Minerva drew from under the sink a heavy black skillet which she slapped down on the counter.

"All right, I will!" shouted the woman at the stove. Snatching up the skillet, she whirled about and swung it against the side of her tormentor's head.

There was a crunching sound, then a metallic clatter as the pan fell to the floor where it skittered halfway across the small kitchen before coming to rest. An expression of surprise briefly touched the countenance of the woman who had been struck, then vanished as she silently crumpled. Jillian, equally silent for a moment, stood there looking down at her sister, then said in a wondering voice, "Oh, my. Now what have I done?"

The Bembridge sisters, identical twins aged seventy-five, occupied a two-bedroom apartment on the top floor of a condominium on Florida's southeast coast. Both were retired high-school teachers —Jillian of chemistry and physics, Minerva of English. Neither had ever married.

They had been living in their apartment now for eight and a half years. The owners of most of the other 149 apartments in the building—those who occupied them the year round, at least—knew them well. Everyone liked and admired them.

"They're so fond of each other," people remarked. "And always together."

True, you seldom saw one without the other. Having no car, they walked daily to a nearby shopping center, taking turns pushing their own shopping cart. When in the afternoon they used the pool for half an hour or so, other users were likely to tell one another what pretty faces and figures the two still had. When young they must have been real beauties.

Then in the evening, before dark, they almost always came down again from their fifteenth-floor apartment, beamed at anyone in the lobby—including whichever security guard happened to be on duty at the desk—and went for a stroll along the beach walk to admire the sea grapes and the water.

In eight and a half years no one in the building had heard them quarrel or even seen them look at each other as though they might like to. It must be true, someone once remarked, that certain identical twins were really one person.

The walls of their apartment knew better, and had for the whole eight and a half years.

"Those books you insist on reading!" Jillian would say in a voice rusty with sarcasm. "How in the world can you believe such rot!" The books referred to were not the novels Minerva sometimes borrowed from the library in the condo's lounge, but volumes ordered from secondhand book dealers. Usually old and costly, they came under the heading of metaphysics—especially the possibility of there being a life after the present one—and to Jillian's scientific mind they were a waste of time and money. Sister Minerva was ridiculed savagely for reading them.

"Tend to your own business," Minerva would snap when sufficiently needled. "At least I'm trying to *learn* something. In case you've entirely forgotten, I taught English, not how to wash out test tubes."

"I did more than wash out test tubes!"

"I doubt it, with your one-track mind."

The truth was they had disliked each other even as children, and were living together now simply because neither, by herself, could have afforded an apartment in such a desirable location. But they did their quarreling in the privacy of their apartment and were careful to keep their voices down. No one knew.

Now in the apartment kitchen Jillian knelt beside her sister and placed an ear to Minerva's breast, listening for a heartbeat. Hearing nothing, she rose and went down the hall to her bedroom to obtain a mirror, which on returning she held close to her sister's mouth. Minerva had stopped breathing, she decided.

"Oh, my," she murmured. "What am I to do with her?"

Her dead or dying sister had been right about one thing; Jillian Bembridge had a one-track mind. Though she sat in the living room now and commanded herself to think, it never occurred to her to invent some explanation for what had happened. To say, for example, that her sister had fallen and struck her head on the stove. She, Jillian, had hit her with the frying pan, and that was that. (The invention was to come later, after she had had much more time to think.)

The first problem, then, was how to dispose of the body. And the second was how to keep the other residents of the building from learning Minerva was gone.

After deciding how to handle both problems, she dragged her sister into the bathroom and went to bed.

In the morning she went to the supermarket but left their cart at home. What she bought was easily carried back in a single large shopping bag. Minerva still lay on the bathroom floor and was now definitely dead—no question about it. At least I waited long enough to be certain, the former chemistry teacher told herself.

Half filling the tub with cold water, she undressed her sister and after something of a struggle succeeded in putting her into it and pushing her down so that she was completely submerged. It made Jillian a little nervous, doing this. They were so much alike in everything but temperament, even weighing almost exactly the same, that it was rather like doing it to herself.

Now she brought from the kitchen one of half a dozen bottles she had bought at the supermarket, and tried to open it. But that was even more difficult than getting the body into the tub had been. The product was a new one, with red-letter warnings on its label. Don't use in garbage disposals. Don't use in toilet bowls. Don't this, don't that. To remove cap, carefully follow instructions. In the end she succeeded in getting it off.

She emptied the whole quart bottle into the tub and decided that would do for the time being. There was no way to hurry this procedure; she would just have to be patient. But then, no one but her sister and herself ever came into the apartment. They had never entertained.

Leaving the bathroom, she turned for one last look at the woman in the tub and at what was happening to the water. Then she firmly closed the door behind her and went into the kitchen to make breakfast. From now on she would have to do *all* the cooking, she reminded herself. Worse luck.

She lost track of the days after that, and of the number of bottles she bought to pour into the tub. The big problem was no longer how to dispose of the body; it was how to keep the residents of the building from knowing there *was* a body.

"My sister and I have decided, Ronnie," she told a carefully chosen security guard, "to be less dependent upon each other. It has occurred to us that if one of us should pass away as we are now, the other might not survive the shock of being left alone."

"A good idea, Miss Jillian," the guard said from behind his lobby desk, where he was more concerned with watching, on his closed-circuit television screen, the entry of a Cadillac into the basement garage.

"I'm Minerva, Ronnie."

He looked up and grinned. "Sorry. I never know which of you is which."

"So what we have decided to do," she went on, "is to go shopping and walking alone for a while. Even to the pool alone. Are we being foolish, do you think? We're seventy-five, you know."

"I think it's a smart move, Miss Minerva."

"Thank you. I just hope people won't become curious and ask too many questions. They're so used to seeing us together."

"Well, if you want me—"

"Would you, Ronnie?" Her smile was bright with gratitude. "I knew I could count on you."

So, of course, it was easy. Minerva and she had never dressed alike. All she had to do was wear her own clothes when she wished to be Jillian and her sister's when she wished to be Minerva. Even in the pool she wore one of Minerva's swimsuits every other afternoon. Soon most of the building's other residents knew of the Bembridge sisters' "experiment" and—yes—admired them for it.

"They're really very astute, you know. Think how many wives are totally helpless when their men die. Husbands, too, when they've been coddled and catered to too much."

Meanwhile, with continued use of the bottles with the difficult tops, and repeated drainings of the tub, nothing much remained of sister Minerva but a skeleton. And when the skeleton was all there was, she began taking the cart again when she went shopping.

There was a time of day just before 9 A.M. when the shopping center was nearly deserted now. The month was July. The winter people had gone back north, and even many of the year-rounders had fled to the mountains of the Carolinas to escape the heat. She carried in the cart each morning one of a collection of large brown paper bags saved from her supermarket shopping, and on reaching the center always went down a lane behind the market.

Just in back of the store was a huge bin for trash that was emptied every few days by a special kind of truck that came around. A mechanical device operated from the driver's seat raised up the bin and emptied it into the truck's bowels, and the vehicle, when full, went off to the city dump to contribute its contents to a landfill.

Each morning as she passed the bin she lackadaisically tossed a bag into it. The hardest things to dispose of were the large leg bones. But she solved that by walking to a hardware store one day and purchasing a hacksaw.

At last the tub was empty, and she was glad because now, after scrubbing it, she would be able to take a bath again. In this building only one bathroom in each apartment had a tub; the other had a shower stall. She never felt right in a shower. But, of course, there wasn't time for a bath just yet. The people in the building were not going to believe forever her story that Minerva and she were struggling to become self-sufficient. Not when for eight and a half years they had done almost everything together.

She still had work to do.

One morning just before daybreak she put a robe and a pair of beach sandals—both belonging to Minerva—into a brown paper bag and walked all the way down the stairs to a door the residents used when going to the beach. There was no need for TV surveillance there; the door was always kept locked and only the owners had keys.

She walked down to the beach, took the robe and sandals out of the bag and dropped them not far from the water's edge, then disposed of the bag itself in a waste container on her way back to the condominium. Letting herself in with her key, she walked the whole fifteen floors back up to her apartment. Not many seventy-five-year-old women could do that, she told herself proudly. *I'm tough, even if dear Minerva did think me stupid.*

An hour later she went back downstairs in the elevator and said to the security guard at the lobby desk, "Ronnie, have you seen my sister?"

"No, Miss Minerva."

"I'm Jillian, Ronnie."

"Sorry, Miss Jillian. Is something wrong?"

"She said she was going for a swim. In the *sea*, if you please, when we haven't done that in ages. I tried to dissuade her, but you know how set she has been lately on becoming totally independent."

"What time was this, Miss Jillian?"

"Just after daybreak."

"She didn't come through the lobby here. I was on duty."

"We always use the service elevator and the side door when we go to the beach, Ronnie."

It would work if she kept her cool, she felt. And she did that, even with the building buzzing for days and the police asking endless questions. After all, a seventy-five-year-old woman shouldn't have insisted on going for a dip in the ocean at a time when the beach would be deserted. And, though the body remained missing, the police had found on the beach a robe and a pair of sandals that belonged to her.

That took care of that.

Now for Minerva's *books.*

She could not have said why, but having such books around the apartment troubled her. They were depressing and she had to get rid of them. Also she ought to dispose of Minerva's clothes, or they would become depressing too.

It was not difficult. The Salvation Army had a collection box at the fire station, within walking distance of the condo. Several trips with the shopping cart were necessary, mostly because Minerva had bought so *many* of the books over the past few years. But in the end she managed it.

Then with all the unpleasantness behind her and nothing more to worry about, she bought a bottle of her favorite wine for an evening of celebration, and after consuming two-thirds of it, decided to take her long-awaited bath.

Removing her clothes, she walked into the bathroom and turned on the water, carefully adjusting the taps to produce a mixture neither too hot nor too cool. She was going to sit in the tub for at least an hour, she promised herself, because a bath ought to be a leisurely experience, relaxing and sensual. And she had certainly earned this one. Dear Minerva had occupied this tub for a much longer time, of course, but that wasn't quite the same, was it? Perhaps because of the wine, she thought that amusing and chuckled over it.

When the depth and temperature of the water pleased her, she went naked to the kitchen and drank the rest of the wine, and had an attack of hiccups when she returned. That was amusing, too, and induced still more chuckles. Dimming the bathroom light to reduce the glare, a ritual of hers on such occasions, she at last stepped daintily into the tub and sat down.

Ah, but it felt good! Closing her eyes, she slid lower until just her head was above water, then kept herself still so the water would become dead flat. It felt so like a caress when it was that way. The only sound in the dimness of the room was that of her own slow breathing.

A familiar voice murmured, "Good evening, sister."

Her eyes shot open and she almost choked on the breath she sucked in. Standing beside the tub was a figure so faint that it seemed little more than a thing of mist—but, mist or no, it had enough substance to be recognizable. It was composed of bones with no flesh on them. As it leaned over her and put forth a skeletal hand, she shrank from it and produced what was meant to be a shriek but came out a mere gurgle.

"I don't think we want you screaming, sister," the voice said softly. "We *never* made loud noises here, did we? Just let me wrap this around you." Taking a towel, the bony fingers drew it tight around Jillian's mouth and knotted it behind her head.

While this was happening, the eyes of the woman in the tub stared up at the skeleton's empty eye sockets and became larger and larger. A paralysis of fear kept her from struggling—or was it the touch of bony fingers on her forehead? She simply sat there trembling from head to foot, the clacking of her teeth filling the room with a kind of death rattle.

"Just wait here now," the voice said. "We're not quite finished yet. I'll be right back, dear."

The misty skeleton turned and walked out of the bathroom, but still the woman in the tub remained immobilized. In less than a moment the figure returned. Now one of the bony hands clutched a bottle with red warnings on its label—one of several left over from before—and with no apparent difficulty the fingers removed the cap.

"Just be quiet now, dear, and this won't take long at all," the voice murmured as a misty hand reached out and inverted the bottle over the bath water.

APPOINTMENT WITH YESTERDAY

GEOFFREY VACE

On the way back to camp that evening, following an afternoon at the seashore, the red-haired boy said, "You guys go ahead, y'hear? Tommy and I got somethin' to do."

"Like what?" he was asked.

"Like never mind. You'll see. Come on, Tommy."

There was still a good hour of daylight left. This was July on Cape Cod. The redhead and little bespectacled Tommy Hibbert, who always did what the redhead wanted, turned off along a sandy footpath, leaving the other six boys of Cabin One to continue along the forest road. All eight were from a Providence, Rhode Island, boys' club, in camp for a month as part of a program for underprivileged youth.

"Boy, will they be surprised when we turn up with it!" said the redhead, whose name was Mark Watson. At fourteen, he was the oldest in Cabin One and naturally the captain. "The only thing is, we have to make sure old Fowler don't see us."

"Will it be dark when we reach camp?"

"Should be, just about."

"What's the problem, then, Markie?"

"The darned thing's *big*. That's what's the problem."

"Oh."

The path they followed was a link between two dirt roads. One road led from a main highway to the camp on the lake. Where the other came from or went to neither boy knew. All they knew was that in an overgrown field by the side of it stood an old Cape Cod cottage, apparently long abandoned, known to all at the camp as the "haunted house." When you came to Camp Wampanoag and heard about the murder from kids who had been to camp before, you had to visit the place. There was a camp rule against it, but you had to go anyway. It was an initiation, kind of.

Approaching the cottage now, red-haired Mark Watson grinned at his protégé. "You scared, Tommy?"

"Not of the house. Only of what'll happen if old Fowler—"

"I tell you he won't know. By the time he even sees what we got, we'll have it fixed up and painted. We'll just tell him we made it."

"Well . . . okay. If you say so."

They trudged through the tall grass to the front door, which made a noise like a stepped-on cat when Mark pushed it open. Had it screeched that way when the robber opened it that night? Probably not. The house was being lived in then by old Mrs. Lazarus, and the hinges wouldn't have been rusty like now.

"I bet he just opened the door real slow," Mark said. "I bet she never even heard him before he squeezed the trigger. Then, pow!"

"What?"

"That's how it must have happened. He was after the money she was supposed to have stashed away here someplace. He just inched this door open"—Mark read mystery stories and intended to write them someday—"and she was sittin' there in that chair with her back to him, rockin' away all unsusspectin', and he shot her."

14

"You sure she was *shot*, Markie?"

"Well, I never heard any different."

"Did you ever ask?"

"No, I never asked. Why would I ask, for Pete's sake? What difference does it make, anyway?"

The younger boy sensed he was making the redhead angry. "Well, gee, all right, Markie, I was just wonderin'."

The grit on the old board floor made scrunchy sounds under Mark's shoes as he walked toward the chair, which was the only piece of furniture in the room. For that matter, it was the only thing in the whole house, he knew. The kitchen, the dining room, the two bedrooms upstairs—all were empty now. Halting beside the chair, he looked around while waiting for the other boy to join him. To tell the truth, he felt a little scared.

But there was nothing to be afraid of, he told himself. It was just a grimy old living room in an abandoned cottage. The walls were yellow and dirty, with crazy cracks running every which way through the faded flowers on their peeling paper. What else could you expect?

"Come on, will you?" he urged his companion.

"This is it?" Tommy said on reaching Mark's side.

"This is it. The old lady was sittin' in this when she was killed. Anyway, that's the story." The chair lay on its side, and Mark leaned over to touch it. "See what I mean? How we can fix it up?"

"Not like it was, we can't."

"We can come close. Anyway, it'll be the chair she was murdered in, even if it don't look exactly the same as then." Reaching down, Mark took hold of its one unbroken arm. "Come on, now. Let's get it out of here!"

It was not an easy task for two boys their age and size. The chair was of Cape Cod pine and fairly heavy. Worse, it was bulky. After a number of tries they settled on a way of carrying it between them with one boy holding the arm, the other an edge of the seat, which was intact. Even so, it kept bumping their legs and thighs, and they had to stop often to rest.

Only once were they forced to move off the road to avoid being seen—or "detected," as the future writer of mystery tales would have put it. They were back on the camp road at the time and heard a pickup coming. "Hey!" Mark hissed in alarm. "It could be Fowler!"

But while the director often did drive the pickup, he was not in it when it passed them. At the wheel was Edgar Nesbit, the middle-aged camp handyman, too interested in sipping from a pint bottle to be aware of the two boys crouching beside their stolen rocking chair in the roadside underbrush.

Edgar almost always had a bottle to sip from—a thing Mr. Darren Fowler, with all his snooping, never seemed to find out. The kids knew but liked Edgar well enough to keep quiet about it. Besides, he didn't get drunk; he just drank.

"All right," Mark chortled as they scrambled back onto the road with their burden. "That's one we don't have to watch out for. Now we only have to get past the others." The others, of course, included Fowler, an assistant director, and several counselors.

But, thanks to the chair, their timing turned out to be excellent, and they arrived at the camp just at dark. Five minutes of waiting behind an old sawdust pile—the place had been a sawmill site once —and they were able almost to stroll to their cabin without danger of being seen. In a welter of excitement, their cabin mates crowded around them.

"There it is!" the redhead gloated, propping the broken chair up so it appeared to be almost usable. "Old lady Lazarus was murdered in this, by gosh, and when we go back to Providence, I'm takin' it with me!"

"How?" someone demanded.

"Never mind how. I'll think of somethin'. But when I start writin' my mystery stories, this is the chair I'll be writin' 'em in."

"Writers use typewriters nowadays, Markie. Even computers."

"All right. I'll think 'em *up* in this chair, then. That's the most important thing—thinkin' 'em up!" He gave the chair a prideful pat, which promptly caused it to fall over on its side as it had been in the front room of the haunted house. "But first we got to fix it up. And fast, before anyone sees it and figures out where it came from."

That night the chair lay in a corner of the cabin, half hidden by the end of the double bunk in which the redhead and his protégé, Tommy, slept. In the morning, after breakfast and chores, Mark went to Edgar Nesbit, the camp handyman, to borrow some tools.

"What you want them for?" About fifty, Nesbit had a beard the color of salt and pepper mixed together in a shaker and eyes so bright blue they looked artificial. He'd been born there on the Cape, less than five miles from the camp.

"I'll show you when we get it done."

"You want them right *now*? You skippin' the swim?"

"We went to the ocean yesterday."

"Okay." Nesbit shrugged to show it made no difference to him. Then he produced, on request, a hammer, a saw, a hand drill, nails and screws, and a screwdriver. When asked for scrap wood, he shrugged again and pointed to an assortment of it on the floor of his workshop.

Mark returned to Cabin One laden and triumphant, and by nightfall the chair had two arms instead of one. Next day it acquired a new rocker and new rungs, though in referring to them as "rungs," the future author admitted he might not be using the proper word. "When I write about this someday, which I intend to, I'll look it up. We don't have time now."

The carpentry finished, back he went to Edgar Nesbit to beg some paint.

"Now, what in the world are you kids doing over there in that cabin?" Edgar demanded. "What you want paint for?"

"We'll show you when it's finished. Please, Edgar? Just a small can of enamel?"

"What color?"

"Well—red." That was the proper color for a murder chair, no?

The following day the old rocking chair, rebuilt and painted fire-engine red, was ready for use, though it looked nothing at all like the one old Mrs. Lazarus had been murdered in.

Now began the games.

With little Tommy Hibbert seated in the chair, solemnly staring at the cabin wall while he rocked, Mark showed the others how the murder must have been committed. Going outside and closing the door behind him, he waited, like the mystery-story writer he intended to be, for suspense to build up inside. Then he silently eased the door open, stepped over the threshold, whipped up his right hand, and said, "Pow!"

Tommy obediently slumped forward in the chair and began groaning.

"You say he was after her money?" one of the other boys said.

"That's the story. People in the village said she had a pile of it hidden away in the house somewhere, though she pretended to be poor."

"Where would an old lady like that get a whole lot of money?"

"Well, she was some kind of witch. Like she told fortunes and stuff."

"There's a Lazarus in the Bible," someone said. "Jesus raised him from the dead."

"That was a *man*, dummy. Anyway, this old lady had a pile of money and this guy, whoever he was, was after it."

"Did he find it?"

"Now, that's a stupid question if I ever heard one. How do we know if he found it or not, when we don't even know who he was?"

"They never arrested nobody?"

"Uh-uh." Mark wagged his head. "They never had a clue."

"Didn't they find a bullet or anything?" someone asked. "If he shot her in the back, like you say, the bullet must have stayed in her or gone through into a wall or somethin'."

From the expression on Mark's face, it was plain to see the future writer of mysteries hadn't thought of that and was annoyed with himself. Luckily he was saved from having to think up a reply when little Tommy Hibbert, still in the chair, suddenly voiced an exclamation.

"Hey! It's moving!"

They all looked at him.

"It's moving!" Tommy propelled himself out of the chair as though it had suddenly become electrified. The leap sent him sprawling to his hands and knees on the cabin floor, where he twitched himself around to look at the chair in astonishment.

The chair was slowly rocking. It continued to rock until Mark reached out and stopped it.

"You're a nut," Mark said. "You rocked it yourself, dummy."

"I did not! I was just sittin' there!"

"You rocked it. Anyone sittin' in a rockin' chair rocks it, even without thinkin'."

"I tell you I didn't," Tommy insisted, though less emphatically than before.

"Look." Mark sat in the chair. "I'll show you."

They watched, some standing within arm's reach, some seated on their bunks. The redhead sat in the chair and nothing happened for what seemed a long time, though surely it was less than a minute.

Then the chair began to rock.

"See?" Mark pushed himself out of it. "You don't know you're doin' it, even. But you do it."

Satisfied, they let the matter drop and began discussing a treasure hunt scheduled for the following day. In charge of that event was the one person in camp they unanimously disliked: the assistant director, Joel Abbott. It was Joel, born in a nearby Cape village, who had gruffly warned all of them to stay away from the house from which Mark and Tommy had removed the chair.

"That house is out of bounds to you kids. And I mean it, you hear?" With his fists on his hips and his head thrust forward like a rooster's, he had snarled his ultimatum. "You go snooping around there, and you'll find yourselves taking the next bus back to Providence!"

Question: Should they boycott the treasure hunt to show the assistant director how little they thought of him?

It was a lively discussion.

But Mark, having retired to his lower bunk, did not enter into it. He sat there with his elbows on his knees and his chin on his fists and gazed at the red rocking chair as though it puzzled him.

His protégé, losing interest in the treasure-hunt talk, retired to the bunk above him, leaned over, and said quietly, "Did you, Markie?"

"Did I what?"

"Make it move? Or did it move by itself, like I said?"

"I dunno." The redhead scratched a corner of his mouth. "I don't *think* I made it move, Tommy, but I dunno."

Now for two days the chair stood in the center of the cabin, and the boys took turns sitting in it. Some said it moved of its own accord; others said they were crazy. Around camp, it became known that the boys of Cabin One had finished a carpentry project, building themselves a rocking chair. The director, Mr. Darren Fowler, came and admired it, praising them for their ingenuity. So did the assistant director, Joel Abbott, and the counselors. None of them recognized the chair as the one from the abandoned home of the murdered Mrs. Lazarus.

Finally, one evening just before dark, Edgar Nesbit, the camp handyman, came to see what had been achieved with his tools, lumber, and paint.

"Well, I'll be gosh darned," he said, gazing at the chair in wonder. His breath betrayed the fact that he had been sipping again.

The boys grinned at one another, and one said, "Give it a try, Edgar. It works real good."

"I bet it does." Edgar eased himself down into it. Then, obviously enjoying himself, he gripped its arms and closed his eyes and began rocking.

Suddenly the chair went all the way back and so did Edgar's head, with something apparently pulling at his hair. His eyes opened wide in bright blue terror and his neck arched up, with his Adam's apple all but popping out of it. And across his neck, just above the Adam's apple, appeared a line of crimson, as though someone had taken a red-ink marking pen and drawn it from under one ear to under the other.

It seemed he tried to scream but couldn't and only made a gurgling, bubbling sound as though his throat had been slashed.

Terrified by what looked like the man's death throes, the boys fled wildly from the cabin. Mark Watson, the future writer of mysteries, was the only one to pause in the doorway and look back.

When they returned with the director and his assistant a few minutes later, the man in the rebuilt rocking chair was dead. The line of red across his throat was already fading. But what was in those brilliant blue eyes would go with him to his grave.

It was terror. Sheer, total, heart-stopping terror.

"This chair!" Mr. Fowler fiercely turned on young Mark Watson. "Did you make it as you said you did?"

"N-no, sir. N-not exactly. We made an old one over."

"Where did it come from?"

"The haunted house, sir."

Mr. Fowler turned in triumph to his assistant. "We seem to have solved an old mystery here, don't we? Even to how it happened. He must have opened the cottage door so quietly she didn't hear him. He walked up behind her and grabbed her by the hair and pulled her head back. He cut her throat."

Still staring at the man in the chair, the assistant director slowly nodded.

"All right," Mr. Fowler said then to the occupants of Cabin One. "You boys may use Cabin Four tonight; those lads went home today. Don't touch anything here. Just clear out with what you'll need."

The boys moved to the other cabin and talked in low tones about what had happened. All agreed that somehow the spirit of the murdered witch-woman must have been waiting there in the rocking chair, for revenge. After all, the Lazarus in the Bible had come back from the dead, hadn't he?

The future writer of mysteries was chided for his invention of the gun.

"You and your 'pow!' Ha!"

But the redhead had no time to waste on foolishness. "Never mind that, you dummies. Don't you see what we got here? This proves that killer never found the old lady's money. He wouldn't have been workin' here as a handyman if he did."

Mouths open, they stared at him.

"What we got to do now," he solemnly told them, "is go back to that old house and do some real detective work."

AT THE
PISTOL'S POINT

E. W. HORNUNG

The church bells were ringing for evensong, croaking across the snow with short, harsh strokes, as though the frost had eaten into the metal and made it hoarse. Outside, the scene had all the cheery sparkle, all the peaceful glamour, of an old-fashioned Christmas card. There was the snow-covered village, there the church-spire coated all down one side, the chancel windows standing out like oil paintings, the silver sickle of a moon, the ideal thatched cottage with the warm, red light breaking from the open door, and the peace of Heaven seemingly pervading and enveloping all. Yet on earth we know that this peace is not; and the door of the ideal cottage had been opened and was shut by a crushed woman, whose husband had but now refused her pennies for the plate, with a curse which followed her into the snow. And the odor prevailing beneath the thatched roof was one of hot brandy-and-water, mingled with the fumes of some rank tobacco.

Old Fitch was over sixty years of age, and the woman on her way to church was his third wife; she had borne him no child, nor had Fitch son or daughter living who would set foot inside his house. He was a singular old man, selfish and sly and dissolute, yet not greatly disliked beyond his own door, and withal a miracle of health and energy for his years. He drank to his heart's content, but he was never drunk, nor was Sunday's bottle ever known to lose him the soft side of Monday's bargain. By trade he was game-dealer, corn-factor, money-lender, and mortgagee of half the village; in appearance, a man of medium height, with bowlegs and immense round shoulders, a hard mouth, shrewd eyes, and wiry hair as white as the snow outside.

The bells ceased, and for a moment there was no sound in the cottage but the song of the kettle on the hob. Then Fitch reached for the brandy-bottle, and brewed himself another steaming bumper. As he watched the sugar dissolve, a few notes from the

21

organ reached his ears, and the old man smiled cynically as he sipped and smacked his lips. At his elbow his tobacco-pipe and the weekly newspaper were ranged with the brandy-bottle, and he was soon in enjoyment of all three. Over the paper Fitch had already fallen asleep after a particularly hearty mid-day meal, but he had not so much as glanced at the most entertaining pages, and he found them now more entertaining than usual. There was a scandal in high life running to several columns, and sub-divided into paragraphs labelled with the most pregnant headlines; the old man's mouth watered as he determined to leave this item to the last. It was not the only one of interest; there were several suicides, an admirable execution, a burglary, and—what? Fitch frowned as his quick eye came tumbling down a paragraph; then all at once grasped out an oath and sat very still. The pipe in his mouth went out, the brandy-and-water was cooling in his glass; you might have heard them singing the psalms in the church hard by; but the old man heard nothing, saw nothing, thought of nothing but the brief paragraph before his eyes.

ESCAPE FROM PORTLAND.
ONE CONVICT KILLED, ANOTHER WOUNDED,
BUT A THIRD GETS CLEAN AWAY.

The greatest excitement was caused at Weymouth yesterday morning on the report being circulated that several convicts had effected their escape from the grounds of the Portland convict establishment. There appears to have been a regularly concerted plan on the part of the prisoners working in one of the outdoor gangs to attempt to regain their liberty, as yesterday morning three convicts bolted simultaneously from their party. They were instantly challenged to stop, but as the order was not complied with, the warders fired several shots. One of the runaways fell dead, and another was so badly wounded that he was immediately recaptured, and is now lying in a precarious condition. The third man, named Henry Cattermole, continued his course despite a succession of shots, and was soon beyond range of the rifles. He was pursued for some distance, but was ultimately lost to view in the thick fog which prevailed. A hue and cry was raised, and search parties continued to scour the neighbourhood long after dark, but up to a late hour his recapture had not been effected. Cattermole will be remembered as the man who was sentenced to death some years ago for the murder of Lord Wolborough's gamekeeper, near Bury St. Edmund's, but who afterwards received the benefit of the doubt involved in the production of a wad which did not fit the convict's gun. In spite of the successful efforts then made on his behalf, however, the authorities at Portland describe Cattermole as a most daring criminal, and one who is only too likely to prove a danger to the community as long as he remains at large.

Fitch stared stupidly at the words for several minutes after he had read them through; it was the last sentence which at length fell into focus with his seeing eye. Henry Cattermole at large! How long had he been at large? It was a Sunday paper, but the Saturday edition, and this was among the latest news. But it said "yesterday morning," and that meant Friday morning last. So Henry Cattermole had been at large since then, and this was the Sunday evening, and that made nearly three days altogether. Another question now forced itself upon the old man's mind; how far was it from Portland prison—to—this—room?

Like most rustics of his generation, old Fitch had no spare knowledge of geography: he knew his own country-side and the road to London, but that was all. Portland he knew to be on the other side of London; it might be ten miles, might be two hundred; but this he felt in his shuddering heart and shaking bones, that near or far, deep snow or no snow, Henry Cattermole was either recaptured or else on his way to that cottage at that moment.

The feeling sucked the blood from the old man's vessels, even as his lips drained the tumbler he had filled with so light a heart. Then for a little he had spurious courage. He leant back in his chair and laughed aloud, but it sounded strangely in the empty cottage; he looked up at the bell-mouthed gun above the chimney-piece, and that gave him greater confidence, for he kept it loaded. He got up and began to whistle, but stopped in the middle of a bar.

"Curse him!" he said aloud, "they should ha' hanged him, and then I never should ha' been held like this. That'll be a good job if they take an' hang him now, for I fare to feel afraid, I do, as long as Harry Cattermole's alive."

Old Fitch opened his door a moment, saw the thin moon shining on the snow, but no living soul abroad, and for once he was in want of a companion; however, the voices of the choir sounded nearer than ever in the frosty air, and heartened him a little as he shut the door again, turned the heavy key, and shot both bolts well home. He was still stooping over the bottom one, when his eyes fell upon a ragged trouser-leg and a stout stocking planted close behind him. It was instantly joined by another ragged leg and another stout stocking. Neither made a sound, for there were no shoes to the cat-like feet; and the stockings were remarkable for a most conspicuous stripe.

The old Fitch knew that his enemy had found him out, and he could not stir. He was waiting for a knife to plunge into the centre of his broad, round back; and when a hand slapped him there instead, he thought for a moment he was stabbed indeed. When he knew that he was not, he turned round, still stooping, in a pitiable attitude, and a new shock greeted him. Could this be Henry Cattermole?

The poacher had been stout and thick-set; the convict was gaunt and lean. The one had been florid and youthful; the other was yellow as parchment, and the stubble on the cropped head and on the fleshless jaw was of a leaden grey.

"That—that ain't Harry Cattermole?" the old man whimpered.

"No, that ain't' but 'twas once, and means to be again! Lead the way in beside the fire. I wish you'd sometimes use that front parlour of yours! I've had it to myself this half-hour, and that's cold."

Old Fitch led the way without a word, walked innocently up to the fire, and suddenly sprang for his gun. He never reached it. The barrel of a revolver, screwed round in his ear, drove him reeling across the floor.

"Silly old fool!" hissed Cattermole. "Did you think I'd come to you unarmed? Sit down on that chair before I blow your brains out."

Fitch obeyed.

"I—I can't make out," he stuttered, "why you fare to come to me at all!"

"O' course you can't," said Cattermole, ironically.

"If I'd been you, I'd ha' run anywhere but where I was known so well."

"You would, would you? Then you knew I'd got out, eh, old man?"

"Just been a-reading about it in this here paper."

"I see—I see. I caught a bit o' what you was a-saying to yourself, just as I was thinking it was a safe thing to come out o' that cold parlour o' yours. So that was me you was locking out, was it? Yet you pretend you don't know why I come! You know well enough. You know—you know!"

The convict had seated himself on the kitchen table, and was glaring down on the trembling old man in the chair. He wore a long overcoat, and under it some pitiful rags. The cropped head and the legs swinging in the striped stockings were the only incriminating features, and old Fitch was glancing from the one to the other, wondering why neither had saved him from this horrible interview. Cattermole read his thoughts, and his eyes gleamed.

"So you think I've come all the way in these here, do you?" he cried, tapping one shin. "I tell you I've walked and walked till my bare legs were frozen, and then sat behind a hedge and slipped these on and rubbed them to life again! Where do you think I got these rotten old duds? Off of a scare-crow in a field, I did! I wasn't going to break into no houses and leave my tracks all along the line. But yesterday I got a long lift in a goods train, or I shouldn't be here now; and last night I did crack a crib for this here overcoat and a bit o' supper, and another for the shooter. That didn't so much matter then. I was within twenty mile of you! Of *you*, you old devil—do you hear?"

Fitch nodded with an ashen face.

"And now do you know why I've come?"

Fitch moistened his blue lips. "To—to murder me!" he whispered, like a dying man.

"That rests with you," said the convict, fondling the weapon.

"What do you want me to do?"

"Confess!"

"Confess what?" whispered Fitch.

"That you swore me away at the trial."

The old man had been holding his breath; he now expelled it with a deep sigh, and taking out a huge red handkerchief, wiped the moisture from his face. Meanwhile, the convict had descried writing materials on a chiffonnier, and placed them on the table beside the brandy-bottle and the tobacco-jar.

"Turn your chair round for writing."

Fitch did so.

"Now take up your pen and write what I tell you. Don't cock your head and look at me! I hear the psalm-singing as well as you do; they've only just got started, and nobody'll come near us for another hour. Pity you didn't go too, isn't it? Now write what I tell you, word for word, or, so help me, you're a stiff 'un!"

Fitch dipped his pen in the ink. After all, what he was about to write would be written under dire intimidation, and nobody would attach any importance to statements so obtained. He squared his elbows to the task.

" 'I, Samuel Fitch,' " began Cattermole, " 'do hereby swear and declare before God Almighty'—before God Almighty, have you got that down?—'that I, Samuel Fitch, did bear false witness against my neighbour, Henry Cattermole, at his trial at Bury Assizes, November 29th, 1887. It is true that I saw both Henry Cattermole and James Savage, his lordship's gamekeeper, in the wood at Wolborough on the night of September 9th in the same year. It is true that I was there by appointment with Savage, as his wife stated in her evidence. It is *not* true that I heard a shot and heard Savage sing out, "Harry Cattermole!" as I came up and before ever I had a word with him. That statement was a deliberate fabrication on my part. The real truth is—' but hold on; I'm likely going too fast for you—I've had it in my head that long! How much have you got down, eh?"

" 'Fabrication on my part,' " repeated old Fitch, in a trembling voice, as he waited for more.

"Good! Now pull yourself together," said Cattermole, suddenly cocking his revolver. " *'The real truth is that I, Samuel Fitch, shot James Savage with my own hand!'* "

Fitch threw down his pen.

"That's a lie," he gasped. "I never did! I won't write it."

The cocked revolver covered him.

"Prefer to die in your chair, eh?"

"Yes."

"I'll give you one minute by your own watch."

Still covering his man, the convict held out his other hand for the watch, and had momentary contact with a cold, damp one as it dropped into his palm. Cattermole placed the watch upon the table where both could see the dial.

"Your minute begins now," said he; and all at once the watch was ticking like an eight-day clock.

Fitch rolled his head from side to side.

"Fifteen seconds," said Cattermole.

The old man's brow was white and spangled like the snow outside.

"Half-time," said Cattermole.

Five, ten, fifteen, twenty seconds passed; then Fitch caught up the pen. "Go on!" he groaned. "I'll write any lie you like; that'll do you no good; no one will believe a word of it." Yet the perspiration was streaming down his face; it splashed upon the paper as he proceeded to write, in trembling characters, at Cattermole's dictation.

" 'The real truth is that I, Samuel Fitch, shot James Savage with my own hand. The circumstances that led to my shooting him I will confess and explain hereafter. When he had fallen I heard a shout and someone running up. I got behind a tree, but I saw Harry

Cattermole, the poacher, trip clean over the body. His gun went off in the air, and when he tried to get up again, I saw he couldn't because he'd twisted his ankle. He never saw me; I slipped away and gave my false evidence, and Harry Cattermole was caught escaping from the wood on his hands and knees, with blood upon his hands and clothes, and an empty gun. I gave evidence against him to stop him giving evidence against me. But this is the whole truth, and nothing but the truth, so help me God!' "

Cattermole paused, Fitch finished writing; again the eyes of the two men met; and those of the elder gleamed with a cunning curiosity.

"How—how did you know?" he asked, lowering his voice and leaning forward as he spoke.

"Two and two," was the reply. "I put 'em together as soon as ever I saw you in the box."

"That'll never be believed—not like this."

"Will it not? Wait a bit; you've not done yet. 'As a proof of what I say'—do you hear me?—'as a proof of what I say, the gun which the wad will fit, that saved Henry Cattermole's life, will be found—' "

Cattermole waited until the old man had caught him up.

"Now," said he, "you finish the sentence for yourself!"

"What?" cried Fitch.

"Write where that gun's to be found—you know—I don't—and then sign your name!"

"But I *don't* know—"

"You do."

"I sold it!"

"You wouldn't dare. You've got that somewhere, I see it in your face. Write down where, and then show me the place; and if you've told a lie—"

The revolver was within a foot of the old man's head, which had fallen forward between his hands. The pen lay blotting the wet paper. Cattermole took the brandy-bottle, poured out a stiff dram, and pushed it under the other's nose.

"Drink!" he cried. "Then write the truth, and sign your name. Maybe they won't hang an old man like you; but, by God, I sha'n't think twice about shooting you if you don't write the truth!"

Fitch gulped down the brandy, took up the pen once more, and was near the end of his own death-warrant, when the convict sprang lightly from the table and stood listening in the centre of the room. Fitch saw him, and listened too. In the church they were singing another hymn; the old man saw by his watch, still lying on the table, that it must be the last hymn, and in a few minutes his wife would be back. But that was not all. There was another sound —a nearer sound—the sound of voices outside the door. The handle was turned—the door pushed—but Fitch himself had locked and bolted it. More whispers; then a loud rat-tat.

"Who is it?" cried Fitch, trembling with excitement, as he started to his feet.

"The police! Let us in, or we break in your door!"

There was no answer. Cattermole was watching the door; suddenly he turned, and there was Fitch in the act of dropping his written confession into the fire. The convict seized it before it caught, and with the other hand hurled the old man back into his chair.

"Finish it," he said below his breath, "or you're a dead man! One or other of us is going to swing! Now, then, under the floor of what room did you hide the gun? Let them hammer, the door is strong. What room was it? Ah, your bedroom! Now sign your name."

A deafening crash; the lock had given; only the bolt held firm.

"Sign!" shrieked Cattermole. A cold ring pressed the old man's temple. He signed his name, and fell forward on the table in a dead faint.

Cattermole blotted the confession, folded it up, strode over to the door, and smilingly flung it open to his pursuers.

THE BEST POLICY

FERENC MOLNÁR

Monsieur Bayout, President of the National Farmers Bank, sent for his secretary Philibert one morning.

"Tell me, Philibert," he said, "who is this man Floriot down at our Perpignan branch?"

"Floriot? . . . That's the cashier. He's acting as manager temporarily. You remember, sir, the old manager, Boucher, died, and we haven't found anyone to put in his place yet. Floriot's looking after things meanwhile. There isn't very much business in Perpignan."

Monsieur Bayout took a letter from his desk. "Well, apparently he's robbing us. I've had this letter from Perpignan. It's anonymous, I admit, but . . ."

He handed Philibert a not very clean sheet of notepaper on which, in a somewhat unformed hand, the following lines were written:

To the President of the National Farmers Bank.
Dear Sir,

We farmers are putting our hard-earned savings in your bank at Perpignan, and one fine day we shall wake up and find it has gone bankrupt and all our savings are lost. It is bound to happen the way things are going on here. You probably don't know that the cashier, Monsieur Floriot, has been embezzling money for months past. He must have put away a tidy packet by now, but of course by the time you high and mighty gentlemen in Paris realize what's going on, all the money will be gone.

"Send an inspector down to Perpignan tomorrow, Philibert," the President said. "But tell him to be tactful, we don't want to upset the man. There's probably no foundation for the story."

Monsieur Floriot, temporary manager of the Perpignan branch, stared at the inspector from Paris with horrified amazement. "Inspect my books?" he echoed. "What, now? In the middle of the month? Without any notification? It's a bit unusual, isn't it?"

The inspector felt sorry for the agitated little man. "There's nothing to worry about, Monsieur Floriot. We do this at all our branches from time to time. The President gets these sudden fits. It's only a formality. I'll be through in half an hour."

"Yes, but people will talk, especially in a small place like this," Floriot wailed. "Everyone will be saying that I've been up to something shady. Think of the disgrace!"

"Nobody's going to know anything about it," the inspector said, a trifle impatiently. "That is, of course, unless you yourself talk. Well, can I see the books now?"

Two days later Philibert entered the President's room. "I'm able to report on the inspector's visit to Perpignan, sir. Everything is in order. Not a single sou missing."

"Good. One really ought not to pay any attention to these disgusting anonymous-letter writers. Thanks, Philibert."

Less than a month later, the President again summoned his secretary. "It's quite ridiculous," he said testily. "But I've had another anonymous letter about Perpignan. The writer declares that the books weren't properly examined. Apparently Floriot made such a song and dance about the whole thing that an accomplice had time to replace the stolen money. We really ought to have gone into the matter more thoroughly."

"Do we have to make another investigation?" Philibert asked ruefully."

The President drummed his fingers on the desk. "I don't like doing it. All the same, it's a duty we owe to our clients. If there is something in it, and people find out afterwards that we were warned, there'll be a nasty scandal. I'm afraid the only thing to do is send the inspector down again. And this time let him do the job thoroughly. I want to clear this up once and for all."

The same day three of the bank's most reliable inspectors set out for Perpignan. This time Monsieur Floriot was really taken by surprise. One of the officials kept guard over him, while the other two carried out a thorough examination of his accounts, lasting over four hours. They found nothing missing, and the books in perfect order.

"I only wish things were as satisfactory in all our branches," the chief inspector said, as he bade farewell to the completely shattered Floriot.

                              *   *   *

A week later: "Monsieur Floriot of Perpignan is waiting to see you, sir." Philibert announced.

Departing from his usual habit, Monsieur Bayout rose and advanced toward his visitor with an outstretched hand.

Floriot, however, gave a stiff little bow. "I've come to hand in my resignation, sir," he said.

"Your resignation? You can't mean that, my dear Floriot. Why?"

"You found it necessary to have my books examined twice running, sir. Naturally it caused a lot of talk. Even though I was proved to be an honest man, it made a bad impression. People are saying there must have been some good reason why the head office sent down twice to have my affairs investigated. My reputation's gone. I'm not a young man, and I have a wife to think of."

Monsieur Bayout was deeply moved. "I'll make it my personal responsibility to see that your name is cleared. Wait a minute, though. . . . The manager's job is still vacant, would you like to have it? No one could doubt your honesty then, could they? Yes, and you'll get a pretty substantial increase in salary, too . . ."

"You really mean . . ." Floriot stammered.

"Of course, of course, my dear fellow. The bank will be fortunate in keeping the services of so conscientious a worker."

Back at his home in Perpignan Pierre Floriot slid his feet into the comfortable felt slippers his wife handed him.

"At last!" he grunted, in a good-humored voice. "What's the use of being an honest man if nobody hears of it? I might have gone on being a cashier for years and years, and the people at the head office would never have known how honest I was."

"They know now!" Madame Floriot beamed, regarding her husband with admiration. "Those letters were a wonderful idea of yours. . . ."

BEYOND REASONABLE DOUBT

ROBERT C. DENNIS

It was a basement place, grimy and smoke-hung, with red check-ered table cloths and on oiled floor. Too many tables were crowded too close together, so that having your drink knocked into your lap by a strange elbow was an ever-present contingency. That sort of place.

A waiter in an apron that could never possibly have been white finally got around to me. "Name it," he said.

"Glennie Tyson still singing here?" I asked.

"You can call it singin'," the waiter said. "An' as far as I know, she's here."

"You've been spending too much time at the Philharmonic," I said disagreeably. "You've lost touch with what the common people like."

"Don't get sore," he protested. "If you like her, she's good. If you don't like her, she ain't. I don't like her. I'm entitled to my opinion, ain't I?" He leaned over confidentially, "Maybe I never listened very good, though. Everytime she sings, I remember she got herself in a big jam a few years ago. Nobody ever found out what really did happen, did they?"

"It never came out," I admitted.

"Some says she did it—some says she didn't. I always wondered. When she first came here to work I use'ta look at her and think, did she or didn't she?" He stared at me expectantly, "I was wonderin', you being an old friend of hers? . . ."

"She never told me," I said evenly, and he went away mumbling to himself to get me a bottle of beer.

I stared around that mean, dismal room, at the glaring center lights and the shadowed corners, the ridiculous little square where no one was dancing, for the simple reason there was no orchestra, and at the dark floor where the oil, covering God knows what

32

stains, was so heavy the bottoms of my shoes were slick. No matter how hard I tried, I couldn't see Glennie in this background.

I shut my eyes and remembered her the first time I saw her, seven million years ago. Seven years ago. She was singing in Mike Nelly's place then, and Mike brought her over to talk to me because I was covering the night spots then and he wanted me to give her a plug. She was that kind of pretty girl, with a placid and deep-set harmony that was more quiet inner glow than structural beauty.

"Gordon Corbitt, Glennie," Mike said. "Be nice to him—but not too nice! There's a limit to what help he can give you."

She slipped into the chair across from me and Mike went away. The first thing she said was, "I don't really need any help."

That was a new approach. "It will only be a mention of you and where you're appearing."

"Oh," she said. "That's all right. Have you heard me sing?"

"Not yet. Are you good?"

"I will be. As good as I need to be." She was very serious about it. "I'll sing in the best places in town someday. Everybody thinks that's a laugh. They don't think I have the talent. But I know." She was serene in her own confidence. "One way or another, I'll get what I want. I always have."

Then I asked her about her background because I sensed it was from there that her overpowering ambition had its genesis. It wasn't really an unusual story; I'd heard of others like it before, and plenty since. A childhood of poverty and hard work. Her father had walked out on her mother, leaving Glennie and two boys. They were six at the time. The mother promptly had a heart attack and never worked again. The problem of existence lay on Glennie's shoulders them.

She got a job as a waitress in a railroad cafe. It didn't pay much and it was hard work, what with the boys to be fed and dressed and sent off to school. Later she was a sales girl, a cashier in a movie house, and finally a model.

"Then I found I had a voice," she explained, "so I got a job singing. I was twenty then, mother had died and my father was married again. He took the boys with him."

She said it as if it were all very right and logical that he should and she was being unreasonable to wish she could have kept them. But she'd been quite lost without them, although, she explained, "They were growing up anyway and didn't really need me."

That was the one and only time she ever mentioned the boys.

Two months after our meeting I asked her to marry me. I was just a struggling reporter then, but I knew in time I'd get to where I could really take care of her.

In that funny, grave way, she said, "Thank you, Gordon. But I'm going to be a big night club star."

It did no good to argue. She had that ambition and until that was settled, one way or the other, I simply had nothing to interest her. I left her alone, finally, waiting till her failure became obvious even to herself.

I stayed away for three months, not seeing her, never hearing anything of her and then one evening I dropped into Mike Nelly's and asked for her.

"Glennie's gettin' married," Mike said.

"Married?" I didn't believe him. "You're crazy! Who to?"

"Lee Vining. Owns the Tampico. Big, handsome guy with a little scar right at the edge of his hair."

"I know him," I said mechanically. Of course she was going to sing at the Tampico. I remembered she had once said she always got where she wanted to go, one way or another.

I got pretty bitter for a while, telling myself I was right about one thing. She hadn't got there on her ability alone. Probably she hadn't gotten anywhere, from the time she wrangled that waitress job at fourteen, on sheer talent. Or maybe the quality of waiting, recognizing and seizing opportunities is talent. I don't know.

I read about her wedding in the papers and the announcement of her opening three weeks later at the Tampico.

She got good reviews. I stayed away, drinking like a camel, until I was suddenly ashamed of myself. Then I dated one of the girls from the paper to make it look right and caught the show one night in November from a ringside table. When Glennie finished her first number, I knew she rated her reviews.

A good band, a flashy setting, and the knowledge that as the boss' wife her job was safe, helped a lot. But she'd improved—or maybe I didn't recognize talent when I saw it. With Glennie I never knew. I was too close to her to know if she was really good.

Lee Vining was there in her dressing room when I went back to see her. His dark face got a shade darker when she ran over and hugged me. It didn't mean a thing, but he didn't like it. She pulled me by the hand across the room. "You know Lee, don't you?"

"Hello, Corbitt," Vining said.

I knew Vining from years back and there was little about him I liked. As Glennie's husband I liked him even less. He had a possessiveness based on an overwhelming ego. The thought that there could be or had ever been another man was pure torture to him. He had a passion for possessing things that lesser mortals could only crave. He wanted people to be envious of him. In this case he ended up being jealous of others because he wasn't certain he possessed Glennie.

I caught my first glimmering of that when he laughed nastily and moved to the door. "I'll leave you in Corbitt's hands, baby. At least he's a man, not a rabbit like your little piano player."

I'd never seen Glennie lose her temper before. I hadn't known one so outwardly placid could flare up so fast. "Tommy isn't a rabbit!" she snapped. "Just because he isn't muscle bound doesn't make him any less a man. And a gentleman, too!"

"A gentleman rabbit," Vining amended and went out, his laugh mocking her.

"Tommy Ameredes," Glennie said, quietly, as if I had a right to know all about it. "A real artist, I think, but he needs confidence in himself."

"How does it feel to be a real artist yourself?" I asked. "The Tampico!"

"I worked hard for this, Gordon," she said, giving me an even stare. "No matter how I got here I've worked hard to rate it. And I've had only a very few complaints on the job of being a wife."

"I wasn't being cynical," I told her. "You're even better than the Tampico. You're still climbing."

"Am I?" she said absently. "That's nice."

That should have been a tip-off. Glennie didn't care. Her career was no longer important. That's what she had said, unwittingly. The desire to get up there on top of the world was gone.

Not that it made any difference to me. She was long past the point where there was anything I could do to help her, even if she would have let me do it. She hadn't let me, I remembered, when she really needed help. But it confused me. I had the feeling I had failed her in some way.

We talked for a few minutes longer and then I left. I thought it was the last time I'd ever be with her. I remember I got drunk again and caught pneumonia in the cold November night but I didn't let Glennie know.

I glanced at my watch and saw there was still five minutes to go. I finished my beer and ordered another because I didn't want the waiter to think I was going to nurse the one bottle through the floor show.

"I don't want you thinkin' I'm tryin' to stick my nose in," he explained when he'd brought the second bottle. "If she done it, it's her business. But it's like answerin' a riddle and lookin' to see if you guessed right—and findin' the answer is missin'! See what I mean? It drives you nutty wonderin', *did* she kill him, or *didn't* she?"

"I know what you mean," I told him. "But I haven't seen her since that time."

He leaned over eagerly. "It's just curiosity," he said. "I admit it. But if you find out, will you give the sign? It's been drivin' me nuts." His tone was pleading. "Her bein' right under my nose all the time, so to speak. You know how it is."

"I know," I said and he took that to mean I'd tell him. We parted then something like friends. . . .

It was a rainy night late in April when Glennie had come to see me in my small apartment. There was a bruise on her cheekbone the size of a silver dollar. She kept her hand over it, trying hard to hide it, but I saw it at once.

"Vining?" I said through clenched teeth, "I'll kill the rotten— Where is he?"

"It's all right, Gordon." She was very embarrassed. "I didn't come for help. I . . . wanted to think quietly. I didn't know where else to go."

I took her coat and made her sit down. "You're not going back," I raged. "If he tries to see you again, so help me, I'll break his back!"

She looked at me almost indifferently. "It was as much my fault, Gordon."

"Was it over Ameredes?" I asked more quietly.

"In a way," she admitted. "There's been nothing wrong between Tommy and me. I've just tried to help him a little. Give him the confidence he needs. He's had a bad time of it, Gordon. He's so— so unworldly."

I knew Vining wouldn't fire the piano player because that wouldn't prove anything. He wanted Glennie to voluntarily re-nounce her interest in Tommy Ameredes in favor of him. That was the only way he would know he possessed her completely. As for Ameredes, I imagined he'd stay as long as Glennie was there.

She curled up on my day-bed. "Just let me think it out," she pleaded. "A little soul searching."

I sat in a big chair and watched her. She lay back, staring up at the ceiling. The rain was still batting at the window and that was the only sound in the room. She didn't speak for so long I finally dozed in my chair. I don't know how long I sat there, half asleep, but finally I came wide awake to find her standing beside my chair staring down at me. She had her coat on.

"You look like a little boy when you're asleep," she said softly, and leaned down and kissed me.

It was the only time, excepting casual good-night kisses, that she'd ever kissed me. She put her arms around me, pillowing my head against her, resting her face in my hair. It was a moment of such ineffable peace and beauty that I knew I had to keep her, no matter what.

"Stay with me," I whispered. "Don't leave me. I need you so."

"You should have called for me when you had pneumonia," she chided softly. "I would have come and taken care of you."

Her arms tightened and I was so positive that she was on the point of saying that she was going to stay, I pulled her down on my lap. "I'll take care of you, darling," I said.

Somehow that broke the web-like spell of the moment. I didn't know why. But she stood up and patted my cheek. "I'm all right now," she said. "I'll know what to do. I guess I didn't really understand myself until tonight."

She went quickly to the door, hesitated, looking back as if momentarily uncertain about something. But all she said was, "You look like a little boy when you're asleep."

The next day Lee Vining's death made every front page in town. He was found, with a bullet in his head, on the floor of his office at the Tampico. A week later Glennie was charged with his murder.

In some ways her trial was the strangest I ever heard of. She pleaded not guilty and then offered absolutely no defense for herself. Her lawyer argued, rather hopelessly, that Vining had accidentally shot himself while cleaning a revolver. He tried to make a point of the time of death, saying it was earlier than the experts estimated. And, if so, she couldn't have shot him, because she was at my apartment during that time.

The prosecutor tried, not very hard, to make her visit to me a rendezvous.

But his real target was the piano player, Tommy Ameredes, a thin, wistful little man with nothing to say. All the details of Glennie's friendship for Tommy came out. She had befriended him—her husband had objected. She wouldn't give him up—Vining had knocked the piano player around more than once. She wanted a divorce and a large settlement, so she could marry Tommy—Vining refused. If she left, she left empty-handed. He made quite a point of Glennie marrying her husband for a chance to sing in his night club. That, he declared, was the only way she could have achieved even that degree of success. If she left Vining, she was finished.

"And so," he thundered, "she took the only alternative. Callously, in cold blood, she put a bullet in her husband's head, so that she would be free!"

The jury stayed out six hours. Then they brought in a verdict of not guilty. In a statement to the newspapers the foreman said the prosecutor had failed to prove beyond a reasonable doubt that it *was* murder.

Right after the trial Glennie phoned me and said she was going to visit with relatives in Canada. She gave up all claim to any of Vining's estate, silencing for a time those who insisted she had gotten away with murder. Later, however, the same critics evolved the theory that she killed Vining in anger after one of his periodic assaults on Tommy Ameredes. But nobody really knew.

We kept up a correspondence for nearly a year but nobody can base a life on impersonal little notes. I tried to forget her. The letters stopped finally and I did forget her except in those lonely hours when a man must live with his thoughts. And at those times I used to visualize how Glennie would come to me.

Then just yesterday I learned she was trying a comeback in a cheesy little dive.

Her voice broke into my thoughts. I'd been so impressed in my reminiscences that I hadn't seen her come out onto the little square of dance floor. She hardly looked seven years older. Maybe up close the signs would be there, but from where I saw she was just as lovely in that placid, quiet way as the day I first saw her in Mike Nelly's place.

Her voice? I don't know. I never could tell whether she had talent or not. I had been in love with her before I heard her sing the first time and I could never be objective about her after that.

She sang three numbers and the applause was long and loud, but it may have been boisterousness rather than enthusiasm. I simply didn't knew whether it portended a successful comeback or not. She took a bow, directed some of the applause to her accompanist, and then walked off.

I didn't follow her. I knew, all at once, that it would do no good to try and help her. I hadn't been able to help her before in time to prevent that grim step she had taken, and I wouldn't be able to now. She didn't need anybody's help. That was what I had failed to understand seven years ago.

I got up and quietly went out into the clean night air, ignoring the reproachful look the friendly waiter sent after me. He felt I was letting him down. Maybe I was. Because now, at last, I thought I knew, beyond even a reasonable doubt, the answer to the question: Had she murdered Lee Vining? But I wasn't going to answer it, not even in the secret niches of my own mind. It wasn't, after all, what I wanted to know. Far more important to me was that I'd found out this night what made Glennie tick.

Her pianist had been a thin man with a wistful, familiar face, who probably looked even more like a little boy when he was asleep. . . .

BLIND DATE

J. LANE LINKLATER

Madge walked toward the bar, past the piano-player. She didn't look at him, and he didn't look at her. It was against the rules for any of the girls to talk to the piano-player. The piano-player, as a matter of fact, didn't look at anybody; he didn't look at anything at all. He didn't even look at sheet music as he played; he didn't have any sheet music. He just sat there, a quiet-looking man with an expressionless face, eyes front, and tapped melody out of the piano keys.

It was past one o'clock in the morning. Pete was alone behind the bar and Madge was the only girl left on duty.

Madge sat down at the bar just as a man came in. The newcomer sat next to her, motioning to Pete to draw two beers and set them up.

The man had been in each night for the last three nights. He was well-dressed, sallow face closely shaved, but his dark eyes were too bright and too fixed in their gaze.

He turned on his stool so that his gaze seemed to take in every inch of Madge's face. "Well," he said eagerly, "how about it, kid?"

"How about what?"

The man said impatiently: "You know what!"

Madge sipped her beer slowly. "What makes you think I'd go with *you*, Moxey?"

"You know you don't mean that. Anyhow, you ought to be getting *some* fun out of life; getting service instead of giving it. I got dough, kid, I *always* got dough. If you was with me, it'd be all fun and no work."

Madge twirled her glass thoughtfully. "You got a good line," she said. "But how about my husband?"

Moxey jeered: "Some husband!"

Madge looked at Moxey. "Ever see him?"

"I don't need to. Anyhow, the way I get it, he went out to sea, didn't he?"

"Sure," said Madge. "He was gone six months. Merchant Marine. But he's back now."

Music was coming from the piano.

"But he still lets you work—"

"Sure," said Madge. "I talked him into that. He gets taken care of, but he's got folks to look out for, and so have I."

"I still think your old man's a punk," said Moxey. "Now if you came with me—"

"My husband," said Madge, "wouldn't like the way you got your arm."

"What he don't know," said Moxey, "won't hurt—"

"Sure, he can't see me," said Madge. Her eyes were half-closed. "But even when he can't see me, and ain't talking to me, he's got a way of telling me things."

Moxey stared at her. "You got too many beers in you," he said.

Madge didn't say anything. The street door opened and two men came in. They mingled in the crowd at first. Both of them looked briefly at Moxey. Unnoticed, they drifted into the dark little room just beyond the piano. There was no one else in there.

They sat down, out of sight. No one could see them from the barroom. They were close to the piano player, but he didn't look at them—just went on playing.

Madge got off the stool, Moxey restrained her. "Have another," he said.

Madge shrugged. Moxey was a customer. She'd have to humor him. Pete showed up and served two more. The small clock on the sideboard said one-forty. The place would close at two. The crowd was thinning out.

Moxey's eyes were suddenly alive. "You're coming with me, kid. You know you are!"

"What's a husband?" whispered Moxey. "Especially a punk that lets you work in a crummy dump like this?"

Madge slid off the stool. "Okay," she said. "But I got to go telephone."

"Okay," Moxey said cheerfully. "But you don't need to tell him where you're going."

Madge disappeared through a rear door. Moxey's gaze was directed into the murky little room beyond the piano player.

Moxey drummed his fingertips on the bar nervously. He wished Madge would hurry back. She wasn't long. And without hesitation she sat on the stool next to Moxey.

"Pete'll close the place in a couple of minutes," she said to Moxey. "Maybe you better go—"

"I'll wait," said Moxey, "for you."

The last customer was leaving.

Pete had the money in a cloth bag close to the cash register. Pretty soon he'd put it in the safe.

Moxey's voice was hoarse now. "You know what, kid? If you hadn't agreed to come with me—I was gonna force you!"

Madge was still smiling. Moxey put a hand on her arm. He seemed very intent. Pete had pulled the blind down over the glass of the street door, was going back behind the bar.

"Okay," said Moxey, in a loud voice.

The piano-player was standing up. As he stood, he lifted his hands in the air. The two men in the dusky room beyond the piano appeared, both holding guns. Moxey, too, had a gun.

Pete's hands went up. One of the gunmen stood against the piano-player; the other covered Pete. Moxey walked behind the bar and took the money bag.

"Easy, huh?" said Moxey.

The two gunmen backed toward the door.

"Okay, kid," Moxey said to Madge. "Here's where you and me start out together."

Madge was still sitting on the stool. She didn't move.

Moxey was impatient. "Come on!"

Madge shook her head slowly. Moxey's face took on a greenish hue. His eyes were a dull glitter. "Turning me down after all, huh? Well, you'll come with me, or you'll never go anywhere!"

Then the street door opened. There were several men on top of the two gunmen.

Moxey roared. His gaze switched rapidly to the doorway, back to Madge again. "Doubled me, huh? Well, you can take this—"

One of the policemen fired. The shot took Moxey's gun out of his hand; for that matter, it seemed to take part of the hand away.

The piano-player was explaining to Pete: "They had me covered from the moment they came in."

"I went out and phoned the cops as soon as I could," Madge said, "after John put me wise."

"Swell work," said Pete. "You two and your musical double-talk. You need a coupla beers."

Madge shook her head. She put her arm about the piano-player's shoulders. "Time to go home, John, honey."

The piano-player turned his head and looked straight at her. The eyes were sightless, but the smile on his face was happy. He dropped a hand toward the piano. With one finger he tapped out three notes, very gently. "Did you understand that?"

The weariness vanished from Madge's face. "Could I miss it? It said: I—love—you."

Brand of Cain

Dan Gordon

They burned the kid with blazing guns. He was in the way so they burned him. They were moving so fast I suppose they didn't know it was a kid. Maybe they didn't care.

The liquor store clerk ran out waving his arms and they took a shot at him as they left. I said, "God . . . " and raced the engine. They piled in fast, and the guy with the gun in my neck didn't move his hand.

"Roll it," he said.

I rolled it. I took them away from there.

There wasn't any trouble from the cars that pretended to follow. They hung far back as if the guys at the wheels were afraid they might overtake us. I twisted the heap around a little, weaving through the narrow suburban streets, then jockeyed out on the boulevard and joined a stream of traffic. They began to talk, then, and I knew we were clear. The boulevard led downtown.

The gun was gone from the back of my neck, but the ape on the front seat with me still had his left arm resting high on the cushion. I said, "Got a cigarette on you?"

He fished for one with his right hand, leaving his left on the seat. In the rear-view mirror I could see Tampa sitting in back with one called Whitey. Tampa started fumbling, too. Catching his eye in the mirror, I said, "Not you, you dirty son." I left it there. I'd have to think of another name. You can't call your *brother* that.

"Kid," said Tampa, grinning, "you push a mean jallopy."

I let up on the gas and the car in back almost piled me. The guy bore down on his horn. "Lay off the big-brother act," I told him. "I don't go for that stuff anymore."

"You will," my brother told me. "You'll pick it up again."

"Never mind. Just keep it rollin'," the guy beside me said.

I gave it a little more gas and moved along with the traffic. The driving was nice and easy. The early morning rat-race was done and the guys with the plushy jobs were beginning to ooze towards their desks.

Tampa and Whitey were counting the money. The ape beside me twisted his head to watch them. "How much did we get?" he said.

"Three hundred," said Tampa.

"Big money," I said.

"It's okay," Tampa agreed.

"A hundred and fifty apiece."

"What?"

"I said you get one hundred and fifty clams, split three ways, for each of the two men you killed."

"Your mouth," my brother said, "has growed since I been away."

Whitey said, "I dunno, Tampa. Your brother's got somethin' there. You're gettin' too sharp with that gun."

"Witnesses," said Tampa. He wasn't sore, like I thought he might be. "Most of the guys that fry get in that spot through not havin' the guts to do a clean job."

Whitey didn't say any more. Afraid of Tampa, I guess. I could understand that. I was afraid of Tampa, too. Always had been. Even when we were kids. Tampa was ten years older than me, and there wasn't an ounce of pity anywhere in him. Things that would make most kids scared or sick, they just made Tampa laugh.

Not that he kicked *me* around much. I learned from watching him work on the other kids. Where he had them beat was he just plain didn't care. It never worried him how bad he hurt the other guy, and a guy who don't give a damn has got an awful edge on the rest of the world. . . .

They had me pull over to the curb three blocks away from the house. I got out and Whitey took the wheel. "You comin' home?" I said to Tampa.

"Later, kid. This heap's hot. We'll have to ditch it soon."

I hadn't known that they'd stolen the car. I thought of the way I'd driven it slow and easy right down through all that traffic. Tampa saw what I was thinking, and laughed.

"Turn off the holy-joe look," Tampa said. "You been driving a stolen car and you held up a liquor store."

"You told me you just wanted to stop in and get a bottle."

"And got one," said Whitey, holding it up. "I grabbed it on the way out."

They all laughed, then. I walked away with my hands in my

44

pockets. Behind me I heard the motor, but the car didn't pass. I guess they made a U-turn. I walked on, thinking, along the familiar neighborhood streets. The cop on the corner spoke to me and I managed to answer him. It was the same cop who'd caught Tampa stealing, nobody knew how many times. The cop liked my father and mother. Told them Tampa was only "passing through a stage."

Tampa had passed through that stage. He'd passed through a lot of stages. Each one was worse than the last. In jail and out of jail, always getting worse. . . . Far down the street I saw my father, going into the building. I slowed down.

I was wondering what to tell the old man.

We live upstairs over the big room where my old man puts out his foreign language paper. There's my father, my mother and me— and Tampa, when he's not in jail.

My father's an honest guy. Dumb, Tampa says. But he's not dumb. Honesty gets in his way. It'll do that in the newspaper business, even a little paper like ours. It knocks your advertising and it cuts down the news you print. My old man always culls the stuff he's not sure of. And when you do that, when you throw away everything that isn't strictly true, you'd be surprised how little news is left.

I looked at our sway-backed truck standing there, loaded down with papers. It didn't make me feel any better. I went in to see the old man.

He was hunched over his desk, writing. Over his shoulder, I saw he was lining up the story of Dave Macker's execution. He had a whole sheet full of Dave's early capers and was leading up to the one they'd grabbed Dave for—the killing of Winky Scanlon.

Dave Macker and Winky Scanlon, and Tampa and Whitey and probably the other tramp who was in the car when he held up the liquor store. They had always traveled together. And Scanlon had finally got his, underneath the pines in the little state park just outside the city limits. Or maybe they'd just dumped him there.

The old man was having trouble with his story. He had headed it in English: Scanlon Killer Executed. I knew that was slowing him down. For no matter how far he went down the page, he must have been remembering that he had seen Tampa that morning—the morning after Scanlon was killed. Being with Tampa in the room, I'd seen the pine needles right away when he dumped them out of his shoes. When Maw saw them littering up the floor, to her it was just more housework. With the old man, it was different. I think the old man caught on.

Now he looked up and shook his head. "I'll have to change it," he said.

"What's the difference, Pop? Dave Macker's killed other guys."

"It may not be quite accurate," my father said. "I'm not at all sure Macker committed the crime for which he is sentenced to die."

I didn't argue with him. For my money, any rap that would eliminate Macker was good for the health of the world. I guess the old man knew that, too, but he wanted it straight in his paper. "Tampa's back," I told him.

He looked glad before he thought, and then he thought and looked grave, "Oh?" he said. "When was he released?"

"Two days ago. They couldn't produce any witnesses. They gave up and let him go."

"Where is he?"

"Around. He's with a couple of friends. They're doing some business right now." I told him that. It was all I could say. Could I tell him his eldest son had shot two people just now? Killed one, maybe both? I couldn't. My father's getting old. He couldn't stand the shock.

I went upstairs to the kitchen. Maw was out shopping somewhere. I ate some cake and drank some milk, then went down the hall to my room.

The door was closed. I opened it. Tampa was sitting on the edge of the bed, smoking and cleaning his gun. He jumped and snarled when I opened the door. When he saw it was me he settled back and went on cleaning the gun.

He looked like a phony actor sitting there on the cheap iron bed, carefully cleaning that gun. Only, I knew he wasn't phony. He was as real as mad dogs come. "When'd you come in?" I asked him.

"Just now. I came in the back. Wanted to brush up before I saw the old man."

Looking at the gun, I said, "Some brushing up. He's writing a story," I added, "for tomorrow's paper. Dave Macker's execution."

Tampa's eyes flickered. "They burn him tonight," he said.

"Late," I said. "It should have been years ago."

He laughed. Always, I'll remember that he laughed. A guy was dying for Tampa's crime, and Tampa could laugh like that. "It ain't what you do," said Tampa. "It's what you get away with."

I felt sick and I turned to get out of the room. I'd forgotten what I came in for.

"Stick around," said Tampa.

I stopped. You did when Tampa talked, even if you were his brother.

"The boys," said Tampa, shoving the little square of oily rag from the back to the front of the gun, "have gone on over to Crestview. There's a little bank over there. It closes at three o'clock. You and I leave here at two-thirty. We're meeting the boys in front of the bank. They'll be drawing some money out."

"Not me," I said quickly.

"You," Tampa said. "Or would you rather I told the old man about that caper this morning?"

"It would kill him," I said, and I wasn't joking. It would be hard for the old man to believe that I'd run into Tampa and those guys on Oliver Street, that I'd said I'd be glad to drive the car if they were going to buy a bottle. What silly notion had been in my head? To save my murdering brother from a drunken-driving charge. . . . "It would kill him," I said again.

Tampa said, "There's your answer."

All over the house I could hear the quiet. Often there's the rumbling noise of the presses running downstairs. Or Maw is in the kitchen, rattling dishes and pans. Not now. All the house—all the world, it seemed to me, was holding its breath, waiting for me to decide to kill my brother. It was patient. The silence held while I thought of calling the cops, thought of a thousand things—and got rid of all those ideas. None of them would work except the cops— and that wouldn't help my old man.

I decided then, and once I knew, the normal sounds came in. I heard the board creak far down the hall. I knew that board. It creaked whenever I came in late. I'd hit it every time. It meant someone had come up the stairs—or someone was going down.

Going to the door, I cracked it, looked at the empty hall.

Nothing. Or if there had been it wasn't there anymore.

"Two-thirty?" I said to Tampa.

"Yeah."

"Meet you here."

He nodded and I went out then, went down to get the car keys. I needed the car to shop around. I was going to buy a gun. The car was gone. So was my father. Maw was still out somewhere. I opened the drawer in my father's desk and looked at the office gun. I hated to take it, knowing it was listed with the cops. They'd get me for killing Tampa if they made just a routine check. I hated to do it, sure. But I didn't have all day. And I might have trouble buying a gun with that wooden look on my face.

* * *

The car he had grabbed was a honey. We took the old road out
of town, with Tampa doing the driving. We didn't talk very much.
Tampa, I guess, had a hangover. I was too busy thinking.

When we topped the hill I could see the park on the other side
of the valley. The pines looked swell, dark blue against the skyline.
The road wound down between the cliffs, dropping down to the
level plateau.

I said, "Tampa. . . ."

"Yeah?"

"Isn't that where Scanlon was killed? In that state park up ahead?"

"So they say."

"I'm askin' you, Tampa."

His head came around for an instant; then we were heading into
a curve and he had to look at the road. "Okay," he said. "You asked
me. So I'll tell you. He was a sorehead. And that's where he got it,
all right."

"But they're going to execute Macker."

"So what? He was there. You can't stay lucky forever."

It had to be now. The curves were behind us and the car was
picking up speed. There wouldn't be another sharp curve until we
came to the park. I said, "No, Tampa. You can't stay lucky forever." I
had the gun out, had it up. . . .

My head hit the windshield when he slammed on the brakes. I
felt my wrist go numb and I knew I had dropped the gun. He swung
the blackjack again and it came down hard on my leg.

"Get out," my brother said. "Get out, you sneaking tramp."

The edge of the road was soft and unsteady. It shifted under my
feet. I stood there, waiting for it, seeing his cruel and sneering
mouth. My ugly, no-good brother. The man I had failed to kill.

"I don't know why I don't plug you," he said, "I'll be back, though,
to make you sorry you ever tried that trick. Right now I haven't got
time. Here," he tossed the gun and it fell on the sand at my feet.
"Learn how to use that thing before you begin to wave it."

The sneer was still on his face after he'd slammed the door. I
didn't stoop to pick up the gun. I watched him drive away.

It was a fine, big car he had stolen. Its tires made a whining,
humming noise as he lined it out down the road. It went out of
sight around the curve, making terrific speed.

It made a fine big crash.

I didn't know what he had hit, but then I saw the smoke. Grabbing the gun, I came up running, running and limping from the lump on my leg where the blackjack had got in its work.

The bend in the road was far away, farther than I'd thought. I made it, finally.

I needn't have hurried. Our sway-backed truck was still blocking the road. There were papers scattered all over and most of the bundles were burning. I couldn't see Tampa's car at all. Near the front of the trick, where he had hit, the flames were thirty feet high.

It is one thing to think of killing your brother, another to know he is dead. I stood there watching the flames, and in back of me the pine trees were making little rustling sounds. I had wished for it, wanted it, but it wasn't making me glad.

I guess I heard the car start. I don't remember now. It was another car, far up the road. It rocketed out from under the trees and streaked out of sight up the hill.

For a little while I thought about that, without coming up with an answer. Then, hearing another car coming, I stumbled off the road, cut back into the trees. I didn't want to see anyone. I wanted to get back to town.

It was almost dark when I made it. Along our street the kids were playing their games, running and screaming as I used to do. Tampa, too, I guess. . . .

The old man was there in the office. He whirled around when I came in. He looked even older, somehow. "Boy," he said, "I was worried. Thank God you got home safe."

"Safe? . . ." I repeated after him. My feet hurt. The soles were burning like fire. Like fire. . . . My head hurt, too, from wondering what to say. "What's the news?" I said.

"Our truck," the old man said. "Somebody stole it today. And two men tried to rob the Crestview bank. I saw them get stopped on the sidewalk."

"Did they?" I kept my eyes away from his, let them drift over the familiar objects in the room. The words on the sheet of paper leaped right up at me. It was the story the old man had been working on when I'd come in early that day. *Scanlon Killer Executed.* . . . "That heading," I said. "I'd leave it the way it is."

My father said, "Would you, son?"

I looked at him, eyes wide when I caught that tone in his voice, remembering the afternoon. I had wanted the car, and the car had been gone long before I left with Tampa. . . . Going to my father, I put my hand on his shoulder. I hadn't ever done that before, but neither of us noticed. "Yeah," I told him, "I'd leave it. I guess that's the best we can do."

His head was pure silver beneath that bright, white light. I took my hands off his shoulder, brushed the pine-needle out of his hair.

THE
BURGLAR'S STORY

W. S. GILBERT

When I became eighteen years of age, my father, a distinguished begging-letter imposter, said to me, "Reginald, I think it is time that you began to think about choosing a profession."

These were ominous words. Since I left Eton, nearly a year before, I had spent my time very pleasantly, and very idly, and I was sorry to see my long holiday drawing to a close. My father had hoped to have sent me to Cambridge (Cambridge was a tradition in our family), but business had been very depressed of late, and a sentence of six months' hard labor had considerably straitened my poor father's resources.

It was necessary—highly necessary—that I should choose a calling. With a sigh of resignation, I admitted as much.

"If you like," said my father, "I will take you in hand, and teach you my profession, and in a few years perhaps, I may take you into partnership; but, to be candid with you, I doubt whether it is a satisfactory calling for an athletic young fellow like you."

"I don't seem to care about it, particularly," said I.

"I'm glad to hear it," said my father; "it's a poor calling for a young man of spirit. Besides, you have to grow gray in the service before people will listen to you. It's all very well as a refuge in old age; but a young fellow is likely to make but a poor hand at it.

Now, I should like to consult your own tastes on so important a matter as the choice of a profession. What do you say? The Army?"

No, I didn't care for the Army.

"Forgery? The Bar? Cornish wrecking?"

"Father," said I, "I should like to be a forger, but I write such an infernal hand."

"A regular Eton hand," said he. "Not plastic enough for forgery; but you could have a writing-master."

"It's as much as I can do to forge my own name. I don't believe I should ever be able to forge anybody else's."

"Anybody's else, you should say, not 'anybody else's.' It's a dreadful barbarism. Eton English."

"No," said I, "I should never make a fortune at it. As to wrecking —why, you know how sea-sick I am."

"You might get over that. Besides, you would deal with wrecks ashore, not wrecks at sea."

"Most of it done in small boats, I'm told. A deal of small boat work. No, I won't be a wrecker. I think I should like to be a burglar."

"Yes," said my father, considering the subject. "Yes, it's a fine manly profession; but it's dangerous, it's highly dangerous."

"Just dangerous enough to be exciting, no more."

"Well," said my father, "if you've a distinct taste for burglary I'll see what can be done."

My dear father was always prompt with pen and ink. That evening he wrote to his old friend Ferdinand Stoneleigh, a burglar of the very highest professional standing, and in a week I was duly and formally articled to him, with a view to ultimate partnership.

I had to work hard under Mr. Stoneleigh.

"Burglary is a jealous mistress," said he. "She will tolerate no rivals. She exacts the undivided devotion of her worshippers."

And so I found it. Every morning at ten o'clock I had to present myself at Stoneleigh's chambers in New Square, Lincoln's Inn, and until twelve I assisted his clerk with the correspondence. At twelve I had to go out prospecting with Stoneleigh, and from two to four I had to devote to finding out all particulars necessary to a scientific burglar in any given house. At first I did this merely for practice, and with no view to an actual attempt. He would tell me off to a house of which he knew all the particulars, and order me to ascertain all about the house and its inmates—their coming and going, the number of their servants, whether any of them were men and, if so, whether they slept in the basement or not, and other details necessary to be known before a burglary could be safely attempted. Then he would compare my information with his own facts, and compliment or blame me, as I might deserve. He was a strict master, but always kind, just, and courteous, as became a highly polished gentleman of the old school. He was one of the last men who habitually wore hessians.

After a year's probation, I accompanied him on several expeditions, and had the happiness to believe that I was of some little use to him. I shot him eventually in the stomach, mistaking him for the master of a house into which we were braking (I had mislaid my dark lantern), and he died on the grand piano. His dying wish was that his compliments might be conveyed to me. I now set up on my own account, and engaged his poor old clerk, who nearly broke his heart at his late master's funeral. Stoneleigh left no family. His money—about £12,000, invested for the most part in American railways—he left to the Society for Providing More Bishops; and his ledgers, daybooks, memoranda, and papers generally he bequeathed to me.

As the chambers required furnishing, I lost no time in commencing my professional duties. I looked through his books for a suitable house to begin upon, and found the following attractive entry:

> Thurloe Square.—No. 102.
> House.—Medium
> Occupant.—John Davis, bachelor.
> Occupation.—Designer of Dados.
> Age.—86
> Physical Peculiarities.—Very feeble; eccentric; drinks; Evangelical; snores.
> Servants.—Two housemaids, one cook.
> Sex.—All female.
> Particulars of Servants.—Pretty housemaid called Rachel; open to attentions. Goes out for beer at 9 P.M.; snores. Ugly housemaid, called Bella; open to attentions; snores. Elderly cook; open to attentions; snores.
> Fastenings.—Chubb's lock on street door, chain, and bolts. Bars to all basement windows. Practicable approach from third room, ground floor, which is shuttered and barred, but bar has no catch, and can be raised with table knife.
> Valuable Contents of House.—Presentation plate from grateful esthetes. Gold repeater. Mulready envelope. Two diamond rings. Complete edition of "Badshaw," from 1834 to present time, 588 volumes, bound in limp calf.

General.—Mr. Davis sleeps second floor front; servants on third floor. Davis goes to bed at ten. No one in basement. Swarms with beetles; otherwise excellent house for purpose.

This seemed to me to be a capital house to try singlehanded. At twelve o'clock that very night I pocketed two crowbars, a bunch of skeleton keys, a centre-bit, a dark lantern, a box of silent matches, some putty, a life-preserver, and a knife; and I set off at once for Thurloe Square. I remember that it snowed heavily. There was at least a foot of snow on the ground, and there was more to come. Poor Stoneleigh's particulars were exact in every detail. I got into the third room on the ground floor without any difficulty, and made my way into the dining-room. There was the presentation plate, sure enough—about 800 ounces, as I reckoned. I collected this, and tied it up so that I could carry it without attracting attention.

Just as I had finished, I heard a slight cough behind me. I turned and saw a dear old silver-haired gentleman in a dressing-gown standing in the doorway. The venerable gentleman covered me with a revolver.

My first impulse was to rush at and brain him with my life-preserver.

"Don't move," said he, "or you're a dead man."

A rather silly remark occurred to me to the effect that if I did move, it would rather prove that I was a live man; but I dismissed it at once as unsuited to the nature of the interview.

"You're a burglar?" said he.

"I have that honor," said I, making for my pistol-pocket.

"Don't move," said he; "I have often wished to have the pleasure of encountering a burglar, in order to be able to test a favorite theory of mine as to how persons of that class should be dealt with. But you mustn't move."

I replied that I should be happy to assist him, if I could do so consistently with a due regard to my own safety.

"Promise me," said I, "that you will allow me to leave the house unmolested when your experiment is at an end?"

"If you will obey me promptly, you shall be at perfect liberty to leave the house."

"You will neither give me into custody, nor take any steps to pursue me?"

"On my honor as a Designer of Dados," said he.

"Good," said I; "go on."

"Stand up," said he, "and stretch out your arms at right angles to your body."

"Suppose I don't?" said I.

"I send a bullet through your left ear," said he.

"But permit me to observe—" said I.

Bang! A ball cut off the lobe of my left ear.

The ear smarted, and I should have liked to attend to it, but under the circumstances I thought it better to comply with the whimsical old gentleman's wishes.

"Very good," said he. "Now do as I tell you, promptly and without a moment's hesitation, or I cut off the lobe of your right ear. Throw me that life-preserver."

"But—"

"Ah, would you?" said he, cocking the revolver.

The "click" decided me. besides, the old gentleman's eccentricity amused me, and I was curious to see how far it would carry him. So I tossed my life-preserver to him. He caught it neatly.

"Now take off your coat and throw it to me."

I took off my coat, and threw it diagonally across the room.

"Now the waistcoat."

I threw the waistcoat to him.

"Boots," said he.

"They are shoes," said I, in some trepidation lest he should take offense when no offense was really intended.

"Shoes then," said he.

I threw my shoes to him.

"Trousers," said he.

"Come, come; I say," exclaimed I.

Bang! The lobe of the other ear came off. With all his eccentricity the old gentleman was a man of his word. He had the trousers, and with them my revolver, which happened to be in the right-hand pocket.

"Now the rest of your drapery."

I threw him the rest of my drapery. He tied up my clothes in the tablecloth; and, telling me that he wouldn't detain me any longer, made for the door with the bundle under his arm.

"Stop," said I. "What is to become of me?"

"Really, I hardly know," said he.

"You promised me my liberty," said I.

"Certainly," said he. "Don't let me trespass any further on your time. You will find the street door open; or, if from force of habit you prefer the window, you will have no difficulty in clearing the area railings."

"But I can't go like this! Won't you give me something to put on?"

"No," said he, "nothing at all. Good night."

The quaint old man left the room with my bundle. I went after him, but I found that he had locked an inner door that led upstairs. The position was really a difficult one to deal with. I couldn't possibly go into the street as I was, and if I remained I should certainly be given into custody in the morning. For some time I looked in vain for something to cover myself with. The hats and great coats were no doubt in the inner hall; at all events, they were not accessible under the circumstances. There was a carpet on the floor, but it was fitted to the recesses of the room and, moreover, a heavy sideboard stood upon it.

However, there were twelve chairs in the room, and it was with no little pleasure I found on the back of each an antimacassar. Twelve antimacassars would go a long way towards covering me, and that was something.

I did my best with the antimacassars, but on reflection I came to the conclusion that they would not help me very much. They certainly covered me, but a gentleman walking through South Kensington at 3 A.M. dressed in nothing whatever but antimacassars, with the snow two feet deep on the ground, would be sure to attract attention. I might pretend that I was doing it for a wager, but who would believe me?

I grew very cold.

I looked out of the window, and presently saw the bull's-eye of a policeman who was wearily plodding through the snow. I felt that my only course was to surrender to him.

"Policeman," said I, from the window, "one word."

"Anything wrong sir?" said he.

"I have been committing a burglary in this house, and shall feel deeply obliged to you if you will kindly take me into custody."

"Nonsense, sir," said he; "you'd better go to bed."

"There is nothing I should like better, but I live in Lincoln's Inn, and I have nothing on but antimacassars; I am almost frozen. Pray take me."

"The street door's open," said he.

"Yes," said I. "Come in and take me, if you will."

He came in. I explained the circumstances to him, and with great difficulty I convinced him that I was in earnest. The good fellow put his own great coat over me, and lent me his own handcuffs. In ten minutes I was thawing myself in Walton Street police station. In ten days I was convicted at the Old Bailey. In ten years I returned from penal servitude.

I found that poor Mr. Davis had gone to his long home in Brompton Cemetery.

For many years I never passed his house without a shudder at the terrible hours I spent in it as his guest. I have often tried to forget the incident I have been relating, and for a long time I tried in vain. Perseverance, however, met with its reward. I continued to try. Gradually one detail after another slipped from memory, and one lovely evening last May I found, to my intense delight, that I had absolutely forgotten all about it.

A BURNING CLUE

E. HOFFMAN PRICE

Do you mean to say," demanded Claire Dennison of her newly widowed sister, Martha Jarvis, "that the insurance company refuses to pay off, simply because you can't prove that Jarvis died before 12 noon instead of some time after that hour?"

"That's exactly it," affirmed Martha, sighing wearily. "You see, the premium hadn't been paid for some time. The extension expired at 12 noon of the very day that his latest playmate called with her pearl-handled light-housekeeping pistol and demanded a show-down. With no insurance, and the house mortgaged to the last shingle, I'm left absolutely broke."

"If that red-headed good-for-nothing hadn't become penitent a minute after she did the first good deed of her life, and then shot herself, we might prove that Jarvis died before noon," thought

Claire; but she said to her sister, "Can't you find *anyone* who heard the shots?"

"Not a soul. There's so much shrubbery around the house, and it's so far from the street—and, you know, a .25 automatic is hardly louder than the snapping of a stick. Claire, there's just no use!"

"But we've got to figure it out, Mart!" insisted Claire. "Let's see— old Aunt Julia says she left the house about half past eleven that morning. How did you know the time?"

"The radio was announcing a domestic science lecture, and Jarvis said, 'Shut the damned thing off!' They checked the broadcasting station, and got the time. She also remembered she had just loaded his pipe. That's it, over there."

Claire followed her sister's gesture, and saw a Turkish water-pipe with its brass fittings, and flexible stem, nearly two yards long, coiled about the neck of the glass water jar.

"She told the coroner all about loading the pipe," resumed Martha. "And how she came back, finding them both 'all daid,' and the pipe turned over, and a hole burned in the rug."

Claire noted the clean-cut, square hole burned through to the warp of the old Persian rug.

"How did that happen?" she wondered.

"When that woman shot him," explained Martha, "he had the pipe stem coiled about his wrist, like he always did. They'd been quarreling before Aunt Julia left. Anyway, she opened fire. And it didn't take much of a move on his part to pull the pipe off the table. The cake of charcoal that keeps the tobacco burning just ate its way into the rug."

Claire's fingernails were turning from rose to dark brown from the smoke of her disregarded cigarette.

"Mart," she said, finally, "call Aunt Julia. I want to talk to her."

For several days Claire pondered on the elusive problem, but in vain.

"Good Lord!" she exclaimed a dozen times over, "why couldn't one shot have stopped his watch, like in a story mystery? All those details, and not one thing to prove he died before noon!"

The deep brand of that last pipe stared up at her from the rug, and mocked her. There was a record of the crime; but it was as vain as the fleeting, spiteful crack of that tiny, deadly pistol which no one had heard. But how use it?

Claire questioned old Aunt Julia over and over again; but the old negress recollected only irrelevant details. But finally, out of the confusion, Claire picked a bit of hope. She phoned her sister's lawyer.

"Mr. Cartwright," she said, "bring the insurance adjuster, and a copy of the testimony of the coroner's inquest—yes, I have something up my sleeve. . . . Please try, anyway. . . . Thank you."

They called the following morning: Cartwright, politely humoring a woman's whim, and utterly hopeless of deriving any benefit from it; and Bartlett, the adjuster, courteous, suave, and determined that his company would not pay $50,000 on any policy that had expired, even if only by five minutes.

"Mr. Cartwright," began Claire, "When did Aunt Julia turn off the radio, the day Mr. Jarvis died?"

The lawyer consulted his file of testimony.

"At 11:32 A.M.," he answered. And then, to Bartlett, "Here it is."

The adjuster nodded. "I'll accept that. It's official."

"And according to the testimony," resumed Claire, "she set his pipe before him at practically the same time."

"Right," admitted Cartwright.

"But I don't see," protested the adjuster.

"Just have patience, Mr. Bartlett," said Claire, sweetly. "Oh, yes, I forgot something. How long could Mr. Jarvis have lived after the shots were fired?"

"Death was practically instantaneous. According to our doctors, he couldn't have lived over a minute, if that long," replied the adjuster. "But—"

"That's fine. Now, Aunt Julia," continued Claire, turning to the old negress, who had entered in response to her ring. "Prepare that pipe, just as you always did."

"This is irrelevant," protested Bartlett. "We're not interested—"

"Oh, but you will be!" enthused Claire, as she smiled at his disgust. "Do step into the kitchen and watch."

Bartlett swallowed his impatience. They all watched Aunt Julia put a square cake of charcoal on the gas burner, then shred a golden brown leaf of Persian tobacco, soak it in water, and wring it dry. She moulded it into a heap, and placed it in the bowl of the pipe. Then with the brass tongs she picked up the glowing charcoal and laid it on the tobacco.

"Take it out in front," directed Claire. "Just where Mr. Jarvis was sitting."

"Really interesting," began Bartlett, ironically. "Still—"

"Might as well see it through," suggested the lawyer.

They sat there, watching the film of white ash accumulate on the surface of the charcoal. Claire put the mouthpiece to her lips, and drew deeply. The pipe gurgled, and bubbled, and a tiny wisp of smoke left her lips. As the charcoal burned, the outer coating of ash fell away.

"Do try it," invited Claire, offering the pipe stem.

Both men hastily refused.

Claire's glance shifted to the clock on the wall. She drew again. Another tiny wisp of smoke. She coiled the flexible stem around her wrist.

"The way they do in Cairo," she explained, with a triumphant glint in her eye. "Like Mr. Jarvis did."

"Mrs. Dennison," protested the impatient adjuster, "I can't see that this is getting us anywhere!"

He rose as if to leave.

"Oh, you don't? Well, Mr. Bartlett, it's about time to show you!" She also rose to her feet.

"Look out!" the men cried in warning. But too late. The flexible stem about her wrist dragged the pipe from the table. The glowing charcoal lay like a great, living ruby on the Persian rug. They smelled the stench of burning wool.

"Let it alone!" commanded Claire, sharply, as Cartwright seized the brass tongs.

They glanced at her, and at each other, and at Claire's sister, and shook their heads significantly.

"Look!" she insisted, ignoring their meaning glances.

She saw them wince as the square of red hot, living fire perceptibly settled as the nap beneath it was consumed. The wanton destruction of that antique fabric had an almost horrible fascination for them. They saw the black, oily distillate from the wool rise up along the edge of the coal. Then the coal shifted again, sinking deeper.

"Mrs. Dennison, are you in your right mind?" demanded Bartlett. "That rug is worth hundreds—"

"Not hundreds," retorted Claire. "Exactly $50,000!"

The adjuster stared, speechless.

Claire seized the brass tongs. There was a perceptible sigh of relief as she picked the hungry destroyer from that rich, old rug. And then silence as they regarded the caked blackness that marked the burn.

"Mr. Bartlett," began Claire, breaking the silence, "compare that burn with the one made when Mr. Jarvis was shot. As you may have noted, I smoked the pipe about ten minutes before I overturned it. The size of the hole I burned will convince you that Jarvis could not have been smoking much longer when he overturned his pipe.

"The cake of charcoal diminishes about a quarter of an inch every ten minutes. Try it.

"And," she concluded, "you see, this rug is worth $50,000!"

"Guess you pay off, Bartlett!" exulted the lawyer.

"You win," admitted the adjuster, as he reached for his pen, and a sheaf of papers.

THE COMPLIMENTS OF THE CHIEF

LINCOLN STEFFENS

The Chief of Police lay on the great, leather-covered sofa in his office alone. He wasn't tired. His barber had shaved him and gone; the mail was attended to; routine business was over for the day. It was pleasant to lie there that way in his shirt sleeves, his collar, cuffs and boots off, and be comfortable. Everything was all right, and for an hour, until noon, the Chief was not to be disturbed.

A light tap at the door and his sergeant came in, a smooth-moving little man, with eyes sometimes light blue and innocent, sometimes dark blue and sharp. The Chief knew no one else would enter then, so he did not look up.

The sergeant showed a card, "Mr. Wayland Morrison Ball," but the Chief wouldn't read.

"Who is it, Mac? What does he want?"

"It's a squeal, Chief, about a gold watch."

"Well, why don't it go to the detective bureau?"

"Just read the name, Banker Ball."

The Chief rose to his feet, hastily pulled on his boots, put on his collar, cuffs, and snapped on his cravat, while the sergeant held the coat. When the Chief had wound down into that, he went to a glass, buttoned up the uniform, touched his hair and went to his roll-top desk. When he was seated, he leaned his head on his hand, put on a dreamy, far-away look, and the sergeant nodded.

"All right, then, send him in," said the Chief.

And so Mr. Ball found him, pondering and absorbed. The sergeant retired.

"Chief Reilly?"

No answer.

"Mr. Reilly, I believe."

The Chief nodded and waved the gentleman to a chair. A minute more of brown study, and the Chief pushed a button three times.

A detective came in and stood beside the desk at attention, till the Chief came out of his preoccupation.

"Where are the men who are working on that jewel robbery now?"

"They are shadowing the thief along the water-front."

"At this moment?"

"At this moment."

"Well, you warn them that the thief will take the Pennsylvania ferry and buy tickets in Jersey City for Washington. Arrest him on this side."

The man saluted and went out.

The Chief seemed satisfied that that case was disposed of. He rose, thought a moment more, and nodded approval. His hand was playing with the banker's card; his eye happened to catch it, read it, then turned slowly up under his heavy brows at the banker who had got up on his feet with the Chief.

"Mr. Ball?"

"Wayland Morrison Ball."

"Banker?"

"Eleventh National Bank."

"Right," the Chief said, slowly nodding his head. "Eleventh National Bank." He went to the window, his back to the banker, then he came about, leaned against his desk.

"Did you ever get back," he said, indifferently, "'the bonds— three, I think, yes, three C. B. & Q's—stolen two years ago?"

"No."

"Might just as well. They were negotiated in Chicago a week before you missed them, got into circulation, and were soon in reputable hands."

The banker was amazed. That case had never been reported to the police. A detective agency was called in, and though its men worked hard, they never got the slightest clew to the thief or the property till the railroad company's transfer clerk caught the bonds at dividend time.

"The boy made a fool mistake, didn't he, taking bonds?" asked the Chief, still rather absently. "Never stole again, I suppose?"

"Why, we never knew who took them," the banker said. "Do you mean to say the thief was an employee? Is an employee?"

"He will never do it again, I think," the Chief said. "I should dismiss all thought of it. Take that chair."

The Chief sat down at his desk, leaned his head in his hand, but this time he set his eyes keenly on the banker's face, all alert and attention.

"Now," he said, "what is the trouble today?"

The banker had gathered himself and was taking the chair indicated. It was near the desk and the light fell on the banker's face; the chief's was in the shadow.

"Robbed?"

"Yes, of a gold watch, given me by my father, and as a present from him I treasure it beyond its true value. But—"

The Chief lifted his hand deprecatingly.

"Where were you and how did it happen?"

"I was crossing the bridge, and—"

"One moment, Mr. Ball. Which way were you going?"

"From Brooklyn here. I hardly ever go to Brooklyn."

"What time did you reach the bridge?"

"Eleven-fifty-five. I know that because I looked at my watch as I took the bridge car. That's how I know I lost it on the bridge. You see—"

"When did you miss the watch?"

"As I stepped off the car on this side."

"The car was crowded, ladies and gentlemen and some workmen. The watch was taken from the chain and the clasp and the chain was put back in place. This was last night?"

The banker was nodding affirmatively to each statement, and his eyes flattered the Chief as he loved to be flattered, by astonishment and wonder shown as a child shows these emotions.

62

"Your name was on the case inside, and your father's?"

"Yes. 'John Henry Ball to his son, Wayland Morrison Ball. Dec. 3, 1879.' It is a heavy hunting case Geneva watch—"

The Chief got up and walked to the window.

"Everybody in the car—except the working people—was talking—"

"Talking and laughing in the several groups—"

Chief Reilly turned back, thinking again.

"Can you be in your office to-morrow at 12:30 o'clock?" he asked at length.

"Yes."

"The watch will be delivered to you then."

The banker knew how to behave in most of the crises of life, but he was uncomfortable now. He would have liked to ask some questions, to express some thanks, to praise the official a little frankly; but the Chief seemed to be absorbed already in something else, so Mr. Ball stepped back, bowing.

"I shall be obliged, Chief Reilly, for this service, I assure you. Good day."

The Chief dropped his head as if mechanically bowing, and the banker reached the door. It opened before him, and he went out to his carriage, which bore him swiftly away to his office.

"Mac," said the Chief, when the sergeant returned to him, "who's working the bridge now?"

"I don't know, unless it's the Keg Kelly mob; but no, you told them to haul off, didn't you?"

"Yes, and after that I warned the Hen and Chickens off."

"Maybe they've gone back."

"Send Thompson in."

Thompson came, hurrying up from court. He was a fat, but clean man of forty, and he looked more like a thief than an actor, for his face, though square and smooth shaven, was red and irregular, with small, damp pink eyes. His "plain clothes" were a bit "tough" in style.

The Chief eyed the detective up and down, slowly, angrily.

"Some of your friends on the bridge have been robbing a friend of mine, Banker Ball. A fine, big gold watch, with the man's name on it."

Thompson moved uneasily from one foot to the other, he rolled his hat around his hand—and he hung his head. He glanced up shiftily twice, as if he thought of an answer, but he made none.

"I want it," said the Chief. "I want you and the watch here at ten o'clock to-morrow morning."

The detective went out. The Chief pulled off his boots, coat and collar and lay down on the lounge.

When Thompson left the Chief's office, he went down in the basement where half a dozen detectives were lounging about. He spoke to them, asking first the same question the Chief put to the sergeant, "Who is working the bridge?" All offered suggestions, and Thompson discussed them with his friends. Then he walked down to the Criminal Court building, where his "side-partner," Tarney, was. Tarney was on the witness stand, so Thompson moved about among the lawyers in the court-room. He spoke to each alone, earnestly, inquiring first, then saying something emphatic. They all seemed to answer in about the same way, each shook his head, lifted his hands helplessly and then nodded. When Tarney was told to "step down," Thompson drew him out into the corridor, and they held a long consultation leaning up against a pillar. They whispered, speaking eagerly, then silent, then enthusiastically again, till they separated.

Tarney, following one clew, visited each court-room in the building and talked with every likely lawyer he saw. He went out into the street and called on other criminal law firms in the neighborhood. Sometimes he met men on the sidewalk with whom he talked. Now and then he stepped into saloons, looked around and either left with a shrug or jumped at some man to whisper to him. This part of his work done, Tarney spent the rest of the day dashing into and out of pawnshops. He never stayed long in a place; just long enough to say a few stern words, make a few gestures, and to write down the one word "Ball."

"The old man wants it, see?" That was the only sentence he spoke aloud.

Thompson went to the bridge. At the New York end he spoke to a man who stood idly watching the crowd, then to a policeman. Each told him something that interested him, but he went on across the bridge afoot, stopping twice on the way over to address ordinary-looking persons. At the Brooklyn end also he addressed men who knew him. A short, swift tour of the pawnshops in lower Brooklyn, and he rode back to New York. He called at several saloons and a few more pawnshops.

"And the old man wants it back," was the way Thompson closed the interviews.

At five minutes to six, Tarney emerged from the crowd in

Twenty-third Street and approached the southeast corner of Sixth Avenue. A big policeman was standing there, but at sight of Tarney, he moved off without a sign of recognition. The detective leaned against the corner. At three minutes to six Thompson arrived. They turned off at once to a restaurant, where Thompson led the way to a corner table, and taking the chair which commanded a view of the whole room, he sat down. Tarney sat opposite him. They ordered a course dinner, with wine, and, saying nothing, ate it. Over the cigars, they exchanged a few words.

"Been to the Hen and Chickens?" Thompson asked.

"Nope. Everywhere else. Left that till tonight. You stop at Kelly's?"

"Nope. No use till to-night."

It was eight o'clock when Thompson, walking alone in the shadow of the tenements on a dark side street, turned suddenly into a noisy saloon. He pushed open the swinging fly doors and stood still between them, holding off a wing in each hand. The room was full of men, some at tables, others at the bar, others again in a back room. All stopped whatever they were doing, and looked at Thompson. There was silence. They stared, and half raised glasses were put down on the bar. The bartender was the first to recover.

" 'Lo, Tom," he said. "Have something?"

A man in the back room went quickly out of the side door. Another followed him slowly.

"Keg here?" Thompson asked.

"Yes," said a voice, and a short, well-dressed man came out of the back room. His face was hard, though the skin was soft and pale, and his hands were long and very fine.

"Want me?" he asked.

Thompson came in and let the doors swing shut.

"No, I don't 'want' nobody," the detective said, smiling a little.

The whole atmosphere of the room changed. The crowd relaxed. Interrupted drinks were swallowed, and liquor flowed, everybody laughed.

"Come here," said Thompson.

He caught Keg Kelly by a buttonhole and drew him into the corner, and Thompson talked for one minute with great firmness.

"And the old man wants it back again," he said at last. "Good night."

The next morning at 9 o'clock Thompson stood on the corner of Mott Street and Houston, Tarney at Mott and Bleecker, with the rear entrance of police headquarters between them. They seemed to be holding receptions. Queer old foreigners, dilapidated loafers, "sports," out-and-out "toughs," went up to them one at a time. Most of them made apologetic gestures, were cursed, and slunk away; a few smiled, spoke a few words and delivered small parcels.

The detectives left their corners simultaneously, and approaching police headquarters, went together down into the basement. There they looked over "the stuff," as they called it, eleven watches of all sizes and shapes. Thompson took off Tarney's hat and held it out while Tarney put his watches in, then he gave it to Tarney while he "unloaded."

" 'Wall,' " he said, "Microwitz wasn't sure of the name. Take it back to him."

Tarney put it in his pocket.

" 'Ball.' Maybe that's it," said Thompson, looking at the next watch, "but it's pretty small. I'll let the old man see it." He kept that. "And here's another 'Ball.' I guess that's it. Keg sent both of these. Beaut', ain't it? Here's a 'Call.' Take it, and this, too. 'Wahl.' Say, here's a 'Hall.' It is a haul, sure enough; regular poem. What's this, another 'Hall.' Those other little ones are n.g. Keep 'em. I'll let the old man take his pick of these two 'Balls.' But I guess this big fellow is the one he passed the word for."

Mr. Wayland Morrison Ball had a few friends in to lunch with him in his office at noon that day. He had promised to show them something interesting, and had explained enough to make them all very much interested to hear more. They looked at the clock when they came in.

"Exactly 12:20, he said," Mr. Ball repeated, "on the minute. He's a remarkable man. Why, I tell you he told me things I didn't know myself—who were in the car, what they did, which ones sang, which ones talked, and—"

A shrewd little broker smiled.

"Well, he did," Mr. Ball insisted. "He even described how the watch was taken off the chain, exactly. And that other case of ours here, you know. He asked me about that, but he thought I knew more than I did. He knows who took the bonds." Mr. Ball lowered his voice. "And we don't know that to this day. He told me what the thief did with them, where they went, through whose hands they passed. It was the most astonishing thing."

The bankers and brokers didn't half believe Ball. They ate of the lunch, drank a sip of tea or water or wine, and glanced up at the clock. Some of them tried to tell detective stories they had read, but Ball said such tales were all rot.

"This is the real thing," he insisted. "Chief Reilly—you ought to have seen the way he looked at me, and the questions he asked—sharp, keen. He's a wonderful man, wonderful. Everything right to the point, every word, every gesture, every glance—"

It was 12:20, and everybody knew it. They were silent, watching the clock or looking at their watches. Some of them stopped eating. The next ten minutes dragged, but they passed, 12:25, 12:26, 27. The men were all nervous now, and serious. At last it was 12:28. There was no sign, and Mr. Ball was anxious, but he smiled confidently. "It isn't time yet," he said.

A minute more crept by; you could hear the clock tick above the ticker. The long hand on the clock moved on slowly till it was against the figure VI; not a sign. it was over the VI.

A rap at the door. Everybody started, and the company laid down their napkins to look, but remembered, and turned their eyes away.

"Come in," said Mr. Ball, raising expectantly.

"Two—two men—gentlemen to see you—"

"Show them in."

The clerk slipped aside. Thompson and Tarney entered side by side, as solemn as undertakers.

"Mr. Ball?" said Thompson, looking at the banker.

"I am Mr. Ball."

"The compliments of Chief Reilly," the detective said. He laid the watch on the table. Then he and Tarney turned and went out.

The watch lay there on the table, every eye fixed upon it. No one moved. The gentlemen glanced around at one another, then up at their host. Mr. Ball smiled a little, rather proudly.

THE
CONFESSION

MAURICE LEVEL

Istood still for a moment before the open door, hesitating, and it was only when the old woman who had been sent to bring me said for the second time, "It is here," that I went in.

At first I could see nothing but the lamp screened by a low-drawn shade; then I distinguished on the wall the motionless shadow of a recumbent body, long and thin, with sharp features. A vague odor of ether floated round me. But for the sound of the rain beating on the slates of the roof and the dull howling of the wind in the empty chimney, the silence was death-like.

"Monsieur," said the old woman gently as she bent over what I now saw was a bed, "Monsieur! . . . the gentleman you asked for is here."

The shadow raised itself, and a faint voice said:

"Very well . . . leave us, Madame . . ."

When she had shut the door after her, the voice went on:

"Come nearer, Monsieur. I am almost blind, I have a buzzing in my ears, and I hear very badly . . . Here, quite close to me, there ought to be a chair . . . Pardon me for having sent for you, but I have something very grave to tell you."

The eyes in the face that craned towards me were wide open in a sort of stare, and he trembled as he faltered:

"But first, are you Monsieur Gernou? Am I speaking to Monsieur Gernou, leader of the bar?"

"Yes."

He sighed as if with relief.

"Then at last I can make my confession. I signed my letter Perier, but that is not my real name. It is possible that if Death, so near me now, had not already changed my face, you might vaguely recognize me. But no matter . . .

"Some years ago, many long years, I was Public Prosecutor for the Republic. I was one of the men of whom people say: 'He has a brilliant future before him,' and I had resolved to have one. I only needed a chance to prove my ability: a case at the assizes gave me that chance. It was in a small town. The crime was one that would not have attracted much attention in Paris, but there it aroused passionate interest, and as I listened to the reading of the accusation I saw there would be a big struggle. The evidence against the prisoner was of the gravest nature, but it lacked the determining factor that will frequently draw a confession from the criminal, or the equivalent of a confession. The man made a desperate defense. A feeling of doubt, almost of sympathy, ran through the court, and you know how great the power of that feeling is.

"But such influences do not affect a magistrate. I answered all the denials by bringing forward facts that made a strong chain of circumstantial evidence. I turned the life of the man inside out and revealed all his weak points and wrongdoings. I gave the jury a vivid description of the crime, and as a hound leads the hunters to the quarry, I ended by pointing to the accused as the criminal. Counsel for the defense answered my arguments, did his best to fight me, but it was useless. I had asked for the head of the man: I got it.

"Any sympathy I might have felt for the prisoner was quickly stifled by pride in my own eloquence. The condemnation was both the victory of the law and a great personal triumph for me.

"I saw the man again on the morning of the execution. I went to watch them wake him and prepare him for the scaffold, and as I looked at his inscrutable face I was suddenly seized with an anguish of mind. Every detail of that sinister hour is still fresh in my memory. He showed no sign of revolt while they bound his arms and shackled his legs. I dared not look at him, for I felt his eyes were fixed on me with an expression of superhuman calm. As he came out of the prison door and faced the guillotine, he cried twice: 'I am innocent!' and the crowds that had been prepared to hiss him suddenly became silent. Then he turned to me and said: 'Watch me die, it will be well worth your while' . . . He embraced the priest and his lawyer . . . He then placed himself unaided on the plank and never flinched during the eternal moment of waiting for the knife. I stood there with my head uncovered. But I, I did not see, having for the moment lost all consciousness of external things.

"During the days that followed my thoughts were too confused for me to understand clearly why I was full of some trouble that seemed to paralyze me. My mind had become obsessed by the death of this man. My colleagues said to me:

" 'It is like that the first time.'

"I believed them, but gradually I became aware that there was a definite reason for my preoccupation: doubt. From the moment I realized this I had no peace of mind. Think of what a magistrate must feel when, after having caused a man to be beheaded, he begins asking himself:

" 'Suppose after all he were not guilty?'

"I fought with all my strength against this idea, trying to convince myself that it was impossible, absurd. I appealed to all that is balanced and logical in my brain and mind, but my reasonings were always cut short by the question: 'What real proof was there?' Then I would think of the last moments of the criminal, would see his calm eyes, would hear his voice. This vision of the scaffold was in my mind one day when someone said to me:

" 'How well he defended himself! It is a wonder he did not get off. . . . Upon my word, if I had not heard your address to the Court I should be inclined to think he was innocent.'

"And so the magic of words, the force of my will to succeed, were what had quieted the hesitations of this man as they had probably triumphed over those of the jury. I alone had been the cause of his death, and if he were innocent I alone was responsible for the monstrous crime of his execution.

"A man does not accuse himself in this way without trying to put up some sort of a defense, without doing something to absolve his conscience, and in order to deliver myself from these paralyzing doubts I went over the case again. While I reread my notes and examined my documents, my conviction became the same as before; but they were *my* notes, *my* documents, the work of my probably prejudiced mind, of my will enslaved by my desire, my need to find him guilty. I studied the other point of view, the questions put to the accused and his answers, the evidence of the witnesses. To be quite sure about some points that had never been very clear, I examined carefully the place where the crime had been committed, the plan of the streets near the house. I took in my hands the weapon the murderer had used, I found new witnesses who had been left out or neglected, and by the time I had gone over all these details twenty times I had come to the definite conclusion, now not to be shaken, that the man was innocent . . . And as if to crown my remorse, a brilliant rise in position was offered me!

"I was very cowardly, Monsieur, for I believed I did enough in tendering my resignation without assigning any reason for it. I traveled. Alas! forgetfulness does not lie at the end of long roads . . . To do something to expiate the irreparable wrong I had caused became my only desire in life. But the man was a vagabond, without family, without friends.

"There was one thing I could have done, the only worthy thing: I could have confessed my mistake. I had not the courage to do it. I was afraid of the anger, the scorn of my colleagues. Finally, I decided that I would try to atone by using my fortune to relieve those who were in great trouble, above all, to help those who were guilty. Who had a better right than I to try to prevent men being condemned?

"I turned my back on all the joys of life, renounced all comfort and ease, took no rest. Forgotten by everyone, I have lived in solitude, and aged prematurely. I have reduced the needs of life to a minimum. For months I have lodged in this attic, and it is here I contracted the illness of which I am dying. I shall die here, I wish to die here . . . And now, Monsieur, I have come to what I want to ask you."

His voice became so low I had to watch his trembling lips to help myself to understand his words.

"I do not wish this story to die with me. I want you to make it known as a lesson for those whose duty it is to punish with justice and not because they are there *to punish in any case;* I want it to help bring the Specter of the Irreparable before the Public Prosecutor when it is his duty to ask for a condemnation."

"I will do as you ask," I assured him.

His face was livid, and his hand shook as he gasped:

"But that is not all. I still have some money that I have not yet had time to distribute among those who have been unfortunate. It is there—in that chest of drawers. I want you to give it to them when I am gone—not in my name, but in that of the man who was executed because of my mistake thirty years ago. Give it to them in the name of Ranaille."

I started.

"Ranaille? But it was I who defended him! I was . . ."

He bowed his head.

"I know. That is why I asked you to come. It was to you I owed this confession. I am Deroux, the Public Prosecutor." He tried to lift his arms towards the ceiling, murmuring: "Ranaille . . . Ranaille . . ."

Did I betray a professional secret? Was I guilty of a breach of rules that ought to be binding? The pitiful spectacle of this dying man drew the truth from me in spite of myself.

"Monsieur Deroux! Monsieur Deroux! Ranaille was guilty . . .

He confessed it as he went to the scaffold . . . He told me when he bid me goodbye there . . ."

But he had already fallen back on the pillow. I have always tried to believe that he heard me.

THE CRIMSON COMPLEX

G. FLEMING-ROBERTS

It was not impulse that made Dorothy Faine bring her roadster to a sliding stop at the corner of Eighth Street. Dorothy Faine never acted on impulse. Being beautiful, she had no motive for developing the vivacity that is supposed to attract men. She thought and moved slowly and accurately. Her emotions were as enduring as a Sunday in July—and as warm. Only Dorothy Faine knew why she tooted her horn invitingly as Detective Sergeant Kerry stepped from the curb at Eighth Street corner. And Dorothy never told.

"I'm going out to Banmar—if you are, Mr. Kerry," she called. Then, she smiled enticingly. She always smiled that way.

Jim Kerry was of one color—red-brown hair and eyes. He always wore red-brown clothes and polished red-brown shoes. He approached the car cautiously—for he was always cautious.

"It's Miss Faine?" He lifted his red-brown hat—a thing almost unheard of among the men of the homicide squad. But then Kerry had not served his apprenticeship on the traffic force. "Of course, I'd be delighted for the lift. I wanted to get out to the hospital as soon as possible."

He sat there, stiffly on the edge of the cushions. A red-brown cigar, unlighted, was fastened between his clean, white teeth.

The girl meshed the gears and raced a Mack truck for the inner traffic belt. "Terrible, isn't it—Mr. Appleard's death?" she said.

"Yes," said Kerry; then, with his usual caution, "murder is always terrible."

"And when I think that he was a patient! It may ruin the future of the hospital. A patient murdered in his bed!" A little shudder passed over the girl.

"Yes," Kerry said again. "You have every interest in the hospital, haven't you, Miss Faine? Not only as chief of nurses, but also because of the young research sensation, Dr. Trenton—"

"No, you have me confused with Nurse Daniels. She is Dr. Trenton's fiancée."

She ran a red traffic signal.

Kerry apologized for his blunder. "It is unfortunate, too. I mean, that Miss Daniels is under considerable suspicion." It was more than suspicion, but Kerry was cautious.

"No!" exclaimed the girl.

Kerry nodded. "You see, she administered the hypodermic that killed Appleard. She used something that caused the old man's blood to clot in his blood vessels—internal suffocation, I suppose you'd say."

"Intravascular clotting," the nurse corrected. "Yes, I heard that Dr. Trenton's new blood-clotting substance—'synthetic cephalin,' he calls it—had been substituted. But I can't conceive of Miss Daniels—"

"You see," Kerry explained, "someone entered Dr. Trenton's lab and took enough of that synthetic stuff from the vial on his desk to make the injection. It was deliberately substituted for the hypodermic prescribed by Dr. Allen. I have not established a motive as yet. It might be that Miss Daniels wanted to prove the worth of her affianced's discovery. Then there is one more—" Kerry was about to say that he had made one more important discovery, but the nurse interrupted.

"But surely, it is an awful fuss to make over an old man who would have died in a few years anyway?" It was the first time Dorothy had said this. She had thought of it several times before. Now that she had said it, she was glad. It sounded like a sort of defense for Margaret Daniels. It was always humane to defend the guilty— even though she hated Margaret Daniels as passionately as she loved Dr. Ralph Trenton.

"The law never considers whether or not a person is too old to live," said Kerry.

A siren screamed at the rear wheel of Dorothy's flying car. A motorcycle drove her to the curb. She pulled up sharply.

"Say, young woman, who do you think you are? That's the third time this week you've run through that traffic light. Think they're put there—" He saw Kerry. He saluted stiffly. "Sorry, sergeant. I didn't recognize you. I'll be more careful after this."

"I would," said Kerry sternly. "You may go on, Miss Faine. Some of these traffic officers are half blind, I believe."

Dorothy hurried her car forward. "That one especially has it in for me," she laughed. "He will have it that my meager earnings are consumed in paying fines for passing red lights. But, you were saying—"

Kerry opened his mouth and shut it quickly. "Some other time, Miss Faine," he said. "Here's the hospital. If you'll just let me out in front. I've a few things to do, but I'll see you later."

"That will be nice," said the girl. She offered one of her lovely smiles. Kerry's cheeks were susceptible. He crimsoned to the eyes.

Dorothy Faine would have given a good deal to know just what Kerry had discovered. As the chief nurse, she felt that she had a right to know everything that went on at the hospital. It was with the idea of pumping Ralph Trenton that she went to the laboratory before going to her desk.

Softly, on her rubber-heeled shoes, she entered the lab. Ralph was at his desk. His hands covered his face. His curly hair straggled over his fingers.

"Ralph, I can't tell you how sorry I am about all this."

Ralph started at the sound of her voice. He looked up. His eyes were haggard and sleepless.

"It's all right, Dorothy," he said weakly. "We all know that Margaret is incapable of such a thing. We simply have to prove that to our thick-headed Irishman."

"You know, Ralph, I'll do anything I can." Dorothy seated herself on the corner of Trenton's desk. She placed a cool, white hand over his hot, moist fist. It seemed but a friendly gesture.

Trenton noticed the coolness and whiteness of her hand. He looked into her face. "Of course, you will. You're a real friend, Dorothy."

More than that. She would have been much more than that. Her blood raced madly. Her eyes entrapped Ralph's eyes and bathed them in dark blue depths. . . .

Phantom wires that enmeshed the nurse and doctor were broken by the sound of shoes clicking in the corridor. Sergeant Kerry entered wrapped in a cloud of cigar smoke.

74

"I've made a very important discovery, Dr. Trenton." He paused in the doorway.

Dorothy slipped from the desk.

Trenton collected his wits.

"You seem to be full of important discoveries today," said the doctor, sarcastically.

Kerry crossed the room and seated himself uninvited at Trenton's desk. He brought a small vial sealed with crimson wax from his pocket. He tapped the vial with his pencil.

"I'm returning your stuff that causes blood clotting in the veins— and kills. I haven't been able to discover why the murderer sealed this vial with red wax when you, Dr. Trenton, say that you left it sealed with green wax."

Trenton shrugged his shoulders. Carelessly, he said, "It is all simple enough. A mere oversight. There were sticks of red, blue, and green wax on my desk. The murderer simply picked up the wrong one."

Kerry was drawing triangles on the desk pad.

Suddenly, his eyes jabbed at Trenton.

"Or perhaps it was only a neat bit of fabrication designed to draw my attention from you, Dr. Trenton."

The doctor flushed angrily. He wanted to say something brilliant and biting, but his lips became dry.

"I'd like to speak to you in private, doctor," Kerry dropped his pencil on the desk and got up.

Dorothy started to leave the room, but Kerry stopped her.

"You remain here, Miss Faine. I'll just step into the hall with Dr. Trenton."

Once in the hall, Kerry seized Trenton by the arm.

"The discovery that I've just made, Dr. Trenton, is that you are sole beneficiary by Mr. Appleard's will. He was your uncle."

Trenton shrugged his shoulders. "I've been aware of that for some time."

"Then why didn't you tell me?" Kerry snapped. "But don't answer. It was because someone who loves you had a motive for killing Appleard in order to marry you. You are now a very rich man, you know."

Ralph flamed. "That isn't true. Why are you so persistent? Margaret couldn't do such a thing. . . . Why, haven't I a stronger motive?"

Kerry nodded shortly. "You have indeed. I'll just make note—"

His hand went to his pocket. "My pencil. . . . I left it on your desk. Wait here, doctor." Kerry turned on his polished heels and reentered the laboratory.

"Nurse Faine," he called from the door, "will you please bring me my pencil—the green one on the desk in front of you?"

"Certainly, sergeant." The girl smiled as she extended the pencil to him.

"Isn't that a pretty shade of green, Miss Faine?" he held the pencil almost lovingly in his hand.

The girl smiled again—still her enticing smile.

Kerry stepped suddenly forward. His eyes sparkled with strange red lights. His two hands closed over the girl's shoulders. His lips came so close to her ear that they brushed on a wisp of her hair. He whispered, "Miss Faine, *you* were the one who substituted the poison for the hypodermic before Miss Daniels administered it. I arrest *you* for the murder of Gregory Appleard. *You* killed him because *you* hated Margaret Daniels; because *you* wanted Dr. Trenton for yourself; because you wanted to marry into the Appleard fortune! And I have the proof!"

The nurse stepped quickly backward. Still, Kerry held her by the shoulders.

"Wh-what do you mean—"

"Simply that my pencil isn't green; it's red. The traffic light this morning was also red. The wax you resealed Dr. Trenton's little bottle with was also red. I mean that you are red and green color-blind, Miss Faine!"

The girl sank limply onto a laboratory stool. A sudden change came over her face. She had become so hideous in those few seconds that, passing her hand across her face, she could feel her ugliness.

THE CUNNING
OF THE SERPENT

HENRY S. WHITEHEAD

The mail came into Carnation twice a week, on Tuesdays and
Fridays. It was brought over from Red Hills, the nearest railroad station twelve miles across the desert, by Joe Sowers, a su-
perannuated cowman. Sowers made the trip to Jim Peterson the
postmaster, keeper of Carnation's chief emporium of general
trade. Therefore, even when he was at home in his rare intervals
of rest from the constant visitations throughout his enormous district, the Bishop of the Niobraras had two heavy days of "inside
work," since his mail receipts were larger than those of any other
citizen of Carnation.

The bishop's mail had another distinction. It contained the only
regular pay-check that came into the little frontier town which was
the geographical center of his work. This was because, being a
missionary bishop, he received his salary from the missionary headquarters in New York once a month. As Jim Peterson was also the
banker, the bishop had fallen into the habit of taking his check to
the storekeeper as soon as he got it, and having it cashed.

This unusual method of receiving one's income had excited much
local comment, and it was well known that Bishop Kent always
carried his check to Peterson's and came out with a roll of two
hundred and fifty dollars, once every month.

This sum was far more than the bishop needed for his simple
requirements, but it made it possible for him to perform a good
many kindly acts with his right hand of which his left hand knew
nothing. The recipients could be counted on to say nothing.

But the case of Rosie, Rosie of the Gopher Hole's Bevy of Blos-
soms, had leaked out some time after Rosie's unexpected departure
for the East. It had leaked out through the ugly mouth of Clark
Shadwell. In a moment of very bad judgment, complicated by a
certain amount of the Gopher Hole's very bad red liquor, poor
Rosie had succumbed to the allurements Shadwell had been holding

out to her, and had abandoned the frying-pan of the Gopher Hole's precarious housing for the fire of Clark Shadwell's tumbledown shack on the edge of town.

Rosie had never ceased to regret this step. But regrets did her no good. Like everybody else in or near Carnation she soon came to know Shadwell for what he was, a truculent, transplanted hill-billy from the Tennessee mountains, a gun-fighter, who, weaned on corn-licker and fed on rat-tail tobacco since before he had teeth, had found the scope of his native land too narrow for his expansive nature. He had come out into the Bad Lands where he would have room to swing a gat, and had picked on Carnation as his habitat. He had made it clear to Rosie that if she ever left him to go back to the Gopher Hole he would get her. This threat had held her through every variety of ill treatment the "pizenest" citizen of Carnation could think up.

One Monday night the bishop had arrived home from a long visitation, and after his usual process of cleaning-up after three weeks away from his famous bath tub, in the alkali-dust, had stepped over to Peterson's for his accumulated mail. There was such a huge stack of it that he had not waited even to cash his check but, intending to do so the next morning, had carried it all home with him.

He was in the midst of this large batch of mail the next morning when a tap on the door interrupted him. He opened the door and Rosie stumbled in. She was weak and sick and half starved, and she was suffering acutely from the effects of the beating Shadwell had administered the night before.

Nobody except the bishop and Rosie, and the Personage up above Who was the bishop's boss, knew what the two said to each other, but about an hour later they came out of the bishop's little house and walked together along Carnation's main street of shacks to Peterson's store. Old Joe Sowers was outside beside his dilapidated buckboard with its pair of rangy cow ponies, and the bishop paused to speak to him.

"Kindly defer your leaving for a few minutes, Mr. Sowers. There will be a passenger going with you to Red Hills."

Old Joe nodded his dusty old head and spat reflectively in the thick dust of the roadway, saying nothing.

The bishop accompanied Rosie into the store, cashed his check and, while the store loafers stood agape, counted out into Rosie's hand ten ten-dollar bills. The loafers followed the oddly assorted pair out in front of the store, and saw the bishop deferentially hand Rosie into the buckboard.

"Take this young lady to the station at Red Hills, if you please," came the bishop's precise voice speaking to old Joe. "Perhaps, too, you will be kind enough to see that she gets her ticket through to New York, and is placed safely on the train."

"Uh-huh," responded old Joe, shifting his quid nervously from one side of his leathern jaws to the other.

The girl looked unutterable things at the little bishop who, removing his hat, bowed to her stiffly, and the buckboard started off at a great rate.

Gravely saluting the men about the store doorway, the bishop turned on his heel, and with a measured tread which he never varied, about twenty-one inches to the step, Reddy Larimore had once reported, walked gravely back to his little adobe house by the creek side.

Ed Hammond, proprietor of the Red Horse Restaurant and Bar, having learned what was in the wind, overtook the little man before he had reached his house. Hammond laid a huge, protective hand on the neat shoulder of the bishop's neatly pressed black coat.

"Land sake, Bishop, y'aint mixin' in on this yere Clark Shadwell's deals, are ye? Goshamighty, man, that cattymount ain't got no respec' fer nothin' ner nobody. They tells me ye're a-helpin' this yere gal o' his'n to get away east. Why, man, he'll jes' plum ruin ye with lead bullets fer that, soon's he knows what ye've ben up to. It's a wonder he haint a-rearin' roun' right now. Why—likely's not he'll be ridin' after 'em an' kill the gal an' old Joe to boot. Hain't ye got no sense?"

The bishop turned on Hammond a cool, level eye.

"Its very good of you, Mr. Hammond, to warn me like this. I appreciate it highly, sir. But there is no immediate likelihood of his doing anything. I am informed by this unfortunate young woman that he is at the present time, drunk, sir, dead drunk in fact.

"She will be aboard the noon train long before he awakens. I have no doubts about her safety. You may be interested to know that I have given her letters to people in New York who will see to her welfare."

"Yeah—but!" Hammond choked at the little man's simplicity. "Look yere, Bishop; I wasn't thinkin' so much about her; only kinda incidental-like. Hits mos'ly you I'm a-thinkin' about. You've gotta live right yere, ain't ye? Well, then, all's I gotta say is, gosh sake, heel yo'self. Kin you do anythin' tall with a gun? I s'pose not. Good land amighty! Hev ye stopped to think what that ——— roarin' son of a gun'll do to you?"

The bishop looked pleasantly up at his big friend who loaned him his dance-hall and bar to conduct services in whenever he spent a Sunday in Carnation. He smiled like a child.

"As I said before, it is extremely kind of you to take this interest, Mr. Hammond. I may tell you that I am not unmindful of my own personal safety. Perhaps you did not know that before I entered the ministry I studied law."

Hammond interrupted. He spoke as a person speaks to a lovable but very inexperienced child.

"Lord love ye, Bishop! This yere aint no question of law. Don't you see? You're dealin'-in with a sharp an' a bad egg. What's this yere Shadwell care 'bout law Good land!"

Ed Hammond threw up his hands in a hopeless gesture. The bishop was incapable of understanding the situation.

The bishop merely continued to smile like a child.

"You misapprehend me, I am afraid, Mr. Hammond. What I meant to convey was only this: That in my study of the law I was frequently confronted with the maxim, 'Never cross a bridge until you come to it!' You see, while I am very grateful to you for your thought of me, yet, after all, we are anticipating, are we not? I fear you are crossing a bridge before arriving at it, Mr. Hammond. Just now Shadwell is in no condition to do anything. He may even remain unaware of what has become of this unfortunate young woman. He is not very popular, is he? There is no occasion for anybody to tell him of my small part in the matter, is there?"

Hammond took his departure abruptly at this point in the conversation. He could not trust himself to speak again without profanity, so strong were his feelings at this moment. He did not wish to use profanity in the bishop's presence.

The bishop continued placidly, twenty-one inches to the step, toward his little house, his mind on his unfinished letters.

Hammond proceeded straight back to Peterson's store, gathered the loafers together, and discharged his mind.

"An' if any of yo' shoats," he ended, "opens yo' traps about it, the old man's cooked, I'm a-tellin' ye; an' if that heppens, by the gosh-amighty, they'll be two more folks full of lead in this yere meetro-polis, the same bein' that there skunk Shadwell an' the saphead that spills a word to him!"

Peterson promised to see to it that old Joe kept his mouth tight shut.

Clark Shadwell's first inquiry took place late that night. He was cold sober when he walked into the Gopher Hole, and he said little. Reluctantly convinced that nobody there knew anything about the subject of his inquiry, he was nonplussed. Shadwell's imagination did not reach the possibility of any one's shipping his light o' love out of town. If she hadn't gone back to her old life at the Gopher Hole she must necessarily be in some other man's house, or dead. As the days succeeded one another, and no evidence of Rosie's being above ground in Carnation, the conviction grew upon him that she must have met accidental death in some form; or, possibly—well, she had more than once hinted at doing away with herself.

The bishop was away from Carnation for several weeks at one stretch, during the rest of the month, and when he returned Shadwell had made up his mind that if he had lost Rosie, at least no other man was hiding her out.

On a certain Tuesday afternoon the bishop and several other persons were in Peterson's store waiting for the contents of old Joe's mail bags to be sorted and distributed. The bishop received his letters and opened the first two or three that came to hand while talking to some of his acquaintances. He glanced through the contents and dropped the envelopes into the waste-box which stood near the central stove.

As soon as he was gone, Clark Shadwell who was present poked at the trash in the waste-box. Then, stooping, he picked out a stamped envelope, which had caught his eye. It was the kind of envelope already stamped, and with three dotted lines in the upper left-hand corner, along with the words: "If not delivered in ———— days, return to ————"

In these blank spaces were written a New York address, and the name, Rose Hollister.

Shadwell spelled this out carefully, then, quickly crumpling the envelope, he dropped it back in the waste-box and, without a word to anybody, walked out of the store and, unhitching his cayuse, loped off in the direction of his shack at the town's edge.

As soon as he was gone, Ed Hammond picked out the crumpled ball and, straightening it out read what Shadwell had read. Then, with a suppressed oath, he started for the bishop's house.

The bishop, urbane as always, listened to his fervid second warning.

Clark Shadwell knew! By Rose Hollister's foolishness, and the bishop's innocence, there was no further concealment possible, and, as Ed graphically imparted it, ——— was about to bust loose.

Was the bishop heeled?

"Goshamighty! Here! Take this! Pack it constant, too! Goshamighty!"

Hammond left, too full of wrath and concern for the bishop's safety to trust himself for further utterance, and the bishop picked up gingerly, and examined curiously, the small, compact, double-barreled derringer he had left on the table.

That evening Doc Ellis had a hurry call to the bishop's house, and the next day the Carnation *Tocsin and Range Bulletin* carried a circumstantial account of how the chief ecclesiastic of the territory had slipped and fallen on the floor of his famous bathroom, the bathroom his predecessor had installed, with a patent ram which pumped water from the creek, and a straining apparatus which removed part of the alkali mud from the water, and broken his right arm. The paper referred to this injury as a compound fracture, this descriptive item being furnished by Carnation's leading scientist, Doc Ellis.

The next day the bishop with his right arm in elaborate splints and a sling concocted of many rolls of bandage, went uncomplainingly about his affairs, and to all inquiries responded with the cheerful statement that his injury was nothing—

"Just nothing at all, thank you."

How he managed for the subsequent days to dress would have puzzled Carnation if Carnation had been critical of such matters. But Carnation wasn't critical and, as Ed Hammond pointed out scornfully to one curious customer of his at the Red Horse—

"That there old bishop don't have to tie no necktie like other Easterners, 'cause he wears one of them purple dickies."

To Hammond's importunities to watch his step, the bishop always returned assurances of his complete immunity from danger, and cited the fact that Shadwell had made no hostile move whatever against him. All Shadwell knew from having read Rosie's envelope was that Rosie had got away to New York and had written to him. There was no necessary connection between those facts and his complicity in her escape.

On Friday of that same week, the bishop received his mail as usual and carried it home with him. Later in the evening he returned to Peterson's store to cash his check. Shadwell and several others were at the store. Peterson handed the bishop his bills, and the bishop placed them with his free left hand in the left-hand pocket of his neatly pressed black trousers, and took his departure after greeting pleasantly everybody in the store.

Shadwell left within a minute afterward, and as there was no one present who could guess that anything was in the wind except Peterson himself, his exit excited no comment whatever. Peterson, greatly worried, and unable to leave because he was alone in the store, sent a boy for Hammond.

Hammond arrived in a minute or two, and Peterson whispered to him that Shadwell had trailed the bishop out.

Hammond sprang out of the door and hurried down the street toward the bishop's house. Past the lighted section of the main street he hastened and broke into a run as soon as he had left this behind him. As he ran he slid his holster around on his belt, and loosened its flap.

The bishop was out of sight, and there was no trace of Shadwell, but Ed had noticed his cayuse still tied to the rail in front of Peterson's when he rushed out, and knew that Shadwell must be afoot, and not far away.

He found the bishop's house in darkness, as he slowed his pace on arriving before it, and looked, with a worried expression, at the unlighted windows. He came nearer, walking stealthily now, his hand on the butt of his forty-five. He started to walk around the house, and as he neared the first corner, he heard Shadwell's voice suddenly and stopped, drawing his gun, just within the concealing shelter of the house's edge.

It occurred to him that at his usual gait the bishop had had just about time to reach his house, and had gone around to the door at the farther side which he commonly used; Shadwell had probably taken the other side of the road, and had managed to pass the bishop on the way, unobserved in the dark. He had been waiting for the bishop around the corner of the house, and had confronted him there. That was it! He, Hammond, had managed to arrive just in time!

Hammond edged himself along against the rough wall of the little house, ready to intervene at an instant's notice.

He heard clearly Shadwell's ugly snarl, low-pitched as it was, around the corner of the house.

"I said shove up yo' han's, ———— yo'! Shove 'em up, now, right sudden—'way up—or I'll blow yo' to ————!"

"But, my dear sir"—it was the bishop's clear voice—"can't you see that it is out of the question? I cannot move my right hand because it is bandaged tight."

"Then shove up yo' good arm—*pronto*, now—yo' mis'ble li'l pup yo'!"

Ed Hammond stepped softly around the corner. He had guessed, correctly, that the bishop would be facing him, Shadwell standing so as to present his back, facing the bishop. He saw Shadwell's back and slouching shoulders, and the little bishop beyond him, his free left hand and arm perpendicular, the huge white bandage which confined the other conspicuous in the dimness of early evening. Shadwell was edging up toward the bishop, his gun held upon him.

What could he be up to, exactly? Then Hammond saw through it. He was intending, first, to secure the roll of bills. When he had once got that safely away from the bishop, he could easily overcome the slightly built, elderly and now disabled little man. He would not risk the sound of a gunshot.

Hammond raised his forty-five.

But he was very unexpectedly interrupted. There came from close at hand a roar which made him jump, and ruined his steady aim.

Shadwell had shot down the little man after all.

Ed plunged forward. A gun was too good for Shadwell. He wanted to get his big powerful hands on him and choke the miserable life out of his worthless carcass.

He stopped, confused in the dim light. The figure which he had dimly perceived as it tottered and fell to the ground in a limp heap lay almost under his feet. It writhed and rolled about, and from it there came a steady stream of profanity.

At a little distance there stood the bishop, busily engaged with his left hand in unwinding the huge bandage from his right hand and arm.

"What the—" gasped Hammond.

"Ah, it is you, is it not, Mr. Hammond?" said the bishop. "You quite startled me, I assure you."

He threw the loosened bandage to the ground and, transferring from his right hand to his left the double-barreled derringer from which a thin wisp of acrid smoke yet rose, he handed the deadly little weapon back to its rightful owner.

"Doctor Ellis was very obliging," remarked the bishop, rubbing his cramped right hand which had just discharged the derringer through the bandage. "He took great pains with this arrangement. You see, Mr. Hammond, I have been for years unused to firearms, and so I could take no chances. That is why I waited until Shadwell came so close that I could hardly miss. I shot him—accurately, I think—through the right shoulder, so as to disable his gun arm. I hope I have not injured him too severely."

Around the corner of the house came a confused group of men, in the lead, Tom Hankins, a deputy sheriff, carrying a lantern in one hand, a glistening blue-barreled forty-five in the other.

"What's all this rannikaboo?" inquired Hankins in a voice of authority.

By the light of the lantern the bystanders envisaged the scene. They looked at the bishop, the bandage on the ground; they sniffed the sharp smell of burned cloth which rose from the crumpled bandages. Hankins, stooping over, hauled the still cursing Shadwell roughly to his feet. His right arm hung helpless. One of the men picked up his undischarged revolver and looked at it curiously.

"You come along with me to the calaboose, Shadwell," said Hankins grimly. "We've had our eyes on you for some time and now I reckon we've got you to rights."

Hankins led away his captive, the other men closing in around them as they wended their way back toward the calaboose.

The bishop looked at Ed Hammond who stood, his jaw hanging, and again the bishop smiled like a happy child.

"I cannot help wishing that I had not been obliged to resort to such an expedient, Mr. Hammond," he remarked, as he picked up the bandages and turned toward his house, "but you may remember that we are exhorted in the Scriptures to combine the harmlessness of doves with the cunning of the serpent! Good evening, Mr. Hammond, and thank you very much."

A DEAD CLUE

DAVID NOWINSON

There was a timid knock upon the door. People who came to visit Nails Sperry didn't usually knock. They walked right in and, if they weren't welcome, they were carried out.

Again a timid knock. Nails Sperry looked down the length of his cigar and grinned. There was only one man who would knock.

"Come in," Nails yelled.

Young Roland Curtis slid hesitantly into the unprepossessing place. The room reeked with the merged fumes of cheap tobacco and cheaper liquor. The one electric light, placed near the door so Nails might see his visitors before they saw him, was covered with dust, casted a wan yellow light as if it, too, felt sick in that foul atmosphere.

These things young Curtis sensed before he saw the man who had sent for him. Nails Sperry sat on the bed looking as hard as his name. He wore a pearl stickpin in his tie. Curtis noticed that.

"Sit down and take a load off your dogs," Nails ordered.

Curtis sat down upon the one chair in the room.

The racketeer stared contemptuously at his guest for a moment. This tall young fellow with the blond hair and the sensitive mouth he had long ago set down as "one of them pretty boys without guts."

"Have a shot of shellac," he invited, dragging a bottle and two glasses from beneath the bed.

He filled the glasses and gave one to Curtis. Curtis sniffed at it and shuddered. In the old days, when his father was alive, there had been bourbon and champagne on the table.

He passed the glass back to Sperry. "Thank you. Don't think I'd better. Too early in the day for me."

Nails spat upon the floor and drank both glasses down. "Never too early for me," he said.

"I don't know why you sent for me," ventured Curtis nervously, "but if it's money, I haven't a cent. You promised me the last time that you wouldn't ask for any more."

"Wait a minute, wait a minute," said Nails. "I'm not asking yet, see? So don't get wise or tomorrow the rags'll be yelling it all over town how your old man chiselled money from the bank before he bumped himself off."

Young Curtis clenched his fists and said nothing. Too late he had discovered how a little knowledge may be a very dangerous thing in the hands of a man like Sperry.

"You still got the pearl necklace, ain't you?" shot out Nails suddenly.

"Yes, but I'm not permitted to dispose of it—as I told you. The will—"

"Yeah, you sobbed out all that hooey before. Well, I don't want you to give me the pearls, see? I just want the use of 'em for a while."

"But why—"

A crafty look came over the racketeer's face.

"Pearls come from oysters, don't they? Oysters are dumb, see? I'm going to send them pearls back to the oysters."

"What do you mean?"

"The rocks are insured, ain't they?"

"Why, yes."

"How much?"

"Fifty thousand dollars. The Runtham Company."

Nails Sperry licked his thin lips. "Fifty grand! Sweet, sweet. Fifty grand from the oysters." His voice changed, took on a menacing note. "Now here's what I want you to do, see? Telephone your jeweler you're sending the pearls through the mail—registered letter, see?—to get the clasp fixed. Then you appoint me your agent to collect and handle all your insurance, see? That's all. I do the rest."

"But the pearls?" protested Curtis weakly.

"You scram home and get 'em for me. I'll give 'em back in three days. Might even give you a cut on my take."

"But how—"

"That's something you wouldn't get hep to," said Nails. "Ever see Mickey Mouse?"

"Of course. Why?"

"Good guy to watch," said Sperry in a tone of dismissal. "Now scram and cart the rocks right up."

When Roland Curtis returned, Nails Sperry ran his hands covetously over the gleaming pearl necklace. Then he handed Curtis a thick brown envelope.

"What's in it?" Curtis inquired.

"That's your pearls, see?" Nails leered. "You'll have that letter registered and you'll send it to your jeweler. Don't try to open it because I know how I fixed it up and you'll screw the works if you fool around, see? Just phone the jeweler and send it right out. In three days you get your pearls and I get my fifty grand, see?"

Roland Curtis didn't see, but he said nothing.

"It's fool-proof, this scheme," boasted Sperry. "It took some work in the old noodle. Now do what I told you."

The blond young man left the room for the second time that morning. . . .

Curtis wanted to open that envelope. A nameless fear stopped him. He wasn't afraid for himself. For Nails to expose what he had threatened, however, besmirching his dead father's name, seemed to Curtis the rankest kind of sacrilege.

The envelope, he thought, was rather thin to hold anything almost as valuable as the necklace. There was something soft inside, as if rolled in cotton. He wondered.

At home, Curtis phoned his jeweler as Nails had instructed. He did something Nails had not instructed, too. He placed the envelope under a large unabridged dictionary to fasten it so that an address might be written more easily. And he signed not his own, but Sperry's name and address before having the letter registered and mailed.

There were three in the delegation that visited Nails Sperry's room next day. Young Roland Curtis led the way. Admitted, he entered, followed by the other two.

Sperry's face darkened as he saw them. "What's the big idea?" he snarled. "Who are those guys?"

"Sorry," said Curtis apologetically. "Awfully rude of me. This is Postal Inspector Danney and this is Federal Agent Smith."

The men bowed. Nails Sperry scowled. He didn't appreciate good manners.

"Well, what do they want here?"

"It's about that letter you sent, Mr. Sperry," said Federal Agent Smith who was a mild little man with sandy hair.

"Me? You're screwy! I didn't send no letter," snarled the racketeer.

"It had your name and address on it," said the mild-mannered Smith. "And besides, what about San Francisco?"

"Well, what about it?"

"In 1929," said Smith reminiscently, "a similar situation occurred in Frisco—with a diamond ring. An insurance company there paid you four thousand dollars because the letter in which you'd mailed the ring for repairing, arrived with a hole in the envelope, explaining the ring's absence. Very neat. There was no substantial evidence at the time, Mr. Nails Sperry, but we've kept you in mind."

The racketeer edged towards the bureau.

"Keep away from there," ordered Smith. A gun flashed in his hand. "You want to give me a chance to finish my story. Inspector Danney will take care of your gun."

Inspector Danney opened the bureau drawer and obliged.

"This letter that should have contained the pearl necklace," continued Smith, "arrived this morning at the Townsend Jewelers. Oddly enough, it contained a dead mouse."

"Dead!" cried Nails hoarsely.

"Yes, it had smothered somehow. Strange, wasn't it? Normally a live mouse gnaws its way out of a letter in a hurry."

"Mickey Mouse would have done a better job," contributed Curtis.

The racketeer wheeled upon him. "Smart, ain't you? Maybe you won't be so smart when I get done talking about what your old man—"

"Where you're going," interrupted the Federal agent softly, "you won't have a chance to talk for a long time. Uncle Sam will see to that. And people don't trust convicts these days."

Inspector Danney, who had been rummaging about the bureau, handed Curtis a string of pearls now.

"Thanks," said Curtis as they led their prisoner away. "You know, they say that pearls come from oysters."

"That's right," agreed Federal Agent Smith. "But oysters are pretty dumb."

DEAD
MAN'S DROP

R. VAN TAYLOR

The sound of the door buzzer didn't merely awaken Carl Munson—it jerked him to an upright position in his sweat-soaked bed. Shading his eyes from the sunlight which streamed through the window, he glanced across at the clock on the dresser. It was ten minutes after three.

Groggily he slipped into a robe. At the dresser he ran a comb through his thinning hair. Then, turning slowly, he walked with hesitant steps into the living room of the shabby apartment.

The buzzer beckoned again.

Munson's hand reached slowly for the latch. Several distinct thoughts filled his mind as he wavered indecisively.

First, it might be that the caller was Middleton. Middleton was the man at the employment agency. As much as Munson disliked the prospect of work, he had gone there several days ago and dropped the word that he was open for the right kind of position. The kind that paid ten times more than a man was worth and would offer an opportunity to knock down plenty on the side. But it wouldn't be Middleton; he'd use the phone.

Second, it was possibly the landlord. Damn him! Munson had told the fat fool that he would pay him his rent in a few days. These money leeches would suck every ounce of blood from a man's body if corpuscles came in the shape of dollar signs.

The buzzer still vibrated in its irritating, impersonal manner.

Then, it could be Barrett.

Munson touched his wet forehead with trembling fingers, trying to erase those agonizing memories—memories of his deal with Barrett and the golden Buddha and a woman's body at the bottom of the Pacific. But this couldn't be Barrett. No. He was still in Honolulu.

Cautiously Munson released the latch and opened the door.

It was Barrett.

Munson cringed, expecting his body to be filled with the ripping, deadly slugs from a pistol. But nothing so fatal took place, only something more puzzling. Barrett stood in the doorway with a good-natured smile on his fleshy face. His six-foot frame was expensively dressed, and beneath his arm he carried a tin box.

"Well, aren't you going to ask me in?" Barrett said.

Munson was completely puzzled. He stepped back quickly. "Yes," he said. "Yes, of course. . . . It's been a long time, Barrett."

"Not so long. Only a year."

Barrett cast an uncritical eye around the room. Munson pulled the edges of his robe tighter over his chest and silently cursed the ragged furniture, dirty ashtrays and messy floor.

Munson stammered, "I—I'm glad to see you. You're looking good."

"Thanks," Barrett replied, extending his hand to shake.

Munson took the hand. A strange vibration shot up his arm. He jerked away rapidly.

Barrett broke into a fit of laughter and at the same time withdrew a small gadget from the palm of his hand. He said, "It gives you quite a scare, doesn't it?"

Munson flushed. "You and your damned jokes! You never will outgrow that kid stuff, will you, Barrett?" Then he added awkwardly, "How about a drink?"

"Sure. Let's have one for old time's sake."

A cabinet stood against the wall. Munson opened it and took out several bottles. Every one of them was empty.

"Have you been drinking lately?" Barrett asked.

"No, it's just that I need to go to a store. I think there's another bottle in the bedroom. I'll go get it."

Munson went into the bedroom. He moved quietly to the dresser and slipped open the top drawer. He pulled out a .32 revolver, dropped it into the pocket of his robe and stuffed a handkerchief on top of it. Immediately he felt a sensation of ease replace his nervous tension.

Grabbing the fifth from the night stand, Munson returned to the living room. "How long are you going to be here?" he asked, pouring a couple of shots.

"That depends. I came over about three weeks ago on the Matsonia and have been staying with some friends out near Stanton Cliffs. Nice place, the cliffs. I go there almost every day, look out over the Pacific and listen to Mildred's voice. It comes with the breakers."

Munson swallowed hard. "How did you know I was here?"

Barrett grinned, "Mildred told me. . . . You thought I was going to kill you, didn't you?"

The color drained from Munson's face. He set the drinks down and turned to Barrett. His hand dropped into the pocket of his robe. His eyes suddenly got narrow.

Barrett continued, "Wouldn't I have grounds for killing you, partner? In case you're rusty, let me review the deal for you.

"A year ago you sold me your half of our clothing store in Honolulu. I paid you $5,000 then with the agreement that I would pay another $5,000 in a year. When you left for the States you took something besides the money. You took my wife. But Mildred never lived to reach this country."

"I didn't have anything to do with that!" Munson protested. "She followed me. I didn't know she was on the ship until we were at sea. I told her that she had made a serious mistake. That she should go back. I thought it was all settled. Then she vanished."

Munson picked up his glass and downed the whiskey. Then he added, "The ship's log reads that she committed suicide by jumping overboard."

"That's a lie. You killed her. Just as I should kill you."

"It was suicide! *You* drove her to it. She couldn't stand you and your damned practical jokes. You were always embarrassing her and her friends. She would have gone with anyone to get away from you!"

Barrett shrugged. "No use getting excited," he said quietly. "Hashing over the past will gain neither of us anything, and besides, I'm here to pay you off."

"You mean you've brought the $5,000 that you still owe me?"

Barrett said, "I failed in Honolulu, went broke. For some reason I couldn't keep my mind on the store. Now there's only one thing of value I have left. It's something you've always wanted and tried to get from me many times. It's easily worth $5,000. In this box, which I have brought with me, you have what is coming to you."

"You don't mean the golden Buddha?"

"After I'm gone you can open it and find out."

"Is it the Buddha?" Munson couldn't help it if his voice sounded greedy. The idol would bring enough money to get him out of the hole. He could get out of this rat-trap, go to some small town and start life over again.

"I didn't say what was in it," Barrett answered. "That's for you to find out."

"You fool."

Munson snatched the box from Barrett. He started to open it.

"Don't!" Barrett shouted.

The warning paralyzed Munson for a second. He laid the box down suspiciously and looked at Barrett, who was now on his feet backing towards the door.

"What's in that box?" Munson demanded. He jerked the pistol from his robe and leveled it at Barrett. "Tell me!"

Barrett reached for the doorknob. "You wouldn't shoot me," he said. "And by the way your hand is trembling. I believe you'd miss me even if you did pull the trigger. You haven't got the guts to be really bad."

"Damn you, Barrett! Tell me what's in that box!"

Munson was pointing his gun at space. Barrett had slipped through the door and silently disappeared down the hall. Munson's arm, which was still pointing the gun, collapsed against his side. Slowly his head turned back to the room and his bewildered gaze fell upon the box.

Munson stood still and thought for a moment. If he had not known Barrett so well, he would have gone to the box and opened it. But Barrett was a very clever man. It would be just like him to turn this whole thing into a big but fatal joke. Barrett could have easily rigged a bomb in the box, or anything else that would do away with him. He wouldn't travel all the way from Honolulu to give the golden Buddha to his worst enemy.

The more Munson thought about it, the more he was convinced that Barrett had something up his sleeve. Carefully picking up the small heavy box, he went into the bathroom and started filling the tub with water. As soon as the tub was full he would submerge it. Then, if it were a bomb, it would be rendered harmless. And if it turned out to be the Buddha, a little water wouldn't hurt it.

While the tub was filling, another thought crossed his mind. What if the water was just the thing to set it off? What if he started to soak the box and then the whole thing blew up in his face? No, he wouldn't use water on the box.

A sensation of helplessness passed through him as he took it back into the living room. His eyes went to the window and a smile formed on his drawn face. *There* was a way of getting rid of it, he thought. Why not toss the thing out of the window and be done with it?

Rapidly he walked to the window. He grasped the box with both hands and started to throw it. In his mind he could clearly see it exploding on the pavement below. Explosion? No! Munson didn't want an explosion here. It would bring an investigation. The police would come. He didn't want to see them.

Perspiration popped out on his face as he tried to think. Maybe he was jumping at conclusions. But he had to be sure. How could he . . .

The telephone rang and Munson flinched.

The sudden noise had frightened him, and his heart was pumping furiously. He set the box down cautiously and went to the phone. Picking up the receiver, he mumbled, "Yes?"

It was Barrett's voice, and he said, "Is that you, Munson?"

"Yes. Where are you?"

"I'm in a bar a couple of blocks down the street." Then he chuckled and added, "You haven't opened the box yet, have you?"

"No. How did you know that?"

"Take all the time you want, Munson. Think it over real carefully. *Think about everything!*"

"Barrett, you've got to tell me! Barrett? Barrett!"

The phone was dead.

Munson grabbed the telephone directory and flipped through the pages. There was only one bar nearby, the Black Cat. He found the number and dialed the phone. A nasal voice answered, "Black Cat. Bartender speaking."

Munson said, "There was a man who used your phone a moment ago. Is he still there?"

"Nope. He just left."

"Could you catch him for me? It's important!"

"Look, mister. I'm here by myself. I can't leave."

"Did he say where he was going?" Munson asked like a plain damn fool.

"People don't tell me their business," the bartender replied impatiently.

Munson dropped the receiver back into the hook. Where was Barrett going? Where, where, *where?*

Stanton Cliffs! Of course, that was it. He had mentioned staying with some friends who lived near there, and that he went to the cliffs every day. But maybe Barrett had given him this information purposely; maybe it was a trap and Barrett wanted to lure him there to kill him in case this infernal machine failed.

Munson's hand tightened on the revolver in his pocket. No, if it were a trap he'd not be the one who would die.

Hurriedly he formed a plan. He would take the box and drive out to the cliffs. If Barrett was there he would force him to tell about the box. But if everything failed he would hurl the thing into the sea. It was an ideal place. The cliffs stood in an isolated location along the coast. If it were a bomb and exploded, no one would be the wiser.

An hour later Munson pulled his blue coupé to a stop at the edge of Stanton Cliffs. It was a barren, desolate place where the earth dropped off into the endless depths of the sea. Looking behind him he could see speeding cars on the highway some three hundred yards away. At this moment he was the only one there.

Munson felt miserable because he had misjudged Barrett's next move. He was filled with indecision. Finally he came to a conclusion. He'd get rid of that damned box and have it off his mind!

Cautiously he removed the box from its secure riding place in the seat of the car. He walked to the edge of the cliffs and peered over the dizzy heights. Two hundred feet down the vertical wall of jagged stone he could see the surf pounding viciously upon the narrow, grey beach. It was a long, long drop.

He tossed the box over the edge and ran back towards the car.

Munson heard the tin box strike stone. There were a series of clashing sounds as it bounced about on the rocks. But no explosion.

Frowning, he walked back to the edge of the cliffs and looked down. He gaped as a tiny, brilliant highlight from yellow metal glistened on the narrow strip of rock and sand below. It was the golden Buddha.

He lowered himself over the edge and started the perilous descent. All he could think about was that idol. It was his! It was money! It was everything he needed!

Halfway down he began to grow tired. His hands were slippery from sweat, and his aching feet could no longer find toeholds in the perpendicular mass of solid rock. He could neither go up—nor down. He became frantic.

Then he heard the motor of an approaching car. He called for help. He yelled for it at the top of his voice.

The distorted shape of a man appeared at the top and gazed languidly at Munson.

It was Barrett.

"Help me!" Munson cried.

"Why should I?" Barrett said. His voice seemed far, far away.

"I'll confess," Munson called back. "I killed Mildred. Killed her because she wouldn't have me. After we were on the ship she told me that you were the one she loved. That she was insane to have left you. She was going back to Honolulu as soon as we docked. I killed her and threw her body overboard. Now help me!"

Barrett stood firm.

"It's all a gag, isn't it?" Munson asked frantically. "It's another one of your jokes. You aroused my suspicions about the box. You knew I'd try to get rid of it. You've had your laugh. Please!"

Barrett didn't move.

Munson screamed, "I can't hold much longer! *Do something!*"

"I've already done it," Barrett answered. "I've paid you off. Only that's not the real Buddha down there. It's just a cheap imitation— like yourself."

And Barrett left.

And Munson's fingers began slipping . . . slipping . . . slipping . . .

DEAD MEN TALK

ERNEST C. AMARAL

The body was sprawled on the floor like a grotesque, inanimate doll discarded by a fickle child. A trickle of blood oozed from its head. It seeped slowly into the dark, uncarpeted floor planking, making it darker still.

The killer had recovered from the first emotional surge of shock that followed completion of his planned crime. He made a careful search of the dead man's bedroom. For days, he had been torn by the fear that his blind employer might have guessed his intentions. The blind had an uncanny ability for sense impressions. It was as if they sent out invisible antennae to perceive waves of emotion.

His search allayed his fears. Everything in the room was placidly and mutely at peace with the world. Nothing screamed a revelation of unnatural horror. The dead man's clothes hung emptily in the closet. The old ship's radio uniform with the gold on the sleeves stood out sharply among the dull, prosaic wear of everyday existence. Over the fireplace mantel, the gleaming fishing rod testified silently to the old man's interests. It had been his pride. An "enchanted wand," he had called it. Fish came to it like iron filings to a magnet. Even his good friend, the sheriff, had gruffly and testily admitted its magical powers as he returned empty-handed beside his laden fishing companion.

The killer left the room. He set about rearranging the picture of death in the kitchen. He lifted the dead man's head then dropped it with a sickening thud against the heavy, metal stand holding the fire-irons. The blood stained it a dull lusterless red like cheap, thin paint. He picked up the poker that had been the murder weapon and washed it in the tin sink of the farmhouse. Returning to the fireplace, he worked it back and forth in the hot ash powder before replacing it in the stand.

He kicked over a footstool. Several other touches completed his work. The picture still held the aura of death. However, instead of murder, it now suggested an unfortunate accident. A blind, old man had tripped and cracked his skull open. It was as simple as that.

The killer now reached down and clawed at several of the bricks forming the hearth. He withdrew the old man's hidden hoard, which he had discovered by accident. The square, metal box contained the money for which he had killed. He went outside and buried it behind the barn. Returning, he checked his setting, a little smile of satisfaction easing the sullen grimness of his mouth. He left, closing the door behind him softly, as if not to jar any piece of his setting out of place. He started out on the long walk to the town. The devoted manservant was going to report the accidental death of his employer to the authorities.

"Hello, Ned."

The startled killer whirled to face the man standing in the doorway. Sheriff Tom Taggart's face was heavy and solemn even in natural repose. Now, an added sadness gave it the morose look of a bloodhound contemplating the enigma of human behavior.

"I just got in from that conference out in Chicago," the sheriff said. "They told me about Bill at the office."

The killer was prepared for this moment. Knowledge of the sheriff's departure had set his murder plan into motion. He nodded silently to the other, secure in the knowledge that the authorities had written off the death as an accident.

The sheriff entered the room, pausing uncertainly in its center. His eyes took in the worn leather chair that had been the old man's favorite.

"I'll miss him, Ned," he said huskily.

He walked into the dead man's bedroom. The other felt a nameless fear coil up tightly inside himself. Unreasoningly, his heart fluttered wildly, like a trapped, panic-stricken bird. He waited for the sheriff to emerge. The moments drew out, and time seemed to be suspended in a vacuum. His eyes were riveted on the bedroom door.

"Sheriff," he croaked hoarsely, "Sheriff, you all right?"

The sheriff appeared in the doorway. "Sorry to leave you like that, Ned. I kinda got lost in thought."

Ned's eyes were held by the long, gleaming rod that was clutched in the sheriff's hand.

"I thought I'd take it along," the sheriff explained. "Bill and I joshed each other so much about it. It will almost feel like having him around again."

Ned shook off the stiff, wary watching that held him. "Sure, Sheriff. I understand," he said. "I guess Bill would have wanted you to have it."

The sheriff crossed to the door. He started to open it, then paused. "What are you going to do?" he asked.

"Guess I'll be moving on," Ned answered casually. "I didn't know what to do about this stuff." He waved at the room's furnishings. "Now that you're here. I guess you'll know how to handle it."

The big, morose man nodded, pinching his lip reflectively. "How soon you going?"

"A day or so."

"I'll drop by before you go." The sheriff went out the door and Ned heard him drive away. Relief flooded over the killer like an insurmountable wave. He dropped weakly into a chair.

Two days later, Ned knelt in the center of the room, tugging at the strap of his suitcase. With a grunt he fastened it and straightened up.

The sound of a car stopping outside held him momentarily still. There was the slam of a door and the crunch of footsteps approaching. The door swung open and Tom Taggart entered.

" 'Lo, Ned." The sheriff's eyes noticed Ned's suitcase. "Leavin'?"

"I was figuring to," Ned answered. Silently, he cursed his luck. He had planned to be gone before the sheriff's arrival.

The sheriff crossed to the suitcase and picked it up. "I'll drop you off. It's the least I can do for a good friend of Bill's."

Ned stared sharply at him. There was a curious edge to the sheriff's voice.

"Comin'?" he called back over his shoulder.

Ned mentally damned his imagination and followed Tom out to the car. They drove off in silence.

Just outside of town, the sheriff spoke. "Got to drop by my office. You don't mind?"

Ned shook his head. A curious sense of desolation swept over him.

They pulled up at the office, a two story red-brick building containing cells for prisoners. Tom Taggart came around to Ned's side and opened the door. "Come on in. I got something to show you."

They entered the building and went into a small room, sparsely furnished with a desk and two chairs. A little, baldheaded man was seated behind the desk.

The sheriff spoke to him. "I'll have that paper now, Pete."

Pete nodded and reached into an open drawer of the desk, silently handing a folded document to the sheriff. He gave it a perfunctory examination then handed it to Ned. "Guess you'll be interested in this," he remarked in an ominously soft voice.

The two stared at each other over the paper. Ned reached dumbly for it and read the black, staring print on the front of the document. Words stood out on the white paper, words that wavered and shimmered like something alive. Ned reached up to wipe away the mist that clouded his eyes. The words came into focus. WARRANT OF ARREST—NED RANDOLPH.

The next half hour was a blank in Ned's mind. There had been the paper, and now it was the cell with a cot in the corner and a high barred window above his head. He sat heavily on the edge of his cot. They knew he had killed his employer. That, he had been able to retain. But how? The question kept plaguing his mind. How?

A shadow fell across his face. He looked up to see the sheriff. His mouth opened.

"You're wondering how we found out, aren't you, Ned?" The

sheriff spoke through the bars. His expression was more doleful than ever. "I don't mind telling you. Bill told us."

Ned looked blankly into the sheriff's eyes. He shook his head in an effort to clear it. "I don't understand."

"Bill left a message."

"He couldn't have. I made sure. I searched everything."

"Everything except the one thing Bill knew I would want," the sheriff rejoined. "You neglected the fishing line, Ned. The reel was tied in a series of knots. That seemed like an odd thing for a fisherman like Bill to do. I noticed the knots had an orderly pattern. After that, it was easy to figure out."

Ned's jaw hung slack and a dazed expression held his face. "Knots? I don't understand."

"Morse code, Ned," the sheriff answered. "Ever hear of it? There are many ways to send a message with it besides tapping out what you want to say. You had a bad break there. You killed a man who had once been a ship's radio officer. He knew—with the uncanny sense of the blind—what you were up to before you committed the crime. He knotted a message on the fishing line knowing that I would want the rod as a keepsake."

"Morse code? Message?"

"The knots represented dots and dashes. It took me a little while to figure out which was which. Want to hear Bill's last words, Ned?" The sheriff withdrew a piece of paper from his pocket. " 'Money under fireplace. Ned knows. Means to kill me.' "

The sheriff looked grimly at the trapped killer. "A message from the grave, Ned. You can kill a man, but that doesn't stop him from talking."

DEATH'S
OLD SWEET SONG

GEORGE WILLIAM RAE

They rode to the prison together, Sam Lester, the big Homicide Lieutenant, and Craig Manton, the girl's lawyer, in Manton's long, sleek car.

"It would pick this night to rain!" Sam Lester said.

Craig Manton had been drinking, and he was in a surly mood. "It doesn't matter," he said. He watched the rain dance on the windshield. "Why do they have to pick *me?*" He spat out suddenly. "*I* don't want to see the damn thing!"

Sam Lester rubbed his blue-tinged jaw. "They're not too bad," he said through his cigarette smoke. "Just a couple jerks against the straps, a little bit of a smell—and it's all over. They're not too bad."

Craig Manton swung his head around. Sweat stood out on his forehead.

"You're used to this," he said. "That's why I wanted you with me. That's why I called you." He turned back to the road. "But a girl. . . ."

"So what?" Sam Lester asked. "She killed a man, didn't she?"

Craig Manton, the girl's lawyer, watched the wet asphalt stream into the headlights beneath the pelting rain.

He licked dry lips, recalling the afternoon that Sam Lester had spent in the lawyer's office when they heard that the governor had refused to grant a stay. . . .

Craig Manton had done the best a lawyer could, but Sam Lester's men had pulled the net too tight.

The girl had been found with the body. The gun was on the floor, where she'd dropped it, her prints on it. Just those two, in her dressing room. They hadn't heard a shot. It was lost in the blaring music. The band leader had gone back to see why she didn't come out for her number. He found her standing over Spook Slade, the man she was supposed to love. Slade had been murdered.

Bluebird was the name she sang under. She had lived up to it, singing the blues as they should be sung, from the heart . . . not the lips.

Sam Lester was a straight dick. He could do nothing but let the cards fall as they would. The girl was found guilty by a jury which couldn't buck those cards. The death penalty was mandatory.

Craig Manton swung the car up before the prison gates.

"Execution witnesses," Sam Lester told the guard who peered through the rain-streaked window. In a moment they were inside, entering the warden's office.

Warden Kelly, a tall man with white hair, pink cheeks, gravely inspected their credentials. His face showed strain. Bluebird was the second woman he'd had in his death house. He knew what it would be like.

Lester and Manton sat on hard chairs, stared at blue-gray walls, stark and clean.

"This is murder," Sam Lester said.

Craig Manton looked at him. "What d'you mean?"

"I mean the girl here is innocent."

"But it was your evidence. . . ." Manton began.

Sam Lester raised a big hand. "I'm a copper, Manton," he said. "I had to go through with it. The evidence forced me to. Still, I think the girl is innocent."

"But you can't prove it," Manton said.

"As I've been telling you all day, Manton, if I could prove it I'd be up with the governor myself."

Manton lighted a cigar, puffed blue smoke up into the hot, sick air of the room.

"I'm not through with this case," Sam Lester said. "Whether the D.A. likes it or not."

Cigarette smoke swirled above the heads of the men in the little room and Sam Lester sat quietly waiting, smoking, talking softly to Craig Manton.

"I had to take her," he said. "All the cards were against her. You knew her defense. 'I didn't kill him. I found him there. Yes, I picked up the gun from the floor where it was, dropped it when I realized. . . . I didn't kill him, he was no good, but I loved him . . .' Then about her past. About Bluebird being strictly a press agent stunt. Her name was Marion Maxon and she came from Groveton, Pennsylvania. Just a kid with a husky voice and a heart that belonged to a no-good hoodlum."

"That was it," Manton said. "What could I do for her? What could any attorney do for her?"

Lester kept talking as if he didn't hear Manton. "About the gun," he said, "there was something about the gun. One piece of evidence that didn't tie in. The D.A. never used it. Had enough, he said. So I kept it. I wondered about it. A funny little thing, just a piece that didn't fit. I kept it and it tantalized me, told me that someone had framed that girl. Someone very smart."

Sam Lester stopped, lighted a cigarette. Watched the smoke fan out from his lips.

Manton was looking at Lester, tight lipped. "You mean you had evidence that you withheld?"

"It wasn't withheld. It was turned over to the D.A. It just didn't fit in."

"What was it?" Manton asked.

Lester didn't have time to answer. He was called to the telephone.

He went into the other room to answer it and Manton sat back, smoking and waiting. . . .

Sam Lester came back with the warden.

"It is time, gentlemen," Warden Kelly said quietly. His humanity was in his eyes; his face was lined. He had a job to do. He was acting in accordance with the dictates of the law. He had no choice.

They went outside then, into the lashing rain, across the prison yard to the Death House, down a long corridor and into the execution chamber. The cub reporter followed, nervously inhaling a bent cigarette.

There were benches for them to sit on beneath a sign marked SILENCE, and the grim instrument of justice at the other end—the chair, stark and fearsome, waiting for the kill.

Sam Lester and Craig Manton sat in the rear row. Despite the sign, Lester still talked in a low soft voice, charged with high excitement.

"My men are giving me a hand," Lester was saying. "That was Sergeant Conroy on the phone. They went over that alley in the rear of the *Blue Moon* again with a fine comb. They found a shell from the .32 that killed Slade! He must've been killed in the alley, carried inside, and the girl is right—she *did* find him that way!"

"It's all theory," Craig Manton said. He was a shrewd lawyer, knew his evidence. "The governor wouldn't—"

"Yeah, I know," Sam Lester said bitterly.

Manton wiped his mouth with the back of his hand. He looked tired, worn.

He took a flask from his pocket, drank deeply. He replaced the flask in his pocket, then carefully wiped his lips with the cobalt-blue handkerchief which he always wore in the breast pocket of his coat.

"Conroy is checking one last lead," Sam Lester said. "If it works out, I'll be able to put the finger on the real killer."

Sam Lester took one more telephone call in the autopsy room off the execution chamber. He was back quickly.

"The warden is calling the governor one last time," he said. "We found out about an angle the D.A.'s investigating attorneys muffed, or passed up. There was another guy. A big shot. He was trying to make a play for Bluebird. I think I can pin it on him. We found out this other guy was being blackmailed by Spook Slade and that he was nearly broke and half-crazy because Bluebird wanted no part of him. He killed Spook Slade and put the frame on Bluebird."

Craig Manton took another drink. "What're they waiting for?" he asked.

Lester said, "The warden. He'll be back in a minute. Then he'll either go on with it or keep her in the cells. It all depends on what the governor says. I tied in that last piece of evidence. The warden knows that, too. That funny little thing that bothered me so much. I tied it in."

Manton said, "I can't stand much more of this."

"It won't be long," Lester said. His dark eyes were half closed. "Take it easy."

Manton had his flask out again. "I can't stand it."

"Take it easy, you got nothing to worry about. You're not going to the chair."

Manton swung around savagely. "No, I'm not. But *she* is."

"Maybe," Sam Lester murmured.

"Maybe—*maybe!* Why don't they get it over with? Damn it, I can't stand it!"

"You're not going to the chair." Lester's voice was a low monotone.

Manton's sullen eyes blazed suddenly. "And damn you, too!" he cried. "You've been playing cat and mouse with me all day! I see it now, you've been sweating me, working on my nerves. I see it now!"

A rumble rose from the men on the benches. They turned and stared at Manton and Lester. Sam Lester was smiling. He said nothing.

"God knows what you've dug up," Manton went on, his voice rising. "You wouldn't let well enough alone. *Let the girl die like I planned for her to die!*"

Manton stopped and stared around, wide-eyed. "Yes, I killed him because he was sucking me dry and keeping her away from me! He had a hold over her. She wouldn't give me a chance. . . ."

Sam Lester was on his feet as were all the men in the execution chamber.

"You were the one who arranged for me to be a witness," Manton screamed at Lester. "You fixed it, didn't you, you devil! Well, you're coming with me!"

A gun glittered in Manton's hand. He swung it toward Sam Lester.

At that instant a sharp blue flame darted from the police positive of Lester's man—the detective who had been masquerading as the cub reporter.

Manton's gun became a great weight in his hand. He dropped it and staggered back, eyes wide. Slowly he folded to the death chamber floor, gasping out his life.

Sam Lester bent over him, "Get the doc," he said tersely.

Lester took the cobalt-blue handkerchief from Manton's breast pocket and an envelope from his own. The blue thread in the envelope matched the blue of the handkerchief.

Sam Lester looked down at Craig Manton.

"It was on the gun, Manton, when you wiped the prints off. Just that blue thread, caught on the sight. Just a little blue thread to tie you up for Hell. . . ."

THE
DEBT COLLECTOR

MAURICE LEVEL

Ravenot, debt collector to the same bank for ten years, was a model employee. Never had there been the least cause to find fault with him. Never had the slightest error been detected in his books.

Living alone, carefully avoiding new acquaintances, keeping out of cafés and without love affairs, he seemed happy, quite content with his lot. If it were sometimes said in his hearing: "It must be a temptation to handle such large sums!" he would reply quietly: "Why? Money that doesn't belong to you is not money."

In the locality in which he lived he was looked upon as a paragon.

On the evening of one collecting day he did not return to his home. The idea of dishonesty never even suggested itself to those who knew him. Possibly a crime had been committed. The police traced his movements during the day. He had presented his bills punctually, and had collected his last sum near the Montrouge Gate about seven o'clock. At the time he had over two hundred thousand francs in his possession. Further than that all trace of him was lost. They scoured the neighborhood and the waste ground that lies near the fortifications; the hovels that are found here and there in the military zone were ransacked; all with no result. As a matter of form they telegraphed in every direction, to every frontier station. But the directors of the bank, as well as the police, had little doubt that he had been lain in wait for, robbed, and thrown into the river. Basing their deductions on certain clues, they were able to state almost positively that the robbery had been planned by professional thieves.

Only one man in Paris shrugged his shoulders when he read about it in the papers; that man was Ravenot.

* * *

Just at the time when the keenest sleuth-hounds of the police were losing his scent, he had reached the Seine by way of the Boulevards extérieurs. Under the arch of a bridge he had dressed himself in some everyday clothes he had left there the night before, had put the two hundred thousand francs in his pocket, and making a bundle of his uniform and satchel, had dropped the whole, weighted with a large stone, into the river and had returned to Paris. He slept at a hotel, and slept well. In a few hours he had become a consummate thief.

Profiting by his start, he might have taken a train across the frontier, but he was too wise to suppose that a few hundred kilometers would put him beyond the reach of the gendarmes, and he had no illusions as to the fate that awaited him. He would most assuredly be arrested. Besides, his plan was a very different one.

When daylight came he enclosed the two hundred thousand francs in an envelope, sealed it with fixed seals, and went to a lawyer.

"Monsieur," said he, "this is why I have come to you: In this envelope I have some securities, papers, that I want to leave in safety. I am going for a long journey and I don't know when I shall return. I should like to leave this packet with you. I suppose you have no objection to my doing so?"

"None whatever. I'll give you a receipt."

He assented, then began to think. A receipt? Where could he put it? To whom entrust it? If he kept it on his person he would certainly lose his deposit. He hesitated, not having foreseen this complication. Then he said easily:

"*Mon Dieu*, I am alone in the world without relations and friends. The journey I intend making is—not without danger. I should run the risk of losing the receipt, or it might be destroyed. Would it not be possible for you to take possession of the packet and place it safely among your documents, and when I return I should merely have to tell you, or your successor, my name?"

"But if I do that . . ."

"State on the receipt that it can only be claimed in this way. At any rate, if there is any risk, it is mine."

"Agreed. What is your name?"

He replied without hesitation:

"Duverger, Henri Duverger."

* * *

When he got back to the street he breathed a sigh of relief. The first part of his program was over. They could clap the handcuffs on him now; the substance of his theft was beyond reach.

He had worked things out with cold deliberation on these lines: on the expiration of his sentence he would claim the deposit. No one would be able to dispute his right to it. Four or five unpleasant years to be gone through, and he would be a rich man. It was preferable to spending his life trudging from door to door collecting debts! He would go to live in the country. To everyone he would be Monsieur Duverger. He would grow old in peace and contentment, known as an honest, charitable man—for he would spend some of the money on others.

He wanted twenty-four hours longer to make sure the numbers of the notes were not known, and reassured on this point, gave himself up, a cigarette between his lips.

Another man in his place would have invented some story. He preferred to tell the truth, to admit the theft. Why waste time? But at his trial, as when he was first charged, it was impossible to drag from him a word about what he had done with the two hundred thousand francs.

He confined himself to saying:

"I don't know. I fell asleep on a bench. . . . In my turn I was robbed."

Thanks to his irreproachable past he was sentenced to only five years' penal servitude. He heard the sentence without moving a muscle. He was thirty-five. At forty he would be free and rich. He considered the confinement a small, necessary sacrifice.

In the prison where he served his sentence he was a model for all the others, just as he had been a model employee. He watched the slow days pass without impatience or anxiety, concerned only about his health.

At last the day of his discharge came. They gave him back his little stock of personal effects, and he left with but one idea in his mind, that of getting to the lawyer. As he walked along he imagined the coming scene.

He would arrive. He would be ushered into the impressive office. Would the lawyer recognize him? He would look in the glass; decidedly he had grown considerably older and no doubt his face bore traces of his experience—No, certainly the lawyer would not recognize him. Ha! Ha! It would add to the humor of the situation. . . .

"What can I do for you, Monsieur?"

"I have come for a deposit I made here five years ago."

"Which deposit? . . . In what name?"

"In the name of Monsieur . . ."

Ravenot stopped suddenly, murmuring:

"How extraordinary . . . I can't remember the name I gave!"

He racked his brains . . . a blank! He sat down on a bench, and feeling that he was growing unnerved, reasoned with himself:

"Come, come; be calm! Monsieur . . . Monsieur . . . It began with . . . which letter? . . .

For an hour he sat lost in thought, straining his memory, groping after something that might suggest a clue. . . . A waste of time. The name danced in front of him, round about him; he saw the letters jump, the syllables vanish . . . Every second he felt that he had it, that it was before his eyes, on his lips. . . . No. At first this only worried him; then it became a sharp irritation that cut into him with a pain that was almost physical. Hot waves ran up and down his back. His muscles contracted; he found it impossible to sit still. His hands began to twitch. He bit his dry lips. He was divided between an impulse to weep and to fight. But the more he focused his attention, the further the name seemed to recede. He struck the ground with his foot, rose and said aloud:

"What's the good of worrying? . . . It only makes things worse. If I leave off thinking about it it will come of itself."

But an obsession cannot be shaken off in this way. In vain he turned his attention to the faces of the passersby, stopped at the shop windows, listened to the street noises; while he listened, unhearing, and looked, unseeing, the great question persisted:

"Monsieur? . . . Monsieur? . . ."

Night came. The streets were deserted. Worn out, he went to a hotel, asked for a room and flung himself fully dressed on the bed. For hours he went on racking his brain. At dawn he fell asleep. It was broad daylight when he awoke. He stretched himself luxuriously, his mind at ease; but in a flash the obsession gripped him again:

"Monsieur? . . . Monsieur? . . .

A new sensation began to dominate his anguish of mind: fear. Fear that he might never remember the name, never. He got up, went out, walked for hours at random, loitering about the office of the lawyer. For the second time night fell. He clutched his head in his hands and groaned:

"I shall go mad!"

A terrible idea had now taken possession of his mind; he had two hundred thousand francs in notes, two hundred thousand francs, acquired by dishonesty, of course, but his, and they were out of his reach. To get them he had undergone five years in prison, and now he could not touch them! The notes were there waiting for him, and one word, a mere word he could not remember, stood, an insuperable barrier, between him and them. He beat with clenched fists on his head, feeling his reason trembling in the balance; he stumbled against lampposts with the sway of a drunken man, tripped over curbstones. It was no longer an obsession or a torment, it had become a frenzy of his whole being, of his brain and of his flesh. He had now become convinced that he would never remember. His imagination conjured up a sardonic laugh that rang in his ears; people in the streets seemed to point at him as he passed. His steps quickened into a run that carried him straight ahead, knocking up against the passersby, oblivious of the traffic. He wished that someone would strike him so that he might strike back; that he might be run over, crushed out of existence. . . .

"Monsieur? . . . Monsieur? . . ."

At his feet the Seine flowed by, a muddy green, spangled with the reflections of the bright stars. He sobbed out: "Monsieur? . . . Oh, that name! . . . That name! . . ."

He went down the steps that led to the water, and lying face downward, worked himself toward the river to cool his face and hands. He was panting . . . the water drew him . . . drew his hot eyes . . . his ears . . . his whole body . . . He felt himself slipping, but unable to cling to the steep bank, he fell. . . . The shock of the cold water set every nerve a-tingle. He struggled . . . thrust out his arms . . . flung his head up . . . went under . . . rose to the surface again, and in a sudden mighty effort, his eyes starting from his head, yelled:

"I've got it! . . . Help! Duverger! Du . . ."

The quay was deserted. The water rippled against the pillars of the bridge; the echo of the somber arch repeated the name in the silence. . . . The river rose and fell lazily; lights danced on it, white and red. . . . A wave a little stronger than the rest licked the bank near the moving rings. . . . All was still.

A Devil's Highball

G. Fleming-Roberts

Fortunately, Gavin Clark considered the whole affair calmly, else the thinning walls of his aorta might have been broken, and its rushing, red cargo of life would have been given up. Since the doctor had told him that he might live nearly a year longer, if he avoided excitement, he had taken everything calmly—even the unfaithfulness of his wife.

Perhaps he had got used to the idea of death. Perhaps that is why he had contemplated murder with greater passiveness than a society woman contemplates another tea.

Since that evening when Clark had unintentionally overheard a conversation between Randolph Shortly and Madeline Clark, he had plotted coldly and impassionately. It was to be simple—this murder, for only simple murders succeed. In the one week that Randolph Shortly had been staying at the Clarks' he had shown himself to be a hog for drink. That fact alone simplified matters. Then at the inquest, it would be called suicide. Clark would see to that.

Gavin Clark took a piece of paper from his pocket and for the eleventh time compared the writing on it with the writing on a letter that Shortly had sent from the mountains. Clark chuckled. He could have made fortunes at forgery, he thought. He had wisely written it on a sheet torn from Shortly's note book. It ran:

Dear Madeline:

What I saw in your eyes last night makes it impossible for me to go on living. Without you, I can't live; yet with you I could never face the sun. There is one honorable way out. I have taken it.

Clark chuckled again. He hadn't attempted a signature. It would have been tricky and entirely unnecessary.

He pocketed the note and drew a small vial from his pocket. The white and red label read:

TRIOXIDE OF ARSENIC—DEADLY POISON!

Rat poison it was and to be used on a rat.

Rat! Clark thought that was putting it rather mild. Had he not been Shortly's best friend, "rat" would have done nicely. But he *had* been Shortly's best friend. It was he, Gavin Clark, who had staked Shortly when Shortly had been broken in health and finance. It was Clark who had sent Shortly to the mountains to regain his health. And Shortly *had* regained his strength. He was now disgustingly healthy—for through the green eyes of a chronic invalid, health is disgusting. This man—this Randolph Shortly, had returned from his mountains to steal another man's wife; and at that, a man who had one foot—nay, more than that, in the grave.

Tonight would be the time. Madeline had to preside at some sort of a club meeting. Shortly would be far gone in drink. Clark would prepare a friendly night-cap that would be a cup of true darkness, and all would be over.

Why hadn't Madeline and Shortly had the decency to wait until he was dead? But no; he was glad he had learned the truth, for now Shortly would pay!

Even at that moment, Clark could make out the voices of Madeline and Randolph coming in low blurred tones from the sun-room. Perhaps they were arranging the details of their flight. He wanted to hear what they were saying; yet he feared that some sentence would arouse passions that would hasten that rupture which spelled death. No; he must live—live to attend Shortly's funeral.

Thus, determined to put eavesdropping beyond temptation, Gavin Clark took up his hat and wandered out into the garden.

Let them talk! He knew the truth.

Unfortunately, Gavin Clark didn't know the truth. Had he listened to that conversation between his wife and Randolph Shortly, the arsenic would have found its way down the kitchen drain; for at the moment that Clark left the garden door, Randolph Shortly was waging the one decisive battle of his pampered life.

"Don't you see, Madeline," Shortly was saying, "I *can't* do this thing to Gavin! Can't you realize what a real friend is? Can you imagine the man you love being weak enough to take advantage of that friendship? Everything that I have I owe to Gavin Clark. Yet, you would have me betray him in order that we might go away together."

He paused, watching the lovely shoulders of this woman; watching every movement of those shoulders, shaking with sobs; trying to watch them as he would have watched the shoulders of a marble statue shaken by a quake.

His victory over himself was complete. He understood her now. She had been a child of love and had become a woman of love. The wound that he had created would soon be healed. He decided to leave on the morning train. He would never see her face again—except in dreams.

Night came quickly for Madeline and Randolph, but slowly for Gavin Clark. Madeline had given up all thoughts of going to her club, but she could not endure her husband's roof for that night. She would go to her sister's for the weekend.

How this decision pleased Gavin Clark! How it relieved Randolph Shortly!

Two hours of cribbage with drinks. Two hours of drinks without cribbage. Four hours all told and Randolph Shortly gazed over the rim of his glass at two Gavin Clarks.

Gavin was a good pal, but there wasn't any use of there being two of him. Now if there had been two Madelines. . . . Shortly's thoughts were becoming tangled.

With a hilarity that was genuine, though not drunken, Clark extended one of two tall glasses towards Shortly.

"Come on, Ran," he urged; "you're not going back on me? Have this last glass with me, won't you? Just what you need to pull you up the stairs."

"S' help me!" Shortly gurgled.

The mud-sloven swine! thought Clark.

"S' help me! Never went back on a pal yet. Not goin' to now."

Clark's right hand held two glasses—two glasses that were Siamese twins. Two swell glasses in one hand. That was funny, Randolph thought.

"Where 'n hell zit?"

"Right here," said Clark, drinking from his own glass.

"Shur?" Shortly seized at the twin glasses with both hands. The liquid slopped as he raised it to his lips.

Clark stood watching the man's Adam's apple slide up and down as he gulped.

"Good stuff!" exclaimed Shortly as he crumpled into his chair, his head and shoulders flopping on the table.

It sounded like the carcass of a dead cat being thrown over the alley fence, thought Clark.

Gavin had no idea that arsenic worked so fast. Perhaps Shortly was only asleep. Anyway, he wouldn't wake up in a long time.

Clark took the empty arsenic vial from his pocket and placed it on the table. Then he took one of Shortly's clammy hands and pressed it against the bottle.

So much for fingerprints! Now for the note!

He placed the scrap of paper on the table near Shortly's glass. Then he tiptoed up the stairs.

He was glad the house was new. He hated creaking floors.

Chuckling softly, he made his way to his own room, undressed, and got into bed. He went to sleep almost instantly—for murderers *do* sleep.

How long Clark slept he did not know. It was still dark when he awoke. But why had he awakened? What was the rushing sound that seemed to come from his pillow, or even from his own ears?

His heart!

The thought boomed on his brain.

But why did it murmur so loudly in his ears? What was that noise —that noise in the hall?

Clark listened intently—as intently as he could with that terrifying lub rushsh—lub rushsh sound in his ears.

There was something walking—walking up and down the hall outside his door. Something that walked as Shortly had walked. It was the same stride that had taken Shortly up the highest peaks of the mountains.

And Shortly was lying dead below, Clark kept repeating. There were four lethal doses of arsenic in his belly!

Gavin stared dry-mouthed at the darkness.

Lub rushsh, went his heart.

He must get up! He must see who walked with Shortly's walk, up and down the hall! Quickly out of bed! Quickly press the light switch! Quickly open the door!

Dry-mouthed, Gavin stared into the dimly lighted hallway.

God! It was Shortly! Shortly's ghost?

Lub rushsh—lub rushsh—rushsh—

Not a cry escaped Gavin Clark's lips as he tottered and fell at Shortly's feet.

Shortly glared half-drunkenly at the clay thing on the floor.

"So you'd poison me, huh? Make out I'd killed myself, huh?"

Clark didn't hear. He would never hear.

"Poison me, would you!" Shortly's voice shook. "Dam' lucky for me I've been taking big doses of arsenic regularly up on those mountains to strengthen my wind and ease my nerves. You get used to that stuff after a while. Gavin, you must be crazy!" He kicked gently at the body.

"Takes all the arsenic in hell to poison an arsenic-eater!"

DOUBLE DEMON

WILLIAM FRYER HARVEY

George Cranstoun put down the newspaper to watch more closely the two women who sat in the shade of the cedar on the far side of the lawn.

He had decided that the time had come to inform them of his decision. Its success would depend on his reading of their characters. Were they, in a word, capable of entertaining the idea of murder? He thought they were.

He looked at his sister Isobel reclining on her chaise lounge, sixty years old, very much an invalid, an aristocrat to her finger tips, used to giving orders, relentless, not unconventional but above conventions, a woman who could keep a secret and proud, devilishly proud. Unprincipled?

Well, if to stick at nothing for a principle was that, he supposed she was. The good name of the family was what Isobel cared for most in the world. Provided that were safe she could be trusted to keep silent.

And Judith? A beautiful woman, Judith. More beautiful since his sister had persuaded her to stop wearing her nurse's uniform. Clever, too, as clever as they make them, and a born actress. She knew how to get her own way right enough and had patience to wait for it. A hard, unscrupulous woman. Isobel had made a mistake in keeping her on when she had really no need for a full-time nurse. Half nurse, half companion was an obviously unsatisfactory arrangement. They were bound to get on each other's nerves.

He wondered sometimes if Judith shared a secret with his sister, and that Isobel hated her for this. So much the better if it were so. It would make his task easier.

There was a movement of the chairs on the other side of the lawn. Isobel was going in to rest. Judith picked up the books and cushions and followed her.

George lit a cigarette. It was hot in the garden, infernally hot. From where he sat in the old stone summer-house his eye took in the long low front of Cranstoun Hall with its white portico. There were too many trees about the house, he told himself. They shut it in on every side except where the gardens sloped down to the park with its lake and templed island. All right perhaps in spring, but in late July the deep green of the foliage was too sombre. Far too many flies about too. A wind ought to blow through the place and there was no breath of wind.

Ah, there was Judith!

He got up and crossed the lawn to meet her.

"What about a stroll in the rock garden?" he said. "There's something I want to talk to you about."

"I don't mind where I go as long as you give me a cigarette. What's the matter, George? You've been moody all day. Is anything worrying you?"

"You can't expect me to be my brightest and best in this infernal heat, but what I've got to say is important, damned important, and you've got to listen. I've loved you now—how long? We can't marry, as things are at present, there's no chance of it."

Judith gave him a curious smile.

"Have I said I wanted to marry you, George?"

"Not in so many words, but we understand each other very well. You've made it clear that you don't want to flirt with me. That's policy."

"Well, perhaps it is."

"Anyhow I love you."

"And if I say that I don't love you?"

"Policy again. You sympathize with me, don't you?"

"I'm awfully sorry for you."

"But you do sympathize. You understand me better than I do

myself. And I've kissed you, not nearly as many times as I want to and as I hope to do, and you've put up with it. Now let's be frank. You are poor, ambitious, unscrupulous. (I know all about your going through my letters.) You've played up to Isobel, making out that she is far worse than she is so that you could keep your job.

"I want you badly and since it's the only way, we must marry. You'd like the job of running this place, and you'd do it damned well. You would make an excellent hostess. Isobel has lost all interest in that side of things, with the result that we are shunned as if we had the plague. We could travel too and rent a villa on the Riviera. You'd enjoy a flutter at Monte Carlo.

"All this to me is a delightful prospect. But I can't marry you while Isobel lives. She treats me like a boy. You know my father left me practically nothing. She got everything; she's rolling in money, and I'm her dependant. She's so madly jealous of me that I can't even invite my friends here without first asking her leave. She grudges me any new acquaintance I might make. She barely lets me out of her sight. You agree?"

They had reached the rock garden. Judith sat down on a seat by the side of a miniature cascade, dabbling her fingers in the cool water.

"You've put the case very clearly, George, but it doesn't seem to get us much further."

"Exactly. We are up against a dead wall. Isobel must go. She's been ill now for months. She can't get much pleasure out of life. Years ago she tried to commit suicide—news to you, but it's true all the same. We can get a great deal of pleasure out of life on certain conditions. I shall help her to go."

"How?" said Judith, still dabbling her fingers in the cool water of the cascade.

George lowered his voice as he told her how.

"And when?" asked Judith.

George told her when.

"And you'll swear," she said after a pause, looking him straight in the eyes, "that it won't be before?"

"Yes, I swear it won't. It may be later because it depends on a number of things. But it won't be before."

"And Isobel won't suspect?"

"No, I shall tell her a story about you. She'll think it's *you* I am going to put out of the way. There's something secretive about Isobel, something she wishes to hide from me, and I think I know what it is. She's jealous of you, she hates you. As I said, she has never got much out of life and you, the daughter of a clerk in Balham, have, and are going to get more.

"So now you know all about it, my beautiful Judith," he went on. "In a year's time you'll hardly know this place. We shall be entertaining the gayest of house parties and you doubtless will be flirting with someone a little more presentable than your friend Dr. Croft. It appeals to you? I see it does. Well, all you have to do is to keep quiet and leave the rest to me. If you have finished washing your hands we will go back to the house."

Dinner that evening was more than usually silent. Judith complained of a headache. Nurse companions are not expected to suffer from headaches. "Too long an exposure to the sun, my dear," said Miss Cranstoun acidly. "You should wear a hat." George did little to keep the conversation going. His interest centered in the decanter.

They adjourned to the library. Judith, refusing coffee, made letter-writing an excuse for an early withdrawal, and the two Cranstouns, brother and sister, were left alone.

"George," said Isobel, "you drank far too much at dinner. You know very well you are supposed to be on a definite regimen. If you can't keep to the amount stipulated we shall have to give up wine altogether. I don't want to do that. The servants will draw their own conclusions, but you can't go on as you have been doing."

"Don't be a fool, Isobel," George replied. "For a clever woman your obtuseness sometimes amazes me. You keep me on the leash, you treat me as a boy, you give me no responsibility, and then expect me to find complete satisfaction in life. But I'm not going to quarrel with you. I have other far more important things to talk about. If I told you I wanted to marry that Wentworth girl what would you say?"

"Impossible, George. You hardly know her."

"That's not my fault. You take such precious care nowadays to prevent our making new friends. You have no objection to her family?"

"Of course not. They are as old as ours. But you can't marry her."

"I'm inclined to agree with you. Judith, for one, would prevent it."

"Judith? What on earth has she got to do with it?"

"More than you think. Judith is a very clever woman and her chief cleverness is in hiding her cleverness. You made a big mistake, Isobel, in keeping her on so long. There was really no need."

"I've certainly been much better the last month, but I'm not well."

"She sees to that."

"Now what exactly do you mean, George?"

"I'm suggesting that Judith, who after all has ample opportunities, takes care, to put it mildly, that your progress should not be too rapid. Do you like her?"

"She is a competent nurse."

"And as a competent nurse she knows the value of drugs. Of course you don't like her, Isobel. You know she gets on your nerves, you know you hate the way she orders the servants about and treats the place as if it belonged to her. She thinks it will some day. I suppose you haven't noticed that she's been setting her cap at me?"

"I don't believe it."

"It's true none the less. At first I rather liked the girl, but when I found that she had been tampering with my letters and was proposing to use blackmail, if necessary, for a lever, I revised my opinion. I can't afford to be blackmailed, Isobel. We can't afford it."

"But George, she has nothing to go on."

"I wish I could think that. You remember that keeper, Carver, whose daughter worked in the dairy? He bought a pub down in Wilton. That's settled all right, I fancy. She won't get much change out of him. But there are other things too. And it seems that my father . . . Well, anyhow, for the sake of the family's good name I've decided that we shan't be troubled with Judith much longer."

"I engaged her, George, and it is I who shall dismiss her."

"I wasn't thinking of dismissing her, not in your way." He cast a glance behind his shoulder and drew his chair nearer to his sister's. "What I really was thinking of was—"

"And why, George," said his sister at last, "do you tell me this?"

"Partly because your help is necessary; much more because I have no wish to go through life with an unshared secret. Yours is a stronger character than mine. We shall need each other's support in the future even more than we have done in the past."

"But Judith; won't she suspect?"

"No. That will be the last thing she will dream of doing."

He told her why.

"And, George," said Miss Cranstoun faintly, "it's a thing I ought to know, it's an awful thing to ask, but . . . when?"

George told her when.

"And now," he said, "I'll say good night. There are one or two things I want to do."

George Cranstoun locked the door of his room, and taking a key from his pocket unlocked a cupboard. He took down a bottle of whisky from the shelf, poured himself out a stiff peg, and drew a pack of patience cards from a drawer in the writing desk. Things on the whole had gone very well. He had been right in his surmise. Judith and Isobel were capable of entertaining the idea of murder. Altogether an intriguing situation.

Very carefully he put out the cards and began his game of Double Demon. It would be a good omen if luck were with him to-night. Eleven o'clock struck, twelve o'clock. The cards would not come out. Half an hour after midnight he went to bed, and when the clock struck one he was sound asleep.

But when the clock struck one Isobel Cranstoun was wide awake. She had locked her bedroom door. Judith Fuller was wide awake. She, too, had locked her bedroom door, but the communicating door between Isobel's room and Judith's was unlocked, unbolted.

George Cranstoun smiled in his sleep.

In the garage at Cranstoun Hall there were three cars, the Daimler, an Austin seven, and a capacious bus-like vehicle built to old Mr. Cranstoun's orders, which, despite the fact that it was supposed to serve a number of useful purposes, was seldom used. George told the chauffeur that it would be wanted early in the afternoon to go into Totbury. Miss Cranstoun had arranged for the indoor and outdoor staff to visit the County Show. They were not perhaps as appreciative as they might have been had the notice been longer. McFarlane would have liked more time to overhaul the engine, the upper housemaid might have arranged for her new dress to have been delivered earlier; the cook, had she known, would have arranged to meet her cousin; Mr. Brown, the head gardener, had some job or other that wanted doing while the fine weather held.

It was, however, characteristic of Miss Cranstoun to make a sudden decision to arrange for other people's pleasure, and Totbury Show had many attractions. Only Woodford the butler, and Mrs. Carlin the housekeeper, chose to remain behind. Mr. George, said Miss Cranstoun, had planned a picnic tea on the island in the lake. They would want only a cold supper.

George spent the morning down by the boathouse, while his sister and Judith took advantage of his absence to hurry over the packing that was necessary for his journey. Each was conscious of a certain restraint, and they worked in silence.

George removed the padlock from the bar that locked the boat-house and got out the punt. It was a good punt, though it badly needed a coat of varnish. The punt was provided with two poles. One was all that would be required, and one paddle. The second pole and paddle he placed in the corner of the boat-house. He brought out cushions from the locker and placed them in the sun to air; then getting into the punt he kept along the reed-fringed side of the lake until he was opposite the island. The island with its solitary poplar and grey stone temple almost hid the hall. Almost but not quite. He could still see the upper rooms of the east wing and the end of the terrace walk. The risk was negligible. From the bank to the island, from the island to the bank, four times he made the double journey, on each occasion varying his approach. Finally, he fixed on his course; the lake was deep enough there and the bottom muddy. It would all happen in the most natural way. Judith, seated at the far end of the punt, would like to try her hand with the pole. Isobel would say that it wasn't really safe to change places out in the lake. They had better wait until they reached the island. But, of course, it would be quite safe if they didn't hurry over it. And then he would lose hold of the pole just as Judith was creeping along, there would be a sudden lurch, and . . . George Cranstoun remembered the pictures he had seen of methods of rescuing the drowning. The method that appealed to him most was that in which the rescuer, swimming on his back supported the head of the drowning person with his hands and held it just above the level of the water. In this case it would be just below.

A gallant attempt at a double rescue.

George Cranstoun smiled.

An early lunch. Then the departure of the bus for Totbury. At half-past two the unexpected arrival of Dr. Croft and another doctor to see Isobel. Judith, of course, has to be present at the interview.

"But why are they so long about it?" thinks George, as he paces the terrace. "There's nothing much the matter with Isobel." He had heard nothing about getting a second opinion. The absurd secretiveness of women. Anyhow, he might as well fill in time by carrying down a few extra cushions to the boat-house.

What was Woodford doing hurrying after him like that, poor old Woodford with that hang-dog face of his?

Dr. Croft would like a word with him in the library? To blazes with Dr. Croft, but he supposed he would have to see the man.

In the library with his back to the empty fireplace, stood Dr. Croft. He did not appear to be at ease, and glanced up at his companion as if he expected him to take the lead. "Dr. Hoylake," he said stiffly, "I don't think you have met him before."

George Cranstoun nodded. He was not interested in Dr. Hoylake.

"It's like this, Mr. Cranstoun," Dr. Croft went on. "We've been having a long talk with Miss Cranstoun, and we have come to the conclusion, and Dr. Hoylake agrees, that for the good of everybody, and not least for your own good, we shall have to make a rather serious break in your life's routine. I don't think it need be for long. Dr. Hoylake, perhaps you would like to explain?"

Dr. Hoylake spoke with slowness and deliberation. George Cranstoun realized what he was saying. He found the idea curiously interesting. It explained much.

As he listened he looked out of the window, across the gardens, across the park, to the lake and the boat-house. Somebody, probably Jackson the head keeper, was quietly putting the punt away.

"Safe for the time being under lock and key," said George Cranstoun. "Well, gentlemen, shall we go?"

EACH NIGHT SHE DIES . . .

WILLIAM BRANDON

The walls in the Kaua Hotel are of bamboo and wood panels. As Jeffrey shaved in the morning he listened to the voices of the man and woman in the adjoining room.

The woman said uneasily, "I wish you'd stop talking about it. It's scary."

"It was only a dream," the man's voice said.

"I think you must have made it up."

A drawer was opened and the man's voice said, "Does this sock have a mate?"

"All husbands are sadists," the woman said.

"Do you know if someone deliberately threw away my socks?"

"You might look in your bag." There was a silence. The woman laughed and said, "Now it makes me feel self-conscious to brush my hair, after that awful dream of yours. You used to say you liked to watch me brush my hair."

"Did you know you put a box of powder in with my socks?"

"Oh, I didn't. It must be yours."

"No it isn't mine. It's yours. It smells to high heaven."

Jeffrey went down to breakfast. He wished he had heard the first part of their conversation. He was curious about the dream with which the man was evidently tormenting his wife. He watched the tourists come and go in the hotel dining room and guessed that this or that sunburned husband and wife might be his unseen neighbors. When he returned to his room in the evening they were gone. Another couple had taken their place. The man's voice sounded querulous and old, and he seemed to be Australian.

In the morning Jeffrey slept late and awakened slowly. He heard the man talking and caught only the words, ". . . it was extraordinarily vivid."

"It gives me the creeps," the woman's voice said.

The man chuckled and said, "I should think it would."

"I do wish you hadn't mentioned it. The things men will carry in their heads."

"Now, my dear, I can't say I thought it up. Simply dreamed it. Altogether different situation." He pronounced it "situwytion." They went out and Jeffrey heard them walk away down the hall. He was extremely interested in their talk of a dream, similar as it was to what he had heard the previous morning. He dressed and went down to the dining room, but he could pick out no one, elderly and Australian, who appeared to resemble the voices he had heard. He was enough intrigued by this dream sequence, he thought, to look up the old gentleman and find some excuse for speaking to him. He went so far as to inquire about the Australians at the desk. The sleek Chinese clerk informed him they were a Mr. and Mrs. Caudle, of New Zealand, sailing at noon aboard the inter-island from Nawiliwili.

"The room is reserved again for tonight," the clerk said. "You do not object? Mrs. Jeffrey is not yet returning from the mainland?"

"Perfectly all right," Jeffrey said. "She won't be back for ten days."

He and his wife had taken the two rooms as a suite, but alone he had no use for both of them. He spent his days on the beach and only slept in the hotel.

"That is very generous," the clerk said. "This is our busiest season."

"Not at all," Jeffrey said affably. "It saves me rent."

He had no opportunity of striking up an acquaintance with the New Zealanders, but the coincidence of dreams occupied his mind for much of the day. He felt frustrated at not having heard what the dreams were about.

He went to bed late but was awake early in the morning. He got up and listened frankly enough at the wall, although he felt that he could scarcely expect to overhear still another discussion of dreams. It was barely sunrise. The green hills of the island were frosted with white mist. All the colors of the world seemed as bright and new as flying sparks. There was no sound from the adjoining room and he decided eventually that last night's reservation had been canceled and that the room was empty. He took a cold shower and was dressing when he heard a woman's voice, a young woman's voice, a childish voice, he thought, say petulantly, "But if you won't tell me I'll always wonder what it was."

A young man's voice said, "You can't tell a dream before breakfast. It's supposed to come true."

"Oh pooh. Drink a glass of water and call that breakfast. And you *were* groaning. You sounded ghastly."

"Well, it was a nightmare."

"But *what* was it?"

Jeffrey moved close to the wall and bent his head, listening.

"Well, it was crazy enough," the young man's voice said unwillingly. "A woman was brushing her hair. I went up behind her and started choking her. She turned around and it was you."

The girl said, "Oh," and after a moment, "I don't see anything so terrible about it. I suppose it's simple dream symbolism and means you feel inferior or something like that."

"Well, it was real as hell, that's all. It was almost as if—well, hell, as if a murder had actually been committed in this room and I could still feel an evil influence here."

Jeffrey's heart gave a heavy thump.

He had planned to wait a week, and this was only the third day. A week would have been better. Safer. Less suspicious.

But a few minutes later he checked out of the hotel. He gave his well-rehearsed explanation to the Chinese clerk, that his wife was not returning to the island, after all, but was meeting him in Honolulu. The clerk was profuse with regrets and alohas but Jeffrey scarcely heard him. He left the hotel and crossed the terrace to the beach and walked toward the airfield. After a few steps he began to run.

EASY KILL

WILLIAM HELLMAN

Rick Haines was a master craftsman. He admitted it. He also admitted to the cleverest brain in the profession; the police hadn't a thing on him because he always planned his jobs well and his plans always worked because they were simple and direct. As now—

He came briskly down the hall, a tall, well-built man, impeccably dressed, carrying a battered brief case. He fore-knew exactly what to do and what to expect when at noon he walked into the fourth-floor office of Acme Finance, and closed the door behind him. The lone occupant, a little gray-haired man, rose hastily and came toward him, said: "I'm sorry sir, but we—"

Rick said not a word. He pushed the little .25 deep under the man's breastbone, fed him two efficient little pills with no more of a report than the pop of bubble-gum, and rolled the body out of sight behind a desk. Then he pulled off the big, black-lensed glasses that were an effective disguise for his small, shrewd eyes, laid his gray fedora on top of them on the desk and went to the unlocked safe where he swiftly and efficiently transferred its more cheering assets to the briefcase. He turned to pick up his hat and glasses and walk out the way he had come, when he froze in amazed disbelief— standing in the open doorway watching him, was a woman. She just stood there with her hand on the knob, a stout, middle-aged woman with gray hair under a little, pertly styled bonnet and blue eyes behind rimless glasses. She was looking at him, her lips parted a little in surprise, as though she had expected to find someone else there.

At the sight of her standing there like that, his well-oiled plans deserted him; he hadn't even remotely considered a chance intrusion. His first wild, blind impulse was to flee, to shoot his way out, but his clever, high-speed brain kept him from making such a fool mistake. He reasoned: she's just standing there, not yelling her head off. So, she just thinks I belong here. I'll get her inside, let her have it, and— He came toward her, smiling, bowing politely.

"Come in, madam," he invited heartily. "We are—"

For a moment longer she just stood there, watching him like a hypnotized bird, shifting her bulk uneasily, trying to see past him into the office. She brought her hands up in a little gesture, as if to make a sign, then suddenly turned and fled.

"Wait!" Rick shouted after her, but she scurried away and was gone before he could grab her. He cursed loud and luridly—she was on to him! He had to catch her and kill her before she got away. She was a living, competent witness who had had plenty of time to memorize his face.

He had the presence of mind to slap his hat on his head, hook his dark glasses on his long nose and grab the briefcase, before he dashed down the hall after her. But the pause had given her time to disappear; he heard the elevator doors clang shut and the car was just dropping out of sight—he knew his ticket to the chair was on it.

He took the stairs in amazing, long-legged strides, almost dropping straight down them. At the street floor, he compelled himself to pause a moment, then go swiftly but sanely through the door into the foyer. The elevator car was loading for another ascent; ahead of him, waddling desperately for the street, was the fat slob who could put the finger on him.

Panic caught at him again. He had to stop her, had to! It was all he could do to keep from shouting at her to stop; he actually started to pull the gun from his pocket to shoot her as she drove ahead through the crowded foyer. She paused once as she came abreast the line of telephone booths, and Rick thought: here it is, she's calling the cops where I can't stop her, here in front of this mob. But she went on, and he guessed without looking that the phones were all busy.

But it was a brief respite at best, a few more steps and she'd be on the street, yelling her head off for a cop. Back in his brain something seemed wrong, for why hadn't she given the alarm before this, to the elevator operator or someone? His quick mind had the answer: she was a woman scared silly and she was beating it for a place of refuge—her home, probably. She'd keep her tongue in silence until she could contact someone she trusted—her old man, likely.

She lumbered out onto the street, paused a moment, while Rick, panicky in his fear and uncertainty, weighed his chances of plugging her right here and running for it, or tailing her. He had no choice; while he hesitated, she popped into a waiting cab and was off down the street.

He had a bad few seconds as he got his car out into traffic, but the drizzling, misty rain helped him, the cabby was a cautious soul and Rick caught up with him two blocks down. He kept close as they threaded through traffic, his eyes glued onto the back glass of the cab, where he could see her huddled and staring back at him repeatedly in her terror.

He smashed the steering wheel a savage blow with his fist and let his rage run free. "The stinking idiot!" he snarled aloud. "I ought to have killed her right there in the office, then I wouldn't have to chase her a couple miles to do it."

They came out onto the wide boulevard and the cab speeded up, but Rick drove carefully, just keeping his quarry in sight; he didn't want to be picked up now. The rain beat steadily against the windshield; the sedate whir of the wiper was company for his thoughts. His master mind was already busily at work planning and as it worked, his rage vanished and his confidence returned. He could handle this job—easy! He'd been right back there—she was holing up somewhere to wait a chance to spill what she'd seen after she got over her terror. And she wouldn't expect the killer to trail her clean out here in the suburbs; she'd figure he was already on the lam. Which was O.K. for Rick Haines.

The cab swung-off the boulevard, went down a quiet, tree-aisled street, lined on both sides by big, box-like houses set back from the sidewalk behind a narrow strip of lawn. Rick swung in, parked the stolen green Chevvy and watched intently; the cab pulled up to the curb half-way down the street, the woman got out, scurried up the walk onto the wide porch. In the half-murk, Rick watched intently and when she used a key instead of ringing the bell, he laughed in pleased confidence, for it meant he had guessed aright— she'd be alone!

He clambered over the seat back, lifted the rear cushion and slid the briefcase back under a mess of papers and old rags he had placed there. He waited a while, then drove boldly down and parked before the house. He got out, swung briskly up the flagstone walk, across the porch and punched the button. He didn't hear the sound of the bell within, so he punched the button again, peering through the curtained glass, and he saw a little light flash off and on somewhere inside in response to his fingered pressure. His lip curled in derision—of all the silly stunts! So the big fool's nerves were too bad to stand the clatter of a bell, eh?

He never had a doubt that his surmise was correct, that she would answer his summons. He waited until she opened the door, stood looking at him enquiringly, then he whipped off the black glasses; she gasped in surprise, her eyes amazed. Her hands came up in a gesture again and before she had the wit to close the door on him, it was too late; he was in the hall, the door closed, the little gun jammed deep against her soft, bulging middle.

Her eyes were big pools of surprised terror.

"Not a peep!" he warned savagely. "So you do recognize me, you blundering idiot! Well, you'll never live to tell it!"

She was paralyzed in her horror, trying desperately to back away from him, her fingers twisting helplessly at her mouth, from which no words would come. He pushed the little gun deeper under her sagging breast, fired twice, the bullets slanting up and to the right. Her clutching fingers clawed at her mouth and face in a gripping spasm of pain and terror; she swayed, then crumpled without a sound.

Rick froze crouching over her, listening—the gun ready in his hand. But no other sound came to him, except somewhere the slow, ponderous ticking of a clock. The shots had made a small noise, like the snapping of a pencil, and perhaps there *was* someone else in another room. He couldn't wait to find out; cautiously he investigated and found no one, and relaxed with a grin.

Swiftly, he executed the rest of his lightning plan. He ransacked the house, turning out drawers and cupboards indiscriminately, spilling their contents in confusion, garnering items of value into a pillow slip.

He came downstairs, dropped the sack of loot with a clatter on the kitchen floor, near the rear exit. He unlocked the door, leaving it partly open, and dropped the little gun nearby. He allowed himself a moment to grin in self-appreciation of his cleverness; the dumb police would lay the crime to a prowler who had killed the woman, ransacked the house, then had been frightened into dropping his loot and escaping out the back door. The little gun could be easily traced to a small-time, misshappen snowbird with a long record.

He went back through the hall to where the woman still lay, a lumpy, sprawling heap. He peered out into the street through the curtain; the rain had stopped, it was wholly deserted and gray in the murky half-light. He put on his glasses, paused, went over and deliberately kicked the woman in the face, laughed and opened the door.

He was half-way through it, when he halted, stunned—a man was coming toward him on the sidewalk, not ten feet from the flagstone walk. A car was parked a little distance behind the Chevvy. Instantly, Rick realized what had happened; he hadn't noticed the other car parked by the trees when he had looked out the curtains, and when he had gone back to kick the woman, the man had got out of it. Who was he? But more important, where was he going? Rick Haines wanted desperately to duck back into the house, but it was too late; the man had seen him.

His master mind came promptly to his rescue. He paused, as though listening to the woman past the edge of the partly open door, said distinctly: "Thank you again, Mrs. Anderson." He almost grinned at the name, he had noticed it on a small plate on her mailbox. He stepped out onto the porch, his hand on the knob holding the door several inches ajar. "I really am sorry. . . ." He paused politely to let her speak, stood listening and nodding, aware that the little man on the sidewalk had slowed, was looking at him curiously. Rick ignored him. "Yes . . . I understand . . . believe me, I'm sorry, too. Well . . ." He laughed ruefully. "Guess I'll have to ask elsewhere. But thank you again. And goodbye," he added gallantly and closed the door behind him, knowing that the spring lock would work.

The little guy on the sidewalk was still looking at him, walking slowly, and a sudden rage flared up in Rick Haines, and he swore silently that he'd be damned if he'd leave a witness this time, no matter how remote the chances of being identified, nor how involved the task of bumping him off. He had cleverly and effectively lulled any suspicions the lug may have had as to his business here, and now to get him into the Chevvy and the rest would be easy. And in his pocket a gun, which he had a license to carry because of his apparent lawful profession, would be enough persuasion. This buzzo was going to die!

He stopped the little man with a word. What a skinny, innocent-looking worm! "Can you please tell me where J. E. Thalmus lives hereabouts?" he asked politely. "Mrs. Anderson tells me she never heard of him at all."

The little man's eye brows went up just a twitch. "Mrs. Anderson said that? Now that is strange—I mean, she has lived here all her life and gets about a lot and knows every soul on this quiet little street. She's a nice woman, Mrs. Anderson; kind and quiet-spoken."

"You know her?" Rick asked and a little alarm bell tinkled back in his brain somewhere. "Yes, she is." Who is this lousy little runt, anyway? Have I seen him some place before? His hand went rigid, hard on the gun in his pocket. He was aware of the little guy's stare, of his quick glance at the bulging hand in his pocket. He laughed. "Well, I guess I'll have to go back for a better address."

He moved a little, looking about to see if any chance window-watcher might see him force the little mug into the Chevvy. Then the peewee surprised him.

"Look," he said suddenly, in a sort of desperate, choked voice, "would you give me a lift downtown?" He laughed ruefully. "That blasted skate of mine there quit on me up the street and I coasted to here."

"Sure, sure!" Rick agreed heartily. "Glad to have you." His heart was singing now—boy, what a break! A solid, hard whack on the buzzo's neck, then drive out along the highway, open the door on that curve and let the body spill out, over the bank in the dark, and into the river below. As simple as that—and the little runt asking for it!

They came down off the quiet, tree-lined street onto the boulevard lanes, then turned west; there were plenty of places along here where he could knock the little guy out before they got into the congested district where traffic was heavy. He'd take it slow. . . .

At an intersection, a cop stood in the renewed drizzle, directing cross-traffic. Rick slowed the car to the required twenty-five; he was too smart to slip up now. But as they approached the officer, the little man suddenly caught at the steering wheel with both hands, heaved with all his puny might. His might was as little as his body, but the maneuver caught Rick off guard because it was totally unexpected. Before his amazed senses could react properly, the wheel spun in his relaxed hands, the car swerved and plowed with a rending crash into an iron trolley pole.

The impact dazed him; for a moment he couldn't move. But the little man had the door open, was out on the street. The cop came over, angry and bawling.

"Watch that man!" the little fellow shrilled. "He's dangerous. He just killed Mrs. John Anderson because he thought she saw him kill my cashier."

My cashier! Rick heard the words and went numb—so he *had* seen the mug before—when he had cased the joint. He started up, but the cop was beside him, the door open, his big service pistol in his mitt. That cop wasn't a coward, but he wasn't a fool either.

"Come out of there, fellow," he said stolidly.

Cold terror revived Rick Haines. "He's a fool," he said furiously. "The jackass asked me for a lift, wrecked my car. I'm a salesman and I called on Mrs. Anderson on business."

"Yes," the little man cut in, dancing in his excitement. "Look, officer, I returned from lunch, found my man dead, the safe looted. I remembered that this is the day of the month that poor Kelly stayed to attend to Mrs. Anderson. She always came at noon when everyone else was out—you see, Officer, she was sort of sensitive about her—her ailment, and Kelly was the only one she would converse with. She came today, stumbled on this guy tapping the till, didn't see poor Kelly, and left because she was unwilling to deal with anyone else! I don't believe she had any idea at all that this thug had killed, but—"

"You libelous little fool!" Rick ranted. He kept his senses by reminding himself that they couldn't pin a thing on him. Sure they'd find her dead, but this runt himself would have to admit she was still alive when they left her! "I never harmed your man, nor Mrs. Anderson. You heard me talking to her when I—"

"Yes," the little man said again. He grinned suddenly. "That's what put me next to you, warned me you were a phoney with something to hide. I came out to talk to Mrs. Anderson because she —well, she can't use the phone. I saw you come out, got a little suspicious, but I'd have to let you go unnoticed—if you hadn't stopped to talk to her. The rest I added up, and when I saw that gun in your fist in your pocket, I was sure. I was sure, too, that the car was stolen, so I deliberately got you to give me a lift so I could—"

"You're a fool!" Rick snarled, but something in the little man's grin put terror in his soul. "Mrs. Anderson was alive when I left her. I talked to her—"

"Sure, but she didn't talk back. She didn't, because she couldn't! That's why she used a door-light instead of a bell—that should have tipped you off, if you saw it. And that's why Kelly alone could talk to her; he alone could talk with his hands! You see, wise guy, Mrs. Anderson did *not* talk to you, because she was a deaf mute, born deaf and dumb!"

Rick's panic possessed him completely then. He forgot everything, even his gun, in his lust for life. He swung around the car, raced in agony for the shielding corner and escape. The policeman's bullet shattered his leg, dropping him screaming to the street.

"Wise guy," the little man said. "Just a death house dummy."

EIGHT DOLLAR MURDER

ROBERT SIDNEY BOWEN

Nick Bass was out of work, broke, and discouraged. His thoughts were becoming vicious. He lived in a furnished room around the corner from a movie theatre and he was three weeks behind in his rent; six dollars. He snorted contemptuously at this small figure. There'd been a day when he'd considered six dollars chicken feed! . . .

It was Saturday night—pay night for most fellows—and he was walking the streets looking for the cheapest food. No matter how carefully he shopped, he couldn't expect his last three dollars to hold out more than a week.

And everything he owned was in pawn, everything but the threadbare clothes on his back. That's how he'd raised the coins he now rubbed together in his greasy pockets. His overcoat, his suitcase, his Sunday suit and shoes—everything except what he had on, and that one thing in his pocket.

The thing bulged, made the tail of his coat stick consciously out, pulled heavily against his thin belt. Somehow, strangely, it comforted him. He was wary of carrying it; to do so was against the law —and yet he was afraid of leaving it at home. His landlady might ransack his room and confiscate it in lieu of the few paltry dollars he owed.

It was a gun; black, shiny, short-barreled but sturdy, a cheap gun, one that he'd had for a long time. And to him it was more than a gun, more than a weapon of destruction. It was a nest egg, a haven of last resort, something he'd put aside for a rainy day. . . .

He walked along, found a brightly lighted chain store, entered, bought a half pound of cheese, four hard rolls, and a pint of milk. With his purchases in a bag, he started home, angry tears in his eyes, resentful of the whole world because of his own need. What he'd seen in the store angered him beyond reparation—fat men and fat women, their pockets filled with money, ordering basketsful of food to take home to stuff themselves and their children. There'd been a time when Nick had spent like that!

In a blind fury he turned the corner by the picture show, brushed carelessly against a line of cheerful people waiting to buy tickets, stumbled across the street and around another corner towards the house in which he lived.

He reached the door, grasped its knob, turned. . . . But it did not open. For a moment he stood there fumbling without understanding. And then he knew. The door was bolted from the inside. He had no key to the outer door, only his room key. Never before had the outer door been locked. It could mean only one thing.

Through the glass he saw his landlady. She had been standing on the other side apparently awaiting his return.

"Let me in," he called.

For a long while she did not answer and then, through the glass, he heard: "Six dollars I want. Three weeks now and you haven't paid me a cent!"

He grabbed the knob, shook the door until its hinges rattled, but it held. He thought of smashing the glass; he thought of the gun. Through the door he said: "Let me in, Mrs. Reilly. Please let me in. I have the money for you. It's in my pocket. I'll pay once I'm inside!"

The latch clicked; the door swung in. He darted past the bulky female figure, down the hall.

As he mounted the carpeted stairs, she called after him: "My money! Where is my money? You lied to me! Enough there is to worry about without the likes of you holding out the rent. And lying!"

"Next week," he promised over his shoulder, "Next Saturday I swear!"

Upstairs he flung himself in his bed, lay there shaking until the sweat of misery popped out of his pores, dried, and chilled him. His room, one flight up, looked across the street to the motion picture theatre. The house entrance was around the corner.

He got up, gazed out of the window at the crowds still pouring into the movies, cursed, and sat down in his single chair.

Slowly he ate hunks of bread daubed with cheese, sipped at the milk to make it last longer. His thoughts were painful. Like a hurt child who sucks its thumb to assuage its grief, he gnawed mopingly at his coarse ration.

He sat there. The movie line shortened. The first show ended. Crowds spilled forth on the sidewalk. He kept on sitting. The second show wound up. . . . One o'clock in the morning and the midnight performance was done.

The lights of the movie marquee went dim, then blinked out. The block, lit only by a street light at its other end, was dark. Through the shadows he saw headlights approach and halt in front of the theatre. He made out the outlines of a heavy-bodied truck.

Two men jumped from its cab. One stepped through the headlight's rays. Nick Bass saw a uniformed body, leather covered legs, and a strong right hand with a pistol swinging loosely from its fingers. The two men went into the theatre. The theatre manager came out with them as far as the door. Each man had a white canvas bag, padlocked. They walked to the rear of the truck. The manager went back in the theatre. The uniformed men opened the rear truck door, tossed in the bags, locked the doors after.

The truck was an armored car! These men had come after the theatre's cash receipts. Money. All that money. People pouring in all day, all week. Every person paying, silver, dollar bills, five dollar bills. Bundles and bags of money!

He deserved theatre tickets, clothes, liquor, food, girls! He'd have them! . . . He had a gun. That was the first step. He could fire the gun. That was the second. Lastly he could make a getaway. . . . Ah, he thought, that's where most of them trip up. Anybody can commit a crime, but most of them get caught.

But he wouldn't get caught! No, sir! He knew a thing or two, had heard smart fellows talk. He knew that those who looked like crooks, acted like crooks, *ran* like crooks, were the ones who ended up in jail. The thing to do was to go about a job as unconcernedly as possible.

He had no record. No one knew of his intentions. No one knew he had a gun. As long as he wasn't seen he could shoot a couple of guys, pick up their money bags, and beat it. But he wouldn't go down the block, or tearing off in a fast car. That was a sure way to apprehension. He had a better plan. . . .

If the armored car came this Saturday night, it came every Saturday. He'd wait until next week, quietly biding his time. He'd sit in his window until after the midnight show was done. He'd wait for the car. Then, as soon as it arrived, he'd go silently down to the street and around the corner. He'd hide until the guard and chauffeur went into the theatre. He'd look up and down the block, be sure all was dark and no one in view. When the guards came out and the theatre manager went back in, he'd step up and without warning take brief aim and fire: once—twice. . . . He'd pick up the money, walk back around the corner to the rooming house entrance, go up to his room. From that point of safety he could watch the arrival of the police . . .

Sunday passed and Monday came. He stayed in his room both days nearly all day long. Monday he went out for a short walk. Returning, he met his landlady in the hall. He did not try to avoid her.

"You don't have to worry now," he told her. "I've got a job—start work soon!"

"Ugh!" was all Mrs. Reilly said, going on with her mopping.

"In a few days I'm going to have plenty of money," he continued. "That little I owe you won't be nothing. I'll be your star roomer!"

Thursday, Friday, Saturday came. He worried a bit during that time. He was afraid the landlady was getting suspicious; she was the suspicious sort. And yet, he comforted himself, she couldn't have gotten wind of his plans. He hadn't revealed them to a soul.

"Bosh!" he told himself. He laughed at his self-created fears. But he *would* have to be careful. That was the very essence of the success he hoped his illicit flower would bear. Even after he got the money he'd have to spend it with caution.

He'd be discreet. After the holdup, after the killing, he'd display a normal amount of interest in it. When talk of it died down he'd move quietly to another neighborhood.

Saturday afternoon, shades drawn, he got out his gun, unloaded it, cleaned it, reloaded it . . . Soon he'd have enough money for the rent all right, he thought while looking at the weapon—a hundred such rents, a thousand such! Eight dollars he owed now. He laughed at the absurd lowness of the amount as compared with what he was going to get! . . .

A footstep sounded in the hall followed by a knock on his door.

He did not answer but hastily, nervously stuffed the gun under his pillow.

Mrs. Reilly's voice chirped out: "I know you're in there, Mr. Bass . . . This is the day you promised me—Saturday. Where's my money?"

He hesitated, then replied: "The days' not over yet, Mrs. Reilly. Don't worry. You'll get it. . . ."

"Humph!" Mrs. Reilly's voice trailed mutteringly after her away from his door and along the corridor. Eagerly he brought out his gun again, toyed with it fondly. . . .

Saturday night! He kept his light off, shades up, to see well out of the window. Watching the crowds emerging after the first movie show, he smiled. He'd be one of them before long, he told himself —money in his pocket, a blonde on his arm. No one would see; no one would suspect.

The midnight show was over; the last of the movie goers came out of the theatre and drifted away. The building went dim, dark, only a single light left burning in the manager's office. The street quieted down. There wasn't a soul in sight.

And then came the headlights, the rumble of the armored car's motor. The heavy vehicle halted before the picture theatre. The two guards got out, went inside.

Creeping out of his room, along the hall, Nick Bass saw a light coming from around a half opened door. It was his landlady's room. Peeping in, he saw her reading beside a table. Her eyes were bent over her paper; he was sure she did not see him. Her being awake was not exactly as he had planned, but it disturbed him only slightly. "Probably sitting up waiting for some other poor devil of a roomer," he told himself. "Makes no difference to me. Her windows ain't on the theatre side of the house. She won't hear the gunshots, won't see . . ."

Slipping down the stairs with only a bare, almost inaudible creak, he proceeded to the street. Beyond the outer door, in the vestibule, he paused, peered up and down the block. All was clear. He rounded the corner, waited. . . .

Three men came out of the theatre. One—the manager—returned. The two guards, white padlocked bags in their hands, started for their car. . . .

Nick Bass fired, once—twice! He heard their screams, groans. He rushed forward, snatched up the bags. They were heavy, weighted with the money for which he'd long yearned. With barely a glance at the bleeding bodies, he waddled across the street, reached the opposite curb and pavement. Rounding the corner, he gained his own doorstep. He saw no one, heard no one. Not until he was well within the shelter of the vestibule was there a sound—a window raised in some house diagonally across.

He was safe, he felt. He stood for a minute collecting himself, quelling the ripple of excitement that ran over him. Then, hearing the whine of a police siren in the distance, approaching, getting nearer, he grabbed the doorknob of the rooming house, twisted. . . .

It did not turn! *It was locked!* . . .

Another moment and he saw Mrs. Reilly's obdurate face behind the glass. He called to her, softly at first, but received no answer. Then, panic stricken, he screamed: "Mrs. Reilly, let me in! Mrs. Reilly, I've got the money!"

He heard her voice through the door: "I want my rent. Four weeks now it's been. Last Saturday you lied to me about having it. Then you promised me this Saturday. Show me the money or I won't open the door!"

He heard sounds behind him, around the corner, the street in an uproar.

He raised the canvas money bags, showing them to his landlady. She did not seem to realize what they were.

Clawing at them, trying to pull off their padlocks, he cried: "Mrs. Reilly, I have the money! I can pay the rent! Let me in. . . . God, let me in!"

But the padlocks wouldn't come off, and Mrs. Reilly didn't move.

Then, madly, he rushed away from the door, to the adjoining house, and to the one next that. He tried doors, found that they didn't yield. A gang of men rounding the corner sent him flying back to his own boarding house. Mrs. Reilly was still behind the glass.

He dropped the money bags, pulled his gun, raised it at her.

A hand from behind knocked the pistol from his grasp.

He was wheeled around by a quick yank at his shoulder. Police men surrounded him. A fleeting ironical thought ripped across his brain: "Thousands I've got locked in these money bags, but the lack of a lousy eight bucks cash-in-hand tripped me up!"

An officer, snapping handcuffs around his extended wrists, said: "This seedy looking guy! If I hadn't seen that gun in his fist and the dough right at his feet, I'd have swore he never had the guts to pull a job like that! . . ."

FERRY SLIP

DON JAMES

They didn't look like bank robbers, Pop Graham thought as he stood beside his gasoline pumps at the crossroads station and eyed the three men. But they fitted the description he'd heard over the radio an hour before.

The man beside the driver opened the door to talk to Pop.

"Which is the Bainstree Ferry road?" he asked.

Pop chewed tobacco thoughtfully. He wondered if they had machine guns and where the money was stored in the car. He waved nonchalantly as the Dickerson brothers went by in their two dump trucks and took the ferry road.

"Them trucks are goin' that way," he said.

"How soon will a ferry leave this side?"

Pop pulled a dollar watch from his pocket and looked at it judiciously. Sam Doonan ran the ferry. Pop and Sam had been friends for a good many years. They played pitch together and once in a while managed a little fishing.

These men in the car had killed a bank cashier this morning. Sam undoubtedly had heard the newscast and descriptions. He had a new fangled battery set on the small ferry and kept it going all the time. Sam was just the sort of darned fool who would recognize these men and then try to do something about it. But, Pop thought, a man can't be a hero against a machine gun.

One of the other men in the car spotted the sign Pop had let Sam put up under his own that said: "Pop's Station."

"The sign says one leaves at 11:50. It's 11:30 now. How far is it, Pop?"

The sign told that, too, but Pop said unnecessarily: "Three miles."

The men in the car exchanged glances. On the highway a battered roadster rattled past toward the ferry slip. Young Hal Liscomb and his girl, Pearl Winders. Nice kids, Pop thought as they waved to him. If Sam Doonan got fooling around with that horse pistol he had on the ferry, these men would cut him to pieces with their fancy guns. No place for two high school kids to be.

"It's pretty slow goin' by the ferry," Pop said. "The highway is closer and faster to get anywhere. Most people usin' the ferry live over that direction is all."

"We can get to the city that way, can't we?" the man by the open car door said.

"You goin' to the city?" Pop asked.

The driver of the car suddenly glared suspiciously at him.

"What's it to you, Pop?" he snapped.

"No need to get riled!" Pop said in disgust. "I was just tryin' to be helpful."

The man by the door grinned. "Sure. Don't pay any attention to him, Pop. He's got a hangover."

Pop wondered if you got a hangover from killing people. These men were smart. They probably figured that police would be watching the main highway farther down the line. They were right about that. State police cars had already gone by, sirens screaming. They'd pick a point where the last of the feeder roads had joined the highway.

No one thought escaping bank robbers would take a ferry. Ferries took time. Once these men crossed the river, they had half a dozen roads to take. They had a good plan.

Down the highway Pete Dinsmore was coming in his battered truck. He'd stop for the regrooved tires Pop had got for him. Then he'd go on down the highway. Pop had a sudden flare of hope, but dismissed it. Pete was too slow-witted to help much.

The man got ready to close the door. Pop shot a stream of tobacco juice to the highway and looked at them.

"There ain't no place to get gas for sixty—seventy miles after you cross the river," he said. "You want to fill up now? You got time before the ferry leaves."

The man in the doorway looked at the driver and they both glanced at the dashboard dial. Pop figured they'd burn up the backroads all the way from Grainsville. An hour and a half of hard driving with hills. They'd be a little short on gas.

The man in the doorway nodded.

"Fill her up, Pop. Make it snappy."

Pete Dinsmore stopped his truck and Pop indicated the tires leaning against the side of the service station.

"Busy," he explained. "Load 'em yourself."

Pop put the hose nozzle in place and started the pump. One of the men got out of the car and leaned against the station in the shade, watching the highway in both directions. He had a hand in a pocket that looked heavy.

Pete loaded his tires and Pop stopped filling the tank to take Pete's money. He returned a dollar.

"I want you to go by way of Hallowells and pick up some old truck tires they got for me," he said. "I want 'em right away. You better hurry. The Dickerson boys and young Liscomb just went down."

The man by the station looked on without interest, satisfied when Pop let the gas flow again.

Pete got in the truck, glanced at a watch, and the truck rumbled off toward the ferry.

Pop finished filling the car tank, carefully wiped spilled gas from the fender, and got the water bucket to fill the radiator.

"Never mind that," the driver barked. "We've only got about ten minutes to make that ferry."

"There's plenty of time," Pop assured him mildly.

He took the ten dollar bill they gave him and wasted a couple of minutes getting change. The car driver glanced at a wrist watch impatiently. The starter ground and the car engine roared into life. The car swerved to the highway and took the ferry road.

"Pete's a fast driver," Pop said thoughtfully. "They won't be able to pass him."

Pop went to the back of the service station and drove out his own weathered car. Carefully he parked it lengthwise across the ferry road and returned to the station.

Pop wondered what Pete would think when Hallowells didn't have any truck tires for him.

He used the crank telephone and asked for the state police.

"Them bank robbers you want," he said. "You hurry up to Pop's place and you'll get 'em. They'll be coming back from the ferry before long. I got the road blocked here."

There was a brief silence as he listened. "They *got* to come back or wait an hour," Pop assured his questioner. "Sam's ferry only holds four cars. He pulls out when he's got 'em. Them robbers are in the *fifth* car this trip. They ain't goin'!"

Pop hung up, took a fresh chew of tobacco, and went in search of his shotgun.

FINAL GAME

HUGH B. CAVE

When the TV voice from the living room told her the football game was nearly over, she left her place at the kitchen stove and went to the cellar door. It was closed, of course. Her daughter always closed it on going down there now. Opening it, Mildred Lacey stood at the top of the steep staircase and called down, "Penny?"

As usual, no answer.

"Penny!"

"Yes, Mommy?"

"Supper's almost ready."

"All right. I'm coming."

She went into the living room then, just in time to see her husband struggle up from his chair in front of the tube. Looking down at the peanuts and empty beer cans on the chairside table, he took time to toss one more fistful of nuts into his mouth before waddling to the set and turning it off. How much did he weigh now, anyway? Two fifty? Two sixty? She had lost track.

"Are you ready for supper, Dan?"

He turned indifferently to look at her, a bear gazing at a fawn. "Yeah, sure. Why not?"

"I'll put it on the table."

Trailing her into the kitchen, he looked with interest at the meatloaf she had taken from the oven, then directed a scowl at the cellar door. Because he almost never shaved; on Sundays now—in fact, seldom even bothered to don a shirt—the scowl was undoubtedly more threatening in appearance than in substance. Certainly there was no great concern in his voice when he said, "She down there again?"

"I told her to come up. Call her, will you?"

He went to the now open door and peered down the flight of steps into the cellar's dimness. Turning back to his wife, he said, "Who's with her?"

"With her?"

"She's got somebody down there. I can hear them talking."

"Uh-uh, Dan. She's just talking to herself. She's been doing that a lot lately."

"What do you mean, lately?"

"Well, the past couple of weeks. I've even had the goofy idea she started on her birthday. Anyway, there's nobody down there."

His scowl genuine now because he was being challenged, Dan turned again and began to descend the steps. They were narrow with no risers—this was an old house in an old part of the city—and on the side away from the wall there was no railing for him to cling to. Twice he nearly lost his balance because his attention was diverted by the sound of his daughter's voice below, and by another voice that belonged, he thought, to a boy about her age. He could not make out what they were saying.

He knew where to look for her, of course. A former owner of the house had turned the far part of its gloomy cellar into a kind of den or hideout, not a place he ever felt like using himself, even when Mildred was down on him, but a retreat Penny seemed more than fond of. He approached it as quietly as he could, hoping to catch some of the conversation before the two children became aware of his intrusion.

"You'll have to help me," he heard the boy's voice say. "I can't do such a thing alone."

"All right," Penny answered, "but we'll talk about it later, okay? I have to go now. Bye."

Dan stepped from behind the furnace and showed himself, then abruptly halted, jabbing his pudgy fists against his sides. This time his scowl used up the whole of his stubbled face and even darkened his eyes.

His daughter was alone, just as Mildred had insisted.

The child knelt with her back to him on an old hooked rug her mother had given her long ago to play on. Her only companion was a doll propped up in front of her. A doll he, Dan Lacey, had given her for her sixth birthday, two weeks ago.

"Who the hell are you talking to?" he said angrily.

Startled, she gave a little jump—at least, her head and shoulders did—then swiftly turned to look up at him. Fright brushed her face as she returned his stare. She had a face like her mother's, soft and pretty almost to the point of being without character, but remarkable for its brilliant blue eyes. She had her mother's blond hair.

"You scared me," she complained.

"Answer my question. Who were you talking to?"

"Only him." She turned to take up the doll. About a foot tall and made of hard plastic, it was dressed in a football uniform and head-gear. Give a girl a boy doll and a boy a girl doll, he thought on buying it. Start 'em young. "I talk to him sometimes when I'm playing," she said.

"I heard two voices, damn it."

"Well, I answer for him in a boy's voice. He can't talk for himself." Dropping the doll, she rose from her knees and took hold of her father's hand. "Shouldn't we go upstairs, Daddy? Supper's ready and you look tired. Your eyes do, anyway. I bet you've been watching football again."

"Why shouldn't I watch football?"

"I don't know. But Mommy says—"

"To hell with what your mother says," he retorted as hand in hand they walked across the cellar to the stairs. "A man works as hard as I do all week has a right to relax on weekends whether she likes it or not. Next time your mother makes a crack about me watching football, you tell her to mind her own damn business."

"You shouldn't swear so much, Daddy."

"And shut up about that, too!"

At supper Dan ate so much of the meatloaf, there was none left when Penny asked if she might have a little more. Mildred produced bread and grape jelly to satisfy her daughter's hunger. Dan was in a mood to be critical, too. His favorite team, the New England Patriots, had lost. "I don't like Penny spending so much time down there in the cellar," he said, scowling across the table at her mother.

"Dan, kids have to play."

"Let her play outdoors, then, with other kids. Not with a doll."

"Dan, *you* gave her the doll."

"All right, I shouldn't have. I was wrong."

"And this neighborhood—"

"What's wrong with the neighborhood? Do we have to be Mr. and Mrs. Rockefeller before our kid can find someone to play with?"

"Daddy," Penny said, "I *do* play with the kids around here. The ones I go to school with, anyhow." She was in the first grade.

"Well then, stop spending so much time in the cellar talking to yourself. It isn't healthy." And, his plate clean, Dan straightarmed himself to his feet and lumbered into the living room, where he turned on the TV and slouched into his chair to watch it again.

In the kitchen Penny helped her mother with the dishes, as usual. "Mommy, did Daddy always watch the television all the time?"

"Well, he always watched the football game, dear. Ever since I've known him, anyway."

"Why?"

"I guess he just likes them."

"Don't you wish he'd stop?"

"We'll, I suppose so. But he won't."

Would he ever? she wondered. No. Dan was a frustrated player, one who had been a star on his high-school team but never good enough to win a college bid and hence never even close to realizing his dream of becoming a pro. When he parked his pounds of flesh in front of the boob tube now, it was Dan Lacey he saw catching those spectacular over-the-shoulder passes or breaking away for touchdowns while the crowds cheered. All the rest of the week he was just an overweight, unhappy man selling cars. And not doing very well at that, either.

"Let me tell you something," Mildred said, knowing the TV in the other room would keep Dan from overhearing. "The very day you were born, honey, your father was watching a football game and almost didn't get me to the hospital on time."

"Really?"

"It's a fact. He knew I was on the verge—and I mean on the *verge*, baby—and do you know what he did? On the way home from work he stopped at a bar, and there was a Notre Dame football game on —it was a Saturday—and when I telephoned where he worked, they didn't know where to reach him. I waited and waited, not knowing what to do—"

"Couldn't you call a taxi?"

"We didn't have that kind of money, baby. The hospital's a long way from here. So I just hung onto myself and waited, and I almost waited too long."

"You mean I might've died?"

"Yes, you could have. It was that close. In fact, I've got something to tell you about that day when you're older. Something I think you ought—" Hearing footsteps in the living room, Mildred fell silent just as Dan came into the kitchen to get a beer from the refrigerator. He gave them a suspicious glance before returning in silence to the television. He always felt, Mildred knew, that when they were talking together they were talking about him.

Sunday again.

"Dan, please come with us. Today is special."

"What's special about it?"

"Dan, I *told* you. Penny's being baptised today."

When they were first married they had attended church together most Sundays. Then he had refused to go during the football season, claiming that by the time they got home and finished the big, leisurely dinner he always demanded on Sundays, the games had begun. In time he had even refused to go during the off season, as he called it.

She had gone. And Penny. But it was not the same, and the Reverend Dawson had only just succeeded in persuading her to have the child baptised. "You owe it to her, Mrs. Lacey. Never mind what your husband thinks."

What Dan thought was clear enough. "Damn it, Milly, I don't like the guy."

"Why?"

"Because I don't like his dumb sermons."

"What's wrong with his sermons?"

"You know what's wrong with them. He's always talking about the hereafter, life after death, rewards and punishments, all that dark-ages crap. Nobody with any sense believes that stuff any more."

"You don't believe in a life after death, Dan?"

"No!"

"I hope you're wrong, Dan. I hope this isn't all we've got."

"What the hell's wrong with what we've got?"

"It isn't enough," she said. "It just isn't enough, Dan. There has to be something better."

"Yeah," he said. "The Pats have to win today; that's what has to be. That Grogan has to throw like he's able to and get some breaks."

She and Penny went to church without him, and the Reverend Dawson baptised Penny in front of the whole congregation, and she was proud. Oh, she was proud. Such a beautiful child Penny was, standing there in her white dress, with her hair aglow and her eyes shining while the minister dipped his fingers in the water and placed them on her brow and said the words. She could almost hear the congregation hold its breath. And when she and Penny got home, Dan did at least put down the Sunday sports section and ask how it had gone.

"Wonderful, Dan. You would have been so proud."

"What'd he preach about?"

"Never mind."

"The same old line, hey?" In a good mood today, he spoke with a grin. "Saint Peter at the pearly gates, with everyone's stats written down in the old record book."

"Well . . . something like that."

"He's got a one-track mind."

"Because he's sincere, Dan. He really believes we should think about it and live accordingly."

"Haw," Dan snorted, and returned his attention to the newspaper.

The Pats were playing Miami. Dan put a six pack of beer and a jar of peanuts on the table beside his chair, folded his hands over his bulging belly, thrust his legs out, and glued his gaze to the tube. Dinner had been roast beef, potatoes, two vegetables, and apple pie with ice cream, but he popped peanuts into his mouth every thirty seconds and had a can of beer in his hand continually.

After the dishes were done, Mildred retired to her bedroom for a nap and Penny went downstairs to her cellar playroom.

The game was nearly over when Penny emerged from the cellar, glanced into the living room at her father—who did not notice her —and went silently along the hall to the bedroom door. Entering the room, she quietly shut the door behind her and went to stand beside the bed on which her mother lay sleeping.

After gazing at Mildred in apparent deep thought for a moment, she reached out and touched her on the shoulder. Mildred awoke with a start.

"Oh, it's you, baby. What do you want?"

"There's something you didn't tell me."

"Something I what?"

"About going to the hospital the day I was born. You didn't tell me I had a brother and he died because Daddy got you there too late."

"What?" Staring in horror, Mildred jerked herself up to a sitting position. "Oh my God, *he's told you!*" she whispered. "He got drunk on that damned beer and told you!"

"Not Daddy." The child shook her head. "Alexander."

"Who?"

"Alexander."

Her eyes widened even more, until they seemed ready to burst. Alexander. Her father's name. Her dead father's name. Dan disliked it, but for once in her life she had stood up to him, insisting that even if only one of the expected twins were a boy he must be called that.

"Where . . ." She stared at her daughter. "Where did you hear that name, baby?"

"He said it's *his* name."

"Who said?"

"My brother."

Her eyes closed and she felt herself falling into a pit of darkness. Falling, falling, and it had no bottom. The day had been such a long one—the baptism, the overlong sermon, the big Sunday dinner and all the cleaning up after it. She slumped back on the bed and did not see her daughter walk out of the room, closing the door behind her again, quiet as a wraith. Did not know that Penny again glanced at her father, in front of the television, as she returned to her playroom in the cellar.

The game ended, but this was a doubleheader Sunday; another contest followed. That one over at last, Dan looked bleary-eyed at his watch. Despite the beer and the peanuts, he was hungry again.

He pushed himself up from his chair and went looking for his wife.

She was awake now. "All right," she said faintly. "I'll fix some supper. Just give me a minute."

"Where's Penny?"

"I don't know. In the cellar, I suppose."

"Damn that room in the cellar. I've got a mind to lock it up!"

Alexander, she thought. She's with Alexander, talking to him, listening to him. I don't think you can lock up that room now, Dan. I think it's too late. Maybe the Reverend Dawson was trying to warn you?

"Come on, get up," Dan said. His favorites had lost both games and he was out of beer to help him bear the grief. Angrily he stormed out of the room to call his daughter.

The door to the cellar was closed. He yanked it open. "Penny!"

As usual, no answer.

"Damn it, Penny, come up out of there!"

"No. I won't." A boy's voice. A *boy's* voice?

He lurched onto the stairs. Stepped on something. Lost his balance and with a hoarse yell went crashing down the steep staircase to the bottom, where the concrete floor stopped his fall with a sound like that of a sledgehammer striking an overripe watermelon.

His overweight body twitched a time or two, then did not move again.

* * *

Following the sound of his yell, Mildred reached the top of the stairs just as her six-year-old daughter appeared at the bottom. Gazing in horror at the motionless form of her husband, at the pool of blood spreading around his head, she watched the child walk around him and climb the stairs toward her. On the third board from the top Penny bent to pick up her doll—flattened now and recognizable only by the football uniform it wore.

"He must have tripped over this, Mommy."

Mildred nodded without knowing she moved her head, her gaze again fixed on the silent shape at the foot of the staircase.

"Over Alexander," Penny said.

Emerging slowly from shock, the woman said, "You've always kept that doll in your playroom. Why did you leave it on the stairs?"

"He told me to, Mommy. He said I had to help."

FIRST KILL

CHET WILLIAMSON

For days now, the hunter had thought about widows and orphaned children, and decided that he would try and see if the man wore a wedding ring. With his 4x Weaver scope, he thought he should be able to catch a glint of gold on the left hand.

However, the Monday after Thanksgiving was often cold in the woods of northern Pennsylvania. Odds were that blaze orange mittens would cover most hands, to be slipped warily off only at the sound of hooves rustling dead leaves. Even then, most men fired rifles with their right hands. A wedding ring would still be covered. Still, he would try to avoid a father, making an effort to show the mercy the earth he loved did not have.

But if he could not see the hand, he would accept whatever target was offered.

* * *

Peter Keats awoke an hour before dawn, pushed in the button of the wind-up alarm clock, and shivered with excitement and the cold. The fire he and his two cabin mates had set the night before in the wood stove was dead, and he was glad he had worn his insulated long underwear in his sleeping bag. He didn't think he could have stood the chilly air against his bare trunk and legs. He woke his friends, slid out of his bunk, and put on two pairs of socks, one cotton, the other heavy wool. He stepped into his thick trousers, then slipped his feet into ankle-high L. L. Bean hunting boots.

Keats was out the front door before the others had disentangled themselves from their sleeping bags. He breathed in the air, reveling in the sharp crispness that stung his throat. He walked up the hill from the cabin to the outhouse, defecated quickly and efficiently, and walked back again, broke the ice in the basin that sat on the railing of the tiny porch, and splashed frigid water on his face. It made him even more wakeful than before.

Back inside, the men joked, ate donuts, and drank the coffee they had made the night before. Then they finished dressing, ending with the heavy coats of safety orange, put wads of toilet paper under their scope covers so the lenses wouldn't fog in the colder outside air, and stepped outside to hunt, and to be hunted.

It took Peter Keats a half hour of walking in near darkness to reach the spot he had chosen the day before, when they had helped each other erect their stands, the elevated platforms in which they would perch and wait for a deer to wander by. One of his friends was a half mile to the northwest, the other a mile south. Keats could easily hear their shots, and if he did he would hold still for five, ten minutes, waiting even more silently in case of a miss or a wounding, in case the deer should run, limp, or drag itself past his stand.

By the time Peter Keats had climbed onto his perch, he could just make out streaks of rose through the ragged treetops to the east. He settled himself, his Remington pump .760 resting across his legs. His feet dangled over the edge of the stand, fifteen feet above the ground. For comfort's sake, Keats had placed a small, flat pillow under the spot where his knees rested against the sharp edge of the stand.

Keats thought that it seemed colder than it had in years before. He rubbed his fingers against each other inside the heavy mittens, and wished that the orange of his jacket was as warm to the touch as it was to the eye. The deer must really be colorblind if that hue didn't startle them. He had heard other hunters say that it appeared white to the deer's eyes. Well, if it did it did. It didn't much matter, and besides, it was the law.

In his fifty years of deer hunting, Peter Keats had always obeyed the law. His father had taught him that when he had given him his first deer rifle at the age of fourteen. One deer a year, no more. No shooting one for your friend, and no shooting a doe in buck season. Keats had done none of those things, simply because he had never been tempted to. And he had never been tempted, because in his half century of what he called hunting, he had never shot, nor had he ever wanted to shoot, a deer.

The pattern was set the first year he went hunting with his father. Keats was positioned next to an oak tree, crouching among the acorns on which the deer loved to feed. His father was a half mile away, and Keats, his heart beating rapidly, waited, waited, feeling youthful erections of excitement come and go. An hour passed, during which Keats stood up several times, stretching his legs. He was standing when he heard the deer approach. He froze, felt the wind on his face from the direction of the sound of breaking leaves, snapping twigs, and saw a buck and two doe push through the brush less than fifty yards away.

He raised his rifle with what felt like the slowness of a watch's second hand, and by the time the buck had cleared the brush, Keats was looking at it through the notch of the open sight. Its smooth coat made it look carved of wood, its brown eyes stared into his like some spirit of the forest, and he felt, holding the deer's life in his fingertip, as though he was defying God, like a vandal in a cathedral. If he pulled the trigger he knew he would violate a far more solemn contract than the one forged between him and his father.

He lowered the gun, and never raised it to a deer again.

Still, he went hunting every year, and patiently bore his fellow hunters' good-natured teasing. He suspected that the old friends he was with now knew the truth, for he no longer even fired a shot or two to make them think he had tried but failed. He had had plenty of chances over the years, and his heart still pounded when he saw a buck approach, pass by him, pause, look up, startled, and run. But he did not lift his loaded rifle to his shoulder.

And it was loaded, always. Every year he went through the ritual of sighting in the rifle at the sportsman's club to which he belonged, cleaning it, taking out the same bullets from the cabinet, bullets that had turned green where lead met brass, and shooting at the targets on the range, until his offhand scores equaled those of men years his junior.

Keats loved the ritual, the preparations, the chance to be with his friends and by himself. His two companions with whom he had come to Potter County shared his love of the outdoors, but he seldom saw them outside of deer season, so that when they did get together there was much to catch up on.

But the solitude was the best part, the sense that there was no one but him in the world to see the sky grow brighter, feel the air become less bitterly cold, behold the dread miracle of winter. He sat and waited, and while he was alert to the sounds of the woods, he also escaped into himself, his past, his thoughts and memories of seasons before.

He thought of his wife, of when they had both been young, though no happier than they were now, of the job at the steel mill he had held for over thirty years before he had retired four years ago, of his church where he served on the budget committee, of his three grandchildren, of the oldest boy, who wanted to go hunting with him next year when he was old enough.

Peter Keats thought of many things as the morning brightened, until the sun slashed bright streaks through the latticework of branches, bathing his orange garb with fire, making him a perfect target.

The hunter saw the man in the tree stand just before 7:30. Ever since dawn he had been moving stealthily, stalking. It was estimated that fifty thousand people would be roaming through the quarter million acres of Potter County's state forests today. Since that averaged out to one hunter per five acres, it was only natural that they would come across each other now and again.

That was what calmed and excited and worried the hunter. It calmed him because no one would take a second look at another man dressed in orange; it excited him because the statistic made it certain that he would find game; and it worried him that the game might be *too* plentiful, tripping over one another in the haste for their own prey. A herd would do the hunter no good. He had to find a single animal, cut off from the rest.

That was when he saw the man in the tree. Thank God, he thought, for the orange. Its warm brightness protected him on the cold ground, marked his targets in the chilly air.

He stepped behind a thick-boled pine tree, and peered out at the man in the tree stand seventy yards away. The man gave no indication that he had seen the hunter.

The hunter slipped the glove from his right hand, put it into his coat pocket, and wadded small bits of wax into his ears. Then he lifted his rifle, a Ruger Model 77, 7 mm. Magnum, and leaned against the tree. He placed his right cheek against the smooth walnut stock, and looked through the Weaver scope with his right eye.

The man in the stand did not fill the field of vision, but the hunter could make out certain details. The man was older, in his sixties, and had probably killed deer for many years. The hunter found a poetic justice in that fact. His hands were mittened, so the hunter could not tell if he wore a ring. Probably married, the hunter thought. He looked like a married man, happy to be alone in the woods. The man had a little gray mustache, and wore glasses with black frames. His booted feet dangled over the edge of the stand, and he swung them back and forth like a child, a movement that any deer would notice immediately. The man did not appear likely to bag a buck this year.

Still, he was hunting deer, so it was the hunter's obligation to hunt him. Maybe he was only a harmless old man who enjoyed sitting in a tree house holding a loaded rifle, but surely he had taken his toll over the years. Now it was payback time.

The hunter flicked off the safety, breathed in icy air, leaned against the tree so that his forehead rubbed roughly against the bark, moved his Ruger in a series of infinitesimal motions until the plain of blaze orange was settled directly under the scope's cross hair. Only then did he place his bare finger on the cold metal of the trigger, let out half his breath in a white puff, hold the rest, and begin, very gently, to squeeze. When he had exerted enough pressure, the firing pin descended, the powder ignited, the bullet left the barrel and flew across the seventy yards in the merest fraction of a second, meeting the man in the tree, expanding the instant it struck the orange jacket, widening as it tore through flesh and muscle and bone. The man flew backwards into a red cloud of himself, and fell from the tree, landing on the dry leaves below like a sack of lime.

The hunter held his pose for a moment, the sound of the explosion reverberating like a great gong. Then he operated the bolt and lowered the rifle so that he still looked through the scope at the man on the ground, ready to fire a second shot at the hint of motion.

There was none. It had been a clean, quick kill.

From the corner of his eye, he had seen the spent shell fly from the ejector, and it took him only a moment to find the gleaming brass amid the floor of dead pine needles. He dropped it into his pocket and walked to the tree stand, pulling the wax wads from his ears. Although he listened intently, he heard no other sounds, neither voices nor footsteps in dead leaves. No, no one would come. No one would leave their stands and jeopardize their own chances of making a kill. It would be safe to do the field dressing.

It was extraordinary, he thought, the damage a single, small projectile could do to a human body. The man had not moved since he had fallen, and the glassy stare told the hunter he was dead. Heart and lungs had been ripped through, and the blood must have ceased its pumping to the brain instantly. He hoped the man had felt little pain, only one, short, sharp, and savage, before he lost consciousness and his life.

The hunter stood for a long time, looking down at the first man he had ever killed, indeed ever even harmed. He thought he had readied himself for it, but no philosophy, no cause firmly and chokingly believed in, had prepared him for this moment. It had prepared him for the stalking, the sighting, even the pulling of the trigger, but not this. He struggled to stop shaking, told himself it was only the cold, that he could not be shaking from emotion because he had none. He was a machine that had functioned as it was supposed to, and would continue to do so.

Again he repeated his manifesto to himself, like a mantra of destruction, all the proper words about the purity of life, the reverence for nature, the abomination of hunting in a country where no one need do so to eat, the thousands of animals wounded and not found, dying slowly and painfully. He thought about the protests he had made with the others, the signs and speeches that had done nothing to slow the annual slaughter, thought about his decision to do more, administer true justice, turn the tables on the hunters, show them all too clearly just what they were doing to another species, going over it again and again in his mind, establishing his alibi, changing his appearance, going far, far from where he lived, to a place where no one knew him, a place rich with human game, where he could make his kill, and show that any species could be preyed upon.

And now he had killed, and now he must continue, be strong, finish the lesson, plant the seeds of legend and terror.

There. He was all right now, ready to do what had to be done.

He propped his Ruger against the tree that held the stand, put on both gloves, and knelt by the side of the dead man. He unsnapped the man's jacket, grasped his neck, hauled him to a sitting position, and removed the sodden mass of cotton shell and goose down. The hole in the man's back was greater than the hunter had imagined.

He let the body flop back onto the bloody leaves, and saw that some blood on the man's small mustache had frozen. It looked, thought the hunter, as though he had cut his lip shaving.

The hunter took a horn-handled knife with a five-inch blade from its sheath, and tried to forget that what lay before him was a human being, tried to think of it only as a slaughtered animal, as the other hunters would think of the deer they had shot.

He cut open the dead man's sweater, shirt, and thermal undershirt, exposing the pallid flesh and the entrance wound to the freezing air. He yanked the upper clothing off the body, then removed the boots and socks, and sliced through the waistband of the trousers, tugging them off, along with the long underwear, until the corpse lay naked on the frozen bed of leaves. The hunter had read over and over about field dressing, and now he would re-create the procedure. It wouldn't be perfect, for the anatomies of deer and men were different. But they would see, and realize, and tell the tale, so that everyone would know there was an avenger in the forest.

A true field dressing would have begun with cutting the penis and scrotum free, then scoring around the anus, but the hunter wanted no hints of sexual psychosis to dilute the true purpose of his act. He left the genitals intact, and instead slipped the razor sharp knife beneath the skin of the lower abdomen. Blade up, he slid the knife through the flesh until it struck the breastbone, exposing a layer of yellow fat and muscle.

He had not reckoned on the fat. It looked greasy and slimy, and although he thought the presence of blood on his gloves would arouse no curiosity, the same could not be said for remnants of fat. So he took off the gloves and laid them next to the butt of his rifle. When he was finished, he would wipe his hands as best he could with the dead leaves.

The incision had drawn back the skin, and the warm, moist organs steamed in the cold air, like clouds rising from a valley. The hunter rolled up his right sleeve, made a few quick, short cuts, and lifted away the fat and the sheet of muscle beneath it. His cold hands nearly burned when he touched the hot, wet innards, and for a moment the steam rose from his hands and forearms. He then cut the diaphragm away from the rib cage, and reached up inside the chest until he found the esophagus and windpipe, both of which he severed, accidentally nicking the palm of his left hand in the confined space. He pulled both tubes back and out, and the lungs, now deflated sacks, followed. It was nearly as easy as the books had said.

A little more cutting of the membranes removed the diaphragm, and in another moment he was able to work the heart free and remove it. Then he reached in with both hands, as though he was embracing the carcass, and lifted most of the viscera out, except for the lower intestine, which was still attached to the anus. He dropped the innards on the leaves, where the smoking, multi-hued mound settled itself like a nest of lazy snakes in sunshine. Then he picked up the knife again, intending to sever the recalcitrant lower bowel, when he heard a crunch of leaves behind him, and a voice. The hunter turned his head and saw, twenty feet away, a man with a gray beard, dressed in blaze orange, holding a rifle pointed at the ground.

When Peter Keats had heard the single shot from the south, he had listened for more, for the signals that he and his friend there had established. If Keats heard one, he could assume it was a single killing shot. If two, a downing shot and a finishing shot. But if three, a miss. His friend's hands were arthritic, especially in the cold, and he could not begin to field-dress a deer. Keats had offered to do the gutting if necessary, and the single shot had told him it was.

It had taken Keats nearly fifteen minutes to walk the mile between the two stands, and when he had seen the figure bent over something red and white he had thought that his friend must have already begun. But he saw quickly that the kneeling man was smaller and narrower through the shoulders than his friend, and Keats walked more quietly, stepping on exposed rocks and patches of pine needles that offered no crisp, betraying resistance.

When he saw his friend, he could not believe it, and said, "God," and stepped on dry leaves. The kneeling man turned then, and looked at him over his right shoulder, and Keats could see his red and glistening hands and forearms.

"What—" Keats began to say, and the man twisted the other way, to his left, toward the tree against which his rifle leaned, stretched, his left hand sliding on the ground as he tried to grasp the rifle's grip with his wet, slippery right hand. He came around toward Keats, one knee on the ground, left leg extended, the barrel bobbing in his efforts to grasp the gun securely.

But before its dark eye could look at Keats, he had raised his Remington, flicked off the safety, and fired before his rifle stopped in motion. The sound of the shot hammered his unprotected ears, and he pressed his eyes shut, waiting to feel the man's bullet tear into him.

The answering shot assaulted his deafened ears, but he felt no pain, and when he opened his eyes he saw the man lying on the ground, still gripping his rifle, blood streaming from a hole in his torn neck like a parasitic serpent escaping its host.

Slowly he lowered his rifle and looked at the two dead men. Then, very softly, he began to cry. He cried for a long time, the hot tears quickly cooling on his stubbly cheeks in the winter air.

Peter Keats had made his first kill.

FLOPHOUSE COURT

HAPSBURG LIEBE

A sort of father confessor to human wreckage off the Big Muddy, was "Sir Henry" Morgan, proprietor of a combination flophouse and soup kitchen—he called it a hotel—in New Orleans' most squalid river-front section. He slept and fed the derelicts when they came to him penniless and hungry, knowing that they'd pay him sometime. His having fallen farther and harder than any of them made him sympathetic. He'd been a great aristocrat in his day. He was still pompous. Hence his nickname, "Sir Henry."

Tonight there was a dick in the house, a squat fellow in the guise of a river-underworld thug, who called himself Frazier. He sat off in a corner of the dimly lighted, unswept lobby and watched the black front doorway with the eyes of a hawk. Unshaven, hard-bitten men came and went; Frazier did not notice them; the man he wanted was not there, as yet. The tall, gray Morgan, sitting back of the ramshackle desk, knew very well that the fellow was a dick. Morgan always knew.

Presently a stranger drifted in, came as soundlessly as a shadow, by way of the rear. He was young, slim, in dark clothing. A pair of very blue eyes burned under the lowdown rim of his soft hat. Leaning across the desk, he breathed shakily: "Are you Mr. Morgan?"

"I most assuredly am, seh. What can I do for you?"

Before the newcomer could answer, another human form approached the desk as soundlessly as a shadow. This was a shawled and slippered hag. The network of lines in her face half concealed a hideous disfigurement of ancient scars. She peered hard at the newcomer's features, then muttered: "It ain't him; no, it ain't him," and vanished.

"Poor old Moll," said Morgan, with much feeling. "Well, seh, what can I do for you?"

The young man with the burning blue eyes glanced uneasily at two passing tatterdemalions, and announced: "I want to see you— private."

For a few seconds of time Morgan watched the disguised officer in the dim corner. Frazier did not look around. Morgan pointed slyly toward the barnlike and now dark room that served as a dining-room. They went in.

"Well, seh?"

The youthful voice was low and strained: "I'm from Memphis, and my name's George Boland, though mos'ly they called me 'Little Tennessee' because I'd come off o' the Little Tennessee River. I was p'izen bad, but I wasn't any crook—jus' buck-wild, y'know. When I tried to straighten up, it was too late. I'd been 'cused o' a lot o' things I didn't do. Then I went to Jim Anderson for advice. Jim runs a little store clost to the water. Said he knowed you, Mr. Morgan. Right?"

"That is correct. Anderson is one of my very good friends. And then, seh?"

"Well," continued the other, "Jim su'gested for me to come to you here in N'Awleens, and he gimme a note to interdooce me to you, and loant me twenty dollars. The note said you'd mebbe loand me another twenty, so I could go to Central America and begin life all over. I snook on the old *Covington Belle* to work my way down the river hustlin' freight; wanted to save my money, y'see, for the long trip. Well, they was a pickpocket aboard. Now listen clost, Mr. Morgan:

"This crook was about my age and size, and awful slick and fast.

157

That night I couldn't sleep, and got up to walk the deck, and I seen him dip into a old man passenger's pocket. Only the three o' us was on that part o' the deck then. Well, the passenger jerked a big gun, but the crook grabbed it, and then he pushed the old man overboard deliberate to keep him from talkin'—and you know what that means?"

"I do, seh. The paddle blades of the wheel mangled and killed the poor fellow, of course. Horrible!"

George Boland, Little Tennessee, went on:

"Like a fool, I jumped the crook, gun and all. He lammed me acrost the head with the gun-barrel, nearly knockin' me out, went through my pockets, and pushed me overboard too! But when I hits water I comes to myself, and swims to beat all. I swam to shore, and caught a freight train at the closest town, and—here I am, half starved to death. The pickpocket got the note I was bringin' to you from Jim Anderson, as well as my twenty dollars. Has he showed up here?"

"No," Sir Henry said. "Come this way, if you please, seh."

He piloted Boland to the patchwork lean-to kitchen, sat Boland down to a great bowl of soup and a plate of buns.

"When you've finished eating, go upstairs and find yourself a bed. I will see you later. Good-night!"

He went back to the lobby.

Frazier, the dick, still sat watching the front entrance like a hawk. This annoyed Morgan a good deal now. He noted then that old Moll the hag had just come in again and was looking closely at the dick.

"It ain't him," she moaned.

"What do you mean?" blurted Frazier. "Are you cracked?"

"Yes, she's cracked," quickly said Morgan, at the desk. He ordered sharply: "You, seh, come here!"

The dick frowned, did not move. A nondescript man rose from a soapbox in deeper shadows, walked to Frazier and glared down at him.

"Sir Henry wants you; didn't you hear? Must I paste yo' face to the back o' yo' neck? Or will you go see what Sir Henry wants?"

Frazier leaped erect, bristling. But he remembered, and smiled. "Oh, all right. My error."

As he bent over the desk, Morgan said: "A new one on the force, aren't you?" There was no answer. Morgan continued: "The older officers know very well that I never fail to tip them off when a criminal comes here. I beg leave to suggest that you return to head-quarters and await word from me. Well, seh?"

Frazier was not pleased at having had his disguise thus pene-trated. But had he been a man of small caliber he would hardly have been a member of the force.

"None of us doubt that you're on the square and level, Sir Henry," he said in undertones. "You see, being a new one, as you guessed, I wanted to show a real willingness to work. I'll stick an hour or so longer, then I'll turn in."

"Do you mind telling me, seh, just whom you are expecting to find here?" very pompously inquired old Morgan.

"Why, no-o-o." Frazier looked to make sure no one listened. "A slim young fellow named George Boland, and nicknamed Little Tennessee. He's wanted pretty badly. Memphis police couldn't get anything on him, so it's up to us. Shipped out for New Orleans on the old *Covington Belle* and turned up missing. Also missing was a rich old Kentuckian named Carnes. The conclusion is that Boland robbed Carnes, killing him in the process, and gave the body to the convenient river. We thought, Sir Henry, that Boland would surely drop in here."

"I see," thoughtfully said Morgan. "I see."

Suddenly Frazier whispered:

"Look, colonel. Know that fellow?"

Just entering the lobby was a slender young man who wore flashy new clothing, carried a cheap new suitcase, and walked with a devil-may-care swagger. He had a pair of bad pale-blue eyes in his head. The shawled and slippered old Moll trailed him in. She tripped spryly to his side, and peered hard at him.

"La, la, la," she creaked. "Too young. But he's a rat, Sir Henry. A yellow rat. You mark my word!"

Her scarred and lined, unbeauteous face upset the swaggering newcomer more than that which she had said. She disappeared like a spirit. The newcomer put his suitcase down at the desk, and inquired uneasily of old Morgan: "Who in hell *was* that?"

"River show girl, forty years ago," quietly explained Sir Henry. "Some drunken brute deliberately broke the bottom of a champagne bottle and threw the bottle at her with an aim that proved damna-bly correct, and she's still looking for him. Cracked, yes, of course. You wish accommodations, seh?"

"I got a note o' interduction here from your friend, Jim Ander-son," the newcomer said, voice unsteady.

Since the flashily dressed one was still more or less upset, he wasn't so cautious as he would have been otherwise. Apparently he hadn't even seen the near-by Frazier. He passed the crumpled note across the desk. Morgan's nimble wits were working fast and hard. He gave the dick a look that registered well.

Sir Henry read Jim Anderson's bold scrawl almost at a glance. He switched his gaze back to the man who had become aware of Frazier's presence and was staring at Frazier in rising suspicion. Sir Henry spoke in tones that were as cold as glacial ice:

"I wish you knew, seh, how it feels to be chopped and mangled by a river stern-wheeler's paddle blades, the paddle blades of the old *Covington Belle,* for instance—Mr. *Boland—*"

The man turned white. His right hand went into his right coatpocket. The dick flashed a badge from under his left lapel, and in that same split second drew his revolver.

"Get 'em up, Boland—quick!" he barked.

The killer fired through his coatpocket. The reports of the two guns were as one report. But Frazier had side-stepped swiftly as he pulled trigger, and the other hadn't.

Frazier spoke coolly.

"One crook less on the Big Muddy. In self-defense, too, so I've no regrets—am not sorry a bit that I didn't go back to headquarters to wait, as you suggested, Sir Henry. Really, I don't believe you could have handled this any better yourself."

Morgan's wise old eyes twinkled.

"Why, no I'm sure I couldn't have handled it any better. And I congratulate you, seh." Sir Henry had known that the killer would come. The killer thought Boland was dead, and the note had meant money.

Sir Henry resolved to see that poor Moll DuBarry had a new dress, at least, for her unwitting aid. Frazier hurried out to the dark street, to phone headquarters.

And George Boland, listening on the dark stairs, smiled.

FLOWERS FOR MR. VECCHI

LARRY ALLAN

Vecchi had just pulled off his shoes, tilted back his chair, and rested his feet in a comfortable position on the radiator when the doorbell rang. Without waiting to pull on his shoes he trotted to the door and threw it open.

"Is this the home of Rudolph Vecchi?" the tall, solemn-faced man standing on the porch asked.

"Yes," Vecchi answered.

"Will you show me where he is, please?" the man said, stepping into the doorway.

"Who?" Vecchi asked, looking at the stranger in surprise.

"Mr. Vecchi, of course!" his visitor explained. "I'm the undertaker and I've come to embalm him."

Vecchi blinked in consternation. For a moment he couldn't speak; then he recovered his voice.

"Are you trying to kid me, or what?" he demanded, blocking the undertaker's effort to enter. "I'm Rudolph Vecchi. Do I look like I need embalming?"

The undertaker, John Stein of Stein's Funeral Parlors, expressed his amazement, and then explained. He had been called on the telephone, told that a Rudolph Vecchi was dead at that address, and had been requested to immediately take the remains for embalming. He was extremely sorry that he had caused Mr. Vecchi any inconvenience, and sincerely glad that Mr. Vecchi was not in need of his professional services.

"Just in case you do have need of my services sometime, however," the undertaker smiled, "I leave my card."

Mr. Vecchi went back to his tilted chair and toe-warming radiator. He cudgeled his brain over the undertaker's curious error. The only explanation, of course, was that someone else with the same name had died and the undertaker had secured the wrong address.

The doorbell rang again before Vecchi had really settled the question in his own mind. Cursing callers who disturbed his evening's rest Vecchi again dog-trotted to the door. A delivery boy with a large, cumbersome package stood waiting. When Vecchi opened the door the boy leaned the package against the door frame and extended his receipt book.

"Sign here, please," he said, running his finger along a blank line in the book.

"For what?" Vecchi demanded.

"Funeral wreath for Mr. Vecchi," the boy explained.

This time Mr. Vecchi nearly suffered a stroke of apoplexy. Recovering, he seized the package, tore the paper covering, and saw that it was a funeral wreath—and tied around it was a purple band with "Rudolph Vecchi" printed in letters of gold!

Vecchi shooed the boy with the wreath away angrily and returned to his tilted chair once more. After thinking it over for a few minutes he decided to take some action. This was going altogether too far. The next thing he knew a hearse would be driving up to his front door!

Vecchi rang up the nearest police station and confided his curious experiences to the desk sergeant on duty. Desk sergeants hear many strange stories, and he promised to send over a man to investigate.

In a few minutes the doorbell clanged again and Vecchi threw it open and peered outside with a quick stretching of his neck. It was the policeman from the station. Vecchi explained what had happened.

"Isn't there something the police can do to fix this thing?" he asked.

"Well now," the policeman answered, "there must be something we can—"

The doorbell rang again.

Vecchi looked at the policeman. The policeman hesitated a moment, then answered the door.

"Is this the home of Rudolph Vecchi, officer?" a man standing on the porch asked.

"It is," the policeman replied.

"Where have they got the body?" the man asked.

Vecchi, standing behind the policeman, grabbed the nearest chair for support. What in the name of all the saints was going on? Vecchi had a curious, chilling feeling running up his spine. He pinched his right leg. It hurt.

The policeman invited the undertaker, from The Funeral Home, in for questioning. It was the same story. A man representing himself as a relative of "the late Mr. Rudolph Vecchi" had telephoned requesting that they come for the body. No, there was no mistake about the address; he had written it down himself just as the man had given it to him on the phone.

When the second undertaker had taken his sorrowful leave Patrolman McGuire expressed his opinion.

"Some practical joker is playing a joke, Mr. Vecchi," he assured him.

"A hell of a joke!" Vecchi exploded. "A joke's a joke, but this is carrying it too far!"

"You're right," Patrolman McGuire answered. "I'll just stick around awhile. Maybe we can trip this smart-aleck up."

They were sitting sampling a bottle of Vecchi's home brew when the doorbell rang the next time.

It was the florist from around the corner with a stand-piece wreath with a white ribbon on which had been printed "Rest In Peace."

Patrolman McGuire sent him away when he was unable to give them any information. Vecchi quickly swallowed a good stiff drink of rye since the beer seemed to have done him little good.

For two hours—until midnight—the doorbell was silent.

"They've had their fun and I guess that's all," Patrolman McGuire declared. "Anyway, it's time for me to go off duty. If they should trouble you any more just ring up the sergeant again. He'll send someone else."

Patrolman McGuire had been gone about five minutes when the doorbell rang.

Vecchi, silently vowing to break the neck of the undertaker, florist or professional pallbearer who might be there, flung open his door.

"I'm a little late," the man standing outside explained. "I really should have been here at nine o'clock, but I was detained. I'm from your old gang in Naples. You double-crosser—"

Vecchi jumped, attempted to slam the door shut, but both shots struck him just over the heart. By the time he had slipped to the floor he was all ready for the next undertaker who would ring the doorbell.

FOOTSTEPS

JUSTIN CASE

Carmody did not hear the broadcast. He was in bed with pen and notebook, listening to his tape recorder and trying to catch the wording of "Chi Chi Bud-O." The trouble with Jamaican folk songs was that people in different parts of the island sang them differently, and some of the patois was all but unintelligible.

He had been collecting folk songs in Jamaica now for nearly a year, but these last half-dozen tapes were giving him trouble.

His housekeeper did hear the broadcast, however. There was a radio in the kitchen where she was preparing his supper. When she came bursting into his room with a paring knife clutched in one hand, Carmody knew something was wrong.

He put his notebook down and frowned at her. "What is it, Mrs. Sheppard?"

"Him did escape, suh!"

"Who has escaped?"

"That Jargie! It was on the radio! Mr. Carmody, him will come straight here to kill you!"

Carmody silenced the recorder on the table beside his bed and looked at her.

"You're sure?" he demanded, then waved a hand impatiently to silence her babbling answer. "Did they say on the radio *when* he escaped?"

"Last night." Her face was gray with terror. "Him could be here *now!*"

"In this rain?"

"No rain can stop that man!" she wailed.

With an effort, Carmody twisted himself on the bed to frown at the room's only window. Through the mist on its bubbly glass he could see water cascading from the edge of the moss-covered roof above. At this time of year such a downpour was likely to continue for days. He knew without asking that the dirt road to the village was washed out; that he could not get there even if he were able to drive. He knew, too, that on a night like this he could not expect the local police to walk three miles to look in on him.

But the housekeeper was right. Jargie would come. Jargie had sworn to get even.

It went back to a day two months ago when Jargie's girl, pretty Gladlyn Henderson, had been found with her throat cut. The whole district knew that Jargie had threatened to "chop" her for paying attention to other men, but no one had said so to the police. They feared Jargie even more than they hated him. Those enormous hands of his had crippled every man who dared to stand up against him.

But he, John Carmody, had gone to the police. The murdered girl had been his housekeeper. He had told them of Jargie's threats and the girl's terror, and his report had led to their discovery of blood under the handle of Jargie's machete. In Kingston, the C.I.D. had proved that the blood was Gladlyn Henderson's. Giant Jargie, swearing vengeance, had been tried, found guilty, and dragged off to prison to face a hanging.

Now he was free again. Coming here. Carmody threw aside the covers and sat upright.

"Crutches," he said, and old Mrs. Sheppard handed them to him. He could not walk much even with them, but it seemed important now to show the old woman he was able to. He hobbled across the room to his typewriter and rolled a sheet of paper into the machine.

He was rusty. He hadn't used the typewriter since smashing his knee in a fall from a horse, the week after Jargie's conviction. He managed a short note, signed it, and sealed it in an envelope.

He handed the envelope to Mrs. Sheppard. "Take this to the village police station, please."

She mumbled something about his supper.

"I can look after myself," he said. "Go on now, before the road gets any worse. I'm asking the corporal to send one of his men here to spend the night. You can come back with him."

She went out of the room shaking her head, and a moment later he heard the front door close. It was already dark out. Would she follow instructions? Probably not. They hated the rain, these people, and most of them were afraid of the dark. She would go home, he supposed, and when she came in the morning she would tell him she had tried to reach the village but the road was out. Anyway, it would get her out of the house.

Struggling to his feet again, he hobbled on the crutches to the front door and locked it, then went down the long, gloomy hall to the kitchen. His supper was on the oil stove. He turned the stove off, ate something, and carried the coffee pot back to his room, spilling some at every bump of the crutches. This place, Glentully, had once been a coffee plantation—a big one for Jamaica. That explained the hugeness of the house, which had nineteen rooms and a maze of corridors on its two levels.

He was out of breath now. He had to sit on the edge of the bed and rest. As he did so, the light over his head suddenly dimmed. He looked up in panic. Electricity here was supplied by a turbine at the river. Sometimes in a hard rain the intake silted up or was choked with leaves. If that happened tonight . . .

The light brightened again. He expelled his pent-up breath in a gust of relief.

Now then, the tapes. There was almost no chance that they would work, but he must use what weapons he had. He dragged himself across the room to the pile of the table, found those he wanted, and carried them back to the machine by the bed. If the power went off, the recorder would still run on its batteries, thank heaven.

Fixing a reel in place, he turned the machine on to be sure the tape was threaded properly. Listened for a few seconds. Shut it off again. Then made himself comfortable on the bed, stared at the open door, and waited. There was no use closing the door. It had no lock.

Nineteen rooms. All of them had windows, but half the sash locks were rusted away or broken. How many outside doors were there in the house? Half a dozen, at least. A determined push would open almost any of them.

He had no gun, of course. Had never owned a gun in his life. Or a machete either. Jargie would have a machete. All the mountain people had them, and kept them razor-sharp with little triangular files. With such a weapon a powerful man could lop a victim's head off at one stroke.

What was that?

A thud, downstairs. He sat up, wincing as the sudden movement brought a stab of pain. His right hand went slowly to the recorder and turned it on. The machine responded with a low hum. He felt for the push-button marked PLAY but did not press it.

It wasn't time. Not yet.

The thud again. A door had opened, then closed. Maybe. Maybe it was just the wind at a window—but there was not enough wind for that, was there? He braced his shoulders against the head of the bed. This was an old, old house. The stairs and floors would creak under the weight of anyone as big as Jargie. But if the back stairs creaked he would not hear them. The door between them and the kitchen was closed.

Somewhere another door squeaked. The kitchen door? Yes, he felt the draft. A draft always came up the back stairs when that door was opened. What he felt was air moving against his face after it flowed like a river down the hall.

A floor board creaked in the hall. He pressed the PLAY button and held his breath.

He had made this first tape months ago at a party in Kingston. Like most such party tapes it was a blur of voices with now and then an outburst of laughter or a moment of silence. He turned the volume up. With a crutch in his hands for a weapon he sat rigid, watching the doorway. Jargie, knowing nothing of tape recorders, would think he had a roomful of visitors. Maybe.

And it was early. Jargie would expect such callers to stay late. Jargie would go away, planning to come again some other time. Maybe.

The tape reels slowly turned. Someone told a joke. Laughter. Silence. "Rum and ginger, darling? Your glass is empty." A roomful of ghosts.

From the hall no sound. Nothing.

The tape ran on and on. It was good for an hour. His eyes burned from staring at the doorway. An hour was forever. Sixty minutes. Sixty times sixty seconds. In any one of which the hulk of Jargie might suddenly fill the doorway.

The tape ran out.

Now was the crucial moment. Now, if Jargie had not gone, it would happen. Carmody reached out to rewind the tape but realized it would fool no one a second time. He held the crutch like a lance aimed at the doorway, and his knuckles turned white with tension.

Suddenly the light over his head flickered. The room went black. All was silent. And then, in the hall, a board creaked.

He dropped the crutch. Throwing himself half off the bed, he seized a second reel of tape and jabbed it blindly at the machine. In the hall, footsteps. Slow footsteps. Jargie was not sure. Jargie was coming to find out. But the hall was long and the darkness confused him.

The tape fought Carmody's fingers. It was a live snake struggling to escape and slither to the floor in the blackness. He caught it in both hands and forced it into place. The footsteps were just outside the door. They were bolder. He could hear a sound of breathing.

PLAY!

The tape turned. The man in the hall took one more step and was in the doorway, peering into the room. But the room was dark. The tape began to sing.

It was a folk song, one of dozens this singer had sung for Carmody. The bold voice filled the room with a wail about a drowning—"Judy Drownded"—but it could have been any song.

In the doorway, nothing. For one, two, three minutes, nothing. Then something metallic clanged to the floor. A thunderclap cry exploded from terror-filled lungs. The ancient floor boards shivered under pounding footsteps, moving away in the night.

The tape was still running when Carmody heard the yell and the shots in the yard. The girl was still singing when Corporal Daley from the village police station strode into the room behind his flashlight, followed by old Mrs. Sheppard. Staring at the bed, surely expecting to find a dead man there, the corporal slowed to a halt.

"But how?" he muttered. "How were you able to—?

He became aware of the song. He scowled at the recorder. "Gladlyn Henderson?" he said. "That *is* Gladlyn, isn't it?"

Carmody could only nod.

On the floor, Jargie's machete glistened in the flashlight beam. The corporal bent to pick it up, then looked at the machine again. "So that is what Jargie was running from. In the dark he thought—"

"Yes," Carmody said.

The girl Jargie had murdered sang on.

FOOTSTEPS IN THE NIGHT

HUGH B. CAVE

Tonight she was late again. With Mrs. Tilford's feeble "Thank you for coming, Angela" still in her ears, she paused in the dim-lit hall only long enough to glance in panic at her watch.

Eleven-fifteen! And she had promised Gil she would meet him at eleven!

She fled down the stairs and out to the sidewalk, desperately hoping to see a cab, even though the fare would take all her money. But cabs didn't cruise on Pine Street at that hour. It was a neighborhood of dingy stores and walk-up tenements such as the one she had just left.

A dark, dreary neighborhood. Lately a dangerous one.

She stood in the doorway, biting her lips and wondering frantically what she should do. Walk? When even the newspapers were warning women not to walk the streets after dark? "Now don't you go home along Pine, Angela," Mrs. Tilford had insisted, lifting herself on one elbow and weakly wagging a finger. "Go up Center to the avenue and take the subway. Center is well lighted."

Please, Gil, don't be angry. But he would be. Only last night he had been furious. "Why do you have to play nursemaid to an old woman anyhow?" he had demanded.

"She can't get out of bed with a broken hip, Gil. And she's a friend. She works with me at the store."

He grumbled, but afterward had relented and kissed her. "Just don't get the idea you're the only girl in the world. Next time I might not wait."

Biting her lip, she stepped from the dark doorway and began walking. She was not fooling herself about Gil Chase. He had faults. But when he said he could have other girls, he was only telling the truth. As for herself, she was no catch for any man. If she hadn't known it by the time she was eighteen and left home, it was

169

not her mother's fault. Mom believed in telling the truth, no matter how it hurt.

What was that behind her? Footsteps?

She turned her head. A man had stepped out of a doorway behind her. A tall man with long arms dangling. Lengthening his stride, he seemed to flow toward her like something in a dream. Dear God! Those stories in the paper! Those two girls!

The clatter of her shoes on the concrete was a drumbeat in the stillness. But when she looked back again, he was still there.

Ahead, only half a block away, was a cross street and a grimy metal lamp-post at the top of which a light glowed like a pale star. If she could reach it ahead of him, there might be a car coming, or people . . .

A man came limping around the corner and she crashed into him.

"My goodness! Vot is the matter vith you?" He lifted her to her feet, a big, solid man with a husky voice that smelled of something he had eaten.

She clung to him and looked back. The dark, flowing figure was nowhere to be seen. "Some—someone was following me!"

"Vere do you go, young lady?"

She told him and he frowned. He was fifty, perhaps, and wore a dark, expensive suit and soft leather slippers. His face was round as a plate and full of concern for her. "Morton Street?" he said. "That is by the little park, no?"

"Yes, yes."

"And vot is your name?"

"Angela Simms."

"An angel, eh? I take the angel home, I t'ink. It is not good for a beautiful young voman to be valking alone at night in this neighborhood. Come."

He walked along beside her, talking. She should be more careful, he said. "I t'ink you have not read the papers lately, little angel. For some girls it vould be safe, perhaps, but for you, no. You are too beautiful. He vaits for beautiful girls, this man."

"Beautiful?" Angela said. "Me?"

"You t'ink you are not, little angel?" He smiled at her. "I tell you so, then. Me you must believe. I am an artist. I make a study of beauty all my life."

The high iron fence surrounding the park was just ahead. His fingers lay gently on her arm as he crossed the street with her. She would have dreaded the park without him; it was small but dark, and the cinder path was lined with shrubs.

But she would have been all right, even alone. Almost at once she saw Gil's car standing at the curb in front of the house, with its parking lights glowing. Her companion saw it, too, and halted.

"Someone is vaiting for you?" he asked.

"Yes. A—a friend."

"Then I say good night, little angel. You vill be safe now."

"Thank you," Angela said. "Oh, thank you!"

She approached the car and saw Gil sprawled on the seat with his head back and his eyes shut. She opened the door and touched him. "Gil," she said. "Gil."

His eyes opened. He looked at his watch. "Go ahead, say it."

"Say what, Gil?"

"You had to play nursemaid again." He sat up. "Let me tell you something. If I hadn't fallen asleep, I wouldn't be here."

"Gil," she said, "you don't understand."

"Are you going to get in? What I ought to do is drive off and—"

"Then drive off," she said.

Had she actually said it? She stepped back with her hand against her mouth. Yes, she had. Without meaning to, without thinking, she had dared.

Gil spoke at last. "What did you say? What was that you said?"

She wondered what had happened to her. Did terror do this to a person? Or was it the old man with the round face wanting to help her, insisting that she was beautiful?

"Okay," Gil was muttering. "So you had a reason for being late. Now for Pete's sake get in and let's go."

"No."

"What?"

"Take out one of your other girls." She stepped away from his hands.

For a minute he only stared. Then he said, "Angie, what's got into you?" and started to squirm himself out of the car. But she had her key in her hand and was climbing the apartment-house steps. Letting herself in, she shut the door behind her.

He returned to the car after a while. It leaped from the curb with an angry roar and went snarling down the street.

At the edge of the little park the man with the round face stopped watching and turned away, gently shaking his head. Hands in pockets, he trudged into darkness, the long fingers of one hand idly caressing a noose of wire.

Good Night, Sweet Alibi

Rufus Bakalor

Gilbert Pitcott, who was known to the grift and law-enforcement professions as "The Ringading Kid," had no business being a con man. He had the appearance of one, which is to say that he looked like a handsome, progressive young businessman. And he was materially successful in the swindle, as witness the fact that he and Diehard Dyson had just roped a visiting Brazilian and fleeced him for the not inconsiderable sum of $300,000. Before taxes, of course.

But Mr. Pitcott, hereinafter referred to as Ringading, was seriously lacking in those strong moral fibers which go into every grifter's makeup. A true blue grifter, all wool and a yard wide, abides by certain professional ethics. Among these are injunctions against the use of violence—except perhaps with a difficult victim—and against the commission of common, thuggish thievery, particularly of a fellow grifter.

As he lay on the bed in his hotel room, smoking a soiled cigarette, Ringading contemplated the violation of both these injunctions. On the deal they had just pulled, he had cleared $120,000. He figured that Diehard Dyson, after cutting in the mob, still had ninety, maybe a hundred, thousand left.

It was Diehard's part of the touch that Ringading wanted, and he wanted it badly. He figured that, with Diehard's money plus his, he could quit the racket for good and maybe open up a nice, respectable nightclub or a nice, legitimate bookie joint. Anyway, he'd find a way to invest the money.

So Diehard had, say, ninety grand, thinking conservatively; and he knew for sure where Diehard had it: with him up at Shay Lake in that little log, porcupine-eaten shack where Diehard always went for fishing, rest and money-counting after a big take.

Ringading worked it all out and decided that it was a sure thing. Ringading was very, very clever. . . .

He checked an address in his memo book and drove to the Runcorne Arms apartment house on Michigan Boulevard. He pressed the buzzer under a card that read *Glorya Easterly* and announced to the throaty contralto inquiry that it was the Ringading Kid on urgent business.

Then he went up.

Glorya Easterly was a sometime showgirl who was gorgeous but greedy. She was very fond of currency and/or possessions readily convertible into same: pearls, the pelts of small fur-bearing animals, precious stones and metals, and the like. She had plenty of them and she wanted more. A lot more. Whether or not she was an elegant fluff is a proposition that has no bearing on this tale.

When Ringading recovered from momentary drowsiness induced by the fumes of *Or et Noir*, he took a chair that Glorya indicated with a jewel-festooned hand.

Glorya fixed him a drink and asked, "Well, Ringading, what's the nature of your urgent business?"

Ringading came right to the point. "How'd you like to make a very soft grand?"

"Love it," said Glorya, leaning forward and breathing a little heavier. "What's the pitch?"

"Just for doing two simple things."

"The simple things are always the best things."

Ringading was silent for a moment and then went on, "I've got to go away on a little trip tomorrow night. But I want it established that I was here, with you, in this apartment, say from eight o'clock until two in the morning."

"A grand for being your alibi?"

"That's it. Only it's got to be an air-tight alibi, air-tight enough to hold water. I'll stage it right. All you got to worry about is following the stage directions."

"Uh-huh," said Glorya. "And where will you be from eight to two?"

"That's the second simple thing in your contract: not to ask any questions."

"Reasonable enough. How do you pay off?"

"Two-fifty to seal it now, and after the job's done, this." He showed her a thousand-dollar savings bond made out to Gilbert Pitcott or Glorya Easterly. "I'll deliver possession of this to you the day after tomorrow. Then you can do what you want with it."

"Sounds all right, but a wee bit cagey. Don't you trust me, Ringading?"

"Sure, I do, up to a point. But Ringading never takes unnecessary chances."

"I just love to do business with you, Ringading."

"And I love to do business with you, Glorya."

"Well, I'm an old, established firm."

Ringading smiled tightly, like an infant with gas on its tummy, counted out two hundred and fifty dollars into Glorya's eager little hand, and said, "I'll see you tomorrow night at eight."

"It's a date."

"By the way," said Ringading, "bruit it about a bit that you'll be entertaining the Ringading Kid here tomorrow night. You know, call up a girl friend and let it drop. That's all you've got to do until we set things up. Say anything you can to plant me here."

"Whatever you say, Ringading. Won't the girls envy me?"

"The thousand is for an alibi," said Ringading. "If I want wisecracks, I'll catch the comic at the Chez Paree."

The next evening, polished and shiny, Ringading wore a brown derby hat, a red cravat, and a Tattersall vest, among other less conspicuous apparel, of course, so that he might be readily identified later.

He walked to the desk in the hotel lobby and told the room clerk, "A rather important call from Detroit may come through for me later. For all others, tell 'em I've checked out. But if the Detroit call comes through, I'll be spending the evening at the Runcorne Arms, apartment one hundred-twelve, care of Miss Glorya Easterly."

He winked elaborately, placed a folded twenty-dollar bill on the desk, and said, "Got that? Runcorne Arms. Miss Glorya Easterly. Better make a note of it so you won't forget."

"I sure won't forget, Mr. Pitcott," said the room clerk. "I wish I had a vest like that."

Then Ringading stopped at the hotel flower shop, and bought seven dozen long-stemmed American beauty roses. "I'll take them with me," he told the befuddled florist. "You write out a card for me. Put: 'To Glorya with love.' Sign it: 'Ringading.' "

Struggling with the roses, Ringading engaged a cab to take him to the Runcorne Arms. When the cab drew up in front of its destination, Ringading handed the cabbie a fifty-dollar bill, and told him to keep the change. "Courtesy of the Ringading Kid," he said, clearly and distinctly.

Sure, it had cost him some money, but the hotel clerk, the florist, and the cabbie would be sure to remember him and surmise his mission. Charge it off to sewing up the alibi with a nice, tight lock-stitch.

When he entered Glorya's apartment, she gasped at the roses that obscured Ringading and cooed, "Oh, Ringading, for me?"

"Yeah."

"Darling! You shouldn't a done it. Just hold on while I run some water in the bathtub."

"Cut the antics and let's get to work. I've got a million things to do tonight."

Ringading had brought with him a small box containing a day's collection of cigarette stubs of his favorite brand. He distributed them liberally in the ash trays in all the rooms of the apartment. He had Glorya mix up a drink and then he planted his fingerprints on the glass. Then he put his fingerprints on various other objects, animate and inanimate. He dropped one of his gloves behind an easy chair, and he left his monogrammed comb in the bathroom.

He stepped to the center of the room, and surveyed, with pardonable pride, what he had wrought.

"Ringading was here!" shouted Glorya.

"That's the general idea," said Ringading. "Now remember, just take it easy until I get in touch with you. All you got to do is pretend I'm here. Get that into your head and don't let anyone ever tell you otherwise."

"Good night, sweet prince," called Glorya as Ringading crawled out the window on to the fire stairs.

"Good night, sweet alibi," rejoined Ringading. . . .

Ringading went down the fire escape stairway and walked four blocks to the place where he had parked his car. He took off his tie, hat and vest and threw them in the back seat. Then he got behind the wheel and started off in a northerly direction, toward Shay Lake and Diehard Dyson's ninety grand, one hundred and ten miles away.

He reached there at a quarter to eleven. By ten to, he had aroused Diehard from his sleep.

When Diehard saw that it was Ringading, he welcomed him heartily. Diehard, as befits a good inside man on the grift, looked like a Wisconsin banker's conception of a Wall Street broker.

"Well, Ringading, what brings you into the wilderness?"

"Got fed up in the city and thought I'd run up here for a change, just for a couple hours. How's the fishing?"

"I wouldn't know," said Diehard. "What're you drinking?"

"Nothing tonight. My stomach . . ." Ringading thought to himself: *Don't touch anything in this place, that's my motto.*

They sat and talked for a while, mostly about the visiting Brazilian and how they had cooled him out.

At last Diehard said, "I don't believe you drove all the way up here just to punch the guff. You're a little too fidgety, even for you. What's up?"

"You're right, Diehard. I've got a lead on an apple that looks good for a hundred G's, maybe more."

"Go on."

"I didn't like to ask you, but I need a bankroll to operate on. I'm cleaned."

"So soon? What's happened to the enterprising Brazilian's investment?"

"You know, Diehard: the ponies, the women, the dice."

"Yes, yes, and yes. It could happen. Ringading, why don't you settle down like me and enjoy the more economical pleasures of life?"

"Maybe I will when I'm an inside man."

Diehard sighed like an indulgent parent and said, "How much do you need?"

"Five thousand should do it."

Diehard rose and walked to the cupboard. "Rope me another sucker like the Brazilian and it's worth it. I'll be back in town Tuesday, same place. So contact me then."

When he reached for a box of corn flakes, Ringading went into action quickly with a blackjack. Diehard never knew what hit him, never knew what hit him again and again and again.

After Diehard stopped jerking, Ringading bent over him and assured himself that Diehard was good and dead. Then he went for the box of corn flakes. And there was the cache, all in five-hundred-dollar bills, as crisp and delectable as the breakfast cereal it was cushioned in.

Ringading stuffed the money in his pockets, took a last look around to see if he had left any tell-tale souvenirs, except for Diehard, and went outside. No one and nothing was stirring outside the cabin, unless you count a highly amateurish choir of crickets. He washed the blackjack clean of fingerprints in the water and then flung it as far as he could into Shay Lake.

There was no reason for him to hide the bills, so he put them in the glove compartment and locked it.

* * *

It was now eleven thirty-five and Ringading began the less tense drive back to Chicago. He wondered how much richer he was on the return trip.

He hit the suburbs of the city at ten to two and decided that he'd better go directly to Glorya's place and check in and out. He had told her two o'clock, and with a crazy dame like Glorya, you couldn't always tell what to expect.

He stopped the car, put on his derby, vest and necktie again, and then continued on at a breakneck clip.

Everyone knows what happens when you exceed the speed limit in Chicago: a squad car nails you. They are very strict about the traffic regulations in Chicago.

So a squad car nailed Ringading. And, what is more, Ringading was prepared to take his ticket like a good citizen and not give the copper any argument.

The policemen peered in the window and exclaimed, "Well, well, well. If this here ain't a pleasant surprise! The Ringading Kid!" He called to his companion at the wheel of the prowl car, "Guess who the cannonball is. The Ringading Kid."

"Maybe I was going a little fast," Ringading put in.

"And that ain't all, Ringading. There's a general call out to pick you up."

"Pick me up? Why?"

"I wouldn't be knowing. But a certain Detective Lieutenant Martin J. Foy is anxious to have a chat with you. And Detective Lieutenant Martin J. Foy is assigned to Homicide, if you take my meaning."

"I don't get it, not at all. My nose is clean."

The policeman stuck his hand in the window, removed Ringading's ignition key, and said, "We'll leave your car just where it is and you come along with us, Clean Nose."

At the precinct station, waiting for Lieutenant Foy, Ringading couldn't dope it out. Something had curdled. But he was sure that he'd left no evidence back at Shay Lake. And just let them try to break down his alibi.

At last, Lieutenant Foy came in and took him to his office. He ushered him to a chair, and offered him a cigarette. "Just a few routine questions, Ringading, if you'll bear with me."

"Sure, sure, Lieutenant. I've got nothing to hide."

"Where were you between, say, ten-fifteen and midnight to-night?"

"If it's O.K. with you, I'd rather not say."

"Why not?"

"Well, to be perfectly frank, Lieutenant, I was with a certain young lady in her apartment during that time." He turned and winked at the several policemen posted about the room. "A fellow's got to have a little fun once in a while."

"I'll give it to you straight, Ringading: there's been a murder and it looks like you're into it up to your neck."

"Hold on, Lieutenant! You can't pin a thing on me and you know it. I had nothing to do with that murder and, what's more, I can prove where I was at the time it was committed. I got witnesses."

The detective smiled like a man having a Swedish rubdown. "So can we, Ringading, and with enough witnesses to do you up nice and brown. I'm warning you now that anything you say can be used against you. Because I'm booking you for the murder of Glorya Easterly. Between ten and midnight tonight, she was killed and robbed in her apartment."

THE GRAVE JOKER

MORRIS COOPER

Mrs. Dolan never nagged. She was just contrary, like the last match in a folder. And since her name on the bottom of a check was the only one recognized by the bank, she always had her own way.

Like the time Mr. Dolan's sister was sick. "Just plain laziness," decided Mrs. Dolan. "What she needs is to go to work. That'll straighten her up. If she's worried about her cough, tell her to cut down on cigarettes."

Everyone was sympathetic with her when Mr. Dolan's sister died of tuberculosis. "Not even a blood relative," they said, "and look at the funeral she paid for. Must have cost a thousand dollars."

And Mr. Dolan? No one noticed him tucked away behind the huge masses of flowers. He just wasn't important enough.

Mrs. Dolan was very upset by the whole affair. "You'd think it was my sister instead of yours," she complained later. "Everything on my shoulders. My friends thought it strange you said nothing."

Mr. Dolan sighed, and Mrs. Dolan snipped: "You're so—" she struggled for the right word, and finally came up with it triumphantly—"so unimportant. No one ever notices you. I'll bet even at your own funeral you'll be the least important thing there."

Mr. Dolan sighed gently again and kept quiet. He knew that she never, never, expected an answer from him.

The first time Mrs. Dolan had played poker, Mr. Dolan made the tactical error of telling her he didn't approve of gambling for high stakes. But that had been when Mr. Dolan was very, very young. And even then, she was contrary. When she had no right to, she would still win.

If someone offered to bet it would be light tomorrow noon, she'd take a gamble, and there probably would be a total eclipse of the sun.

Tonight, Mr. Dolan didn't want to go to the party; he was tired and lonely.

"I'm not going alone," Mrs. Dolan declared. "I'd be the laughing stock of everyone there."

Mr. Dolan sighed and went for his topcoat.

He offered to drive, and automatically held the door open while she got behind the wheel. He walked around the car and got in beside her. It was a little chilly, so he started to roll the window up.

She snapped, "Leave it down." And added, "There'll be a lot of smart, sophisticated people there tonight. So don't say anything. Just sit."

Mr. Dolan closed his eyes while she drove. He thought of his son—he thought of him a lot lately, and always as *his* son. Years ago he had stopped thinking of her as a mother. If it ever crossed his mind, it was only to wonder that the miracle of her becoming a mother could have transpired.

Of course his son was dead and buried with thousands of other soldiers who would never come home, but that didn't matter to Mr. Dolan. He could always close his eyes and be with him.

Mr. Dolan was sorry he hadn't been able to see his son before he went overseas. He had wired home for money to fly. All he had was a five-day leave and he couldn't make it by train.

Mrs. Dolan had decided that flying was too extravagant. "He can come home next month," she had said. But next month never came. He would never come home.

A gentle smile touched Mr. Dolan's lips. Soon he would be with his son forever. Six months, the doctor had told him. A year at the most. And Mr. Dolan had a plan for those remaining months. He was going to where his son slept. He could get a little cottage near him, and every day he would be able to have a long visit with him and his buddies.

But Mrs. Dolan must never know of this plan. This was a secret Mr. Dolan kept locked in his heart.

The party was gay and reckless. Mr. Dolan sat in a corner chair, alone and unwatched. There was poker and dice and some threw knives at the wall. Someone offered to hold his hand up as a target. Mr. Dolan closed his eyes and dreamed.

The loud voice of a man woke Mr. Dolan. He listened.

"Lots of people play it," the voice was saying. "And it's a fascinating gamble." He held up a shiny revolver and picked a cartridge from the handful that lay on the table. "It's simple." He slipped the cartridge home and spun the cylinder. "One bullet. Six to one odds."

He put the muzzle to his temple. There was an empty click, and Mr. Dolan could hear the explosions of pent-up breath. Two or three others tried it. And that same empty click. Then the game paled and the crowd wandered off. Mr. Dolan closed his eyes.

Mrs. Dolan shook her husband. She snapped, "At least you can stay awake and pretend you're enjoying yourself." She saw him looking at the table on which the revolver lay. "What's that for?" she asked.

The man who had started the game came up. "You missed all the fun," he said. Mrs. Dolan listened and saw her husband shake his head.

She laughed. "That sounds like fun." Mr. Dolan touched her arm and she pulled away. She was always contrary.

"Look, everyone." She held the revolver and spun the cylinder.

180

"Anyone want to lay odds?" Mrs. Dolan laughed and put the muzzle of the shiny gun in her mouth.

Then she pulled the trigger.

Later, the police were very severe. A lieutenant of detectives gave them a harsh lecture. But there wasn't much he could do.

And, besides, if anyone had seen Mr. Dolan take out five cartridges from the revolver before the police arrived, he never thought the fact important enough to volunteer the information.

GRAVEYARD RACE

ANDREW FELL

They were talking about murder. Both of them knew it, even while they were still skirting around the edges of the subject. In Tom Wilson's penthouse, forty floors above New York, Wilson's wife, Felicia, and his confidential assistant, Harrison Baldwin, were talking about murder—Tom Wilson's murder.

Felicia, cool and beautiful in a silver evening gown, sat at the baby grand with her fingers resting on the keys. Harry Baldwin slouched against the doorway leading to the terrace—big, shock-haired and hot in his two-hundred-dollar dinner jacket. He lit a cigarette carefully, and they looked at each other with the look two people give who know each other very well.

"Look, darling," Baldwin said, when the cigarette was burning, "you're sure Tom said that? That he was going to sell Wilson Air Conditioning and Refrigeration and retire to a simple life in the country with you?"

"With me and the kiddies—when they come," Felicia said, her voice subdued. "He's tired of working just to make money. He wants to spend more time up in Maine hunting. He wants to spend more time with me—lots more. He's afraid he's been neglecting me. He's afraid I've been lonely."

She shuddered.

"He's fifty, pot-bellied and bald, and he can't talk about anything but baseball, deer hunting and refrigeration." She smiled wryly. "And he's afraid he's been neglecting me. God! I've been able to stand him only because he's been working eighteen hours a day. If I had him all to myself I'd go stark mad in a month."

Baldwin nodded and tossed his cigarette out over the terrace into the dark September night.

"I understand, darling," he said mockingly. "Also, if Tom sells the business, he'll lose most of his investment. I don't know what will be left, but the income won't buy you diamonds, pearls and a fifteen-room penthouse on Park Avenue."

"It'll affect you too," Felicia said. "You'll be out of a job. The new owner would have his own confidential assistant. It might be hard to get another job as good again."

"I know it. On the other hand, if I were running the business, I'd have it clearing a million a year inside five years."

"I'm sure of it," Felicia said. "Darling, how would you like to be running the business?"

"I'd like it fine. What do you suggest?"

"If Tom died—" her fingers touched the keys lightly; a single minor chord trembled in the room and echoed out— "I'd inherit the firm. I'd make you general manager."

"Would you? And would you marry me?"

Felicia nodded slowly. Then she smiled.

"I suppose I'd have to, darling," she said.

Baldwin lit another cigarette, absently, and stared down at the green-gold fire of the tip. "He'd have to die quite soon, to do any good," he commented. He looked up and caught her gaze. For a long moment they stared at each other.

Felicia had come from a poverty-stricken Southern town and deliberately married wealth, he knew—and he admired her skill in doing it. Harry Baldwin had come from the East Side slums and worked his way up with tactics that even in the slums would have been dirty; Felicia knew it and admired his dexterity at not getting caught.

"I'm very tired of Tom," Felicia said. "*Very* tired."

"So am I," Baldwin said. "I've been tired of him for five years. But he's been a living. Now he's not going to be a living any more. So?"

"So what?"

"What's the rest of it? You haven't said this much without having a lot more in your mind."

"How well you know me, darling. But then, you should, shouldn't you? I was thinking of Tom's beautiful hunting lodge in Maine, built only last year. He keeps wanting me to go up there with him to get away from this heat. But I hate the woods. Yet it seems a shame to let the place go to waste."

"And you intend to go up there with Tom?"

"No, darling. *You* are going up with Tom. Next Saturday. I'll follow on Monday."

"You have it all arranged?"

"Practically. I'll talk Tom into it when he comes home tonight."

"I see. Then what?"

"Before Monday comes, Harry darling, don't you think that Tom could have a hunting accident. Or be cleaning a gun when it goes off? Or something?"

Baldwin was silent for a long moment. Then at last he nodded slowly, watching Felicia's face.

"Yes, my dear," he said. "I think that Tom will have a hunting accident, or be cleaning a gun when it goes off, or—something."

Tom Wilson—Thomas T. Wilson, air conditioning, cold storage and deep-freeze units—stood on the terrace of his hunting lodge, wearing loud slacks, an even louder jacket, a thirty-dollar Scotch wool scarf around his throat, breathing deeply of the cool, pine-scented air.

"This is the life, Harry!" he said with satisfaction. "When I retire this is where I'm coming to live. I should have been a country boy. If I hadn't been born into a family with a lot of rich connections, like Aunt Minetta, I probably never would have tried to make money. Been a lot happier if I hadn't, too."

Baldwin, towering over the pudgy, baldheaded man beside him, did not crack a smile.

"That's the way it goes, Mr. Wilson," he said solemnly. "Say, did you see that? That was a deer then! A six-point buck!"

"Where?" Tom Wilson yelled. "Where, Harry?"

"Down by the stand of cedars. It's gone now. But I bet we could bag one tomorrow before Mrs. Wilson gets here!

"You think we could?" The fat little man's eyes glistened. "That would be something. That's why I built this place. Imagine being able to have fresh venison the whole year round, right out of your own cellar."

"Why don't we get up early and have a try?" Harry Baldwin asked, watching the little man from the corner of his eye.

"By Godfrey, we will!" Tom Wilson exploded. "Come on, Harry, let's go into the gun room and get down a couple of rifles. We can give them a good cleaning and have a little target practice before the sun goes down."

They headed for the gun room, where the clock on the wall said just exactly five. . . .

The clock in the New York penthouse said five, too, when the phone call came. Long distance from Boston for Mr. Thomas Wilson. Felicia took it, her voice cool and soft.

"I'm sorry, he's not in," she said gently into the mouthpiece. "Who's calling, please?"

"This is Charlie Ivors, Mrs. Wilson," a man's voice said. "Of Ivors and Clark. We're attorneys for your husband's aunt, Minetta Wilson."

"Oh, of course!" Felicia's cool tones warmed up at the name. Aunt Minetta! Worth two million dollars—as Tom had often commented —all of it willed to a home for wayward girls!

"Mrs. Wilson, it's extremely urgent that I contact Mr. Wilson," the lawyer on the phone said. "His aunt had a stroke this morning. She's dying in the hospital."

"Dying?"

"Yes, slowly but surely. She may last eight hours, or a week. No longer. But she's altered her will. We've just finished changing it to make Mr. Wilson the beneficiary."

"Harry—his aunt's beneficiary?" For once in her life Felicia Wilson had difficulty speaking. "But I thought she was leaving everything to some home."

"She was, but she changed her mind. Now she's leaving it all to your husband. And she'd like to see him before she dies—just for a moment."

"Of course. Mr. Ivors, I'm terribly sorry, but he's away. The heat was making him feel miserable, and he's gone off for a short vacation. I don't know just where."

"If you can possibly locate him, please do, Mrs. Wilson. Get him up to Boston at once. It won't make any difference about the legacy, but she does want to see him."

"I will. I'll make every effort to find him."

"Thank you very much. And tell him to take care of himself."

The lawyer chuckled—a dry, legal chuckle. "It wouldn't do for anything to happen to him now. He has to survive his aunt to inherit, of course. If anything happened to him before she died the money would go to charity after all. Well, good-bye, Mrs. Wilson."

"Good-bye."

Felicia Wilson hung up, her face flushed, her heart pounding. Two million dollars—if Aunt Minetta died first. But if Tom died first . . .

She snatched up the phone again and gave long distance the Maine number.

"And keep ringing until they answer, operator! It's a matter of life and death!"

"Now here's a beautiful gun," Tom Wilson said fondly, patting the handmade Swiss .350 with the telescope sights. "It practically aims itself. Say, Harry, isn't that the phone ringing?"

Baldwin turned his head in annoyance. His nerves were tight and his face flushed, for all the easiness of his manner. He'd cut close to the line plenty of times in his career, but he'd never stepped over it into the dark region of murder. He knew exactly what he was going to do and say; he had no doubts, but he was nervous. And he had no desire to talk to anyone on a telephone just now.

"Yes, you're right. Phone back in the library is ringing, Mr. Wilson."

"Thought I heard it a minute ago. Why don't you answer it?"

"It's probably for you—on business. Why don't we let it ring? You're here for a rest!"

"That's right, I am." The little, baldheaded man looked sulky. "I told them at the office not to call me on any account. All right—the heck with it! Let it ring until they get tired."

Behind them, in the library beyond the gun room, the phone kept shrilling, mechanical, untiring, relentless. Harry Baldwin closed his ears to it. Wilson was seated in a light, comfortable cane chair, the rifle across his knees, a glass of Scotch and soda at his elbow. Baldwin picked up a long-barrelled target pistol from the table beside him and held it out carelessly toward Wilson.

"Here's a good gun for target practice," he said. "Helps sharpen the eye."

"A pistol!" Wilson said. "Can't hit a thing with them."

"Oh, you can if you're close enough," Baldwin said. "And a .22 will kill if your aim is good enough."

"Sooner use a pea-shooter!" his employer sniffed. "Say, that telephone is getting on my nerves. Go shut it off—tell 'em I'm dead or something, and can't come to the phone."

"I'll do that," Harry Baldwin said roughly. "I'll see that you aren't bothered!"

He pulled the trigger, and the little gun went *pop* in a surprised manner. Flame scorched Wilson's tweed jacket. The fat, bald man looked up at Harry Baldwin, and his mouth opened accusingly. But the words he wanted to say died with him. The gun muzzle had only been six inches from his heart, and even as his mouth opened, he died.

With a convulsive motion, Wilson jerked in the chair, stiffened, then lay back limply, his chin lolling on his chest. A little trickle of red began to dampen his gaudy jacket.

With satisfaction Baldwin stared down at the dead man. Then he carefully wiped the revolver and laid it in the dead man's lap, touching the limp finger tips to it in many places. He was reaching for the cleaning tools, to put them on the table at the dead man's elbow to complete the picture, when the harsh shrilling of the telephone beat back into his consciousness again. For a minute he had managed to ignore it. Now it rasped into his brain like a dentist's drill.

"Shut up!" he roared at it, then, with long strides, crossed into the library and snatched up the receiver.

"Hello!" he shouted. "What is it?"

"Harry!" Across the miles Felicia's voice was more agitated than he had ever known it. "Harry! Don't do anything! You mustn't! Not yet!"

"Don't do anything?" Baldwin said stupidly, staring back through the connecting door at the top of the bald head which lolled to one side. "What're you talking about?"

"Harry, listen!" The words that raced along the copper wires at first made no sense; then comprehension came. "So you see, Harry, Tom has to be alive when his aunt dies, to inherit. Do you understand me? *Tom must stay alive until after his aunt dies!* Harry, are you still there? Say something!"

"Yes, I'm still here." Harry Baldwin's mind was racing as it never had before. Two million dollars depended on the question of which death came first—and the wrong death had come first! If they had waited a week, the money would have gone to Tom—and then to Felicia. But now it was too late! Tom Wilson sat in there, dead, and in Boston, hundreds of miles away, an old lady lay in a hospital bed, dying, but still alive . . . still alive. . . .

"Harry, what is it? What's wrong?"

"Listen, Felicia." They had to speak guardedly. You never could tell when the operator was listening in, out here in the sticks. "I understand everything. But it's done, do you hear? It's done!"

"Done! Oh, no!"

"Get hold of yourself. I'll think of something. I already have a plan."

"A plan?"

"I'll call you back later. That much money is worth fighting for. I'm going to fight for it. Now hang up. Don't try to call me again. Remember, I'll call you later!"

He heard a click as Felicia hung up the receiver in New York. Then he hung up himself. Slowly he recrossed into the gun room and stared down at the silent figure of the dead man who, alive, was worth two million dollars to them. There was no stiffening yet—that would not come for hours. But already the wet crimson stain on Tom Wilson's jacket was drying.

Harry Baldwin took a deep breath. Then he got busy. . . .

The mantel clock said eight as Felicia Wilson, the lines of strain around her eyes showing even in the subdued light of her bedroom, crushed another cigarette into a saucer piled high with them. She was reaching for a fresh pack when the phone rang.

"Felicia? It's Harry. Be careful what you say."

"Harry! Yes, of course! Where are you?"

"I'm in Bangor. I'm driving down to Boston tonight and coming on to New York by plane. We have to have a conference."

"Of course. But—what have you done. About *him?*"

"I've arranged things. When that lawyer calls again, say Tom is off on a cruise with a friend; you can't possibly reach him. Stall them off until after the old lady dies."

"But what about Tom?"

"Tom's all right. I've taken care of him. The accident is going to happen *after* Aunt Minetta dies. Do you hear? *After* she dies!"

"But how can you manage such a thing?"

"I can't tell you on the phone. I'll be there in the morning. Then we'll talk. Now good-by and don't worry."

"But Harry—"

In the phone booth in a bar in Bangor, Harry Baldwin hung up with a silent curse for women's insistence. But as he got into his car, he was grinning at the thought of Tom Wilson, dead, but waiting for death to play a return engagement with him tomorrow or the next day or next week.

From time to time he chuckled to himself as he raced southward through the night.

He was chuckling when, just outside Boston, his car turned a corner to find a truck on the wrong side of the road.

He had no time even to stop laughing before he hit. Then metal screamed rendingly, and everything went black and silent. In the hospital he managed to whisper Felicia's name and phone number. Then for many hours blackness claimed him again. But he was conscious when she got there—a tiny spark of consciousness deep down in his twisted and broken body. . . .

They showed her into the room and the figure in the bed did not move as she entered.

Only the eyes turned toward her.

"Mr. Baldwin—Mrs. Wilson is here," the nurse said to the silent figure. And in a whisper to Felicia, "He can barely speak. It's his spine. There is no hope."

Then she withdrew to just outside the door.

Felicia dropped to her knees by the bed and put her lips close to Baldwin's ear.

"Harry," she said, and her voice was no longer either cool or gentle. "What did you do with him? With Tom? What was your plan?"

Harry Baldwin closed his eyes, then opened them again. His lips twisted with anguished effort.

"He—" he said clearly. "He—"

"Yes, Harry!" Felicia's voice was frantic. "What was your plan?"

"Accident . . . cleaning a pistol," Harry Baldwin said, the sweat standing out on his forehead.

"Yes, but then what? What did you do with him after I phoned?"

"Hid . . . the body. Produce it . . . after the aunt . . . dies."

"But where? Where?" The handkerchief between Felicia's fingers ripped across. "Tell me, Harry, where?"

"Hid the body . . . hid it . . ." The words faltered. The breathing ceased, caught again, ceased, caught again. No more words came.

"Nurse! Nurse!"

The nurse took one look, then ran for the doctor. But Baldwin died on the operating table half an hour later, without speaking another word.

* * *

"Well, lady, I've showed you over th' hull lodge, attic to cellar, all but this one room, an' I'll show it to you soon's I find a key on this dad-blamed ring to fit.

"Sure it's in fine condition. Sure's my name's Eph Plumly, you c'd move in right this minute. Been kept ready to live in ever since Miz' Wilson went off to South America three years ago. She said to keep th' furnace goin' an' th' 'lectricity turned on. Didn't want th' house to run down. But she didn't want anybody goin' inside it, neither. 'Cept me, an' I only been in enough to check th' fuel oil and order more.

"For fifty thousand this here place is a dead steal. Only four year old an' only used one season. For a girl's summer camp it couldn't be beat. Got a private lake, private woods, dandy hunting—guess that don't interest you—private road, automatic oil heat, automatic refrigeration system, automatic laundry machine, everything. House works practically by itself—you just push buttons.

"Why's it goin' so cheap? Lady that owned it, Miz' Wilson, just died in South America. One o' them tropic diseases. Estate wants to sell it off. You're th' first party 'cept me to be inside since she left— 'cept for th' search party that looked for Mr. Tom Wilson but couldn't find him, right after he disappeared.

"Yep, that was a prime mystery. Mr. Wilson, he disappeared. Mr. Baldwin, his secretary, he run into a truck and killed hisself th' same night. Miz' Wilson, she didn't have no idea what become of Mr. Wilson; she give him up fer dead. An' down in Boston there's two million dollars can't go to nobody because they don't know where on earth or anyplace else Mr. Wilson is, livin' or dead.

"But there, I'm gabbin' too much. Mr. Lamb, th' real estate man, he tole me to just show you this place, to keep my mouth shut, an' not to act any dumber than I have to. Now I got this door open— come on in. This here is th' cold storage room. See that thermometer? Temperature's twenty in here. Empty now, but you c'd pile it full o' sides of beef or venison, an' not a pound would ever spoil on you.

"That was Mr. Wilson's idea. He was bugs about huntin'. He wanted to keep venison down here to have th' whole year around. He was in' th' refrigeration business, so he put th' finest danged cold storage room an' quick-freeze unit made into this house.

"I'll show you. This little door here in th' corner—it opens into th' quick-freeze room. You shove a whole deer in there, close th' door, an' she's friz solid inside twenty minutes.

"Here th' door comes now—see how thick it is? An' th' light goes

on inside an' everything. . . . Lady! Lady, what're you screamin'
for? You're hurtin' my ears! Why, jeepus creepus, it's Mr. Tom Wilson!

"Lady, *please* stop that screamin'. Mr. Wilson ain't going to hurt
you. By grab, he sure looks in prime condition. Never see nothing
like it. Three years he's been sitting in his easy chair in that quick-
freeze room, that pistol on his lap, waitin' to be found—but if we
was to take an' thaw him out, you'd think he'd just died this afternoon. Fool any doctor in Maine—I'll be a ground hog if he
wouldn't . . . !

"Lady, just you quiet down an' I'll call the sheriff."

THE GUY WHO
HEARD MURDER

FRANCIS K. ALLAN

N o," Bill said as the little guy reached toward the shelf of sherry.
"I want a bottle of champagne tonight. Domestic, but something nice. It's an anniversary, see?" And he grinned.

The little guy cocked an eyebrow. "Lemme guess. The first wedding mile-post, maybe?" The little guy wasn't dumb. He could see
Bill Harley's grease-stained fingers and the holes in the pawn-broker
coat. He knew Bill from six months ago—worked for the Fifth
Avenue Coach Company, mechanic, and strictly a two-buck cash
man.

"Yeah. It *is* the first. How did you know?"

"Just had a hunch." The little guy took down a six-ninety bottle
and, for some reason, he called it five. Just once. Just because Bill's
eyes were tired but bright, and his face was young and hungry. And
it *was* too damned high for a bunch of grapes, anyway. Six-
ninety. . . .

190

It was snowing and Bill thought of a song as he walked along Third Avenue. Shadows of night sprawled down from the massive El beams, and he whistled the song: something about love and the sands of Hawaii. It didn't mean anything, except that he was happy. And that was something almost new. His fingers counted the bills in his pocket. Twenty-eight left from the forty-four a week. That meant only five for the cigar-box this week. Five added to a hundred and eighty five. . . .

God, it took a long time, he thought.

It happened much too quickly, then. The kid—just a little kid, no more than four years old—ran after the dog that had pulled away from the woman. The woman cried out, and the dog barked gaily, and the little kid toddled in a half-run off the curb, calling to 'Bitsy.' And that was when the cab turned the corner. Fast. And it seemed much faster in the night-shadows, with the yellow fenders looming tough and hard, and the little kid stumbling there. The woman screamed and the dog bounded gaily back to the sidewalk. The little kid didn't. Bill had one second, one jump, a few feet to leap and grasp and sprawl across the car tracks with the kid in his arm.

He made it, and the package smashed as he fell. The champagne . . . All gone on the pavement, he thought queerly, and a lean cool pain stuck into his hand. Then the kid was crying. The cabby was swearing softly. The woman was holding the kid and saying how wonderful. The champagne was spreading across the snow, and the bottle stuck jaggedly from the broken bag. The drops of blood dripped from Bill's wrist. Pretty deep, he thought. And no champagne for Linda.

It was one of those things that happen and end in a minute in Manhattan. The snow kept falling. The cab was gone, and the kid and the woman were gone. Bill was holding his handkerchief around his wrist and the blood kept coming—hard. He remembered the place—just down the block from the apartment. A shabby little office, it looked like. He even remembered the name: Dr. I. Felcamp. He passed the place every day.

"And another five bucks," he said wearily. "*Nothing* for the box." And if you were like Bill, five bucks was the difference between fear and a song of Hawaii. *The box was so damned important.* Like a race against the trap of fate.

He walked quickly. He pushed open the door into the shabby apartment building, and opened the door into Dr. Felcamp's suite on the main floor. It was almost dark in this room. The only light was a dim milky glow that filtered through the glass of an inner door. Bill heard a voice speaking in the room, then a voice answered softly—both men's voices—". . . most successful operation," one voice was saying.

Bill hesitated, then sank down on the shadowy form of a leatherette couch. The hand was still bleeding and bad, he could see. He remembered the bracelet with the gift-wrapping in his pocket. From Bill to Linda, it was engraved. But the silver-and-blue paper was already crushed and dirty. It wouldn't do.

He tore it away from the box and took out the slender bracelet. Soiled and ugly, he thought as he looked at the wrapping. Just like a day had been soiled and ugly, nine months ago. Like an omen.

"Just take a look," a dry voice was saying inside the inner office. "Put the picture up by that mirror. It's the best job I ever did. Nose. Ears. Eyebrows. And now that you've dyed your hair. Nobody will ever know. You're a new man, Red."

"Yeah. The guy from Mexico, let's say. Mr. Juan from Monterrey." A laugh hardened in the low voice. "I think I'll try the puss out at the Tango Club. Maybe tonight." There was a pause, then the low voice became metallic. "Well, Doc, you should have gone to Hollywood. You might have lived longer. And I've got a last dance with Connie, too."

"Oh, I get along. I—Red! What are you—" the voice was raw.

"*Nobody* should know about my face, Doc. Sorry."

"That knife! Don't you—*Don't!* Doooo . . ." The cry ended in a strangled burble. The low laugh came again, and something soft and heavy bumped the floor.

Bill's muscles snapped. He choked. He jerked erect. The bracelet tinkled to the floor and rolled. A floor-board squealed in the inner office. Bill grasped the outer door, jerked it open and slammed it behind him as he ran. He heard the running feet behind him. Faster and faster he ran through the snow and darkness, and the truth burned deep in his mind: Doctor Felcamp had been killed—knifed to death!

Home . . . Go home . . . Home to the shelter of Linda!

And at last the night was quiet behind him. At last he was climbing the dust-scented stairs to the fourth-floor walk-up. She kissed him.

"You're late," she whispered. "You don't even know what day this is? No?" Her eyes were darkly shining and her lips were soft. "You—Bill! You're so— And your hand! What happened, Bill?"

"It was—Just a kid. A little kid ran into the street. That was all." He tried to calm his voice. In the mirror he saw his thin face—pale and damp with perspiration, and his dark hair was tumbled. He'd lost his hat.

"But let me see your hand. It— Oh, it's *deep*, Bill!" she cried. "I'll get a doctor. Lie down and let me—"

"No, you can't! I mean, not now. Just fix it yourself. Just—"

"But it's deep, don't you see? Maybe a vein or an artery. You—"

"But doctors sometimes ask questions and . . ." He stopped abruptly. Linda's dark eyes were still and frightened. Suddenly he felt shallow and crumbling inside. He fumbled for the chair and sank down. "Feel sick. . . . Must have bled more than—Linda, wait!" he cried as she opened the door. He tried to think. It would have been all right—just a cut hand and simple. But now Felcamp was dead, maybe, and less than a block away. The gift wrapping-paper with fingerprints was in that front room. And blood on it. Cops would think. They'd ask questions and finally it would all come out and—

"Linda! Don't call a doc—" he cried. But she was gone and her heels made a light staccato down the stairs. He started up and the room tilted lazily. He grasped the chair and sank down again. Dimly he became aware of the rich scent of cooking onions. And champagne, he thought. But the champagne was gone, he reminded himself. Hard to remember. Funny, what a cut and a little blood could do. Maybe it was never eating lunch, too. It left you feeling fuzzy, sometimes. . . .

The scent of onions turned thick and smoky. The clock beat out its restless rhythm. Now there were two clocks clamoring. Two lights swimming in the ceiling. Two windows instead of one. And it seemed so long ago. Linda was gone. Where? . . . Oh, yeah. Doctor . . . Questions. . . .

So you saved a child and didn't wait for the police? . . . Very old, don't you think? . . . And you say your name is Bill Harley? . . . Let me see. Funny, you know, but I was in Boston about nine months ago. There was a little piece in the paper about a young fellow by that name. Night-manager of a parking garage, he was. Yeah . . . Seems a customer left a diamond ring in the pocket of a car one night. Then it was gone. Harley was gone, too. They found the place where he'd sold it for five hundred dollars. Yeah. And you say your name is Bill Harley?

"But I *had* to! I *had* to!" Bill shouted. "She was sick and I had to!

193

Linda was sick! And I'm saving money. In that cigar-box, see? It'll take a long time, but I'm going to pay it back! And I didn't kill Felcamp! I stole the ring, but I didn't kill—"

The echoing of his raw shouts blasted back from the walls and reality crashed about him. He was standing in the middle of the room, his fists clenched and his face draining perspiration. And he was utterly alone and the onions were burning. He moved his hand across his eyes and held onto a chair-back. Dimly he heard the knocking at the door, then it was pushed open. A broad baldheaded man peered in.

"Hey, Harley, everything okay with you folks? I thought I heard something sounded like—Hey, what's on your hand, pal?"

It wasn't a cop, Bill realized slowly. It was just McGuire, the guy that took care of the building. Just McGuire. Nice Irishman . . .

"Hey, you don't look none too good. . . ." Bill heard McGuire's voice fade off into a tinkling sound. It was going to be good to sleep. . . .

Someone kept saying, "Just make him swallow that soup. My Land, he's thin as a rail. . . . Looks peeked to me." And somebody said, "Gimme another strip of that adhesive tape. Jeeze, what a slice he gave hisself."

He opened his eyes and saw them—McGuire and his busy little wife, and the fat guy named Lucas from the first floor. "Linda?" he whispered. McGuire poured more soup down his throat. It was thick and fire-hot, and it dragged the walls of his stomach together.

"And now you are getting out of here, wife. And also Lucas," McGuire said. "All out and along with you, now."

The door closed. McGuire walked back to the bed and scratched his leathery jowls. "Now, as neighbor to neighbor, I would say we should talk. First, is there trouble with the missus?"

"Not trouble. She . . . She went out to get a doctor for my hand."

"You are not telling it all to McGuire." He stuck a scrap of cigar in his yellowed teeth. "An hour ago I'm pulling off my undershirt, putting away my shoes, and turning on the radio. Then I hear footsteps down the stairs—your wife's; a man can tell. Next I hear a man's soft voice asking, 'Does someone named Linda live here?' And the voice, being your wife's, answered who she was. The soft voice said, 'You dropped your bracelet back there, sweetheart, while you were listening too hard. And you've still got blood on your hand, too. Leave us take a stroll.' And so, me being not dressed, I watched from the window. See, first I heard a sob like someone was choking, then I saw a man carrying her across the sidewalk into a car. And that was the facts of it, sure."

"He took Linda!" Bill jerked erect. "He followed me! But it was too dark, and he couldn't tell if it was a man or woman! He thinks *she* was wearing the bracelet, and he thinks *she* heard what he said. Oh, my God!"

"And what did he say?" McGuire asked in a steam-roller voice.

"I don't—don't remember exactly. In Dr. Felcamp's office before he killed Felcamp. His name was Red and Felcamp had operated on his face. Then he must have killed Felcamp, and I heard him laughing about having a last dance with Conrad. I ran because I didn't want the cops—" Bill bit off his words. McGuire looked at him with gin-watery eyes. But the eyes were bright and swift behind their haze.

"A last dance with Conrad . . . Red . . ." he echoed. Suddenly he stood up. "Rum-soaked they called me, huh!" he chortled. "I know a thing or two! Felcamp, the old rascal. And a guy named Red for a last dance with Conrad! . . . Change your shirt. Harley, Get a clean suit if you've got one. There's a chance. Maybe Red will just cool your wife off and test her later to see if she talked to anybody. That's the only chance! But change clothes fast. I'll be waiting at my apartment. Hurry!"

It was hard to dress with only one hand, and the room kept tilting around the rims of his eyes. And his brain kept screaming its mute thunder: Linda was gone, and Red had taken her! . . . Where?

You've got to understand that Bill was a frightened guy. Not fat with money or hard with wisdom or tough with being around. Just a thin-faced guy with black hair and nice dark eyes, and young enough to fear . . .

McGuire had on a battered derby and patched overcoat when Bill reached his apartment. "Got to hurry," he panted. He was already sweating. He took a last pull from straight-gin. "Felcamp's dead. Twice in the heart, once in the throat. No loss, I would say. And I am asking you, honest as an Irishman to another, just tell me what's hiding behind your eyes, Harley?"

Bill told him the story in the cab, after McGuire had said, "Tango Studio on Seventh Avenue."

"I never told Linda. It was when I was working in the parking garage in Boston, and Linda came to New York to meet her brother. He'd been in the army overseas, see? And then he left to go home to Memphis, and I got the telegram from the hospital here in New

York. It said she, Linda, was in the hospital with a ruptured appendix. I . . . God, I didn't know. I was scared and we . . . we'd just been married three months. I tried to draw money ahead, but the guy at the garage just said what the hell. Then this guy named Laslo brought his car in, and drunk like almost always. I saw him toss the ring into the glove compartment. Then he went across the street to the dice game. I got to thinking. I mean . . . it seemed right, just that minute. The ring didn't mean a damn thing to him, and it could mean . . . well, life and death. Don't you see?"

"Go on. The ring and then what?"

I sold it. Five hundred dollars and came to New York. They found out about it. I . . . But I'm going to pay it back. There's a cigar-box at home. Ten dollars a week. I'm saving that, but—But don't you understand? If the cops knew about me being at Felcamp's, and then about this other thing in Boston . . . Don't you see?" he asked.

"You think I am always nursing a furnace for eighty greens a month?" McGuire asked bleakly. "Once I am with the Safe-and-Loft Squad, and simply because I need a brandy to spark my heart—" He stopped as the cab stopped. "Are you free with a buck?"

Bill paid. McGuire laid his gin-scented lips against Bill's ear. "This is it, like I know my name is McGuire. Conrad, see, runs this tango school, but he gets too rich for it to be honest. A few citizens have remarked that a little cocaine passes between the hostesses and the favored customers. Now . . ." And his whisper became a sandpapery rasp above the traffic. "Two years ago, before I am heaved off, I know a guy named Red Lindello that handles the ship-to-shore route for Conrad. But Red is too easy with a thirty-eight, and a gambler in Belleview sings a line or two before he checks out. Mostly it is about Red, who shot him. And quite oddly, before anybody can arrest Red, he vanishes."

"You think he went into hiding?"

"You citizens are so naive. A nice word I learned. Yes, Red went into hiding, I would say, because murder-raps make a lad talk so freely. And Conrad would not care for unlimited conversation by an old friend. But now Red is patched and new-faced. Apparently he is ambitious and wishes to live and grow wealthy on Conrad's pitch. So let us walk upstairs and have a short-rye. But very silently. Follow me."

"But Linda—I don't give a damn about anything but—"

"Let us be frank, Harley," he sighed. "We have one prayer for the missus. Namely: Red may not be sure she didn't tell someone else about his new face. He thinks she knows a lot and maybe told. So he may have stuck her away for later persuasion. We hope." He opened the door into a vast music-throbbing room. Slender girls, ivory-faced and ruby-lipped, swayed in the arms of smoky-eyed men. A bar was crowded at one end of the huge room.

"Two ryes," McGuire ordered. "Will you satisfy the bill?" he asked delicately. He gargled down his drink and punched Bill's chest. "Over there. The man with a face like a tired cat—that is Conrad."

Bill looked. He was a thin man with yellow-white hair, drooping eyes, and an in-slooping chin. He swayed on the balls of his feet and seemed to dream. A waiter touched his arm and whispered. Conrad nodded and drifted toward a side door.

"I will observe and suggest," McGuire was saying. "Perhaps you will advance another rye?" His eye-lids were at half-mast.

Bill laid out another dollar, but his eyes were locked on Conrad. Abruptly he put down his glass and moved through the swaying crowd toward the side door. Suddenly he stopped. A lean black-haired man with thick ears hurried out of a telephone booth, glanced around him, and darted through the doorway.

When Bill opened the door, soft footsteps on a pitch-dark stairway was the only sound to be heard.

Bill climbed the stairs and the backs of his knees ached.

He climbed the last step. He stopped at the door and listened. There was not a sound within the room. Carefully he struck a match and looked around. Along the dusty wall was a line of quart beer bottles. One of them would have to do.

He held the bottle-neck in sticky fingers and with his bandaged hand he turned the knob. Slowly the door swung inward on darkness and silence. He listened, hearing first the drum-beat of his own pulse, then a movement of feet in another room. "Very slow now, Connie. Right down these steps," said the same soft voice. "And I'm right behind you."

Bill felt his way across the room, into a long hall where a light glowed in the distance. He followed the light through a blue-and-gray office where a wall-safe was open and empty. He found another door and a fire-escape leading down to a dark court. And he heard the dual footsteps below, first on the steel steps, then on the concrete of the court.

He heard a motor choke and roar deeply, and he saw the long coupe moving into Seventh Avenue as he hurried out of the court.

*   *   *

The cabby said, "Sure, Mack. Cinch." He kept behind the coupe as it turned east. At Second Avenue it turned uptown again. Near the bridge at Fifty-seventh Street, the coupe burrowed into a dark side-street and the light went off.

The building looked vacant where the coupe was parked. The ground-floor windows were boarded-up. The main door was padlocked. A short flight of steps led down to a basement door. The latch moved at his touch and the scent of dust and oil flowed through his nostrils. The sound of footsteps echoed.

Bill's knees kept wanting to fold and his stomach kept wanting to crumble. Perspiration turned salty in the corner of his eye as he felt his way through the darkness. And at last a margin of light gleamed under a closed door. He stopped, and the soft voice was speaking inside:

"And you're right sure, sweetheart, you didn't do any talking?"

"I didn't talk. I told you and told you. I didn't talk."

Bill's heart drummed upward in his throat. *It was Linda!*

Bill grasped the knob and hurled the door open. There was one instant in which to see it—the lamp on the table, Conrad unconscious on the floor, the glistening blade of the knife in the lean man's hand, and Linda in the chair.

The lean man spun around. The knife flashed as it dropped to the floor and his hand was like a striking snake—striking toward his pocket, leaping back with the automatic. The red dark of flame licked from the muzzle and the cool needle of pain stung Bill's shoulder. The beer bottle made a flashing arc across the room and smashed into the lamp. There was a soft-hiss of flame, a brilliance of livid tongues licking upward as the oil spread, then a cry as the leaping flame found the woolly coat of the thin man.

The next ten seconds lived forever. The lean man kept screaming. The gun kept blasting in his hand, and his eyes seemed to draw the flame inside them. They blazed and his teeth shone and the veins showed in his ears. Then his tie became a swift ripple of fire that ringed his throat and his scream became a liquid bubble of saliva and fire. In the next instant he was a mass of fire that threshed toward the door. His fingernails gnawed at the knob. He staggered. He fell. He tried one last time to scream, and in the midst of the scream came a futile sob and silence.

Bill plunged across the room, past the mounting flames, and he tore at the ropes about Linda's ankles. The fire licked his feet and burned his cheeks, and then—then at last they were running. They were running together, past the choking scent of the burning man, past the heat.

McGuire was shouting.

"In there, boys! I've got 'em trapped, right in there!"

The rest of it was in the papers. The Ajax Brandy Company gave McGuire a job as nightwatchman and the *Banner* paid him fifty dollars for his personal account of the deadly struggle. And Laslo, a Boston gambler, came down with a case of champagne. He said he never had worn the ring, anyway. Unlucky. And he hadn't lost a bet since the ring got lifted.

THE HARD-LUCK KID

GEOFFREY VACE

Almost from the beginning, Willie Elliot's luck was bad.

At the age of nine, seeing an aquarium in a pet shop, he saved his paper route money until he could afford one. Then he concocted a net out of cheesecloth and a coathanger, went to the local pond, and captured eleven small swimming things to put into it.

By week's end his aquarium had drawn half the kids in the neighborhood to the Elliots' rumpus room. Then on Monday morning he walked into that room and found it in pieces on the floor and his brother Joe's cat sitting there beside it, licking her chops.

Joe was a year older than Willie and always got top billing in the Elliot household. Ask their father Matthew about his two sons and he would say, "Well, now, they're both okay, of course, but Joe *is* better looking and smarter." Ask their mother Evelyn and she would say, "Well, we *planned* for Joe, you know. Willie was sort of an accident."

The cat that knocked over the aquarium and devoured its inhabitants that day was a reddish brown female tabby striped somewhat like a tiger. About six months old, she was called Miss Susie. Joe had seen her cavorting in the window of the same pet shop in which younger brother Willie had encountered the aquarium. "Hey, that's a neat cat!" Joe said. So, of course, his parents decided he adored animals and ought to have one for a pet.

Brother Willie, be it noted, had to acquire the aquarium with his own hard-earned money, but Joe got the cat as a gift.

As it happened, Joe lost interest in the cat in less than a week, so Willie was the one who fed her and kept her litterbox clean.

Willie got the short end of the stick again when he was fourteen and in high school. That year he discovered a bright, shiny trumpet in a pawnshop window and saw it as a magic means of becoming more popular. If he could teach himself to play it and get into the school band, hey, there was no telling what his future might be. A skinny, somewhat frail kid at that point, he hadn't a prayer of making the football team, on which brother Joe was already a hotshot quarterback. Nor, being somewhat on the homely side, was he anywhere near as popular with girls, who fluttered around Joe like hummingbirds at a feeder.

So with money saved from mowing neighbors' lawns and shoveling snow out of neighbors' driveways, Willie secretly bought the trumpet and a book on the art of trumpet playing and began practicing.

Not openly, of course. He knew his parents would never stand for that. But any time his parents and brother were absent from the house, he would climb the pull-down stairs to the attic and snatch the instrument from its hiding place there and work on it. Usually he sat on an old ladderback chair under the single bare bulb that provided light to read the books by, and Miss Susie, following him up, would lie contentedly on an old discarded couch and adoringly watch him. She didn't seem to mind the sour notes. Not even in the beginning when they were pretty frequent.

But the very day Willie worked up courage enough to reveal his ownership of the trumpet and his intention of trying out for the band, he developed a sore lip. A lip so horrendously sore that Dr. Breckenridge, the family's physician, proclaimed trumpet playing forever out of bounds. And brother Joe, indifferently lifting the instrument to *his* lips, discovered *he* had the natural talent of a Louis Armstrong.

Joe had no desire to be in the band, of course. He was too busy being a football hero. But once more Willie had to resign himself to playing second fiddle.

So it went, again and again, down through the years. The only member of the Elliot household who seemed to understand Willie's feelings was Miss Susie. But that, Willie figured, was probably only because he was the one who always looked after her and took her to the vet when she wasn't feeling right. He always knew when she wasn't feeling right. She only had to look at him.

When Willie was nineteen, Miss Susie was ten and a half but, due to his unflagging care, was still as bright-eyed and bushy-tailed as a kitten. "If you were to bring her to me as a stray and ask me her age, I would probably guess four or five," the vet said one day, fondly patting Willie on the back. That was the year Willie fell in love.

A high school graduate now, he had a job selling used cars while brother Joe was in college on a football scholarship. The young lady came in one day to look at cars. Her name was—I'm sorry, but you'll have to accept the coincidence—her name was Susan. She actually introduced herself after Willie had talked to her awhile. "What's your name, anyway?" she said right out of the blue. "I mean —I'm Susan Wetherby."

"My name is Willie Elliot," said he, blushing.

He didn't sell her a car. In fact, he ended up whispering to her that nothing on the lot was really what she wanted. But he did take her to the movies that night. And so it began.

Right from the start Susan was a hit with the family, as well she should have been. The same age as Willie, she worked as a salesperson in a downtown department store and had deep blue eyes, lovely auburn hair, and a figure any model would have been proud of.

Most of all she was sweet and unsophisticated—exactly the right sort of girl for a man like Willie.

But one Sunday, six months later, just when Willie was on the verge of asking her to marry him, something happened. Susan was a regular at the Elliots' Sunday dinner table by then, and was expected. But half an hour before she arrived, while helping Mom in the kitchen, Dad suddenly clapped a hand to his chest, turned white as the fridge, and collapsed onto a chair.

"Matthew! What's the matter?" Mom cried in alarm, rushing over to him.

"My heart," he gasped. "I think it's my heart."

"Willie!" Mom cried. "Call Dr. Breckenridge!"

Willie did that, and the doctor wasted no words. "Take him to the hospital, Willie. I'll meet you there," he said briskly.

Of course Mom insisted on going, too. So brother Joe was at home alone when Susan arrived.

Dad's problem turned out to be nothing more serious than indigestion, but something happened in the Elliot home during the two hours Willie and his parents were absent. What it was, Willie never found out. But from that Sunday on, Susan was no longer exclusively Willie's girl.

Brother Joe began inviting himself along when they went places, like to a movie or the library, or even to McDonald's for a hamburger. Unfortunately, Joe was almost always around, too, because the college he attended was in the city and he lived at home.

After he got his degree and a job with a local but world-renowned high-tech research organization, Joe gradually took Willie's place as Susan's escort, and Willie was again second fiddle.

One night after the three of them had been to a basketball game and the brothers were back home, Joe walked into Willie's room without knocking and closed the door behind him. Mom and Dad were in the living room, watching an old Fred Astaire–Ginger Rogers movie on TV.

Willie had his pajamas on and was about to climb into bed. Joe, still dressed, walked over to a chair and straddled it backwards, with both arms draped along its top and a scowl on his handsome face. "Willie, we have to talk," he said.

"No, we don't," replied Willie. "Because I already know what you're going to say."

"Huh?"

"You want to take her away from me, don't you? You want to marry her."

"How'd you know?"

Willie only shrugged.

"Well, hey, kid, I'm sorry," Joe said. "But she fell in love with me and I couldn't stop her, y'know? I mean it just happened."

"And you want me to butt out," Willie said.

"Well, yeah. You know how it is."

"All right, I will."

Joe said, "Thanks, kid. You're a pal," and walked over to rumple Willie's hair before leaving the room. The door clicked shut behind him.

Miss Susie had been stretched out on Willie's bed while the

brothers talked. Now, when Willie got into bed and reached up to turn off the lamp by which he usually read himself to sleep, the tiger-striped tabby did an unusual thing.

She had been sleeping with Willie for years, normally outside the covers at the foot of the bed, sort of snuggled up against Willie's feet. Tonight she walked up to the head of the bed, wormed herself in *under* the covers, and snuggled against his chest. As if she had understood every word.

When his tears at last stopped flowing, Willie fell asleep with one arm around her.

Susan—the other Susan—asked Willie's forgiveness the very next day. Walking into the used-car establishment where he worked, she tried to find words to explain what had happened. She hadn't meant to fall in love with Joe, she said. She hadn't wanted to. She still loved Willie and always would. "B-but I couldn't help myself," she stammered. "I don't know why, but I just couldn't."

Willie told her he understood. And, in a way, he did. After all, he'd been the underdog, the wannabe, the left-behind all his life, always stumbling along in brother Joe's shadow. What had happened wasn't her fault. "We can still be good friends," he said, kissing her on the cheek.

She told him she and Joe had set a wedding date. They were to be married September fifteenth, just short of two months away. "And Joe wants you to be best man, Willie dear," she said. "Will you? Please?"

"Do *you* want me to?" Willie asked.

"Well . . . yes. Of course."

"Okay," he said sadly. "If it's for you."

"And will you tell him, Willie?" she begged. "Will you tell him this evening?"

"I'll tell him," Willie promised.

Brother Joe was in the basement that evening when Willie reluctantly decided the time was right to keep his promise. He was in the rumpus room in which, years before, Miss Susie had knocked over the aquarium.

Since Joe's acquisition of a degree in advanced physics and his affiliation with the world-renowned research organization, that room had been radically altered. Joe had completely taken it over and transformed it into his personal workroom, all others kindly keep out. For months he had worked evenings on a mysterious project that no one else in the family was allowed to approach.

It just about covered the entire top of what had been the family ping-pong table, and resembled something in a science fiction movie.

Nearing the end of the project this evening, Joe made some final adjustments on two parts of the machine that resembled old fashioned telegraph keys, the kind that send out dots and dashes when tapped, except that one of these was bright red, the other green. Then he adjusted a tubelike arrangement that resembled a blowgun. And finally he walked down to the end of the table where stood a box of Kellogg's cornflakes.

Picking that up, he carried it a few steps farther and placed it on a folding metal chair which he then lined up with the blowgun thing.

"Come on now," he whispered fiercely. "Work!"

Back he went to the ping-pong table, where, after peering at the chair and the cornflakes box for a few seconds, he tapped the red key with a fingertip.

There followed a low buzzing sound, almost inaudible, that lasted—Joe timed it with the sweep-second hand on his wristwatch —for exactly seventeen seconds. When it ceased, the chair was no more than half an inch high and the box of cornflakes on it was no bigger than a speck of dust.

Joe strode to the chair and looked down at it for a few seconds but did not try to pick it up. Satisfied, he returned to his machine and pressed the green telegraph key.

Again the buzzing sound lasted exactly seventeen seconds. Then —presto!—the chair and the box of cereal on it were their old selves again.

"Hey, hey!" Joe exulted, clasping his hands over his head and leaping two feet off the floor. "Got it! At last!"

He tried again, this time with a game-winning football from a trophy case. After seventeen seconds the chair was reduced in size as before and the football became no bigger than a mustard seed, but both returned obediently to normal size when he touched the green key to restore them.

Then he took a black leather wallet from his pocket and placed *that* on the chair, not the least deterred by the fact that it contained over a hundred dollars in bills. And after reducing it to an object almost too small to be visible, his shrink machine successfully brought it back intact.

At that moment, while he was looking about for something else on which to test his invention, there came a knock on the lab door.

"Yes?" Joe said impatiently. "Who is it?"

"Me. Willie. May I come in?"

The words "No, I'm busy" got as far as the tip of Joe's tongue but no farther. A gleam came into his eyes. "Sure, Willie, if you want to," he said amiably.

The door opened and Willie stepped in, followed by Miss Susie. Joe saw the cat slink in between Willie's feet but was too excited to care. "What is it, Willie?" he asked. "Whatcha want, pal?"

"I'd like to talk, if you don't mind."

"Sure, buddy, why not?" Striding toward him, Joe put a hand on the kid brother's shoulder and turned him toward the chair on which he had placed the Kellogg's cornflakes, the football, and the wallet. "Sit down, Willie," he said. "What's on your mind?"

Willie obediently sat and began talking—about the wedding and how Susan had asked him to be best man. Nodding and saying things like "Uh-huh, sure, of course, Willie," Joe casually strolled back to the apparatus on the ping-pong table.

Standing there, he surreptitiously reached for the red button while saying, "Well, of *course* I want you to be best man, Willie! Who else would I even think of? You're my only brother, for God's sake."

His finger touched the red button and the buzzing began.

Miss Susie, following the whole cunning procedure with her eyes and ears, at once voiced an ear-splitting shriek and launched herself. Like a Patriot missile fired at one of Saddam Hussein's Scuds, she slammed into Willie's chest and knocked him clean off the chair onto the floor. Knocked the chair over, too. All in mid-flight, so to speak, for she wound up a dozen feet away with her tail twice its normal thickness and her teeth gleaming in a snarl that would have done credit to a Bengal tiger.

With a "damn!" of utter disgust and annoyance, Joe left his place at the machine and strode forward to pick up the chair and put Willie back on it. The machine continued to buzz.

Thirteen seconds. Fourteen. Fifteen.

Joe reached the chair and leaned forward to grab it. Seven or eight feet away, Willie was still on the floor, too dazed from his fall to do more than lie there.

Sixteen.

Joe banged the chair down on its four legs, upright, and turned toward Willie.

Seventeen.

Both Joe and the chair were suddenly the size of figures in a doll house. A very small doll house. Very.

Willie at that moment was struggling to get to his feet. He did not see Miss Susie emerge from under the ping-pong table and pounce. He was making so much noise, he did not even hear the *crunch* as her jaws clicked shut. All he knew, when he got to his feet, was that the machine on the ping-pong table had stopped buzzing and his brother Joe had suddenly vanished, and that his beloved cat was sitting there beside a very tiny replica of the chair that he, Willie, had occupied a moment before.

And Miss Susie was licking her chops as she always did after a hearty meal.

No one ever solved the mystery of the disappearance of Joe Elliot. The papers ran stories on it. A TV program about unsolved mysteries did a segment on it. The producers of a well-known talk show even urged Willie and Susan—married by then—to appear on the show and discuss it, and the money they were paid helped them furnish their new home.

The general belief is that while Willie lay in a daze on the rumpus room floor, just after Miss Susie knocked him off his chair, Joe decided he did not want to marry Susan after all and seized that opportunity to take a walk. A long one.

The day after Joe's disappearance Miss Susie, the tabby, seemed to have a problem of some kind with her digestion, and of course Willie took her to the vet. "If I didn't know you better, Willie," the vet said, "I'd have to guess you gave her something unsafe to eat like, say, some cat food that had gone bad. What really happened, probably, is that she ate a bug or something, as even the best of cats sometimes do." But Miss Susie got over it and is living happily now with Willie and Susan in their above-mentioned new home on the other side of town.

Not knowing what the apparatus on the ping-pong table was or what to do with it, Mr. and Mrs. Elliot eventually dismantled it and disposed of it for a few dollars at a garage sale. At the same time they sold the tiny chair for a quarter, not knowing what that was either.

Today, six months after Joe's disappearance, Susan teaches school and Willie still sells cars. But he sells new ones at a top-rated dealer's now, and displays a confidence that seems certain to win him an early promotion.

You never can tell, can you? As the poet John Gay once wrote:

> *Life is a jest, and all things show it;*
> *I thought so once, but now I know it.*

A Helping Hand

Rufus Bakalor

While he was arranging Floyd Venn in his chair for a haircut, the barber asked in a positive tone, "Only use the clippers in the back, Floyd?"

"Clippers all over this time, Mr. Cartwright," replied Floyd with a little smile.

"You mean clippers on the *sides*, too?"

"No, I mean all over. I mean, I want *all* my hair cut off—all of it, right down to the follicles."

"Right down to the follicles," repeated the barber, shaking his head with disbelief.

"And such lovely, black, curly hair, too!"

"It's got something to do with a story, Mr. Cartwright," explained Floyd. "Just go ahead and clip away. I know what I'm doing."

"Oh, well, if it's a story—" said the barber, flourishing his clippers for a trial spin in the air. "You're the doctor, Floyd. I'll bet this one'll be a dinger."

"I wouldn't like to say, just yet. It's only a gimmick I have to authenticate."

After the shearing, Floyd went to the Variety Store, where he purchased a bottle of black india ink, a packet of sewing needles, and an indelible pencil.

"Another story, Floyd?" asked the proprietor.

"That's about the size of it, Mr. Buckman," he replied casually.

Then Floyd hurried home to start the supper.

When Lily, his wife, returned from work, Floyd met her at the door, wobbling his head and beaming broadly.

Lily noticed the condition of his head with only passing interest and asked, "What are we having for supper tonight, Floyd?"

"Wieners and sauerkraut," Floyd said peevishly. "Aren't you going to ask me why I've had all my hair cut off?"

"I suppose you're authenticating a gimmick for another story."

"You suppose right. But *what* a gimmick! I'll bet other detective story writers' wives show a little more interest in their husbands' work than you do. I don't get any encouragement from *you*."

"All right," said Lily wearily. "What is it this time?"

The almost complete lack of enthusiasm on Lily's part did not deter Floyd. With considerable agitation, he explained, "Let me start by saying that I want you to write a message on the top of my head, partly in india ink, partly with a wetted indelible pencil, and partly scratched in with a needle."

"What kind of a message?"

"*Any* kind of a message," said Floyd impatiently. "This gimmick I've dreamed up, see? Maybe I'll make it a spy story or something. Maybe it'll be one of a series. Anyway, the secret message has got to get through, see? The courier's head is shaved and the message is written on it, see? Then his hair grows back, concealing the message, see? When the courier gets to where he's got to go, his hair is cut off again and there's your secret message!"

"Why cut his hair off? Why couldn't he just remember the message?"

Floyd threw his arms out in a gesture of hopelessness. "Why? Why? Why? Well, there's a little matter of a writer's creative imagination involved. Believe me, I can jimmy the circumstances so that the only logical place for the secret message is on top of the courier's head." He paused for a moment and then threw at her, "The courier can speak only English. The message is in Esperanto!"

"I see."

"Anyway, be that as it may, I want to see what material is most satisfactory for writing the message, what effect the growth of the hair has on each of them, how long it takes the hair to grow again, whether complete concealment is effected, et cetera, et cetera."

After supper, Floyd knelt before her, and Lily, successively using the instruments he had furnished, printed clearly on his pate:

Whoso diggeth a pit shall fall therein.

That evening, while Floyd was pacing the den floor, generating more crime-story plots, Lily sat in the living room, as she often did, thinking wistfully of the old, more normal days before Floyd had sold his first story to *Incredible Detective*.

He had been a teller at the New Haydock State Bank and they had lived fairly comfortably. Mr. Jeffrey, the president of the bank, had been very fond of Floyd and had intimated that he was next in line for the assistant cashiership.

Then Floyd had written a short story which he titled "Death at Dawn." *Incredible Detective* sent him a check for all rights to it, retitled it "Good Mourning," and published it.

From the day Floyd got the letter of acceptance, he was a changed man. He bought a new typewriter and a tweed sport coat, quit his job at the bank and decided to devote all his time to being a writer. He was sincere. He wrote a lot of stories and, moreover, he sold some of them. But the recognition and emolument he hoped for were slow in coming. Eventually, Lily had talked Mr. Jeffrey into giving her Floyd's old job at the bank, while he stayed at home, keeping house and writing stories. Actually, their economic position was the same as it had always been, except that their relationship was slightly askew.

It pained Lily that Floyd took his writing so seriously and, in doing so, had little time for the amenities of married life. He jabbered plots and gimmicks at her incessantly, until her brain was numbed to them. She would never forget the night he had found her reading a rival author's mystery and descended upon her with the indignant fury of one betrayed.

It pained her, too, to know that the town laughed at Floyd Venn. His "authenticating gimmicks" was a community joke. There was the time he lay under water at the bathing beach for an hour, breathing through a tube stuck in his mouth, to test an escape gimmick. And the time he had sewed himself up in a flour sack at the grain elevator. And the time he was missing for two days, and she found him in the trunk of Mr. Jeffrey's automobile, living on wax crayons, authenticating a hideout.

The house was rigged with his contrivances: booby traps, apparatuses for doing something in a room while outside it and with the door locked, devices for appearing to be present in one room while actually in another.

If the Venns had visitors, Floyd was likely to beg one of them to hit him so that he could determine the natural way a struck man falls, or ask them to assume the roles of killers and corpses while he constructed a crime. But not many people had the courage to visit the Venns any more.

Lily pondered these things, and added to them the most recent incident of her coming home to find that her writer-husband had had all his hair shorn off. She rose and began to pace the floor, her head bowed in thought.

On her way home from the bank the next afternoon, Lily stopped at Wilson's Hardware Store and asked to see some rope.

"What you want it for, Mrs. Venn?" asked Mr. Wilson. "Clothesline?"

"Well, no. It's for Floyd. He just asked me to get him about twenty feet of slender, but stout, rope."

"Floyd's plotting out another story, eh? Well, I could suggest sash cord, but I won't." He held up an end of quarter-inch manila rope. "If Floyd's looking for a good strong, slender rope for his story, this here's his baby. Ain't so thick, but it's got a breaking strength of 600 pounds."

"This looks like just what he had in mind," said Lily, carefully examining the rope. "Will you please write that descriptive information—about the breaking strength and all—on the saleslip? Floyd usually likes to know all about it."

That evening, Lily tilted her head shyly and said to Floyd across the supper table, "I suppose you'll only laugh at me, Floyd, but I've thought of a gimmick for a story."

"You?" said Floyd with surprise.

"Here's the caper, Floyd. A man is found hanged in his basement. It looks like suicide. It seems like suicide. Everyone thinks it's suicide. Even the coroner's jury finds that it's suicide. But—"

"—but the clever detective smells something fishy!" Floyd concluded.

"Exactly. But the clever detective sees something that the others have missed. One little slip-up someplace."

Floyd grew excited. "And through it he pins the murder on the killer. Say, that's not bad, not bad at all."

"Only, I guess it really isn't such a good gimmick after all. How'd we ever figure out what that slip-up could be?"

"How, indeed?" said Floyd.

"No, Floyd. No! no! no! I know what you're thinking, and I won't permit it. You'd hurt yourself."

"Hurt myself, indeed. It would only be for a moment and don't you worry, I'd always be able to grab on to the beam so that the rope wouldn't be tight around my neck. Now, if I only had a suitable length of slender, but stout, rope."

"Well, I did notice some nice manila rope in the basement," said Lily. "But I won't permit you to risk your life for a silly plot."

Before she had finished, Floyd was on his way to the basement. She followed him.

When he had arranged everything, Floyd took out his memorandum book and made some notes:

Slip-up in Hanging. What way stool fall kicked from under? Upturned? How body dec. hang? Where knot after weight appl'd?

He gave the notes to Lily to read so that she could be watching for the details. "I believe that in regular hangings death occurs when the neck breaks from the sudden jerk. *That* I want to avoid," he said pensively.

Lily pleaded with him to give up the project. But she knew it was useless. He had that look in his eye.

"However, if I let myself down slowly, I would only strangle myself. But, of course, if I keep hold onto the beam above me, I won't. There's really nothing to it."

It was a fairly simple matter for Lily. He did cling tenaciously to the beam, and she had a little difficulty prying his fingers off, but it was nothing to speak of.

She paused at the bottom of the stairs and surveyed the scene: the upturned stool, Floyd's memorandum book lying on the floor containing the notes that were the equivalent of a suicide message, and Floyd's lifeless body hanging so that she could read the printing on his shaven head.

She went upstairs, washed the supper dishes, and tidied up the rooms. Then she applied fresh make-up, adjusted the seams in her hose and ran out into the street, screaming for help.

How to
Show a Corpse

Johanas L. Bouma

It was almost too late when I found out what kind of a guy my old man really was. Almost, I said. I felt good. This was one time the old man wasn't going to have to show me.

It was cold there in the park. There was a wind. It was eleven o'clock, and there wasn't a star in the sky. I pulled the collar of the old topcoat up around my ears, wondering why Kay didn't show up. She'd gone to visit a girl friend at the boarding house where she used to stay. She'd promised to meet me at eleven. It was going to be like old times. Women! I didn't grimace when I thought it. I was in love with my wife.

We'd dug that mad idea of robbery out of our systems. Easy money. Nuts. One robbery leads to another, and old man murder is hunched at the end of the trail waiting to pounce. I tell you I felt clean.

I walked back and forth along the graveled path, remembering little bits of wisdom the old man had taught me and that I hadn't been able to appreciate until tonight.

"Mike Polomsky, that dumb foreigner," the kids used to call him. What they didn't know!

I remember how that one time, right after we came over from the old country, he caught me swiping some coins from the dresser drawer. He was there when I turned around, a big man with sloping shoulders and a gaunt frame that would never fit his clothes. He smiled, but I didn't know then what that smile meant, that it held tolerance and patience and a dogged belief in what was right and what was wrong.

"Little Pete," he said softly. "This you do is a very bad thing. The money, it is nothing. It is nothing what your mother she would think, or your big brother or sister." He squatted down, elbows on knees, and took my hand and tapped it against my chest. "It is here, little Pete," he continued. "It is something to you in here. What you do bad you carry here, and sometimes make big lump like sickness."

I hated to have him talk to me that way. "Why don't you beat me?" I screamed.

He shook his head, his eyes looking patiently into mine. "No, little Pete. To beat a boy proves nothing. It is to show him that helps."

He'd always show us kids when we did something wrong. Show us, you understand, not tell us. Like the time I took the quarter he'd given me and played the slot machine down at the pool hall. He came up and watched me put the last nickel in.

"To play the machine is nothing, little Pete," he said gently. "But it is foolish. I will show you." He went over and got a dollar's worth of nickels and put them all in the machine. He got back two. "You see? It is foolish."

He gave me the two nickels for the movies.

When Mom died it nearly finished the old man. Then one time my brother Joey got mixed up with an older gang, and one day the cops grabbed him. Right away my old man was down at the station. He stayed in there about an hour, and when he left he had Joey with him. He sent him upstate to work on a farm. Joey has a place of his own now.

He quit the docks then and took a night watchman's job at the Brill Cement Co., only four blocks from our place. I was out of school, a husky kid for my age, and I went down and joined the longshoremen's union. I hated working the docks. I wanted something better than what the old man'd had, so at night I studied drafting through a correspondence course. I had a lot of plans, and they weren't all on paper, either.

Then I met Kay.

Her maiden name had been Kilpatrick, and she'd been secretary to Mr. Brill at the cement works. I'd gone down there one evening to bring the old man his midnight supper. She'd worked late that evening. The old man was in the outer office, and when I handed him the lunch bucket she came in.

She was small, with long, dark hair that turned inward at her shoulders in a fat roll. She was wearing a yellow dress that clung, and her nylons shimmered. She had a graceful, racy look about her that made my throat thicken. Her eyes danced when she saw me.

She pinched the old man on the cheek and said, "Aren't you going to introduce us, Pop?"

It made me mad the way he shook her off. It was the first time I ever saw his eyes go angry, and when he finally introduced us, I knew he didn't like doing it. After we talked a bit, I asked could I take her home. That was fine, and it was fine too when I kissed her good night.

I saw her the next night, and the next. The old man found out about that and he didn't like it. He didn't say anything right off, but one day he tried to tell me she wasn't any good.

"She's from bad people, little Pete," he said sadly. "She would pull you down, spoil you for what you are trying to do."

"Where'n the hell am I at now?" I shouted at him. "A lousy laboring job and living in a shack because you never could afford anything better. And what do you know about her people? She's an orphan. They've been dead for fifteen years."

"I have heard from her. She used to go with a bad gang."

"Go ahead, queer it. The first decent girl I've met, and you want to queer it. Show me where I am wrong. Go ahead and show me. You've shown me everything else."

"Maybe some day," he said heavily, "you will understand."

"You'd show a corpse if you thought it would do any good," I yelled.

Three weeks later we slipped across the state line and were married.

I remember the honeymoon. We had a week at the lake, and it was all the moonlight and roses stuff you hear about. But I found out a couple of things. She liked money, and she liked better to spend it. I had three hundred saved up, and she went through it in five days.

And she told me about having gone with Charlie Fowler.

I knew Charlie. He'd run in the same gang with Joey. He was a cheap, flashy punk who'd made nickels rolling drunks and running errands for the big boys. He was supposed to be a small-time big-shot now, taking whatever he could get his pasty hands on.

I didn't like her telling me about him. As far as I was concerned that part of her life was finished. And then I got the queer feeling that she enjoyed telling me and watching me squirm. Her eyes'd get that cat look, flat and watchful like a cat's eyes get when it's teasing a mouse. But about the time I'd get ready to bust, she'd go all soft in my arms and press her body against mine. Then she'd ask was I jealous. I'd forget everything then but about us two being together, and how much I loved her, and how nothing in the world could ever separate us.

She'd quit her job and given up the room at the boarding house. We tried to find an apartment. Sure, the housing shortage, so we had to move in with the old man. He'd added a couple extra rooms to the shack since he'd bought it, and all in all it wasn't a bad set-up. And we had the place to ourselves after the old man had his supper and left for work.

Then the longshoremen pulled a strike.

Two weeks and it was still going strong, and we were broke. I had to quit the drafting course because I couldn't meet the payments. One evening while the three of us were having dinner, the old man asked me how was I doing with the drafting. I told him.

"Look, pop, we're gonna have to cuff you for board and room for a couple weeks. At least until this strike is settled."

He waved it aside. "It is nothing," he said. "And the money for the lessons I will pay. You learn it well, Pete. Some day you will be a big man."

He gave me the money for the course and a ten spot besides.

He'd quit calling me "little Pete" right after Kay and I were married. I took the money, thinking what a swell old guy he was. And then I saw how Kay had a mean look in her eye, but she didn't say anything until after he left.

"You're stupid to take money from that old fool," she yelled. "It's nothing but a cheap handout."

"You ought to be damn glad he offered it," I flared. I threw the ten spot across the table. "Take it for a new dress, you appreciative tiger."

She grabbed the bill and tore it in half. There was some sort of hate in her face that frightened me. She went into our room, and when she came out she was wearing her coat. I heard the front door slam. She didn't come back until after midnight.

It kept up like that for another week. And then one day I came home from picket duty and found Charlie Fowler there with her.

I threw him out.

"What're you doing letting that guy hang around," I yelled at her. "If I ever catch you with that guy again, I'll kill him and you too."

"Charlie gets along," she threw back at me. "A new car last week, and what have you got?"

"Sure, maybe you married the wrong guy."

"Maybe I did."

Then she started to cry and I couldn't stand that, and the next thing I was over there making up to her.

"What do you want to go and act like that for?"

"I don't know," she sniffled. "It's just that I get so tired of having nothing."

That night was fine. I got a catch in my throat watching the way the moonlight touched her face, and the way her hair was fanned around the pillow. I watched her for a long time, wondering if there wasn't some way a guy could latch on to a bagful of cash. I couldn't think of a way. I buried my face in the curve of her neck. It was warm and pulsing and alive. She stroked my hair.

"Pete?"

"Yeah, honey."

"Wouldn't it be wonderful if we had enough money so that you could go to a good school for a couple of years and really learn drafting? I don't mean any cheap thing like this course you're taking, but something really good that would guarantee you a future."

"Be swell, honey. Got four or five thousand handy?"

She didn't say anything for a while. Then: "I know a place where we can get that much, Pete. Maybe more."

"Yeah. Sure. Remember I'm no vet, honey, and no loans on account of no collateral."

"It wouldn't be a loan, Pete."

"Huh?"

"I know where we can lay our hands on it. Every Saturday at the cement works—"

I sat up. "Say! What're you talking about?"

She came close to me. "It's an idea, Pete. Just an idea. But it means a break. We haven't had any breaks, Pete."

"Get rid of that idea," I snapped. "Leave that kind of stuff to your old friend Charlie."

"I don't want Charlie. I want you."

Her face was that close. She whispered it. I got faint and dizzy from loving her so much, and I knew all hell couldn't stop me from giving her what she wanted.

She said, "We'll need a plan, Pete."

"All right, shoot."

"They sell a lot of stuff there on Saturdays. People come in with trucks and buy cement, gravel and sand maybe to lay a driveway or build a fence. Farmers come in from the country and buy paint and stuff Brill sells on the side. Some Saturdays they take in seven or eight thousand."

"Where do they keep it?"

"The safe is in Brill's office. I remembered the combination when I left."

For a second I got a glimpse of what a heller she really was.

"You mean you planned this thing all along?"

"I just remembered, that's all. Besides, it's nothing but an old tin box—"

"They probably changed the combination. They always do when an employee leaves."

"I thought of that. Look. Mr. Brill used to couldn't remember the combination, so he'd write it on the underside of his top desk drawer."

"Boy, you notice everything."

"Sure," she said. "He didn't think I knew. But just to be on the safe side, in case he hasn't written the new one, I thought we'd have Charlie in on it. He could open that box—"

"Nothing doing," I yelled. "This is strictly between us. And say, this is the only time, you understand? No more after this one."

She kissed me. "Sure, Pete."

"And one more thing. We pull this some Saturday when that Bailey fellow works in pop's place. And no rough stuff."

"He has next Saturday night off. And we don't want to get hurt and we don't want Bailey to get hurt. But we'd better take the .45."

The .45 was an automatic Joey had given me when he returned from overseas. I said, "I guess we can take it. There are only three shells left in the clip, but we won't really use it anyhow."

"You'd better draw up a plan," she said. "Maybe we can work it so Bailey'll be at the other end of the yard when we pull it."

I knew most of the layout, and what I didn't know Kay did. I drew a regular plan showing all the stations the watchman had to make and when he had to make them. We planned it for eleven o'clock. I could get us inside easy, and at that time Bailey would be on his rounds and clean at the other end of the yard. I drew it up neat, as if it were a regular building plan, and then we acted out every move we figured to make.

I never saw anyone as excited as Kay. She seemed to glow with some kind of energy I had never noticed before. I was frightened, just plain frightened. I'd get the shakes just thinking about it and would jump like a rabbit when something happened. Like the time I thought the plan had been moved.

I'd put it in with the drafting lessons I was working on, and each night I'd pull it out and we'd go all over it again.

"Kay! You touch our plan?"

She came running in from the kitchen. "I didn't touch it. Do you suppose—"

"Christ!"

I ran through the stack again. Lesson one, two and three and all the rest of them. And at the bottom of each one my name signed with a flourish. And then I found it, but we had a big argument about her touching it.

Saturday night came too soon for me.

"Say, pop, Kay and I thought we'd go for a long walk this evening, maybe take in a movie. Like to come with us?"

We knew he didn't like much to walk, and that he rarely went to a movie, but we wanted to find out what he was planning on, and we didn't want to come right out and ask him.

The old man grinned. "Too much walking I do on the job, and tonight is the job again. Bailey he no feel good, sick. I take his place."

I went as cold as a corpse ready for burial. I saw Kay stiffen.

I watched him shove the .38 revolver he always carried on the job in his coat pocket. I couldn't meet his eyes; I felt rotten, like the time he'd caught me swiping the money.

"To carry this I do not like," he said, slapping the pocket that had the butt of the revolver sticking out of it. "To use it—" He smiled a little sadly and waved good night.

I wondered how much he suspected, and then I began to feel kind of relieved. I told Kay, "Well, I guess that washes us up."

"Maybe next week—"

"Nothing doing," I said. "I couldn't stand another week of this. And you couldn't stand it. We'd be like cats and dogs."

"Maybe it's better this way."

"Jeez, I am glad it's over. We were nuts."

"I've got to get off alone somewhere," Kay said. She was nervous, and she kept walking up and down the kitchen. Then she went into our room and came out wearing her coat. She said, "I am going for a walk."

"I'll go with you."

She shook her head. "For this once I've got to have it out with myself. Sometimes things run that way. Being together now will just make us feel sorry for each other."

"I guess you're right."

"I'll tell you what. I'll drop over to the boarding house later on and visit with Nell." She kissed me then and told me to meet her in the park.

It was eleven-thirty. I'd given her a half hour, so I cut for home. I remembered that the plan was still in with my drafting lessons. I had to get rid of it, and quick.

The house was still dark. I went inside and turned on all the lights and got some coffee going in the kitchen. Then I went to hang my topcoat in the closet. I tossed it onto a hook next to the leather shoulder holster, and I stiffened.

The .45 automatic was gone from the holster.

I looked for the plan. That too was gone. I began to feel a thin blade of fear cut through my guts. The front door slammed. I turned off the bedroom lights and stepped toward the front room.

"Kay," I said.

She was facing away from me, and when I spoke her shoulders jerked and her body became a great silent scream. She turned. She looked grey, like a cat's face is grey, her eyes green and round and glistening like a cat's eyes.

Her bag was on the couch, an oversized handbag with a fancy plastic clasp. I moved toward the couch, but not fast enough. She grabbed the bag and she hissed, "Keep away from me, damn you!"

I felt the skin go tight across my cheekbones. Something worked on my insides. They were cement. I took a step. She moved back until her shoulders touched the wall. She fumbled with the bag, her eyes never leaving my face. And then she was looking through me, past me, and her mouth opened and her lips drew back across her teeth and some sort of gibberish croak came from her throat.

I hadn't heard the old man come in.

He was standing inside the door, holding his coat tightly across his middle, his shoulders hunched, his face the color of wet paper, like the blood had long ago left it. The .38 hung from his right hand.

Kay was still backed against the wall. A shudder ran through her. She shoved her hand inside the bag. It came out holding the .45 automatic. And then she screamed, "You filthy old man! Go away!" Then she began to laugh. "They'll get Pete. I left the plan down there. It's got his name on it, and I'll swear to it—"

"Kay," I yelled. "For God's sake, Kay—"

"Little Pete."

I twisted a look at the old man. His voice was hollow but far-reaching. He was looking at Kay and shaking his head. His hand came from under the coat. It was clenched. The fingers opened. A crumpled sheet of paper fell to the floor.

Kay's face sagged. Her mouth hung loose. She looked at the paper, looked at the automatic, looked at the old man. Her eyes began to gleam. I moved toward her. I was too late. She shot him twice, and the third time the trigger snapped—empty.

A terrible jagged cry shot through me. The bullets had slammed him back against the door jamb. The coat dropped from his arm. His shirt front was one mass of blood. And then I knew he'd already taken a slug in his guts, taken it before he took the last two, taken it probably in Brill's office and then walked four blocks with it bleeding his life out.

"Pop!" I cried.

His face was fighting the pain, but he smiled a little. A sad smile. And then he brought the gun up and Kay cried, "Oh, my God!" and then he shot her.

I watched her fall, watched the stain spread across the front of her dress. The old man kind of sighed and slid to the floor. I was down there with him, holding him in my arms and bawling like a baby.

"Little Pete," he whispered, "get rid of paper. She and Charlie, they did this thing."

Then he died like that in my arms.

It was a grey day, and a raw wind whistled through the row of poplars that lined the cemetery. The grave looked mean and ugly, and I tried to keep my eyes away from it, but then I'd see the slate-colored pile of dirt, and that'd be just as bad.

Behind me I could feel that deep, heavy silence that comes with a funeral crowd. A lot of them were the old man's friends. I hadn't known he had so many. And then the newspapers had played it up. They said he'd died a hero. The police had found Charlie in Brigg's office. Dead. They said I was the fall guy. They said Charlie and she had planned it, that the old man had shot Charlie and then followed Kay home and shot her too. What they didn't know was why he followed her home.

I wasn't the fall guy. The old man had been the fall guy. If Bailey hadn't been sick that night it wouldn't have happened. I stood there thinking that, and how the old man had saved my skin. And I wasn't worth it. God, I wasn't worth it.

Then it was over, and I turned and listened to the consolations. Someone touched my arm. It was Bailey.

"I feel responsible," he said. "Pete, I'm awfully sorry. I should have worked that night."

It made me mad. "You couldn't help being sick."

"Sick?" he said. "I wasn't sick, Pete. He came over and asked to switch nights. I told him it was all right with me."

A blinding white light struck across my eyes, and suddenly it seemed the old man was standing in front of me, and he was saying, "It is to show that helps, little Pete."

And then I knew it was only the sunlight breaking through the clouds that had blinded me. About the other I don't know. I don't want to know.

All I know is that the old man showed me for the last time.

I HOPE THEY'RE WORRIED

DON JAMES

They didn't know that I was within a few yards of them. As far as they were concerned, they were alone on the boat landing. They didn't have any reason to know that I was sitting in the sun behind the small shack where we stored gasoline.

I could sit there, out of sight, and look across the blue water of Flathead Lake beneath the cloudless Montana sky and listen to every word they said.

It was all interesting because Joan and her husband, Stanley, were quarreling about me.

"This time it's certain to work!" Stanley insisted.

"Like the other time?" she asked sarcastically.

"That was a mistake."

"It was stupidity," she snapped. "You hired a gunman at an outrageous price, sent him to South America to kill my dear step-brother, John Marshal, so that I can inherit a million dollars, and what happened?"

"I know what happened," Stanley said angrily. "Stop harping about it!"

"Your gunman murdered some man named Mike Harvey, got killed himself trying to get away, and it all makes John inquisitive enough to come home for the first time in twenty years. So now we have him on our hands—a stranger that I can't even remember—finding out how we've been spending the family money, and obviously about to cut me completely out of his will and off the allowance list. Oh, you're brilliant! A brilliant husband!"

At least they knew how I felt about their chiseling on the family fortune that had been entrusted to me. And they suspected that I had an idea why the killer had shown up in South America.

Out on the lake a trout jumped. Waves slapped against the landing. And in back of me Stanley Leed shot off his mouth to his wife in pure anger. I didn't bother to listen to all of it. I was waiting for him to pick up the first thread again. He did after a few moments.

"Now shut up and listen to my plan," he snapped.

She shut up because there was silence and then he began to talk again.

But I wasn't that lucky. They were walking away as he talked and I only caught the first words:

"The easiest way to get rid of him is to make it look like an accident. Here's how we'll do it. . . ."

They walked out of my hearing then.

I waited half an hour watching the trout jump. The sun was hot and lazy. Music came faintly across the broad expanse of the grounds and I knew that they were up in the lodge where they couldn't see me.

I dived into the water and swam for a while. That was why I had gone down there in the first place. Overhearing their conversation was just a bonus—a bonus for murder.

When I came out I dried myself in the sun and went back to the lodge in a roundabout way. They didn't hear me come in and I dressed in my room and walked down into the living room that looked like the lobby of a resort hotel. They were playing the radio and drinking highballs. I greeted them casually and mixed myself a drink.

"Took a nap," I explained indifferently.

Stanley smiled the charming smile he usually wore and Joan stood and stretched.

"The Hawkins are driving over for dinner," she announced. "I'd better make sure the cook knows. It's almost three o'clock."

We watched her leave the room, a neatly built young woman wearing slacks and sweater that probably cost more than Stanley was capable of earning in a month. But that didn't bother them. They had been on the Marshal gravy train a long time.

"Do you miss South America?" Stanley asked pleasantly.

"A little."

"After New York, this country makes a good relief," he grinned.

"A good place to spend the summer," I agreed and stood. "I think I'll take a run into Kalispell," I added.

He nodded. "The station wagon's out in front. You may as well take that. It will be simpler."

I kept my face deadpan, but already the little warning bells were ringing. "Make it look like an accident," he'd said. The road to Kalispell was tough until you hit the paved highway. There were plenty of places where a car could go off and plunge down a hundred feet into the lake. Brake rods can be filed through to slivers, steering gears can be gimmicked.

"No. I think I'll take the sedan. It's faster," I said and watched his face for a sign of disappointment.

I didn't see it. He shrugged and mixed himself another drink.

"Pick up some cigarettes if you think of it," he said. "We're about out."

I got the sedan out and drove carefully into Kalispell, thinking things through. Suddenly I realized that it wasn't going to be too pleasant waiting for someone to try to murder me. I wondered what would happen if I looked up the sheriff and told him the story of what I'd heard.

I decided it wouldn't do much good. Cops aren't interested in murders until there are bodies, and anything I said that I'd heard could be refuted by both of them. I'd have to stand my word against theirs. Besides, I wanted to handle this thing.

I drove down Kalispell's main street and parked in front of the Montana Hotel. I went in search of the largest office building and looked at the names listed in the entrance. I picked the first one that read "Attorney" after the name. This was going to be a simple job. Any attorney would do.

It took about forty-five minutes to complete my business and I stopped at a cocktail lounge and had two drinks. There was a girl bartender who gave me a smile when I said the records listed on the juke box were old.

"Some like it that way," she said.

I played the same piece five times and she caught it.

"You must like South America," she told me. "You've played 'Flying Down To Rio' five times."

I grinned. "I like music."

"I like it slow and sweet," she said.

Slow like a funeral march, I thought. That's me—a prospective funeral. But it wasn't funny. I shivered and asked for a carton of cigarettes to take with me.

I left the place, had the sedan gassed and tires checked, and drove back to the lodge. I noticed that the station wagon was in the garage.

The Hawkinses had arrived and already were well into the martinis. Everyone was having a good time when I went in. It looked like a good party.

Sue Hawkins was tight enough to make a play for me and Pete, her husband, was tight enough not to care. He and Joan were dancing while Stanley matched drinks with Clara Hawkins, Pete's sister, whom they obviously had brought along for me.

By the time it was time to eat, most of them didn't want food. Drinking dinner seemed like a good idea and the cook looked disgusted when I went into the kitchen and got something more substantial than martinis. I ate plenty to keep sober.

It was just getting dark when Joan pulled me to one side.

"Let's have a big party, John!" she suggested. "Clara's birthday is this week. Let's have a surprise party for her!"

"Why not!" I agreed. The little bells were ringing again. Those warning bells.

"Why don't you get the station wagon and go down and collect the Lindseys and Wheelers?" she suggested. "You could slip out and no one would notice."

The light in her eyes wasn't from martinis and the little bells became gongs ringing like a four alarm fire.

I let her think that I hadn't had that meal to keep me sober.

"That," I said owlishly, "is an excellent idea. We'll throw one hell of a party."

"You can go out the back way," she whispered.

As I left I saw her exchange a glance with her husband. It was as if they were saying, "There goes the corpse."

I went out to the garage and got a flashlight from the sedan. Down on my knees I flashed it under the old station wagon. It had brake rods and there was a neat, clean, filed notch two-thirds through one.

I straightened up and said some obscene, unpleasant things under my breath. That's how it makes you feel when someone plans to murder you and you find out how and when, and where.

Joan looked angry when I went back to the house, but I grabbed a drink fast and grinned at her.

"Too many drinks to drive," I told her. "Got a better idea. Going to call Kalispell and have a taxi bring them out."

She let it go at that. There wasn't anything else to do. But she didn't like it. She didn't like it at all.

Clara Hawkins got me in the study and let me know she wanted to be kissed. The party was rolling good and I didn't mind kissing her. She wasn't planning to murder me. Joan and Stanley were planning that.

By ten o'clock it was more than a party. It was getting to be a brawl. That was when I went upstairs and finished what I had to do there. A few moments later no one saw me walk down to the gardener's shack and then to the boat landing. I had to do some things there, too.

Going back to the house, I thought how it might have been if I hadn't overheard the conversation at the dock, and if I had taken the station wagon in the afteroon or even later.

It probably would have happened on the long down grade that ended with the sharp right turn. A foot pressed hard on the brake pedal, the sudden feeling of release as the rod broke and then the spurting forward of the car. The curve had never been banked properly. That would help.

It was a straight hundred foot drop to boulders at the lake's edge.

That was how close I had come to dying.

By the time I reached the house the martinis were out of my system and I wanted to do something that I knew wouldn't do. I wanted to walk up to Stanley Leed and smash my fist into his face, to beat him to a battered mass of flesh and bone and then throw him out on the gravel of the drive and throw his wife after him.

That was what I wanted to do, but somehow I didn't.

Instead I danced a couple of times with a girl in jodhpurs who had come with the crowd that arrived in the taxi. She kept saying what a wonderful man she thought Stanley Leed was. It made me a little sick. I felt like shaking her and telling her something about murder.

It was quite a party. A party with death as the unseen guest and a couple of people with murder in their hearts who were throwing it.

I kept my end of it up. I danced and drank and did my share of necking with the others. I had to make it look right. Anyhow, you may as well. You're a corpse soon enough. And Marshal money was paying the bills. A man and a woman with murder in their hearts were throwing the party, but I signed the checks. Even for the brake rod they'd filed almost in two; the steel-etched invitation to death.

Meanwhile I had a job to do. I wanted to gage things right. When the time came, I did it with a slight swaying and a surliness as if the drinks were talking and I was plastered.

I simply told them to hell with the party, that I was going out in the boat.

Sue Hawkins wanted to go with me and I leered at her so that her husband took care of that, although he had to break away from Joan to do it.

"My wife isn't going out in any boat with a damned wolf!" he said thickly.

So I took a healthy swing at him. They dragged us apart.

No one wanted to go with me after that.

No one followed me to the dock, either. I got in the launch and started the motor. I let its roar wake up the night and the mountains and the animals that probably wondered what was going on. I let people in the other lodges near the lake hear it. I wanted them to know that I was going out on the lake.

Then I shoved off and headed out over the water. It's a big lake with plenty of room. I even enjoyed it because the moon had come up and the night was warm. It made me think a little of South America and I wondered if the bar girl in the Kalispell cocktail lounge was playing "Flying Down To Rio."

Suddenly I laughed. Not a pleasant laugh. A low, bitter one. I was thinking of John Marshal's corpse.

After a while I drew in close to the shore on the other side of the lake and shut off the motor. The boat glided in beside the dock I'd noticed days before. The lodge behind it was dark and empty, its windows were heavily boarded.

I took some things out of the launch and then went to work with the stuff I'd picked up at the gardener's shack.

I wedged a couple of cushions under the wheel and made certain that they were solid. I started the motor again. Then I lit a match, carefully shielding it, and applied it to the split end of the fuse I'd already picked up in the shack.

I had to jump fast so that I wouldn't land in water as the launch headed out toward the center of the lake. Standing on the shore among trees I watched it, a lonely looking launch speeding over the lake.

It must have been a thousand yards off the shore when the fire in the fuse hit the stump-blasting dynamite I'd planted in the gas tank.

There was a blinding explosion and parts of the launch went up and came down splashing into the waters of the Flathead.

In a few minutes lights began to come on in lodges across the lake. I saw a door open in the lodge I'd just left and then figures came out on the grass in the moonlight.

Quietly I slipped into the shadows of trees and headed for the highway, lugging the bag I'd packed and brought down to the launch earlier.

It was a long hike before me to Whitefish where I could catch the Empire Builder as it came through on the way to Spokane. But I had to hike it. I didn't want anyone to see me until I'd slipped onto the train and was buying a ticket from the conductor.

It's hard to bury a living corpse.

I stayed in Seattle a week, which was long enough to get the whole story from the newspapers. The story about John Marshal's death when his launch mysteriously blew up on Flathead Lake. The fruitless efforts to find his body. Then the strange part about how John Marshal had changed his will that afternoon in a Kalispell attorney's office cutting his step-sister and her husband completely out of the picture and leaving them penniless. About Marshal's bequest of all his estate and its proceeds to an obscure hospital in South America with which he had been working in tracing down a jungle fever.

All in all, the newspaper did a good job of covering the story and I learned all I wanted to know.

By telegram I booked passage to South America from San Francisco under the name of John Michael Harvey, as my passport read but as few people knew me; the same passport I'd used when I came home.

In an isolated spot on the Amazon there was a grave that held John Marshal and the name Mike Harvey was on the headboard above it. I doubted if anyone would ever question the natives about it.

The natives had watched me bury John Marshal and plant the headboard over his grave.

When I had set it up, I turned to them and explained.

"If they ever ask," I said, "tell them this is where Mike Harvey is buried. Tell them John Marshal buried him here."

The night before, John Marshal had lived three hours after Leed's gunman had shot him and after my very own gun had killed the gunman.

The gunman had confronted John and had told John who sent him; that he was going to kill John. He was very sure of himself. My coming into the tent had disturbed his aim just before I shot him, but his aim had been good enough.

Good enough that John died, but not before we'd talked and he'd asked me to go back in his name and find out what was happening and to square things.

He hadn't been home for years. No one there knew him. Joan had been a baby when he left. And I'd lived so closely to him that I knew as much about his life as I did about mine. I could take his place. I even looked like him with the same general coloring and build.

"If you want the money keep it," he whispered and tried to keep the blood off his lips. "Too much involved for a new will drawn here to stand. They'd think you did it. Out here in the jungle. Take my identification-papers. Practice signature . . . that's all they've seen of me . . . twenty years. Don't let Joan—Stanley get money . . . find out, Mike . . ."

That was when he died, the blood finally gushing from his mouth as I held him in my arms, tears streaming down my face. That guy was part of me.

So I took his name and gave him mine, and I came back—Mike Harvey with revenge in my heart.

The attorneys for the estate smiled when I joked that twenty years makes a difference in a man's looks. None of them remembered John Marshal, anyhow. He hadn't been important when he left.

I knew John's business as well as he had. It was one of the things we had to discuss during the lonesome jungle days and nights. I discussed plenty of it with the attorneys and I signed papers.

I'd practiced the signature all the way up. It passed.

No one mentioned a look at passports, nor fingerprints, nor positive identification. I got by with it. That was the way I'd carefully planned it. They accepted me as John Marshal who had come back after twenty years.

When Joan and Stanley asked why I had returned, I simply told them that my associate and best friend, Mike Harvey, had been shot by a stranger who was killed trying to escape. I'd decided to come home and check up on things.

That's it, except that before I left Seattle I found an auto parts shop and bought a brake rod like the one on the old familiar station wagon.

I borrowed a file and carefully notched the rod like another rod I'd seen. Then I wrapped it and sent it without a return address to Mr. and Mrs. Stanley Leed, Kalispell, Montana.

I hope it worries them for the rest of their lives.

IF THE SHOE FITS

KEN LEWIS

My headlights picked up Freddie Church, the screwball lip of Hollywood, less than five hours after the grand jury indicted Oscar Sampsel for coercion and blackmail. He was scurrying along Sunset Boulevard as though someone had given him a running hot-foot.

I wondered whether his feet hurt or whether his phrenetic gait was merely the natural outgrowth of perpetual agitation. Out of court, Freddie always seemed agitated. And vague, bewildered, and ineffectual. Privately, he looked more like a startled rabbit than a top-notch criminal mouthpiece. But then, privately, he wasn't before a jury.

Anyway, something about the anguished quiver of his jib nose and pushbutton chin made me decide to give him a break. I slid the coupe to the curb and called: "Hiya, chum. Who switched feet on you?"

He paused in midstride to glare at the pointed toes of his black dress oxfords, then his harassed eyes clouded with recognition and he rushed toward me.

"Feet? Feet? *Fate!* That's what brought us together, Lieutenant! You've simply got to help me find him!"

"Find who? Charlie Ross?"

He ignored that. "Why, find Lucky, of course! Haven't you heard? Don't you know the awful thing they've done, indicting Oscar Sampsel on Lucky's testimony?"

My brows arched. "What's your kid brother got to do with the Sampsel case?"

I took the crumpled L of newsprint he handed me and shoved it under the dash light.

It was the tail-end of an item clipped from one of last week's papers, detailing the information that the district attorney had called upon one Byron H. "Lucky" Church, well-known Hollywood broker, shortly before placing certain evidence against Oscar W. Sampsel, actors' agent, with the grand jury. Block-penciled in the margin was the succinct comment: YOU KNOW BETTER THAN THAT, FRIEND. GET AMNESIA—BUT QUICK!

I whistled and handed back the clipping. "This has all the sweet simplicity of Sampsel's little pal, Ricco," I said. "I hope Lucky had sense enough to wipe his nose after that."

Freddie shuddered. "It was too late!" he wailed. "He'd already signed the deposition! When Miss Fischer told him that Sampsel was trying to force her to sign him as her agent, Lucky simply boiled over!"

I thought of Priscilla Fischer, the rising young starlet currently engaged to Lucky Church, and began to get the picture. Ostensibly, Oscar Sampsel was a run-of-the-mill Hollywood ten-percenter. Actually, he was an expert blackmailer who used the dirt he dug up on the stars' private lives to chisel in on their fabulous paychecks as an agent.

"Well," I grunted, "if there's anything unkosher in Pris's private past, I'll eat my shiny brass buttons come next St. Swithin's Day."

Freddie collapsed into the seat beside me. "What does it matter," he moaned, "with Ricco on Lucky's trail? We've simply got to find him first, Lieutenant Gilligan! I thought perhaps Trogo's Bar—"

I saw what he meant. There were two reasons why no one had

ever blown a whistle on Sampsel before. One was the fact that he usually had the goods in black and white before he put the squeeze on a victim. The second, and most important, was his highly efficient little one-man protective agency.

The agency's name was Ricco—no one had ever heard him called by any other—and he specialized in accidents. Sometimes they were fatal, sometimes merely disfiguring, but almost always they were disastrous to the career of anyone who incurred his boss's displeasure.

You saw him sometimes slipping along in fat Oscar's wake, a small gray, metallic-eyed shadow, thin lips pursed, white hands immobile. And sometimes you didn't see him at all. Sometimes you just felt him, lurking somewhere behind the scenes within easy reach of his patron's wheezy voice.

If Ricco was on the prowl for Lucky Church, then this time I could appreciate Freddie's agitation.

"Trogo's Bar it is, chum," I said.

The neons along the Sunset Strip were splashing the early dark with surrealism as I nudged the coupe to the curb opposite the hole-in-the-wall drinkery. For some absurd reason Freddie insisted on doing the leg work while I covered the street entrance, and as I watched his spindly figure hitch through the door, I thought about the other half of the Brothers Church.

Lucky was the younger of the two, and the breadwinner. He'd started as a penny-ante gambler in his teens, run up a surprising score before he was twenty, and then had discovered the vast legalized roulette of the stock market.

He was a smart operator, and more than one moneyed maharajah of the galloping tintypes now beat a regular path to his brokerage office. The resultant commissions permitted him such luxuries as an Italian-style villa in the Hollywood hills, a fiancée like Pris Fischer, and an older brother like Freddie.

I had seen Freddie work. I knew that, when placed before a jury, the rabbit became a lion, the sardine a shark, the sparrow a veritable legal eagle. The watery eyes became clear and flashing, the apparently fumbling mind as cold and incisive as a steel trap, the fluttery voice, alternately as mellow as a con man's, persuasive as a hypnotist's, moving as a demagogue's. Under the influence of Freddie's closing pleas, hardbitten judges were wont to paw for their pocket handkerchiefs, and sobbing juries to acquit triple poisoners or take up collections to give axe murderers a new start in life.

231

I was still contemplating the strange Jekyll-Hyde aspect of the little shyster's personality when the police radio dispatcher at the Hollywood sheriff's sub-station began to make noises in my dashboard receiver.

The noises were directed at Lieutenant Beau Gilligan, Homicide, so for the next few minutes I forgot all about Freddie. But when he hobbled from Trogo's Bar moments later, dolorously shaking his head, I was able to greet him with a bracing grin.

"Cheer up, chum," I said. "Your worries are over. Ricco was located ten minutes ago in your garage."

"But—but I don't understand. We had to sell the Cadillac. We have no garage now—"

"Sure you do," I soothed. "That big five-stall job behind the villa. Remember?"

He shook his head bewilderingly. "But we don't live at the villa any more. Not for almost a week. The lease ran out and we—we decided we didn't like the place well enough to renew it. What was Ricco doing up there?"

"Nothing," I told him. "Just lying there. There's a rumor that his skull was bashed in by a defective garage door. Shall we go?"

Half a mile back along Sunset, Freddie plucked hesitantly at my elbow. "If—if there's no special hurry, Lieutenant," he stammered. "I wonder if we could drop by the Elite Hotel a moment. . . ."

I shook my head, knowing what bothered him.

"There's no use worrying now," I said gruffly, swinging the coupe onto Crescent Heights Boulevard. "If Ricco was still looking for Lucky when he got it, well and good. If he'd already found him— well, there's still no use worrying about it now."

Ten minutes later, a narrow, looping side-street brought us to a white pile of architecture overlooking the milky way of valley lights below.

Aside from a lone prowl car in the drive, the bulk of the homicide hierarchy was apparently still on its way. I beached the coupe behind the radio car, loped through an intervening rose garden toward the garages at the rear.

Freddie was trudging virtuously along the graveled semi-circle to my left when I reached the uniformed deputy guarding the garage.

"Nolan," I acknowledged. "Who tipped us?"

"Dame in the next house up the hill. Thought she heard a scream down here and phoned in."

I shined my flash at the white expanse of garage door behind him. The door, an overhead type, had caught about six inches above ground level. Two gray-clad legs, backside up, protruded from the crack beneath it.

Freddie came up, saw the legs, gurgled unhappily and stepped back, perching on one foot like a distressed stork. "Any other way inside?" I asked.

Nolan nodded and led us to a small side door in the left garage wall. "Ain't been used much," he pointed out. "Farther from the house. Guess they mostly came and went through the big door."

Light from a ceiling bulb inside spilled bleakly across oil-smudged concrete, glinted from rusty tools lining the walls. It bathed in light a gray bundle with a red-and-black melon attached which sprawled against the crack at the bottom of the far door, its position matching that of the legs outside.

The bundle was Ricco's torso—the melon, his head. The black was hair—the red, something that looked like ketchup but wasn't.

"Door's steel, Lieutenant," Nolan said. "Operates automatically. Electric eye in a post outside opens it, pushbutton just inside the wall there shuts it. Speed controlled by those spring balances under the roof. Only the spring that's s'posed to keep it from bangin' down has worked loose. You can see it hangin' there. . . . Looks like the door fell on his head when he reached back from outside to push the release button. Busted his skull, knocked him flat an' pinned him across the hips as it came on down."

I tiptoed gingerly along the wall, knelt by the corpse. Then I shook my head. "The door might have knocked him out, even cracked his skull," I said, "but it never made that round, ragged hole in his crown. Better start frisking the grounds for the proverbial blunt instrument, Sergeant."

I was studying a pair of rubber heelprints caught in a pool of crankcase sludge beyond the body as he sighed and went out.

Freddie peered around the edge of the side door, stared greenly at the corpse. "F-find anything, Lieutenant?"

I pointed to the heelprints. The tread of the left one was almost completely worn off, while the right appeared to be new. "Fresh," I said. "No dust on 'em, though the rest of the puddle's fuzzy with it."

Freddie bent forward to look at them, blinked rapidly three times and looked away.

"Ricco's?"

"Too big."

"The—the murderer's, then?"

I nodded.

"But, who—"

I eyed him silently for a long moment. "I think we both know that," I said at last, gently. "Lucky told me once about his right leg. Meningitis, wasn't it, as a kid? He'd learned to cover up the slight difference in length by walking almost entirely on the ball of his right foot. That explains why that heel's so little worn."

Nolan appeared abruptly in the side door swinging a ball-peen hammer. The ball at one end of its head looked as though it had been dipped in a mixture of putty and red lacquer. "Found this in the weeds outside," he announced.

I examined it thoughtfully. "Brains," I said. "Good work, Nolan. Sounds like the others coming, now. Hold 'em off a minute, will you?"

He nodded and went out whistling. I suspected that he'd misunderstood my allusion to brains.

Freddie was gnawing his lower lip. His eyes swung unwillingly to the hammer, and for a minute I thought he was going to lose his supper. Then, in mid-heave, his jaw clamped shut and he stopped shaking. His watery eyes cleared, his jib nose jutted out, and his voice deepened resonantly.

"You'll never make it stick, Lieutenant!" he warned me theatrically. "I see it all, now—a clear case of self-defense if ever there was one! Somehow Ricco found out our new address. Disguising his voice, he phoned Lucky, announced himself as the new tenant here, and lured him out here on some pretense of irregularity about the way we'd left the place. He meant to kill him in the garage, then make it look like an accident caused by that broken door spring. But somehow Lucky sensed a trap, armed himself with that hammer, and, in defending himself, accidentally killed his attacker instead—"

My grin stopped him. I suddenly felt a lot better, hearing him spout off in his best courtroom manner that way. "If anybody can sell that to a jury, it's you," I said. "But personally, I'm not interested. My job's just to bring them in. What happens to them after that is the D.A.'s worry."

He eyed me austerely. "I feel it my duty to warn you, Lieutenant. Any mistreatment of my client at the hands of the police will promptly be reported to the proper authorities."

"Sure, sure," I grinned. "Let's go find him, first."

* * *

The Elite Hotel was one of the shabbier walkups in one of the more rundown districts of East Hollywood. A hard-eyed landlady leered after us speculatively as we mounted the stairs to Room 313.

The door scraped back at Freddie's shove, and a lean, tousled figure in red pajamas stirred on the bed inside, opened one dark eye.

"Oh, Beau. Greetings. So Hollywood's favorite bloodhound has tracked us to our gruesome lair! I hope you're alone in that—"

Freddie fled toward him. "Don't say a word, not a word!" he shrilled. "Gilligan's going to arrest you for the murder of Sampsel's man, Ricco. You simply mustn't talk till I say so, Lucky!"

The second dark eye opened. "What the hell—"

"Please, Lucky! You've got to listen to me. I know about these things! It looks bad now, but I'll take care of it, all right. Don't worry. We'll talk it all over, privately, after Gilligan has you booked—"

Lucky Church stared at his brother as though insanity had suddenly cropped out in the family. Then, gradually, the bewilderment in the black eyes was veiled behind the set, inscrutable mask of the professional gambler.

"Right, Lieutenant?"

"Right," I nodded.

With a prodigious sigh, Freddie sank into an overstuffed chair beside the bed, reached unconsciously for his shoelaces. Then he stiffened, his eyes darting toward me nervously.

"Go ahead, Freddie. Take 'em off," I said. "They don't fit worth a damn, do they? They've been bothering you all night."

"Take—what off, Lieutenant?"

"Lucky's shoes, of course. The ones that made those heelprints in the garage oil. Sorry I couldn't stop by and let you change 'em on the way to the villa."

The thin, high overtones of panic began to edge his words. "Why, Lieutenant, whatever makes you think—" Lucky's barely audible gasp of recognition cut him off.

Freddie's watery eyes jittered miserably across the carpet. "It's not what you think, Lucky!" he babbled. "Honest it's not! It's not what you think it is at all!"

"I don't think anything—yet," Lucky said grimly. "I haven't seen enough cards."

"Well, I think," I said. "Believe it or not, Freddie, sometimes thinking is almost a frequent occurrence with me. You've been hopping around all night as if you'd been given a hotfoot. And you were damned careful to stick to the drive, back there at the villa. You didn't want to leave any heelprints in the soft turf beneath the roses—heelprints that could definitely be traced to you.

"So I think, for instance, that when I picked you up on Sunset you weren't heading for Trogo's Bar in search of Lucky, at all. You were heading for the nearest bus stop, hoping to get back here and change shoes before Ricco's body was found.

"I think you planned to kill him as soon as you heard the newscast about Sampsel's indictment. You knew that he'd head for the villa as soon as it got dark, believing Lucky still lived there, and when he found nobody home he'd probably make for the garage, planning to wait there till Lucky returned and gave him a chance to stage his fatal 'accident.'

"So you merely went up and hid in the garage first, conked him with the hammer when he showed up, then jimmied the door spring so it would look as if he'd been caught by one of his own infernal contraptions. And you wore Lucky's shoes to throw us off the trail, in case any doubt arose later."

Freddie had slumped to his knees beside the bed. "No—no!" he sobbed. "Believe me, Lucky, I didn't plan to involve you at all! I knew my feet hurt, but I didn't know why till Gilligan called attention to them back there on Sunset. Then I looked down and saw that in my excitement I'd put on your shoes by mistake when I ran out of the apartment. I was taking a bath when the newscast came over and—"

He turned to me. "I'll admit I went up there hoping to find Ricco," he said dully. "But I didn't mean to kill him—not at first. I was going to make a deal—offer to defend Sampsel in Superior Court. I'd figured out a way to get Lucky's deposition ruled out as evidence, and I was going to promise that Lucky wouldn't testify in person, if only Ricco'd lay off us.

"I hid in the garage, like you said. But I—I was scared stiff. I didn't know what he might do when he found me, whether he'd even give me a chance to talk. By the time I finally heard a noise in the drive outside, I didn't want any part of the setup any more. . . .

"I'd purposely left the main garage door up. Now, in my panic, I frantically pushed the release button, hoping to shut it again before he could reach me. But I was too late. I didn't know how close he'd got, creeping up on me that way in the dark. And the door didn't come down slowly, as it should have. I guess that spring really had worked loose by itself. Anyway, it fell. . . ." He shuddered.

"He must have just started through when it hit him—knocked him flat, pinned him there on the floor, his head bleeding. . . . I lifted his wrist. I couldn't feel any pulse. I twisted him enough to put my ear against his chest. I couldn't hear his heart at all. I felt wonderful. . . .

"And then another thought hit me. What if he wasn't really dead, after all? What if he was just stunned? I didn't know enough about such things to be sure. I looked down at him lying there on the floor, so quiet now, so harmless—for the moment. And I thought what would happen if he ever got up again.

"I'd lost my chance to bargain with him. I knew that. He'd never trust me now, after what happened. He'd go right on hunting for Lucky, and sooner or later he'd find him. And then Lucky would die, no matter what I tried to do to stop it. I saw the hammer hanging on the wall, and I thought what a filthy little rat Ricco really was, and—well—he looked dead enough, all right. But it seemed a shame not to make sure. . . ." His voice trailed off to a whisper.

I studied him ironically for a long moment. "He was no more of a rat than a dozen others you've got off scot free in court," I said. "You know that, don't you?"

His face fell. "Yes, I—I suppose so. But it just seemed like a kind of a game, then. It didn't seem like this, at all. Honest, Lieutenant, I'll never again have anything to do with a m-murderer."

I nodded. "You're right about that, anyway," I said grimly. "Oh, I believe your story, all right. Even the part about the busted door spring. After all, those things do happen. But you'll never be able to make a jury believe it—not even you."

His eyes shifted wretchedly. "I know. But when I saw those heel-prints, and knew you already suspected Lucky, I was sure I could get him off O.K. Well, it's over, now. And I'm glad. Somehow I'm glad it's really me going to jail, instead of Lucky." He held up his wrists for the cuffs. "Do your duty, Lieutenant," he said.

I scratched my ear. "I'm trying," I said, "to decide just what it is. When you knocked off that lousy little creep tonight, you did more for the cause of justice than you and your kind have ever done in a thousand court appearances. It doesn't seem right to arrest a man for a thing like that. . . . I've got a good notion to take Lucky in, after all, and let you spring him with that self-defense plea you dreamed up back in the garage."

His eyes began to shine again. "The case'll never even reach the manslaughter stage, Lieutenant! I promise!"

He was right. The case, in fact, never got beyond the inquest. The coroner's jury found that Alonzo Ricco—they'd dug up a first name for him somewhere—had met his death while attempting to commit a homicide. Lucky wasn't even held.

So Freddie Church, the screwball lip of Hollywood, had won another phony case. I felt a lot better about it when the coroner informed me privately that Ricco really had been dead before the hammer hit him.

I was also highly gratified to note the following question in a local gossip column two weeks later:

> What rising filmland mouthpiece has given up his successful criminal law practice to take a job in the legal department of one of our major studios?

It was the first time I'd ever known the answer to one of those things. And me a detective!

IMPERFECT ALIBI

D. L. CHAMPION

By the standards of almost anyone else, Herman Phillips was a punk, a potential killer and an unredeemed bum. According to his own lights he was a big shot who, at the moment, stood half way up the ladder of success.

Three months ago he had been a poolroom hanger-on in Columbus, Ohio. He had a dozen petty holdups to his credit, a few assaults, and a possible murder. But, as he often regretted, he had no future. He seemed destined to remain a small town second rater, miles removed from the big money.

But now he felt like a stock clerk who has been promoted to vice president of the firm in a single afternoon. A chance meeting, sheer luck and a few bold words had put him on Willy Magness' payroll.

Willy Magness to Herman Phillips was what Abe Lincoln was to most lads his age. A hero, sitting high on a pedestal to which few could aspire. Next to the mayor, Willy ran New York. And there was a school of thought which insisted that the mayor had just a little less influence than Willy.

Herman had dwelt in the big town for three months. Each week he had drawn a handsome salary from Willy Magness. Thus far he had been asked for nothing in return.

Herman looked around the city and found it satisfying. He invested in a gaudy hotel suite and an even more gaudy show girl. Elaine was blond, tall and flashier than anything Herman Phillips had ever observed on the corner of Broad and High Streets of the city which gave him birth.

All in all, Herman was happy. There was a single, not too big, fly in the ointment. Elaine was not exclusively Herman's property. Her other gentleman friend was, apparently, a man of means, limousines and a charge account at Cartier's. There was too much dough involved for Elaine to ditch him entirely for Herman's love alone.

Then there came the day when Herman was given his first assignment. Willy Magness sent for him. Lolling behind a huge desk, an expensive cigar in his mouth, the racketeer regarded his latest henchman.

"Herman," he said. "I got a job for you."

"O.K.," said Herman. "Just name it and it's done."

"There's a guy called Harrigan," said Magness. "He's a private lawyer working for a reform society. He's got some papers which will prove embarrassing to a political friend of mine. He works late at night. I'll give you the office address. I want you to pay him a visit."

Herman nodded. He recalled the gangster lingo he had read in the magazines. "So I rub him out?"

"You do not," said Willy Magness. "You can slug him, if you like. You might even knock out a tooth or two. My political friend will be grateful for that. Then take the papers. They'll be in a brief case in the upper right hand drawer of his desk. You'll arrive there at eleven o'clock."

"O.K.," said Herman airily. "I'll get there around eleven."

"You will not," said Willy Magness. "You'll get there at precisely eleven. That'll fit in best with your alibi."

"Alibi?" said Herman Phillips. In Columbus, Ohio, minor assault was managed without much attention to detail.

"Alibi," said Willy Magness. "The D.A.'ll know damned well this was my work. I want every boy of mine to have a sound alibi so that nothing can be pinned on us. You know Frank Carver?"

Herman nodded. Frank Carver was a political force who, because he was a pillar of the church, effectively kidded the public into accepting him as a solid, respectable citizen.

There was another reason he remembered Carver. He had met him on the same night he had first met Elaine—at a party in Magness' apartment.

"O.K.," said Magness. "You and I were at Carver's apartment between eleven and one tonight. The elevator boy will swear he took us up. Carver will attest that we were there. Got it?"

"Sure," said Herman. "I got it."

"All right," said Magness. "Get going."

Herman Phillips carried out his assignment with ease, facility and a feeling of well being. Slugging an elderly lawyer across the skull with a revolver barrel, loosening two of his teeth, was not a perilous undertaking. Herman felt rather like a German company which had just slaughtered four Poles.

Then, as he left the office building and started for home, an idea struck him.

This was the night that Elaine went night-clubbing with her elderly admirer. He knew, too, that the girl would first drive to her apartment to change her clothes after the show. They would arrive sometime shortly after midnight.

Since he already had a cast-iron alibi, reasoned Herman, why not knock his rival off right now?

It seemed foolproof. He took the subway to 72nd Street and stationed himself in the shadows of a brownstone house entrance two doors away from the apartment building where Elaine lived. He thrust his hand deep into his pocket and caressed the butt of his automatic.

A few moments later the limousine drove up. A man, clad in evening clothes disembarked, his back to Herman, and helped

Elaine from the machine. Herman, his little eyes cold, his lips set into a grim line, stepped out quickly from his cover.

He took the automatic from his pocket, lifted it, and fired twice. Then he turned on his heel and ran like hell back to the subway station. Eight minutes later, he was half a mile away, sitting calmly in the elaborate living room of his Broadway hotel suite.

He poured himself a slug of Bourbon. He lighted a cigar. He donned a dressing gown and paced up and down over his luxurious carpet. He felt like a conquering hero. His ego reared itself. He had slugged a guy and committed murder. And no one could touch him —ever. Herman Phillips had achieved everything he had ever dreamed of. He was a big shot.

He was a little drunk when the knock came at the door. He smiled confidently and opened it. Two men stood outside. One was wide and short, the other tall and thin. They both wore good suits and gave off that air of authority which means the law.

Herman grinned expansively and invited them in. The tall and thin man said: "You Herman Phillips?"

Herman bowed, proudly admitted his identity.

"You know a dame called Elaine Roberts?" asked the wide, short man.

Herman's grin grew broader and he admitted that, also.

"O.K.," said the thin man. "That's all we wanted to know. Get your drawers on and come along with us."

"For what?"

"Murder. There was a guy killed outside this Elaine dame's joint a few hours ago. We know you're her boy friend. You're coming with us."

Herman's grin grew positively angelic. "What time did you say this murder took place?"

"Twelve ten."

"Go away," said Herman. "I got an alibi. A perfect alibi."

"Yeah?" said the wide, short man unbelievingly.

"Yeah," said Herman smugly. "Willy Magness and me was up to Frank Carver's place tonight. From eleven till one. I got a dozen witnesses who can vouch for me."

"Carver?" said the tall thin copper. "Did you say Carver?"

Herman Phillips nodded. Then both his visitors burst into uncontrolled laughter.

Herman regarded them in bewilderment.

"What are you laughing at? I told you I got a dozen witnesses."

The wide, short man, stopped laughing. "You ain't got Carver," he said. "He's dead. He was killed at twelve ten. That's the guy whose murder we're holding you for, Herman."

They dragged Herman downstairs into the taxicab. Somehow he was suddenly incapable of walking.

IN THE BAG

CAREY BARNETT

He watched the girl for at least thirty seconds before deciding to put his foot on the brake-pedal. Hitch-hikers in Florida were nearly as plentiful as palm trees. But she was young to be thumbing a ride at four-thirty in the morning, so he stopped.

"Been on the road all night, sweetheart?"

She shook her head. She was all of five three, weighed easily a hundred pounds, and was scared. Cute though, he decided, despite the lines of fatigue marring her pale face.

"I left Miami at three o'clock," she said, and timidly added, "My room rent wasn't paid, so I had to get up before the landlady did."

He leaned out and took the suitcase from her hand. Its weight surprised him. Gently, so that the battered cardboard would not burst open, he swung it onto the rear seat. The girl got in beside him and pulled the door shut.

"Half frozen, aren't you?" he observed. Florida mornings could be cold sometimes, and the ragged red sweater she wore could not be very warming.

"Uh-huh. A little."

She was going home, she said. She had gone to Miami to meet someone but failed to make the connection. Then she had tried to find work, but Miami was full of girls looking for work. Her name was Matalee.

"Mine," he said, "is Jim Smith. I'm a salesman." Actually it was Art Mace and he worked for the government and was in Florida trying to help stem the northward flow of drugs from that busy port-of-entry. The suitcase, the hour and the girl had aroused his suspicion.

Drugs could be transported that way. You never knew what the dealers would come up with next.

Thinking about it, he drove along at a steady forty mile an hour clip, casually studying his passenger. Presently he said, "That's a heavy bag you've got."

She had picked up a magazine and was frowning at it. "Do you read this?"

He chuckled. The magazine was called *Lonely?* and it had arrived in his mail months ago, along with other such junk. Many a dreary evening had been made less dreary by his correspondence with some of the lonely souls listed in it.

"My hobby," he admitted. "You meet the queerest people."

"Do you?"

"My first letter was a blind stab in the dark, to a girl who called herself Constant Heart and quoted Confucius. 'And I know why our breathing is nothing more than a perpetual sigh,' says she. I guess it's the hellion in me. Other lads collect postage stamps."

He grinned at her.

The girl only stared. Perhaps she, too, was thinking about the suitcase.

"You're too young to appreciate such stuff," he said. "How old are you?"

"Nineteen."

"Sweet nineteen. One of my lonely hearts said she was that age. Many an ardent letter I banged out to her on the old portable. Georgia gal. So help me, I even sent her a photo."

"What was her name?"

"Darned if I remember. She mostly signed herself *Lover.*"

There was a small silence.

"Are you going far?" she asked after a while.

"West Palm Beach. I do a lot of business in West Palm. Sold five thousand yellow shirts there last trip."

"I guess you're a good salesman." She smiled. "I mean, with your line you could sell anything."

He laughed. She seemed to be a nice kid.

But you never could tell, could you? She was just the type the runners might use. So young and innocent. He'd still have to look at that suitcase when she got out of the car.

In West Palm he stopped the car and turned to her. "I guess this is where we part company. It sure has been nice knowing you. Hey, a girl as cute as you ought to be way up around Jacksonville by dark. Take this, so you'll have a place to sleep tonight."

She took the bill and thanked him.

He leaned over the seat and grabbed the suitcase, almost sure, now, that he knew what was in it. When you'd been on the job as long as he had, you got so you could tell.

"No," she said quickly. "Let me."

"Huh?"

"It's all ready to fall apart!"

His jaw tightened. "Lady," said Art Mace, "you've been riding with the wrong guy. You played your cards wrong. I was wise to you from the start."

Getting out, she didn't reach again for the bag but stood very still on the sidewalk, watching while he dragged it from the car and plunked it down on the curb.

"I happen to know all about girls like you," Art Mace said.

On one knee he yanked the battered bag open and pulled out slacks, dresses, pink underwear, shoes, and then, with a grunt of satisfaction, a worn leather box once used for stationery.

"Believe me, lady, I know all about this racket."

The girl had not spoken. She only stared at his hands as they opened the box and lifted out a pack of letters and a photograph. When he slowly raised his head and looked up at her, her eyes were wet.

"You might at least have remembered my name," she said.

INCENSE STICKS

ERNEST LEONG

Song Li Djien hated his upstairs neighbors, the Lings. He decided this as he lay in bed, waiting for sleep to come and knowing it wouldn't. And it was all the Lings' fault.

The *Dai Lo* (the "Elder Brother" from the Ho Tong Association) had set him up in the studio apartment when he arrived in America months ago. He shared the place with two other immigrants. They, like Song, worked at Ho's Wet Wash Company under the bridge. The bed was used in eight-hour shifts and Song was fortunate to have the night shift to rest, so his personal habits wouldn't change much—or so he had thought at the time.

It had taken Song almost all that time to become accustomed to the sound of Grandmother Ling pacing back and forth, sobbing and talking to herself, usually about money worries from the little he could understand. Sometimes the mother would comfort her, though he hadn't heard her in a while. That wasn't so bad, but then the father would come home, and the evening would end in an eruption of yelling and wailing over their situation. When it was really bad, May, their eight-year-old daughter, would come down the fire escape, and stay with Song until things quieted down. Sometimes she'd drift off to sleep in his arms, and Song would nod off too.

"C'mon," Song muttered in Cantonese at the white ceiling, "someone say something!"

But all was still tonight. It was the third night in a row like this, and it was driving him crazy. He silently cursed the bad luck that made him an unwilling noise addict, cursed the Lings, cursed his mother and wife who made him come to America, the Mountain of Gold, especially now, when China was battling the Americans in Korea.

No one here likes the Chinese, and who could blame them? he mused. While I come here looking for that mountain of gold, a world away my countrymen are trying to kill American devils. Yes, it was very bad joss to be here now, Song decided.

Song threw the covers off, flicked a Camel expertly out of the pack, lit it, and went to the open window. He sighed, stared blankly out at the huge white face of Virginia Mayo painted on a billboard across the street. Song knew no other white people except her. It had taken weeks before he was able to decipher her name, and that was only because the ad for the same cigarettes ran in the *Chinese Journal*. He cocked his head, studied the bright, blond hair, brilliant white teeth, and the ivory hand delicately holding a lit cigarette inches from her thin red lips. He reached the same conclusion he did every night as he looked at her blue eyes. They were cold, distant, looking right through him as if he were invisible.

"Why so cold?" he asked her. "Afraid I'll steal the gold in your hair?"

Song blew a long line of smoke in her direction, stared the smoke as it broke up over the street. He scanned the rest of the street, which even at this late hour was teeming with humanity. Song glanced at, but hardly noticed two men in fedoras and zoot suits standing underneath the street lamp at the corner, looking up, apparently right at him.

On the other hand, it could be worse, he decided. At least I have a room to myself. If I'd come over now, maybe I'd be packed in one of those warehouses by the water, and have to sleep in a big room with fifty others around me. And Elder Brother has taken a liking to me, promised to help bring my family over as soon as I've saved enough. My joss isn't all bad.

Song suddenly raised his head, sniffed at the air. Incense. The Lings had lit incense sticks again, another new ritual Song would have to become accustomed to. He flicked his cigarette butt out the window, angrily slammed the window shut. The two men at the corner watched this with silent impassivity.

He climbed back into bed, resumed staring at the ceiling. Damn those Lings, he thought to himself. But even as he said this to himself, his eyelids slowly grew heavier. His breathing also became deeper, slower, and soon he was sound asleep. Perhaps it was because a familiar sound had returned which finally put him to sleep: the sound of someone upstairs, pacing and sobbing.

Song slowly opened his eyes, stared blarily towards the curtains rustling in the breeze. A tiny silhouette was blocking his view of Virginia Mayo.

"I'm scared," the silhouette said, its small, child's voice squeaking hoarsely.

"May?"

Song propped himself on an elbow. He hardly noticed that the incense aroma was stronger as he reached for another Camel, lit it. He beckoned to her. But May stayed by the window, her tiny fists clutching the curtain. He could sense her wide brown eyes staring, studying him through the darkness. The moonlight streaming in framed her in its white, eerie glow, giving her skin a blanched appearance.

"Your parents fighting again?" he asked in Toysan, the dialect the Lings spoke.

May shook her head. "I haven't seen my mother for a week," she whispered.

She sniffed, and her breathing became choked and halting, as she fought a losing battle to hold back tears. Song went over to her, put an arm around her. He stroked her short, round hair. Her mother must've given her that haircut before she disappeared, he mused idly. With a soup bowl over the head, same as my mother did for me.

"What is it, little sister?" he whispered gently in her ear. She said nothing, just sobbed softly into his chest. Song frowned, pitying her and yet also irritated about being awakened. "What have you done?"

"Me?" she squeaked. "I didn't do anything! It's my father!"

Song nodded reassuringly, stroked her hair. He frowned at her comment, but decided not to press any further. He watched her as she cried.

My daughter's three years younger than this one, he thought. That makes Song Poo-Yi five. Five! She can walk and talk now, but when I left, she was smaller than my pillow!

Would she know him? Song wondered. No, that wasn't the question. Would she accept him was more like it. Would his family like America? Could they live like this? Definitely not. Song made a mental note to speak to Elder Brother about a bigger apartment just for him and his family, like the Lings have. Elder Brother would help. He'd said so, in fact. When the right time comes, he would lend Song whatever he needed.

"Soon I'll have a bigger place," he said aloud.

He smiled at May, who had stopped crying. She was now hiccuping uncontrollably.

"Don't make me go back there," she said between hiccups. "Let me sleep here."

"All right," he said soothingly, "all right."

He guided May to the bed, and she climbed obediently in. Song remained on one knee by her, sang a Cantonese lullaby to her about a Chinese wife who pined for her husband, while the husband sold their crops in the town.

She fell asleep within moments. Song studied her round, smooth face, thought again about his own daughter. Through the ceiling came the muffled sounds of sobbing again.

He got up, walked slowly to the window. His nostrils flared as he became aware of the incense. He clambered quietly onto the fire escape.

"I have to speak to Mr. Ling," he muttered at Virginia Mayo as he climbed the metal stairs. "May isn't my problem."

The two men at the corner silently watched him. The fat one started to move forward, but the thin one held him back, shaking his head. He guided his partner out of sight, around the corner.

Song blinked. Even with the moonlight, it took him a moment to adjust to the darkness of the Lings' apartment. He climbed into the living room through the open window.

He covered his nose with his T-shirt as he muffled a cough. The smell of incense was overpowering. Song retreated to the window, where he inhaled the night air deeply. When he felt better, he took out a handkerchief, tied it over his lower face.

As Song tiptoed further in, the sobbing became louder. He could even make out a Toysan phrase every now and then: "my fault . . . I'll join you soon . . . I had to . . . had to . . ."

Song cursed as he touched a creaky floorboard. He gently raised his foot up, corrected his course. He kept his eyes focused on the slit of light from the bedroom door just a few feet to the right.

Next to the front door just ahead of him was a wall mirror. Song stopped, looked at his reflection a moment. I look just like a bandit in those Western movies, he thought. His hand flashed down to his hip, as he practiced a phantom quick draw. His eyes slanted up as he grinned boyishly behind his mask.

He looked back at the door, straightened from his gunfighter's crouch. With a last look back at Virginia Mayo for confidence, Song strode quickly, but still quietly, to the door. He knocked gently, twice.

"Mr. Ling?" he said in a low but audible voice. He turned the knob, slowly opened it. "We must talk."

The door creaked back on its hinges as more of the room became visible to Song. The lone lamp threw out a dull, yellow glow over the flowered wallpaper. The door swung farther back, and he saw a bed, a prone figure and a man's leg, seated.

"I'm sorry to disturb you," Song began, "You don't know me, but I'm from . . ."

There was no sound, no warning beforehand, like he'd seen Western gunfighters get before the final shootout. There was just the blinding flash of orange, a puff of smoke, and the rancid smell of burned gunpowder. Song felt as if the whole left side of his head had been set ablaze, as he was spun completely around by the bullet, and smashed headlong into the wall. Vaguely, as if from a great distance, Song heard footsteps on the creaking floor, as a heavy, oppressive darkness forced his eyelids shut.

"Don't move, or I'll blow the rest of your head off."

The voice sounded far off, like a man shouting from a hilltop. The darkness gradually broke apart, giving way to a liquid red, and the male voice speaking in Toysan sounded much closer. Song opened his eyes, winced as dozens of needles seemed to be sticking him on the left side of his face. There was a pounding noise that Song thought was in his head until Ling got up.

"Remember, don't move," Ling said, pocketing his gun, as he moved toward the front door.

Song cautiously raised his hand to his brow: it felt sticky. His fingers were wet with dark blood. He could vaguely hear Ling at the front door, reassuring some neighbor that everything was all right, to go back to sleep. Ling returned.

"Where's your partner?" Ling snapped at him. "I know you assassins always work in pairs."

Song felt the cold muzzle of a revolver shoved under his jaw. Ling spoke again, this time slowly, deliberately.

"Where—is—he?"

"I—I'm no assassin," Song gasped back. "I'm Song, your neighbor." Song forced his eyes up, so he looked right at the man towering over him. "Your daughter is downstairs in my room now, Mr. Ling."

Ling's eyes narrowed. He relaxed the muzzle from Song's jaw very slightly.

"You're lying." But Ling's voice lacked conviction.

Song started to shake his head, grunted from the sharp pain this caused.

"No, she's down there," he replied. "Go see for yourself if you want."

"Sure, you'd like me to go out on the fire escape so your friend can take a shot at me, wouldn't you?"

Song suppressed a belch. Right now, he didn't care if he was killed or not. Waves of nausea swept through him, and he felt like he was going to be sick right there, from his spinning head and the burning incense sticks. Ling sat back, motioned with his gun for Song to sit up as well, which he did, with great effort.

"If you're my neighbor, why haven't I ever seen you before?"

"I work at Ho's Wet Wash Company, from 8 in the morning til 10 at night," Song explained. "Then I come straight home to sleep."

"What's my daughter's name?"

"May," Song replied. "Check her room. She's not there."

Ling got slowly up, edged to the door, peered down the hall.

"May!" he called out. No answer. "May!" He repeated, louder. "Don't move."

Ling inched into the hallway, moved down it. Song laughed glumly at this last command. He looked over at the body lying on the bed.

She was old and thin, and her skin shrivelled. Her lips were webbed shut, as if the age lines were bits of thread sewn around her mouth. She wore a white blouse (as if she were expecting death, Song mused), and her hands were folded neatly over her chest.

Did he kill her? Song wondered. Slowly, his mind was getting clearer, as the intensity of the pain let up. What assassins would be after him?

"Am I next?" he asked aloud. He let out a huge breath, trying desperately to figure it all out. What will become of my family if I die? Will I get a decent burial? Song's mind was racing now, as he tried to find a solution. None came, except that he must escape. He tried getting up, fell back down, just as Ling came back. His gun was down at his side, and he looked sheepish.

"Who did you say you were again?" Ling asked.

"Song Li Djien," Song told him. "I'm not an assassin."

"I know," Ling said timidly. "I looked out the window. Those two men are gone."

Ling stiffened, as a sudden thought flashed through him.

"May!"

He ran out again. Song shut his eyes, put his head back against the wall. Why had he come? he angrily asked himself through gritted teeth. Just mind your own business next time. If there's a next time. . . .

Ling came back. He was out of breath and sweating, but there was a relieved look on his face.

"She's safe," he announced. "Still sleeping in your bed."

He bent by Song, gently pressed the handkerchief to his head. Song flinched, but didn't resist. Ling continued to dab.

"I—I had no idea," Ling continued. "I thought you were one of them."

"One of who?"

"Those two men were sent here to kill me by Elder Brother," Ling stated simply. Song blinked, frowned at him.

"Why would he want you killed?" Song asked.

"Because I owe him money. Few weeks ago, my mother was very ill. We thought she'd die, and she probably would have, unless she got special medical care. But that's very expensive, and I had to borrow from Elder Brother. I have to the end of this week to pay him back, with interest."

Ling stopped, sighed.

"We could barely get by with what I made and her social security," Ling continued, nodding at the body. "And there's still May to take care of. I still need those social security checks to take care of her!"

"So no one knows she's . . ."

Ling looked up at him, shook his head.

"Where's your wife?" Song asked.

"Elder Brother took my wife," Ling said. His voice and lower lip began to quiver. It broke when he spoke of his wife. "I actually should've paid him last week. He gave me the extra days when I asked him, but took her as security. If I don't have the money by then, he said he'd kill me and take everything."

Song stared at him dully, his jaw open.

"Elder Brother would never do anything like that!" Song declared firmly. "He only wants to help us."

Ling laughed harshly. He stopped dabbing Song's head. "Help us do what?"

"To—to . . ." Song stopped. He struggled to think. Elder Brother had always been so friendly, so helpful . . . but after all, they were all Chinese, brothers of the skin, strangers in a strange land. Yet no one else had helped. Only Elder Brother . . .

"I better call a doctor for you," Ling said, getting up.

Song suddenly reached out, grabbed Ling's wrist. Ling winced with pain. Song studied Ling's face. He looks sincere, he thought to himself. No. He's crazy. Look what he's doing, burning incense and weeping over his mother's body when she should be buried and her soul allowed to ascend to Heaven. What *did* Elder Brother want?

"What happened to her?" Song asked, nodding at the corpse.

Ling turned slowly to look at the drawn face of the old woman. He sadly shook his head.

"She thought she could help us by killing herself," he said, sighing heavily. "She heard about how American companies pay life insurance if you die, and she thought she could repay our debt this way. But they don't pay if it's a suicide," Ling said. "She didn't know that."

An angry look flashed momentarily in his eyes.

"Why didn't she speak to me?" he asked, frustrated. "We could've found another way. Any way's better than that way."

"Then you didn't kill her," she began.

They looked up: May was at the door, staring at them.

"May!" Ling cried out. He leaped towards his daughter, covered her eyes. "Don't look!"

May tried to pry her father's hand from her face.

"Let me see," she asked with surprising calmness.

Ling looked frantically back at Song, as if for approval. Song nodded at him, and Ling took his hand away. May went to the corpse, studied it with innocent curiosity, her brown eyes taking in every detail. Ling came up behind her, put a hand on her shoulder.

"She did it for us, child," he spoke gently. May said nothing, just studied the corpse. Then, on an impulse, she turned and threw herself into her father's arms, sobbing softly.

Using the wall again for support, Song worked his way to a standing posture with an audible grunt. He swayed uncertainly, and the dizziness was as bad as ever, but he managed to hold that position. Ling looked up at him.

"Song," he began. "I'm so sorry."

Song looked dully at them. He held his head as if to keep it from flying apart.

"It's not your fault," Song said.

"Let me call you a doctor," Ling said, and he started to rise, May still in his arms. Song shook his head, waved his hand at him to remain. He turned, and limped slowly to the hall.

"Where you going?" Ling called out.

"To get some answers," Song replied. He walked back through

the living room, to the window, swung himself out to the fire escape. He looked across the street: the two men were there again.

Song swayed as he tried to descend the fire escape, but with each step, his feet seemed to turn to lead, and his head buzzed like a swarm of bees. The oppressive darkness was beginning to descend again. But even through the blinding pain, Song thought about Elder Brother, about his family, about America. I can't bring them over, he thought desperately. Not until I get answers. I must see Elder Brother, speak to him face to face. I must know what he wants. . . .

Four more steps, Song thought. Through the dark curtain of green spots, he could just make them out. Move, he commanded his legs. Find the next step. His left leg slid out reluctantly, his foot stabbed into empty space. . . .

He missed the step, and Song fell headlong to the landing. The two men watched this quietly, impassively. They looked at each other, the fat one pointing and nudging his skinny partner. They began to cross the street, when a female passerby, looking up at the fire escape, screamed and pointed at Song's unconscious body. As heads began to appear at open windows, the two stopped in the middle of the street. They exchanged glances again, looked one last time, longingly it seemed, at the fire escape, and retreated back around the corner.

An ambulance and two police cars arrived. While two policemen tried to calm the neighbors and extract information, the ambulance men and the other police broke down Song's door, picked Song up from the fire escape, placed him on a stretcher, and struggled to bring him as gently and quickly as possible to the street. Song awoke, his eyes wild. He grabbed at the mens' arms, asking in Cantonese, was it better to leave his family in China? What should he do now?

The men spoke soothingly to him in English, promising he'd get help soon. They descended to the street, which was even more crowded than usual. It seemed like the whole block was up and out on the street.

The only apartment door that remained shut tight, and the only ones not out on the street, were the Lings.

AN INGENIOUS DEFENSE

ANONYMOUS

Mr. Serjeant Vaughan (afterwards Mr. Justice Vaughan), while on his way to Chelmsford assizes, met with an intelligent and pleasant fellow-passenger on the coach. What happened on this occasion is narrated by Mr. James Grant in his book on *The Bench and the Bar*. Mr. Serjeant Vaughan was, on such occasions, very fond of what he used to call a little agreeable chat with any talkative person he chanced to meet. He was not long in ascertaining from his companion that he also was going to the Chelmsford assizes, which were to be held on the following day.

"As a juryman, no doubt?" said Mr. Vaughan.

"No, sir, not as a juryman," said the other.

"Oh, as a witness, I should have said."

"Not as a witness either—I wish it were as pleasant as that."

"Oh, I see how it is: you are the prosecutor in some case which is painful to your feelings. However, such things will happen—there is no help for them."

"You are still wrong in your conjecture, sir. I am going to pay away money for a relative who has a case at the assizes."

"Ah, that's it! Very unpleasant, certainly, to pay money," observed the learned serjeant.

"It is, indeed, for those who have little to spare," observed the other.

"It is not a very serious amount, I hope?"

"Why, the magnitude of the sum, you know, depends on the resources of the party who makes the payment."

"Very true, certainly very true," said Mr. Serjeant Vaughan.

254

"The sum is £500, which, to one of my limited means, is a very large sum indeed."

"Oh, but perhaps you expect to be repaid later?"

"That is most uncertain. It depends entirely on whether my relative, who is an innkeeper, succeeds in business or not."

"Well, it is undoubtedly a hard case," observed Mr. Serjeant Vaughan, with a serious and emphatic air.

"Ay, you would certainly say so, if you only knew it all."

"Indeed! Are there any peculiar circumstances in the case?"

"There are, indeed," answered the other, with something between a sigh and a groan.

"Is the matter a secret?" inquired Mr. Serjeant Vaughan, his curiosity now wound up to no ordinary pitch.

"Not in the least," said the other. "I'll tell you the whole affair if you don't think it tiresome."

"I am all anxiety to hear it," said the learned gentleman.

"Well, then," said the other, "about six weeks ago a respectable corn dealer of London, while on his way to Chelmsford, met, on the coach, with two persons who were perfect strangers to him. The strangers soon entered into conversation with him, and having learned the object of the corn dealer's visit to Chelmsford, said that they also were going there on a precisely similar errand—namely, to make some purchases of corn. After some further conversation, it was suggested by one of the strangers that it would be much better for all three if they could come to a mutual understanding as to what amount of purchases they should make—for if they went into the market 'slapdash' and without any understanding, the result would be that in so small a place as Chelmsford they would simply cause the prices to rise; whereas by operating slowly and in concert that would be avoided.

"The second stranger pretended to approve highly of this suggestion and further proposed, in order to show that no one had the advantage of the other, that they should all three deposit their money in the hands of the respectable landlord of the principal inn, taking care that they did so in the presence of witnesses, and that special instructions should be given to the landlord not to give up a farthing to anyone until all three returned together to receive the whole. The first stranger then added that if the landlord violated the special instructions, he—the landlord—would be held responsible.

"The London merchant, knowing the landlord of the inn to be a man of undoubted respectability—the landlord is my relative, you understand—at once assented to the proposal, and each of the three accordingly placed in the landlord's hands, under the circumstances stated, £250—making £750 in all."

"Well," observed Mr. Serjeant Vaughan, "you certainly interest me in your singular story. And what was the result?"

"Why, this: scarcely had the three men left the inn a minute, when one of the two strangers—the one who had been the spokesman with the landlord and had made all the arrangements with him —came running back, and said that, on second thought, they had all come to the conclusion that it would be better to make their purchases as early in the day as possible, and that consequently the other two had desired him to return and get the money."

"And your relative, the landlord, gave him the whole sum?" interposed Mr. Serjeant Vaughan.

"He did, indeed—unfortunately for himself and for me," answered the other.

"And what followed?" inquired the learned gentleman, eagerly.

"Why the other stranger and the London merchant returned about an hour later and demanded their money—£250 each."

"When the landlord, of course, told them he had given it all to the first stranger?"

"He did."

"On which, I suppose, the second stranger and the merchant are now bringing action against the landlord?"

"Precisely so. And seeing that defense is useless, inasmuch as the landlord delivered the money to one when his instructions were peremptory not to deliver it until all three were present, my relative is allowing the action to go undefended. The money must be paid to the sharper—for both strangers, as events have proved, were sharpers—and also to the London merchant."

"And you really have made up your mind to pay it?"

"Oh, certainly—there is no help for it."

"I am a barrister and I will be happy to defend the case for the poor landlord gratuitously."

The other tendered him a thousand thanks for his kindness, but expressed his apprehensions that all efforts at defense would be perfectly useless.

"We shall see," said the serjeant, "we shall see. You and your relative the landlord will call on me this evening at eight o'clock, to arrange for the defense tomorrow."

Tomorrow came and the case was duly called in court. The poor innkeeper, acting on the advice of Mr. Vaughan, but not perceiving in what way he could be benefited by it, defended the case. Everything proceeded so favorably for the prosecution for some time that even though every person in court deeply sympathized with the unfortunate landlord, they saw no possibility of any result other than a verdict against him.

But Mr. Serjeant Vaughan, when the case for the prosecution was closed, rose and said, "Now, gentlemen of the jury, you have heard the evidence adduced. You have seen it proved by unimpeachable witnesses that the defendant received the most positive instructions from all three not to deliver up the money, or any part of it, to any of the parties except in the presence of all. Gentlemen, my client has got the money in his possession, and is ready to give it when *all three parties* come to demand it. Let the absent party present himself, in company with the other two, and everyone will have his money returned to him."

The prosecution looked amazed. The verdict was, of course, for the defendant. It is unnecessary to add that the man who had absconded with the money never returned, and that consequently the landlord never had to pay a farthing of the amount.

It might have been more equitable to share the loss of the honest corn dealer, but a London merchant deserved to pay *something* for his experience.

INTO THE LION'S DEN

WILLIAM F. NOLAN

Before she could scream, his right hand closed over her mouth. Grinning, he drove a knee into her stomach and stepped quickly back, letting her spill writhing to the floor at his feet. He watched her gasp for breath.

Like a fish out of water, he thought, like a damn fish out of water.

He took off his blue service cap and wiped sweat from the leather band. Hot. Damned hot. He looked down at the girl. She was rolling, bumping the furniture, fighting to breathe. She wouldn't be able to scream until she got her breath back, and by then . . .

He moved to a chair across the small living room and opened a black leather toolbag he'd placed there. He hesitated, looking back at her.

"For you," he said, smiling over his shoulder. "Just for you."

He slowly withdrew a long-bladed hunting knife from the bag and held it up for her to see.

She emitted small gasping sounds; her eyes bugged and her mouth opened and closed, chopping at air.

You're not beautiful anyway, he thought, moving toward her with the knife. Pretty, but not beautiful. Beautiful women shouldn't die. Too rare. Sad to see beauty die. But, you . . .

He stood above her, looking down. Face all red and puffy. No lipstick. Not even pretty any more. No prize package when she'd opened the door. If she'd been beautiful he would have gone on, told her he'd made a mistake, and gone on to the next apartment. But, she was *nothing*. Hair in pin curls. Apron. Nothing.

He knelt, caught her arm and pulled her to him. "Don't worry," he told her. "This will be quick."

He did not stop smiling.

"A Mr. Pruyn out front, sir. Says he's here about the Sloane case."

"Send him in," said Lieutenant Norman Bendix. He sighed and leaned back wearily in his swivel chair.

Hell, he thought, another one. My four-year-old kid could come in here and give me better stories. Stabbed her to death with my crayons, Daddy. Nuts!

Fifteen years with the force and he'd talked to dozens of Dopey Joes who "confessed" to unsolved murders they'd read about in the papers. Phonies. All phony as a fiver with Ben Franklin's kisser on it. Oh, once he'd struck oil. Guy turned out to be telling the truth. All the facts checked out. Freak. Murderers are not likely to come in and tell the police all about how they did it. Usually it's a guy with a souped-up imagination and a few drinks too many under his belt. This Sloane case was a prime example. Five "confessions" already. Five duds.

Marcia Sloane. Twenty-seven. Housewife. Dead in her apartment. Broad daylight. Throat cut. No motives. No clues. Husband at work. Nobody saw anybody. Score to date: zero.

Bendix swore. Damn the papers! Rags. Splash gore all over the front page. All the gory details. *Except*, thought Bendix, the little ones, the ones that count. At least they didn't get those. Like the fact that the Sloane girl had exactly twenty-one cuts on her body below the throat; like the fact that her stomach bore a large bruise. She'd been kicked, and kicked hard, before her death. Little details —that only the killer would know. So, what happens? So a half-dozen addled pin-heads rush in to "confess" and *I'm* the boy that has to listen. Mr. Ears. Well, Norm kid, somebody's got to listen. Part of the daily grind. So, listen.

Lieutenant Norman Bendix shook out a cigarette, lit it, and watched the office door open.

"Here he is, Lieutenant."

Bendix leaned forward across the desk, folding his hands. The cigarette jerked with his words. "Come in, Mr. Pruyn."

A small man stood uneasily before the desk, bald, smiling nervously, twisting a gray felt hat in his hands.

In his early thirties, guessed Bendix. Probably a recluse. Lives alone in a small apartment. No hobbies. Broods a lot. They don't have to say a word. I can spot one a mile away.

"Are you the gentleman I'm to see about my murder?" asked the small man. His voice was high and uncertain. He blinked rapidly behind thick-rimmed glasses.

"That's right, Mr. Pruyn. Bendix is my name. Lieutenant Bendix. Won't you sit down?"

Bendix indicated a chair near the desk.

"Pruyn. Like in sign," said the bald little man. "Everyone mispronounces it, you know. An easy name to get wrong, I suppose. But, it's Pruyn. Emery T. Pruyn." He sat down.

"Well, Mr. Pruyn." Bendix was careful to get the name right. "Want to go ahead?"

"Uh—I *do* hope you are the correct gentleman. I should hate to repeat it all to someone else. I abhor repetition, you know." He blinked at Bendix.

"Believe me, I'm your man. Please go ahead with your story."

Sure, Bendix thought, rave away, Mr. Pruyn. This office lacks one damned important item: a leather couch. He offered the small man a cigarette.

"Oh, no. No, thank you, Lieutenant. I don't smoke."

Or *murder,* either, Bendix added in his mind. All you do, Blinky, is read the papers.

"Is it true, Lieutenant, that the police have absolutely no clues to work on?"

"That's what it said in the papers. They get the facts, Mr. Pruyn."

"Yes. Well—I was naturally curious as to the job I had done." He paused to adjust his glasses. "May I assure you, from the outset, that I am indeed the guilty party. The crime of murder is on *my* hands."

Bendix nodded. Okay, Blinky, I'm impressed.

"I—uh—suppose you'll want to take my story down on tape or however you—"

Bendix smiled. "Officer Barnhart will take down what you say. Learned shorthand in junior high, didn't you, Pete?"

Barnhart grinned from the back of the room.

Emery Pruyn glanced nervously over his shoulder at the uniformed policeman seated near the door. "Oh," he said. "I didn't realize that the officer had remained. I thought that he—left."

"He's *very* quiet," said Bendix, exhaling a cloud of pale blue cigarette smoke. "Please go on with your story, Mr. Pruyn."

"Of course. Yes. Well—I know I don't *look* like a murderer, Lieutenant Bendix, but then—" he chuckled softly, "—we seldom look like what we really are. Murderers, after all, can look like anybody."

Bendix fought back a yawn. Why do these jokers pick late afternoon to unload? God, he was hungry. If I let this character ramble on, I'll be here all night. Helen will blow her stack if I'm late for dinner again. Better pep things up. Ask him some leading questions.

"Just how did you get into the Sloane apartment?"

"Disguise," said Pruyn with a shy smile. He sat forward in the leather chair. "I posed as a television man."

"You mean a television repair man?"

"Oh, no. Then I should never have gained entry since I had no way of knowing whether or not Mrs. Sloane *needed* a repair man. No, I took the role of a television representative. I told Mrs. Sloane that her name had been chosen at random, along with four others in that vicinity, for a free enhancer."

"Enhancer?"

"To enhance the color range in her television set. I just made it up, out of my imagination."

"I see. She let you in?"

"Oh, yes. She was utterly convinced, grateful that her name had been chosen, all excited and talking fast. You know, like women do."

Bendix nodded.

"Told me to come right in, that her husband would be delighted when he got home and found out what she'd won. Said it would be a wonderful surprise for him." Mr. Pruyn smiled. "I walked right in carrying my bag and wearing some blue coveralls and a cap I'd bought the day before. Oh—do you want the name and address of the clothing store in order to verify—"

"That won't be necessary at the moment," Bendix cut in. "Just tell us about the crime first. We'll have plenty of time to pick up the details later."

"Oh, well, fine. I just thought—well, I put down my bag and—"

"Bag?"

"Yes. I carry a wrench and things in the bag."

"What for?"

"To use as murder weapons," smiled Pruyn, blinking. "I like to take them all along each time and select the one that fits."

"How do you mean?"

"Fits the personality. I simply choose the weapon which is, in my opinion, best suited. Each person has a distinctive personality."

"Then—" Bendix watched the little man's eyes behind the heavy lenses. "—you've killed before."

"Oh, of *course*, Lieutenant. Five times prior to Mrs. Sloane. Five ladies."

"And why have you waited until now to come to the police? Why haven't you confessed before?"

"Because I chose not to. Because my goal had not been reached."

"Which was?"

"An even six. In the beginning I determined to kill exactly six women and then give myself up. Which I have done. Every man should have a goal in life. Mine was six murders."

"I see. Well—to get back to Mrs. Sloane. What happened after she let you in?"

"I put down my bag and walked back to her."

"Where was she?"

"In the middle of the room, watching me. Smiling. Very friendly. Asking me questions about how the enhancer worked. Not suspecting a thing. Not until . . ."

"Until what, Mr. Pruyn?"

"Until I wouldn't answer her. I just stood in front of her, smiling, not saying a word. Just standing there."

"What did she do?"

"Got nervous. Quit smiling. Asked me why I wasn't working on the set. But, I didn't say anything. I just watched the fear grow in her eyes." The little man paused; he was sweating, breathing hard now. "Fear is a really wonderful thing to watch in the eyes of a woman, Lieutenant, a *lovely* thing to watch."

"Go on."

"When she reached a certain point I knew she'd scream. So, just before she did, I clapped one hand over her mouth and kicked her."

Bendix drew in his breath sharply. "What did you say you did?" he demanded.

"I said I *kicked* her—in the stomach—to knock the wind out of her. Then she couldn't scream." Pruyn chuckled softly, shaking his bald head. "It was fine. Fine."

Bendix stubbed out his cigarette. Maybe, he thought, just maybe . . . "*Then* what?"

"I walked to the bag and selected the knife. Long blade. Good steel. Then I walked back to Mrs. Sloane and cut her throat. It was very rewarding. A goal well conquered."

"Is that all?" Bendix asked, watching Pruyn's eyes.

Because if he tells me about twenty-one cuts, then he's our boy, thought Bendix. The kick in the stomach could be, just *could* be, something he'd figured out for himself. It's done in the movies all the time. But, if he tells me about the cuts . . .

"Oh, there's more, Lieutenant. Naturally, I rolled her over and left my trademark."

"What kind of trademark?"

The small man grinned shyly behind the thick glasses. "Like the Sign of the Saint—or the Mark of Zorro," he said. "My initials. On her back. E. T. P. Emery T. Pruyn."

Bendix eased back in his chair, sighed, ran a slow tongue around his lips and shook out a fresh cigarette.

"Then I removed her ears." He looked proud. "For my collection. I have six nice pairs now."

"Wouldn't have them *with* you, I don't suppose?"

"Oh, no, Lieutenant. I keep them at home—in an attractive silver box in my dresser. Do you want to hear the rest of my story?"

"Sure. Go on."

"Next, I took all of Mrs. Sloane's perfume and emptied it in the kitchen sink. Four bottles."

Like hell you did, thought Bendix. He recalled the small pink bottles of perfume on Mrs. Sloane's dressing table—three quarters full.

"I can't stand cheap perfume. Poured it all out. Every drop. Then

I cut all her nightgowns to ribbons. Nightgowns are *foul*, don't you agree? They smother the body. I burned the pieces before I left."

"That's it, eh?"

"Yes. Then I went home. That was three days ago. I arranged my affairs, put things in order and came here, to you. I'm ready for my cell."

"No cell, Mr. Pruyn."

"What do you mean, Lieutenant?" Emery Pruyn's lower lip began to tremble. He stood up. "I—I don't understand."

"I mean you can go home now. Come back tomorrow. Around nine. We'll get the other details in the morning. Then, we'll see."

"But, I—I—'

"Goodnight, Mr. Pruyn. Officer Barnhart will show you out."

From the door of his office, Norman Bendix watched the two figures recede down the narrow hall.

An odd one, he thought, a *real* odd one.

Emery Pruyn pulled the Buick out of the police parking lot and eased the big car into the evening flow of traffic.

So easy, he thought, so wonderfully exciting and easy, his sortie into the lion's den. The excitement of it was very much like the excitement with the knife. Delicious, the way he'd included that bit about the kick in the stomach. Dangerous, but brilliant. The false confession performed by a master!

Emery Pruyn smiled as he drove, remembering the look on the Lieutenant's face when he'd mentioned the kick. Absolutely delicious! Well, more excitement was ahead.

Much more.

IT'S
YOUR NECK

GEORGE WILLIAM RAE

I'll tell you we make no pretense to extra brains here in Danton,
but sometimes we can be right smart when the notion strikes.

Now take the slicin' a Marthee Regulus—That mornin' I was
more tired'n usual cause I'd spent the night in the jailhouse charged
with bein' drunk and disorderly. It wasn't new. I'd done it before.

I was tired, but I went downta the shop bright'n early as usual.
Before I put on a clean starched coat I dusted around and tidied up a
bit, as it was Saturday.

I set out my barberin' tools, clippers, thinnin' shears, tonics and
so on, then set to honin' my two razors. One thing I always saw to
personal was the honin' a my two razors.

I take pride in the right-smart way I can handle a razor. If it's not
honed by someone with the right know-how it just don't slice.

Well, that morning, as usual, Jedge was first in an' I shaved him
up proper. He didn't ask for a massage, so I didn't suggest it. One
thing 'bout the barberin' business I do detest is the sellin' a "extras"
by purrin' inta a customer's ear that he should have a rub or an
expensive lotion or suchlike. One thing I never did do.

Well, Jedge tole me. "Too bad 'bout Marthee," he said to me.

"How?" I asked.

"Ain't ya heard 'bout the slicin' a Marthee?" Jedge said.

"Jedge," I said, "Make sense."

"Why, Willie Jones' boy went overta Marthee Regulus' place'n
found her liein' in a poola blood liketa a lake," Jedge said.

"No!" I said.

"Throat slit from ear ta ear."

Well I hadn't heard about it, I told him.

I had his cheeks and mustache done, and began on the throat an'
neck. Ain't conceit. I can clean a neck with the best of 'em.

See, I always begin on the left side an' have a special wayta pull
the skin down so's the whiskers stand straight up an' the razor slices

264

against the roots—clean an' pretty an' fast, too. Oh, I take pride in my shavin's. Ain't many can handle a razor like I can.

When I'd cleaned him good and scalded a little color inta his face with a real hot towel, Jedge told me, "Willie Jones' boy found her all right. She was cold dead, they say. Sheriff Woods said she'd been dead all night long. Poor thing. Such a quiet-livin' body, too."

I wiped up my razor real careful and put it away.

"Yes, she was a quiet poor-thing," I said to Jedge.

"Sheriff Woods called it murder," Jedge said.

"Murder?" I said.

After that I was busy putting perfumed water on his face, wipin' it good an' dry an' powderin' it up proper-like.

The Jedge got up. "God help the butcher that did the awful thing," he said, an' went out.

I tidied up a bit more an' soon a coupla haircuts walked in. One waited while I worked on the other. They didn't say much. But they looked white-mad and what little they did say was enough.

Warren Pollard, he's the grain man downta the co-op, an' Jimmy Rucker, he's the owner of a big farm.

"It's a Gawd-awful thing that our women can't be left tuh live in peace, even," Pollard said.

"Yes, it sure is an awful thing," Rucker said.

"What you referrin' to, gents?" I asked.

"The slicin' a Marthee Regulus," they told me. "Allow as the feller that did 'er'll be right sorry he did."

The way he said it made my blood run cold, an' I'm no coward, long's a razor's within reach.

"Quick justice's the thing," Ruckus said.

Pollard, who was in the chair right then, swung around and they looked at each other. Both a them was tremblin' mad. "Jedge Lynch'd teach him," Pollard said.

After that they kept quiet and I didn't say anythin'. I'll tell you why. I hate one thing in the barberin' business an' that's a long-talkin' barber. Leave the talkin' ta womenfolks, radio announcers, so on. Talkin' barbers I do detest.

They went out together. One waited for the other. After that, as usual, it was quiet an' I read the morning paper an' yawned a lot an' finally stood with my hands behind me lookin' out a the window at Main street.

Nothin' much on Main street. A few stores, the co-op, the hotel across the street with some cane chairs dozin' in the sun.

As I looked out, I noticed a crowd collectin' outside a Phil Mallory's Pool Emporium which set catty-corner from my shop down Main street. They was a lot of them. Some a them was the reg'lar idlers, bums you might say, but Pollard an' Rucker an' Sheilds an' Jonesie—you wouldn't call them bums.

I'll tell you, Jedge Lynch is a cold fella to have around your home-town. I shivered. I don't generally, but I did this time an', as I say, I'm no coward.

Then I dusted again, as business seemed to be collapsed, an' I'm a fella that likes to keep busy. One thing I detest in the barberin' business is a barber who warms his back-side in slack time 'stead a puttin' it to good use for his own benefit.

Ten-fifteen. Sheriff John Woods walked in. John Woods is a big fella. They don't come with shoulders like John's got, too often—nor with his great strength.

"Mornin' John," I said. He'd put me in his jailhouse last night but that wasn't much. I'd been drunk, is all. Oh I'd raised hell with the boy that ran the Danton Tavern, you might say. All I said was that booze is bad for the kidneys. An' what d'ya think? They bounced me! Well, I raised hell an' in I went. Drunk an' disorderly. What d'ya think a that?

"Mornin' Rance," he said.

"Shave, John?" I asked. Let bygones be bygones, I thought. I won't act mad 'cause he run me in.

"Yeh," John said.

I lathered up. "Why so glum?" I asked him, brushin' his cheeks.

"I'm only one man," he answered. "Wish I was a hundred."

"Why so?" I asked. "What's up, John?"

He looked at me. "Don't you know?" he said.

Then I caught on. "Oh *them*." I said glancin' out a the window.

They was more a them now. They was more a them, an' they was collectin' in those awful little groups that men always collect in when somethin' horrible is in the air. I'll tell you it's an icy wind to have whistling around your home-town. I began to feel like I'd never felt before.

"Plannin' on doin' anything to stop 'em?" I asked John.

"If I was a hundred men, I could," he said. "I called the militia. But that takes time. They don't know how fast Judge Lynch gets elected."

I'll tell you I know John Woods—since we was boys I've known him. I'll tell you he's no fool. He knows when he's licked.

"Who're they huntin', John?" I asked working my fingers inta the lather on his cheeks, chin an' throat.

"Don't know," he said detached.

"It's on accounta the slicin'?" I asked.

"Yes, you know Rance," he told me.

I took up my newest razor—the one the drummer sold me a year or so previous. He said it was genuine surgical steel, the kind they use in scalpels. It was a good one. None better. I stropped it good.

"Bad 'bout Marthee," John said.

"Very," I said.

"Bad life she had."

"Don't I know," I said.

Outside, the crowd was growin' faster'n a litter a wildcats.

"Yes, you know," he told me.

Then I knew why John Woods was gettin' a shave in the middle a Jedge Lynch's election.

"Yes," I said, trying the slicin' edge on my thumb. "Yes, I know John," I told him. The blade wasn't quite right yet. I stropped it some more. I wouldn't use a dull slicin' edge.

"Marthee Regulus," John said. Then he paused like he was thinking, an' swallowed again. The skin was sure taut on his throat, all right. "She had nothin' but misery," John said. "She was plenty good, but she had nothin' but misery. First it was her Paw, drunk an' all. Then it was his dyin' sickness, drawn out an' all. Then it was her havin' ta marry that city fella an' her baby dyin' an all. Yes an' she coulda had happiness, too. It could a been different."

"Yet it could," I said.

"The city fella runnin' away an' leavin' her an' never showin' back —that was the worst a all," he said.

"Yes, that was the worst," I said.

I began on the left cheek. John was quiet now, an' there was only three sounds in the whole world, you might say. The scrapin' a my razor, the tickin' a the pendulum clock and the murmur a the boys outside electin' Jedge Lynch.

"She coulda had much better," John said as I snapped off the first row a lather onta the piece a newspaper on his chest. Suddenly he was lookin' me right in the eye, funny-like.

"She coulda married *you*, Rance," John said. "You always did love 'er."

"She could a," I said. "But she never did give me moren' a hello now an' again."

"What about last night?" he shot at me.

I lifted the razor off his cheek fast-like. *"How?"* I asked.

"You was seen leavin' her place last night 'bout seven, Rance," John said. "She was sliced at six, six-thirty."

"Indeed?" I said.

I began shavin' him again. One thing I don't like in the barberin' business is a barber that gets excitable.

"You've seen her lately more'n you think people know about, Rance. You'n I are friends. Don't deny it."

"I ain't denyin'," I said.

Just then it seemed's though Jedge Lynch won the election, cause the boys headed for the jailhouse with a growlin' quietness that made my scalp creep. Oh, I'm no coward, but I can't deny I was sorry for the poor devil they'd find in that jailhouse.

"You still got that darky-boy in the jailhouse—the one you pinched last night?" I asked John.

"Yes," he said through white lips. "My God, they'll string *him* for it sure."

"Sure they will," I said commencin' on John's mustache. "Jedge Lynch'll string the likeliest one, John."

Nobody outside now. The sound a poundin' commenced, though, from the direction a the jailhouse. They probably got a rammin'-pole from Healy's woodyard down near there.

The jailhouse was stout. It would take plenty a pounding to bust in the door. The place was fairly new—just built five years ago. 'Bout the time that city fella ran away an' left poor Marthee Regulus.

"Nothin' *I* can do," John said. "God knows that boy is innocent."

He looked at me. I was beginnin' on the left side a his throat as I usually do.

Suddenly John Woods said in a choking voice, "It isn't right! He's innocent!"

"Is he?" I said.

John looked at me. His lips curled and his teeth showed—just like animals do.

"I came here to do it," he said. "I tell you, Rance, you're under arrest."

"An' I tell you, John," I said, "you're under a surgical steel slicin' edge."

We looked at each other. He didn't stare me down.

"You sliced her 'cause she wouldn't have you," he hissed through his teeth. "You did it, Rance. I arrest you. You're guilty."

I looked at him. I felt my heart whangin' against my ribs like that ram was goin' against the jailhouse door.

Sudden-like, the rammin' stopped, an' I knew they was inside the jailhouse.

John said, "I got a gun in my fist."

Ever feel a slicin'-edge begin ta bite inta your throat? Well I'll tell ya, John Woods did then.

I skipped around behind him quick-like. "Drop it," I said to him in the mirror, holding the slicin'-edge closer.

He looked at me an' said. "For crysakes don't." But he knew I would. He dropped it.

"Don't stir, John," I said, pullin' the whitecloth off.

In a while the distant murmur from the direction a the jailhouse grew louder. They was comin' out.

First thing they was inta the shop, Pollard leadin'. They had the darky boy with 'em. The rest a Jedge Lynch's electors stuffed inta the shop an' bulged out inta the street.

When they seen the way I had John Woods, they stopped talkin' an' stood stock-still. You coulda heard a hair fall to the floor.

"You find it?" I asked them. They nodded soberly.

John watched them in the mirror.

"Right under the bull-pen in the jailhouse," Rucker said. "The boy here had a dozen holes pounded down inta the cement. Somethin' awful is in that cement."

"A soft thing," I said. They nodded.

"That's why I got arrested last night," I said. " 'Cause I'd seen what he'd done ta Marthee. I had a suspicion somethin' awful was buried under that bull-pen. Other times I'd been arrested, I'd noticed an awful smell in that jailhouse."

They looked at me. They was so shocked that the lynchin' fire gone out a them.

"He did it for her land," I said. "He's tried an' tried ta buy it, but she wouldn't sell. Same reason he killed her husband, the city fella, then spread the story the man'd run away. Marthee never did believe the man'd run away."

They looked at me. "So it's Marthee's husband's under the jailhouse floor?" they said.

"Been there for years," I said. "I suspicioned it recently an' was plannin' another way ta catch the killer. Then he did that awful thing last night."

They looked at the darky-boy.

"He'll have to do some fast talkin' now, I'll tell ya," Rucker said.

"You chisel thing an' hammah is in the jailhouse," the boy said to me. I could see he'd remember the chilly breath a Jedge Lynch on his neck for years.

"Thanks for diggin' in there, boy." I said. "You was smart to do what I told you."

Then they all looked at John Woods, lying there under my razor. I'll tell you he found out how smart we could be in Danton when the notion struck. He didn't move much under the slicin' edge—no sir.

"We'll save him for the chair, boys," I said, "What do you say?"

"Save him for the chair," they said. "Don't let him get away."

I'll tell you he wasn't getting away from me—*ever!*

JACKIE WON'T BE HOME

DANE GREGORY

It was the eighth time she had called that day. I didn't even have to ask who it was; I'd been expecting the call. I juggled the transmitter and said, "Hello . . . hello, Mrs. French," doing my best to put a there-there-everything-will-be-all-right note in my voice. It wasn't easy. The morning extra was spread across the desk in front of me.

She said, "Jackie isn't home yet, Phil."

She had a nice voice. Even now, with the thin glassy edge of panic on it, you knew it for the voice of a thoroughly nice person—the kind of woman that men like Dave French do not deserve but frequently seem to get.

I sketched a bizarre doodle on my desk-pad and said, "I—well,

I'm sorry to hear that, Mrs. French. But I'm sure everything will be all right. Do you want me to connect you with Dave's—with Mr. French's office?"

"I guess not, Phil. You can take my message in to him. Just say that Jackie won't be—" She stopped. "Just say that Jackie isn't home yet."

I waited for the *clac* of a broken connection. There wasn't any, and the silence ached like a hollow tooth, and I knew she wanted me to say something reassuring whether I meant it or not.

I tried. "I wouldn't worry too much about it, Mrs. French. Eight hours is quite a while for a kid to be away from home, but you know how kids are at that age. They go for a stroll, and they get interested in various things, and the hours just sort of skip by without their noticing it. Or maybe they know they're a little late and are afraid to come home and face the music. I wouldn't worry too much. Jackie's all right."

Her voice was very faint. "Jackie has a healthy appetite. Phil—he wouldn't have missed his lunch for anything. And his—his dog came home exactly six hours ago. But thanks, anyhow. . . . I'm glad Dave has a man for a—a private secretary. Men are more comforting, somehow, at a time like this."

My ears went hot and I said, "Well—uh—thank you." Being a nice person, she wouldn't know why Dave preferred masculine secretaries. A blonde with beautiful legs would probably have lured more clients, but blondes with beautiful legs frequently hear too much and talk too much about what they hear. Dave wouldn't have liked that. As it was, he managed to stay only a jump or so ahead of disbarment proceedings.

I said again, "Well, thanks, Mrs. French," and she said, "Thank *you*, Phil," and we hung up.

I didn't go in to see Dave for a minute or two. I simply sat there trying to keep my eyes off the newspaper and thinking about the tight, restrained panic in Eileen French's voice. And about small Jackie French, eight years old, who had once given me three meat-agates as a gesture of esteem. I even remembered that the marbles were still in one pocket of my light gray suit.

I wasn't any sentimentalist; two years of Dave French's society had done the same thing to me that twenty minutes of boiling does to an egg. I rarely if ever got wet-eyed and maudlin about kids in the aggregate, many of whom seemed to me almost as unpleasant as adults. But I had liked Jackie French. He had tight yellow curls that made a neat frame for his small, serious brow, and his eyes were dark and candid like his mother's, and he'd never been a kid of whom people said, "Now if that child were *mine*, I'd . . ."

Thinking about him now, I had to look down at the newspaper again. And there was the headline that had been slapping me in the eyes at three-minute intervals throughout the day: MACHINE-GUNNERS SLAY WOMAN, CHILD!

And underneath it, a story that began like this:

> Local crime claimed a frightful toll this morning when machine-gun fire from a speeding sedan cut down a woman and a small boy near the intersection of Eighth and Walnut. The woman has been identified as (Miss) Rose Voight, 27, a notorious underworld character; but the body of the child—described by police as extremely fair, well-dressed, and seven or eight years of age—is still at the city morgue awaiting identification.
>
> According to an eye-witness who narrowly escaped death himself, the boy was playing near the corner and was inadvertently caught in the withering hail of bullets aimed at Miss Voight. The crime occurred at about 8:30 A.M. No arrests have been made. . . .

It was a big story and naturally there was more of it. But I couldn't take any more. I was thinking about Jackie, and how he always left the house for a stroll in the early morning; and I was remembering for the hundredth time that there were only about eight blocks between the French home and the intersection of Eighth and Walnut. Not much of a walk for a kid with sturdy legs. . . . My eyes skipped to the secondary banner-line of the day, which was all about Nazi planes shoveling carloads of death onto London. It occurred to me that there ought to be one country in the world where kids could go out with their dogs and play in the sunlight.

I got up and moved to the door of Dave's private office. It was a smug mahogany door with the words D. J. FRENCH, ATT'Y on it in raised white letters, and it opened into an immense sound-proofed room where chromium, leather and broadloom meshed in a surprisingly beautiful pattern. Dave French sat behind acres of desk and looked at nothing at all. His white, square hands were flat on the desk top. His white, square face was as expressionless as a cube of sugar. But there were shadows in his eyes and under them, and at that moment I found myself capable of a deep pity for him. He looked like an old and tired caliph.

"Well, Phil?"

I said, "There've been a couple of telephone calls in the past few minutes."

"And?"

I decided to give it to him the hard way; at that, it's sometimes the kindest way to dispense bad news. "One was from McLemore of the police, and he pulled the usual line about not wanting to waste the taxpayers' money. He says they can't afford to organize a city-wide search for Jackie when there's a chance that—well, Dave, he thinks you or Mrs. French ought to go down and see if you can identify the child at the—Of course, there's not one chance in thousands that it *is* Jackie."

Dave French said, "Not yet, Phil."

"But McLemore thinks—"

"To hell with what McLemore thinks." He said it without an exclamation point; his voice was as flat and expressionless as his face. "I won't go. I won't let Eileen go. Not yet, Phil. Why is it that some people are always so eager to know the worst?"

"But suppose it isn't the worst? It would take a load off—"

He slapped the desk-top and his eyes went dark and hot. "We'll wait a while, I said. The other call?"

"It was from your wife. She asked me to tell you that—"

Dave French said flatly, "That Jackie isn't home yet."

I nodded.

Dave French reached slowly across the desk. He opened the silver humidor and took out a black cigar that looked like a toy blimp. His hands were quite steady as he put it between his lips and held the desk-set lighter to it. He said, "Wait a minute, Phil. Don't go. You're a smart boy—the smartest secretary I ever had, I guess. Tell me something, Phil. Do you believe in—well, fundamental ironies?"

I said, "In *what?*"

"The hang-Haaman-thereon formula. The hoist-with-your-own-petard formula. The biter bit—that kind of thing. . . . I guess I still haven't made myself clear." He pointed the cigar at me. "In other words, Phil, do you believe that there is a certain inexorable law of recompense—or of retribution, rather—that trips men into the pits they dig for others?"

I wasn't quite so sorry for him now. Not many men would have sat around discussing abstractions at a time like that. I said, "I don't know much about it, Dave, but if it's a law that applies to eight-year-old kids I think it ought to be repealed. Did you want anything else?"

Something like a smile skimmed across his lips. "Always the materialist, aren't you, Phil? Well, well—never mind. You called Sam Crowder and his boys according to my instructions?"

I said, "Yes."

"You told them I wanted to see them in regard to a certain important business matter?"

I nodded, incapable of any pity whatever for him now. "They're coming right over."

"I thought they would." This time the smile caught his lips and hung on, and I had never wanted to hit a man so badly in my life. "Yes, Phil, I rather thought they would. They need me, you know."

"As much as you need them," I reminded him.

"Quite so," said Dave French, and blew a great billowing cloud of smoke. "Dissimulation is not one of your many talents, Phil, and I take it that you disapprove of my clients. Well, this time I shall not ask you to share the same roof with them. When they arrive, simply escort them into my office and then absent yourself for a while. Go for a walk. Buy yourself a drink or an ice cream cone. Go to some corner lot and watch the kids playing base—" He stopped. "Well, anyhow, go somewhere. The fact is, we'll want to be alone."

"I know just how you feel," I said, and let the smug mahogany door slap shut behind me.

They arrived about ten minutes later. There was Samuel Crowder, the Mr. Big of the outfit, who came in rolling his stomach and shaking his pink flews and looking somewhat like a cartload of sofa cushions. You knew that there'd have been egg on his vest if he had worn one. Behind him was Al Genna, thin and taut as a 'cello string, with polished yellow cheekbones and a corvine nose that bisected lips no thicker than a dime. And there was young Johnnie Bedell, whose clothes always seemed to melt in your mouth and whose round collegiate face looked as harmless as parchesi until he happened to furl his eyelashes. Something about his eyes reminded me of the meat-agates Jackie French had given me.

They all said, "Hello, Phil," and I said "Hello" and ushered them into Dave's office. Then I put on my hat and went outside feeling as if I'd dipped my hands in fresh angleworms clear up to the elbows.

The air was good. An April squall sweet with the foretaste of rain went prowling down State Street, curiously picking up hats and skirts and old candy wrappers as it prowled. I liked the feel of it against my face. But this was the month of spring vacation, and there were also lots of kids on the street, and every kid I saw made me think of Jackie.

I turned east and headed for the building that housed the city morgue.

I didn't want to go. Nobody, not even McLemore, had suggested that I go. But I was pretty tired of the situation as it stood—almost as tired as I was of Dave French's stoical resignation to it. The whole thing was stretching my nerves from here to there, and I could only guess what it was doing to Eileen French.

I think I deserved ten for effort. I did my best. But my feet started putting on weight before I'd covered half a block, and they were all but immovable by the time I'd reached the morgue. I couldn't go in; and I mean just that. There are certain psychological stymies as solid as a wall.

I turned around and plodded west to State Street, understanding Dave French a little better than I had. I still didn't like him; but when a man faces something unendurable he can hardly be blamed for granting himself minute-to-minute reprieves. I smoked a couple of sour cigarettes and went back to the office.

The phone on my desk was sending sharp, anxious trills through the emptiness. I picked it up and said, "Hello! Hello, Mrs. French!" and then my fingers went pudgy and damp on the transmitter.

She'd had more courage than Dave French and I. Or less endurance, maybe. She was calling from home, but she'd been to the morgue—and she told me about it in a voice I'd never heard before.

I kept saying, "Yes. Yes. I'll let him know right away, Mrs. French. Right away." My fingers shook the handset into its cradle and I went in to see Dave French.

He said, "Hello, Phil." I looked around the office and couldn't think of anything to say but, "Hello." Under the circumstances, it was probably the weirdest thing I'd ever said.

"I wasn't expecting you back quite so early. I'm glad you're here, though."

The square block of face was as stolid as ever, but his voice was slightly more amiable now. He sat as usual behind vast reaches of desk, a fountain-pen poised in his blunt-tipped fingers. But the sheet of paper in front of him was blank.

I said, "Dave, you—" The stench of cordite choked the words

back into my throat, and I could only stand there looking around me.

The room was no longer beautiful. Sam Crowder's body made a grotesque round hummock in the middle of the rug; there was a bullet-hole just below his left eye and he had died as untidily as he had lived. Not far from Crowder lay young Johnnie Bedell, his soft hands joined across a stain in the handkerchief pocket of his coat. Al Genna sat dejectedly in an easy chair near Dave's desk. His slack face leaned toward spread knees so that he seemed to be staring at the blue automatic that had slipped from his fingers; but there was no trace of interest in his eyes.

Dave French said quietly, "Don't stand there and gape, Phil. It ought to be obvious enough that they're dead. I killed them."

"But, Dave—"

"Can't you figure it out? Rose Voight was going to be the star witness in the district attorney's case against Crowder on vice charges. I knew who was to blame for the—the killings. They knew I knew. That was why they came over, Phil—they thought I was going to rig an alibi for them. They hadn't heard about . . . Jackie."

I said, "Dave. Listen, Dave . . ."

"They knew they could count on me because I'd saved them before. But for me, Sam Crowder would have got life under the Baumes law three years ago. But for me, Genna and Bedell would long since have been gassed like the mad dogs they were. I was responsible for their existence, Phil, and that makes me as much a murderer as—"

"Dave!" I said huskily. "Let me talk, damn it! Your wife called a minute ago. . . . She—she'd been down there."

He sat quite still, his eyes steady on mine. "Jackie?"

"No. The—body had been identified just a little while before she got there. I—she told me the boy's name, but it's slipped my mind now. His mother had left him in the care of a governess, and the governess had kept a date with her boy-friend, and—well, the kid wandered. And—"

"What about Jackie?"

"I'm telling you, man! When your wife got home, she found him waiting there for her. He'd been playing"—I swallowed—"been playing cops and robbers with some other kids, and they locked him up in an old shed-building. Then they heard the shots on Walnut Street and went rushing over the way kids do. What with all the excitement, they forgot about Jackie—and it wasn't until late this afternoon that one of them remembered him."

There was silence like a hole in time. Then Dave French said, "Thanks, Phil," as if I'd had something to do with it. He gestured vaguely. "I—thanks. . . . But this was an obligation, you know. It would have had to be done anyway. A kid is a kid, no matter whose he is. And I was already pretty tired of—things."

I said, "It'll be all right, Dave. No court in the world would convict you of—"

He didn't seem to hear. "I'm not leaving much of a legacy for Jackie, Phil. I know that. But some day you might tell him that I . . . left him a city that was a little safer for him and . . . for others like him. I guess it's a sort of legacy, at that. Tell him for me, will you, Phil?"

I said, "Why, sure, Dave. Sure," and I'm going to keep my promise. I owe that much to Dave French. I'd never liked him as much as I did that moment—as his body slumped sideways and I saw what Genna's bullets had done to him. . . .

Jeff Peters as a Personal Magnet

O. Henry

Jeff Peters has been engaged in as many schemes for making money as there are recipes for cooking rice in Charleston, S.C.

Best of all I like to hear him tell of his earlier days when he sold liniments and cough cures on street corners, living hand to mouth, heart to heart with the people, throwing heads or tails with fortune for his last coin.

"I struck Fisher Hill, Arkansaw," said he, "in buckskin suit, moccasins, long hair and a thirty-carat diamond ring that I got from an actor in Texarkana. I don't know what he ever did with the pocket knife I swapped him for it.

"I was Dr. Waugh-hoo, the celebrated Indian medicine man. I carried only one best bet just then, and that was Resurrection Bitters. It was made of life-giving plants and herbs accidentally discovered by Ta-qua-la, the beautiful wife of the chief of the Choctaw Nation, while gathering truck to garnish a platter of boiled dog for the annual corn dance.

"Business hadn't been good at the last town, so I only had five dollars. I went to the Fisher Hill druggist and he credited me for a half-gross of eight ounce bottles and corks. I had the labels and ingredients in my valise, left over from the last town. Life began to look rosy again after I got in my hotel room with the water running from the tap, and the Resurrection Bitters lining up on the table by the dozen.

"Fake? No, sir. There was two dollars' worth of fluid extract of cinchona and a dime's worth of aniline in that half-gross of bitters. I've gone through towns years afterwards and had folks ask for 'em again.

"I hired a wagon that night and commenced selling the bitters on Main Street. Fisher Hill was a low, malarial town; and a compound hypothetical pneumo-cardiac anti-scorbutic tonic was just what I diagnosed the crowd as needing. The bitters started off like sweetbreads-on-toast at a vegetarian dinner. I had sold two dozen at fifty cents apiece when I felt somebody pull my coat tail. I knew what that meant; so I climbed down and sneaked a five-dollar bill into the hand of a man with a German silver star on his lapel.

" 'Constable,' says I, 'it's a fine night.'

" 'Have you got a city license,' he asked, 'to sell this illegitimate essence of spooju that you flatter by the name of medicine?'

" 'I have not,' says I. 'I didn't know you had a city. If I can find it tomorrow I'll take one out if it's necessary.'

" 'I'll have to close you up till you do,' says the constable.

"I quit selling and went back to the hotel. I was talking to the landlord about it.

" 'Oh, you won't stand no show in Fisher Hill,' says he. 'Dr. Hoskins, the only doctor here, is a brother-in-law of the Mayor, and they won't allow no fake doctors to practice in town.'

" 'I don't practice medicine,' says I, 'I've got a State peddler's license, and I take out a city one wherever they demand it.'

"I went to the Mayor's office the next morning and they told me he hadn't showed up yet. They didn't know when he'd be down. So Doc Waugh-hoo hunches down again in a hotel chair and lights a jimpson-weed regalia, and waits.

"By and by a young man in a blue necktie slips into the chair next to me and asks the time.

"'Half-past ten' says I, 'and you are Andy Tucker. I've seen you work. Wasn't it you that put up the Great Cupid Combination package on the Southern States? Let's see, it was a Chilian diamond engagement ring, a wedding ring, a potato masher, a bottle of soothing syrup and Dorothy Vernon—all for fifty cents.'

"Andy was pleased to hear that I remembered him. He was a good street man; and he was more than that—he respected his profession, and he was satisfied with 300 per cent profit. He had plenty of offers to go into the illegitimate drug and garden seed business; but he was never to be tempted off of the straight path.

"I wanted a partner, so Andy and me agreed to go out together. I told him about the situation on Fisher Hill and how finances was low on account of the local mixture of politics and jalap. Andy had just got in on the train that morning. He was pretty low himself, and was going to canvass the town for a few dollars to build a new battleship by popular subscription at Eureka Springs. So we went out and sat on the porch and talked it over.

"The next morning at eleven o'clock when I was sitting there alone, an Uncle Tom shuffles into the hotel and asks for the doctor to come and see Judge Banks, who, it seems, was the mayor and a mighty sick man.

" 'I'm no doctor,' says I. 'Why don't you go and get the doctor?'

" 'Boss,' says he, 'Doc Hoskin am done gone twenty miles in the country to see some sick persons. He's de only doctor in de town, and Massa Banks am powerful bad off. He sent me to ax you to please, suh, come.'

" 'As man to man,' says I, 'I'll go and look him over.' So I put a bottle of Resurrection Bitters in my pocket and goes up on the hill to the mayor's mansion, the finest house in town, with a mansard roof and two cast-iron dogs on the lawn.

"This Mayor Banks was in bed all but his whiskers and feet. He was making internal noises that would have had everybody in San Francisco hiking for the parks. A young man was standing by the bed holding a cup of water.

" 'Doc,' says the Mayor. 'I'm awful sick. I'm about to die. Can't you do nothing for me?'

" 'Mr. Mayor,' says I, 'I'm not a regular preordained disciple of S. Q. Lapius, I never took a course in a medical college,' says I. 'I've just come as a fellow man to see if I could be of any assistance.'

" 'I'm deeply obliged,' says he. 'Doc Waugh-hoo, this is my nephew, Mr. Biddle. He has tried to alleviate my distress, but without success. Oh, Lordy! Ow-ow-ow!!' he sings out.

"I nods at Mr. Biddle and sets down by the bed and feels the mayor's pulse. 'Let me see your liver—your tongue, I mean,' says I. Then I turns up the lids of his eyes and looks close at the pupils of 'em.

" 'How long have you been sick?' I asked.

" 'I was taken down—ow-ouch—last night,' says the Mayor. 'Gimme something for it, Doc, won't you?'

" 'Mr. Fiddle,' says I, 'raise the window shade a bit, will you?'

" 'Biddle,' says the young man. 'Do you feel like you could eat some ham and eggs, Uncle James?'

" 'Mr. Mayor,' says I, after laying my ear to his right shoulder blade and listening, 'you've got a bad attack of super-inflammation of the right clavicle of the harpsichord!'

" 'Good Lord!' says he, with a groan. 'Can't you rub something on it, or set it or anything?'

"I picks up my hat and starts for the door.

" 'You ain't going, Doc?' says the Mayor with a howl. 'You ain't going away and leave me to die with this—superfluity of the clapboards, are you?'

" 'Common humanity, Dr. Whoa-ha,' says Mr. Biddle, 'ought to prevent your deserting a fellow-human in distress.'

" 'Dr. Waugh-hoo, when you get through plowing,' says I. And then I walks back to the bed and throws back my long hair.

" 'Mr. Mayor,' says I, 'there is only one hope for you. Drugs will do you no good. But there is another power higher yet, although drugs are high enough,' says I.

" 'And what is that?' says he.

" 'Scientific demonstrations,' says I. 'The triumph of mind over sarsaparilla. The belief that there is no pain and sickness except what is produced when we ain't feeling well. Declare yourself in arrears. Demonstrate.'

" 'What is this paraphernalia you speak of, Doc?' says the Mayor. 'You ain't a Socialist, are you?'

" 'I am speaking,' says I, 'of the great doctrine of psychic financiering—of the enlightened school of long-distance, subconscientious treatment of fallacies and meningitis—of that wonderful in-door sport known as personal magnetism.'

" 'Can you work it, Doc?' asks the Mayor.

" 'I'm one of the Sole Sanhedrims and Ostensible Hooplas of the Inner Pulpit,' says I. 'The lame talk and the blind rubber whenever I make a pass at 'em. I am a medium, a coloratura hypnotist and a spirituous control. It was only through me at the recent seances at Ann Arbor that the last president of the Vinegar Bitters Company could revisit the earth to communicate with his sister Jane. You see me peddling medicine on the streets,' says I, 'to the poor. I don't practice personal magnetism on them. I do not drag it in the dust,' says I, 'because they haven't got the dust.'

" 'Will you treat my case?' asks the Mayor.

" 'Listen,' says I. 'I've had a good deal of trouble with medical societies everywhere I've been. I don't practice medicine. But, to save your life, I'll give you the psychic treatment if you'll agree as mayor not to push the license question.'

" 'Of course I will,' says he. 'And now get to work, Doc, for them pains are coming on again.'

" 'My fee will be $250.00, cure guaranteed in two treatments says I.

" 'All right,' says the Mayor. 'I'll pay it. I guess my life's worth that much.'

"I sat down by the bed and looked him straight in the eye.

" 'Now,' says I, 'get your mind off the disease. You ain't sick. You haven't got a heart or a clavicle or a funny bone or brains or anything. You haven't got any pain. Declare error. Now you feel the pain that you didn't have leaving, don't you?'

" 'I do feel some little better, Doc,' says the Mayor, 'darned if I don't. Now state a few lines about my not having this swelling in my left side, and I think I could be propped up and have some sausage and buckwheat cakes.'

"I made a few passes with my hands.

" 'Now,' says I, 'the inflammation's gone. The right lobe of the perihelion has subsided. You're getting sleepy. You can't hold your eyes open any longer. For the present the disease is checked. Now, you are asleep.'

"The Mayor shut his eyes slowly and began to snore.

" 'You observe, Mr. Tiddle,' says I, 'the wonder of modern science.'

" 'Biddle,' says he. 'When will you give uncle the rest of the treatment, Dr. Pooh-pooh?'

" 'Waugh-hoo,' says I. 'I'll come back at eleven to-morrow. When he wakes up give him eight drops of turpentine and three pounds of steak. Good morning.'

"The next morning I went back on time. 'Well, Mr. Riddle,' says I, when he opened the bedroom door, 'and how is uncle this morning?'

" 'He seems much better,' says the young man.

"The Mayor's color and pulse was fine. I gave him another treatment, and he said the last of the pain left him.

" 'Now,' says I, 'you'd better stay in bed for a day or two, and you'll be all right. It's a good thing I happened to be in Fisher Hill, Mr. Mayor,' says I, 'for all the remedies in the cornucopia that the regular schools of medicine use couldn't have saved you. And now that error has flew and pain proved a perjurer, let's allude to a cheerfuller subject—say the fee of $250. No checks, please, I hate to write my name on the back of a check almost as bad as I do on the front.'

" 'I've got the cash here,' says the Mayor, pulling a pocket book from under his pillow.

"He counts out five fifty-dollar notes and holds 'em in his hand.

" 'Bring the receipt,' he says to Biddle.

"I signed the receipt and the Mayor handed me the money. I put it in my inside pocket careful.

" 'Now do your duty, officer,' says the Mayor, grinning much unlike a sick man.

"Mr. Biddle lays his hand on my arm.

" 'You're under arrest, Dr. Waugh-hoo, alias Peters,' says he, 'for practising medicine without authority under the State law.'

" 'Who are you?' I asks.

" 'I'll tell you who he is,' says the Mayor, sitting up in bed. 'He's a detective employed by the State Medical Society. He's been following you over five counties. He came to me yesterday and we fixed up this scheme to catch you. I guess you won't do any more doctoring around these parts, Mr. Fakir. What was it you said I had, Doc?' the Mayor laughs, 'compound—well it wasn't softening of the brain, I guess, anyway.'

" 'A detective,' says I.

" 'Correct,' says Biddle. 'I'll have to turn you over to the sheriff.'

" 'Let's see you do it,' says I, and I grabs Biddle by the throat and half throws him out the window, but he pulls a gun and sticks it under my chin, and I stand still. Then he puts handcuffs on me, and takes the money out of my pocket.

" 'I witness,' says he, 'that they're the same bills that you and I marked, Judge Banks. I'll turn them over to the sheriff when we get to his office, and he'll send you a receipt. They'll have to be used as evidence in the case.'

" 'All right, Mr. Biddle,' says the Mayor. 'And now, Doc Waugh-hoo,' he goes on, 'why don't you demonstrate? Can't you pull the cork out of your magnetism with your teeth and hocus-pocus them handcuffs off?'

" 'Come on, officer,' says I, dignified. 'I may as well make the best of it.' And then I turns to old Banks and rattles my chains.

" 'Mr. Mayor,' says I, 'the time will come soon when you'll believe that personal magnetism is a success. And you'll be sure that it succeeded in this case, too.'

"And I guess it did.

"When we got nearly to the gate, I says: 'We might meet somebody now, Andy. I reckon you better take 'em off, and———' Hey? Why, of course it was Andy Tucker. That was his scheme; and that's how we got the capital to go into business together."

THE JOB

JOE R. LANSDALE

Bower pulled the sun visor down and looked in the mirror there and said, "You know, hadn't been for the travel, I'd have done all right. I could even shake my ass like him. I tell you, it drove the women wild. You should have seen em."

"Don't shake it for me," Kelly said. "I don't want to see it. Things I got to do are tough enough without having to see that."

Bower pushed the visor back. The light turned green. Kelly put the gas to the car and they went up and over a hill and turned right on Melroy.

"Guess maybe you do look like him," Kelly said. "During his fatter days, when he was on the drugs and the peanut butter."

"Yeah, but these pocks on my cheeks messes it up some. When I was on stage I had makeup on em. I looked okay then."

They stopped at a stop sign and Kelly got out a cigarette and pushed in the lighter.

"A nigger nearly tail-ended me here once," Kelly said. "Just come barreling down on me." He took the lighter and lit his smoke. "Scared the piss out of me. I got him out of his car and popped him some. I bet he was one careful nigger from then on." He pulled away from the stop sign and cruised.

"You done one like this before? I know you've done it, but like this?"

"Not just like this. But I done some things might surprise you. You getting nervous on me?"

"I'm all right. You know, thing made me quit the Elvis imitating was travel, cause one night on the road I was staying in this cheap motel, and it wasn't heated too good. I'd had those kinds of rooms before, and I always carried couple of space heaters in the trunk of the car with the rest of my junk, you know. I got them plugged in, and I was still cold, so I pulled the mattress on the floor by the heaters. I woke up and was on fire. I had been so worn out I'd gone to sleep in my Elvis outfit. That was the end of my best white jumpsuit, you know, like he wore with the gold glitter and all. I must have been funny on fire like that, hopping around the room beating it out. When I got that suit off I was burned like the way you get when you been out in the sun too long."

"You gonna be able to do this?"

"Did I say I couldn't?"

"You're nervous. I can tell way you talk."

"A little. I always get nervous before I go on stage too, but I always come through. Crowd came to see Elvis, by god, they got Elvis. I used to sign autographs with his name. People wanted it like that. They wanted to pretend, see."

"Women mostly?"

"Uh huh."

"What were they, say, fifty-five?"

"They were all ages. Some of them were pretty young."

"Ever fuck any of am?"

"Sure, I got plenty. Sing a little Love Me Tender to them in the bedroom and they'd do whatever I wanted."

"Was it the old ones you was fucking?"

"I didn't fuck no real old ones, no. Whose idea is it to do things this way, anyhow?"

"Boss, of course. You think he lets me plan this stuff? He don't want them chinks muscling in on the shrimping and all."

"I don't know, we fought for these guys. It seems a little funny."

"Reason we lost the war over there is not being able to tell one chink from another and all of them being the way they are. I think we should have nuked the whole goddamned place. Went over there when it cooled down and stopped glowing, put in a fucking Disneyland or something."

They were moving out of the city now, picking up speed.

"I don't see why we don't just whack this guy outright and not do it this way," Bower said. "This seems kind of funny."

"No one's asking you. You come on a job, you do it. Boss wants some chink to suffer, so he's gonna suffer. Not like he didn't get some warnings or nothing. Boss wants him to take it hard."

"Maybe this isn't a smart thing on account of it may not bother chinks like it'd bother us. They're different about stuff like this, all the things they've seen."

"It'll bother him," Kelly said. "And if it don't, that ain't our problem. We got a job to do and we're gonna do it. Whatever comes after comes after. Boss wants us to do different next time, we do different. Whatever he wants we do it. He's the one paying."

They were out of the city now and to the left of the highway they could see the glint of the sea through a line of scrubby trees.

"How're we gonna know?" Bower said. "One chink looks like another."

"I got a photograph. This one's got a burn scar on the face. Everything's timed. Boss has been planning this. He had some of the guys watch and take notes. It's all set up."

"Why us?"

"Me because I've done some things before. You because he wants to see what you're made of. I'm kind of here as your nurse maid."

"I don't need anybody to see that I do what I'm supposed to do."

They drove past a lot of boats pulled up to a dock. They drove into a small town called Wilborn. They turned a corner at Catlow Street.

"It's down here a ways," Kelly said. "You got your knife? You left your knife and brought your comb, I'm gonna whack you."

Bower got the knife out of his pocket. "Thing's got a lot of blades, some utility stuff. Even a comb."

"Christ, you're gonna do it with a Boy Scout knife?"

"Utility knife. The blade I want is plenty sharp, you'll see. Why couldn't we use a gun? That wouldn't be as messy. A lot easier."

"Boss wants it messy. He wants the chink to think about it some. He wants them to pack their stuff on their boats and sail back to chink land. Either that, or they can pay their percentages like everyone else. He lets the chinks get away with things, everyone'll want to get away with things."

They pulled over to the curb. Down the street was a school. Kelly looked at his watch.

"Maybe if it was a nigger," Bower said.

"Chink, nigger, what's the difference?"

They could hear a bell ringing. After five minutes they saw kids going out to the curb to get on the buses parked there. A few kids came down the sidewalk toward them. One of them was a Vietnamese girl about eight years old. The left side of her face was scarred.

"Won't they remember me?" Bower said.

"Kids? Naw. Nobody knows you around here. Get rid of that Elvis look and you'll be okay."

"It don't seem right. In front of these kids and all. I think we ought to whack her father."

"No one's paying you to think, Elvis. Do what you're supposed to do. I have to do it and you'll wish you had."

Bower opened the utility knife and got out of the car. He held the knife by his leg and walked around front, leaned on the hood just as the Vietnamese girl came up. He said, "Hey, kid, come here a minute." His voice got thick. "Elvis wants to show you something."

KERRIGAN

EDWIN BAIRD

The beefy man sprawled at the lunchroom counter, munching a hamburger and drinking coffee. He looked over the thick brim of his cup at the girl.

The girl sat on a box behind the counter. It was a high wooden box, used by her in lieu of a chair, and, sitting on it, she could watch the highway in both directions.

"You been waitin' five years for this guy," said the man. "How much longer you gonna wait?"

"Five more years, if necessary. But I think," she said, looking intently at the highway, "it won't be more than five minutes now."

He turned and followed the direction of her gaze. At a bend in the road, a man had appeared, hurrying this way, yet moving furtively, like a man pursued.

The beefy man turned back to the girl. "What was this guy sent up for?" he asked.

"Nothing!" she said emphatically. "He was framed and railroaded. He was absolutely innocent. And even if he weren't," she passionately declared, "I'd still wait for him."

The beefy man took a bite of hamburger and looked at her and shook his head. "You're sure nuts about this—what's his name?"

"Kerrigan," she murmured, her brown eyes on the approaching man. She seemed to breathe the name to herself. "Kerrigan," she softly whispered.

"Kerrigan, eh?" said the beefy man, his mouth full of hamburger. "Oh, yeah. I remember now—Kerrigan Mulcahy. He got a ten-year stretch, as I recall, and I guess he *was* railroaded at that."

The girl's level brown eyes, still on the road, suddenly dilated. The man in the road had quickened his steps and was running toward the lunchroom, looking back over his shoulder.

Now he was at the lunchroom door. He stood in the doorway, panting heavily. He was a gaunt man in prison denim. He looked frantically about and saw the girl on the box.

"Mattie!" he gasped, and started toward her.

But in that instant a fusillade of shots rang from the road and the man pitched forward, dead.

The beefy man, mouth bulging with food, had swung round on his stool just as the man in prison clothes dropped dead across the threshold.

He gaped froggishly.

A state police car had stopped outside. A squad of officers, guns drawn, tumbled from the car and came pounding toward the lunchroom. Two of them loomed in the doorway. One prodded the convict's lifeless body.

"Got this one all right," he muttered. He looked at the beefy man, then spoke to the girl: "Prison break, Miss. Ten inmates escaped. We'll have to search this place."

The girl, still seated on the wooden box, was watching them steadily. Hatred blazed in her narrowed brown eyes.

"You murderers!" she said between bared teeth. "Killing a defenseless man like that! You—"

"Sorry, Miss." The officer turned to the beefy man. "You see anybody 'round here?"

"Naw." The beefy man aimed a stubby finger at the slain convict. "But there's the guy she was lookin' for. I heard him call her name. And she's been waitin' five years for him!" He fished a coin from his leather jacket and dropped it on the counter. He looked at the girl. "Tough break, Mattie." Then he stood up. "Well, I'll be on my way."

"Not so fast," said the officer. "Stay right where you are till I tell you to go." He spoke to his companion: "Keep an eye on this fellow, Bill. Joe, you and Jim look around outside while I search this joint."

He stepped over the body on the threshold and strode inside.

The girl, still sitting on the box, crossed her knees and watched him scornfully.

He came behind the counter, poked beneath it, looked in a linen hamper, then went to the kitchen. She heard him moving about, poking in the pantry and the china closet; and then he went outdoors and around the side of the house.

He appeared again at the front door and stooped over the dead man lying there.

"All right, Bill; lend me a hand."

He did not speak to the girl, nor did he look at her.

She sat on the box, watching him stonily. She saw him and his brother officer lift the body of the man they had killed, and carry it outside and dumped it into the back of their car. The other two officers joined them, and they all climbed in and the car backed and turned and went whining off down the highway.

The beefy man still sat at the counter. He was picking his teeth with a broken match and watching the girl.

"Tough luck, Mattie," he said. "Waiting five years for a guy, only to see him rubbed out like that! Right before your eyes. Then carted off like a dead dog! . . . But my proposition still stands, Mattie. Any time you wanta hook up with me . . ."

His voice wandered to a stop. She was looking at him in cold silence, and her expression seemed to say:

"Get out of here, you mugg!"

"Well, I'll be on my way," he said, and got heavily to his feet. "So long, Mattie."

She saw him go outside and climb up behind the wheel of his truck. She watched the truck, as she had watched the police car, until it vanished down the highway.

Then, for the first time, she stood up. She went to the front door, looked sharply up and down the road, then closed the door and locked it. She went to the back door, looked around outside, and closed and locked that, too.

And then she came back to the high wooden box she had been sitting on.

With a quick movement, she tipped it over.

And there on the floor, looking up at her, was a rugged young man in prison denim.

"I thought they'd never go," said the girl. "It seemed another five years, Kerrigan."

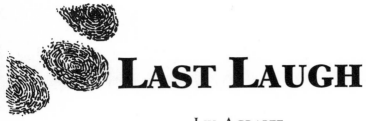

LAST LAUGH

LIX AGRABEE

It's the damnedest joke. I'm going to die laughing. . . .

Ella is little and soft and plump, and her mouth was crushed velvet under mine. I was crazy about her, and I couldn't believe my luck when she actually consented to keep house for me. Funny thing—even as I watch her leaning there against the table, blowing perfumed cigarette smoke into my perspiring face, I can't say I'm really sorry for any of it. It was worth it while it lasted. After a lifetime of Emily, Ella was worth it. It's like trying to live with a gaunt, spitting old alley cat, then having a silky, purring Persian to pet.

You don't see women like Ella in hayseed towns like this one very often. Usually they marry young, enchanted by a haystack, a full moon and some young farmer. Or they go off to the big city. Or run off with a traveling salesman who eventually runs out on them.

I could hardly sleep nights for thinking about her after she came to spend a vacation at old lady Harkinson's boarding house, though I did wonder why in the world she had picked Orrinville. It's not even one of those picturesque post-card villages one reads about in travel books and such.

I know now why she came here, but I didn't then.

I don't think anyone in town was surprised when they heard that Emily had picked up and walked to Blorr Junction, caught the train and left me, as she'd always threatened to do. I think, too, that they were secretly pleased when they found out she'd gone. Don't get me wrong. They all liked me, but there wasn't a soul who could deny the hatred they had for Emily. She caused more trouble with her tongue than you could believe possible, created eternal friction with her spiteful gossip and general vindictiveness, and broke up at least two homes that I know of. So that I think there was a sigh of relief, and perhaps a prayer of thanksgiving for my sake.

"Don't know how you ever stood her," Tom McCracken said to me on Main Street. "Beggin' your pardon, but she were a mean, cantankerous person, weren't she?"

"Oh, well, it takes all kinds, you know Tom," I said feebly. It didn't seem right to say anything against her.

"Hear tell that Widder Stone at the boarding house has her eye on you." He grinned, smirking just a trifle to show his man-of-the-world status and his complete understanding.

"Well, I can't very well think of getting married again, can I? I'm not free."

"Who said anything about getting married?" Tom cackled, spewing a stream of tobacco juice to the side of the boardwalk. "Maybe she'd like to come keep house for you." He winked with pleasure. "Gus Larsen gets away with it, even if the Ladies Aid don't like it. After all, they can't prove nothin', can they? Man's got a right to keep a housekeeper, ain't he?"

So after a while Ella Stone came to keep house. Everybody in town took a sort of sneaking joy out of it, remembering nosy Emily and her spiced tongue and the years of nagging misery she'd put me through.

I'm not kicking about the way things turned out. As I say, it was worth it while it lasted. Even at the beginning I couldn't understand why Ella with the gleaming hair—though after a while I noticed it was dark at the roots—and the dimpled satin hands, saw anything in me, taciturn, hardbitten Lute Brown. She wasn't extravagant. Even when she discovered the box where years of savings had accumulated, she didn't beg for pretty things and such stuff. Of course, there was method in her madness. But I never guessed, never dreamed.

I thought my breakfast coffee tasted a mite bitter, but Ella curled up on my knee, nuzzling my neck like a playful kitten, running her hands through my sparse gray hair and—well, I'd have swallowed hemlock without noticing anything much out of the ordinary about it.

Then the pains began. I dismissed them for a while, but when they got so bad I couldn't get off the living room couch, I told Ella she'd better get old Doc Bradley to come up and see me.

Her eyes went wide. "Honey-pet—is it really that bad? Here, darling, perhaps a massage will make the nasty old pains go away."

But I was in agony. Soon I moved away from the smooth little hand that was caressing my body so gently. "Afraid I'll have to have the doctor, Ella. Go see if he's around."

She went out, and the minutes ticked away. I staggered to the window to see if they were coming, fell in a crumpled heap on the floor, then managed to pull myself up again. For a second I didn't know what to think. There she was, sitting in the frayed old hammock between the oak trees, a cigarette going at intervals in her full, pouting mouth, a dull curl of smoke twisting around a scarlet-tipped finger, a sandaled foot swinging free and accentuating the curve of a silken leg.

I hung there, doubled up. It was impossible for me to go for help. It was too late for that. It was too late for a lot of things. I saw everything, understood everything. I saw why a woman of her sort would come to a little town, where it is comparatively easy to become friendly enough to pick up a good thing when you see it. She'd be very comfortable with me out of the way. But—how did she expect to get away with it?

I guess she saw me there, for she came to her feet with a satisfied smile, ground the cigarette out beneath her toe, and sauntered in. She was safe. It was too late for me to do anything for myself, or to her. She knew it, and she knew I knew it.

"How you feeling now, Lute?" Perfectly relaxed, I thought wonderingly. She sounded as though this were old stuff to her, to get mixed up with an old fellow, then get rid of him for what she could get out of it.

And so it was I found out. Sitting on the edge of the table she told me about herself, smoking, watching me with waiting eyes, just as though we were simply trying to pass the time away. She had lived on a farm in an isolated area within a hundred and fifty miles of Orrinville. . . .

"I got damn sick of having nothing—no nice clothes, no fun, no nothing. . . ." So she had conceived the idea that she had so successfully carried into execution. "You're the third old gaffer I've done business with—after all, these are extended business trips and nothing more," she said, laughing in indulgent amusement at herself. "This is the last time though. I've enough now to keep myself in all the luxuries I want for the rest of my life. Thanks, Lute, for how you've helped me."

How did she get away with it? Simple. "I took them—I'll take you—back with me. You'll just disappear, and so will I, as far as Orrinville is concerned."

How would she take me back? "I'm not so foolish as not to have that all planned out," she gurgled, delighted at her own cleverness. "I'll do what I've done before—it's a cinch I couldn't leave you here. If there's no body, no evidence of foul play, and, most important, no suspicion of it, everyone will take it for granted we left town, and no one will wonder over much."

"But—but how," I gasped. I was in a tortured agony, but that iron will of mine kept me going until I could straighten this fantastic maze out. Ella! Silly, giggling, delicious Ella—a professional murderess! "Bury me?"

She seemed irritated by my thick-headedness. "Don't be foolish —how could I do that? There isn't a minute when some nosy busybody isn't watching this house, titillated by what they all suspect is true, but can't prove! Bury you? How could I here? Back home, there's any number of places for that, where you could never be found. But here? Hah! And it's a sure thing that there's no place in this house for me to get rid of you."

Her satisfied smile grew until it was a genuine laugh. She was inflated by her own ego. Are all murderers like that? Do they think they can get away with it? Because, of course, I see now, it simply can't be done.

"I'm going to put you in that huge iron-bound trunk up there at the back of that smelly attic of yours. I discovered it one day when I was hunting around to see if I could avoid buying a trunk—that's a dangerous thing to have to do. I'll take no other luggage, so there'll be no suspicion aroused, and in an hour Tom can take me to Blodd Junction—he's already promised. By tonight you'll be sleeping in a permanent bed—far away from Orrinville. There'll be nothing here to show—"

She was gabbling away with the details, but I wasn't listening. Her eyes widened as I started to laugh. Even with the wracking pains, it still sounded like a laugh—a groaning, horrible caricature of a laugh.

I can't help it. It's the damnedest joke I ever heard. And I am, I really am, going to die laughing. You see, she's not going to be able to get me in the trunk. Emily's in there now.

LET NATURE
TAKE ITS CORPSE

C. WILLIAM HARRISON

Eph knew a stranger was coming to camp half an hour before the man made his appearance. Knowing this required no great amount of intellectual discernment. As a matter of fact there were many times when you could ask Eph what state he lived in, and he would have been at a loss to give the correct answer. Some of the local wags have replied that Eph lived in a state of constant confusion. Which was not entirely wrong, at that.

In the hazy recesses of Eph's brain there was no room for complicated problems. When he needed food he prepared it as simply and easily as possible. When he needed sleep, he slept.

And when the crows clamored over around Turkey ridge, as they just had a few minutes ago, it meant a stranger was at the edge of the swamp. It had always been so, and Eph never questioned it—or worried about it. It had to be a stranger because Professor Carthage was too woods-wise to cause such a disturbance among the crows. It was as simple as that.

He paused briefly to listen to the crows, and then returned stolidly to his work of pulling a few of the weeds out of his small garden patch.

His crude shack and scrubby garden were on a low knoll that thrust up from the swamp, and all round him down below were murky waters and treacherous stretches of marsh. He worked thoughtlessly at his weeding. He had never bothered to do this before, but the Professor had said his cabbage and turnips and tomatoes would grow better if the weeds were removed. So Eph unquestioningly pulled weeds.

A chicken hawk rose suddenly out of the underbrush near the lightning-scarred beech tree, and so Eph knew the stranger was coming into the swamp. The trail, as thin and uncertain as a shadow, passed near the foot of the beech, and no stranger to the swamp could have found or followed that crooked path without help. Therefore Eph knew Professor Carthage was with the stranger, guiding him to Eph's camp.

The two men came out of the marsh and approached the knoll on which was Eph's shack. Eph watched them indifferently. In his vague way he liked the little professor, and equally vaguely he resented the intrusion of the stranger.

Professor Carthage was a small thin man with thick white hair and a surprisingly deep voice. He slipped the bulging pack-sack from his narrow shoulders.

"Forage for the human animal, Eph. Bacon, flour, beans—manna from Morganville, and enough to last us a week." But he wasn't a man to give more than fragmentary interest to food. He waved his ever-present butterfly net.

"Caught this fellow on that hummock east of Bear Wallow. A beauty, Eph, an exceptionally fine specimen of the *Euproctis chrysor-rhoea.*"

Eph squinted through the close-meshed netting. "Ha?"

"Browntail Moth, to you," Professor Carthage said.

A thought struggled through the placid waters of Eph's mind. "You write Miz Carthage in town, Professor?"

The little man said with amused severity, "I told you to remind me to write my wife *before* I left for town, not after I got back."

Eph shook his big head uncertainly. "I guess I must've forgot."

Professor Carthage smiled. "But I didn't. I wrote the letter, and now Mrs. Carthage will feel confident I'm in my hotel room writing a profound paper on the caterpillars native to the north-central states. She'd have a hemorrhage if she knew where I really am. She thinks my health can't stand hunting specimens in a swamp."

He seemed to remember for the first time the stranger he had brought into the swamp with him.

He said, "Eph, this is Mr. Johnson. I met him in town, and he asked me to bring him here. He wants to hire you to dig some peat moss for him."

Johnson was not tall, but there was a suggestion of toughness and leashed energy in his compact shape. He stood somewhat back from Professor Carthage, and he didn't smile when he was introduced. He had quick dark eyes that were strangely humid in their restlessness; his mouth was thin and long.

Eph thrust out his hand. "H'lo."

Johnson didn't seem to see his hand. Eph let it sag uncertainly to his side.

Johnson said, "Quite a place you've got here. I don't imagine you have many visitors."

Eph considered this dully. Professor Carthage said with a chuckle, "Not in this swamp. I imagine I'm the first visitor Eph ever had out here. With the exception of you, of course."

A shadowy thought suggested to Eph that Johnson seemed oddly pleased with this information. But it was a thought that slid into Eph's mind and out again without leaving a mark.

He said, "You want to buy peat moss, ha?"

"Yeah." But the man's eyes were on the thin strand of wire stretching across the shingle roof of Eph's shack. "You got a radio here?"

"Ha?"

"A radio?"

"Uh-huh." Eph thought the man seemed displeased by this information. "But the batteries are dead, and it ain't much good."

A faint smile traced the stranger's thin mouth. "That's too bad." But he didn't seem to think it was too bad.

"The batteries went dead last night," Eph said. "You like radios, Mr. Johnson?"

"Sure."

"I like radios too. I like to hear music on them."

Mr. Johnson looked at Professor Carthage, and winked. "I like music, too." He seemed to think something was funny, and Eph couldn't understand it.

Eph said, "Last night the music was pretty. Then the music stopped and some feller said something about a bank or postoffice being robbed up around—I don't rightly remember what town it was."

"Greenfield," Professor Carthage said.

Eph was unaccountably disturbed by some quality in Johnson's dry question. "You know about that holdup?"

"Just what I read in the papers while I was in town this morning."

Eph wished the stranger would go away. He felt more at ease when he was alone or with Professor Carthage. There was something about this stranger that made Eph feel as he did when he sensed the danger of quicksand out in the swamp. He didn't know what made him feel that way. He just wished the stranger was gone.

Johnson's softness asked, "What did you read about that holdup?"

Professor Carthage was bent, rummaging in the sack. "The usual newspaper account. A bandit held up the Greenfield bank yesterday afternoon. He killed the teller, and got away with an undetermined amount of cash. Before the teller died, he described the crook as medium tall, well dressed, and using a gun with a broken butt plate. The killer was believed to have fled in this direction."

The Professor found what he was looking for, a greasy brown-paper sack. He looked at Eph. "Where's Skipper? I brought him some bones."

Eph grinned broadly. "Skip like bones." He waved his big hand vaguely in the direction of the swamp. "Skip's out there someplace. Huntin', I guess." He pursed his lips, and sent a whistle echoing through the marshes.

It was just a little terrier with muddy feet and burr-tangled hair. The dog came bounding up the knoll, saw the stranger, and began barking challengingly. Johnson put his hand in his coat pocket.

Eph said, "Skip's all right. He ain't never bit nobody, and he don't see no strangers out here. Just let him sniff you, Mr. Johnson, and he'll be all right."

Johnson swore gratingly. "I don't like dogs. Keep him away."

Eph said, "He likes to play big, Skip does. But he won't bite, mister."

The dog walked stiff-legged toward the stranger, hackles raised, growling out his challenge. Johnson's hand came out of his pocket, gripping a blued automatic by its barrel. He bent and lunged toward the dog with sudden violence. His hand raised, and whipped down. The terrier yelped only once. The gun butt clubbed down again.

The stranger straightened and spun, holding his gun level. "I told you to call him off," he said harshly. "I don't like dogs."

Professor Carthage was looking at the broken butt plate on the automatic. He raised his eyes. "Why—why, you're that murderer!"

The killer's laugh was a raw thing. "That makes you know too much, pop." His dark eyes were humid with mockery. "It ain't good to know too much about a guy the cops are hunting, pop. I suppose you're going to turn me in now."

Professor Carthage was a mild little man whose world of science had not prepared him for the cruel realities of the civilization he lived in. To him crime was a thing to be read about and deplored but which never came into his personal life.

He should have been afraid, but he wasn't. He was a harmless little man who didn't know enough about the realities of life to be afraid. He should have known the futility of trying to get away. But he didn't.

"Indeed I shall report you, sir!"

He went down the weedy slope of the knoll, a small man hurrying to bring justice to a wanted murderer. He didn't once glance back over his shoulder. It didn't occur to him that such things as violence and murder could ever touch him.

He started along the narrow path that bridged the swamp waters, and it was there that the bullet struck him between his shoulders. He fell face down in the stagnant water and didn't move.

What had happened was slow sinking into the hazy depths of Eph's brain. When realization finally came full and strong into him, he could show only a simple man's childlike resentment.

"You killed my Skip, and he never hurt anybody in his life." He put his dull eyes on the murderer. "You killed Professor Carthage, and he was good to Eph. You shouldn't ought to have done that, mister."

He brought up his huge hands. He said heavily, "Now Eph will kill you. Eph never hurt anybody before, but Eph is going to make you dead."

The killer said with brittle harshness. "You big ox, I've got the gun, see! You try anything with me, I'll put a slug in your guts. You're big, but you're not bigger than a bullet. Get that into your thick head, and don't forget it."

Slow-dawning realization of danger halted Eph's advance. But fear never got to him. He looked at his big hands, and he looked at the killer, and a crafty light stirred sluggishly in his resenting eyes.

Johnson said corrosively, "We're going to stay here in this camp, just you and me. You're going to cook meals, if you know enough to cook, and if you ever try to slip away I'm going to put a bullet in your stomach. No one will ever look for me here, and I'm staying until the pressure is off."

Eph said heavily, "Sometime Eph is going to make you dead like Skip and Professor Carthage. You just wait and see, mister."

Eph made his break the next morning. There was no great cunning in what he did. He walked out of his shack, the killer following him warily. He paused at the crest of the knoll where he had dug the graves for Skipper and Professor Carthage. He paused to gaze down at the fresh-turned earth, the dim recesses of his mind awed by the swiftness with which death can replace life. He wished he could hear Skip's excited barking again when he treed a 'possum. He wished he could again see Professor Carthage's slight shape prowling through the swamp trails after an elusive butterfly for his collection.

Behind him the killer said, "The same thing can happen to you, pal-o. Keep that tucked away in whatever you use for a brain."

Eph turned heavily. "You wouldn't kill Eph. You say you would, but you wouldn't."

"Just try me and see, pal-o."

"Only big Eph knows the trail out of the swamp. You make Eph dead and you can't get out alone."

Johnson said malevolently, "I'd rather rot in here than let you bring the cops in after me." He showed his gun, and the tawny glint of danger was in his dark eyes. "Get back to the shack, dumbo."

"Eph wants to walk."

The big man turned his back on the gun. He went down the knoll's slope, and moved onto the path that bridged dark stagnant water. The killer followed, silently watchful.

The sun rays had been bitter on the shadeless knoll, but here beneath the green roof of the swamp trees it was quite cool. The air was stale and clogged with the heavy wetness of the marshes, and the dank smell of decay was everywhere. Turtles, disturbed by the passing of the two men, slid down muddy banks into the stagnant waters, and somewhere not far away a bird ribboned the silence with its raucous cry.

"Any snakes in here?"

"Copperheads and moccasins."

Johnson's eyes narrowed. "So that's your pitch! You're hoping you can walk me around in here until I get snake bit. It won't work, dumbo. We're going back."

Eph kept walking.

Johnson said harshly, "I said we're going back, damn you!"

Eph's walking had carried a low-hanging limb with him, and suddenly he released it. The branch lashed Johnson's face, and he heard the sound of the big man's heavy running. He cursed savagely, broke clear of the limbs, and jerked up his gun.

He fired, and saw Eph stumble. But the big man kept running. Johnson broke into a run. Limbs clawed at him, and he fought through tangles of brush, goaded on by the red lust to kill.

He fired again, and knew his bullet had found its mark in Eph's leg, but he couldn't stop the big man. Eph's direction changed sharply, turning his flight across a low grassy knoll. Johnson fired again, but he hurried his shot and missed. He sprinted on to the knoll.

"You damn fool, you can't get away!"

Even the dim working of Eph's mind must have told the big man that. But he kept running heavily, limping and weakened by hurt. The knoll ended on a cutbank, and there was water beyond, broken a short distance out by a narrow spit of sand. Another island lay past that.

Ephs' leap overshot the sand spit, and he splashed heavily in the muddy water. He slogged on toward the island.

The killer ran to the edge of the cutbank. He shouted harshly, "I've got one more bullet left in this gun, but I've got plenty more back at camp. Come back here, damn you. You ain't got a chance to get away now."

Eph kept moving on.

"Then I'll come after you," Johnson swore.

The sand spit curled like a bent finger jutting out from the island. Johnson leaped for the sand, and his judgment of the distance was good. It was too good.

The killer struck the sand, but there was nothing dry and solid to it. It seemed to melt away as he touched it, and he plunged to his hips in loose, heavy wetness. He cursed and struggled with swift panic plunging through his brain.

"For God's sake, man, do something! Pull me out of here."

"You made my Skip dead, Mister Johnson. You shouldn't ought to have done that."

"I'll give you enough money to buy a dozen dogs. Get something and pull me out."

"You made Professor Carthage dead, Mister Johnson."

The offer of money could not argue against big Eph's simple condemnation. The gritty wetness was rising across the killer's chest, swiftly and inexorably toward his shoulders, his neck, his face.

He leveled his gun on big Eph. "Damn you, I'll kill you! I've got one more bullet in this gun. I'll put it through your guts if you don't help me!"

But Eph did not move. And the killer did not shoot. He had only one more bullet in his gun, and he could not wait until the quicksand locked all air from his lungs.

Only one more bullet, and the killer could not wait. . . .

THE
LETTERS OF
HALPIN CHALMERS

PETER CANNON

I'm glad you've come," said Ida Carstairs. She was sitting by the
window beneath the pagoda-shaped bird cage, her face nuzzled
by Max, her pet conure. Little had changed in the three years since
I had last stopped in, to pick them up for the drive to the Halpin
Chalmers centennial conference. About the cluttered living room,
displayed on walls or tables, were the dusty souvenirs and tattered
testimonials I had come to know over countless visits, the tokens of
a long career that had brought its share of recognition but limited
financial gain. If anything the place looked tidier and neater than in
the past, thanks to the current services of a series of home atten-
dants—and of course emptier. When earlier in the month I had
seen the obituary in the *Partridgeville Gazette*, I had decided that it was
time to put aside our differences, that I should pay my respects to
the widow.

And then there were the letters, the letters of Halpin Chalmers
to his best friend, Fred Carstairs, to whom he wrote almost daily
during his prolific Brooklyn period. Having recently received the
contract for the first critical biography (provisionally titled *Secret
Watcher: The Life and Strange Death of Halpin Chalmers*), I was determined
at long last to lay my hands on these priceless epistles from the pen
of America's foremost author of the occult.

"I knew you'd come, Peter," said Ida Carstairs. "Please sit down."
She gestured at Fred's old wheelchair.

For a woman in her late eighties Ida was in remarkably good
shape, as strong in body as her husband had been frail. With no
sign of strain she rose and lifted Max off her shoulder and into his
cage.

"Fred's last months were very difficult," she said. "After he got out of the hospital he wouldn't let anyone touch him. And his language! Such words I had never heard out of his mouth before. He was no longer my sweet little Fredela."

I had known that Fred had been hospitalized, that for a time he had even been placed in the psycho ward.

"His pain wasn't just physical, Peter. 'Why doesn't anyone come see me?' he'd cry. 'I'm so lonely.' "

Why indeed? Why didn't the fans—and certainly Fred had his own followers, apart from those who cared only about his connection with his more illustrious friend—line up at his bedside to comfort him in his final days? Partridgeville may be off the beaten track, but I believed it when she said no one came. The sad truth is they stayed away, we all stayed away, because of her.

"He was so unworldly, my beloved," she said, mercifully not mentioning my own neglect of Fred, "like Prince Myshkin in Dostoyevsky's *The Idiot*."

As fond as she genuinely was of her late husband, in my experience she could never stand him getting all the attention, even if that attention was motivated out of a regard more for the occult tales of Halpin Chalmers than for the occult tales of Fred Carstairs. I alone of the Chalmersians recognized that the key to Fred lay through Ida. I alone knew of the existence of the Chalmers letters, secreted in a musty old trunk I had managed to inspect in Fred's bedroom while pretending to go to the bathroom during one of my earlier visits. So over the years I listened for hours to her wild and fantastic stories of her glamorous youth on the stage and to her grandiose dreams of future travels and triumphs, if only to gain a few minutes with Fred—who might if I was lucky drop a fresh, precious nugget or two concerning Halpin Chalmers all those decades ago.

But I could take only so much. My patience ran out in 1991, the year of the Chalmers centennial. I had written Ida a letter politely suggesting that she stay home while I drove Fred to Brooklyn to be the guest of honor at the 100th-birthday celebration weekend. But she didn't take the hint. She had insisted on going too—with her parrot. Those who attended need not be reminded how her antics (and those of her bird) on more than one occasion disrupted the proceedings. She defied me. She had to pay the price. As a consequence I ceased my visits to Fred. I refused to return her phone calls.

"You know, Peter, Fred and I were not all that well matched. My friends, people in the theatre, wondered what I saw in him. He was so shy. At parties he hardly said anything."

As a matter of fact, he hadn't said a whole lot at the centenary either, apart from parroting the same tired anecdotes about Chalmers he'd been repeating for more than sixty years, ever since his fellow author's premature death in 1928. His semi-senile performance there should have been Fred's last bow. No one had expected the venerable occultist to reach his own century or beyond. (While the obituary had reported he died at 100, he was really 101, having shaved a year off his age at some point in his career. To one correspondent Chalmers clearly states that his boyhood pal was born in 1893, not 1894.) But he astonished everyone by surviving another three years. In the meantime, I concentrated on producing shorter critical works for *Chalmers Studies* and other learned journals, knowing that sooner or later I would get my chance at the letters in Fred Carstairs' trunk.

The Chalmers letters to Carstairs! What a trove! A few teasing extracts, a mere fraction of the total, had been published in the *Collected Letters of Halpin Chalmers*. Literally hundreds of virgin pages had yet to meet the feasting eyes of the Chalmers scholar. Why hadn't their recipient sold them? In his declining years, before he fell and couldn't leave their Central Square apartment, Fred had consigned other items in his occult collection to a local second-hand bookdealer, including his copy of *The Secret Watcher*, inscribed by Chalmers himself. I know; I was the one who had picked up this treasure at a price so enviable I forbear from citing the figure. Had he tried to sell off the letters, whether piecemeal or as a lot, my informant, the proprietor of the Angell Hill Bookshop, would have alerted me immediately.

As much as he could have used the money, did Fred deliberately keep the Chalmers letters to himself out of spite? Whenever I hinted at their existence, he pretended not to understand. In face of such coyness I decided early on not to push the matter, instead to adopt a waiting policy, hoping to gain his confidence and eventually the prize that would secure my own name as the world's leading authority on Halpin Chalmers.

"Nobody knew he was a writer. He certainly didn't dress like one. Let me tell you, Peter, before he broke his hip he used to go out in that shabby coat of his and do the shopping. When he sat down to rest, strangers would put a dollar in his hand, thinking he was a homeless person! Can you imagine, Fred Carstairs, the great occult author, mistaken for a homeless person!"

If it can be said that Chalmers died before his time, then Carstairs lived beyond his time—long after his time. At his death Chalmers was at the peak of his powers. His posthumously published work established his reputation as the supreme practitioner of the genre. His heirs are rich today from the royalties generated by the millions of copies of his books still in print. On the other hand, Carstairs in his prime never achieved more than a workmanlike competence. In his old age he was honored more for his longevity than for any lasting contributions to the field. During the occult resurgence of the late 1960s and 1970s he enjoyed a revival of sorts, but by the 1980s and early 1990s he could expect only the rare anthology appearance, or possibly a foreign rights sale, to supplement the monthly social security checks that supported him and his wife and their bird in their golden years.

To be fair to Fred, he could be perfectly candid about his own lack of genius relative to his best friend's. One has only to read that sketchy, rambling, error-riddled, if often charming memoir of his, written in his dotage, *Halpin Chalmers: Voyager of Other and Many Dimensions*, to appreciate the man's modesty. And yet, and yet, there must have been times when he deeply resented his old friend—when the interviewers, their indifference to Fred Carstairs only too evident, asked him just one question too many about Halpin Chalmers.

"He lived in this dump of a town all his life and they completely ignored him. But Fred's big-shot celebrity-author friend, that turd, they named for him that fancy housing development in Mulligan Wood!"

Both writers had grown up in Partridgeville, but Chalmers had left that provincial New England city and settled in Brooklyn, to compose the masterpieces on which his fame rests today. As for Carstairs, he had remained in Partridgeville, where nothing newsworthy had occurred since the death of Halpin Chalmers, brutally and mysteriously murdered at age thirty-seven during a short homecoming sojourn. Fred, in fact, had been the last person to see him alive, though he had apparently been no more illuminating when questioned by the police at the time than in 1976 when I first queried him on the subject. (To another correspondent Chalmers records his frustration over his friend's tendency to mix things up—a tendency that did not improve with age.) This was soon after I moved to Partridgeville, where I had been quite fortunate to find a one-bedroom condo in the then newly erected Halpin Chalmers Estates.

"Occult writers, bah! Such people—no class, no culture," Ida continued. "But what did I know? It was only a month after we met that we decided to elope."

Fred and Ida had married late in life, after a brief courtship in New York, he for the first time, she for the fourth or fifth (she was always vague about how many husbands she'd had). Fred had brought his bride back to Partridgeville, a place that she grew to despise and that she loved to abuse almost as much as occult writers. But I had heard the story of their tragicomic marriage a thousand times before. I could care less, especially now. All that mattered was obtaining the letters. At the next pause in the monologue I excused myself and headed down the hall.

Proceeding past the bathroom door I entered Fred's dank, curtained bedroom, hoping to find it unchanged since my last snooping expedition. It was in one essential: the ancient trunk still rested at the foot of the bed. While feigning to listen to Ida, I had conceived a plan—to remove the letters a bundle at a time, to slip them into my jacket or the bookbag I habitually carried. In the coming weeks and months I would visit Ida regularly. I was forgiven; we were, after all, friends again. I wished I had thought of this expedient long before, and wondered at my past scruples. But time had not seemed of the essence, until I received permission from the Chalmers estate for the biography—which would be a lesser thing without ample quotations from the Chalmers letters to Carstairs. I didn't want to disappoint the heirs.

From the living room I could hear Ida conferring heatedly, in French, with the Haitian home attendant. The moment had come to act. As before, no lock secured the rusty clasp of the trunk. My heart in my mouth, I raised the lid. There was the same stale, musty odor I remembered, though somewhat less pungent than previously. I could dimly see—I could see nothing! Or rather, almost nothing. On the bottom lay a few scattered sheets. I seized an envelope, and as I peered closely at the familiar handwritten scrawl, behind me I heard a squawk.

I turned and saw Ida in the doorway, her pet parrot on her shoulder.

"We knew you wanted those letters, Peter. Fred and I often talked about it. It was so obvious. My little 'idiot' said he was going to reward you for your kindness by leaving you the letters after he died. It was to be a surprise. But then, for no good reason, after that horrible trip to Brooklyn, you stopped coming. Then Fredela got ill and I tried to call you and you still wouldn't come. You, the most faithful and loyal of all the Chalmerdesians!"

305

I made no apologies. All I could do was stammer something about the letters and their value.

"Oh, yes, I knew we could sell for a pretty penny such drek. Fools! But at our age, what did we need for cash? Because Fred was a fighter he protested at first when I said I had a better use for them. From his wheelchair, though, he couldn't really go against my will. In the end he went along."

I followed her back into the living room, hoping against hope that she had simply removed the letters of Halpin Chalmers to elsewhere in the apartment.

"The supply has nearly run out, so I'll have to go back to using old newspapers." She placed the conure inside the pagoda-shaped cage and shut the door. "There, I bet you didn't realize Max was also a critic!"

THE MAN OF THE KNIFE

ALEXANDRE DUMAS

There dwells in Ferdj' Ouah a Sheik named Bou Akas ben Achour. It is one of the most ancient names in the country, so we find it in the history of the dynasties of the Arabs and Berbers of Ibu Khaldoun.

Bou Akas is 49 years of age. He dresses like the Kabyles; that is, in a gandoura of wool girt with a leathern belt, and fastened around the head with a slender cord. He carries a pair of pistols in his shoulder-belt, at his left side the Kabyle flissa, and, hanging from his neck, a little black knife. Before him walks a Negro, carrying his gun, and at his side bounds a large greyhound.

When a tribe in the vicinity of the twelve tribes over which he rules occasions him any loss, he deigns not to march against it, but is satisfied with sending his Negro to the principal village, where the Negro shows the gun of Bou Akas, and the injury is repaired.

There are in his pay two or three tolbas who read the Koran to the people. Every person passing by his dwelling on a pilgrimage to Mecca receives three francs and at the Sheik's expense remains in Ferdj' Ouah as long as he pleases. But should Bou Akas learn that he has had to do with a false pilgrim, he sends emissaries to overtake the man wherever he may be, and they, on the spot, turn him over on his face, and give him twenty blows of the bastinado on the soles of his feet.

Bou Akas sometimes dines 300 persons, but instead of partaking of the repast, he walks around among his guests with a stick in his hand, marshalling his domestics; then, if there is anything left, he eats, but the very last.

When the Governor of Constantina, the only man whose supremacy he acknowledges, sends him a traveler, according to whether the traveler is a man of note, or the recommendation is pressing, Bou Akas presents him with his gun, his dog, or his knife. If he presents his gun, the traveler shoulders it; if his dog, the traveler holds it in leash; if his knife, the traveler suspends it from his neck. With one or another of these talismans, each of which bears with it the degree of honor to be rendered, the traveler passes through the twelve tribes without incurring the slightest danger. Everywhere he is fed and lodged for nothing, for he is the guest of Bou Akas. When he leaves Ferdj' Ouah, it is sufficient for him to deliver the knife, the dog, or the gun to the first Arab that he meets. The Arab, if hunting, stops; if tilling the ground, he quits his plough; if in the bosom of his family, he departs; and taking the knife, the dog, or the gun, returns it to Bou Akas.

In fact, the little black-handled knife is very well known; so well known, that it has given its name to Bou Akas—Bou d'Jenoui, or The Man of the Knife. It is with this knife that Bou Akas cuts off people's heads when, for the sake of prompt justice, he thinks fit to decapitate with his own hand.

When Bou Akas succeeded to his possessions, there were a great number of thieves in the country. He found means to exterminate them. He dressed himself like a simple merchant, then dropped a douro, taking care not to lose sight of it. A lost douro does not remain long on the ground. If he who picked it up pocketed it, Bou Akas made a sign to his chiaous, disguised like himself, to arrest the culprit. The chiaous, knowing the Sheik's intention in regard to the culprit, beheaded him without more ado. The effect of this rigor is such that there is a saying among the Arabs that a child of twelve years of age wearing a golden crown could pass through the tribes of Bou Akas without a finger's being raised to steal it.

One day Bou Akas heard mentioned that the Cadi of one of his twelve tribes rendered judgments worthy of King Solomon. Like another Haroun al Raschid, he wished to decide for himself the truth of the stories which were told him. Consequently, he set out in the guise of an ordinary horseman, without the arms which usually distinguished him, without any emblem of rank, nor any followers, and mounted on a blood-horse about which nothing betrayed that it belonged to so great a Chief.

It so chanced that, on the day of his arrival at the thrice-happy city where the Cadi sat in judgment, there was a Fair, and, in consequence of that, the Court was in session. It so chanced also— Mahomet watches over his servants in all things—that at the gate of the city Bou Akas met a cripple, who, hanging upon his burnoose, as the poor man hung upon the cloak of St. Martin, asked him for alms. Bou Akas gave the alms, as behooves an honest Musselman to do, but the cripple continued to cling to him.

"What do you want?" asked Bou Akas. "You have solicited alms, and I bestowed them on you."

"Yes," replied the cripple; "but the Law does not say only, 'Thou shalt bestow alms on thy brother,' but, in addition, 'Thou shalt do for thy brother all in thy power.' "

"Well, what can I do for you?" inquired Bou Akas.

"You can save me, poor wretch that I am, from being crushed under the feet of the men, the mules, and the camels, which will not fail to happen if I risk myself in the city."

"And how can I prevent that?"

"By taking me up behind you, and carrying me to the market-place, where I have business."

"Be it so," said Bou Akas, and lifting up the cripple, he helped him to mount behind. The operation was accomplished with some difficulty, but it was at last done. The two men on the single horse traversed the city, not without exciting general curiosity. They arrived at the market-place.

"Is it here that you wished to go?" inquired Bou Akas of the cripple.

"Yes."

"Then dismount," said the Sheik.

"Dismount yourself."

"To help you down, very well!"

"No, to let me have the horse."

"Why? Wherefore should I let you have the horse?" said the astonished Sheik.

"Because the horse is mine."

"Ah, indeed! We shall soon see about that!"

"Listen, and consider," said the cripple.

"I am listening, and I will consider afterward."

"We are in the city of the just Cadi."

"I know it," assented the Sheik.

"You intend to prosecute me before him?"

"It is extremely probable."

"Now, do you think that when he sees us two—you with your sturdy legs, which God has destined for walking and fatigue, me with my broken legs—think you, I say, that he will decide that the horse belongs to the one of the two travelers who has the greater need of it?"

"If he say so," replied Bou Akas, "he will no longer be the just Cadi, for his decision will be wrong."

"They call him the just Cadi," rejoined the cripple, laughing, "but they do not call him the infallible Cadi."

"Upon my word!" said Bou Akas to himself, "here is a fine chance for me to judge the Judge." Then he said aloud, "Come on, let us go before the Cadi."

Bou Akas made his way through the throng, leading his horse, on whose back the cripple clung like an ape; and presented himself before the tribunal where the Judge, according to the custom in the East, publicly dispensed justice.

Two cases were before the Court, and of course took precedence. Bou Akas obtained a place among the audience, and listened. The first case was a suit between a taleb and a peasant—that is to say, a savant and a laborer. The point in question was in reference to the savant's wife, with whom the peasant had eloped, and whom he maintained to be his, in opposition to the savant, who claimed her. The woman would not acknowledge either of the men to be her husband, or rather she acknowledged both; which circumstance rendered the affair embarrassing to the last degree. The Judge heard both parties, reflected an instant, and said:

"Leave the woman with me, and return tomorrow."

The savant and the laborer each bowed and withdrew.

The second case now came on. This was a suit between a butcher and an oil merchant. The oil merchant was covered with oil, and the butcher was besmeared with blood. The following was the butcher's story:

"I went to buy oil at this man's house. In paying for the oil, with which he had filled my bottle, I took from my purse a handful of money. This money tempted him. He seized me by the wrist. I cried thief, but he would not let go of me, and we came together before you—I clasping my money in my hand, he grasping my wrist. Now, I swear by Mahomet that this man is a liar when he says that I stole his money, for in truth the money is mine."

The following was the oil merchant's story:

"This man came to buy a bottle of oil at my house. When the bottle was full, he said to me, 'Have you change for a gold piece?' I then felt in my pocket, drew out my hand full of money, and put the money down on the sill of my shop. He snatched it up, and was about to go with both it and my oil, when I caught him by the wrist, and cried thief. In spite of my cries, he would not return my money, and I have brought him here, that you may decide between us. Now, I swear by Mahomet that this man is a liar when he says that I stole his money, for in truth the money is mine."

The Judge made each of the men, complainant and defendant, repeat his charge. Neither varied. Then the Judge pondered a moment and said:

"Leave the money with me and return tomorrow."

The butcher deposited in a fold of the Judge's robe the money of which he had never relinquished his hold; whereupon the two men bowed, and each went his way.

It was now the turn of Bou Akas and the cripple.

"My lord Cadi," said Bou Akas, "I have just come from a distant city, with the intention of buying goods at this mart. At the gate of the city I met this cripple, who at first asked me for alms, and finally begged me to allow him to mount behind me; telling me that, if he risked himself in the streets, he, poor wretch, feared he should be crushed under the feet of the men, the mules, and the camels. Thereupon, I gave him alms, and mounted him behind me. Having arrived at the market-place, he would not alight, saying that the horse which I rode belonged to him; and when I threatened him with the law, 'Bah!' he replied. 'The Cadi is too sensible a man not to know that the horse is the property of that one of us who cannot travel without a horse!' This is the affair, in all sincerity, my lord Cadi, I swear it by Mahomet."

"My Lord Cadi," responded the cripple, "I was going on business to the market of the city, and mounted on this horse, which is mine, when I saw, seated by the wayside, this man, who seemed about to expire. I approached him, and inquired whether he had met with any accident. 'No accident has befallen me,' he replied, 'but I am overcome with fatigue, and if you are charitable, you will convey me to the city, where I have business. After reaching the market-place, I will dismount, praying Mahomet to bestow upon him who aided me all that he could desire.' I did as this man requested, but my astonishment was great, when, having arrived at the market-place, he bade me dismount, telling me that the horse was his. At this strange threat, I brought him before you, that you might judge between us. This is the matter, in all sincerity, I swear by Mahomet."

The Cadi made each repeat his deposition, then having reflected an instant, he said:

"Leave the horse with me, and return tomorrow."

The horse was delivered to the Cadi, and Bou Akas and the cripple retired.

The next day, not only the parties immediately interested, but also a great number of the curious, were present in Court.

The Cadi followed the order of precedence observed the first day. The taleb and the peasant were summoned.

"Here," said the Cadi to the taleb, "here is your wife; take her away, she is really yours." Then turning toward his chiaouses, and pointing out the peasant, he said: "Give that man fifty strokes of the bastinado on the soles of his feet."

The case of the oil merchant and the butcher was then called up.

"Here," said the Cadi to the butcher, "here is your money; you did really take it out of your pocket, and it never belonged to that man." Then turning toward his chiaouses, and pointing out the oil merchant, he said: "Give that man fifty strokes of the bastinado on the soles of his feet."

The third case was now called, and Bou Akas and the cripple approached.

"Could you recognize your horse among twenty horses?" inquired the Judge of Bou Akas.

"Yes, my lord Judge," replied Bou Akas and the cripple with one accord.

"Then come with me," said the Judge to Bou Akas, and they went out.

Bou Akas recognized his horse among twenty horses.

"Very well!" said the Judge. "Go and wait in Court, and send me your opponent."

Bou Akas returned to the Court, and awaited the Cadi's return.

The cripple repaired to the stable as quickly as his bad legs would allow him to go. As his eyes were good, he went straight up to the horse, and pointed it out.

"Very well!" said the Judge. "Rejoin me in Court."

The Cadi resumed his seat on his mat, and everyone waited impatiently for the cripple, who in the course of five minutes returned out of breath.

"The horse is yours," said the Cadi to Bou Akas. "Go take it from the stable." Then addressing his chiaouses and pointing out the cripple, he said: "Give that man fifty strokes of the bastinado on the back."

On returning home, the Cadi found Bou Akas waiting for him.

"Are you dissatisfied?" he inquired.

"No, the very reverse," answered the Sheik; "but I wished to see you, to ask by what inspiration you render justice, for I doubt not that your two other decisions were as correct as the one in my case."

"It is very simple, my lord," said the Judge. "You observed that I kept for one night the woman, the money, and the horse. At midnight I had the woman awakened and brought to me, and I said to her, 'Replenish my inkstand.' Then she, like a woman who had performed the same office a hundred times in her life, took my inkglass, washed it, replaced it in the stand, and poured fresh ink into it. I said to myself immediately, 'If you were the wife of the peasant, you would not know how to clean an inkstand; therefore you are the taleb's wife.' "

"Be it so," said Bou Akas. "So much for the woman, but what about the money?"

"The money; that is another thing," replied the Judge. "Did you notice that the merchant was covered with oil, and his hands were greasy?"

"Yes, certainly."

"Very well! I took the money and placed it in a vase full of water. This morning I looked at the water. Not a particle of oil had risen to the surface. I therefore said to myself, 'This money is the butcher's, not the oil merchant's. If it had been the oil merchant's, it would have been greasy, and the oil would have risen to the surface of the water.' "

Bou Akas again inclined his head. "Good," said he; "so much for the money, but what about my horse?"

"Ah! that is another thing, and until this morning, I was puzzled."

"Then the cripple was not able to recognize the horse?" suggested Bou Akas.

"Oh, yes indeed, he recognized it."

"Well?"

"By conducting each of you in turn to the stable, I did not wish to ascertain which one would recognize the horse, but *which one the horse would recognize!* Now, when you approached the horse, it neighed; when the cripple approached the horse, it kicked. Then I said to myself, 'The horse belongs to him who has the good legs, and not to the cripple.' And I delivered it to you."

Bou Akas pondered for a moment, and then said: "The Lord is with you; it is you who should be in my place. I am sure, at least, that you are worthy to be Sheik, but I am not so sure that I am fit to be Cadi."

MANY HAPPY RETURNS

JUSTIN CASE

The house was an old one on an old road, miles from anywhere, but the freshly painted sign by its driveway—TOURISTS' REST—was as reassuring as a cleric's smile of welcome.

"Let's," Grace Martin said, squeezing her husband's hand. "There's no telling what we might find!"

Their car was already bulging with antiques collected in six states, but Tom Martin didn't care. He had just acquired his M.A., a teaching job at a highly regarded prep school, and a beautiful bride. "Done," he agreed without hesitation.

The warped and weathered door creaked open as they wriggled from the car. A man as old as they had expected, with a crown of white hair glowing in the dusk, limped down the rickety steps to greet them. An equally old woman, doll-dainty, smiled and nodded in the doorway.

It was the woman who escorted the newlyweds to their upstairs room. "Our name is Wiggin," she said, "but please call me Anna. And when you've freshened up, do come down for tea."

Grace Martin became enthusiastic about the massive four-poster bed while her husband irreverently bounced on it and pronounced it comfortable. They "freshened up" by lamplight and went downstairs to a dim parlor filled with antiques and the smell of age.

Anna Wiggin poured tea into fine old cups, and her husband Jasper, in reply to Grace Martin's question, said in a cracked voice, "No, we do not collect antiques. Not really. We have just acquired these things as we needed them."

"You are only just married, you two," Anna said with her smile. "I can always tell."

"Five days," Grace admitted.

"You are very young," Jasper said.

"Not so young. I'm twenty-two. Tom is twenty-four."

The old man moved his head up and down as if to say he had made a guess and the guess was correct. He did not say how old he and Anna were. He did remark, "I am a little older than my wife, also," then sipped his tea and added, "You must tell Anna your birthdays. She will read your futures."

"By our birthdays?" Grace Martin said.

"Oh, yes."

"How can you do that, Mrs. Wiggin?"

"I can do it." The doll-woman leaned closer, nodding and nodding. "When were you born, my dear?"

"May eleventh."

"It won't work, you know," Tom Martin said with a grin. "She—" Then puzzled by the old woman's expression, he was silent.

Jasper rose from his chair and placed his hands on his wife's frail shoulders. Though all but transparent in the lamplight, the hands were strong and long-fingered. "Now, Anna," he said softly, "do not be excited."

Grace Martin sent a half-frightened glance at her husband and said, "Is there something special about that date?"

"It is Anna's birthday also."

"Oh, how nice! We *are* special, then, aren't we?"

"Don't go putting on airs," Tom Martin chided. "You're forgetting—"

"Now, darling, don't spoil it."

"I will get some more tea," the old man said. "Fresh cups, too. We must have a toast."

The others were joking about the birthday when he returned from the kitchen with a tray. Placing four full cups on the table, he sat down again. The lamplight splashed his shadow on a wall as he raised a hand and said, "To the day that gave us two such lovely ladies."

They laughed and drank.

"You see, my dear," the old man said to his wife, "it never fails."

"What never fails?" Tom Martin asked.

"Only yesterday Anna was saying we would have to leave this house and find another. So few travelers use this old road any more. And even with many guests we sometimes wait years, of course."

"Wait for what?" Tom said.

"They have to have the same birthday, you see."

Tom nodded solemnly. It was past the old folks' bedtime, he supposed. When you were that old, a break with custom could make the mind a bit fuzzy. "Well, of course—" He started to rise. Grace and he had had a long day too, more than three hundred miles of driving.

"Wait, please," Jasper Wiggin said. "It is only fair that you understand."

With a tolerant smile Tom sank down again.

"There is a mathematical master plan, you see," the old man said. "Each day so many people are born, so many die. The plan insures a balance."

"Really?" Tom suppressed a yawn.

"I can simplify it for you, I think, if you will pay close attention. Each date—that is to say, each eleventh of May or ninth of June or sixth of December and so forth—is a compartment in time. Now suppose a thousand people are born today, to take their place with all the thousands born on this date in previous years. If the plan were perfect, all those born today would live exactly a year longer than those born one year ago, and so on. You follow me?"

"Uh-huh," Tom said sleepily.

"But the plan is not perfect. There is a thinning out through sickness and accidents—there has been from the beginning—and as a consequence, some of those born today will die before the expiration date, and others will live beyond it to maintain the balance."

"Sure," Tom mumbled.

"Each time compartment in each of the time zones is controlled this way. Life moves according to mathematics, just as the stars do."

"Remarkable," Tom said. Across the table his wife Grace was practically asleep. "What about the normal increase in population?"

"Oh, that's accounted for. So are wars, plagues, and things of that sort. If we had more time, I could make it all quite clear."

"You discovered this yourself, Mr. Wiggin?"

"Oh, no. There was a man from Europe staying with us one summer—a mathematical genius named Marek Dziok. Not in this house, of course; we have moved many times since then. Dziok had an accident—he was very old, and one night he fell down the stairs, poor man—but before he died, he took us into his confidence."

"I see."

"You don't believe me?" Jasper Wiggin said. "Dziok was writing a book—a philosophy based on his mathematics. He never finished it. But I have the manuscript . . ." He left his chair and limped to a bookcase, from which he lifted out a thin, paper-bound sheaf of papers. "Perhaps you would like—but no, you won't have time." Shaking his head, he put the sheaf of pages back.

"I guess I'd better take my wife to bed," Tom Martin said. "She's asleep."

"Yes, it works faster on women."

"What works faster?"

"The powder."

"You mean you put something—" Staring at his wife, Tom placed his hands flat on the table and pushed himself erect. It required enormous effort. "You mean—"

"You haven't been listening, have you?" the old man complained sadly. "And I've tried so hard to explain. Your wife and mine share the same time compartment, don't you see? You know yourself by now that Anna and I are much older than people get to be *naturally*. There's only the one way to do it."

"By—by killing off—"

"Precisely."

"And you think you're going to kill *Grace?*"

"It's been nineteen years since the last one for Anna," the old man sighed. "Hasn't it, dear?"

The doll-woman nodded, "Jasper has been luckier. He had one eight years ago."

"You're crazy!" Tom Martin shouted. "Both of you, you're crazy! Grace, wake up! We're getting out of here!" But when he leaned across the table to shake his wife awake, his legs went limp. He collapsed onto his chair. His head fell on his hands.

After a moment he was able with terrible concentration to bring the faces of Jasper and Anna Wiggin into focus again. There was something he had to remember—something he or they had said earlier, or he should have said but hadn't . . .

"It won't hurt, you know," the old man was saying sympathetically. "You'll both be asleep."

"Both . . . both . . ."

"Oh, yes. We'll have to kill you too, of course. Otherwise, you'd tell."

"Wait," Tom whispered. The room was filling with shadows now. "Wait . . ."

"But it won't be a waste, your dying. Somebody in *your* compartment will benefit, you know. Somebody with your birthday."

"Birthday," Tom repeated. That was it—birthday. "You're wrong about Grace—about—her—birthday." He made a supreme effort to get the words out before it was too late. "I tried—to tell you. She wasn't born May eleventh—"

"Oh, come now, Mr. Martin," the old man said sadly.

"No, no, it's true! She was born May eleventh in *Manila*. The Philippines. Her father taught—taught college there. Different—time—zone. Don't you see? A whole—day—different—"

The room went dark. In the darkness, though, he thought he heard the old woman begin to weep, and was sure he heard the old man saying, "Now, now, Anna, don't do that. There will be another one before too long."

Then nothing . . .

He was in the big four-poster bed when a shaft of sunlight wakened him. His wife lay asleep at his side. Their clothes were neatly folded on chairs.

Tom yawned and sat up. His wife opened her eyes and said, "Hi."

"You know something? I don't remember going to bed last night," Tom said.

"Neither do I."

"I don't remember getting undressed or folding my clothes like that. Grace"—he was frowning now—"I *never* fold my clothes. You know that."

"All I remember," she said with a yawn, "is getting sleepy at the table." She looked at her watch. "Anyway, we'd better be moving. It's after nine."

When they were ready to go they walked downstairs together, Tom carrying their suitcases. Anna Wiggin came from the parlor to greet them. "Did you sleep well?" she asked, peering into their faces.

"I'll say we did," Tom said.

"You were both so tired," Anna said, nodding. "Won't you have breakfast before you go?"

They said no, thanks, they were late as it was, and Tom took out his wallet to pay for their night's lodging. Anna said wait, please, she would get her husband, he was out in the field. So Tom and Grace Martin went to their car with the suitcases and Tom went back into the house alone.

It came back to him when he walked into the parlor and saw the table and the tea service and the extra cups. The extra cups! At first it was fuzzy and confused; then it sharpened and he remembered everything—just as Grace had remembered everything up to the time of *her* falling asleep.

He snatched the sheaf of papers from the bookcase. It was indeed a manuscript, handwritten and yellowed with age. Its title was *The Mathematics of Life* and its author was Marek Dziok.

Under the author's name, in a different hand, was written: *Born 1613. Died (by accident) 1802.*

There was a sound of footsteps in the kitchen. Tom thrust the manuscript inside his shirt and quickly stepped away from the bookcase.

"You know, I'm still sleepy," his wife said later as their car purred along a parkway. "It must have been that house. They were nice old people, though, weren't they?"

"Remarkable," Tom said.

"I wonder how old they really are."

Tom did not answer. He had already finished his figuring and now he was thinking of the pilfered manuscript inside his shirt. That, too, was remarkable. With the information it contained, a man could live a long time.

Of course, it was all pretty weird and sinister. Nevertheless . . .

In spite of himself, he began to think about birthdays—his wife's and his own.

MARKED
IN RED

RALPH POWERS

The back room of Retti's grew dangerously quiet as Tip Marbury entered. It was a long room cluttered with tables and chairs and with the slouched figures of men and women. Cigarette smoke eddied in shifting layers and through it two pasty-faced waiters in dirty jackets moved like fish in a milky aquarium.

A girl at a corner table spoke nasally, breathing the silence.

"There's that hot-foot dick again! Why don't somebody throw him out on his ear?"

Marbury grinned and nodded his head and grinned again. But he could feel hard bright eyes stabbing through the smoke, hostile and curious.

He crossed the room quickly on the balls of his feet and stopped in front of the man who stood propped against the farthermost door with a cigarette hung on his lower lip. The man stared at him with silent disapproval.

"Hello, Retti," said Marbury.

Retti, the speakeasy proprietor, spoke softly without taking the cigarette from his lips.

"Are you gonna spend every night wit' us, chief?"

"I told you I had a steer, Retti. I said there was a guy comes here I wanted to meet."

"Who?"

Marbury stared at Retti's sloe-black eyes, his thin lips and his slicked-down hair.

"Duke Hadden," he said. "He got out of stir yesterday. I thought he might show up in your place. You haven't seen him have you?"

For a moment Retti looked sidewise across the room. Then he shook his head.

"No, he ain't showed up."

Marbury glanced where Retti's eyes had swiveled and his lips spread in a sudden pleased smile.

"I see his moll's here though," he said. "Stella Rusano! He used to pal around with her in the old days."

"Yeah, they were both sent up. She got out first."

"And she's been waiting ever since," said Marbury. "I think I'll have a little chin with her, Retti. Maybe Hadden will drop in later."

He walked across the floor again to the table where the girl was sitting alone and as he did so he studied her face intently.

It was a hard little face, chalk-white under the overhead lamp, with a painted red slit of a mouth. But it wasn't all bad. There were hints of softness in the eyes. Hints of strength in the small, pointed chin.

Marbury nodded and grinned at her, and eased himself into a seat at her side. Her lips hardly moved. She was staring straight down at her whisky glass, fingering the edge of it.

"You've got a hell of a nerve," she said.

"So have you, coming here—with the Beckerman case not cleaned up. Where's Hadden?"

"I'd like to know!"

There was something in her voice that made his head jerk around; made him look at her with sharp intentness. All the softness had left her eyes now. Her mouth was a straight, bitter line.

"Tell me some more," he said. But she only shook her head.

"Waitin' for the split, eh? And Hadden hasn't shown up."

"You know everything," the girl sneered.

Her tone gave her away. He knew he was on the right track. Burke Hadden and she had both done time for the same job—the Beckerman jewel robbery. They'd been caught red-handed with some of the small stuff, pins and things—but the big grab, the blue-white rocks, had never been located.

"Listen, kid," he said. "Why don't you stay away from that guy? You was pretty straight till you started playing around with him."

The girl shrugged her slim shoulders. Her mouth grew hard and ugly.

"He can't—double-cross—me."

She bit the words out slowly and Marbury, looking down at her, saw that she was shaking. She opened the small, bright-colored handbag she carried and began fumbling for a package of butts. Marbury started to offer her one of his, then suddenly he made a grab for her wrist.

"Hold on, sister! What you got there?"

* * *

He was looking down at her lap, looking into the handbag that the girl tried to snap shut. Then his hand dived in and his fingers came out holding a small, gleaming revolver.

"So—you've started going around heeled?"

She tried to snatch the gun from him, but he held her off.

"Gimme that, you big, pussy-footing shamus. You ain't gonna run me in for—"

He shook his head.

"I could, but I won't. It's you I'm thinking of, kid. You just got out of stir a month ago. Why don't you try goin' straight for a while?"

"I will after—"

"After what?"

"Never mind—but lemme have my gun, Marbury. I ain't gonna shoot anybody—it's only for protection."

"Yeah?"

"Yeah!"

His eyes were shrewd and kindly as he stared down at her sullen face. The same face he remembered when she was just one of Rusano's kids, roller skating in front of her dad's grocery store down on Sullivan Street. The same kid who'd swiped apples to give to him, back when he was a rookie cop, and who'd tripped him up on the sidewalk a couple of times and made him sweat and swear.

Then she'd disappeared for years and he hadn't seen her again till she'd turned up as Burke Hadden's moll, tough and hard as they made 'em.

But somehow, looking at her now, he still saw that knock-kneed, funny-faced little kid who'd handed him apples.

"I'm getting sentimental," he said huskily, "but you know I won't run you in. How are you on dough?"

"I spent my last five bucks for that cannon. Retti's givin' me credit till Burke comes."

"Till he comes," said Marbury slowly and saw the girl's eyelids flicker. He fished in his pocket then, drew out a thin wallet and peeled off five one-dollar bills.

"Here's a loan," he said. "It ain't much, but it will help till you get a job."

She shook her head first, then took the bills. But her hand came back with the fingers open.

"Gimme that gun. Be a sport. You wasn't so bad when you was a cop, Marbury."

"You win," he said, and stuck the gun back into her sweaty little hand.

He ordered himself a glass of beer, drank it and eased out of his seat.

"I'll be seein' you," he said. "Be a good kid, and don't do anything I wouldn't."

He left the iron-grated door of the speakeasy, walked down the block, then turned and came back on the other side where the shadows were thicker. He ducked into the doorway of an empty house and waited, eyes slanted on Retti's place.

Patience was one of Tip Marbury's strong points.

It was nearly two hours before Stella Rusano came out. She was still alone and when the light from a street lamp fell on her pale little face there was a look there that he didn't like.

She teetered down the block on her high-heeled shoes. A couple of prowling youths made catcalls at her, but she didn't seem to hear. She signaled a taxi at the corner and got in.

"There goes one of my bucks. She's getting high-toned for a dame who's broke."

He came out of his doorway at a run and loped down the block toward the corner. Headlights of another cab goggled up the street. He raised a big paw and signaled, waiting till the taxi slid in to the curb.

"Keep that other bus in sight," he said to the driver.

Then he settled back and lit a cigarette. It might be a bum steer he was on, but it was worth trying. The cab eased into Seventh Avenue and headed uptown.

At Twentieth Street the taxi ahead swung left and headed for the river. Marbury's cab followed, past garages, cheap apartments, a theological seminary, and on into a block of run-down rooming houses.

"Slow down," said Marbury suddenly. He saw that the cab ahead was doing the same. Stella Rusano was bending forward in her seat, looking out of the side window, staring at the house numbers.

"She's a bad kid to welch on," he muttered. "I think this guy Burke Hadden has made a mistake."

If he could locate the Beckerman diamonds he knew his own stock would go up at headquarters. But he was going to see that Stella Rusano wasn't implicated.

The cab ahead stopped and the girl got out. She paid her fare and started walking. Marbury got out, too, and followed her.

He kept well behind, but not too far. He saw her turn into a gate halfway down the block and go up the front stoop of a house. He saw her press a bell button, and then disappear. And he crossed the street and slouched along, getting the number of the house.

It was hard to figure what to do next. Hadden might be inside, or he might not. It wasn't her own place or she wouldn't have spent so much time looking at the numbers. She might be just nosing around, or she might have followed a hot tip.

Marbury waited on the corner, puffing a cigarette, eyes slanted back. A half hour passed and he began to get restless. Another fifteen minutes and he was uneasy. Then he snapped into sudden alertness.

An old woman with stringy hair and a wrinkled face was running down the steps of the house Stella Rusano had gone in. She turned on her flat heels and started shuffling up the block where the light of a cigar store showed. She was walking faster, Marbury figured, than a dame of her age should.

He crossed the street at a quick angle and stepped in front of her.

"What's your hurry, mother?"

The old woman started and looked up at him with suspicion in her watery eyes, and he saw that she was breathing hard.

"None of your business, mister. Get out of my way—I gotta find a phone."

He opened the edge of his coat and let the light of the arc lamp gleam on his first-grade detective's badge. The old woman stared at it, stepped back and spoke in a croaking voice.

"There's been a shooting in my house. I heard a girl scream. The door was locked and I couldn't get in. I was gonna call the cops—but you'll do."

"Come on, mother."

He took her arm and began pulling her back, making her heels flap and her breath come in gasps. Then he snatched the key from her hand and ran up the stoop ahead of her.

"First floor rear," she panted.

He walked down a dark, stuffy hallway, came to a door and palmed the knob; but it was locked as she had said. The old woman came hobbling up to him and he jerked a question at her.

"Ain't you got a key?"

She made sweeping motions with her calloused hands.

"It won't go in, mister. The fella left his key on the inside."

"The fella?"

"Yeah—Burney Hampden—the gent that had the room."

"Burney Hampden—that's what he calls himself now is it? He was always dumb about his monikers."

Marbury stepped back then, turned a muscular shoulder to the door and lunged forward. The old woman made complaining cluckings with her tongue. The door cracked and Marbury lunged again. Wood snapped this time and he pitched into the room.

His gun was out, in his hand; but he didn't need to use it. One light was burning and Stella Rusano lay on the floor. Beyond her he saw an open window, and he ran to that. Then he saw that it was only a six-foot drop to the yard. There was a fence with a door in it and that was open, too, and the night was dark and silent.

He turned back into the room and stared down at the girl. Her face was even whiter than it had been and the front of her dress was discolored and soggy. He didn't need to look twice to see that she was dead. A man's necktie hung over the back of a chair, and the three drawers in the bureau were open, showing that somebody had made a quick getaway.

"The louse," said Marbury harshly. "The dirty louse!"

He stared at Stella Rusano. She didn't look much now like the little knock-kneed kid he remembered. She looked like what she was—a moll who had got hers. But there were runs in the stockings that covered her thin legs, and there were coppery lights in her dark, wavy hair, and Marbury swallowed hard. He wasn't as tough as he liked to appear.

Then he bent forward and swore under his breath.

"What the hell?" he said.

Stella Rusano's handbag was open. The gun was still in it. Burke Hadden hadn't given her a chance to use it. But a dollar bill, one of those that Marbury had given her, was lying on the floor, and the girl's white, still fingers near it held her lip-stick. She'd used the lip-stick—drawn a red, irregular line down the back of the bill, until the bullet lodged close to her heart had stopped her. She'd been trying to tell somebody something.

With his face screwed into a puzzled knot Marbury picked up the bill and studied it.

"She knew she was getting ready to croak," he muttered. "She knew I'd turn up when the call went in to headquarters. What did she want?"

He slid a big hand across his forehead and rubbed the end of his nose. Then he drew a cigarette from the package in his pocket and squeezed the tobacco out of it slowly, letting it dribble on the floor.

"What did you want, kid?" he muttered again. "What were you tryin' to tell me?"

He shook his head, staring at the bill, angry with himself. Then suddenly he jumped and turned on the old landlady.

"Stay here, mother. I'll put that call in to the cops for you—and when they come tell them that Tip Marbury's working on the case. Tell them he's got a hot steer."

His eyes were bright now and his face was hard. He went out of the room, through the hall and down the steps at a lope, and headed for the corner cigar store. He snapped into a telephone booth, took down the receiver and put in a call to headquarters.

"Marbury speaking. Stella Rusano, Hadden's moll, has just been bumped off. I'm going after Hadden now—the guy that did it."

He gave the street and house number and heard the desk sergeant's excited query.

"Where is Hadden?"

"Where I'm going to get him—and the Beckerman rocks."

Marbury grinned humorlessly then and hung up. He spent a minute thumbing through a telephone directory, found what he was after, and went out into the street. He signalled another cab and gave the driver an address in Jersey City.

"Make it snappy," he said, "there's a boat sailing and a guy on it I want to see."

He fumed as they crossed on the ferry, but the driver made up for lost time when they reached the other side. He turned left, sped along the river front and came to a screeching stop in front of a dock with a long shed on it.

Marbury dived into the shed, ran up a covered gangplank and on board a twin-funneled steamer that was tied up alongside the pier. He went to the purser's office and flashed his badge.

"Lemme see the passenger list."

When the startled young man behind the window shoved it to him he ran a thick finger down the long columns of names. Then he clicked his tongue.

"It wouldn't be Hampden this time. No—Horner Burkley—the dumb egg!"

He turned and crooked his finger at a steward.

"Take me to Horner Burkley's cabin—nine twenty-two."

The steward started off and Marbury followed, fingering the gun in his right coat pocket. When the steward stopped at a stateroom door he took the gun out and thrust its blunt nose forward purposely. The steward started to knock, but Marbury pushed the door open and jumped inside.

A big man with sharp features whirled around, glaring. His hand started to move toward his pocket.

"Don't do it, Mr. Burkley-Hampden-Hadden—it wouldn't do you any good. Stick 'em up—you lousy murderer!"

The big man's face went white and his hands up.

"Now," said Marbury, "I'm gonna give you some new jewelry to play with—since you like it so much."

He took a pair of jingling handcuffs from his pocket and snapped them on the big man's wrists. Then he snapped open the suitcase that rested on the lower berth and searched through it till he came to a small, flat package wrapped in soft leather. He undid it and stared at the glistening heap of sparklers, diamond necklaces, rings and bracelets worth a quarter of a million—the Beckerman jewels. Hadden spoke between clenched teeth, his eyes dark with fury.

"Who tipped you off—how did you know?"

"That girl-friend of yours. She was dead, but she left a message for me." Marbury shook his head slowly. "You're dumb about two things, Hadden—those tricky names you pick and the frails you pal around with—and try to double-cross. You ought to of known that you couldn't welch on a kid like Stella Rusano and get away with it. Here's the note she left."

Marbury reached into his pocket and pulled out the dollar bill with the red line on it that Stella Rusano had drawn with her dying fingers. He held it close to Hadden's uncomprehending eyes.

"I don't get you, Marbury," the big man grated. "What kind of a gag—"

"She outwitted you, Hadden—made you look like the dumb, murdering, double-crossing cluck you are. You taunted her, didn't you—told her you were sailing tonight, even showed her your passport? Then when she asked for her share of the split you gave her lead instead. And the game kid stayed alive long enough to tell me where to find you."

Marbury raised his hand then and pointed to the side of the suitcase that rested on the bunk. There was a big label on it, put there by the steamship company, and it proclaimed to the world at large what Stella Rusano's dying message had meant. Hadden's jaw sagged as he read the words:

"Dollar Steamship Line, Inc."

Marbury was nodding slowly.

"Yeah, she drew a line right through the middle of the bill—get it? 'Dollar Line'—and told me where to find you just as though she'd written it on a board fence in letters six feet high."

A MATTER OF PROOF

GROVER BRINKMAN

Something was moving far up the dusty St. Croix Road. Old Jim Fargo laboriously tied a second knot in the bandage on his throbbing, badly infected finger, and shuffled inside his peeled-log shack to get his telescope. Presently he came out to the porch again, poured some antiseptic solution on the crude bandage, then carefully focused the ancient glass. He stared long and earnestly, until he was quite sure the black dot, now rapidly growing larger, was an automobile. When he put down the glass he seemed suddenly weary, and dejected in spirit.

However, when the low-slung sedan finally jolted to a stop in front of his disreputable abode, Old Jim had again assumed a nonchalant attitude. He hummed an old Creole chant as he awkwardly pared potatoes, trying valiantly to keep his sore finger out of the way.

Three strangers slid out of the car and came up to the porch. They were dark-skinned and shifty-eyed. They acted nervous and ill at ease.

The taller of the three flipped back his coat for an instant, just long enough to flash a badge. Old Jim noted the bulge of shoulder holsters.

"We're looking for a guy," the tall man said bluntly. "We're officers from upstate. They told us back at St. Croix that you were the only old-time hermit in this area who knew the Okefenokee. We was wondering if you happened to see anyone come down the bayou."

Old Jim stopped his paring, spat derisively over the broken porch rail.

"I ain't paid much attention to the bayou, or anything else," he said evasively, waving a fly off his bandage. "Been too busy tryin' to save this blamed finger from gangrene."

"We trailed this guy to St. Croix. We're certain he was heading for the swamp. If he was, wouldn't he go in by way of the bayou?"

"Mebbe. And then agin, mebbe not. What kind of a guy was this feller?"

"He's a big man—must weigh all of 225. A surgeon by profession, red-headed, and his eyes are blue like robins' eggs—"

Something clattered to the porch floor. Old Jim tried mightily to steady his good hand as he picked up his paring knife. When he looked up, however, his weatherbeaten old face had the immobility of a faro dealer.

"Big guy, you say? Hell, if he's thet heavy, the bog's got 'im by now." He sent tobacco juice over the railing again. "Nobody can go into this part of the Okefenok' less'n you're a pint-sized runt like me. Know thet, don't you?"

The tall man was scowling. "They told us as much in St. Croix. That's why we came all the way out here. You're the only guy who can go in and get this fellow."

Old Jim perked up his head. "I ain't no man-catcher, mister. Besides, if this guy is a hard egg, I'm liable to stop a bullet—"

"There isn't much danger," the tall man returned. "Doctors don't carry guns. Besides, if your theory is right, he's liable to be a mile down in the bog by now."

Old Jim nodded. There was no way out, evidently. Laboriously he slipped into hipboots, donned a dirty old hat. "I'll go," he said wearily, "but it's liable to take hours. Better come up an' cook some grub. There's sweet potatoes ready, an' a squirrel—"

The tall man peeled off a bill from an overly fat roll. Old Jim was scowling, rubbing an imaginary bite on the top of his cranium, as the tall man crammed the bill inside a pocket of his dirty vest.

"We've got to get this guy, see?" the tall man persisted. The statement undeniably was an order.

"Scared I'll bring 'im out dead," Old Jim argued. "If he don't know the swamp, some varmint'll git 'im, even if the bog don't."

"Just so we have some proof," the tall man concluded. "Some positive proof."

Minutes later, Old Jim was poling his scarred pirogue down the bayou, following the black waterlane that led into the heart of the swamp. There was a hard, steely light in his watery old eyes as he poled deeper into the treacherous bog. From time to time he spat derisively into the brackish water, as if ridding his mouth of some extremely bitter taste. . . .

The scorching July sun was well past the meridian when he finally came out of the swamp. He was alone. The trio shuffled down to the muddy bayou edge to meet him.

"I found 'im," Old Jim began, wiping his brow, "but I can't git 'im out. He's in the bog. Must have floundered right onto a big cottonmouth. Can't move 'im, for the bog won't hold me up thet long, and my one hand's no good. Was wonderin'—"

"Nix on that!" the tall man interrupted. "Not on your life! If the bog won't hold you, how could any of us go in? We're all heavier than you."

The tall man scowled as he pondered, tossed a pebble idly into the tepid stream. "All we need is some evidence that this guy is actually dead—some positive, undisputable proof."

"Proof?" echoed Old Jim, "you mean—"

He left the sentence unfinished, turned back to his boat, grimacing at the pain in his puffed finger.

Without further parley he started poling his battered pirogue back into the Okefenokee. But now a whimsical smile lingered on his leathery face despite his pain.

Finally he grounded the pirogue on a low mud bank, whistled softly. A giant of a young man came splashing through the slush and bramble toward the boat. He was mud-spattered, dirty, haggard, but his blue eyes burned with an intense light that changed and softened as the older man approached.

"They want some proof you're dead, Nat," Old Jim said.

A film of fear suddenly veiled the eyes of the younger man. "Take them my class ring, clothing—anything," he began feverishly.

"That wouldn't do. The tall one would catch on."

"He's too damned smart." Nat Fargo wiped clammy sweat off his freckled brow. "Watch him like a hawk, Dad. Don't even hint we're kin. He thinks I come from the Everglades instead of the Okefenokee. He's a snake, and he'll try to get me if it takes a lifetime. All his mob are behind bars, excepting these three. My evidence put them there."

"Calm down!" Old Jim said, scratching his seedy old head in bafflement. "We'll figure out somethin'. You're safe here. Nobody knows 'bout the cabin on the island but me an' you. You can stay here till the law catches up with these birds, and that shouldn't be long. Let's see. . . ."

A pair of whippoorwills was circling high above the mirror-like surface of the bayou, cutting mad capers in the cobalt sky, when Old Jim came out of the swamp for the second time.

"Here's your proof," he told the tall man. "Positive proof."

As the trio gathered around the oil-cloth-covered table in his kitchen, he unwrapped his red handkerchief. The tall man took one look, prodded gingerly with the tip of a pencil until he was certain of the insignia on that gold band. Then he turned away without a word. His two henchmen made wry faces and hurried outside.

When the last exhausts of the big car dimmed into the distance, Old Jim smiled.

"Thet son o' mine'll be the greatest doc in the world some day," he soliloquized, as he studied his bandaged hand. "Takin' off thet old rotten finger didn't hurt a bit!"

MIND OVER MAYHEM

MACK REYNOLDS

The others had straggled out one by one and I was the only remaining customer. The bartender drifted down and wiped the bar in front of me listlessly, and yawned.

"Why the hell don't you go home, Jerry?" he asked conversationally.

I put the tabloid I'd been glancing at to one side and grinned at him. "Haven't got a home, Sam; just a hotel room with four walls and a bed and a chair or two and a couple hundred pocket books. I'd rather sit here and look at you."

He leaned on the bar before me and said, "You oughta get married, Jerry. Why don't you ask that girl . . . what was her name? The blonde, pretty little girl."

"Frances."

"Yeah, that's right. Frances. Why don't you ask her to marry you?"

I twisted my glass on the bar, lifted it over to a new spot, twisted it again and then again, making small wet circles.

"I did," I said. "A couple of months ago I asked her, 'Why don't we get married, Frances?' "

"Well, what'd she say?" Sam asked, yawning again.

"She just laughed and said, 'Who'd have either of us, Jerry?' "

Sam snorted. "I've heard that one before."

"It's almost two o'clock. You can't expect me to be original this time of the night."

A guy came in and took a stool two down from me and Sam walked over to him.

"Only fifteen minutes to go," Sam said. "What'll it be?"

"Bourbon," the stranger told him. "You gents like to have one with me?"

Usually the guy who comes into a bar the last few minutes before closing has already been drinking pretty heavy; he's been put out of a place that shuts up early and he's looking for that last drink that's suddenly become so important. This guy was an exception; he was cold sober. About thirty, which makes him a few years younger than me and maybe twenty years younger than Sam, he was neatly dressed and had an air of sharpness that seemed out of place this time of night.

"Thanks," I told him. "I could use another beer."

Sam poured the stranger's whiskey, drew my beer and then got himself a glass of vermouth, which is the only stuff I've ever seen Sam drink.

Sam said, *"Prosit."*

The stranger said, *"Skoal."*

I said, "Here's how," and we all started working on our drinks.

I said something about the weather and they both agreed and

everybody lapsed into silence. After a minute or two, the stranger started looking at the tabloid I'd discarded.

Finally he laughed and said, "Did you see this item about the old lady that socked some punk who was trying to hold up her liquor store? She slugged him with a bottle of Scotch."

Sam said, "Did it break the bottle? She would've saved money if she'd used something cheaper."

"Every once in a while you read something like that," I said. "That old doll must be a terror. I'd hate to be her old man."

The stranger finished off his drink and ordered another. Sam glanced up at the clock, saw we had time, and said this one was on him. I had another beer.

"The guy was an amateur," the stranger said. "If he'd had any sense, he wouldn't have tried anything on the old lady."

"Hell," I said, "How'd he know, when he pulled the gun on her, that she was going to haul off and conk him with a bottle? It was just one of life's little surprises."

"He should've sized her up before pulling the caper. If he'd taken his time, he could've seen she was the type that'd blow her top and start screaming, or throwing things or some such. Five minutes of analyzing her character and he would've seen he'd better go somewhere else."

"Maybe you're right," Sam said argumentatively, "but how would he go about analyzing her character in just the few minutes time he'd have? He couldn't hang around the store very long or it'd look suspicious and she'd be calling for the cops."

"You wouldn't need very long," the stranger told him. "You can size a person up in just a few minutes by the way they walk and talk and by their gestures—that sort of stuff."

I grinned. "Okay. Size me up. If you were analyzing my character, would you go ahead and stick me up or not?"

He smiled back. "Sure I would. You're the easy-going type. Even if you had much money on you, and you probably never have, you wouldn't think it was worth taking a chance on getting yourself killed."

Sam grunted, "That sounds like Jerry, all right. How about me?"

The stranger flicked his hand almost disdainfully. "You're easy. I'd take a chance on you right off the bat. You'd be scared stiff at the first sight of a gun."

The old boy was irritated. "Where'd you get that idea?"

"It's the little things I watch," the stranger said. "Like the fact that you crook your little finger when you pick up your glass. A thing like that tells a lot."

Sam had been just about ready to take a sip from his vermouth. Sure enough, the little finger was crooked. It looked sort of ridiculous on the part of a big burly guy like Sam.

Sam snorted.

The easy-going smile left the stranger's face. He put his right hand in a pocket and brought out a snub-nosed revolver.

His voice was chilly now. "Let's try the experiment out," he said. "This is it. Fork it over, gents."

I said, "I'll be damned," and got my hands up in a hurry. "Take it easy, buddy—sometimes those things go off," I told him nervously.

He smiled a little, contemptuous smile at me and waggled the gun at Sam. "You too, big boy," he snapped. "Put 'em up."

Sam stood there, his two beefy red hands on the bar, and stared blankly at the gunman for a long moment. Finally he gave a deep sigh, and began to make his way around the end of the bar.

"Hold it," the stranger said sharply. "Get back to that cash register and—"

"In your hat," Sam said, coming toward him.

"Take it easy, Sam!" I warned him shrilly, expecting to hear the gun's roar at any split second.

But he kept advancing.

A muscle was twitching in the gunman's neck; his finger began to tighten on the trigger. "You're asking for it," he snarled.

"And over your ears," Sam said, and reached out suddenly and hit the guy sharply across the wrist with the edge of his hand. The gun dropped to the floor, and Sam stooped quickly and scooped it up with his left hand.

"Call a cop, Jerry," Sam told me softly, keeping the gunman covered. He made his way around the end of the bar again, and took his old place.

I went down to the other end of the room, where Sam has a pay phone booth, and shakily made the call.

By the time I came back I was boiling, I was so mad. "You conceited crackpot," I snapped at Sam. "Just because he said you'd be yellow in an emergency, you didn't have to show off like that."

The gunman had slumped back onto a stool, perspiration standing out heavily on his forehead. He started to say something, but then shut up.

Sam shrugged. "There wasn't any danger of his shooting. Any guy with enough brains to figure out that character analysis stunt before pulling his stickups has too much sense to kill a man. He wouldn't want to risk a murder rap. As it is, he'll only get sent up for a year or so."

He picked up his vermouth glass and finished his drink. I noticed that he still crooked his little finger. He saw my eyes on it and grinned wryly. He held it out so that I could see a small white scar running along the knuckle.

"Piece of shell fragment creased it back during the first war. Haven't been able to bend that finger since," he said.

MINE HOST— THE GHOST

COSTA CAROUSSO

The heat had been unbearable all day. But now, a breath of air was stirring. Pedestrians looked hopefully at masses of clouds forming on the horizon. Presently, thunderheads swelled toward the zenith, cutting off the sun. Yellow squares of light began to show against the black walls of the office buildings. Muted rumblings sounded. The clouds merged overhead and sank downward.

"Like the first dawn of creation," I said to myself, looking through the window.

"Or the first dawn of doom!"

I wheeled sharply. I hadn't heard the man arrive at my side. I wasn't aware that I had spoken aloud. He was a gnarled little gnome of a man. His hair was white and his little eyes were black and bright.

"You'll forgive me," he said politely, "for presuming to read your mind?"

I nodded, still puzzled.

"It was not difficult," he said. "I have learned that a young writer invariably thinks in trite phrases at first. It occurred to me that you were comparing the scene before us to the popular conception of the first dawn of creation, so I hazarded an alternative."

"How did you know I was a writer?" I said, nettled.

A mischievous smile tugged at the old man's lips, but his voice was bland. "I asked our esteemed bartender," he said, nodding toward George. "Would you join me in a drink?"

At that moment the storm broke. Thunder crashed through the room. Rain streaked down the windows till it was impossible to distinguish anything outside. Pitiless lightning blasted the sky apart.

It would be hours before I'd want to go out, and besides, I felt that a writer could pick up something useful from one of these old timers. I agreed to join him and we sat down.

"I haven't seen a storm like this for eight or nine years," I said. "Since the summer lightning struck the old Hollingway mansion and killed the three Hollingway cousins."

My host sipped his Scotch-and-soda appreciatively. "Lightning didn't strike the Hollingway place," he said.

Now everyone knew that lightning had struck the Hollingway place and burned it to cinders along with the three cousins who were inside. So if this ancient little man believed in a different version, I wanted to hear it.

"What did happen?" I asked.

"It was set afire deliberately," the old man said. He stirred his drink carefully, then raised it to his lips. "By a ghost." He looked at me, obviously enjoying my impatience.

"Come now," I said. "Surely you don't expect me to believe in ghosts."

"No," said the old man. "The point is—the Hollingways did."

My curiosity was itching, but at the same time I was detached enough to realize that the old man had a superb gift for story telling. "You should have been a writer," I said.

"I was," he answered. Thunder crashed outside. The old man smiled.

"Go on," I prompted. "The Hollingway house wasn't struck by lightning; it was set afire by a ghost. The Hollingways weren't killed accidentally; they were murdered."

"That," said the old man, "is something that you'll have to decide for yourself." He looked at his glass, which was empty, so I told George to bring the bottle. I sat back to listen to his story. He told it well—so well that I could see the rain glistening down the walls of the Hollingway mansion; see the headlights of Eric Hollingway's car as it wound up the half-mile bluestone driveway bordered by dark trees. . . .

Eric slammed shut the door of his car and turned up the collar of his coat. Flashes of lightning grotesquely illuminated the empty house. In another moment it was lost in the darkness and rain. Eric ran toward the steps, cursed when he stumbled. Then his huge fist was turning the key, pushing the heavy door inward. He snapped on the switch and brilliance flooded the room. He went from one room to another, turning on the lights, looking into the closets, searching beneath the beds and behind the furniture. Finally he went downstairs and paced the floor.

Half an hour later he ground out his fourth cigarette and looked at the telegram again. COME TO THE COUNTRY HOUSE TONIGHT, it said.

A noise sounded on the porch. A moment later his cousin Jim was standing before the door. Water streamed from his clothes and made a puddle at his feet.

"Well, here I am," he said. "What do you want?"

"What do I want! What do you want?"

"Nothing," said Jim. "I got your telegram and I came." He held the pale yellow slip to Eric.

Eric read it. It was the same as his. "What made you think I sent it?"

"Well," said Jim. "The whole thing was your idea in the first place, so I figured—"

"My idea!" Eric roared. "Cut that stuff. All of us were in on it. And you know it!"

"Of course we were," said Jim. "Don't get excited. If you didn't send that telegram, Perce must have."

"Yeah," said Eric. "But why doesn't he show up?"

Jim lit a cigarette and tossed the match into the fireplace. "I wish I had a drink," he said.

"Take it easy on the drinks," growled Eric. "Someday you'll shoot your mouth off and then we'll all be sunk."

Jim's lips tightened, then he opened them to speak. "Some day—" he began. The door creaked open and Perce stood dripping on the threshold.

"What happened?" he asked. "What's up?"

"Didn't you send those wires?" Jim asked.

"No," said Perce. "I thought that—" He took a telegram from his pocket and handed it to Jim. "I got one, too. I didn't—"

"I'll be damned!" snarled Eric.

Thunder crashed against the house. Lightning stabbed at the windows. The rain beat an incessant tattoo upon the roof. The room was silent save for the breathing of the three men.

"Maybe Kelston sent them," suggested Jim. "Maybe he wanted to talk to us about the will."

"Why wouldn't he sign his name, then?" asked Perce. "And why come all the way out here?"

"You've got me," said Eric. "Do you think that shyster suspects anything?"

"For God's sake, watch what you're saying," warned Perce.

"It's all right," said Eric. "I searched this place from top to bottom when I came in. Nobody's here."

"I don't like it," said Perce. "I'm getting out." He moved toward the door.

"Wait a minute," said Eric. "Kelston will probably show up."

Perce's hand was on the doornob. He turned, his face colorless. "It's locked!"

Jim and Eric sprang forward. Eric seized the knob, turned it one way and then the other. Then he grasped it with both hands and heaved with all his body. The door didn't budge.

Jim sprang to the window and threw it open. Wind lashed the curtains, rain splashed on the floor. Jim said, "Good Lord!"

"What!" shouted Perce.

"Bars," said Jim. "Inch-thick bars."

"The devil you say!" bellowed Eric, shouldering Perce aside and leaping forward. Fear was in his face when he turned.

"You and Perce take the upstairs rooms," ordered Eric. "I'll take the downstairs and the cellar."

"Let's all go together," said Jim.

"What's the matter," sneered Eric. "Scared?"

"No, I'm not scared," said Jim. "And lay off me. Someday you're going to push things too far and I'll—"

"You'll what?" asked Eric.

"Cut it out, you two," said Perce.

"What I meant," said Jim, "was that we all ought to search this place carefully. Maybe someone planted a dictaphone. This looks like a sly police trick."

"Oh," said Eric. "Yeah, that sounds like a good idea. I never thought of that."

"No brains and all brawn," said Jim.

"Shut up, you guys," said Perce. "And be careful what you say. I don't like this."

"Come on," said Eric, moving toward the cellar stairs.

The storm receded with rumbling growls, then awakened with even greater fury. Branches lashed the house; lightning threw eerie shadows against the windows.

"Well," said Eric. "There's no dictaphone."

"There's no way out, either," said Jim.

"The phone!" said Perce. "Why didn't I think of the phone!" He leaped forward and snatched up the receiver. He jiggled the hook. The other two men pressed in close. Finally Perce let the phone slip from his fingers. "Dead," he whispered.

"All right, Eric," said Jim. "What's next?" His voice was hard.

Eric looked up, bewilderment on his heavy face. "I don't get it," he said. "What do you mean?"

"I mean how much of our cut do you want—to let us out of here alive? Or is Perce with you on this?"

The bewilderment on Eric's face slowly changed to understanding; the understanding exploded into rage. "Why, you dirty little—" he bellowed, lunging forward. "I'll break every—"

Jim ducked beneath Eric's flailing arms and grabbed his legs. They crashed to the floor together. "Hold him, Perce!" he shouted. "Hold him before he gets his gun!"

Perce waited uncertainly for a moment. Then he dived in. One of Eric's thrashing heels caught him in the chest and sent him reeling across the room. Eric's hands closed on Jim's throat.

"Perce! He'll kill us both! Quick!"

Perce got unsteadily to his feet, then jumped at Eric's back. He got a strangle hold and twisted. Jim struggled free and pinned back Eric's arms. Perce kept squeezing till Eric began to choke. "No!" he coughed. "Stop. Haven't any gun!"

Perce stopped choking him and searched him while Jim held down his arms. Finally he stood up. "Let him go," he said. "He hasn't got a gun."

"Well, don't try anything like that again," warned Jim. "Perce and I can finish you."

Eric struggled to his feet and sank into a chair. His lips were bleeding and he wiped away the blood with the back of his hand. "You damn fools," he said. "I didn't have anything to do with this."

Neither of the two men met his eyes. He looked at Perce and then at Jim. "Don't you believe me?"

"I don't believe anyone when that much money is concerned,"

said Jim. "You were here first. How do we know you didn't fix up this place and send those telegrams?"

"And then lock the door from the outside?" jeered Eric. "Don't be ridiculous. You're supposed to be the brilliant Hollingway."

Jim was silent for a moment, then he turned to Perce. "You were the last one in here," he said. "You made this trap. You—"

Perce stepped back slowly. He watched Jim advance toward him and looked to see what Eric would do. "No! I swear I didn't. Eric, you've got to believe me!"

Thunder crashed against the house. The lights went out. Silence held the room.

"I suppose he cut the wires, too," said Eric. "Don't be so damn suspicious, Jim. We're not trying to double-cross you."

"The lights don't prove a thing," said Jim. "The storm did that. I'm not trusting anybody."

"Cut the jaw," said Eric, "and let's see if we can find some candles."

Hurried footsteps sounded on the rug. Then Perce screamed "Look! Lights! Anderson's place has lights, and it's on the same line!"

"Someone cut the wires," whispered Eric. "Someone . . ."

Perce slammed himself against the door and pounded on it with his fists. "Let me out of here," he screamed. "Let me out of here! Let me out!"

"That's no good," said Eric. "I'm going to see if I can find a candle." He stumbled against a chair and cursed. He lit a match and walked into the hall. Perce fell into a chair and covered his face with his hands. Jim stood nearby, motionless.

"Find anything?" Perce asked, when Eric came back.

"I got a candle," Eric said. "But it won't last very long." He came in holding the candle in front of him. The spasmodic light deepened the lines on his drawn face, outlined his eyes with cavernous shadows. His face was like a mask of fear. He set the candle on the mantle and then drew back.

The three men were seated far apart. They didn't speak. Their eyes darted from the flickering flame to one another. Their hands were clenched. A wrist watch inexorably counted the tickings of eternity. Eric was the first to move. "Got to see a man," he said, rising to his feet. His words were strained.

Jim watched him out of the corner of his eyes and glared back at Perce. The sound of Eric's feet faded into silence. The silence was shattered by a gasping scream. Eric came pounding back.

"I saw him," he said. There was no expression in his words. "I saw him."

"Saw whom?" snarled Jim.

"I saw Uncle John!"

"No!" screamed Perce. "No!"

"I saw him. Upstairs in the hall. He was standing there looking at me."

"Don't be a damn fool," said Jim. "He's dead."

"I know," said Eric. "This thing was dead, too. It didn't move. It didn't speak. It just stood there."

"It's your imagination," said Jim.

Eric shook his head. "No. I saw it."

"I'm going to see it," said Jim. He began moving toward the stairs. Then he stopped and turned. "Come on, Perce," he said. "We'll both go. Just to prove Eric's wrong."

"I don't want to see it," said Perce. But he rose slowly to his feet and went to Jim. "I don't want to see it. I want to prove to myself that there's nothing there." They walked off together.

Eric covered his face with his hands. His hands tightened convulsively when he heard Perce scream. He got up and met Perce and Jim in the hall.

"You saw it," said Eric.

"Yes," said Jim. "It just stood there."

"But he's dead," said Perce. "He's dead."

"I know," said Eric. "I gave him enough to kill ten like him."

"I saw him in his coffin," said Jim. "I saw him in his grave. I saw him buried under six feet of ground, and the dead don't walk again."

The candle guttered and went out.

Finally the rain stopped and there was no sound at all. Then there was the soft rustling of cloth and the sound of feet moving across the carpet; a gasp and a groan.

"He's dead," said Jim. "Eric's dead."

"You killed him," said Perce.

"Yes," said Jim. "Because he killed Uncle John. Now maybe the thing is satisfied. Now maybe it will go away."

"Light a match," said Perce.

Jim lit a match. It showed Eric sitting in his chair, leaning slightly forward. The light of the match reflected from the knife blade in his throat, just below the ear. Then the match went out.

"You killed him because you want all the money," said Perce. "You're going to kill me, too."

"No," said Jim. "I left the knife there. I killed him so the thing would go away. I don't want the money."

"Light another match," said Perce.

Jim lit another match. His face was haggard and his eyes were wild. His features wore the slackness of an idiot's.

Perce lifted the gun and aimed between Jim's eyes. Then he pulled the trigger.

"You wanted all the money," he said. "You were going to kill me, too. Now I'll get all the money." The echoes quieted and died.

Footsteps sounded upstairs in the hall. Then on the stairs.

"It's coming down," said Perce. "It's coming down to get me." He laughed. "It won't get me," he said. He lifted the gun to his head. "It won't get me." The gun roared. . . .

I poured a stiff drink from the bottle and drank it straight. The old man was looking at me, waiting for me to speak.

"That makes a hell of a good story," I said, searching in my mind for what name he used to write under.

"But of course you refuse to accept it as the truth," he said.

"Naturally, I don't believe in ghosts," I shrugged.

The old man smiled tolerantly. "At first Eric and Jim and Perce didn't believe in them either. But when tension developed in their minds, they finally did—and went mad."

"But you said this Uncle John was dead," I protested.

"No," he corrected me. "*They* said he was dead. What actually happened was that the heart medicine he was taking acted as an antidote to the poison they gave him, and he only became very sick.

"With all his money it was easy to have a sculptor make a wax effigy of him to be buried. The rest was relatively simple."

It still made a good story, but all I had seen in the Hollingway tragedy was the bare fact that a house had been struck by lightning and burned to the ground, with three unfortunate men trapped inside.

"What about the fire?" I asked. "You forgot to explain about the fire."

"Oh, that! Well, the whole mess was pretty sickening, and if the newspapers got hold of it, it would have been nauseating, so I punctured the oil tank down in the cellar and attached a long fuse to it."

"*You!*"

"I? Did I say *I*? Pardon me. A slip of the tongue. I meant Uncle

John." He smiled at me benevolently. "Fancy me doing a thing like that."

But suddenly it struck me that there was only one writer whose mind was capable of thinking up a situation like that. His name had been J. J. Drake. And J. J. Drake was the pen-name used by a mild little man called John Hollingway.

MOTIVE

AUGUST DERLETH

Eliphas Jackson could have been summed up in a few words: middle-aged, timid, going bald. He wore glasses over mild, watery blue eyes, and had blond hair around his bald spot. He dressed neatly, whether following his profession or not, and was surprised when people took an interest in him. But he appreciated it very much. He did not have much companionship and was always somewhat lonely.

So when the elderly traveler who had come to the hotel only a little while after he himself had come invited him to his room for a little talk, he accepted readily enough and eyed his acquaintance anew: a bluff, red-faced man, with twinkling eyes and graying moustache. Probably in clothes. There was nothing distinctive about him.

Jackson was talked at effusively, waved expansively to a chair, and had the slightly disagreeable sensation of having a newspaper fanned under his nose.

"Murch is the name, sir," his red-faced host said jovially. "Just plain Murch. It's not much of a name, but it'll do."

Jackson smiled. "It's not as common as Jackson," he said almost apologetically.

"Perhaps not," conceded Murch. "But I don't know that I'd a lot rather have a common name like that. It's a good sound name, whatever you say."

He bustled about and got out a siphon and some glasses, explaining that he had been experimenting with some Sauterne—"Gassing it a bit," he said, but it tasted good enough. Of course, if Jackson were a connoisseur, or something like that, he wouldn't care for it.

Jackson tried it gingerly and admitted that it was good.

Murch settled himself into a chair which fitted him too snugly and waved the paper at him again. "Been reading about these queer murders," he said. "Awful stuff, I call it."

"You mean those people dying in the small towns around here?" Jackson asked.

Murch nodded. "One in almost every town so far, right up the line to here. Seems to be working along this route, and it wouldn't surprise me if one hit this town, too—but I hope not until I get out of it." He giggled.

Jackson reflected briefly that he had a vaguely disgusting giggle.

Murch leaned confidentially over the table. "You know, Jackson, I've got a theory—a great theory about those crimes," he said. "I'll bet I could tell you just how they were done."

Jackson looked polite. "Could you?" he asked.

"I could," affirmed Murch gravely.

"The papers said the police didn't have any clues," mused Jackson thoughtfully.

"Well, it's true they hadn't much to go on. Take that first murder now—an old woman. Like a bolt out of the blue, it was. She'd no relatives, no money to leave, nothing; there was absolutely no motive. Nothing to be gained by her death. I can well imagine the police were baffled on that one especially. It was the lack of motive —that always gets them, you know. They go looking for it right off, and when they can't find it, most of the time they're lost right at the start. At that, I don't know that the second didn't puzzle them still more. Young man that time, remember? They couldn't find a shred of motive that time, either. And no connection among the six who died."

"Have they found a motive in any?" inquired Jackson.

"Not one," replied Murch proudly, and then leaned forward again to add, "But I have. I've found a motive for every one of them!"

Jackson looked at him a little more closely. The twinkling quality seemed to have left Murch's eyes, and a light seemed to glow from behind them. There was something hard and glittering about them. It was uncanny and disturbing. A breath of uneasiness fanned up in Jackson.

"Really," he said.

"I have," repeated Murch.

Jackson waited.

"Going around the way I do," continued Murch, "I found out that every town where a murder was committed was visited by a medicine show. A one-man show on a one-night stand. The fellow sold some kind of laxative pills by the box; cheap, too. Well, sir, in one of those boxes in each town, that man put a poison pill. Cyanide— that's what the autopsies showed on these bodies, remember? He didn't know who'd get that poison pill; but he didn't care. He'd be safely out of there before anything happened, and in that way, no one would ever suspect, because he never sold more than one poison pill in a town."

"But there's no sense to it," protested Jackson.

"Of course not," agreed Murch instantly. "But that's the way it was done. I'll bet on it. I'll bet the police have been making inquiries and traced some of the cyanide. Fellow wasn't shrewd enough, but they'll find him, they'll find him, all right, you mark my words!"

"They will?"

"They most certainly will. It's only a matter of time. But I'll bet they won't guess at the motive until the last, and then if they'll look up that fellow's ancestry, they'll find proof and trace of it." He leaned over and tapped Jackson's knee, and his voice dropped to a harsh whisper. "You see, the fellow's a murderer of the worst kind, and it's very likely he doesn't know it."

Jackson was fascinated against his will. He stared at the remarkable hardness of his companion's eyes until he felt his mouth go dry. Unaccountably, he felt himself loathing this sinister fellow-traveler, he felt a revulsion rising within him, and he wanted desperately to escape. But he did not move. He licked his lips tentatively and asked in a whisper as low as Murch's,

"How so? How so he doesn't know it?"

"It's the motive," said Murch triumphantly. "That's the secret!"

"And what—what is the motive?"

"You'd never guess, not in a hundred years," said Murch. "I'll tell you how I've got it figured out. The man's a homicidal maniac, that's what. Every little while he has to kill someone. It's a strange kind of mania—he might know what's the matter with him, and he might not. Ten to one, he doesn't. It works like this—Every little while a sort of spell comes over him; he becomes someone else for that time and he has to kill someone. Do you understand that, Jackson? He simply must kill someone, or he must put into operation a plan to kill someone. Most of the time when they're like that, they get violent; they take up a knife or pistol and go after the first person they see. But sometimes it's different; sometimes they work secretly. Like this man now, this fellow who's done all these murders and got away with it. Take him, now—can you guess what happens to him?"

Jackson shook his head mutely, his eyes almost afraid to leave Murch's face. He saw that his companion was perspiring.

"Well, he gets a spell like that, and he likely gets it when he's making his pills. He makes them all, you know, and when he gets such a spell, he's a dangerous maniac, the worst kind. And he makes one pill up with deadly poison in it, only one; and he puts it in one of the boxes to be sold in the next town—or if he makes them up for several towns, he puts one poison pill in each batch. If he expects to sell twenty boxes, he puts a pill in one of them. That's the way he does it. Once he's done that, he'll be satisfied; he doesn't know who'll get that pill, but he knows that somebody will die by his hand. And very likely, once it's done, he forgets all about it. He comes out of his spell, and he never knows what happened. He sees his pills done, but he doesn't know that somewhere among those boxes are scattered deadly poison pills. He's had his spell, you see, and like as not he's imagined all the suffering and agony those poor people are going through before they die. But after he's done the pills, he forgets; he's as sane as you and I."

The theory held Jackson almost as strongly as Murch's hypnotic eyes. His uneasiness had congealed into terror, but no sign of it passed his lips.

"If he doesn't know it," he began, "how can they prove it to him? What can they do to him?"

"They'll lock him up in an asylum—keep him in solitary, most likely, dark all the time. It'll be hell on him, being sane most of the time, sane as you and I, but it's the only thing to do."

Jackson caught what seemed to him a rising light in Murch's eyes; Murch was looking at him so strangely that his uneasiness and terror thrust sharply up within him, and he got up suddenly, mumbling that he had to go to his own room, that he had some letters to answer and had to get at them.

Murch waved the paper after him jovially enough but made no move to stop him.

Once in his own room again, Jackson shuddered. He sat down as if still under the influence of Murch's baleful eyes, and picked up a letter he had already read once that day—from the board chairman of the next village.

Dear Mr. Jackson:
We enclose herewith our permit as per your payment of the seventeenth for a one-night stand of your medicine show in our village on the night of the twenty-third . . .

What was it Murch had said? *Homicidal mania.*

He got up quite calmly and drew himself a glass of water. Then he brought his stack of pills to the table and began methodically going over them, going over the small boxes, one by one.

In the seventh one he found a pill somewhat different from the others—a little darker where the sugar coating had begun to crack and peel slightly.

He looked at it, took it out, and held it in his palm.

Then he pushed the box away, got up and pulled over the glass of water.

He took the pill and sat down to wait.

MURDER
IN BRONZE

HERBERT L. MCNARY

Mr. Brickley walked into the office of Mr. Jennings. If there is any foundation for the adage that successful business partnerships are built upon contrast the firm of Jennings & Brickley, dental supplies, should be flourishing, even in these times. Oliver Jennings knew the dental supply business from the roots up and Bert Brickley knew how to get customers.

Mr. Brickley, short and rotund, and garbed in an eye-catching gray mixture, entered by the corridor door. The partners maintained separate offices in the same suite and there was a connecting door between the two offices, but Brickley had misplaced the key.

He undoubtedly could find it if he put his mind to the task, but such minor details annoyed him.

Jennings, crossing towards the filing cabinets with papers in hand, looked up over his spectacles. He, too, was short, about the same height as Brickley, but not nearly so plump. He was mild, meek, a typical business drudge with pale eyes and thinning gray hair.

"Did you want something Bert?"

"No, nothing particular," answered the partner, toying with a cigar, his small dark eyes squinting through the smoke, "just having my office floor oiled."

The senior partner frowned. "Have that done every week, don't you?"

"Well, I got stuck with that oil. Might as well use it. Besides I like to have my place looking—impressive."

Jennings surveyed the unpretentious furnishings of his office defensively. Despite the fact the funds came from the same account the two offices contrasted just as severely as the two partners.

"Hmm, as long as it's serviceable, that's all that counts."

"Well, you know how it is. The people who come into my office —well, we have to make a show." It was an old argument, but the senior partner recognized the fundamental truth. Money had to be spent to make money, only Bert had extravagant habits he should curtail in times like these. Jennings tugged at one of the drawers in the tall wooden file case and grumbled in exasperation as it stuck. He almost pulled the case over before he yanked the drawer open.

"You ought to get a new one of those," suggested Brickley. "It's out of date—"

"Can't afford it," snapped Jennings testily. He inserted the papers in the file and turned around.

"And while on the subject, Bert, we've got to put a little more pressure on our accounts."

Brickley waved the expensive cigar. "Oh, we can't be too hard on the dentists. People owe them money and take their time paying. We've got to be indulgent."

"Still, we ought to be getting more than we have." Jennings went to the closet for his coat and hat. He lunched between twelve and one while his junior partner, who arrived later in the morning and presumably had a later breakfast, went to lunch from one to two.

"I met Dr. Wynant yesterday," continued Jennings, pulling on his coat carefully because of torn sleeve lining and not observing that his partner stiffened tensely. "I mentioned our account with him casually, and he said he felt certain he had settled with you."

"Well, you know Wynant," protested Brickley with a short laugh. "No head for business. He probably *thinks* he made payment. Not that he isn't good. I'll drop around and see him this afternoon."

"He is going up to Maine on a two weeks' hunting trip," said Jennings curtly. "That is what gets under my skin. If they can afford hunting trips they can afford to pay their bills."

"Right," agreed Brickley and seemed anxious to change the subject. He knew how to do so. He crossed to Jennings' desk and picked up a book.

"New one? And on Caesar, too."

Jennings frowned uneasily. "Why—it's a first edition. A real bargain."

"How much?" challenged the junior partner.

"Er—three hundred—but you don't understand."

"Sure I do. We all have our weaknesses. With me it's clothes and showy things. With you it's anything connected with Caesar."

"After all, it affords me enjoyment," said Jennings a bit tartly. "Are you coming?"

The senior partner locked the door behind them and stepped into the outer office. It was his custom to lock his door when leaving. Any phone calls would come through the switchboard and could be transferred to Brickley.

Bert Brickley went into his office, richly furnished in mahogany, and sat down to think, rolling his cigar thoughtfully in his mouth and occasionally doing some figuring on a pad.

When the senior partner returned from lunch, Bert Brickley departed immediately. He did not go directly to his favorite dining place but crossed to the Avenue where he liked to stroll leisurely as though very much a part of this atmosphere of luxury; smiling and bowing at the least provocation and gazing into the art shops with all the appearance of a connoisseur. But today he hurried rather than strolled; and he did little bowing and smiling. But he did, however, gaze in a shop window displaying antiques and pieces of art. If his memory served him right—yes, there it was!

The junior partner of Jennings & Brickley stepped inside and made a purchase.

Bert Brickley's phone buzzed. Jennings was on the other end of an inside call.

"Bert, come in here at once. There's—well, come in here."

Brickley went into the senior partner's office, passing through the outer office as usual to do so. He found, in addition to the perplexed senior partner, two deliverymen and a large crate.

"Bert, do you know anything about this? What did we ever order from Bentino's? That's an art shop."

"It's a little surprise from me," smiled the junior partner, rubbing spatulate fingers. "A real bargain I knew you would appreciate. Open it, boys. I'll need your help."

The two deliverymen went to work on the box and soon had the top removed. Carefully they separated the packing and then with difficulty lifted out a heavy bronze bust.

"Julius Caesar—almost in the flesh," exclaimed the junior partner, spreading his hands. Jennings said nothing immediately. His sagging lips denoted mingled emotions. Of course the younger partner could not distinguish the enormous gulf between rare editions and manuscripts on Caesar and this grotesque monstrosity in bronze; yet, Bert meant well, and Jennings was too gentle to offend.

"It's—it's very thoughtful of you, Bert. You shouldn't have spent your money this way. Er—I was wondering what I would do with it—"

"Put it right up here," suggested the junior partner, indicating the filing cabinet. "Come on, boys, give me a lift."

The senior partner was about to protest. To have that with him all day long forecasted torture; but on second thought he realized that if he did not keep it here he would have to bring it home and keep it exposed where Bert could see it any time he dropped in. No, better to have it here where he would be engrossed in work and able to forget about it; and with it reposing on the file cabinet his back would be to it most of the day. Even when he went to the cabinet he would have to look up almost deliberately to see it. After a time he could devise some excuse to get rid of the gift.

About a week following this exposition of generosity on the part of Bert Brickley, the junior partner returned from luncheon to find the office force in a state of confusion.

"Oh, Mr. Brickley—Mr. Brickley," moaned Miss Stevens, the old maidish secretary, "something dreadful has happened. There has been an accident."

"An accident?"

"Yes. Mr. Jennings. He's been killed. I phoned the police. Perhaps I shouldn't. Maybe I should have waited."

"You did exactly right, Miss Stevens. We'll let them take entire charge when they come."

"They are here."

"Here?" exclaimed Brickley. "Er—they must have been very prompt."

The junior partner stepped into Jennings' office. A tall, somewhat gawky young chap in blue uniform stood at the door; probably the policeman picked up at the corner. At Jennings' desk sat a middle-aged man in drab civilians. His round face denoted curiosity rather than shrewdness as Brickley entered.

"I'm the junior partner," announced Brickley. "Miss Stevens told me there had been an accident. Is it—serious?"

"Yeah, pretty serious," said the headquarters man. "He's dead. That ain't official, of course. I have to wait for the coroner. But if he ain't dead I never saw a stiff."

Brickley peered past the desk. There on the floor near the filing cabinet lay the huddled form of the senior partner with matted blood in the thin gray hair. Near by on the floor reposed the up-ended bronze statue of Caesar.

"When did it happen?" asked Brickley.

"About quarter past one, if the dame outside phoned immediately like she said. She heard the crash and rushed in."

"I was to lunch. My office is next to this—"

"Yeah. I was there. Sit down, Mr. Brickley. I want some facts. We gotta turn in a report."

The junior partner took the other chair near the desk, careful to turn his back to the gruesome sight. There wasn't much to tell about Jennings. His age. Lived alone. No near relatives—

The headquarters man's feet went up on the desk as he tilted back in his chair. He saw Brickley frown.

"Seems natural to put my feet on the desk. It helps to think. Blood rushes to the head, or maybe it's the brains. Try it." The gray, level eyes seemed suddenly impelling. Brickley felt confused. "Try it," repeated the detective, "an' see if I ain't right."

Almost as if hypnotized Brickley obeyed. His feet lifted to desk in a fashion similar to the detective's. If Jennings could see this lack of dignity. . . .

"Think any better?"

"I—I can't say that I do."

"Well, just think back over the last couple of hours. Say between 12 and 1. Maybe I can help. Jennings, here, goes to lunch. You come in that door. Yeah, I know it ain't used much. You lost the key. But it was used recent. There's fingerprints. Too blurred to be read, but damp enough to show they were placed there recent. Fat fingers have a way of sweating.

"Then the last page of this report on the desk is missing. Jennings comes in; wonders where it can be, and finally goes to the file. Maybe he's mad. He don't look up and notice that the statue is balanced on the edge, havin' been shifted that way while he was out to lunch. He jerks open the drawer. It sticks anyway. I tried it. Down comes—who is it? Napoleon? Well, it don't matter. He did a complete job."

Brickley had been staring open-mouthed. Now he recovered his composure.

"Why—why, this is preposterous! Just because there are a few fingerprints on the door—"

"Fingerprints—hell! *Heel prints!* You're kind of short, Brickley, and you had to stand on a chair to fix that statue. You left your mark. Yours is the only office that was oiled recently; and besides these heels that you're so kindly showin' me are peculiar. Must be expensive. Well, there's an impression of one of them on the chair. No wonder I asked Miss Stevens if you bought that statue.

"Don't know the motive; but I've a hunch that if I impound the books I'll find it. I'm impoundin' them shoes, too. You'll have to come along in your stocking feet."

But just then Brickley looked as if he would have to go on a stretcher.

MUSHROOMS

CHET WILLIAMSON

When 3-Ball and X-Too got on the train, they walked immediately to the last car, X-Too in the lead. 3-Ball was glad, since it gave him a chance to watch X-Too move, and X-Too moved about as def as any brother he'd ever seen, even with a piece on his hip. The piece made X-Too move even cleaner than usual, thrusting out his hip to the left as if to make up for the uneven balance the pistol caused.

They didn't pass any cops on the way, and there was nobody in the last car except a tall and stringy blind kid with shades and one of those long white canes with the red tip. He was sitting near the center of the car, his head back, blind eyes looking up. Looked a little like Stevie Wonder, 3-Ball thought, wondering if the blind brother could be a musician.

"Think he's a musician?" he asked X-Too.

X-Too gave him The Look. "Whatta fuck you talkin'?" he said.

"Blind homeboy. Look like Stevie Wonder."

"Well, I look like fuckin' Ice Cube, only badder, and I don't rap. Now stop talkin' shit."

They sat down at the very back of the car, which ran across a section of dead track, throwing the train into total darkness and stopping the noisy fans for five seconds. "Wonder if that home know when that happens," said 3-Ball when the lights and fans came on again.

"What?"

"When it gets dark in here."

"How he know? Homeboy's blind."

"Well, y'know, sometimes they can tell between light 'n dark."

X-Too didn't say anything, just kept looking at the door at the front of the car. Finally he spoke. "We ice that motherfucker soon's he come in. Don't give him no chance to grab his own piece."

"Yeah. Smoke 'im in the fuckin' feet."

"Not the feet *first*, asshole. Fuckin' *head* first, or chest. *Then* his feet." X-Too nodded. "Right in his goddam Air Jordans, home. Nail his feet to the cross with bullets."

Lord Jake-Ay was the man they were about to kill. Jake-Ay had been the one who had shot Luther JD dead, then shit in his suede Fila hightops and jammed them back on Luther JD's feet, leaving him lying in an alley with shoes full of crap. On top of that, Jake-Ay had pissed on Luther JD's colors. It had been stupid of Jake-Ay, but everybody knew that Jake-Ay was stupid, even Jeango, the Blews' main man, but he kept Jake-Ay around anyway, since Jake-Ay would smoke anyone anytime.

Well, now X-Too and 3-Ball would smoke Jake-Ay.

They knew that he got on every night at the third stop past where they got on, always at the same time, after he got done pushing rock in the Van Norris Street arcade, got on and headed uptown to chill with Jeango. 3-Ball thought they'd grab his take, but maybe not. It would be some def gesture, leaving the money on him, just banging his feet until they were bloody stumps of dirty white leather and muscle and bone. The Blews would get the message all right. All the boys in the hood would know it was The Chillin Crew. And no shit and no piss. That kind of jive was for animals like Jake-Ay.

David heard the voices at the end of the car. Two young black men. They spoke seldom, and although they made no attempt to talk quietly, the sound of the train prevented his picking out more than the occasional word.

He felt the train begin to stop, and knew they must be just below the theatre district, although he could not see the walls of the tunnel pass by more slowly until the individual bricks and the name of the station were discernible. When he felt the train stop and heard the doors slide open, he started to loudly whistle, "Stop in the Name of Love."

"What the motherfuck . . ." he heard one of the young men say, but kept whistling, thinking about Nancy and how hard it was going to be for her. He had been blind from birth, but to learn what it was like when you were in your twenties—damn, that was tough.

He kept whistling, heard the door at the front of the car rasp open, heard the scrape of a cane on the floor, heard her call his name, tentatively, and with no little fear. "David?"

"Here, Nancy," he said. "Fifth seat back on the right."

The cane stuttered along, and he felt the vibration as she grasped the edge of each seat, counting. "That's right, here," he said when he heard her beside him.

Just as she sat, the train lurched and started, as she fell against him. He felt something strike his thigh and clatter to the floor. Unerringly he leaned forward and skimmed his fingers just above the linoleum, immediately contacting her sunglasses. As he lifted them, he could feel that they were the type with side panels, allowing no one to peer in. He took her hand and placed the left stem into it.

"Thanks," she said.

"Get down okay from your apartment?"

"Yeah. But God, it was rough. Getting down the street to the station was scary, but once I was down here, finding the right platform . . ." She sighed with a shudder. "I must have asked half a dozen people. I feel so much at the mercy of just anybody."

"You'll get over it," he told her. "It's rough at the start."

"I don't know how it could get any rougher," she said.

"Fuck, man," X-Too said.

"What?"

"Thought that blind fuck be off by now. 'Stead he meet some bitch."

"She fly, though," 3-Ball said, then added, " 'Cept she blind."

"Wouldn't stop me. Fly's fly. Head down, butt up, don't matter they see or not. Bust her butt."

"We do that?" asked 3-Ball, trying not to sound anxious.

"Shit, no. We bangin' Lord Jake-Ay tonight, not pussy. Wish they get off, though."

"Got another stop. Maybe they will."

"They don't, we tromp 'em down we have to. They just mushrooms."

"Yeah." 3-Ball chuckled. "Mushrooms." He thought it would be a pity, though, to burn a bitch that good looking. "You know, I seen her somewhere," he said after a moment's thought. "Ain't she that bitch inna commercial—for that, what the fuck, secretary school or somethin'?"

"What trash you talkin'? Blind secretaries?"

"Nah . . ."

"How them bitches type? Got Braille typewriters?"

"Nah, nah, they ain't *blind* secretaries."

"Then what that bitch be sellin' for 'em? Motherfucker, but you dumb."

"She fly enough to do commercials," 3-Ball insisted.

"Yeah, fuck, sellin' canes." X-Too glared at the couple. "They don't get off the next stop, they need more than canes. Fuckin' mushrooms. Smash 'em. Cold smoke 'em."

The lights and the fans went off, started again. The train began to slow.

"You hear those guys?" David asked Nancy.

"What guys?"

"Two homeboys in the back of the car. Left side."

"How do you know that?"

"Heard them talking. You'll hear when we stop now."

The train shivered to a halt. The doors slid open, but David heard no one get on or off. The men in the back were silent, and

David thought he sensed a tension in them. When the doors closed, he heard only a few words, one of which was "mushrooms."

Mushrooms. They were hardly talking about fungi, David thought, so it must have been innocent bystanders they were referring to. But what the hell, it was probably just gang talk, bravado. He had heard enough of it growing up in the projects. If the two had been planning to do anything to him and Nancy they probably would have done it by now.

David had little fear of the trains. He'd been robbed before, but he had always been cooperative and never been hurt. He always carried twenty dollars with him. It was no more than he could afford to lose, and just enough to satisfy a mugger.

"I hear them now," Nancy whispered.

David heard them too. Their voices were pitched lower now, and from their tone he knew he had been right about the tension he had sensed. But he had heard it all before, and if he had left a subway car every time he heard those tight, choppy tones, he would have had to cab everywhere. Maybe they were on their way to a drug deal, or, hell, maybe just a date. People could get edgy about a lot of little things.

"I hear them," Nancy repeated, "but I can't tell exactly where they are. How do you know?"

"Same way I knew where to get your sunglasses. Get a sense from the sound of things. I know—aurally—what a subway car's like, how the sounds bounce off the walls, how many rows, how many seats. And something close, like your glasses, well, that's easy. Most sighted people could do it, they put their mind to it. They drop things in the dark, they poke around for a while. But if they'd just listen to it hit, even something little, they could reach right for it."

"Um. That's neat. I really appreciate you helping me like this, David."

"No problem." David smiled, and hoped she could sense it. He had helped a lot of people like Nancy who came to the Blind Association. He always enjoyed it, showing people the ropes, fascinating them with his abilities and teaching them to do the same kind of thing. He just hoped it would do her some good.

The train jerked, and began to move.

"Shoulda told 'em to get off, maybe," said 3-Ball.

X-Too frowned even deeper than before. "Hell, we make 'em get off, they's a cop at the next stop. They don't get off in time, fuck 'em. Maybe we bust caps on 'em, they don't get smoked before."

3-Ball sat back and tried to relax, but it was hard. He heard that Lord Jake-Ay had an Uzi, though Luther JD had been smoked with a .38. X-Too had an Uzi too, but only used it to cap homes from cars. It was too big to carry around. What X-Too had tonight was a .44 magnum, its six and a half inch barrel jammed down his pants leg next to his dick. It was still a big gun, big enough to tear off Jake-Ay's feet once they smoked him dead.

'Course maybe they could shoot him so that he didn't die right away, but could feel his toes being blown off. 3-Ball grinned at the thought, and his hand went inside his bright red jacket, to his waistband and his own pistol, a sweet little Colt Cobra that X-Too called a pussy gun. That hadn't stopped 3-Ball from capping three Blews with it in as many months. And tonight, Jake-Ay.

Then he looked at the man and woman sitting halfway up the car, and thought he should tell them, tell them now before the train stopped, so that they could get off right away, before Jake-Ay got on and the shooting started. He knew mushrooms were mushrooms, but damn, there was no point in blind people being hurt. After all, they hadn't seen him or X-Too, couldn't make any I.D.

He stood up and started to walk toward them, but X-Too's shout stopped him. "3-Ball! Whatta fuck you doin'?"

"I'm just—"

"Get yo' ass back here. *Sid*down!"

3-Ball shambled the few feet back to where X-Too sat. When he looked behind him, he saw that the man and woman were cocking their heads as if listening to the rebuke. 3-Ball sat down and said softly, "Man, don't dis me in front of them people, okay?"

"Fuck, they can't see, they don't know I dissed you."

"Still, man . . . I just wanted to tell them to get off fast, the train stop. You know, 'fore Jake-Ay get on."

"Well, that was dumbfuck. What you care? They start walkin' off, Jake-Ay use 'em for cover comin' in, now that's fuckin' brighta you. Just leave 'em where they sittin'." X-Too looked out the window at the dark rushing past. " 'Sides, we gotta cap 'em anyway."

"What? Why?"

"They heard your name. I call it."

3-Ball could only see X-Too's reflection in the dirty glass, but thought that the dark line of X-Too's mouth was smiling. Maybe X-Too called his name on purpose. Sometimes 3-Ball thought that X-Too just liked smoking people, it didn't matter who. Yeah, maybe he did it on purpose.

"Damn," 3-Ball said. "Thassa shame, have to waste a fly piece of pussy like that."

"Accidents happen," said X-Too, still looking out the window.

When the train started to slow, X-Too and 3-Ball didn't wait until it stopped to take out their pistols. X-Too slid his .44 from his pants slow, a smooth smile on his face, like he was slipping out his dick to show a bitch. 3-Ball just tugged his Cobra from his waistband, and out it came, the grips getting wet fast from the sweat on his palms. "Watch the side," X-Too said. "I take the front."

Finally the train stopped, and the doors opened, but no one came in. After half a minute the doors closed again, the train started rolling. "Ain't comin' in the side," said 3-Ball.

"Shut up," X-Too said, his yellow glare fixed on the window of the door at the front of the car. "I see 'im."

Now 3-Ball saw him too, and they both slouched down so that only the tops of their capped heads were visible over the seat in front of them. Jake-Ay slammed a fist against the door, smashing it open, and came into their car. He was wearing a heavy leather coat and a Kangol whose brim hid his eyes.

X-Too's first shot took him by surprise, giving him no time to draw his gun. It hit him in the left shoulder, slamming him back against the edge of the door.

The sudden motion made 3-Ball's shot miss, and he saw blood and more splatter from the rip in Jake-Ay's leather coat. Then Jake-Ay dove into the corner, flipped back his coat with his good arm, and 3-Ball knew why Jake-Ay's coat was so huge. It had to be to keep an Uzi under it.

X-Too stood up to get off a second shot just as Jake-Ay let loose with the Uzi. It spat a trail of bullets across the width of the car, and 3-Ball ducked down behind the seat. The last thing he saw had been the blind man and woman dropping, and he wondered if they had been hit, then decided they hadn't, because he would have seen their heads pop.

Then he heard X-Too's .44 roar again, and X-Too's voice screaming, and the Uzi stop chattering, and when he looked he saw X-Too falling down on top of him like a big black tree, and he caught him, one Crew catching another, and felt a hot wetness in X-Too's belly, and heard X-Too moan, "Fuck, fuck, *mother*fuck," over and over like some dumb, simple rap.

3-Ball staggered to his feet, his Cobra up and pointing toward the end of the car, but Lord Jake-Ay's face beneath the Kangol looked like grape jelly, and he wasn't moving. The Uzi lay silent across his lap.

Now X-Too was saying something that 3-Ball couldn't make out, something that sounded like X-Too was trying to whistle through his teeth. 3-Ball leaned across, and X-Too grabbed him with the hand that wasn't holding his insides.

"Feet," X-Too said. "Feet . . . shoot his . . . motherfuck . . . feet. Use the Uzi . . ."

3-Ball nodded, climbed over X-Too, and ran down to the end of the car, his Cobra trained on Jake-Ay just in case. As he passed their seat, he saw the man and woman crouched behind the seat, probably wondering what the hell was happening.

He grabbed the Uzi, stuck the Cobra in his belt, stood over Jake-Ay's body, and fired into the dead man's feet. The bullets went through the floor of the car, and blood, ripped muscle, and bone shards spattered his own clean hightops, but he kept smoking until the Uzi was empty, and Jake-Ay's right foot was only pink pulp. There wasn't even that much left of the severed right foot, most of which had been smashed down through the floor onto the tracks.

Then 3-Ball put the empty weapon under his arm, and trotted back to X-Too. X-Too's face was ashy, and blood and something yellow was seeping through his fingers where he held them against his stomach.

"Now . . . cap the mushrooms," he rasped. ". . . then get me out . . ."

The train was starting to slow for the next stop, and 3-Ball knew he'd have to be quick. He set the Uzi next to X-Too, yanked the Cobra from his belt, walked up to the seat, and lifted the gun to fire.

But when he saw the girl's face, so pretty even though masked by sunglasses, he hesitated for just a moment, just long enough for the train to cross a rough switch and lurch savagely, so that he nearly fell, and the pistol slipped from his sweating, trembling hand. He saw it spinning down into the dark space between the man and the woman, and the image locked in his sight as they hit dead track, and all the lights in the car went out.

David had heard the shots, the running footsteps, then the same coming back, had heard them stop beside him and Nancy, had heard the gun hit the floor and slide across it.

He reached down, to the right, and grasped it with his right hand, took Nancy's hand with his left, pressed it against her palm, said, "Do it," praying that she would.

Then he felt the gun wrenched away from him, and heard her sunglasses clatter again on the floor. This time he didn't reach down to pick them up.

In three seconds, when the lights came back on, 3-Ball found himself unarmed, and the bitch with the gun in her hands, swinging it in his direction. Blind or not, he wasn't taking any chances. If he grabbed it, she'd sure as hell pull the trigger, and the way the damn piece was waggling in his direction, he didn't want to risk it. So he moved back slow, watching the black muzzle like a blind eye.

Then he heard a voice roar, *"Geddown!"* and he hit the floor, scuttling back toward X-Too, thinking that if he got X-Too's .44 he could smoke the bitch. But then he heard his gun go off in the bitch's hand, and saw X-Too's gun come thudding down into the aisle, along with X-Too's shoulders and head, part of which had been blown away by the crosscut bullets with which 3-Ball kept his Cobra loaded. Damn, he thought, not bad cappin' for a blind bitch.

3-Ball kept crawling toward the .44, now only eight feet away, moving as silently as he could so the bitch wouldn't hear him. He had halved the distance between himself and the gun, when he heard footsteps behind him. He turned, looked, and froze when he saw the woman standing, her face and the Cobra pointing in his direction. Her sunglasses had come off, and he could see her eyes now, blue and real pretty for blind eyes.

But it was all right. As long as she didn't hear him, he could grab that gun, take sweet, slow aim, and drop her like a sack of shit. He made himself look away from her, and kept crawling.

"Stop," she said. Her voice was real pretty, even shaking like it was, but he just smiled and kept crawling toward the gun, now nearly within his reach.

"Stop," she said again. *"Stop, red jacket!"*

Red jacket? The words froze him. How'd the bitch know what he had on, unless . . .

He turned and looked up at her, at her bright, blue, pretty eyes that he damn well *knew* he'd seen on the TV, staring at him, seeing him . . .

Yeah. Really *seeing* him.

"Stop," she said again, in the voice he'd heard telling all about that secretarial school.

But he couldn't stop. Not this close. And he turned and reached for the gun, grabbed it, brought it around, and then the bullet smashed into him and he went blind and deaf and dumb for always.

When the police got on at the next stop, they found three dead men and two people alive, one blind man, one sighted woman. One of the cops helped the woman pick up the things that had fallen out of her bag. The last thing he found was a script of a play entitled *Wait Until Dark*.

"Did you get enough of a lesson for tonight?" David asked Nancy when they finally left the hospital.

"Yes," she said, holding his arm in hers, guiding him down the strange steps, over the strange sidewalk, toward a corner where they could catch a cab.

"Sedative helping?" he asked her, thinking that he felt a lot calmer now. But he hadn't killed anyone.

"I think so. I'm still shaky. God, what a nightmare. A bad dream that got worse. Let's sit down. Just for a minute. My knees are still trembling." They sat on a bench, but she still held David's arm.

"I thought I was playing, you know?" said Nancy, almost to herself. "Like a game. Sensually slumming. But now I feel like being blind is . . . as much of a craft as acting. Even an art. How you ever found that gun, just grabbed it so fast . . . I never could have found it in the dark that way."

David turned toward her. "Mushrooms were meant for the dark," he said, and she gave a little laugh, then stopped, as if angry with herself for being flippant after what she had done.

"I found it," David said, then added slowly, softly, "But I couldn't have shot them."

"No. No. You couldn't see them."

Now he was even quieter. "I didn't say that."

She said nothing, then released his arm. When she spoke again, her words were chill and distant. "God. It must be hard to be blind."

"Maybe we should all be blind," David said. "It makes it a lot harder to kill people."

Nancy looked at him for a long time. Though he couldn't see her, he felt her eyes on him. By the time the cab drove by, it had grown colder, and no less dark.

New Blood

Gary Lovisi

He only had one more to go. One more and he'd be in the record books. One more and he'd be Number One! One more and he'd be the greatest of them all.

But it wasn't easy. With every killing the cops closed in on him more and more. The noose circled and constricted. His scent grew warmer and the chances of getting caught came closer. And he still had so much work to do. So much left unfinished.

It wasn't as easy as all the papers made it look either. No one seemed to understand. The victims, they all had to be just right. They couldn't be just anyone. That was the hard part and it was getting impossible now. There weren't that many accessible nurses in the city hospital system. Everyone was on the lookout. They were all so careful now, and the police were watching. Many of the best prospects didn't even go to work anymore. It made it hard to find out where they lived. Many others were guarded day and night. He knew. He checked. They were not accessible.

He preferred long-haired blondes. He knew he'd have to get at least one more of these to break his record. The papers said it all in big bold headlines:

NURSE KILLER STILL AT LARGE!
12 NURSES SLAIN IN 12 WEEKS!
TERROR GRIPS THE CITY!
WHO WILL BE NUMBER 13?

It was not easy. One nurse a week. Twelve long weeks. He'd wanted to give up weeks ago. Stop it all. Maybe turn himself in? He had actually hoped to get caught—but then the record stared him in the face—the newspapers and TV news played it up so big— he was *almost* the greatest mass serial murderer of nurses of all time —it was a challenge he could not ignore. But enough musings. He had work to do. Tonight was the last night of the thirteenth week. He'd have to do it tonight. It must be tonight. He had to stay on schedule.

* * *

He found another nurse. He had this one picked out since yesterday. He'd followed her. Watched her. Found her address where she lived on First Street in Park Slope. It was a short walk from where she worked at the Medical Center. The giant Methodist Hospital had plenty of nurses to choose from. But too many were Puerto Rican, a lot were black or from the islands, too many were Indian or Paki. All not right. Then there was this nice Irish blonde. And she was just right.

He'd noticed her. Her hair so long. So blonde. He'd never seen her before at the hospital. He figured she was new. She was. He liked that. Laughed about it in his twisted mind. New blood. He needed new blood.

He stalked her. She was a harmless young doe. He was the big bad wolf. He felt the sharpness of his knife, as he did so he touched himself, feeling himself grow. He anticipated the time. It would be very soon now.

This was just what he needed. A new girl. She was one of the prettiest he'd ever had this way. He was getting more excited minute by minute. Anticipating.

Moving fast he followed her down the dark and lonely streets.

She looked back now! Thought she saw someone. He ducked behind a stoop, she saw nothing and kept walking. He followed again.

She reached Number 127. He'd cased the apartment building yesterday. There were ten floors. Her place was on the seventh floor, apartment 7A. He moved in quickly and carefully behind her.

She startled, jumped.

"Oh, hi, I'm sorry," he said so cordially, with such a smile, "I know I've got the key here somewhere. . . ."

She turned, she looked at him. Sized him up. Wrong.

She held the door for him. Smiled.

She smiled! He liked that!

"You're the guy from 8C, Mr. . . . ?"

"Sure. Johnson. Can never find my key."

She held the door open for him to enter the building. They walked together to the elevator. They got in the elevator together.

She pressed 7.

He remembered just in time and pressed 8.

She relaxed.

He got that weird feeling. Kept quiet. Watched her without

letting her see him watching her. She turned and smiled. He smiled back.

The doors opened on the seventh floor. She got out and walked across the hall to her door. He watched her put her key into the door. Turn the knob. Saw the door open a crack and before she could open it farther—before the elevator doors closed and took him up to the eighth floor—he was upon her. Pushing her into the apartment. Throwing her down to the floor. Closing the door behind him. Locking it quickly. Tight shut. Like a vault. So she could never escape. Never!

Then he turned to the girl. Blonde. Long hair. Pretty. Very pretty. Laying on the floor at the other end of the room. Motionless. She was all his now.

She was laying there face down. She still didn't move. He came closer to her. The shadows of the dark room making his movements mysterious. Fearsome.

He touched himself in anticipation. Looking at her laying there. Helpless. Touching himself. Imagining.

He drew out the knife. It was long, sharp, the steel called out to him.

And then the lights went on! From out of nowhere a dozen armed men came at him. Knocking the knife from his hand. Grabbing him tightly. Holding him roughly with guns to his head while they frisked him for other weapons. He could not move.

The girl got up from the floor then. She took off the long blonde wig. Her real hair was short and black.

She held out the wig, "Here. Is this what you were after!"

"Liar!" he yelled at her, "You were so pretty. Instead you're just a disappointment like all the others."

"All those others you've killed?" she asked.

He didn't speak.

The girl held his knife so he could see it. "This is what you used to torture them. Such a terrible weapon. Why?"

He was quiet for a second, then smiled, said, "I know my rights. I want to see a lawyer. You can arrest me, but I don't have to tell you anything."

The girl smiled back, "Why darling, what makes you think we're the police?"

NIMBLE
FINGERS

W. RYERSON JOHNSON

This much I knew: that Laramie had succeeded in opening the safe at 114 Rue Lovais, Paris, and had disappeared with the famous Voutir ruby.

Beyond that I knew nothing. A newspaper dispatch from Paris had been my source of information. That had been three weeks before. And I had had no word from Laramie since the night he sailed from New York. Frankly, I was worried.

Laramie was a new man in our select little crowd. We knew his record, of course, before ever we admitted him to our circle. That he was a brilliant and successful worker could not be denied. But, though we had the greatest respect for his prowess, we did not entirely approve of his methods, which were erratic, daring, and sensational to an extreme. He was an inveterate gambler—a magnificent bluffer. He would take a dozen chances where there was but need of taking one.

Once for a whole day he accompanied a detective who was out on his trail. He went the entire rounds, reported with him at headquarters, and returned at night with the dick's identification papers as a souvenir. He was as elated over the feat as if he had lifted a string of pearls.

Harwell censured him severely, but what was the use? Laramie only smiled, shrugged his lithe shoulders; went out the next day with the same dick and returned that evening with a new .45 blue-steel automatic. It was his way. He liked the excitement, he said. After that we took his escapades more or less as a matter of course. He *was* devilish clever.

We had planned the Voutir affair together, Laramie and I, the day before he sailed for France. He was to secure the ruby, and get it past the customs officials in whatever manner seemed expedient. I was to be of use only in disposing of the stone for a straight cash payment, after Laramie should get it into my hands. The profits, as always, were to be divided according to our respective risks in the enterprise.

And now it was three weeks, according to the newspapers, since Laramie had secured the well-known ruby. He should have been in New York before this. I stood gazing moodily out of the window. As I have said before, I was worried. The police of two continents were looking for the man. And he was given to taking such useless daredevil chances. Then, too, Laramie was, in a way, untried. True, he had always played square before. But this was his first really big job with us, and—Well, it was three weeks now. He should have been here in two at the most.

A taxi pulled up to the curb in front of the house and stopped with a jerk. A man stepped out.

"Laramie!" I cried, joyously, impulsively, to myself.

But, even as my lips formed the word, some of my old fears returned. It was Laramie, all right. But not the dashing, care-free Laramie of a month before. His old swagger was gone. As he turned toward the house he walked bent over, like an old man. It was with undisguised apprehension that I met him at the door and grasped his hand.

"Right in here, Laramie," I said.

He sank into a chair, wearily, as I looked to him eagerly for some sign. He gave me no satisfaction. I was alarmed. The man looked bad, worn, clearly haggard. White skin, hollow cheeks, dark circles under the eyes, all told of wearing days, sleepless nights, trouble. Or was it worry? My heart seemed to stop beating. Had he failed? Could he be holding out on us?

"Well, how's everything?" I asked, as casually as possible.

He answered, his eyes half closed, gazing at the floor:

"They hounded me from the moment I got the stone. Day and night—I couldn't shake 'em. It was hell."

He spoke jerkily, with apparent effort.

"I couldn't get a ship out of France. Tried on both coasts. Narrow escape both times. Managed to make it through Spain to Lisbon. Got an old tub, the *Queen Ann*, for New York. Young French dick got the ship, too, at the last minute."

He was speaking more evenly now.

"I bought off the wireless operator. It was hide-and-seek between the Frenchman and myself, all the way across. I used a disguise for the first couple days. But he was wise. Night and day we played the game. It just about wore me out.

"I was near all in to start with, you know, from a week's hounding around the continent. I took his gat away from him, though, a couple days out of New York."

Laramie, for the first time raising his eyes from the floor, smiled grimly at the recollection.

"Had a little peace then. Pitched the gat overboard, of course, before we made New York, and his papers too. I couldn't use 'em. They've got me tagged at the custom's office.

"When we docked, I no sooner stepped ashore than a dick and a customs officer grabbed me and rushed me to an inspection office at the end of the pier.

" 'We won't have to hold you here long, Laramie,' the customs guy says, grinning. 'Just long enough to go through your clothes. See you haven't any baggage.'

"I admitted readily enough that I was Laramie; they knew it, anyway. But I pretended to be wholly at a loss as to the reason I was being held. And when they ordered me to strip I protested, naturally; asked them how they got that way; told them to go to the devil.

"They stripped me themselves, then, and stood me in a corner of the room. They looked in my mouth, my ears. They combed carefully through my hair. After a long time in which they finally satisfied themselves that there was no ruby concealed on my body, they started in on my clothes.

"Garment by garment, they scrutinized every square inch of them. They ripped open my belt and necktie and pulled the padding out of the shoulders of my coat. They jerked the sweatband from my hat. Look at my shoes!—heels pulled off and toes cut clear through.

"It was nearly two hours before they tossed me my clothes in disgust and allowed me to dress. Oh, yes, they were good enough to lend me a bathrobe, and they wrote me out a check for my ruined clothes, too.

" 'Well, you're free, Laramie,' the inspector growled. 'That Paris wire was the bunk. The ruby's not on you.'

"So I dressed, and then in a roundabout way came here." He lowered his voice with an air of finality and his weary eyes again sought the floor.

I was disappointed—bitterly disappointed. Why had not Harwell seen through this blunderer? He had insisted that I do this job with him. And the man had failed! Doubtless he had attempted to pull the old plant trick. I turned on him, savagely.

"Why did you do it, man? You've been in the game long enough to know better than that. Why, that's amateur stuff, rank amateur. They've got it now. It doesn't matter where on the boat you hid it, in the stateroom or out of the stateroom—they've got it now."

Laramie spoke sharply, his features hardening, a glow in his dull eyes. "What do you mean, amateur stuff? Who said anything about hiding it on the boat? I'm not quite hopeless, you know."

Then his manner changed. He regarded me, a curious expression on his face. "Did I ever mention to you, Johnson, that I once played in vaudeville? I did, for several years," he went on, not waiting for me to reply. "I used to pull guinea pigs out of my hat, palm coins, do all sorts of sleight of hand, you know."

He smiled.

I was furious.

"Guinea pigs?" I railed. "Guinea pigs be damned! What's that to do with smuggling in the Voutir ruby, you fool?"

"The Voutir ruby, as you know, is perfectly flat on one side, and round—about the size of a quarter," he said, still smiling. "It has nothing to do with guinea pigs, particularly. *But remember what I said about sleight of hand and palming coins?*"

I stared at him, incredulously. "Then," I gasped, "then—you mean—"

He said not a word. Slowly he extended his arm and opened his hand.

The ruby lay in his palm.

No Flowers
for Henry

CARL HUGHES

The Shaws were in their kitchen, doing the dinner dishes, when the car turned into their driveway between the high mounts of snow. Henry took off his apron. "Here they are," he said, partly to his wife Alice and partly to the nondescript yellow tomcat, Bertie, who sat there on a kitchen chair.

It was only fair, he thought, to warn Bertie that his most voluble critic, Marguerite Bensinger, was arriving. In fact, he had had a little talk with Bertie earlier, about not being too offended by the things Marguerite was likely to say.

Henry knew, of course, that Bertie understood him. From the day the old boy had strolled into the yard to be adopted, the two had been able to communicate.

"You let them in, dear," Henry's wife said. "I don't want Sis to see my kitchen looking like this."

Henry went down the hall and pressed his forehead against the rectangle of glass in the upper third of the front door. He did not open the door at once, knowing the cold would chill him and he might shiver for as long as ten minutes. The cold affected him that way all the time now.

He did not wait for the Bensingers to ring the bell, however. When he saw them through the glass, he drew the door open.

"Welcome back to the frigid north," Henry said. Actually, his sister-in-law and her husband had returned three weeks ago from their Caribbean vacation, but this was the first time he had seen them. They had been too busy to visit, although the two sisters had talked at least once a day, at some length, on the telephone.

Carl Bensinger grinned and shifted his slide-projector case to his left hand so he could grasp Henry's outthrust hand with his right. They were the best of friends. "Frigid is the word," he agreed. "Henry, you lucky old buzzard, wait'll I tell you what—"

"For heaven's sake, go on *in!*" His wife gave him a push. "Do you want them to pay for heating the whole outdoors?" Like a performing bear in her bulky fur coat and high fur hat, she followed Carl over the threshold. "Where's Alice?" she demanded.

"In here, Sis," Alice Shaw called from the kitchen. "Come see my new refrigerator when you get your things off."

Marguerite Bensinger watched Henry hang her coat in the front-hall closet, then handed him her fur hat and went down the hall to the kitchen. Her husband frowned at Henry while shrugging his coat off. "You bought a refrigerator?"

Henry only nodded.

"What for? I thought you were all set to sell this place."

"Well," Henry said, "your wife's been talking to Alice, and we see a lot of problems." He picked up Carl's projector case and steered Carl into the living room. "I'm glad you brought this. Ours isn't working right."

"What do you mean, a lot of problems? What problems?"

"Oh, you know."

Carl backed up to an overstuffed chair and seated himself, still peering at Henry and still frowning. "No, I don't know. When you sold the florist shop you were like a kid getting out of school. You were all steamed up about leaving this lousy climate and going down there to Jamaica and growing flowers. What's wrong?"

Henry sat, too. "Nothing's wrong, Carl. Not *wrong*. Nothing's even decided yet. It's just that—"

"They hike the price on you? Man, if they did, I wouldn't blame them. That's a beautiful place you've got lined up there, Henry. We rented a car in Kingston and drove out for a look, and I want to tell you those Blue Mountains are really something. The house, too. *Did* they up the price?"

"No. It's not that."

"Then what is it, for Pete's sake? You were in seventh heaven about this thing when Marguerite and I went down there on our vacation."

"Well, I'm fifty-five years old, you know."

"What the hell's that got to do with it?"

"Alice, too. She's almost that age, Carl. Marguerite's been reminding her. It would mean starting all over—"

Henry paused to reach down and stroke his cat, who had wandered in from the kitchen. The cat rubbed its face against his hand and went over to Carl, who looked down with a grin and said, "Hi, you old buzzard. How's the world treating you?"

"Meow," said Bertie, strolling on to a favorite spot under the coffee table.

"As I was saying," Henry said, "It would mean starting all over in a strange place, finding new friends and getting used to new things and—well, you know. There'd be a certain amount of risk, too. There's no risk if I just retire."

"You're out of your mind," Carl said. "Look, Henry. I went into some of those flower shops in Kingston and checked on prices. In Montego Bay, too. They get a fortune for flowers there. A man like you, with your know-how, would have it made." He leaned forward to point a finger at Henry's chest. "What will you do if you *retire*, for Pete's sake?"

"Well, Alice thinks I could take up golf."

"You? *Golf?*"

"Or fishing or something. There are lots of things a man can do, Carl. Growing flowers is hard work. I don't believe you realize how hard it is. If you'd spent practically your whole life in the business as I have, you—"

"You should say 'whole entirely life,' " Carl corrected, grinning.

"What?"

"That's how they talk in Jamaica. I asked a higgler in Kingston what something cost, and she said I could have the whole entirely thing for so much."

"Oh." Henry turned his head, thinking his wife had called him. She had not, though. The two women were in a bedroom now, and Alice was only talking to her sister.

"You don't mean it!" Alice said. "Why, that's just what Henry and I have been looking for, to go with this new wallpaper!"

Carl Bensinger frowned at Henry. "You papered the bedroom over?"

"Alice got a good buy at Hallowell's. Marguerite phoned her about it." Henry studied the back of his right hand. "The old paper *was* pretty shabby, I guess."

"And what are you looking for to go with it?"

"Huh?"

"She just said—"

"Oh. Spreads. We need new bedspreads now, Marguerite said."

"You going to do the whole house over?"

"Oh, I don't suppose we—"

The women came into the room then, and Carl Bensinger said how about looking at the slides he had brought over. Carl was an avid photographer. A good one, too.

"We're dying to see them," Alice said. "Aren't we, Henry?"

Henry said they were, and began to set up the screen while Carl arranged the projector and slides on a table. While the men were thus occupied, Henry's cat, Bertie, came out from under the coffee table in front of the divan, where the women had seated themselves. He sat there with his head atilt, studying Marguerite. If he understood what people said—as Henry swore he did—he had no reason to be fond of her.

She did it again now, while gazing down at him with an expression of total dislike. "You are just about the ugliest cat I have ever seen," she said slowly and distinctly. "The very ugliest." Then to Henry she said, "If you must have a cat around the house, Henry, can't you at least get one with some breeding?"

"He's got breeding enough for me," Henry said. "Bertie's a real smart cat."

"He's nothing but an alley cat, and you know it."

"The book I bought says he's a Domestic Short-Hair," Henry countered, fiddling with the screen.

"Good grief," Marguerite snorted. Then as Bertie took a step toward her: "Don't you come near me, you grubby beast! You're just an old flea-bag."

"Not a flea on him," Henry said.

"Well, I don't care. He looks like a worn-out yellow rug."

Henry finished adjusting the screen and moved over to a light switch. With a nod to Carl, he put the lights out and sat down. He did not sit on the divan with the sisters. He sat on a chair in a corner.

The first slides were of the hotel where Marguerite and Carl had stayed in Kingston, and then there were two of a Jamaican policeman with red stripes on his pants directing traffic at a busy downtown intersection. Carl said he never hoped to see a more efficient policeman. Marguerite said it was true, but of course he had to be efficient because the traffic was just ghastly.

There was a picture of a man dragging a block of ice along a sidewalk, on a rope, and Carl said by the time the poor guy got it home it probably would not be big enough to chill a rum punch. Marguerite said that was true because Jamaica was so wickedly hot, but he would be better off without the rum punch because everybody in Jamaica drank too much, all the time.

Then, dramatically, Carl said, "Now watch this, Henry! I don't think you saw anything like this when you were there!" And the screen was full of blue flowers.

"Aren't they something?" Carl said. "Women were selling them on the *sidewalk*, Henry, in some stalls right by the court house. If you ever wondered about growing flowers there, you've got your answer now. What are they, you know?"

Henry leaned forward on his chair. "Agapanthus. Lilies of the Nile."

"They grow them up in the mountains, the woman told us. Right up where you . . . here, this shot shows the stalls and the women. I had to get back a way."

"And he almost got run over," Marguerite said. "They drive on the *left* there and he was looking the wrong way. You wouldn't catch me driving in a crazy country like that, I can tell you."

"You get used to it," Carl said. "Now here's the car we rented: one of those little English jobs. And here's the mountain road to the place you're buying, Henry. I guess I don't have to tell you that, huh?"

"Just looking at it scares me half to death," Marguerite said.

"Oh, it isn't that bad. Just a bit winding is all." Carl showed some more pictures of the road, then paused again. "Now!" he said. "Here's your house, Henry, and what a marvelous old house it is! How old is it, anyway?"

"Ninety-three years," Henry said from his chair in the darkness.

"The plumbing is certainly old enough," Marguerite said. "If you could call it plumbing."

"Here's the view from the porch," Carl said. "Man, look at those mountains! They make you feel—"

"The trouble is, you get tired of just a view," Marguerite said.

"You know, you could actually *hear* those mountains," Carl said. "Everything up there was so still, you could almost hear things *growing*."

"We asked if you could get TV there," Marguerite said, "but nobody seemed to know. They said almost nobody *had* TV because you have to make your own electricity with a generator or something. But I don't suppose the reception would be any good, anyway. Even the radio reception wasn't too good, because of the mountains. I don't know what in the world you'd do for entertainment, Alice. Carl, show the ones of Montego Bay."

"Just a second," Carl said. "Henry, here's a shot of an interesting old guy we met on the property, and a cat he said belonged to him. He said you stopped to look at some flowers in his yard, and the two of you got to talking, and you promised him a job." The slide showed a solemn black man in blue denim shirt and pants standing on the veranda steps of the 93-year-old house, with a cat as yellow as Bertie curled around his left ankle. "He said his name was Manny."

"Yes. Emmanuel. And the cat's name is Emilina." Henry leaned forward and thrust his right hand into the beam of light from the projector. "He gave me this piece of serpentine. Said it came from the property. Just for the fun of it, I had Kartin the jeweler mount it for me."

Glowing eerily in the light, on a plain silver band on Henry's third finger, was a greenish stone the size of a flattened pea.

Carl leaned forward to look at it. "Why'd he do that, Henry?"

"Well, he said he was an obeah man."

"Isn't that a kind of voodoo?" Marguerite asked.

"Not exactly. They both originated in Africa, he told me, but voodoo is a ceremonial thing while an obeah person works alone. In this case, with a cat."

"You mean that's an obeah cat in the picture?" Carl said.

"Well, Emmanuel said he and Emilina were one."

"Just like you and *your* awful cat—is that what you're saying?" Marguerite said. "And you actually wear that ring?"

"Oh, he doesn't wear it all the time," Alice intruded with a little laugh of embarrassment. "He just put it on this evening because you two were coming. You know—a conversation piece."

"He told me," Henry said, "if I ever needed his help, all I had to do was rub the stone. Like that fellow with the lamp in the Arabian Nights."

"I should think you'd be afraid to have a man like that working for you," Marguerite said. "I know *I* wouldn't hire such a person."

"Oh, come on," Henry said. "You know I don't believe in voodoo or obeah or any of that stuff. He was just a nice old guy with a wonderfully green thumb."

"You haven't tried the ring, then?" Carl said.

"Of course not. What do you take me for?"

"Please, Carl," Marguerite said impatiently, "Alice wants to see Montego Bay. She didn't get there. Henry was too wrapped up in his flowers."

Carl glanced at Henry but Henry stayed silent, so with a shrug he put a stack of slides aside and showed pictures of the north-coast tourist town, running through them mechanically while the two women commented on the clothes being worn by the tourists. Then after a pause Carl said, "Well, that's it, I guess. Anything you'd like to see again, anyone?"

Henry said, "Could I see those shots of King Street again, Carl? You suppose?"

"The flower vendors? Sure!"

"He means the policeman," Marguerite said quickly. "He's not really interested in flowers any more. Are you, Henry?"

Henry's voice was a long time coming out of the darkness. When it came, it sounded as though he were shivering as he had at the front door, though the room was warm enough. "I guess it isn't important." Reaching out to put a light on, he stood up. "Shall we have a drink?"

His wife's sigh seemed to be one of relief, and she nodded. Carl said, "Rum for me, please, Henry. I'm a convert now."

Henry turned to his sister-in-law. "And you, Marguerite? The usual?"

"You don't mind, do you, Henry? I know it's a lot of bother, using the blender just for me."

"No bother," Henry said.

Bertie, his yellow cat, silently trailed him into the kitchen.

The blender whirred on the kitchen counter for a while, and then Henry came back with drinks on a tray. It was a lovely, two-toned tray of Jamaica's most beautiful wood, blue mahoe. After serving the two sisters and Carl, he returned to his chair, lifted his own glass, and said in a voice filled with resignation, "Well . . . here's to not growing flowers in Jamaica."

"Now, Henry," his wife protested.

"Henry, you're crazy to give it up," Carl Bensinger said.

Marguerite emptied her glass without comment, then suddenly sucked in a noisy breath and let the glass drop to the carpet while clutching her throat with both hands. Her eyes became the size of half dollars and in trying desperately to speak, she nearly fell off her chair.

Henry and Carl rushed to her and got her to her feet. They led her into a bedroom and made her lie down. But still she struggled to speak as though someone had stuffed a gag into her mouth and she could not get a word out past it.

Henry's wife frantically called a nearby hospital.

An ambulance came. Alice rode in it with her sister, holding Marguerite's hand, while Henry and Carl followed in a car. When Marguerite was released two hours later, she was still unable to talk though otherwise quite all right.

She never did talk again, though a dozen doctors and psychiatrists took turns telling her there was absolutely nothing physically wrong with her.

One day months later, while Henry's wife Alice was visiting her speechless sister at the latter's home, Carl Bensinger and Henry sat in Henry's living room watching football on TV. When a beer commercial came on, Carl suddenly rose and shut the TV off.

"All right, Henry," Carl said. "Before I ask the obvious, just let me say you actually did me a pretty big favor, and I'm grateful. It's been real peaceful around my house since that night we showed the Jamaican slides. Now come clean. Tell me the truth. What did you put in Marguerite's drink that night?"

Henry shook his head. "Nothing."

"Oh, come on now, Henry. Maybe you fooled the medics, but you can't fool me. What—"

"I didn't do a thing, I tell you," Henry said. "I was running the blender to make Marguerite's drink, see? All of a sudden Bertie here" —he nodded toward the yellow cat lying at his feet—"jumped up on the counter and rubbed his head against my hand. Well, not my hand, actually. Against *this*."

Henry tapped the serpentine stone on his ring.

"And when he did it, I heard old Emmanuel's voice in my head, clear as I can hear yours right now, asking me how he could help."

"And?" Carl said, wide-eyed.

"I said, 'Just make her shut up.' That's all. I swear it. 'Just make her shut up.' I only wanted some relief, man. I don't think I meant it to be forever."

NOBODY,
THAT'S WHO

WILLIAM F. NOLAN

Look, Danny, you're my lawyer, aren't you? Can't you get me *out* of this? Hell, it's all crazy, it's a frame. Sure, I can go all over it again for you if that'll help. Sure, right from the beginning outside her apartment.

Well, like I said, I didn't really have anything *definite* to go on. I mean, I had this kind of hunch is all. Just a feeling that she was playing house with some other guy while I footed the bill. When I get a strong hunch on something I usually play it out. So that night I decided to stick around after leaving her apartment. Just in case. I kissed her like nothing was wrong and pretended to leave. But I only took the elevator down one floor, then climbed the stairs back to her apartment. I posted myself down at the end of the hall where it was plenty dark, where I figured I wouldn't be seen. And, by God, I didn't have long to wait, either. Maybe ten, fifteen minutes. Then along comes this guy. Like I told you, I never did get a look at his face. Wore a hat pulled down low and the collar of his topcoat was turned up all the way round, so I couldn't make out any features. Just a tall guy in a dark blue outfit.

Anyway, he tapped on the door, quiet like, two shorts and a long, and she opened it while he slipped inside. Now that was two o'clock on the nose. I checked my wrist watch, because I wanted to see just how long he'd stay in there with her. Hell, I felt like rushing in there and catching the pair of them at it, but I'd have to break the damn door down to do it and by that time he'd be long gone down the fire escape outside her window. So I decided to see just how long he'd stay.

Figured I couldn't hang around in the hall. Too suspicious in case the house dick came along, or maybe another hotel guest or some-body. I knew this guy would have to cross the lobby on his way out, so I took the elevator down and planted myself in a leather chair by the doors and waited. Just waited it out for him. I didn't know, right then, just what the hell I'd do when he finally showed. I was boiling, I'll admit. I hate being played for a sucker. That really ate into me. I mean, after the way I'd set her up and all. I just sat there in that chair and boiled.

Finally, two hours later, the elevator door slides back and he steps out. Same guy. Same dark blue outfit, hat and all. And, damn it, I *still* couldn't make out what he looked like. My chair was too far back and the lobby was pretty dark by then. I would have had to catch him and knock off that hat of his to really get a look, but what the hell, *she* was the one I wanted, not him. So I let him go. That was my first big mistake.

Then I got the idea about scaring her. I mean, I wanted to teach her a lesson. Shake her up good. Not hurt her, understand, just scare her. Sure, I had every right in the world to work her over for two-timing me, but I decided not to lay a hand on her. I figured why play it dumb and get myself in hot water with the law.

So I took the stairs up to her apartment. Four flights, just enough to wind me, get me to breathing hard like I was half nuts, you know. Figured that would help.

I tapped on her door, soft, the same way he had. Two shorts and a long. I knew she'd be plenty surprised to see me—and she sure was. She thought her lover boy had come back until she got a look at me. Then she tried to shut the door in my face, but I just pushed hard and forced my way inside.

"Whatta you want?" she says, and starts backing away from me toward the bed.

I didn't say a damn thing, just stood there looking mean, breathing hard and ragged. She let out a gasp, a kind of little choking sound. Then she dropped on the bed and curled up there, watching me like I was some kind of animal.

I locked the door behind me, then went over to the open window and shut and locked it. Like maybe I was going to do something that I didn't want anyone else to hear.

Oh, she was scared, all right, *plenty* scared. She didn't know what the hell I'd do next. I could see her eyes shining out at me from the bed, wild and wide. She had on a pink and blue shortie nightgown and her legs were all drawn up under it. She looked like a rabbit you catch in the headlights of your car, kind of frozen with fear.

I eased down into a chair by the window, where she could see my face in the reflection of the outside neon. Then I thought of a beautiful touch.

I began to scrape my fingernails. You know, just sitting there quiet in that chair, with the red and yellow neon lighting my face, breathing slow and hard—and scraping each nail with one of those sharp little silver files. Listen, that threw the fear of God into her. She figured I was just waiting till I finished the last nail before I went for her, so she was as still as a cat. Just her eyes moved, watching me.

Well, this went on for maybe ten minutes. Then she began to see I was bluffing, that I wasn't going to try anything. She sat up and dug out her cigarettes. She lit one, with the pillow propped up behind her. Then she tried some bluffing on her own.

"What's the idea?" she said. "Why the big spook routine?"

"I know all about your boy friend," I told her. "I saw him come in and I saw him come out."

"So what?" she snapped. "So a guy spends a couple of hours in my apartment."

The goddam nerve of her! Here I'd set her up in this place of her own, bought her some nice clothes and things and always treated her fine. And this is what she gives me. I'm telling you, it knocked me out. Then I asked her if she denied sleeping with this guy.

"He made a few passes and we wrestled around some, that's all," she told me.

Oh, sure. I believed that was all like I believed there wasn't any moon in the sky.

When she saw I wasn't having any she got sore. Her whole face changed. I mean, she suddenly turned hard, like some two-bit hustler. All the softness went fast and it was like I was seeing her for the first time with the shell off. She knew the game was finished and she didn't give a damn.

Then I got the full treatment. She began to laugh at me like I was a fool.

"You're not very bright," she told me in that new hard voice of hers. "Sure I had some kicks with this guy. Why? Because I'm fed up with playing around with you, that's why."

Then she told me that this other guy was a real *man*—not just a weak excuse for one—and that one like him was worth ten of me.

God, but she had nerve! Wasn't afraid of me at all by then. Not at all.

And I didn't intend to touch her. She wasn't worth it. Maybe I *was* the dumb cluck she made me out to be. Maybe I deserved what I was getting. I was as sore as hell at myself for playing along with her.

"I'm finished," I said. "This is the end of the line for us."

She just kept on laughing. Told me the sooner I got out the happier she'd be.

And here's where the crazy part starts. I was on my way to the door when it opened—and there, outlined against the light from the hall, was this guy of hers in the blue coat. And right away I saw something glint in his hand and I knew he had a gun.

It was all real freaky. He'd done the same thing I'd done. Come back, I mean. He'd probably seen my car parked in the hotel lot and recognized it. Had come back up and heard our voices outside the door. Figured she was playing *him* for the chump. Hell, it was all mixed up ten ways from Sunday.

Well, this guy didn't give either of us a chance to say a damn thing. Just stood there for a split second, long enough to make out the girl good and clear. Then he just pumped two slugs into her, one, two. Just that quick. Slammed the door and he was gone. Only first he tossed in his gun and it landed right at my feet on the rug.

That's when I *really* played it dumb. I actually picked the damn thing up and looked at it. Now, I've seen guys do that in the movies maybe fifty times and I always figured it was phony. No innocent party, I told myself, would ever pick up a murder weapon and get his fingerprints all over it. But I swear that's just what I did. Who knows why? Shock, I guess. The shock was terrible, the kind you get after a real bad auto accident. I was trembling, I remember, and weak all over.

I knew she was dead without even walking over to her. Nobody could miss at that kind of range. So I just stood there holding on to that damn gun and looking down at it while the outside hall filled up with people.

Next thing I know, somebody is pounding like hell on the door and yelling for me to open up. Oh, I dropped the gun quick enough then, all right. I knew I was a goner if they found me in here with her body, so I unlocked the window and took off down the fire escape.

What else is there to tell? The cops were waiting for me when I dropped into the alley—and I guess I sure looked guilty enough. I told them about the other guy in the blue get-up, but they just grinned and treated me like I was already on my way to the chair.

Hell, Danny, can't you find this guy? *He* killed her, not me. I never even touched her that morning. I don't know what this guy looks like, but he's *got* to be found. What chance have I got without him? Who's going to believe my story?

I'll tell you. Nobody, that's who.

Start looking for this guy, will you? He could be almost any-body. A mutual friend maybe. Hell, Danny, *You* knew her—and I've seen *you* wearing a dark blue topcoat. And . . . the guy's about your height, too.

Just do one thing for me, will you? Quit grinning like that. That's the way the damn cops grinned at me.

Will you *quit* it?

NUMB

WAYNE A. HAROLD

Bert Jacobs couldn't believe it when the young black man whipped out the gun, right in front of the library.

The kid was shaking in his dirty jacket, droplets of rain trapped in his unruly hair. The crack rock blazed in his dead eyes.

He waved the gun for emphasis. "Gimme your wallet."

Bert put up his hands. "Look, I don't have my wallet on me. I was just studying. I didn't think that I'd *need* it."

The mugger shook his addled head, seemed confused. Finally, he exhaled a short burst of air from his runny nostrils. "Well, you *did*," he said, then he squeezed the trigger.

There was a hot cloud of gas, a short burst of flame, then the bullet struck Bert in the chest. There was no pain. For a split second, Bert thought that the gun was full of blanks.

Then he looked down at his chest.

His forehead started to sweat and he wanted to vomit. He looked up at the mugger. "You *bastard*."

The young predator's jaw dropped. He threw the gun to the wet pavement, started running.

Bert gazed down at his hands; they were bluish, clammy.

He started after his attacker.

The thug sped across the street. Bert was close behind. He

tramped through a puddle and cold water splashed up on his leg. His head felt fuzzy. Numb.

For a split second he thought that he was five years old again, tearing through the massive puddles that always formed in his Grandma's back yard after a heavy rain.

On the street, in the present, he shook his head, tried to concentrate on running.

The mugger shot toward East 12th Street.

There were a few people out, despite the late hour and the rainy weather. The thug collided into a bag lady, knocked her down to the wet pavement. On her butt, her humble belongings scattered around her, she cursed him. He quickly regained his footing, started fleeing again. He passed through a pair of spike-headed punk kids who were hanging out in front of an alternative music bar.

Down half a block, Bert shouted to them. "Stop him! *Stop* him! He *shot* me!"

The kids looked at the thug (who was rapidly disappearing down the sidewalk), then back at Bert, confusion showing in their bleary eyes.

Bert sped past them.

He suddenly remembered the sick kitten that he found outside once, when he was a young teenager. It was screaming in pain, dying of some unknown ailment. Bert carried it to a clear, grassy area, started to clean the mucous from its eyes. Just as he was ready to wipe it away with his handkerchief, he saw that the mucous was moving. It was maggots. Flies had laid thousands of eggs in the helpless kitten's eyes, ears, and mouth, and now the tiny maggots were burrowing through its head, causing it unbearable pain.

Tears streaming down his face, young Bert found a heavy rock and lifted it high. . . .

He was breathing hard now. Without the numbness, his legs would have long since tired. Just ahead of him, the young mugger looked bushed. Not to mention scared. Bert kept after him, left, right, left, right.

"G-Get away from me!" the mugger shouted back.

The chase continued, now down South Prospect. There were three hookers on a corner up ahead, one of them a thin black girl with a beehive hairdo, the other two dumpy, white, and unattractive. "Whoa," the black girl exclaimed, seeing what was heading their way.

"Stop him!" Bert screamed. "He just *shot* me!"

One of the white girls grabbed the black girl's arm. "Stay out of it, Lee. Might be big trouble."

The black girl frowned.

Frustrated, Bert tapped into his final resources and poured on the speed. He drew closer, ever closer, reached out with his arm, almost able to touch his attacker. . . .

In his mind he saw himself on the high school football field, chasing a running back from the rival team. He knew that Jeannie was in the stands, hating football because she thought that it was pointless and stupid, but getting excited all the same, dry washing her hands as Bert moved in for the kill. . . .

Jeannie. They were engaged to be married. One month away. One month.

Bert was starting to despair. His attacker was getting away from him.

The black hooker was still frowning. "That white boy said that the black boy *shot* him."

The other fat hooker agreed with her peer. "You don't need no more hassles, Lee. Let 'em go by."

Lee sighed. "Hell with that."

She stuck her thin leg out and tripped the young black man. He hit the pavement. Hard.

The other two hookers stepped back.

Bert was on him in no time flat. He beat him with his fists, over and over again. "You bastard! How does *this* feel? You like *this?*" Both of them were screaming, crying. Finally, his fists bloody, Bert quit.

Lee ran over to Bert. "Hey, man. You okay?"

Hunched over his attacker, Bert coughed up blood. "He *shot* me. Wasn't gonna let him get a . . . *away* with it. Call cops. Gun over . . . on Euclid. Right in front of . . . *library.*"

She bent over, took his hand. "Your chest—it's bleeding."

"Yeah," Bert replied. "I was . . . studying." His eyes closed.

He was at the drive-in, making love to Jeannie for the first time. They had both been virgins. In the back of his dad's old Ford, they tried to keep their heads down, out of the line of sight of the other cars. They were giggling, both of them tickled by each other's nervous incompetence.

On the street, Bert laughed out loud.

"What's so funny?" Lee asked.

He grinned stupidly, let out a gurgle, then dropped dead on the spot.

The homicide detective was a tall black man with a totally shaven head. He was questioning Lee. Behind them, the Mobile Crime Unit was burning the midnight oil, sketching, photographing, and tagging away with reckless abandon. The unfortunate object of all their attention was Bert, who lay on the pavement, as dead as the concrete.

The detective forced a grin. "Workin' late tonight, Lee?"

She lifted an eyebrow. "Ain't illegal to step out for a walk, Klohn. I'm free, black, and over twenty-one. . . ."

"*Way* over," Klohn added with a smile.

Lee shook her head, smiled back.

They glanced over at Bert's body. Both of them stopped smiling.

"Chased him down, huh?" Klohn asked.

"Yeah. Said the other kid shot him in front of the library."

"We just sent a patrolman over there. If there's a gun, he'll find it."

"Think it'll have fingerprints on it?"

"Probably," Klohn replied. "But that don't matter much. The kid's in the back of the patrol car, confessin' up a storm. Stupid crackbaby's scared to death."

Lee pulled her green leather jacket tight around her to keep out the chill. "Can't believe it. That white boy runnin' all that way, bein' all shot up an' everything."

"It happens, Lee. Not often, but it happens. Sometimes they don't even *realize* that they've been shot. It's from the *shock*. Turns them numb and they can't even feel the pain. Then, a few minutes later, they just konk out."

Lee wiped a tear from her eye. "That sucks. He was just a kid."

"Yeah," Klohn replied. "But he was stubborn like a man."

ON A
DARK OCTOBER

JOE R. LANSDALE

The October night was dark and cool. The rain was thick. The moon was hidden behind dark clouds that occasionally flashed with lightning, and the sky rumbled as if it were a big belly that was hungry and needed filling.

A white Chrysler New Yorker came down the street and pulled up next to the curb. The driver killed the engine and the lights, turned to look at the building that sat on the block, an ugly tin thing with a weak light bulb shielded by a tin-hat shade over a fading sign that read BOB'S GARAGE. For a moment the driver sat unmoving, then he reached over, picked up the newspaper-wrapped package on the seat and put it in his lap. He opened it slowly. Inside was a shiny, oily, black-handled, ball peen hammer.

He lifted the hammer, touched the head of it to his free palm. It left a small smudge of grease there. He closed his hand, opened it, rubbed his fingers together. It felt just like . . . but he didn't want to think of that. It would all happen soon enough.

He put the hammer back in the papers, rewrapped it, wiped his fingers on the outside of the package. He pulled a raincoat from the back seat and put it across his lap. Then, with hands resting idly on the wheel, he sat silently.

A late model blue Ford pulled in front of him, left a space at the garage's drive, and parked. No one got out. The man in the Chrysler did not move.

Five minutes passed and another car, a late model Chevy, parked directly behind the Chrysler. Shortly thereafter three more cars arrived, all of them were late models. None of them blocked the drive. No one got out.

Another five minutes skulked by before a white van with MERTZ'S MEATS AND BUTCHER SHOP written on the side pulled around the Chrysler, then backed up the drive, almost to the garage door. A man wearing a hooded raincoat and carrying a package got out of the van, walked to the back and opened it.

The blue Ford's door opened, and a man dressed similarly, carrying a package under his arm, got out and went up the driveway. The two men nodded at one another. The man who had gotten out of the Ford unlocked the garage and slid the door back.

Car doors opened. Men dressed in raincoats, carrying packages, got out and walked to the back of the van. A couple of them had flashlights and they flashed them in the back of the vehicle, gave the others a good view of what was there—a burlap-wrapped, rope-bound bundle that wiggled and groaned.

The man who had been driving the van said, "Get it out."

Two of the men handed their packages to their comrades and climbed inside, picked up the squirming bundle, carried it into the garage. The others followed. The man from the Ford closed the door.

Except for the beams of the two flashlights, they stood close together in the darkness, like strands of flesh that had suddenly been pulled into a knot. The two with the bundle broke away from the others, and with their comrades directing their path with the beams of their flashlights, they carried the bundle to the grease rack and placed it between two wheel ramps. When that was finished, the two who had carried the bundle returned to join the others, to reform that tight knot of flesh.

Outside the rain was pounding the roof like tossed lug bolts. Lightning danced through the half-dozen small, barred windows. Wind shook the tin garage with a sound like a rattlesnake tail quivering for the strike, then passed on.

No one spoke for awhile. They just looked at the bundle. The bundle thrashed about and the moaning from it was louder than ever.

"All right," the man from the van said.

They removed their clothes, hung them on pegs on the wall, pulled their raincoats on.

The man who had been driving the blue Ford—after looking carefully into the darkness—went to the grease rack. There was a paper bag on one of the ramps. Earlier in the day he had placed it there himself. He opened it and took out a handful of candles and a book of matches. Using a match to guide him, he placed the candles down the length of the ramps, lighting them as he went. When he was finished, the garage glowed with a soft amber light. Except for the rear of the building. It was very dark there.

The man with the candles stopped suddenly, a match flame wavering between his fingertips. The hackles on the back of his neck stood up. He could hear movement from the dark part of the garage. He shook the match out quickly and joined the others. Together, the group unwrapped their packages and gripped the contents firmly in their hands—hammers, brake-over handles, crowbars, heavy wrenches. Then all of them stood looking toward the back of the garage, where something heavy and sluggish moved.

The sound of the garage clock—a huge thing with DRINK COCA-COLA emblazoned on its face—was like the ticking of a time bomb. It was one minute to midnight.

Beneath the clock, visible from time to time when the glow of the candles was whipped that way by the draft, was a calendar. It read OCTOBER and had a picture of a smiling boy wearing overalls, standing amidst a field of pumpkins. The 31st was circled in red.

Eyes drifted to the bundle between the ramps now. It had stopped squirming. The sound it was making was not quite a moan. The man from the van nodded at one of the men, the one who had driven the Chrysler. The Chrysler man went to the bundle and worked the ropes loose, folded back the burlap. A frightened black youth, bound by leather straps and gagged with a sock and a bandanna, looked up at him wide-eyed. The man from the Chrysler avoided looking back. The youth started squirming, grunting, and thrashing. Blood beaded around his wrists where the leather was tied, boiled out from around the loop fastened to his neck; when he kicked, it boiled faster because the strand had been drawn around his neck, behind his back and tied off at his ankles.

There came a sound from the rear of the garage again, louder than before. It was followed by a sudden sigh that might have been the wind working its way between the rafters.

The van driver stepped forward, spoke loudly to the back of the garage. "We got something for you, hear me? Just like always we're doing our part. You do yours. I guess that's all I got to say. Things will be the same come next October. In your name, I reckon."

For a moment—just a moment—there was a glimmer of a shape when the candles caught a draft and wafted their bright heads in that direction. The man from the van stepped back quickly. "In your name," he repeated. He turned to the men. "Like always, now. Don't get the head until the very end. Make it last."

The faces of the men took on an expression of grimness, as if they were all playing a part in a theatric production and had been

386

told to look that way. They hoisted their tools and moved toward the youth.

What they did took a long time.

When they finished, the thing that had been the young black man looked like a gigantic hunk of raw liver that had been chewed up and spat out. The raincoats of the men were covered in a spray of blood and brains. They were panting.

"Okay," said the man from the van.

They took off their raincoats, tossed them in a metal bin near the grease rack, wiped the blood from their hands, faces, ankles and feet with shop rags, tossed those in the bin and put on their clothes.

The van driver yelled to the back of the garage. "All yours. Keep the years good, huh?"

They went out of there and the man from the Ford locked the garage door. Tomorrow he would come to work as always. There would be no corpse to worry about, and a quick dose of gasoline and a match would take care of the contents in the bin. Rain ran down his back and made him shiver.

Each of the men went out to their cars without speaking. Tonight they would all go home to their young, attractive wives and tomorrow they would all go to their prosperous businesses and they would not think of this night again. Until next October.

They drove away. Lightning flashed. The wind howled. The rain beat the garage like a cat-o'-nine-tails. And inside there were loud sucking sounds punctuated by grunts of joy.

ONE MAN'S POISON

CURT HAMLIN

The sign rather amused Mr. Petten. He thought it clever. He saw it, of course. His eyes were small, deep-set in his fat cheeks like halved grapes pushed into a bowl of lumpy gruel, but those eyes missed very little. It wasn't the big sign that interested him. That was simply the name—HARITH'S—lettered in tarnished gilt over the door. The other was quite small, a footnote done in black paint at a lower corner of the single display window.

PRESCRIPTIONS FOR DIFFICULT CASES

Chuckling to himself, he pushed open the door and waddled inside.

The outer room of the place was no more than six-by-eight, empty except for an elderly, straight-backed chair that leaned wearily against one wall. At the back were a grilled window and a narrow doorway with a swinging door. Mr. Petten moved over and peered between the bars of the window. Inside, a dark young man in a white, linen coat was hunched over a table, inking entries into a large ledger. He raised his head as Mr. Petten stared in at him, and nodded pleasantly.

"Yes?"

"I'm George Petten," said Mr. Petten ponderously.

"Petten?" The young man marked his place in the ledger and closed it slowly, his eyes thoughtful. "Petten. Yes. Of course. Petten." He rose and came through the swinging door, blotting ink-stained fingers with a wad of cotton. "What can I do for you?"

"I want to see the manager."

"I'm the manager," said the young man, "and the druggist, and the clerk. In short, I own the place."

Mr. Petten scowled and shuffled his thick, broad feet uncertainly. "I expected someone older."

388

The young man rolled the cotton into a ball and tucked it neatly away in a trouser pocket. "My dear sir," he said gently, "I studied for years under my father. Since his death I have discovered a good many things even he didn't know. You have nothing to worry about. Absolutely nothing." He grasped Mr. Petten by one arm and urged him through the swinging door. "We can talk more comfortably in here. Also, it's absolutely private."

The inner room was as crowded as the outer had been bare. The walls were tiered by narrow shelves, all of them lined with bottles, jars, and flasks. There was a large sink, the drainboards on either side of it littered with a variety of chemical equipment.

The dark young man brought out a second chair, dusted it lightly with the sleeve of his jacket, and pushed it into place. "I'm interested to know how you heard of me."

Lowering himself, Mr. Petten waved a plump, vague hand. "Somebody told me. I'm not sure who it was. At a party, I think."

"You don't remember?"

"No. Does it make a difference?"

"I hardly think so," said the young man, smiling a soft smile. "No, I hardly think so. Not in this case. Well, now." He folded his hands on the table top and leaned over them. "If you'll please tell me about your problem."

Mr. Petten's eyebrows curled like furry caterpillars. "I'll do no such damned thing. I came here to buy something. You're here to sell it to me. I'll buy it and leave. That's the end of it."

"Don't be an ass," the young man said calmly. "I'm a specialist. A specialist has to know the facts. Cases differ. A member of the family, for example, is quite a different problem from, say, a casual acquaintance. Even you should be able to see that."

Mr. Petten reddened and puffed angry lips. "It's both."

"Two?" asked the young man. "Well! You *have* a tidy little project for yourself, haven't you?" He pulled at one earlobe, regarding Mr. Petten with interest. "Go on."

"The rest of it's none of your damned business."

"If it wasn't my business," snapped the young man sharply, "you wouldn't be here. If you won't be reasonable, get out. I've work to do."

Reopening the ledger, he picked up his pen and set to making entries in a careful, neat hand.

Mr. Petten fumed. He sucked his teeth. He blew out his cheeks.

He tapped the tips of his fingers ominously on his paunchy middle. "All right," he finally muttered. "Have it your way."

"Eh?"

"I said have it your way. I'll tell you. Only this makes you an accessory before the fact. Don't forget that."

The young man smiled a little and closed the ledger again. "I'll take that chance."

"Damned right you will," said Mr. Petten. "Damned right. Now. The first one's my wife. Marion. She's twenty-seven. We've been married three years. I bought her and paid for her. That's the way I do business. Put my money on the line and take delivery. All I expect is a fair return on my investment. Get what I mean?"

The young man murmured smiling agreement.

"Right," said Mr. Petten. "Fair return. Only I'm not getting it. There's another man."

"Ah."

"Get what I mean?"

"Perfectly."

"I was thinking," said Mr. Petten, "of poison. Something that couldn't be traced."

The young man put back his head and gave a short, hard laugh. "My dear sir," he chuckled, "you've been reading these murder books. There's no poison known that can't be found by an expert analyst. Now in my father's day . . ." He broke off to stare reminiscently at the ceiling, then shrugged his shoulders. "However, that's neither here nor there. The fact is, the science of detection has advanced beyond all reasonable bounds. What used to be a simple problem in murder is no longer simple. Quite the contrary."

"Um." Mr. Petten gloomily regarded the floor.

"Don't worry," said the young man. "I'll fix you up with something. Let me see. Does your wife—Marion, I think you said her name was—like any particular kind of food?"

"Food?"

"Yes. Like fish. Or mushrooms. Or—"

"Mushrooms," said Mr. Petten. "She's crazy about mushrooms."

"Excellent."

"Eh?"

"I said that was excellent. Now then. The—er—gentleman in question? Is he also fond of mushrooms?"

"Him? He's the one that got her started on them. Never used to have the blasted things. Now we have them all the time. Having them tonight." Mr. Petten spat. "Never touch them myself."

"Better and better." The young man gave his hands a brisk, cheerful rubbing. "Tell me—does the gentleman come often to dinner?"

"He comes," Mr. Petten said sourly, "every night. Every single, blasted night of the week."

"And tonight you're having mushrooms?"

"I said so, didn't I?"

"Fine," said the young man, rising from his chair. "Tonight, Mr. Petten, you eat mushrooms along with the rest of them. Don't forget. That's important."

He went to the rear of the room, opened a cabinet and fumbled about inside. Coming back, he placed two small vials on the table in front of Mr. Petten. One was red, the other blue, and each contained a liquid of uncertain color. "The red one," he explained, "contains muscarine. And some other things. Muscarine is a mushroom poison."

Mr. Petten poked at the red vial with a suspicious forefinger. "How does it taste?"

"Very pleasant," said the young man. "An old recipe of my father's. And simple to use. You just pour it into the mushroom sauce. It does the rest."

Mr. Petten's face went suddenly pale. "But if I eat—"

The young man chuckled. "You'd better let me finish. Listen. If three people eat a meal, and two of them die while the third remains perfectly all right, the police are going to get suspicious. But if the third one gets sick, even though he doesn't die, there's no particular reason for suspicion. The point is, Mr. Petten, you get sick but you don't die." He indicated the blue vial. "That's where the other stuff comes in."

Mr. Petten prodded the blue vial. "What is it?"

"An antidote," said the young man. "A really remarkable antidote. Different. You take it *before* you take the poison. At least six hours before. That way, no one can ever suspect you've taken it. By the time you eat the mushrooms, all traces of this will have vanished." He pushed the two vials together and stepped back, beaming. "That," he said, "will be five hundred dollars. For both of them."

Mr. Petten reared up in his chair. "What!"

"Very moderate, I think," the young man stated.

"It's outrageous," shouted Mr. Petten. "It's highway robbery. It's—"

"Of course," the young man said gently, "you could always use a gun. The only thing is, the police have such an embarrassing way with guns."

"Look here." Mr. Petten pounded the table with a fat, forceful hand. "I don't believe in buying pigs in a poke. For all I know those damned things may be filled with common tap water."

The soft, wise smile curled on the young man's lips. "You could try one of them," he suggested. "The red one, for example. I'm sure—"

"I'll do no such thing," Mr. Petten snapped. "Now you listen to me. I'm a business man. I'll make you a business proposition. I'll pay you a hundred dollars now. If the stuff works the way you say, I'll pay you the remainder. You can trust me."

The young man hesitated a long moment. Finally he nodded wearily. "All right. It's a deal."

"Cash," said Mr. Petten. He reached for a plump wallet, laid out five twenties, and picked up the two vials. "Fair and square. Cash."

They walked together through the outer room. Mr. Petten went into the street. The young man stood in the doorway. Mr. Petten jerked a thumb at the gold-lettered sign. "Harith. That you?"

The young man shook his head. "He was the original owner," he said. "He—uh—died. My father never would change the name. He always said that Harith kind of started him out in this business. In a way, that is. He was quite sentimental about it." He giggled.

"Oh," said Mr. Petten. "Well. See you again."

The young man raised his hand. "Good-bye, my friend."

Waddling down the street, Mr. Petten was quite pleased with himself. He blew a toneless tune through fat, pursed lips. The vials clinked pleasantly in his pocket. He was thinking he'd turned a nice piece of business. Two murders, and at fifty dollars a throw. "Afterwards," he told himself, "he can whistle for the rest. But he won't whistle loud. Not that one. Not when he's an accessory before the fact." He smiled grimly.

Back in his office, with the door securely locked, he uncorked the blue vial and poured its contents down his throat.

After Mr. Petten left, the dark young man returned slowly to the rear room of his shop. He thought it unlikely that he would ever see Mr. Petten again, certainly not after he swallowed the contents of the vial—poison. He thought that very probably Mr. Petten wasn't entirely honest, anyway. Even alive, he probably wouldn't have paid the remainder of his bill. Shaking his head, the dark young man bent again over the big ledger. A few minutes later he took an empty statement blank from the drawer of the table. In a neat, orderly hand he wrote:

For Services Rendered $500.00

He got out the telephone book, leafed through it, and carefully copied out the address.

Mrs. Marion Petten
1930 N. Lindenwald Rd.
City

THE PIGEON DROP

MICHAEL A. BLACK

Laura had stationed herself outside, just to the right of the re-volving doors. She could look through the big plate-glass windows and study the people inside the bank, sizing them up. Picking the right one—that was the key. The all-important first step. If you got the right pigeon, everything else would fall right into place.

Through the window she saw Andrea, her partner, stand up. She had been sitting inside near the row of lobby chairs, and standing up was the signal if she saw a good prospect making a large deposit or withdrawal. Laura then saw the woman that Andrea had indicated exiting through the revolving glass doors.

The mark was older, and a bit on the plump side, with thick, somewhat old-fashioned glasses perched on her nose. Her flowered dress had a clean but well-worn look to it.

Good, thought Laura. One that's too stingy to buy new clothes. Probably worth a bundle.

She got up and began walking parallel with the woman, just slightly ahead of her.

The older lady stopped when Laura turned and smiled disarmingly.

"Excuse me," Laura said, in her perfectly affected Southern drawl. "Could you help me?"

"Why I'll certainly try, dear," the older woman said, smiling back.

"My name's Laura."

"I'm Mildred. Mildred Castle."

"Oh, my mother's name was Mildred," Laura lied. "Perhaps you knew her. Mildred Stone?"

"No," Mrs. Castle said, shaking her head. "I don't believe so."

"Oh, anyway," said Laura. "I've just moved up here from Tennessee, and I found this envelope with all kinds of money in it, along with this funny note. Can you read it?"

She handed Mildred the note after giving her a quick glimpse of the cash roll. Actually it was a hundred dollar bill wrapped around a large wad of ones, inside a large manila-colored envelope.

"This looks like shorthand, dear," said Mildred looking at the note.

Laura scratched the side of her head, which was the signal for Andrea, who was already walking in their direction, to steer toward them.

Laura looked up and pointed to Andrea, who looked rather prim and proper in a gray business suit.

"Oh, she looks like a secretary," Laura said. "Excuse me. Could you help us?"

Andrea raised her eyebrows demurely as she approached.

"Yes?"

"I'm Laura and this is Mildred. We've found a bunch of money and this note, but it's in shorthand. Can you read it?"

Pausing to take out her glasses, Andrea took the note. Her brow furrowed as she read it, then she looked up at them.

"Where did you get this?" she asked. "This note says the money is proceeds from illegal gambling."

"Goodness," said Laura, feigning surprise. "What should we do?"

Andrea removed her spectacles and put them in her purse. "Well, whatever you decide, it's doubtful the money could, or even should, be returned to its owner."

"That's true," Laura said, giving Mildred's face a quick scan to see if they were drawing her in.

"Have you counted the money?" Andrea asked. "How much is there?"

"Yes I have. It's fifty thousand dollars," Laura said, emphasizing each word.

"Merciful heavens," Mildred said.

"Why don't we all three keep the money?" Laura blurted impetuously. "We can split it three ways. Is that legal?"

"Well," said Andrea. "I'm a legal secretary. My boss is a lawyer in that building." She gestured, indicating one of the tall structures behind them. "I could go call him."

Laura looked anxiously at Mrs. Castle. This was the second hook. If the pigeon went along with this phase, they were usually in for the rest.

"What do you think, Mildred?" she asked.

"Well," Mildred said slowly, "I suppose it wouldn't hurt to ask."

Andrea told them that she'd be right back, and went through the revolving doors of the bank building. She went to the pay phones in the lobby near the elevators. While she was gone Laura sat down with Mildred on one of the stone benches and flipped to the pictures of two small children in her wallet. Their father, she explained, was a fireman who had recently been killed in the line of duty. She took out a picture of an old boyfriend to show Mildred, and even managed to produce a convenient tear drop to roll down her cheek.

"I moved back here so we'd be close to his folks," Laura said. "To give the kids a chance to know their grandparents."

"That's nice, dear. I certainly treasure mine."

"Oh, you're a grandmother," Laura said solicitously. "Do you have their pictures?" Her job at this point was to keep the pigeon talking until Andrea returned for the rest of the set-up.

But Mrs. Castle made it easy for her, pulling out pictures of her grandchildren and telling Laura all those little stories that she really couldn't care less about.

After a few minutes Andrea came back through the revolving doors, walking briskly now, as if eager to share her newly obtained knowledge.

"My boss said it's legal for us to split the money, but we should register the serial numbers and wait thirty days," she said. "That's the legal time limit for claiming lost items."

"Register the serial numbers?" asked Laura quizzically.

Andrea nodded. She was speaking rapidly now, the way somebody does when they're speaking about a complex subject that, to them, is routine.

"My boss can do that for us," she said. "What he does suggest is that he hold onto the money in the mean time."

"Ah, I don't know about that," Laura said hesitantly.

"Well, if you're worried," Andrea continued, "we can each put up a certain percentage of what's in the envelope, as . . . good-faith money. And at the end of the thirty days, we can legally split up the money."

Laura narrowed her eyes slightly and glanced at each of them. "Mildred, I trust you. Why don't you hold the money? Would you have any objections to that?" she said, turning toward Andrea.

Andrea took in a long breath before she answered.

"Maybe the best thing to do is for each of us to put up the good-faith money," she said. "Say like I give you a certain percentage of what's in the envelope. . . ."

"Oh, I see. That way nobody would cash in the money before the thirty days," Laura said. "Sure, I'm willing to do that. Mildred, how about you? I think that's fair, don't you?"

"I would agree with that," Mildred said slowly. Then added, "There's an old saying: Sometimes it takes money to make money."

Oh, this is great, thought Laura. An old saying, my ass. She'd have to remember that one for the next mark.

"So if I put up, say, ten thousand," Andrea said, trying to gauge how much they could make on this one, "could you each match that?"

At this point the pigeons were usually worried at the prospect of the money slipping away. And they were also confused by all the double talk but hesitant to admit it, lest they appear stupid.

"I've got my insurance money," Laura said. "Mildred?"

"Like I said, it takes money. . . ." Mildred said, showing them a denture-perfect smile. "I just need to make a withdrawal."

"This sounds like a wonderful opportunity," Laura said. "Doesn't it, Mildred?"

Mildred flashed her smile again. "Yes, dear, it certainly does."

"Well, like I said, I was just on my way to deposit some insurance settlement money," said Laura. "I can't pass up a chance like this. My kids are gonna be so happy."

"She's a widow," Mildred said, as if she and Laura were old friends. "Her husband was a fireman."

Great, thought Laura, she's so caught up in the story the rest will go like clockwork.

"Well, I bank down the street," Andrea said, smiling with a venal gleam in her eye. "It's agreed then? We each put up ten thousand, and Mildred can hold the envelope for thirty days?"

"Oh, Mildred," said Laura. "Let's all do it. It's like a dream come true."

"It certainly does sound like a great opportunity," said Mildred, smiling back at her. "Let's just step back inside the bank, and I'll be right back with my third," she said.

Andrea and Laura exchanged surreptitious winks. Just like clockwork. The only thing they had to do to complete the scam was switch the envelopes once they had Mildred's "good-faith money" in it. Then, after a quick excuse to disappear for a moment, they'd slip away to their car, which was parked on the other side of the building.

Usually, Laura would go to the car to get her money while Andrea went to telephone her boss again. They'd leave the pigeon sitting there holding what she thought was the envelope with all the money in it, for safekeeping. By the time the mark finally opened it and discovered that it only contained cut-up newspaper, Laura and Andrea would be long gone with the real cash.

Mrs. Castle went to the glass desks that held the bank withdrawal slips as Andrea and Laura watched from the lobby, turning so they'd be out of the range of the surveillance cameras. The old woman wrote out her withdrawal slip and walked to the tellers' window. Laura glanced furtively over her shoulder. The teller moved with a ponderous slowness, but it always seemed that way. The waiting was the hardest when the pigeon drop was almost complete.

Finally, Mildred moved toward them, a well stuffed envelope in her hand. As she approached, she smiled conspiratorially.

"I've got my share," she said.

"Good. Let me put it in this big manila one," Laura said.

Mildred handed over her heavily stuffed envelope, and Laura stuck it inside the large 8 × 10 manila envelope. Stuffing it in her large purse, she turned slightly away from Mrs. Castle for a moment as she looked at Andrea.

"Nothing left to do but see your boss, right?" Laura said.

"Wait, is your money inside?" Andrea asked, pointing to Laura's purse.

"Oh no, it isn't," she said. "I was keeping it in the trunk of my car until I'd decided on a bank." Laura opened her purse, withdrew the dummy manila envelope, and handed it to Mrs. Castle. "Here, Mildred, why don't you hold the money until I run out to my car?"

"All right," Mildred said. The big envelope felt stuffed.

As Laura moved toward the doors Mrs. Castle trailed close behind her. Andrea said she wanted to visit the ladies' room before going to her bank and went toward the washrooms. Laura smiled at Mrs. Castle as she stepped inside the revolving doors.

"I'll be right back, Mildred," she said.

"I doubt it, dear," answered Mrs. Castle.

As the door swished around Mildred bent down and deftly slipped the heavily padded envelope in between the door frame and the edge of the thick glass cylinder in which the doors revolved. Laura jolted to a stop, trapped inside. She pushed forward, but the door wouldn't move with the envelope binding it. Nor could she push the door backwards against the gears.

"Mildred," Laura said, desperation edging into her voice. "Take that out of the door."

Mrs. Castle ignored her and whistled loudly, gesturing for the bank security guard. As he approached, Mildred pointed to the ladies' room.

"I've got this one. The other one's in there, wearing a gray suit. The cops are on the way," she said. "Now move your butt."

The detective watched as both Laura and Andrea were handcuffed and placed into the back of the squad car. Then he turned to Mildred.

"Mrs. Castle, I'd like to thank you for catching another one of these bunco teams for us."

Mildred smiled and patted his arm.

"That's perfectly all right, Detective Meyers," she said. "Just doing my civic duty, as usual. Now, when's the court date?"

The detective told her, then scratched his head.

"You know, ma'am, your note to the teller for her to call us was enough. You didn't need to trap them for us."

"This way I figured it'd be a stronger case," said Mildred. "No way they're gonna beat this one, right?"

"Yes, ma'am," the detective said. "Instructing the teller to record the serial numbers on the bills you gave to her will probably assure a conviction, but, Mrs. Castle, what I mean is, it's kinda dangerous for civilians to get too involved in police business."

"Civilians," Mildred said with a smile. "Just whose collar do you think this *is*, sonny?"

A QUARTER
FOR CRAZY EDDIE

WILL MURRAY

They tell me I could make more money robbing banks or holding up liquor stores, especially drifting as much as I do. I know that. I also know that's not for me. I'm a regular guy with old-fashioned ideas about working. It's just that I'm a little unorthodox in the way I go about it.

This time it was Boston. The company's name was the Dyna Corporation. According to their want ad, they manufactured electronic components for the Automatic Testing Industry and needed stock help. Perfect.

The Dyna Corporation was an old twelve-story building on Summer Street. I was waiting outside before they opened for business, and before any other applicants showed up.

The interview was routine. I called myself "Carl Shaner" on the application—keeping my first name as I always do—and claimed my only prior work experience was ten years as a shipper for the mythical Highsound Stereo Component Company in Baltimore. Employers don't expect falsified credentials and they almost never check out-of-state references.

A big jowly guy named Salwak took my application. I answered the usual questions and did my best to create a good impression. I had deliberately undervalued myself on the application. That was the hook.

"According to this," Salwak said, "your last employer went out of business."

"Yes, that's true," I told him. "I couldn't find another job down home—it's that bad there—so I'm trying to make a new start here in Boston." I tried to sound down and out.

Salwak looked at the application again, then proceeded to fill me in on the company.

"We manufacture state of the art circuit boards. These boards are used in automatic testing equipment of all types. They are small, but very delicate and expensive. Your duties will be to help maintain our regular inventory and you will be responsible for shipping hardware to our customers."

"Sounds right up my alley," I said.

Salwak nodded. "The position starts at $3.40 an hour."

The ad had said $3.70 an hour.

"Fine," I said.

"In that case, Mr. Shaner," Salwak beamed, "I think you are exactly the individual we are looking for. You start tomorrow. Report to Mr. Roberts at the dock."

The next day I reported to Shipping and Receiving at eight sharp. Jerry Roberts, a bluff character who reminded me of a Keystone Kop, was in charge. The rest of the crew were a predictable bunch. Tony Cellini was the jokester of the group—there's one in every place. Lance Royston was quiet, black, and smart as a whip. He really should have been in charge, but the smart ones never are. If I ever retire from this game, I might write a book about the people I've worked with. They're part of what I enjoy about this.

I fitted in without any trouble. I always do. The work was easy. We were the low men on the Dyna totem pole, which didn't surprise me. Shipping and Receiving was in the basement, out of sight, and our loading dock was in the rear alley, which was below street level. Finished printed circuit boards—PC boards for short—came down to us in plastic bags for storage or shipping. Whatever went on upstairs, it didn't concern us much. The shipping crew kept apart from what Jerry called the "boy geniuses" upstairs. We didn't even eat in the company cafeteria. Instead, we ate at a neighborhood bar or sent out. That was how I first met Crazy Eddie.

It was on my second day. The buzzer had announced lunch.

"Where are we eating today?" I asked Jerry.

"I sent out for it. Pizza. I hope you like it with onions and peppers."

"I can handle it," I grinned. The pizza arrived almost immediately, brought by a vacant-faced kid who might have been anywhere from 16 to 26. He handed the pizza to Tony and stuck out his hand, palm up.

"Hey, hey," he said. "Gimme a quarter."

"Here you go, Eddie."

The kid's eyes got wide and a sappy grin spread over his face. He scooped up the coin with a pudgy hand. He turned to Lance next and repeated his demand. Lance gave him a quarter. So did Jerry. Then he came up to me.

"Gimme a quarter." His eyes were fish-gray. I hesitated.

"Go ahead, man," Lance said.

I dug into my pocket. The kid was grinning and bouncing on his feet. "C'mon, get it up. Get it up." He gave me the willies.

I pulled out a fifty-cent piece. "Here, take four bits," I said. Anything to get rid of him.

The kid took the coin, looked it over once, and dropped it in the alley dirt. "C'mon, get it up," he said again.

"Give Eddie a *quarter*," Tony told me. "He only takes quarters."

I fumbled out a quarter. He took it and skipped away, grinning and shaking the quarters in his cupped hands like a five-year-old.

"That's Crazy Eddie," Jerry told me as we sat on the dock to eat. "He's been in and out of institutions most of his life, but he's harmless. Goes around begging quarters off people—that's how he makes his living. When he's around, we send him out for food and pay him in quarters. He's sort of a tradition around here, so we try to take care of him."

"The reason he wouldn't take your fifty cents," Lance put in, "was because he doesn't understand money. He just knows that a quarter will buy him a candy bar, and that's all he cares about."

I picked up my half dollar and finished my lunch. "Crazy."

We saw Crazy Eddie about twice a week, and I sort of got used to his idiot grin. He has to be one of the strangest characters I've met in this game. If I ever write that book, I told myself, Crazy Eddie's going to be in it.

Yeah, he sure is.

It was at the end of the first week that I met John Grodin. John worked upstairs in Design, but he was a maverick and welcome in Shipping. He had lunch with us whenever he got fed up with the upstairs crowd. When he did, we would get in a few hands of poker.

I made a point of getting to know John. I liked him and he had the inside track at Dyna.

"Just what do you do up there all day, John?" I asked.

Most people don't show much interest in what others do for a living. Consequently, when someone does, the floodgates open.

John launched into a long explanation of how he mocked up PC board designs with mylar sheets and pressure-sensitive tape to simulate circuitry. The boards were used the way computers are used to test car performance. John designed the custom boards for special equipment, he told me.

"Worth a lot of money?" I asked.

"The regular boards you guys store aren't worth more than a few hundred dollars each, but some of the custom PC boards cost heavy bread, let me tell you. I'm working on a design now that will be worth a cool five grand."

I whistled. "What do you make them out of—platinum?"

"No, the parts are just fiberglass and copper solder." John got a board and took it out of its plastic bag. It was about the size of a ruler, except that it was made out of green plastic.

"See how thin these circuit lines are? The tolerances are unbelievable. This is art."

"Are these things worth anything to anyone outside of the companies you make them for?"

"Sure," John said. "Any number of people would love to get their hands on some of our designs. Some other computer outfit who can't afford our boards. Or our competition. A thief could do well for himself if he had connections in the industry."

I smiled to myself. I had hopes of being that thief.

The weeks slid by and I slipped into the routine. The work was simple. The regular stock boards were kept in a locked storage cage. The custom jobs, when they were being held before shipping, were kept in individual combination lockers in another cage. I knew all the combinations—it was my job.

In the meantime I pumped the others as much as I could. It was Jerry's job to lock up at night, so I learned about the alarm and where the keys were kept. From Lance I found out that the night security guard mainly patrolled the upper floors. The Dyna Corporation was shaping up very nicely.

One night I checked out the place under actual "working" conditions. I entered the alley behind Dyna after eleven on a Saturday night, walking at a quick pace past the dim bulbs glowing over the rows of loading platforms and service doors—as if I had taken a wrong turn and was anxious to find my way back. It looked perfectly deserted. Then a foot kicked a pebble somewhere in front of me and a voice said, "Hey, hey!"

I froze. There was someone there I couldn't make out in the dark. When he said, "Get it up," I recognized Crazy Eddie's voice. Sure enough, he stepped into the dim light.

I let out a pent breath. "Hi, Eddie."

"Gimme a quarter," he grinned. I flipped him a quarter. He caught it and went past me. He didn't say thank you—he never does. I got out of that alley in a hurry, making a mental note to carry a quarter for Crazy Eddie—just in case—when the job became ripe.

I had been there almost seven weeks when the opportunity of a lifetime came. I almost didn't take it. I hadn't set up a fence yet and, worse, I hadn't put in my three months. I always put in at least three months before I make my move. Paying my dues, so to speak.

It happened over lunch. John Grodin came down looking harried.

"Just finished five board designs for a jet-engine test unit," he informed me. "Man, were they *tough*. I figure that by the time they add up all the costs of redesigning and experimentation, those boards will cost the contractor $25,000 each."

I munched on my burger to cover my excitement. Throwing in some of the random stock, I could walk off with more than $150,000 in the trunk of my car. I could worry about a fence later.

"When are they going out?" I asked John. Everything depended on his answer.

"Tomorrow morning. They're being loaded and inspected now. You should have them by three for packing."

The boards came down at 2:30. They didn't look any different from any of the zillion other boards that had passed through my hands, but the amber plastic and copper circuitry might as well have been solid gold. I stored them carefully.

When five o'clock came, I pretended to misplace a shipping form. I told the others to go ahead, that I would lock up. Just like that. Why not? I was a trusted co-worker. They didn't know it was good-bye, not good night.

I disconnected the alarm first. Then I punched out, shut off the lights, and left by the service door, taking the ring of keys that hung beside it with me.

I drove home wearing a grin as big as Crazy Eddie's.

I had dinner, watched the news, and waited. It was going to be a cinch. Only one thing bothered me—I hadn't put in my three months' time. I was superstitious about that, but I put it out of my mind. If I unloaded those boards right, I could be in Las Vegas inside of a month. I always went to Vegas after a job.

At ten o'clock I eased my car into the alley behind Dyna and parked beside the dock. I got in through the service door with the key.

Once inside, it was just a matter of unlocking the storage cages and working the combination lockers. I carried the five special boards out first. Then I got the rest of the custom boards and some of the inventory stock. Everything fitted into the trunk.

I reset the alarm, replaced the keys, and shut the service door behind me. Simple, no? Yes, but I had put in almost two months at Dyna to make it that simple. The whole thing had taken 20 minutes. I made for the car, feeling only a little tightness in my gut.

Then the alley turned white with light. I ducked instinctively. A prowl car had turned the corner, moving slowly with its flashers off.

No time to start the car. I ran. Car doors slammed open and shut behind me. Heavy feet pounded. I heard a shout as I cut around a corner.

Damn the luck! They must have been late on their regular patrol. I ducked into a passage between two buildings, and around a corner. Breathing more from nerves than effort, I stopped to get my bearings.

A voice from the shadows said, "Get it up!" and my heart stopped.

Then I recognized that voice. It was Crazy Eddie, a foolish grin on his loose face and his white hand outstretched. "Hey, hey! Gimme a quarter," he demanded. I couldn't have been more scared if those two cops had jumped out of the shadows.

The heavy feet sounded again. I got an idea. Then I felt sick. I had forgotten to check my change! I dug into my pocket frantically, finally pulled out a quarter by feel.

"Here, Eddie. When those cops come, tell them I went the other way, understand?" Eddie nodded vacantly. Running the opposite way, I turned into a blind alley. I waited, listening, my gut like a drum. Crazy Eddie would steer the cops the other way and I'd be home free—maybe I could get back to the car.

I heard a voice order, "Hold it!"

"Wait, Joe. It's Crazy Eddie. He's okay. Hey, Eddie, did you see a guy run this way? Yeah? Which way did he go?"

Crazy Eddie mumbled something I couldn't hear, but I did hear the cops trot away. It worked. I waited some more, then peered out. Crazy Eddie was still standing there. He looked confused, but he didn't matter any more. I legged down the street and around the corner.

The two cops were waiting for me with guns drawn. "Right there, buddy," one of them ordered. I put my hands up—there was nothing else to do. They frisked me against a wall and read me my rights. Crazy Eddie came to watch. When I saw his face, I knew he'd tipped them off.

"What the hell's the matter with you?" I yelled at him. "I gave you your damn quarter! Why'd you do it?"

One of the cops looked at me funny. The other one told him,

"Crazy Eddie will do almost anything for a quarter, but he has no use for any other kind of money." He walked down the street, and came back with something shiny he'd picked off the pavement.

"Looks like you made a common mistake, pal." He held up a Susan B. Anthony silver dollar to the light.

THE RAFFLE

WAYNE D. DUNDEE

I waited until the operator hung up in disgust, after telling me repeatedly and with growing impatience that no one at the random long distance number I'd given her was willing to accept charges for the call.

"Did you tell them this is urgent—an emergency?" I wailed loudly into the dead pay phone.

I gave it a beat, like I was listening to her say something back, then held the mouthpiece out a little farther and raised my voice a couple more notches, loud enough this time to be heard even above the plinkety-twang of the godawful hillbilly music playing on the juke box. "Yeah, well, thanks a whole fucking heap, operator," I hollered. "You're about as compassionate as that tightwad damn brother of mine. To hell with you and him both, then!"

I returned the phone to its cradle with a loud bang and stormed back toward my stool at the bar. I could feel different sets of eyes following me, exactly the way I wanted them to. I didn't look back at any of them, just set my face in the frustratedly pissed-off expression I wanted them all to see and made for the stool.

Angie sat on the one next to it, waiting.

I dropped onto the seat, grabbed the half-empty glass of beer I'd left behind, tipped it up, and drained it.

"Bad luck, baby?" Angie wanted to know.

"Do I look like I had any *good* luck?" I snapped, keeping the act going.

"That high and mighty brother of yours . . . you should have known he wouldn't lift a finger to help. Let alone spend a dime."

"Lousy tightwad wouldn't even take a collect call to hear what the problem was." I brought the empty glass down heavily on the bartop. "Rotten cheap bastard!"

The fat, sweaty bartender waddled over. "Keep a little tighter lid on it, buddy, whatya say? Everybody in here's got their own share of grief, they ain't interested in hearing you cuss about yours."

Outside, the wind slapped late summer rain against the roof and windows and carried the growl of rolling thunder.

I dragged my palm down over my face, like a guy with the weight of the world grinding him under. I said, "You know the old saying that goes, 'Ever had one of those days?' Well, I've had a whole string of *nothing but* 'one of those days,' mister. A fella gets chafed pretty damn raw after a while, so you'll have to excuse me all to hell and gone if my lousy attitude is spoiling the mood for anybody else."

"Take it easy, baby," Angie said.

"I'm cool," I told her.

"That's the way," the bartender said. "Just keep cool."

Like that's what he was doing, the fat slob. His eyes were dull slits in folds of pasty white blubber and he was unable to stop them from gazing down the front of Angie's dress. Of course, paying attention to the way Angie's curves filled out her rain-soaked dress was exactly what we wanted every guy in the place to be doing, but I didn't need lard-ass there behind the stick to get so overheated by the display he'd have a stroke or something; he was the key to getting the whole gig off on the right foot, making it work or not.

"How about another beer?" he said to me, finally managing to tear his gaze away from Angie's cleavage. But not for long. "And how about you, ma'am—another sloe gin?"

We both told him yeah and he set to work fixing us up.

The tavern was your typical country junction joint, located where a county blacktop crossed a neglected stretch of two-lane highway between a couple jerkwater little towns that were hell and gone away from any decent-sized city. The whole area seemed heavy into pig farming, judging by the barnyard layouts and the billboard advertising, not to mention the smell that had hung in the steamy air ahead of the storm. The gin joint was a place where the blue-collar hicks came to swill beer, shoot a little pool, listen to pathetic cowboy music, talk big, and pretend their lives were right on track. A place ripe for making a quick score but one where I'd damn sure go buggy if I had to spend more than a couple hours.

"On the house," the bartender said, returning to set fresh drinks in front of us. "The spell of bad luck it sounds like you're having, you need to catch a break, even if it's only a small one."

One of the men a ways down the bar, a whiskery old coot who looked to be pushing eighty or so, said, "What's so small about a freebie? I started coming here when you was still crapping yellow, Andy Torple—hell, before that, before you were even a gleam in your old man's eye—and in all the time since you took up behind that bar you never once offered *me* a round on the house."

"No, and I don't intend to," the bartender replied good-naturedly. "I might get you spoiled, Gleason, and before I knew it you'd come to expect a freebie every forty or fifty years."

"I'd know better than to expect anything from a cheapskate like you," the old man groused. "I see now the only way to get any decent treatment around here is to be built like a brick you-know-what."

The bartender—Andy, the old guy had called him—actually blushed a little bit. But that didn't stop him from glomming another eyeful of Angie's swelling breasts as he said, "Don't pay no attention to Gleason. He's so damn old his brain dried up and turned to dust sometime back in the fifties."

"Don't worry about it," Angie said, showing him a microsecond of her full candlepower smile. "Thanks for the drinks, all the same. That was sweet of you."

Andy blushed even more and I made a silent bet with myself that he might actually say something as corny as, "Shucks, it was nothing." But he didn't. Instead, though, he came up with a question almost as lame. "You folks ain't from around here, are you?"

"Not on your life," I said. "Strictly passing through."

"We're on our way to Tulsa," Angie added. Then, after a perfectly timed pause and with just the right dejected tone in her voice, she tacked on, "Well, at least we *were.*"

"What do you mean 'were'?" Andy wanted to know.

I knew then she had him hooked. From that point, she could have gone into a spiel about gross bodily functions or a lecture on the mating rituals of the South American pissant and he would have hung on her every word. Him and practically everybody else in the joint. Over the click of pool balls and the blare of the juke box—and in spite of what the bartender had said earlier about nobody wanting to hear our problems—the dozen or so other customers, all men, were straining pretty obviously to catch what was going on. Us being strangers could have accounted for a certain amount of that; one of us looking the way Angie did made it unanimous.

Angie answered the bartender's question with a kind of forlorn sigh. "I don't see how we can make it now. Not in time, anyway. Milo's got this really great job waiting in Tulsa, see—the break we've been needing—but he's got to be able to start right away. We were deadheading straight on through. Then our car broke down. That's why we showed up here all soppy wet and everything, we had to walk in the rain from back up the road. Milo says the car needs a-a . . ." She looked flustered and turned to me. "What did you call it, baby?"

"Transmission," I muttered. "Damn thing's been acting up. Finally went."

Andy looked hopeful. "Hey, there's a really good service station in Cottonville. Only a few miles from here. I bet they could fix your car easy, get at it first thing in the morning and maybe have you going again before noon tomorrow. Wouldn't the start of your job wait that long?"

I gave him a look like you'd give a kid who just handed you a rotten report card. "You don't listen too good, do you? I told you I'm coming off a whole string of shitty luck. I had barely enough money for gas to make Tulsa, and I had to go in hock for that. You know what an automatic transmission—even a rebuilt one—is likely to run? You could line up service stations from hell to breakfast, pal, but it wouldn't do me any good because I'm tapped out and I got nowhere to turn. You heard my luck on the phone—I can't even get anybody to take a call." I let out a raspy laugh. "Let's face it, things just haven't been going my way and they're not ready to change yet. Not in Tulsa, and sure as hell not here."

Angie put her hand on my arm. "Don't be so down, baby. Something will work out. We always got each other."

"Sure," I said. "Sure."

The bartender just stood there looking kind of sad and confused. Sad because he had a soft heart and the chump really wished he could say or do something to help; confused because to his mind having a lady who looked like Angie ought to be enough good luck for any man.

"Look, pal," I said to him. "I appreciate your concern and the free drinks and all, really. But could you . . . well, not crowd us right at the moment. We got some things to work out here, just the two of us. You understand, right?"

He held up his hands. "Sure, mister. I didn't mean to pry or anything. You go on and take your time." He started to back away, his eyes unable to keep from lingering on Angie. "Just holler if you need anything."

Outside, lightning split the night and made the windows blink rapid bursts of brilliant silver.

Angie and I sat sort of hunkered over our drinks, our soaked clothes and slumped shoulders showing two people nearly worn to a frazzle by adversity. Her hand was very warm on my arm. We talked low, making sure nobody was close enough to hear.

"The fat sucker bought every damn word of it," Angie was saying, an edge of disdain in her voice.

"They almost always do," I reminded her. "Only difference is, this one seems a little more genuinely concerned about our plight."

"As far as I could tell, the main thing he was concerned about was getting a look at my tits."

"I don't blame him."

She smiled slyly. "It makes you hot, doesn't it? Seeing the suckers get all jazzed up over me, knowing you're the only one getting what they're all wanting so bad."

"That better be the way it is."

"What's that supposed to mean?"

"You figure it out."

I tipped up my beer and used the motion as an opportunity to survey the room once more. Counting the bartender, there were eleven guys present. Eleven marks. I'd figured on more, even for a weeknight, but the storm was probably keeping some of the less dedicated drinkers at home. Twenty was about the right number. Not too many to manage, but enough to assure a decent take.

Too late to do anything about it now, though. We'd put time into this, had it all set up. The only thing left was to play it out and settle for what we got.

Lowering my drink, I said to Angie, "The bartender's made the rounds. Those that didn't already hear what we were telling him, know by now all about our situation. I can see in their eyes that none of the jerks feel a bit sorry for me. They're all wondering the same thing: What does such a knockout chick see in such a loser?"

"When you talk mean to me, I sometimes wonder myself what I see in you."

"Knock that shit off. We're in the middle of a gig here, we got no time for tender feelings." I put my hand over hers. "In about ten seconds, jerk your arm away and give out a loud *No*. Make them think we're arguing about something, let them wonder what it is."

"I know the routine. We've been through it enough times."

"Then do it."

She jerked her arm away and said sharply, "No!"

I put my arm around her and pulled her closer, held her tight against me. "Good job. That got their attention."

"Maybe I wasn't acting."

"Everybody in the world spends ninety-nine percent of their lives acting. Most of them just never figure it out."

"That's what you always say."

I kept track of things in the reflection off the bottle-strewn wall mirror behind the bar. "Okay, they've settled back down. They can see you're not struggling so they figure we made up over whatever caused you to try and jerk away. In a little bit now, it'll be time to make your trip to the juke box."

"I hate that part. Hate their eyes all over me."

"Who's kidding who, you little tease. You love it, and we both know it."

The sly smile again. "You prick."

"I just tell it like it is."

"You want me to put on a show for these rubes? Fine. You got it. Just sit back and watch me work." She scooped a handful of quarters from the change scattered in front of me, slid off her stool, walked over to the juke box.

Well, *walked* doesn't quite say it. With the rain-soaked dress hugging every inch of her like a layer of paint, she sort of slithered and jiggled her way across the floor in a manner that threatened to singe every eyeball in the place. Once at the machine, she leaned slowly over to peer more closely at the song selections, in the process striking a wildly provocative pose with her fine ass jutted out like a highway sign. Even Gleason, the ancient old grump seated down the bar from me, perked up at the display.

I sipped some of my beer and let them drool over her for a while. Let their minds start to conjure up fantasies that would play right into my hands when I made the next move.

I waited until Angie's first selection was playing and she'd started to switch her fine ass to the beat while she took her time pondering another choice. By then all the marks were wearing slack-jawed expressions and staring as openly as front-row customers in a grind house.

410

I had to wave my arms like a windmill to get the bartender's attention. He trudged over to see what I wanted.

"Another beer?"

"In a minute, maybe. What I need first is a word or two with you." I held my voice in a kind of conspiratorial hush.

Andy looked uncertain. "About what?"

"Listen. You own this place, right?"

"Free and clear. My old man left it to me and I take good care of it."

"Good, good. Then you got nobody to answer to if it came to making what you might call, well, a controversial decision."

"I guess not. What do you mean?" He aimed the question at me but he couldn't keep his eyes off Angie over at the juke box.

I dragged my hand down over my face again, laying on the act of somebody struggling with a real dilemma. "This isn't easy to bring up, I want you to understand. But you already know the fix I'm in. . . ."

Andy gave a firm shake of his head. "Come on, mister, if this is about a loan or something you can't expect me to—"

"Hell, I'm not talking about a loan," I cut him off. "I'm talking about nothing more than a little game of chance. A raffle. Held right here, tonight, in your place. A chance for me to raise the money I so desperately need, a chance for you and your customers to win a mighty fine prize."

His piggy little eyes turned skeptical and just a bit smug. "And what would this 'mighty fine prize' be that you've got to raffle?"

I gave him smug right back. "You've been gawking at it ever since I brought it in here. You and every other swinging dick in this place."

It took him about half a minute to get it. When he finally did, his jaw practically dropped onto the bartop. "Sweet Jesus. You mean . . . *her?* You mean the prize is your lady?"

"Winner gets half an hour with Angie. Do whatever he wants. You've got some kind of back room here, don't you? A cot maybe? If not, there are a couple pickups outside with camper shells. I guarantee the setting won't really matter. A half hour with Angie—no matter where—any man will think he's in paradise."

"Are you serious? Jesus, mister. It's hard to believe anybody would . . ."

"It's my only chance to make Tulsa in time. And Tulsa may be my only chance of keeping Angie for much longer at all. I can live with what we got to do. So can she. You and your customers sure haven't minded drooling and staring at her ever since she walked in. But if you're a bunch of Bible-thumpers by day, or goody-goods of some other cut who only sneak peeks and are afraid of a chance to get it on for real, then I guess I read you wrong and we can forget it. We'll find some other way—"

"No. No, no. Nobody said that. Jeez, give me a minute to catch up with all this. Nothing like this has ever happened to me before."

"I'm guessing the guys here are all regulars. You know them all, right? I'd have to have your word that none of them will go running to the law afterward, or that none of them are kinky in some way Angie's got to worry about in case they win."

"You got no worry about any of that. I know all these boys. Well, all but that young fella in the back shooting eight ball. He's some biker passing through, waiting out the storm. Sure don't have to worry about his type running to the law."

"You up for it, then?" I asked him point blank. "I can't afford to offer you a cut, but think what it'll do for business if you let word get around. Not just tonight, but from now on. Guys you never saw before will start stopping in just to hear you tell the story. And they'll keep coming back because they'll be hoping they're lucky enough to have lightning strike again while they're here. You *do* reckon the boys we got on hand tonight are willing to try and get lucky, don't you?"

He grinned wolfishly. "Are you kidding? Look at the way they're all looking at her. Who can blame them? And who in his right mind wouldn't go for a chance at . . . well, something so fine."

I reached across the bar and clapped a hand onto his meaty shoulder. "Good, good. Here's the way we'll work it then. . . ."

I drew twenty squares on a sheet of paper, numbered each one. While I was doing that, Andy, the bartender, went around and explained to the others what was up. Every one of them was eager to participate. It would cost them twenty-five bucks a square. They could pick their number, first come first serve. I'd write their name in the square carrying the number of their choice. When the sheet was full, I'd cut it up, drop the squares into a hat, draw out the winner. Everything in plain sight, everything above board.

The squares went almost faster than I could take money and write in names. Andy alone bought four of them, a hundred bucks' worth, and just shelling out the dough made him as flushed and sweaty as if he'd already had the sex he was gambling on. Old Gleason, who must have had a hell of a lot more steam stored up in him than you'd ever guess, antied up for two chances. Some of the others were also willing to increase their odds by buying two. By the time it was done, I had five hundred bucks and a sheetful of filled-in squares in front of me.

Through it all, Angie remained off by herself at one end of the bar. Calmly smoking a cigarette and sipping sloe gin. Cool and aloof, like a queen bitch in heat waiting for a winner to emerge from the pack of hounds snarling after her scent.

The place went quiet as a tomb while I held the hat at arms' length in one hand, reached in with the other, swirled the bits of paper, then withdrew one. Or so most of them thought. The piece of paper I held up and began to unfold had actually been deftly palmed back when I was cutting up the squares and dropping them into the hat to begin with.

"Number twelve," I read aloud. "Sam Stone."

Everybody started looking at one another. Their expressions were perplexed. They didn't seem to recognize the name.

Then the young biker with the sullen eyes and the mane of wheat-colored hair pushed his way through. "That'd be me."

A general groan of despair and a handful of curses rolled out of the pack of slump-shouldered losers.

"You're a lucky man, son," I said, looking into his eyes. Sam Stone. Stoney, we'd taken to calling him shortly after he joined our crew back in Kansas City. He'd proven himself to be sharp, a fast learner. Lately I'd taken to wondering just *how fast* on the uptake he might be. I wondered exactly what him and Angie did during those half-hour chunks of time they spent alone together whenever we ran this scam, playing out the rigged "win" while I waited somewhere else with the sorry remains of whatever flock we'd just fleeced.

"Yeah, sometimes I do get lucky." Stoney replied now, meeting my gaze evenly.

A deeply disappointed Andy pointed the way to the back room and Stoney and Angie disappeared through the doorway.

The rest of us didn't have much to say while we waited. A couple of the players finished their drinks and left.

Eventually Andy came over by me. "Now that you got yourself some money, you be wanting the name of that service station I told you about?"

I shook my head. "Don't think so. Figure the quickest way is for us to catch a ride to the nearest town with a train or bus station and go on into Tulsa that way."

"What about your car?"

"The junk parts off it probably wouldn't be worth the price of towing. I don't much care what happens to it."

"Guess you won't be needing it where you're going anyway."

"Tulsa, you mean?"

"Uh-uh. Not exactly."

The warning was there in his voice but I wasn't quick enough to catch on. Not before I got grabbed from behind by two of the others, two burly farmer types. My arms were pinned to my sides, my chest slammed hard against the edge of the bar. There was no sense in struggling. I've never been very physical, I get by on my wits.

"What the hell gives?" I demanded.

"The jig is up, you phony fucker—that's what gives," Andy sneered, leaning across the bar and shoving his fat face close to mine.

The two guys holding me jerked me around in time to see Angie and Stoney being shoved from the back room by two other guys— the same two I thought had left. One of the guys was flashing a pistol. Stoney's hands were tied behind his back with a torn and knotted strip of bar towel. Both he and Angie were bare from the waist up. Their two captors might have peeled Angie for a cheap thrill, but that wouldn't explain Stoney being partly undressed. What it meant was that the two of them had started to strip each other before they got interrupted. I felt a sickening anger toward both of them and the guilty look in Angie's eyes when she tried to meet mine only made it worse.

"We had you sharpies spotted from the minute you walked in," Andy was saying, continuing to sneer. "Old Gleason here was off visiting relatives in Missouri last month and heard stories about you three recently pulling this stunt in several rural counties over that way. The folks involved only figured out they'd been scammed after they got to comparing notes. Gleason recognized you from the descriptions they gave, and clued the rest of us in on what you were up to."

"Why'd you go so far along with it, then?" I said.

"Just to make sure, sonny," Gleason answered. "Just to make damn sure."

"So what now? I suppose the cops are on their way."

Andy wagged a scolding finger at me. "Oh, no. You made me promise no one would run to the law, remember?"

"You've obviously got something in mind. You trying to say you've put together some kind of half-assed lynch mob?"

"No!" Angie cried. "Do something, Milo. Offer them money. Pay them whatever it takes."

Andy chuckled. "Don't worry, little lady, we ain't going to lynch nobody. And it ain't money we want in payment . . . but it's something else you got plenty of."

Angie's eyes went big. "No!"

"We're going to take what we already paid for, that's all. You tried to cheat us, so now we remove the risk. Everybody gets to be a winner."

Stoney tried to say something but Andy backhanded him with surprising viciousness. When he was through, breathing hard from the exertion and breaking into a fresh sweat, the bartender turned to old Gleason. "You earned top honors, old man, you and your eagle eyes. Take her in the back again. Then it'll be my turn."

Angie started to tremble, too scared to resist.

"Don't try to fight him, lady, he's a lot stronger than he looks. And if we have to, there's plenty of us willing to come hold you down for him."

Gleason laughed nastily. "That'll be the day, when I need any of you young whelps to hold a girl down *for me.*" He shoved Angie roughly ahead of him and followed her into the back room.

After the door had closed, Andy motioned for Stoney to be dragged over closer to where I was. When that was done, he said, "Now for you two bastards."

He motioned again and a tall, gangly, tow-headed man stepped up to stand next to him. "This here's Homer Dobbins. Homer might not look like much to a couple of sharpies like you two, but it happens he's a successful local businessman. And he's got a real special skill. Almost like fate, him being on hand tonight. Homer runs the local hog market, see, has for years . . . and in that time he's become the champeen hog nutter in all of Caliboros County."

Something icy clutched my insides.

"We ain't going to run to the law," Andy continued. "But we're by-God going to have us some justice. And since you two were fixing to screw every one of us like you already screwed who knows how many other trusting old country boys before this, we decided the only right thing to square all of that is to fix it so you don't screw nothing ever again. . . . Show 'em, Homer."

Grinning, Homer held up two gleaming blades; a straight razor and what looked like a curved linoleum cutter.

I heard somebody start to scream and it took a minute to realize it was me. More hands grabbed me, pulled me down, pressed my shoulders to the floor and began yanking my limbs spread-eagled. I caught a final fleeting glimpse of Homer's grinning face and glittery blades before he knelt down and went out of sight behind the heads and shoulders of the guys pinning my legs.

In the background, fat Andy was cackling. "Spread em wide, Milo baby!"

The only hope I had left was that I could stay conscious long enough for the satisfaction of hearing that bastard Stoney do some screaming too.

A REAL NICE GUY

WILLIAM F. NOLAN

Warm sun.
      A summer afternoon.

The sniper emerged from the roof door, walking easily, carrying a custom-leather guncase.

Opened the case.

Assembled the weapon.

Loaded it.

Sighted the street below.

Adjusted the focus.

Waited.

There was no hurry.

No hurry at all.

He was famous, yet no one knew his name. There were portraits of him printed in dozens of newspapers and magazines; he'd even made the cover of *Time*. But no one had really seen his face. The portraits were composites, drawn by frustrated police artists, based on the few misleading descriptions given by witnesses who claimed to have seen him leaving a building or jumping from a roof, or driving from the target area in a stolen automobile. But no two descriptions matched.

One witness described a chunky man of average height with a dark beard and cap. Another described a thin, extremely tall man with a bushy head of hair and a thick mustache. A third description pegged him as balding, paunchy and wearing heavy hornrims. On *Time*'s cover, a large blood-soaked question mark replaced his features—above the words WHO IS HE?

Reporters had given him many names: "The Phantom Sniper" . . . "The Deadly Ghost" . . . "The Silent Slayer" . . . and his personal favorite, "The Master of Whispering Death." This was often shortened to "Deathmaster," but he liked the full title; it was fresh and poetic—and *accurate*.

He *was* a master. He never missed a target, never wasted a shot. He was cool and nerveless and smooth, and totally without conscience. And death indeed whispered from his silenced weapon: a dry snap of the trigger, a muffled pop, and the target dropped as though struck down by the fist of God.

They were *always* targets, never people. Men, women, children. Young, middle-aged, old. Strong ones. Weak ones. Healthy or crippled. Black or white. Rich or poor. Targets—all of them.

He considered himself a successful sharpshooter, demonstrating his unique skill in a world teeming with three billion moving targets placed there for his amusement. Day and night, city by city, state by state, they were always there, ready for his gun, for the sudden whispering death from its barrel. An endless supply just for him.

Each city street was his personal shooting gallery.

But he was careful. Very careful. He never killed twice in the same city. He switched weapons. He never used a car more than once. He never wore the same clothes twice on a shoot. Even the shoes would be discarded; he wore a fresh pair for each target run. And, usually, he was never seen at all.

He thought of it as a sport.

A game.

A run.

A vocation.

A skill.

But never murder.

* * *

His name was Jimmie Prescott and he was thirty-one years of age. Five foot ten. Slight build. Platform shoes could add three inches and body pillows up to fifty pounds. He had thinning brown hair framing a bland, unmemorable face. He shaved twice daily— but the case of wigs, beards and mustaches he always carried easily disguised the shape of his mouth, chin and skull. Sometimes he would wear a skin-colored fleshcap for baldness, or use heavy glasses—though his sight was perfect. Once, for a lark, he had worn a black eye patch. He would walk in a crouch; or stride with a sailor's swagger, or assume a limp. Each disguise amused him, helped make life more challenging. Each was a small work of art, flawlessly executed.

Jimmie was a perfectionist.

And he was clean: no police record. Never arrested. No set of his prints on file, no dossier.

He had a great deal of money (inherited) with no need or incli-nation to earn more. He had spent his lifetime honing his consider-able skills: he was an expert on weaponry, car theft, body-combat, police procedures; he made it a strict rule to memorize the street system of each city he entered before embarking on a shoot. And once his target was down he knew exactly how to leave the area. The proper escape route was essential.

Jimmie was a knowledgeable historian in his field: he had made a thorough study of snipers, and held them all in cold contempt. Not a worthwhile one in the lot. They *deserved* to be caught; they were fools and idiots and blunderers, often acting out of neurotic impulse or psychotic emotion. Even the hired professionals drew Jimmie's ire—since these were men who espoused political causes or who worked for government money. Jimmie had no cause, nor would he ever allow himself to be bought like a pig on the market.

He considered himself quite sane. Lacking moral conscience, he did not suffer from a guilt complex. Nor did he operate from a basic hatred of humankind, as did so many of the warped criminals he had studied.

Basically, Jimmie liked people, got along fine with them on a casual basis. He hated no one. (Except his parents, but they were long dead and something he did not think about anymore.) He was incapable of love or friendship, but felt no need for either. Jimmie depended only on himself; he had learned to do that from child-hood. He was, therefore, a loner by choice, and made it a rule (Jimmie had many rules) never to date the same female twice, no matter how sexually appealing she might be. Man-woman relationships were a weakness, a form of dangerous self-indulgence he carefully avoided.

In sum, Jimmie Prescott didn't need anyone. He had himself, his skills, his weapons and his targets. More than enough for a full, rich life. He did not drink or smoke. (Oh, a bit of vintage wine in a good restaurant was always welcome, but he had never been drunk in his life.) He jogged each day, morning and evening, and worked out twice a week in the local gym in whatever city he was visiting. A trim, healthy body was an absolute necessity in his specialized career. Jimmie left nothing to chance. He was not a gambler and took no joy in risk.

A few times things had been close: a roof door that had jammed shut in Detroit after a kill, forcing him to make a perilous between-buildings leap . . . an engine that died during a police chase in Portland, causing him to abandon his car . . . an intense struggle with an off-duty patrolman in Indianapolis who'd witnessed a shot. The fellow had been tough, and dispatching him was physically difficult; Jimmie finally snapped his neck—but it had been close.

He kept a neat, handwritten record of each shoot in his tooled-leather notebook: state, city, name of street, weather, time of day, sex, age and skin color of target. Under "Comments," he would add pertinent facts, including the make and year of the stolen car he had driven, and the type of disguise he had utilized. Each item of clothing worn was listed. And if he experienced any problem in exiting the target area this would also be noted. Thus, each shoot was critically analyzed upon completion—as a football coach might dissect a game after it had been played.

The only random factor was the target. Pre-selection spoiled the freshness, the *purity* of the act. Jimmie liked to surprise himself. Which shall it be: that young girl in red, laughing up at her boyfriend? The old newsman on the corner? The school kid skipping homeward with books under his arm? Or, perhaps, the beefy, bored truckdriver, sitting idly in his cab, waiting for the light to change?

Selection was always a big part of the challenge.

And *this* time . . .

A male. Strong looking. Well dressed. Businessman with a briefcase, in his late forties. Hair beginning to silver at the temples. He'd just left the drugstore; probably stopped there to pick up something for his wife. Maybe she'd called to remind him at lunch.

Moving toward the corner. Walking briskly.

Yes, *this* one. By all means, this one.

Range: three hundred yards.

Adjust sight focus.

Rifle stock tight against right shoulder.

Finger inside guard, poised at trigger.

Cheek firm against wooden gunstock; eye to rubber scopepiece.

Line crosshairs on target.

Steady breathing.

Tighten trigger finger slowly.

Fire!

The man dropped forward to the walk like a clubbed animal, dead before he struck the pavement. Someone screamed. A child began to cry. A man shouted.

Pleasant, familiar sounds to Jimmie Prescott.

Calmly, he took apart his weapon, cased it, then carefully dusted his trousers. (Rooftops were often grimy, and although he would soon discard the trousers he liked to present a neat, well-tailored appearance—but only when the disguise called for it. What a marvelous, ill-smelling bum he had become in New Orleans; he smiled thinly, thinking about how truly offensive he was on that occasion.)

He walked through the roof exit to the elevator.

Within ten minutes he had cleared central Baltimore—and booked the next flight to the West Coast.

Aboard the jet, he relaxed. In the soft, warm, humming interior of the airliner, he grew drowsy . . . closed his eyes.

And had The Dream again.

The Dream was the only disturbing element in Jimmie Prescott's life. He invariably thought of it that way: The Dream. Never as *a* dream. Always about a large metropolitan city where chaos reigned —with buses running over babies in the street, and people falling down sewer holes and through plate glass store windows. Violent and disturbing. He was never threatened in The Dream, never personally involved in the chaos around him. Merely a mute witness to it.

He would tell himself, this was only *fantasy*, a thing deep inside his sleeping mind; it would go away once he awakened and then he could ignore it, put it out of his thoughts, bury it as he had buried the hatred for his father and mother.

Perhaps he had *other* dreams. Surely he did. But The Dream was the one he woke to, again and again, emerging from the chaos of the city with sweat on his cheeks and forehead, his breath tight and shallow in his chest, his heart thudding wildly.

"Are you all right?" a passenger across the aisle was asking him. "Shall I call somebody?"

"I'm fine," said Jimmie, sitting up straight. "No problem."

"You look kinda shaky."

"No, I'm fine. But thank you for your concern."

And he put The Dream away once again, as a gun is put away in its case.

In Los Angeles, having studied the city quite thoroughly, Jimmie took a cab directly into Hollywood. The fare was steep, but money was never an issue in Jimmie's life; he paid well for services rendered, with no regrets.

He got off at Highland, on Hollywood Boulevard, and walked toward the Chinese Theater.

He wanted two things: food and sexual satisfaction.

First, he would select an attractive female, take her to dinner and then to his motel room (he'd booked one from the airport) where he would have sex. Jimmie never called it lovemaking, a *silly* word. It was always just sex, plain and simple and quickly over. He was capable of arousing a woman if he chose to do so, of bringing her to full passion and release, but he seldom bothered. His performance was always an act; the ritual bored him. Only the result counted.

He disliked prostitutes and seldom selected one. Too jaded. Too worldly. And never to be trusted. Given time, and his natural charm, he was usually able to pick up an out-of-town girl, impress her with an excellent and very expensive meal at a posh restaurant, and guide her firmly into bed.

This night, in Hollywood, the seduction was easily accomplished.

Jimmie spotted a supple, soft-faced girl in the forecourt of the Chinese. She was wandering from one celebrity footprint to another, leaning to examine a particular signature in the cement.

As she bent forward, her breasts flowed full, pressing against the soft linen dress she wore—and Jimmie told himself, she's the one for tonight. A young, awestruck out-of-towner. Perfect.

He moved toward her.

"I just *love* European food," said Janet.

"That's good," said Jimmie Prescott. "I rather fancy it myself."

She smiled at him across the table, a glowing all-American girl from Ohio named Janet Louise Lakeley. They were sitting in a small, very chic French restaurant off La Cienega, with soft lighting and open-country decor.

"I can't read a word of this," Janet said when the menu was handed to her. "I thought they always had the food listed in English, too, like movie subtitles."

"Some places don't," said Jimmie quietly. "I'll order for us both. You'll be pleased. The sole is excellent here."

"Oh, I love fish," she said. "I could eat a ton of fish."

He pressed her hand. "That's nice."

"My head is swimming. I shouldn't have had that Scotch on an empty stomach," she said. "Are we having wine with dinner?"

"Of course," said Jimmie.

"I don't know anything about wine," she told him, "but I love champagne. That's wine, isn't it?"

He smiled with a faint upcurve of his thin lips.

"Trust me," he said. "You'll enjoy what I select."

"I'm sure I will."

The food was ordered and served—and Jimmie was pleased to see that his tastes had, once again, proven sound. The meal was superb, the wine was bracing and the girl was sexually stimulating. Essentially brainless, but that didn't really matter to Jimmie. She was what he wanted.

Then she began to talk about the sniper killings.

"Forty people in just a year and two months," she said. "And all gunned down by the same madman. Aren't they *ever* going to catch him?"

"The actual target total is forty-one," he corrected her. "And what makes you so sure the sniper is a male? Could be a woman."

She shook her head. "Whoever heard of a woman sniper?"

"There have been many," said Jimmie. "In Russia today there are several hundred trained female snipers. Some European governments have traditionally utilized females in this capacity."

"I don't mean women *soldiers*," she said. "I mean your nutso shoot-'em-in-the-street sniper. Always guys. Every time. Like that kid in Texas that shot all the people from the tower."

"Apparently you've never heard of Francine Stearn."

"Nope. Who was she?"

"Probably the most famous female sniper. Killed a dozen school-children in Pittsburgh one weekend in late July, 1970. One shot each. To the head. She was a very accurate shootist."

"Never heard of her."

"After she was captured, *Esquire* did a rather probing psychological profile on her."

"Well, I really don't read a lot," she admitted. "Except Gothic romances. I just can't get *enough* of those." She giggled. "Guess you could say I'm addicted."

"I'm not familiar with the genre."

"Anyway," she continued, "I know this sniper is a guy."

"How do you know?"

"Female intuition. I trust it. It never fails me. And it tells me that the Phantom Sniper is a man."

He was amused. "What else does it tell you?"

"That he's probably messed up in the head. Maybe beaten as a kid. Something like that. He's *got* to be a nutcase."

"You could be wrong there, too," Jimmie told her. "Not all law-breakers are mentally unbalanced."

"This 'Deathmaster' guy is, and I'm convinced of it."

"You're a strongly opinionated young woman."

"Mom always said that." She sipped her wine, nodded. "Yeah, I guess I am." She frowned, turning the glass slowly in her long-fingered hand. "Do you think they'll ever catch him?"

"I somehow doubt it," Jimmie declared. "No one seems to have a clear description of him. And he always manages to elude the police. Leaves no clues. Apparently selects his subjects at random. No motive to tie him to. No consistent M.O."

"What's that?"

"Method of operation. Most criminals tend to repeat the same basic pattern in their crimes. But not this fellow. He keeps surprising people. Never know where he'll pop up next, or who his target will be. Difficult to catch a man like that."

"You call them 'subjects' and 'targets'—but they're *people!* Innocent men and women and children. You make them sound like . . . like cutouts in a shooting gallery!"

"Perhaps I do," he admitted, smiling. "It's simply that we have different modes of expression."

"I say they'll get him eventually. He can't go on just butchering innocent people forever."

"No one goes on forever," said Jimmie Prescott.

She put down her wineglass, leaned toward him. "Know what bothers me most about the sniper?"

"What?"

"The fact that his kind of act attracts copycats. Other sickos with a screw loose who read about him and want to imitate him. Arson is like that. One big fire in the papers and suddenly all the other wacko firebugs start their *own* fires. It gets 'em going. The sniper is like that."

"If some mentally disturbed individual is motivated to kill stupidly and without thought or preparation by something he or she reads in the newspaper then the sniper himself cannot be blamed for such abnormal behavior."

"You call what *he* does normal?"

"I . . . uh . . . didn't say that. I was simply refuting your theory."

She frowned. "Then who *is* to blame? I think that guy should be caught and—"

"And what?" Jimmie fixed his cool gray eyes on her. "What would you do if you suddenly discovered who he was . . . where to find him?"

"Call the police, naturally. Like anybody."

"Wouldn't you be curious about him, about the kind of person he is? Wouldn't you *question* him first, try to understand him?"

"You don't question an animal who kills! Which is what he is. I'd like to see him gassed or hanged. . . . You don't *talk* to a twisted creep like that!"

She had made him angry. His lips tightened. He was no longer amused with this conversation; the word game had turned sour. This girl was gross and stupid and insensitive. Take her to bed and be done with it. Use her body—but no words. No more words. He'd had quite enough of those from her.

"Check, please," he said to the waiter.

It was at his motel, after sex, that Jimmie decided to kill her. Her insulting tirade echoed and re-echoed in his mind. She must be punished for it.

In this special case he felt justified in breaking one of his rules: never pre-select a target. She told him that she worked the afternoon shift at a clothing store on Vine. And he knew where she lived, a few blocks from work. She walked to the store each afternoon.

He would take her home and return the next day. When she left her apartment building he would dispatch her from a roof across the street. Once this plan had settled into place in the mind of Jimmie Prescott he relaxed, allowing the tension of the evening to drain away.

By tomorrow night he'd be in Tucson, and Janet Lakeley would be dead.

Warm sun.

A summer afternoon.

The sniper emerged from the roof door, walking easily, carrying a custom-leather guncase.

Opened the case.

Assembled the weapon.

Loaded it.

Sighted the street below.

Adjusted the focus.

Waited.

Target now exiting.

Walking along street toward corner.

Adjust sight focus.

Finger on trigger.

Cheek against stock.

Eye to scope.

Crosshairs direct on target.

Fire!

Jimmie felt something like a fist strike his stomach. A sudden, shocking blow. Winded, he looked down in amazement at the blood pulsing steadily from his shirtfront.

I'm hit! Someone has actually—

Another blow—but this one stopped all thought, taking his head apart. No more shock. No more amazement.

No more Jimmie.

She put away the weapon, annoyed at herself. *Two* shots! The Phantom Sniper, whoever he was, never fired more than once. But *he* was exceptional. She got goosebumps, just thinking about him.

Well, maybe next time she could drop her target in one. Anybody can miscalculate a shot. Nobody's perfect.

She left the roof area, walking calmly, took the elevator down to the garage, stowed her guncase in the trunk of the stolen Mustang and drove away from the motel.

Poor Jimmie, she thought. It was just his bad luck to meet *me*. But that's the way it goes.

Janet Lakeley had a rule, and she never broke it: when you bed down a guy in a new town you always target him the next day. She sighed. Usually it didn't bother her. Most of them were bastards. But not Jimmie. She'd enjoyed talking to him, playing her word games with him . . . bedding him. She was sorry he had to go.

He seemed like a real nice guy.

RED RUNS
THE TIDE

JOHN P. FORAN

The yacht basin nestled peacefully at the foot of green hills dotted with white, where fresh-water streams foamed over rocky ledges and flowed down to join the river's march to the salty sea. About thirty yachts, ranging in size from the river cruiser, *Judy-Ann*, to the ocean-going *Corsair*, were tied to buoys in the basin.

The tide pinned a police launch against the dock that was used as a landing and fueling station. A cop stood on the dock, guarding what was left of David Salisbury after nine days under the rotted wooden hulk that lifted out of the water south of the basin. A weathered tarpaulin protected the body from the heat of the sun.

Sergeant Eaton, of the marine division, sat in a wicker chair on the clubhouse porch. Despite the heat, his ruddy face was placid and his pale blue eyes were deceptively tranquil.

"Pretty," he murmured. "Like a marine toyland."

"Some toys," said Syd Bohm, his engineer. "A hundred grand and you own the *Corsair;* or, if you don't have that kind of dough, you murder Salisbury and marry his widow." He was younger and leaner than Eaton. The heat of the sun and the waiting kept him mopping nervously at his thin face. "What's keeping them?" Irritably he pushed away from the porch rail. "This sun is murder—"

He stopped as two cars, a big black limousine and a small and somewhat battered sedan, came through the basin's gate and drove over to the dock. A big, florid man got out of the limousine and helped a dark-haired woman alight. A slender man carrying a small, black bag got out of the sedan.

"Well, at least Phil's on time for once," growled Syd. "Now if he can forget he's a deck hand and make like a medical examiner—"

"Don't worry about Phil," said Eaton placidly. "Did you turn the wire recorder on?"

"Yeah." Syd checked his watch. "Got 'bout twenty-five minutes to run. I shifted it. It's under the couch in the commodore's office. Ran the wires out the window and around to the beam right over your head. You can hear a whisper on the porch."

Eaton watched what was going on down on the dock. Phil stood to one side while the cop knelt down and lifted a corner of the tarpaulin. The woman took a look at the body. A thin scream floated up to the porch as she recoiled and buried her face in the florid man's shoulder. He held her close for a moment, then turned toward the clubhouse. Phil set his bag on the dock, knelt down and went to work.

"Sarge, are you sure this is going to work?" Syd wiped his thin neck with quick, nervous gestures. "I mean, testing a ship's boiler water is one thing, but river water—hell, why not leave it to the shoreside detectives? It's their job anyway."

"It's a job for men who know the river and its ways," Eaton commented quietly.

"Yes, but—" Syd frowned and went on uneasily: "Remember it was La Salle who kicked up such a fuss last winter when brass fittings were stolen from the basin—like he owned a dozen yachts. And he knows the chief personally."

"Easy, now." Eaton got up as La Salle led Mrs. Salisbury up the porch steps. "Sorry to put you through such a grisly ordeal," he said, sounding very solicitous. "A body bloated by the river is a sickening sight."

Mrs. Salisbury shuddered violently. Her heavy-boned face was white and the skin was taut about a full, sensuous mouth. Her dark eyes were tortured.

La Salle glared at Eaton as he helped her into one of the wicker chairs. "I remember you now," he rasped. "The sergeant who couldn't catch those petty thieves last winter. You're much more effective at torturing women, aren't you?"

Behind La Salle, Syd winced.

Eaton took it calmly. "Just a few questions," he said, and before La Salle could interrupt. "I know, you've answered so many questions already. But now we want to know just how friendly you and Mrs. Salisbury were before her husband was drowned."

Mrs. Salisbury gasped.

"That's a damnable insinuation!" La Salle leaned toward Eaton, his full face livid. "Everybody, including the chief of police, knew that Grace and David and I were friends, close friends. David took many business trips for weeks at a time. He *wanted* me to entertain Grace." He stopped abruptly, staring past Eaton and down to the dock where Phil was working a hand pump. "What's that man doing?"

Without taking his eyes from Mrs. Salisbury, Eaton said, "The medical examiner is making a test for us. When did you last see your husband, Mrs. Salisbury?"

"It isn't possible to test a body that's been in the water over a week," snapped La Salle. "The chief's own personal physician discussed that with us last night."

"It's possible," said Eaton negligently, "to test the salt content of the water that went into Salisbury's lungs."

"And what'll that prove?"

"The exact hour he was drowned."

Eaton turned his attention back to Mrs. Salisbury. She was sitting stiffly erect, her hands white on the arms of the wicker chair. She glanced nervously at La Salle before speaking.

"David got home about eleven that night—a few minutes after. He'd been on the *Corsair* with Harold making up a list of pilot charts for a trip down the coast and across the Gulf of Mexico. I promised to stop off at the hydrographic office and pick them up for him the first thing in the morning."

"You three were taking the trip?"

"No. David owned a refinery down in Texas City and he was arranging the trip for a group of prospective buyers. He was almost asleep when he remembered the list on the *Corsair*. Despite my protests he insisted upon getting dressed and going back for it."

"What time was that?"

"Almost two in the morning."

Eaton turned to La Salle, who said angrily, "We've been over all this with the chief of police. The watchman admitted he was out cold in the clubhouse locker room. He'd found a bottle of whiskey—"

"A very convenient bottle," murmured Eaton.

La Salle's eyes narrowed. "So David took the launch out to the *Corsair*," he went on. "He fell overboard and drowned. That's obvious because the launch was found adrift the next morning, and the tide carried his body down to the old wreck and trapped it under the rotting beams where you grappled for it." His voice was like a whip flaying Eaton, while he kept glancing down to the dock where Phil was packing his bag. "And I've already testified that I left here with David about twenty minutes before eleven and went straight to my hotel. The doorman and elevator operator have corroborated that."

"And they also admitted that you—or anyone else in the hotel—could have slipped out the back way." Without giving La Salle a chance to answer, he turned and watched Phil come toward the clubhouse.

There was a tense silence as Phil came up the steps. Looking at Eaton, he asked, "Would you like me to complete the test right here?"

Eaton nodded. Syd picked up a wicker table and set it in front of Phil. They watched in silence as Phil opened the black bag and took out a wooden rack holding three glass tubes half filled with transparent liquid.

Uncorking the tubes, Phil explained, "This first tube contains a sample of high tide water. You see, when the tide sweeps in from the ocean the river has a maximum salt content, but at ebb tide —this middle sample—the fresh-water streams flowing down out of the hills reduce the salt content. This third tube contains fluid taken from the dead man's lungs."

He took a bottle out of the bag. "This is potassium chromate. I'm going to put an equal amount into each tube and the water in each will turn yellow. Now, a solution of silver nitrate. The resultant color will tell us the salt content of each sample."

They watched him squeeze drops of nitrate into the first test tube. The yellow changed to orange, then to pink, which deepened to a bloody red. He shifted the dropper to the low tide sample, and this time the yellow changed to pink.

Eaton held up a hand as Phil poised the dropper over the fluid taken from Salisbury's lungs. "High tide was at nine the evening Salisbury drowned." He took a newspaper clipping out of his pocket and handed it to La Salle. "You can check the tide with that. If Salisbury was drowned after two in the morning," he went on, "the sample taken from his lungs will match the low tide sample."

He sat back, and nodded to Phil. Syd held his handkerchief against a damp cheek, not daring to breathe.

"Here goes," said Phil. He squeezed drops of nitrate into the third tube and the fluid changed slowly from yellow to orange. More nitrate and the orange merged into pink, then deepened to red.

"Sergeant!" Syd's voice smashed the silence. "It matches the high tide water. Salisbury couldn't have drowned at two in the morning!"

Grace Salisbury's dark eyes were fastened in horror upon the bloody test tube. La Salle held the clipping clenched in one hand, his florid face set hard. Eaton's eyes flicked to Phil, then to Grace.

"You look ill, Mrs. Salisbury," said Phil. "Better come inside and rest a while." Syd pushed against the back of the wicker chair and Mrs. Salisbury jerked forward. Phil took her arm, and urged her to her feet. Syd moved swiftly between the chairs, cutting La Salle out of it. He took Mrs. Salisbury's other arm and they led her inside.

Eaton leaned forward. "This must be quite a shock, Mr. La Salle." His voice was low and sympathetic. "But we figured it from the beginning."

La Salle turned back to Eaton, anger pushing shock out of his eyes.

"We were pretty certain Salisbury discovered he'd left the chart list on board the moment he got home and saw his wife. She was going to take the list to the hydrographic office, wasn't she?"

"What the hell does that have to do with it?"

"When Salisbury insisted upon coming back for it," Eaton continued, "his wife decided to come along. The watchman was drunk, so they took the launch out themselves. We figure Salisbury slipped and fell in the river as he was tying up to the *Corsair*. Then Mrs. Salisbury saw her chance—"

"That's ridiculous!" La Salle's voice was blustery, but lacking anger. "Mrs. Salisbury wouldn't have the physical strength—"

"She's an expert swimmer."

"Yes, but—"

"How much does a body weigh in water?" Eaton spread his hands. "There's no way out. Salisbury was drowned at high tide. It has to be Mrs. Salisbury."

"But high tide was at nine, not at eleven-twenty, the earliest they could have come back here."

Eaton shrugged. "Have you forgotten that the tide takes a couple of hours to turn? Face it, Mr. La Salle. When Salisbury fell in the river, he wasn't the husband she'd loved, but a hateful business executive who kept depriving her of the love and affection she craved."

La Salle licked his lower lip. Speculation moved in his eyes, then in his voice. "Naturally, it wasn't premeditated. The sudden temptation, all the loneliness and frustration sweeping over her—temporary insanity—"

"A jury would understand," said Eaton softly. "Perhaps forgive."

Mrs. Salisbury suddenly appeared on the porch. Eaton didn't look up. La Salle's first warning was an angry blast. "You miserable coward! I heard every word over the wire recorder in the commodore's office. You'd sell me out—"

"Shut up, Grace!" La Salle was on his feet, dismayed. "They're trying to trap us!"

"They can't trap me!" she shot back. "You drowned my husband. You took his body over to the sunken wreck and pushed him under it. Then you forced me to alibi for you."

"That's a lie! David was still alive when we left here. He went home to you. You've admitted it in front of dozens of witnesses."

"Liar!" screamed Mrs. Salisbury. "Liar! Liar!"

"Take them away," said Eaton wearily.

Syd flipped the wheel hard over as Phil hopped on board with the bowline in his hands. When the launch was headed for the basin entrance, he glanced over his shoulder. Eaton was in the stern, his legs braced, a placid look on his ruddy face.

"Old poker face." Syd grinned. "I'd have bet two to one La Salle would have guessed we were using two high tide samples."

"Anyone but a murderer," said Eaton, "who was worried about the salt content of the water he'd forced his victim to swallow."

THE RED SAIL

LESTER DENT

He came out on the dock with long steps, putting his feet down hard. Two women tourists had just smiled at him, but he had not noticed, although it was unusual for him to be unaware when a woman noticed him. Some perspiration, the result of excitement, stood on his face.

The sloop was tied to the dock. She was a grandma among boats, but not a very large grandma. The boat was about thirty-six feet long, and a little on the shabby side.

He jumped on the old sloop.

"Ahoy, Charlie," he called.

The young man who put his head out of the cabin companionway was thin, stooped. He wore glasses that magnified his eyes. His chin was small. He was very young, a boy. Twenty, perhaps.

"Say, I don't know you," he said nervously.

The bigger, browner man walked toward him, saying "Better get down in the cabin, Charlie, where we can talk."

Charlie stumbled back into the cabin, alarmed.

The big man took a pair of handcuffs out of his hip pocket. He sat on one of the two bunks in the tiny boat cabin. He swung the handcuffs from one hand and said, "Edna didn't come back, did she, Charlie?"

Charlie swallowed. He couldn't seem to take his eyes off the handcuffs.

"Well, Edna won't be back, Charlie. You might as well know that right off," the big man said.

The blood began to leave Charlie's face.

The handcuffs clinked as the big man tossed them from one hard brown hand to the other. It was the only sound in the cabin.

"Tough on you, at that," the big man said dryly. "You must have loved her. I guess nothing but love would take a hotel clerk and change him around the way you've been changed."

"Who—who are you?" Charlie gasped.

The big man ignored the question and asked, "Ever go to the Indian Village and watch the Seminole wrestle the alligator, Charlie?"

"Huh?" said Charlie. "What?"

"You should go sometime and watch the show. The guy throws the alligator, then rubs it with his hand, kind of soothing like, until he calms it down. Then he gets right out of the pen and away from that alligator. You should have done that with Edna."

Charlie's eyes filled with misery.

"Take Lee Wanuck," the big man said. "That Lee—you don't know Lee Wanuck, Edna's ex-husband, do you?"

"No," said Charlie. "He was—"

"He was in the penitentiary before you met Edna, I know."

"Who are you?" Charlie said bitterly. "And what right have you—"

"Edna was pretty sick of it all when you met her. She was full of crime doesn't pay and all of that stuff. You felt sorry for the kid at first, eh Charlie? And the sorry feeling hatched out and was love. That the way it happened, wasn't it? That was the line she gave you, wasn't it?"

"What right—"

The big man interrupted, "Edna said she wanted a home, kids, peace, comfort, security, so on and so on. You were the guy to give 'em to her. So she married you."

A kind of inner light flashed over Charlie's face. "She wanted them!"

The big man showed his teeth unpleasantly.

"Sure, kid," he said. "Sure—in a pig's eye."

"Damn you!" Charlie cried. "I don't know who you are, but you're as wrong as can be."

"Take Lee Wanuck. Now Edna is Lee Wanuck's kind. The girl of a thief, a cheap crook. She can't settle down. Her feet began to itch, didn't they, right after you were married? She wanted to go to Kansas City. So you went to Kansas City to humor her. And then you went to Arizona, to New Mexico, then down to Florida. You know what she was doing, Charlie? She was tearing you loose from your roots. She was working on you—trying to make you a no-good like Lee Wanuck. She's clever, isn't she?"

"No!" Charlie said hoarsely. "You're wrong!"

The big man laughed suddenly. The laugh was so humorless it could have been bones rattling.

"Oh, stop it! What kind of fool are you, anyway?" he said violently.

Charlie was shaking. "You liar!" Charlie said. "You awful liar! We went to Arizona for my health. New Mexico, too. I was rejected for the army. I was rejected for the army, the navy, everything. We were trying to build up my health, that's why we went to Arizona."

Charlie had clenched his fists with vehemence. "My health is why we came here, too."

The big man jangled his handcuffs. "You poor, blind stupe," he said.

Charlie shuddered and stared at the man.

The big man said, "Last night there was a guy down here wanting you to smuggle refugees in from Cuba."

Charlie froze.

"Friend of Edna's, wasn't he?" the big man said.

"No," Charlie said hoarsely. "No, he only knew her when she was married to Lee Wanuck, was all."

The big man snorted and said, "Charlie, you can be thrown in jail right now. Just that guy being on your boat and propositioning you is enough. Enough to jail you."

There was no sound in the boat now, no sound at all, except the little waves slapping the side of the boat hull, making tiny licking noises.

"You poor sucker," the big man said.

Charlie buried his face in his hands.

The big man stared at him, and shook his head slowly, and said, 'They teach us something in the F.B.I. training course, something that goes about like this: The law is primarily interested in reforming men. We want to prevent men from becoming criminals." He was silent. He cleared his throat a time or two.

He put the handcuffs back in his pocket.

"Beat it, Charlie," he said.

Charlie took his face out of his hands. "What?"

"Vamoose," the big man said. "I don't think you're a crook at heart."

"You—you've arrested Edna?" Charlie asked hoarsely.

"Vamoose," the big man said.

Charlie left. He got out of the boat and fled down the dock. He even forgot his hat.

When Charlie was out of sight, the big man walked around looking over the old boat. He was grinning thinly.

A woman came down the dock. She was slender, about twenty, and radiant. She didn't look radiant when she saw the big man.

"Hello, Edna," the man said. "Charlie is gone. Charlie won't be back. Charlie has scrammed."

"Lee!" The girl's eyes were frightened. "Lee Wanuck."

The big man started at her, and suddenly the evil of the man was all over him.

"Charlie won't be back," he said. "I owed you a paying-off for being too damned good for me—and so Charlie won't be back."

The girl turned white. "You—you—"

"I paid you off," the big man said, and began laughing his ugly, bone-rattling laugh. But that stopped when he saw Charlie again.

Charlie was coming. He had a cop with him. Charlie pointed and said, "That's Lee Wanuck, an ex-convict, officer. I think he knows something about an alien-smuggling plan, or anyway one of his pals tried to hire our boat for some such thing yesterday." The cop arrested Wanuck.

Then Charlie grinned at Edna, and put his arm around her tenderly. "I knew he was Wanuck," he explained. "Nobody else could be so wrong about you, darling."

A RETRIEVED REFORMATION

O. HENRY

A guard came to the prison shoe-shop, where Jimmy Valentine was assiduously stitching uppers, and escorted him to the front office. There the warden handed Jimmy his pardon, which had been signed that morning by the governor. Jimmy took it in a tired kind of way. He had served nearly ten months of a four-year sentence. He had expected to stay only about three months, at the longest. When a man with as many friends on the outside as Jimmy Valentine had is received in the "stir" it is hardly worth while to cut his hair.

"Now, Valentine," said the warden, "you'll go out in the morning. Brace up, and make a man of yourself. You're not a bad fellow at heart. Stop cracking safes, and live straight."

"Me?" said Jimmy, in surprise. "Why, I never cracked a safe in my life."

"Oh, no," laughed the warden. "Of course not. Let's see, now. How was it you happened to get sent up on that Springfield job? Was it because you wouldn't prove an alibi for fear of compromising somebody in extremely high-toned society? Or was it simply a case of a mean old jury that had it in for you? It's always one or the other with you innocent victims."

"Me?" said Jimmy, still blankly virtuous. "Why, warden, I never was in Springfield in my life!"

"Take him back, Cronin," smiled the warden, "and fix him up with outgoing clothes. Unlock him at seven in the morning, and let him come to the bull-pen. Better think over my advice, Valentine."

At a quarter past seven on the next morning Jimmy stood in the warden's outer office. He had on a suit of the villainously fitting, ready-made clothes and a pair of the stiff, squeaky shoes that the state furnishes to its discharged compulsory guests.

The clerk handed him a railroad ticket and the five-dollar bill with which the law expected him to rehabilitate himself into good citizenship and prosperity. The warden gave him a cigar, and shook hands. Valentine, 9762, was chronicled on the books "Pardoned by Governor," and Mr. James Valentine walked out into the sunshine.

Disregarding the song of the birds, the waving green trees, and the smell of the flowers, Jimmy headed straight for a restaurant. There he tasted the first sweet joys of liberty in the shape of a broiled chicken and a bottle of white wine—followed by a cigar a grade better than the one the warden had given him. From there he proceeded leisurely to the depot. He tossed a quarter into the hat of a blind man sitting by the door, and boarded his train. Three hours set him down in a little town near the state line. He went to the café of one Mike Dolan and shook hands with Mike, who was alone behind the bar.

"Sorry we couldn't make it sooner, Jimmy, me boy," said Mike. "But we had that protest from Springfield to buck against, and the governor nearly balked. Feeling all right?"

"Fine," said Jimmy. "Got my key?"

He got his key and went upstairs, unlocking the door of a room at the rear. Everything was just as he had left it. There on the floor was still Ben Price's collar-button that had been torn from that eminent detective's shirt-band when they had overpowered Jimmy to arrest him.

Pulling out from the wall a folding-bed, Jimmy slid back a panel in the wall and dragged out a dust-covered suitcase. He opened this and gazed fondly at the finest set of burglar's tools in the East. It was a complete set, made of specially tempered steel, the latest designs in drills, punches, braces and bits, jimmies, clamps, and augers, with two or three novelties invented by Jimmy himself, in which he took pride. Over nine hundred dollars they had cost him to have made at ———, a place where they make such things for the profession.

In half an hour Jimmy went downstairs and through the café. He was now dressed in tasteful and well-fitting clothes, and carried his dusted and cleaned suitcase in his hand.

"Got anything on?" asked Mike Dolan, genially.

"Me?" said Jimmy, in a puzzled tone. "I don't understand. I'm representing the New York Amalgamated Short Snap Biscuit Cracker and Frazzled Wheat Company."

This statement delighted Mike to such an extent that Jimmy had to take a seltzer-and-milk on the spot. He never touched "hard" drinks.

A week after the release of Valentine, 9762, there was a neat job of safe-burglary done in Richmond, Indiana, with no clue to the author. A scant eight hundred dollars was all that was secured. Two weeks after that a patented, improved, burglar-proof safe in Logansport was opened like a cheese to the tune of fifteen hundred dollars, currency; securities and silver untouched. That began to interest the rogue-catchers. Then an old-fashioned bank-safe in Jefferson City became active and threw out of its crater an eruption of banknotes amounting to five thousand dollars. The losses were now high enough to bring the matter up into Ben Price's class of work. By comparing notes, a remarkable similarity in the methods of the burglaries was noticed. Ben Price investigated the scenes of the robberies, and was heard to remark:

"That's Dandy Jim Valentine's autograph. He's resumed business. Look at that combination knob—jerked out as easy as pulling up a radish in wet weather. He's got the only clamps that can do it. And look how clean those tumblers were punched out! Jimmy never has to drill but one hole. Yes, I guess I want Mr. Valentine. He'll do his bit next time without any short-time or clemency foolishness."

Ben Price knew Jimmy's habits. He had learned them while working up the Springfield case. Long jumps, quick get-aways, no confederates, and a taste for good society—these ways had helped Mr. Valentine to become noted as a successful dodger of retribution. It was given out that Ben Price had taken up the trail of the elusive cracksman, and other people with burglar-proof safes felt more at ease.

One afternoon Jimmy Valentine and his suitcase climbed out of the mail-hack in Elmore, a little town five miles off the railroad down in the black-jack country of Arkansas. Jimmy, looking like an athletic young senior just home from college, went down the board sidewalk toward the hotel.

A young lady crossed the street, passed him at the corner and entered a door over which was the sign "The Elmore Bank." Jimmy Valentine looked into her eyes, forgot what he was, and became another man. She lowered her eyes and colored slightly. Young men of Jimmy's style and looks were scarce in Elmore.

Jimmy collared a boy that was loafing on the steps of the bank as if he were one of the stock-holders, and began to ask him questions about the town, feeding him dimes at intervals. By and by the young lady came out, looking royally unconscious of the young man with the suitcase, and went her way.

"Isn't that young lady Miss Polly Simpson?" asked Jimmy, with specious guile.

"Naw," said the boy. "She's Annabel Adams. Her pa owns this bank. What'd you come to Elmore for? Is that a good watch-chain? I'm going to get a bulldog. Got any more dimes?"

Jimmy went to the Palmer Hotel, registered as Ralph D. Spencer, and engaged a room. He leaned on the desk and declared his platform to the clerk. He said he had come to Elmore to look for a location to go into business. How was the shoe business, now, in the town? He had thought of the shoe business. Was there an opening?

The clerk was impressed by the clothes and manner of Jimmy. He, himself, was something of a pattern of fashion to the thinly gilded youth of Elmore, but he now perceived his shortcomings. While trying to figure out Jimmy's manner of tying his four-in-hand he cordially gave information.

Yes, there ought to be a good opening in the shoe line. There wasn't an exclusive shoe-store in the place. The dry-goods and general stores handled them. Business in all lines was fairly good. Hoped Mr. Spencer would decide to locate in Elmore. He would find it a pleasant town to live in, and the people very sociable.

Mr. Spencer thought he would stop over in the town a few days and look over the situation. No, the clerk needn't call the boy. He would carry up his suitcase, himself; it was rather heavy.

Mr. Ralph Spencer, the phoenix that arose from Jimmy Valentine's ashes—ashes left by the flame of a sudden and alternative attack of love—remained in Elmore, and prospered. He opened a shoe-store and secured a good run of trade.

Socially he was also a success, and made many friends. And he accomplished the wish of his heart. He met Miss Annabel Adams, and became more and more captivated by her charms.

At the end of a year the situation of Mr. Ralph Spencer was this: he had won the respect of the community, his shoe-store was flourishing, and he and Annabel were engaged to be married in two weeks. Mr. Adams, the typical, plodding, country banker, approved of Spencer. Annabel's pride in him almost equalled her affection. He was as much at home in the family of Mr. Adams and that of Annabel's married sister as if he were already a member.

One day Jimmy sat down in his room and wrote this letter, which he mailed to the safe address of one of his old friends in St. Louis:

Dear Old Pal:

I want you to be at Sullivan's place, in Little Rock, next Wednesday night at nine o'clock. I want you to wind up some little matters for me. And, also, I want to make you a present of my kit of tools. I know you'll be glad to get them—you couldn't duplicate the lot for a thousand dollars. Say, Billy, I've quit the old business—a year ago. I've got a nice store. I'm making an honest living, and I'm going to marry the finest girl on earth two weeks from now. It's the only life, Billy—the straight one. I wouldn't touch a dollar of another man's money now for a million. After I get married I'm going to sell out and go West, where there won't be so much danger of having old scores brought up against me. I tell you, Billy, she's an angel. She believes in me; and I wouldn't do another crooked thing for the whole world. Be sure to be at Sully's, for I must see you. I'll bring along the tools with me.

Your old friend,
Jimmy

On the Monday night after Jimmy wrote this letter, Ben Price jogged unobtrusively into Elmore in a livery buggy. He lounged about town in his quiet way until he found out what he wanted to know. From the drug-store across the street from Spencer's shoe-store he got a good look at Ralph D. Spencer.

"Going to marry the banker's daughter are you, Jimmy?" said Ben to himself, softly. "Well, I don't know!"

The next morning Jimmy took breakfast at the Adamses. He was going to Little Rock that day to order his wedding-suit and buy something nice for Annabel. That would be the first time he had left town since he came to Elmore. It had been more than a year now since those last professional "jobs," and he thought he could safely venture out.

After breakfast quite a family party went down town together—Mr. Adams, Annabel, Jimmy, and Annabel's married sister with her two little girls, aged five and nine. They came by the hotel where Jimmy still boarded, and he ran up to his room and brought along his suitcase. Then they went on to the bank. There stood Jimmy's horse and buggy and Dolph Gibson, who was going to drive him over to the railroad station.

All went inside the high, carved oak railings into the banking-room—Jimmy included, for Mr. Adams's future son-in-law was welcome anywhere. The clerks were pleased to be greeted by the good-looking, agreeable young man who was going to marry Miss Annabel. Jimmy set his suitcase down. Annabel, whose heart was bubbling with happiness and lively youth, put on Jimmy's hat and picked up the suitcase. "Wouldn't I make a nice drummer?" said Annabel. "My! Ralph, how heavy it is. Feels like it was full of gold bricks."

"Lot of nickel-plated shoe-horns in there," said Jimmy, cooly, "that I'm going to return. Thought I'd save express charges by taking them up. I'm getting awfully economical."

The Elmore Bank had just put in a new safe and vault. Mr. Adams was very proud of it, and insisted on an inspection by every one. The vault was a small one, but it had a new patented door. It fastened with three solid steel bolts thrown simultaneously with a single handle, and had a time-lock. Mr. Adams beamingly explained its workings to Mr. Spencer, who showed a courteous but not too intelligent interest. The two children, May and Agatha, were delighted by the shining metal and funny clock and knobs.

While they were thus engaged Ben Price sauntered in and leaned on his elbow, looking casually inside between the railings. He told the teller that he didn't want anything; he was just waiting for a man he knew.

Suddenly there was a scream or two from the women, and a commotion. Unperceived by the elders, May, the nine-year-old girl, in a spirit of play, had shut Agatha in the vault. She had then shot the bolts and turned the knob of the combination as she had seen Mr. Adams do.

The old banker sprang to the handle and tugged at it for a moment. "The door can't be opened," he groaned. "The clock hasn't been wound nor the combination set."

Agatha's mother screamed again, hysterically.

"Hush!" said Mr. Adams, raising his trembling hand. "All be quiet for a moment, Agatha!" he called as loudly as he could: "Listen to me." During the following silence they could just hear the faint sound of the child wildly shrieking in the dark vault in a panic of terror.

"My precious darling!" wailed the mother. "She will die of fright! Open the door! Oh, break it open! Can't you men do something?"

"There isn't a man nearer than Little Rock who can open that door," said Mr. Adams, in a shaky voice. "My God! Spencer, what shall we do? That child—she can't stand it long in there. There isn't enough air, and, besides, she'll go into convulsions from fright."

Agatha's mother, frantic now, beat the door of the vault with her hands. Somebody wildly suggested dynamite. Annabel turned to Jimmy, her large eyes full of anguish, but not yet despairing. To a woman nothing seems quite impossible to the powers of the man she worships.

"Can't you do something, Ralph—*try*, won't you?"

He looked at her with a queer, soft smile on his lips and in his keen eyes.

"Annabel," he said, "give me that rose you are wearing, will you?"

Hardly believing that she heard him aright, she unpinned the bud from the bosom of her dress, and placed it in his hand. Jimmy stuffed it into his vest-pocket, threw off his coat and pulled up his shirtsleeves. With that act Ralph D. Spencer passed away and Jimmy Valentine took his place.

"Get away from the door, all of you," he commanded, shortly.

He set his suitcase on the table, and opened it out flat. From that time on he seemed to be unconscious of the presence of any one else. He laid out the shining, queer implements swiftly and orderly, whistling softly to himself as he always did when at work. In a deep silence and immovable, the others watched him as if under a spell.

In a minute Jimmy's pet drill was biting smoothly into the steel door. In ten minutes—breaking his own burglarious record—he threw back the bolts and opened the door.

Agatha, almost collapsed, but safe, was gathered into her mother's arms.

Jimmy Valentine put on his coat, and walked outside the railings toward the front door. As he went he thought he heard a far-away voice that he once knew call "Ralph!" But he never hesitated.

At the door a big man stood somewhat in his way.

"Hello, Ben!" said Jimmy, still with his strange smile. "Got around at last, have you? Well, let's go. I don't know that it makes much difference, now."

And then Ben Price acted rather strangely.

"Guess you're mistaken, Mr. Spencer," he said. "Don't believe I recognize you. Your buggy's waiting for you, ain't it?"

And Ben Price turned and strolled down the street.

SACRIFICE

C. J. HENDERSON

Herbert sat at the kitchen table, unable to eat. The television before him blared on and on—its icy glow ruining his digestion, stealing appetite from his empty stomach. He had turned it on, hoping the scheduled comedy might take his mind away from the world around him. Herbert had forgotten the news briefs which started off every hour. He pulled at a hangnail while the screen assailed him.

CHOC-O-CAKES INJECTED WITH CYANIDE—TEN DEAD IN JERSEY NURSERY SCHOOL . . .

The television sat at the end of the metal table, its cord trailing off somewhere into the books on the shelf behind it. Beaming out at Herbert, it offended him daily, taunting him with ever-increasing numbers of blandly different unthinkables, daring him to turn it off —to even turn away.

"I won't," he thought. "No matter what it makes up. I won't give in."

Herbert unfolded his arms and pushed his rapidly cooling Kraft Macaroni & Cheese Deluxe Dinner away from himself, down the table—out of reach.

NO CLUES IN THE WILMERDING REST HOME ARSON CASE . . .

Somehow, he just did not feel like eating.

"There's no avoiding it," he admitted. "I just haven't done enough."

Herbert shuddered at the thought. He wondered if enough could be done—if *anyone* could do enough. He had tried. God—how he had tried. At least, he thought he had. Each time the world had escalated its attempts to cave in on itself, so had his efforts to put things aright. More sacrifices—a greater effort . . .

MORE AT ELEVEN ON THE . . .

442

Reaching out, straining to reach to the end of the table, he clicked the set off in mid-tragedy, chewing at his nails as he wondered at it all.

Mary had decided to cut her hair again, shorter than the last time. She snipped at it randomly—without any thought set aside for style or appearance. Although she had not left much the last time, she did manage to find some loose bits to clip—shears pressed into the sides of her head, angling after this fast-growing follicle or that one. Looking at herself in the mirror, staring at her handiwork, she wished she had not thrown out every last cigarette—was glad that she did.

In the end, it had been such a little thing to give up. Anything to get back at the radio.

> FOUR MORE WINTER WAR CASUALTIES WERE DISCOVERED TODAY, FROZEN TO DEATH IN THEIR HOMES, VICTIMS NOT ONLY OF THE COLD, BUT OF THE CITY'S MERCILESS UTILITY BARONS . . .

Anything to keep her mind off the world locked outside her door. She had passed on going to the play with Frank, even though she did like him and he had seemed very secure about the whole thing. Something had warned her, however. Something had let her know that the streets just were not the place for her to be. Something made with Japanese technology and German plastic bought on Canal Street for ten dollars that nightly turned the key in the lock of her warm, secure cell.

> . . . TAKING HIS OWN LIFE AFTER KILLING HIS WIFE AND THREE GIRLS . . .

She had not noticed over the last months—not really—how her hair had started getting shorter, and then shorter, and her nails, shorter, and her meals, smaller, and well, who really needs cigarettes, anyway—I mean, the way the world is—

Joe had heard enough. The nightly news had only been a rehash of the slop that had poured out over him from his paper on the way home—more details dripping off the pages and out of the set like broiling fat falling into a fire. It was bad enough that everyone in the office had been talking about it. *Talking*. There was a euphemism for it—

"You mean those people in El Paso?"

"Yeah. They stuffed the drugs inside ketchup bottles."

"Four dead—right?"

"Yeah. Pretty spicy stuff, huh?"

And then the laughter. Four dead in the morning. By the train ride home, and the evening paper, two more had died, making all the jokes funnier by fifty percent.

Turning the TV off with the fingers remaining on his right hand, Joe left the den, heading for his bedroom. No wife waited anymore. Even his dog had deserted him, frightened by the morose, continually cynical atmosphere that had settled around his master and then spread outward through his home and all the things in and around it.

"Maybe Lucky didn't run away. Maybe he was only stolen," Joe whispered to himself. "Or killed."

Forsaking his bed, Joe pulled a blanket from it and then curled on the floor in the black, shivering in his chilly darkness. Duty now for the future, he thought, smiling weakly, trying to fit the edges of his blanket around and under his rear end and his feet.

Herbert sat in the kitchen, still at the table. Tears ran down his face—slow but unstoppable. Nothing he ever did was enough. Maybe the axe would help—maybe. But, if he was wrong, said the little voice in the back of his head, there would be no second chance.

"No second chance?" he asked the air in a small, confused voice. What could he be thinking? There was always a second chance. Clicking his set back on, he watched the small white dot in the center grow in size.

MORE BOMBINGS IN THE CENTRAL LOWLANDS FORCE UN TROOPS TO . . .

The picture faded away as he clicked the screen back to blackness.

"There's no reason for all of this," he thought. "I've just got to make a bigger sacrifice. Something they'll all notice. Something worth the effort."

Lifting himself from his chair, he went to the drawer in his desk where the tools were. He considered the chisel and several of the planes for a long moment before shutting the drawer again. Then, turning to the umbrella stand next to him, Herbert pulled free the saw standing in it, bracing his leg against the chair next to his dresser.

After the eye-crushing pain of the first few strokes, he suddenly found he could not move the saw. Forcing his eyes open, he spotted the problem immediately. Pulling the blade upward, he untangled the pant threads caught in its teeth. Then, with a path cleared, he set back to work, grimly clamping his jaws and bubbling lips together, gamely sawing stroke after stroke, ignoring the swooshing sound and the bone powder and the blood until he had finished his work and had toppled to the floor.

"Maybe that," he thought. "Maybe they'll notice that."

But, even as he fell off into unconsciousness, Mary's radio kept reporting its grim fascinations, and Herbert just kept wondering, as did Joe and the army of their fellows—all sawing away—just how much grist the mill demanded.

THE SAPIENT MONKEY

HEADON HILL

I would advise every person whose duties take him into the field of "private enquiry" to go steadily through the daily papers the first thing every morning. Personally I have found the practice most useful, for there are not many *causes célèbres* in which my services are not enlisted on one side or the other, and by this method I am always up in my main facts before I am summoned to assist. When I read the account of the proceedings at Bow Street against Franklin Gale in connection with the Tudways' bank robbery, I remember thinking that on the face of it there never was a clearer case against a misguided young man.

Condensed for the sake of brevity, the police-court report disclosed the following state of things:

Franklin Gale, clerk, aged twenty-three, in the employment of Messrs. Tudways, the well-known private bankers of the Strand, was brought up on a warrant charged with stealing the sum of £500— being the moneys of his employers. Mr. James Spruce, assistant cashier at the bank, gave evidence to the effect that he missed the money from his till on the afternoon of July 22. On making up his cash for the day he discovered that he was short of £300 worth of notes and £200 in gold. He had no idea how the amount had been abstracted. The prisoner was an assistant bookkeeper at the bank, and had access behind the counter. Detective-sergeant Simmons said that the case had been placed in his hands for the purpose of tracing the stolen notes. He had ascertained that one of them—of the value of £5—had been paid to Messrs. Crosthwaite & Co., tailors, of New Bond Street, on July 27th, by Franklin Gale. As a result, he had applied for a warrant, and had arrested the prisoner. The latter was remanded for a week, at the end of which period it was expected that further evidence would be forthcoming.

I had hardly finished reading the report when a telegram was put into my hands demanding my immediate presence at "Rosemount," Twickenham. From the address given, and from the name of "Gale" appended to the despatch, I concluded that the affair at Tudways' Bank was the cause of the summons. I had little doubt that I was to be retained in the interests of the prisoner, and my surmise proved correct.

"Rosemount" was by no means the usual kind of abode from which the ordinary run of bank clerks come gaily trooping into the great City in shoals by the early trains. There was nothing of cheap gentility about the "pleasant suburban residence standing in its own grounds of an acre," as the house-agent would say—with its lawns sloping down to the river, shaded by mulberry and chestnut trees, and plentifully garnished with the noble flower which gave it half its name. "Rosemount" was assuredly the home either of some prosperous merchant or of a private gentleman, and when I crossed its threshold I did so quite prepared for the fuller enlightenment which was to follow. Mr. Franklin Gale was evidently not one of the struggling genus bank clerk, but must be the son of well-to-do people, and not yet flown from the parent nest. When I left my office I had thought that I was bound on a forlorn hope, but at the sight of "Rosemount"—my first real "touch" of the case—my spirits revived. Why should a young man living amid such signs of wealth want to rob his employers? Of course I recognized that the youth of the prisoner precluded the probability of the place being his own. Had he been older, I should have reversed the argument. "Rosemount" in the actual occupation of a middle-aged bank clerk would have been prima-facie evidence of a tendency to outrun the constable.

I was shown into a well-appointed library, where I was received by a tall, silver-haired old gentleman of ruddy complexion, who had apparently been pacing the floor in a state of agitation. His warm greeting towards me—a perfect stranger—had the air of one who clutches at a straw.

"I have sent for you to prove my son's innocence, Mr. Zambra," he said. "Franklin no more stole that money than I did. In the first place, he didn't want it; and, secondly, if he had been ever so pushed for cash, he would rather have cut off his right hand than put it into his employer's till. Besides, if these thick-headed policemen were bound to lock one of us up, it ought to have been me. The five-pound note with which Franklin paid his tailor was one—so he assures me, and I believe him—which I gave him myself."

"Perhaps you would give me the facts in detail?" I replied.

"As to the robbery, both my son and I are as much in the dark as old Tudway himself," Mr. Gale proceeded. "Franklin tells me that Spruce, the cashier, is accredited to be a most careful man, and the very last to leave his till to take care of itself. The facts that came out in evidence are perfectly true. Franklin's desk is close to the counter, and the note identified as one of the missing ones was certainly paid by him to Crosthwaite & Co., of New Bond Street, a few days after the robbery. It bears his endorsement, so there can be no doubt about that.

"So much for their side of the case. Ours is, I must confess, from a legal point of view, much weaker, and lies in my son's assertion of innocence, coupled with the knowledge of myself and his mother and his sisters that he is incapable of such a crime. Franklin insists that the note he paid to Crosthwaite & Co., the tailors, was one that I gave him on the morning of the 22nd. I remember perfectly well giving him a five-pound note at breakfast on that day, just before he left for town, so that he must have had it several hours before the robbery was committed. Franklin says that he had no other banknotes between the 22nd and 27th, and that he cannot, therefore, be mistaken. The note which I gave him I got fresh from my own bankers a day or two before, together with some others; and here is the most unfortunate point in the case. The solicitor whom I have engaged to defend Franklin has made the necessary enquiries at my bankers, and finds that the note paid to the tailors is *not* one of those which I drew from the bank."

"Did not your son take notice of the number of the note you gave him?" I asked.

"Unfortunately, no. He is too much worried about the numbers of notes at his business, he says, to note those which are his own property. He simply sticks to it that he knows it must be the same note because he had no other."

In the slang of the day, Mr. Franklin Gale's story seemed a little too thin. There was the evidence of Tudways that the note paid to the tailor was one of those stolen from them, and there was the evidence of Mr. Gale, senior's, bankers that it was not one of those handed to their client. What was the use of the prisoner protesting in the face of this that he had paid his tailor with his father's present? The notes stolen from Tudways were, I remembered reading, consecutive ones of a series, so that the possibility of young Gale having at the bank changed his father's gift for another note, which was subsequently stolen, was knocked on the head. Besides, he maintained that it was the *same* note.

"I should like to know something of your son's circumstances and position," I said, trying to divest the question of any air of suspicion it might have implied.

"I am glad you asked me that," returned Mr. Gale, "for it touches the very essence of the whole case. My son's circumstances and position are such that were he the most unprincipled scoundrel in creation he would have been nothing less than an idiot to have done this thing. Franklin is not on the footing of an ordinary bank clerk, Mr. Zambra. I am a rich man, and can afford to give him anything in reason, though he is too good a lad ever to have taken advantage of me. Tudway is an old friend of mine, and I got him to take Franklin into the bank with a view to a partnership. Everything was going on swimmingly towards that end: the boy had perfected himself in his duties, and made himself valuable; I was prepared to invest a certain amount of capital on his behalf; and, lastly, Tudway, who lives next door to me here, got so fond of him that he allowed Franklin to become engaged to his daughter Maud. Would any young man in his senses go and steal a paltry £500 under such circumstances as that?"

I thought not, but I did not say so yet.

"What are Mr. Tudway's views about the robbery?" I asked.

"Tudway is an old fool," replied Mr. Gale. "He believes what the police tell him, and the police tell him that Franklin is guilty. I have no patience with him. I ordered him out of this house last night. He had the audacity to come and offer not to press the charge if the boy would confess."

"And Miss Tudway?"

"Ah! she's a brick. Maud sticks to him like a true woman. But what is the use of our sticking to him against such evidence?" broke down poor Mr. Gale, impotently. "Can you, Mr. Zambra, give us a crumb of hope?"

Before I could reply there was a knock at the library door, and a tall, graceful girl entered the room. Her face bore traces of weeping, and she looked anxious and dejected; but I could see that she was naturally quick and intelligent.

"I have just run over to see if there is any fresh news this morning," she said, with an enquiring glance at me.

"This is Mr. Zambra, my dear, come to help us," said Mr. Gale; "and this," he continued, turning to me, "is Miss Maud Tudway. We are all enlisted in the same cause."

"You will be able to prove Mr. Franklin Gale's innocence, sir?" she exclaimed.

"I hope so," I said; "and the best way to do it will be to trace the robbery to its real author. Has Mr. Franklin any suspicions on that head?"

"He is as much puzzled as we are," said Miss Tudway. "I went with Mr. Gale here to see him in that horrible place yesterday, and he said there was absolutely no one in the bank he cared to suspect. But he *must* get off the next time he appears. My evidence ought to do that. I saw with my own eyes that he had only one £5 note in his purse on the 25th—that is two days before he paid the tailor, and three days after the robbery."

"I am afraid that won't help us much," I said. "You see, he might easily have had the missing notes elsewhere. But tell me, under what circumstances did you see the £5 note?"

"There was a garden party at our house," replied Miss Tudway, "and Franklin was there. During the afternoon a man came to the gate with an accordion and a performing monkey, and asked permission to show the monkey's tricks. We had the man in, and after the monkey had done a lot of clever things the man said that the animal could tell a good banknote from a 'flash' one. He was provided with spurious notes for the purpose; would any gentlemen lend him a good note for a minute, just to show the trick? The man was quite close to Franklin, who was sitting next to me. Franklin, seeing the man's hand held out towards him, took out his purse and handed him a note, at the same time calling my attention to the fact that it was his only one, and laughingly saying that he hoped the man was honest. The sham note and the good one were placed before the monkey, who at once tore up the bad note and handed the good one back to Franklin."

"This is more important than it seems," I said, after a moment's review of the whole case. "I must find that man with the monkey, but it bids fair to be difficult. There are so many of them in that line of business."

Miss Tudway smiled for the first time during the interview.

"It is possible that I may be of use to you there," she said. "I go in for amateur photography, and I thought that the man and his monkey made so good a 'subject' that I insisted on taking him before he left. Shall I fetch the photograph?"

"By all means," I said. "Photography is of the greatest use to me in my work. I generally arrange it myself, but if you have chanced to take the right picture for me in this case so much the better."

Miss Tudway hurried across to her father's house and quickly returned with the photograph. It was a fair effort for an amateur, and portrayed an individual of the usual seedy stamp, equipped with a huge accordion and a small monkey secured by a string. With this in my hand it would only be a matter of time before I found the itinerant juggler who had presented himself at the Tudways' garden party, and I took my leave of old Mr. Gale and Miss Maud in a much more hopeful frame of mind. Every circumstance outside the terrible array of actual evidence pointed to my client's innocence, and if this evidence had been manufactured for the purpose, I felt certain that the "monkey man" had had a hand in it.

On arriving at my office I summoned one of my assistants—a veteran of doubtful antecedents—who owns to no other name than "Old Jemmy." Old Jemmy's particular line of business is a thorough knowledge of the slums and the folk who dwell there; and I knew that after an hour or two on Saffron Hill my ferret, armed with the photograph, would bring me the information I wanted. Towards evening Old Jemmy came in with his report, to the effect that the "party" I was after was to be found in the top attic of 7 Little Didman's Fields, Hatton Garden, just recovering from the effects of a prolonged spree.

"He's been drunk for three or four days, the landlord told me," Old Jemmy said. "Had a stroke of luck, it seems, but he is expected to go on tramp tomorrow, now his coin has given out. His name is Pietro Schilizzi."

I knew I was on the right scent now, and that the "monkey man" had been made the instrument of *changing* the note which Franklin Gale had lent him for one of the stolen ones. A quick cab took me to Little Didman's Fields in a quarter of an hour, and I was soon standing inside the doorway of a pestilential apartment on the top floor of No. 7, which had been pointed out to me as the abode of Pietro Schilizzi. A succession of snores from a heap of rags in a corner told me the whereabouts of the occupier. I went over, and shaking him roughly by the shoulder, said in Italian:

"Pietro, I want you to tell me about that little juggle with a banknote at Twickenham the other day. You will be well rewarded."

The fellow rubbed his eyes in half-drunken astonishment, but there certainly was no guilty fear about him as he replied:

"Certainly, signor; anything for money. There was nothing wrong about the note, was there? Anyhow, I acted innocently in the matter."

"No one finds fault with you," I said; "but see, here is a five-pound note. It shall be yours if you will tell me exactly what happened."

"I was with my monkey up at Highgate the other evening," Mr. Schilizzi began, "and was showing Jacko's trick of telling a good note from a bad one. It was a small house in the Napier Road. After I had finished, the gentleman took me into a public house and stood me a drink. He wanted me to do something for him, he said. He had a young friend who was careless, and never took the number of notes, and he wanted to teach him a lesson. He had a bet about the number of a note, he said. Would I go down to Twickenham next day to a house he described, where there was to be a party, and do my trick with the monkey? I was to borrow a note from the young gentleman, and then, instead of giving him back his own note after the performance, I was to substitute one which the Highgate gentleman gave me for the purpose. He met me at Twickenham next day, and came behind the garden wall to point out the young gentleman to me. I managed it just as the Highgate gentleman wanted, and he gave me a couple of pounds for my pains. I have done no wrong; the note I gave back was a good one."

"Yes," I said, "but it happens to have been stolen. Put on your hat and show me where this man lives in Highgate."

The Napier Road was a shabby street of dingy houses, with a public house at the corner. Pietro stopped about half-way down the row and pointed out No. 21.

"That is where the gentleman lives," he said.

We retraced our steps to the corner public house.

"Can you tell me who lives at No. 21?" I asked of the landlord, who happened to be in the bar.

"Certainly," was the answer; "it is Mr. James Spruce—a good customer of mine, and the best billiard player hereabouts. He is a cashier at Messrs. Tudways' bank, in the Strand, I believe."

It all came out at the trial—not of Franklin Gale, but of James Spruce, the fraudulent cashier. Spruce had himself abstracted the notes and gold entrusted to him, and his guilty conscience telling him that he might be suspected, he had cast about for a means of throwing suspicion on some other person. Chancing to witness the performance of Pietro's monkey, he had grasped the opportunity for foisting one of the stolen notes on Franklin Gale, knowing that sooner or later it would be traced to him. The other notes he had intended to hold over till it was safe to send them out of the country; but the gold was the principal object of his theft.

Mr. Tudway, the banker, was, I hear, so cut up about the false accusation that he had made against his favourite that he insisted on Franklin joining him as a partner at once, and the marriage is to take place before very long. I am also told that the photograph of the "monkey man," handsomely enlarged and mounted, will form one of the mural decorations of the young couple.

SIDE DOOR TO HELL

CYRIL PLUNKETT

The medical examiner paused to talk a moment, despite the rain. "A shot through the heart, Nelson," the M. E. said. "I've placed the time of death two hours ago, at eight or thereabouts."

Jan Nelson's throat was tight and aching. "Any clues?"

"Well," the M. E. said, "one or two things that look promising. Inspector Cray has all the dope. He's waiting for you, Nelson."

"Thanks, I'll go right in." Nelson turned away.

There was a terraced lawn, and deep within it a massive stone building, gray and shapeless in the darkness. The lights on either side of the doorway seemed strangely dim.

"Be very sure," he'd said. *"Cris, don't gamble with our lives, our happiness."* Nelson's mind was filled with Cris, the wonder of her—and the doubt he'd known for months.

He walked stiffly, like a fighter after listening to the count of ten. Tall, with the leanness of a man high-strung, he was stooped a very little, as though the weighty problems of his office—District Attorney—were, indeed, pounds upon his back.

He went inside, then, into the tension of official business, past uniformed police, and reporters pressing for a statement. Naturally, Sordell's murder was big. Sordell had been big-time, an artist whose cover girls were internationally known.

Inspector Cray was in the studio living room, a broadly built man, massive. He was busy with dictation. He waved and said, "Hello, Mr. Nelson. Be with you in a minute." And then, to the patrolman taking notes: "According to the statement of employees, Sordell furnished keys to the side street door, at the bottom of the stairway, allegedly that certain people, female, could come and go at any time, unseen." He turned back to Nelson. "We're good till morning on this one. You know Sordell?"

"By reputation," Nelson said.

Cray's stare was long and irritating. "Well, I can take that word either way and still be right. That's the pattern. Too many girls. Anyway, one of them was here tonight. The switchboard operator and elevator boy both tagged her."

"They know her? They know her name?" Nelson interrupted, queerly.

"That's right," said Cray. "It's Shaw. Catherine Shaw—we've found her address scrawled in Sordell's phone book. Here's the way we reconstruct it: Sordell was seated at his desk, being threatened, maybe. He got up fast, because the chair legs made deep scars in the carpet. He came around the desk, and that's when the bullet got him."

Cray pointed to the chalked outline on the floor, marking where the body had fallen. And then Jan Nelson saw beyond the outline. Nelson saw the drawing, and his heart started thumping in his breast. The pastel upon the desk was a mauve monochrome on illustration board, and recently finished, for no fixative had been applied. The study was of a girl, and her hair was partly smudged, as though the artist's hand had smeared it. And the girl wore a mask, but little else. Behind the mask her eyes smiled archly, invitingly.

"Worries me, that picture." Cray slowly thumbed up and down his jaw. "I've a hunch it's important. Maybe the smear—I don't know. Maybe those erased particles lying on the floor. An artist wouldn't smear his own work, brushing it off. An artist wouldn't do a thing like *that*."

The muscles tightened in Nelson's jaw. "About this girl, Inspector?"

For a moment Cray didn't answer. Then he said, "She was up here about five minutes. She left in a hurry—looking scared, according to the witnesses. I've already sent a man to watch her address. Care to run out there with me?"

"Yes," Nelson said. "I'll be glad to."

They rode a police car, in the back seat, with a detective named Simms at the wheel. Cray and Simms got to talking of the war, but Nelson was silent and frowning. He was thinking of a curious thing, a lipstick. He was thinking of Cris. . . .

They'd met at a party, a year back, in midsummer. She was like someone da Vinci might have painted, or like the girl you dream of. You looked at her and it was like listening to Wagnerian opera. She was the girl millions saw on billboards and the pages of the magazines.

Looking back, the amazing thing was that she had found him at all worthy of her interest. He was thirty-eight, and the war had passed him by; but he was a man whose name was repeatedly appearing in the newspapers—and so. . . .

"Cris, be sure," he'd said, that night, weeks later. "Be so very sure first. I can't be intense tonight, a month—and then casual afterward. I'm not that way. It's all or nothing, Cris. I won't share you. You can't go on with your career. I won't pick up a magazine and see you there. It's got to be the way *I* want it, Cris—for life."

The police car made a sudden turn and Cray's voice broke into Nelson's thoughts abruptly. "By the way," Cray said, "how is *Mrs.* Nelson?"

Nelson stiffened. "Thanks, she's fine."

A moment passed. Cray seemed to be considering. "Model, wasn't she?"

They were passing beneath a street lamp, and Nelson saw Cray's eyes. Cray was looking at him, and he felt helpless, very small like a mouse in a dusty corner. From the distance a bell tolled, deep toned and dismal.

They left Simms outside. They talked to the buxom landlady at Catherine Shaw's address. The landlady said, "Miss Shaw? I don't believe she's in. Is it—business?"

"Police business," said Cray.

"Not—not Cathy!"

Cray said, "We'll take a little look at her room."

So they saw Cathy Shaw's room, and it was cretonne and white linen; not at all the velvet that had been Sordell's. The note was crumpled in a wastebasket. Cray found it and handed it to Nelson.

"Dear Mr. Sordell," Nelson read. *"I've argued with myself whether to see or write you, but in either case the answer is the same. I hate you—"* That was all that had been written.

Cray reclaimed the note, put it in his pocket and began questioning the landlady. Nelson went into the hall, went downstairs. There was a phone just below the stairs. He stood before it, one hand in his coat pocket; and then he removed the hand and the small bright object clasped in it—a lipstick, gold and initialed with tiny jewels. For a moment he stared at the lipstick blankly. He sighed as he dialed Erie-7700.

The whispered ringing on the other end seemed within his brain. He counted with the rings, and with the breathless spaces. But Cris didn't answer. A footfall sounded behind him suddenly. Nelson put the receiver back on its hook, shoved his clenched hand in his pocket.

Cray said from the stairs, "We're going two blocks up the street. To see a lad named Farraday."

They drove the two blocks, and the bell was tolling dismally again, the quarter hour, fifteen after eleven. The door to Farraday's room cracked open slowly at Cray's knock.

He was young, thin. Nineteen, perhaps. He wore slacks and a polo shirt, and he was smoking a cigarette. The room was blue with smoke. Farraday, all right. He looked frightened.

Cray said, "You'd better let us in."

"Police?"

"That's right."

Cray pushed the door, and there *she* was, behind it. Cretonne and white linen. She wasn't wearing that, but she was in her teens, with eyes that were great blue pools, and she was blonde, her slender body beautiful. Catherine Shaw.

Nelson closed the door and sat down as Cray crossed the room. Cray stood facing into the room.

"Let's put the cards down," Cray said. "Just what happened to-night, Miss Shaw?"

She looked at Farraday, and then at Nelson, and her whole body trembled. Cray sighed and swung around a little. "Well, how about you, Farraday? Been here all evening?"

Farraday flung himself into a chair. He was watching Cray warily, but the overflowing ash tray on the end table occupied him a moment. He brushed the loose ash to the floor. "Yes, of course," he said. "Why?"

"Nothing to hide, either of you?"

Farraday laughed shortly. "That's a good one."

Cray didn't smile. He said, "We've found the letter Miss Shaw began to Sordell."

She gasped and put both hands to her face. Farraday's cheeks were chalk-white and he seemed scarcely to be breathing. He shot out of the chair. Cray made a motion to check him, but Farraday straight-armed Cray, spun away from him and darted for the door. He reached the door ahead of Nelson, slammed it in Nelson's face. They heard him running down the stairs.

Cathy Shaw moaned. Cray said, "Get your coat, girlie, and come along with us."

"But—" she began. Cray had turned his back to her. He was saying reproachfully, "You might have been a little quicker, Mr. Nelson. Won't matter though. Won't matter. I expected something like this. Simms will nab him." He turned around again. "Ready, girlie?"

When they reached the front door the detective, Simms, was sitting on the steps with Farraday, handcuffed to him.

"We'll take 'em both in for questioning," Cray said. Simms walked with Miss Shaw and Farraday, between them, down the walk to the squad car.

"Coming, Mr. Nelson?" Cray said.

Nelson shrugged off his preoccupation, shook his head. "I'll catch a cab," he said.

But he walked, to compromise with time, in fear of time. Twice he stopped to phone, at a drugstore, at a restaurant. *Erie-7700 . . . Erie-7700.* There was no answer either time, and therefore Cris was not at home. Nelson sat a long while in the restaurant, thinking, staring into the past.

At first he hadn't believed there could be such happiness, in the plans he made with Cris, in their marriage, in living with her afterward. Their suite had a broad, revealing view of the rivers meeting to conceive the sea, it was a very special suite, high above the city and well beyond Nelson's means, but one always set a jewel in gold and that's the way he felt about it. He'd awaken each day and look at her—her eyes closed still, in sleep; or at her photograph in the double frame with his, smiling at his own stern expression, her dark head tilted back in a pose altogether glamorous. And he'd sigh and think: *Jan, boy, you've won her.*

But the job, he knew from the beginning, was going to be to *keep* her.

It had been purely accidental that his cab arrived home one night as hers was ready to depart. She was wearing black, something very slim and modish. This was back a few weeks, in cool September, the anniversary month of their marriage. His first thought had been to try to head her off—she'd expected him to return quite late that night—but within a block or two his mind had clouded. He'd followed her uptown. Presently her cab stopped before an imposing building; a side entrance—and she had a key.

"Drive around the block," Nelson told the cabbie.

He'd stared, unseeing. Numb and cold, yet burning, knowing now the ugly, moving plan of things. "Keep driving," he'd said to the cabbie. Anywhere—"

Nelson looked up, now, at the counterman standing before him, and he took a deep breath. He ordered coffee—and drank it black, and then he rose from the counter stool. He left the restaurant. The time was nearing two A.M. when he reached home.

The door was unlocked, and his heart quickened. He opened the door—to stop short and stiffen. Inspector Cray sat there in the living room. Alone. Cray's eyes were very keen. Nelson saw this keenness and momentarily hated it.

"I thought you'd be along soon," Cray said. He was opening a fresh pack of cigarettes. "You know how it is with homicide. A good officer must have an answer for everything. Well, an answer's been missing."

"Indeed?" said Nelson.

Cray offered the pack. "Smoke?"

Nelson shook his head. He sat down.

"I had a talk with your wife tonight," Cray said. "At headquarters."

The smoke was drifting past Cray's watchful eyes. Nelson saw the smoke apart. He wet his lips but didn't speak.

"I've got a photographic mind," Cray said. "That drawing on Sordell's desk worried me. I had a feeling I knew who the model was, and it wasn't Catherine Shaw. It wasn't naive—you know?"

Still Nelson did not answer and Cray smiled a very little.

"Funny thing. I thought you'd say, 'Hello Inspector. How about a drink?' . . ."

"Skip the small talk, Inspector."

Cray shrugged. "All right. You followed your wife to Sordell's tonight?"

"You raise your voice. Is that a question?"

Cray dropped ash in the tray. "Question mark or period—does it matter? We're not getting anywhere, Nelson. And it's late. I'm tired. I never intended to waste time in small talk. But you're in a black mood, and—"

"We can skip my mood too, Inspector."

Cray sighed and shook his head. "No, we can't. A cop can't overlook even a thing like that. But I will pass it by a minute and go on to the missing lipstick."

Nelson's gaze shot up. "Lipstick?" He met Cray's cold stare, and a moment passed, and then he said, "I see." His shoulders sagged, and he looked down at his hands. "Yes, Inspector, as a matter of fact, I did follow my wife tonight. I've followed her many nights, recently. But tonight—I smoked a cigarette, outside, after she went in. I was going in. I'd got an impression of the key she carried. I'd made a decision—but nevermind that, it's unimportant. Cris reappeared very soon, three or four minutes. She went away, and I went in, and Sordell—"

Nelson paused and came out of his chair and suddenly began pacing. "You're a cute one, Inspector. Suppose I say I found Sordell dead?"

"Did you?" Cray cut in softly.

Nelson ignored the interruption. "Suppose I do say that—the case against me switches to my wife. Well, damn you, Cray, I *could* confess to killing Sordell. I could do that and make it stick—to shield my wife. But I won't. You understand that Cray, I won't! I've gone through a hell of doubt tonight. I admit it. I found my wife's lipstick lying near Sordell's body. I picked up the lipstick. No question about it being hers; I'd bought it myself. Her initials were on it. But I picked up the lipstick, and the inference, finding it there, was —but to hell with the inference! I know Cris. I believe in her. I didn't kill Sordell, and Cris didn't, and I'll fight you all the way, Cray, to prove that—"

Nelson stopped, puzzled and wary, for Cray was chuckling.

"It's all right," Cray said. "That's all I wanted to know. Mrs. Nelson says she lost a lipstick; we found no lipstick. Did Farraday take it? Or someone else we hadn't tied into the case yet? You see how I had to know. Anyway, Farraday's our boy."

Cray put out his cigarette and rose. "He didn't like Sordell's propositions, or what he figured Sordell had demanded of his girl friend. He lifted her key to get in, and she chose the same time— and without her key, necessarily the front entrance—to see Sordell and tell him where to get off at. Remember me pointing out that pastel crayon dust, and the smudge on Sordell's drawing? Maybe you saw Farraday brush ash from the end table up there in his room? Well, it looked like a nervous habit; you know, brushing things like lint and such to the floor. So I played the hunch and had Farraday's room searched. We picked up a pair of beige gloves and the left glove showed a crayon smear."

"Cris—?" Nelson prompted, unsteadily.

There was a small sound behind him. He turned. Cris was standing in the bedroom doorway. Her eyes were very bright, glistening.

She began speaking swiftly, as though his silence frightened her. "Jan, my first fear was for you. I—I guessed that you'd found out I was seeing Sordell, and—but I knew Inspector Cray would help us. I went to him. I didn't fear him." A knuckle cracked; the skin above her knuckles showed white. "I—I'd dropped my purse, at the shock

459

of finding Sordell dead, and I didn't miss the lipstick until later. Then I went right down to see Inspector Cray—"

She seemed suddenly surprised to find that she was back where she had started from. Her pause was awkward, pleading. "But Jan, you—you believed in me—"

There were tears and she was in his arms, warm and wonderful. His lips were buried in her hair. The hall door had closed on Cray, but they hadn't noticed.

"Jan," came her muffled voice, "it's just that I was lonely. I've been working again. I've been modeling for Sordell, and nothing else—"

He said, "Don't worry. I suppose every man who marries beauty has to fight it out with doubt. But I'm glad I won, Cris."

THE SILVER PROTECTOR

ELLIS PARKER BUTLER

When our new suburban house was completed, I took Sarah out to see it, and she liked it all but the stairs.

"Edgar," she said, when she had ascended to the second floor, "I don't know whether it is imagination or not, but it seems to me that these stairs are funny, some way. I can't understand it. They are not a long flight, and they are not unusually steep, but they seem to be unusually wearying. I never knew a short flight to tire me so, and I have climbed many flights in the six years we have lived in apartments."

"Perhaps, Sarah," I said, with mild dissimulation, "you are unusually tired today."

The fact was that I had planned those stairs myself, and for a particular reason I had made the rise of each step three inches more than the customary height, and in this way I had saved two steps. I had also made the tread of the steps unusually narrow; and the reason was that I had found, from long experience, that stair carpet wears first on the tread of the steps, where the foot falls. By making the steps tall enough to save two, and by making the tread narrow, I reduced the wear on the carpet to a minimum. I believe in economy where it is possible. For the same reason I had the stair banisters made wide, with a saddle-like top to the newel post, to tempt my son and daughter to slide downstairs. The less they used the stairs, the longer the carpet would last.

I need hardly say that Sarah has a fear of burglars; most women have. As for myself, I prefer not to meet a burglar. It is all very well to get up in the night and prowl about with a pistol in one hand, seeking to eliminate the life of a burglar, and some men may like it; but I am of a very excitable nature, and I am sure that if I did find a burglar and succeeded in shooting him, I should be in such an excited state that I could not sleep again that night—and no man can afford to lose his night's rest.

There are other objections to shooting a burglar in the house, and these objections apply with double force when the house and its furnishings are entirely new. Although some of the rugs in our house were red, not all of them were; and I had no guarantee that if I shot a burglar he would lie down on a red rug and bleed to death. A burglar does not consider one's feelings, and would be quite as apt to bleed on a green rug, and spoil it, as not. Until burglarizing is properly regulated and burglars are educated, as they should be, in technical burglary schools, we cannot hope that a shot burglar will staunch his wound until he can find a red rug to lie down on.

And there are still other objections to shooting a burglar. If all burglars were fat, one of these would be removed; but perhaps a thin burglar might get in front of my revolver, and in that case the bullet would be likely to go right through him and continue on its way, and perhaps break a mirror or a cut-glass dish. I am a thin man myself, and if a burglar shot at me he might damage some of our things in the same way.

I thought all these things over when we decided to build in the suburbs, for Sarah is very nervous about burglars, and makes me get up at the slightest noise and go poking about. Only the fact that no burglar had ever entered our apartment at night had prevented what might have been a serious accident to a burglar, for I made it a rule, when Sarah wakened me on such occasions, to waste no time, but to go through the rooms as hastily as possible and get back to bed; and at the speed I traveled I might have bumped into a burglar in the dark and knocked him over, and his head might have struck some hard object, causing concussion of the brain; and as a burglar has a small brain, a small amount of concussion might have ruined it entirely. But as I am a slight man it might have been my brain that got concussed. A father of a family has to think of these things.

The nervousness of Sarah regarding burglars had led me in this way to study the subject carefully, and my adoption of jet-black pajamas as nightwear was not due to cowardice on my part. I properly reasoned that if a burglar tried to shoot me while I was rushing around the house after him in the darkness, a suit of black pajamas would somewhat spoil his aim, and, not being able to see me, he would not shoot at all. In this way I should save Sarah the nerve shock that would follow the explosion of a pistol in the house. For Sarah was very much more afraid of pistols than of burglars. I am sure there were only two reasons why I had never killed a burglar with a pistol: one was that no burglar had ever entered our apartment, and the other was that I never had a pistol.

But I knew that one is much less protected in a suburb than in the city, and when I decided to build I studied the burglar protection matter most carefully. I said nothing to Sarah about it, for fear it would upset her nerves, but for months I considered every method that seemed to have any merit, and that would avoid getting a burglar's blood—or mine—spattered around on our new furnishings. I desired some method by which I could finish up a burglar properly without having to leave my bed, for although Sarah is brave enough in sending me out of bed to catch a burglar, I knew she must suffer severe nerve strain during the time I was wandering about in the dark. Her objection to explosives had also to be considered, and I really had to exercise my brain more than common before I hit upon what I may now consider the only perfect method of handling burglars.

Several things coincided to suggest my method. One of these was Sarah's foolish notion that our silver must, every night, be brought from the dining-room and deposited under our bed. This I considered a most foolhardy tempting of fate. It coaxed any burglar who ordinarily would have quietly taken the silver from the dining-room, and have then gone away peacefully, to enter our room. The knowledge that I lay in bed ready at any time to spring out upon him would make him prepare his revolver, and his nervousness might make him shoot me, which would quite upset Sarah's nerves. I told Sarah so, but she had a hereditary instinct for bringing the silver to the bedroom, and insisted. I saw that in the suburban house this would be continued as "bringing the silver upstairs," and a trial of my carpet-saving stairs suggested to me my burglar-defeating plan. I had the apparatus built into the house, and I had the house planned to accommodate the apparatus.

For several months after we moved into the house I had no burglars, but I felt no fear of them in any event. I was prepared for them.

In order not to make Sarah nervous, I explained to her that my invention of a silver-elevator was merely a time-saving device. From the top of the dining-room sideboard I ran upright tracks through the ceiling to the back of the hall above, and in these I placed a glass case which could be run up and down the tracks like a dumb-waiter. All our servant had to do when she had washed the silver was to put it in the glass case, and I had attached to the top of the case a stout steel cable which ran to the ceiling of the hall above, over a pulley, and so to our bedroom, which was at the front of the hall upstairs. By this means I could, when I was in bed, pull the cable, and the glass case of silver would rise to the second floor. Our bedroom door opened upon the hall, and from the bed I could see the glass case; but in order that I might be sure that the silver was there I put a small electric light in the case and kept it burning all night.

Sarah was delighted with this arrangement, for in the morning all I had to do was to play out the steel cable and the silver would descend to the dining-room, and the maid could have the table all set by the time breakfast was ready. Not once did Sarah have a suspicion that all this was not merely a household economy, but my burglar trap.

On the sixth of August, at 2 o'clock in the morning, Sarah awakened me, and I immediately sat straight up in bed. There was an undoubtable noise of sawing, and I knew at once that a burglar was entering our home. Sarah was trembling, and I knew she was getting nervous.

"Sarah," I said, in a whisper, "be calm! There is not the least danger. I have been expecting this for some time, and I only hope the burglar has no dependent family or poor old mother to support. Whatever happens, be calm and keep perfectly quiet."

With that I released the steel cable from the head of my bed and let the glass case full of silver slide noiselessly to the sideboard.

"Edgar!" whispered Sarah in agonized tones, "are you *giving* him our silver?"

"Sarah!" I whispered sternly, "remember what I have just said. Be calm and keep perfectly quiet." And I would say no more.

In a very short time I heard the window below us open softly, and I knew the burglar was entering the parlor from the side porch. I counted twenty, which I had figured would be the time required for him to reach the dining-room, and then, when I was sure he must have seen the silver shining in the glass case, I slowly pulled on the steel cable and raised case and silver to the hall above. Sarah began to whisper to me, but I silenced her.

What I had expected happened. The burglar, seeing the silver rise through the ceiling, left the dining-room and went into the hall. There, from the foot of the stairs, he could see the case glowing in the hall above, and without hesitation he mounted the stairs. As he reached the top I had a good view of him, for he was silhouetted against the light that glowed from the silver case. He was a most brutal looking fellow of the prizefighting type, but I almost laughed aloud when I saw his build. He was short and chunky. As he stepped forward to grasp the silver case, I let the steel cable run through my fingers, and the case and its precious contents slid noiselessly down to the dining-room. For only one instant the burglar seemed disconcerted, then he turned and ran downstairs again.

This time I did not wait so long to draw up the silver. I hardly gave him time to reach the dining-room door before I jerked the cable, and the case was glowing in the upper hall. The burglar immediately stopped, turned, and mounted the stairs, but just as he reached the top I let the silver slide down again, and he had to turn and descend. Hardly had he reached the bottom step before I had the silver once more in the upper hall.

The burglar was a gritty fellow and was not to be so easily defeated. With some word which I could not catch, but which I have no doubt was profane, or at least vulgar, he dashed up the stairs, and just as his hand touched the case I let the silver drop to the dining-room. I smiled as I saw his next move. He carefully removed his coat and vest, rolled up his sleeves, and took off his collar. This evidently meant that he intended to get the silver if it took the whole night, and nothing could have pleased me more. I lay in my comfortable bed fairly shaking with suppressed laughter, and had to stuff a corner of a pillow in my mouth to smother the sound of my mirth. I did not allow the least pity for the fellow to weaken my nerve.

A low, long screech from the hall told me that I had a man of uncommon brain to contend with, for I knew the sound came from his hands drawing along the banister, and that to husband his strength and to save time, he was now sliding down. But this did not disconcert me. It pleased me. *The quicker he went down, the oftener he would have to walk up.*

For half an hour I played with him, giving him just time to get down to the foot of the stairs before I raised the silver, and just time to reach the top before I lowered it, and then I grew tired of the sport—for it was nothing else to me—and decided to finish him off. I was getting sleepy, but it was evident that the burglar was not, and I was a little afraid I might fall asleep and thus defeat myself. The burglar had that advantage because he was used to night work. So I quickened my movements a little. When the burglar slid down I gave him just time to see the silver rise through the ceiling, and when he climbed the stairs I only allowed him to see it descend through the floor. In this way I made him double his pace, and as I quickened my movements I soon had him dashing up the stairs and sliding down again as if for a wager. I did not give him a moment for rest, and he was soon panting terribly and beginning to stumble; but with almost superhuman nerve he kept up the chase. He was an unusually tough burglar.

But quick as he was I was always quicker, and a glimpse of the glowing case was all I let him have at either end of his climb or slide. No sooner was he down than it was up, and no sooner was the case up than he was after it. In this way I kept increasing his speed until it was something terrific, and the whole house shook. But still his speed increased. I saw then that I had brought him to the place I had prepared for, where he had but one object in life, and that was to beat the case up or downstairs; and as I was now so sleepy I could hardly keep my eyes open, I did what I had intended to do from the first. I lowered the case until it was exactly *halfway* between the ceiling of the dining-room and the floor of the hall above—and turned out the electric light. I then tied the steel cable securely to the head of my bed, turned over, and went to sleep, lulled by the shaking of the house as the burglar dashed up and down the stairs.

Just how long this continued I do not know, for my sleep was deep and dreamless, but I should judge that the burglar ran himself to death sometime between half-past 3 and a quarter after 4. So great had been his efforts that when I went to remove him I did not recognize him at all. When I had last seen him in the glow of the glass silver case he had been a stout, chunky fellow, and now his remains were those of an emaciated man. He must have run off one hundred and twenty pounds of flesh before he gave out.

Only one thing clouded my triumph. Our silver consisted of but half a dozen each of knives, forks, and spoons, a butter knife, and a sugar spoon, all plated, and worth probably ten dollars, and to save this I had made the burglar wear to rags a Wilton stair carpet worth fifty-nine dollars. But I have now corrected this. I have bought one hundred and fifty dollars' worth of silver.

THE
SLAVE-MAKER

EDGAR WALLACE

Once upon a time, in those absurd days of war, when the laws governing the sanctity of human life were temporarily suspended, Captain Henry Arthur Milton, making a reconnaissance to the northwest of Baghdad, saw the solitary figure of a man lying in the desert land. By his side was a dead camel.

Dipping his ship down to take a closer view, the flying officer saw the man's hand raised feebly as though signaling for help.

Captain Milton shut off his engines and five minutes later had landed and was examining the wounded man—a person of some importance, to judge by the trappings of his camel and his own raiment.

He had been shot in the shoulder, was half delirious with thirst, and proved to be one Ibn el Masjik. He had been wounded in a skirmish with British troops, and after his rescuer had made him comfortable El Masjik had a request to make.

"I am the chief of a fighting clan and I could not survive the disgrace of being taken prisoner. Therefore I ask you as a favor that you take me to the city of my father, and I will give you my parole

466

that I will not fight against your people, nor shall any of my tribe fight."

Milton spoke Arabic as though it were his mother-tongue. He was also a man of unconventional habits, and although he had no more authority to carry out the wishes of his prisoner than he had to take upon himself the command of the British Army in Mesopotamia, he did not hesitate.

His airplane made a journey of a hundred and seventy miles, landed within half a mile of the walled city of Khor. And at some risk to himself—for the local inhabitants were unaware of his errand of mercy—delivered the wounded man to the care of his friends.

"Come to me when this war is ended," said Ibn el Masjik, "and, though all the world be against you, I shall be for you. If you are poor, I will make you rich. My father's city is for your asking."

This time he spoke in English, for he had in his youth been educated at a preparatory school in Bournemouth.

Henry Arthur Milton remembered this promise some years later, when he was hard pressed, and for six months was the guest of Ibn el Masjik.

The white-walled city of Khor stood on the edge of the wilderness, and time had passed it by. Raiding parties went out unashamed and returned laden with booty and slaves. Milton saw men and women sold in the market-place, saw life unchanged from what it had been in the days when Mahomet's uncle was guardian of the Kaaba, and the Prophet's disciples were praying in Medina.

One night Henry Arthur expostulated about certain practices, and the thin, ascetic face of Ibn el Masjik lit up in a smile. He tossed a half-smoked cigarette into a silver vase, lit another, and settled himself more comfortably on the cushions.

"My friend," he said, "it is a far cry to Bournemouth, Hampshire. Slavery is merely a name for service, and it is a matter of form whether it takes the shape you see here in Khor, or in some dingy northern town where men and women have to leave their beds at the sound of a whistle and hurry through rain and sleet to the prison-houses you call factories. My slaves are more pleasantly treated: they have the sunshine; they are well fed; they sleep in their own houses."

He was perfectly frank about the traffic. There was a little port on the Red Sea where one could buy, under the very noses of a British administration, this kind of artisan—at a price.

"Not always can I buy what I desire," he explained. "My women

ask me all the time for such a man, and where may he be found?"
He sighed heavily. "Yes, the West is creeping upon us, and Kemal's
new law concerning women has reached even here."

He shrugged his shoulders, smoothed his white silken robe more
decorously about his knees, and smiled reminiscently.

"I do not object. There is a piquancy in the new custom which is
very amusing. And we differ from most other tribes in that our
women are never veiled, and have rights of choice."

After Milton came back to Western Europe he frequently corre-
sponded with his blood brother, and at the back of his mind he
always had Khor as a final sanctuary in case things went wrong.

The police might suspect that Henry Arthur Milton, whom they
called The Ringer, had many homes, but they did not know where.
Certainly they did not know about the place in Norbury where he
spent a great part of his time.

There was a small garden at the back of the house which he
cultivated, and across the dividing wall it often happened that
he discussed with his neighbor such mundane matters as the depre-
dations of cats.

He had few opportunities, for Captain Oring, that gray-bearded
man who had dreamed for forty years of a shore life, was captain of
a small tramp vessel which traded between London and Suez. He
was not only captain but part proprietor, he and his sons holding
three-quarters of the shares in his little vessel.

One of the "boys" was his chief officer, another his chief engineer, a third attended to the business end in London. He had, also,
a daughter, a floridly pretty girl, who kept the home for her brother
and did an immense amount of housework in such time as she could
spare from the cinemas.

On an occasion when The Ringer was absent from London the
girl disappeared. Her father was at sea, and it was from him, months
later, that The Ringer heard the story.

Captain Oring did not tell him coherently—it was not the sort
of story that a father could tell straightforwardly—and Henry Arthur Milton listened to the broken narrative with a cold-blooded-
ness which was his chief characteristic.

"My boy found her after a lot of trouble . . . she's with my
sister now, in the country. Naturally, I've tried to find the people.
But what chance have I got in London? I can't go to the police. . . . I don't want her name in the papers, do I? If I ever meet
this man . . ."

"You won't," said The Ringer. "But perhaps I shall—I travel about a lot."

(In the neighborhood Henry Arthur Milton was registered as Mr. Ernest Oppenton, and his profession was described as "commercial traveler.")

Captain Oring went away to sea, with his sons and his grief and his patched-up little steamer; and Henry Arthur Milton had certain urgent business which took him to Berlin—so urgent that you might imagine that the matter of Lucy Oring had entirely slipped from his mind.

But nothing ever escaped him, and on his return to London he became a great frequenter of that type of West End club which appears on, and is struck from, the register so very rapidly that you might not know it had ever existed.

He overheard a little; waiters told him some things. It is extraordinary how confidential an Italian waiter will become to a man who speaks his language. Women told him most of all, for he paid for drinks with great munificence.

On a certain afternoon a scene was enacted at one of the great London terminals which was so commonplace that only very keen observation would have noted it as being out of the ordinary.

The nice-looking old lady with the white hair and the cameo brooch saw the train come slowly along the platform of Victoria Station, and moved nearer to the barrier.

Presently, the passengers began to trickle past the ticket-collector, not in the hurried way of suburban season-ticket holders, but with the leisure which is peculiar to travellers from a distance. She watched carefully, and after a while she saw the pretty girl with the black suitcase. She was dressed in dark brown and carried in her other hand a bunch of autumnal flowers.

The nice old lady intercepted her.

"My dear, are you Miss Clayford? I thought so! I am Mrs. Graddle. I thought I would come along and see you safely across London."

The girl nodded gratefully.

"I was wondering what I should do. Are you from the agency?"

The nice old lady smiled.

"Oh, dear no! But a friend of mine at the agency keeps me informed about the engagements. I like to do what I can for young people. Now, you must come along and have tea with me. I understand it is a perfectly awful place you are going to! Forty pounds a year for a nursery governess is scandalous! And in a little country village where there is nothing to see and nothing to do . . . !"

She rattled on as she accompanied the girl through the booking-hall to the station yard, and Elsie Clayford listened dismally. Forty pounds a year was a small sum, but she understood that her new employers were very nice people, and that the home was comfortable. It was her first engagement.

"I'd like you to stay a few days with me," said Mrs. Graddle, as she signalled a cab. "I've got a lovely little house in St. John's Wood, and we have young society. I have already telephoned to Lady Shene, and she agrees. You might do a theatre or two. . . ."

Elsie had not the vaguest idea who Mrs. Graddle was. She guessed that the old lady was a member of one of those organizations which undertake the care of young girls. It was a matter for satisfaction that such societies existed.

For instance, as she had met her white-haired guardian she had noticed a lank-looking man with long black hair and large horn-rimmed spectacles; and this sinister-looking individual had looked at her so oddly that she felt a queer little thrill of fear. And now he was standing at her elbow as the cab drew up at the curb.

"Get in, my dear," said Mrs. Graddle, as Elsie pushed in her suitcase. The girl obeyed, and the old lady was following when the man with the spectacles caught her arm, and, drawing her gently aside, shut the cab door.

"King's Cross," he said to the driver, and, still holding Mrs. Graddle's arm, he pushed his head through the open window space. "Your train leaves at 5:32. Lady Shene will probably meet you at Welwyn Station. Have you money for the cab fare?"

"Ye-es," said the panic-stricken Elsie.

"Good. Don't talk to people unless you know them; especially angelic old birds like this one."

He waved the cab on.

"What's the idea?" demanded Mrs. Graddle, breathlessly.

The man had already called another cab.

"Get in," he said. She obeyed tremblingly. The man followed.

"I've told him to drive through the park. I'll drop you at the end of Birdcage Walk."

"I've a good mind to give you in charge!" There was a whimper in the old woman's voice. "Who do you think you are?" He did not answer this question.

"You've been convicted twice—once in Leeds and Manchester,"

he said, "and for a number of offences. You get acquainted with somebody in a registry office who keeps you supplied with information regarding the movement of servants. I understand that you're not above touting and using the cinemas to discover stage-struck girls."

"You can't prove anything," she interrupted. "And even if you arrest me—but you're not going to do a thing like that."

She opened her bag with trembling fingers, groped in the interior and took out a wad of banknotes.

"Be a good man and don't make any trouble," she pleaded.

The Ringer took the notes from her hand, counted them deliberately.

"Sixty-five pounds doesn't seem a very adequate bribe," he remarked.

She opened an inner purse, and sorted out two notes, each for a hundred pounds.

"That's all I've got." Old Mrs. Graddle was inclined to be hysterical. "You 'busies' can't keep your noses out of anything!"

The Ringer tapped at the window and the cab stopped. It was now raining heavily, and there were few pedestrians about.

"Have you any children?" he asked.

"No," she said quickly.

"Apart from the beastliness of your job, do you ever realize what it feels like to be a father or a mother, to be waiting and hoping for somebody to come back . . . to be uncertain about their fate?"

"I don't want any argument with you," she said, with surprising savagery for so picturesque an old lady. "You've got your money, and that's all you care about! I've got no children."

"I think you're right," he said, cryptically, and opened the door for her.

"Let him drive on to the Tube station," she demanded; but he shook his head.

"You can get out and walk. You'll be wet through, probably, and die—and if you do I shan't stop laughing!"

She said something which no angelic old lady should have said. The Ringer smiled. As she moved quickly toward Parliament Square, he paid the cabman.

"Turn round and go back," he said.

And he slipped on a mackintosh which he carried over his arm, took off his glasses, and wiped away his small mustache before the cabman had turned the nose of his machine in the other direction.

He was taking no risks—the more so since he was well aware for what destination Mrs. Graddle was bound.

In the circumstances she went to a lot of unnecessary trouble in taking an Underground train to South Kensington and doubling back by taxi. Eventually she reached her pleasant home in St. John's Wood in a condition of semi-exhaustion.

It was a very nice house, with a beautiful dancing floor; this was necessary, for Mrs. Graddle gave select parties. The peculiar servants she employed were decorating the ballroom when she arrived, but she was not interested in the coming festivities of the evening.

She went upstairs to the small study, where her son was eating greasy toast and reading the evening newspaper.

"Hullo! Did you get her?" he asked pleasantly.

He was a lethargic man of thirty, heavy-featured, heavy-eyed, and decidedly plump. On one finger he wore a diamond ring of great value; stones sparkled from his ornate cravat. He listened while she told her breathless story, stroking his small mustache.

"That's pretty bad," he said. "Who was he? Do you know him? A 'busy?' It's awkward—damned awkward! They know about the Leeds and the Manchester affair too; that's rotten!"

He had reason for his perturbation. Only by the skin of his teeth had he succeeded in keeping clear of the Manchester charge, and it would have been much more serious for him than for his mother.

"What are you scared about—I paid the feller, didn't I?" She rang the bell viciously, and when the servant came: "We shan't want the room for that girl; she's not coming," she snapped, and when the servant had closed the door: "For God's sake don't sit there shaking like a jelly, Julian! There's nothing to be afraid of!"

But Julian thought there were many things to be afraid of, and enumerated a few.

"I've been dreading this," he quavered, "ever since that Oring girl was found. Let's go down into the country, mother—what about Margate? We could stay there for a month or two till this affair blew over?—"

"It has blown over," she interrupted, and went upstairs to change from her street clothes, which were most uncomfortably damp.

Julian Graddle never felt less like following his legitimate profession. He had to go into the West End to attend to two clients, for he was a ladies' hairdresser—an extremely useful trade to his mother: for women gossip to one another. They talk of servants who are leaving them, of girls who have got into scrapes. Some of his mother's best "finds" had been located by Julian in the course of his working day.

He was certainly not at his best after a series of sharp admonitions from his best client—a lady whose temper was by no means equable. And he went to his second call more rattled than ever. The next day he had to attend at the shop which employed him, and he lived on tenterhooks, growing bolder, however, as the day progressed without a sign of a policeman.

In the evening, as he was leaving, the clerk at the desk handed him a slip of paper.

"Miss Smith, 34, Grine Mews, telephoned for you specially."

He frowned at the paper, but the time was convenient. "Six-thirty," said the note. "Miss Smith, very urgent. Pay on completion of work."

He was not at all surprised to be called to a mews. So many fashionable people had converted garages into artistic flats.

The occupant of 34, Grine Mews, was obviously terminating her occupation. There was a board displayed, informing the world that "this handsome and commodious flat" was to let. He knocked at the narrow door, which was immediately opened.

"Come in," said a man's voice pleasantly. "Are you the hairdresser? Miss Smith has been waiting for you."

Julian stumped wheezily up the steep stairs. They were uncarpeted, and so was the landing above. There was also the queer smell which attaches to houses that have been long unfurnished. Possibly Miss Smith was only just moving in.

His conductor opened a door.

"This way. It is rather dark, but I'll get a light."

Julian entered unsuspectingly. The door slammed behind him—then there was a click, and a bare lamp hanging from the ceiling glowed dimly. The room was empty of furniture; the floor and mantelpiece were covered with dust. Over the little window a heavy horse-rug had been fastened with forks.

"Don't move," said the stranger.

His face was covered with a half-mask: a habit of The Ringer's when he was not wearing disguise.

"If you raise a bleat I shall shoot you through the stomach, and you will die in great agony," he said, calmly; and Julian's face went green at the sight of the pistol in the man's hand.

"What—what—?" he began.

"Don't ask questions. Go through that doorway."

Like a man in a dream, the prisoner obeyed. The inner room had a rickety table and a dark-colored sofa, evidently left by a former tenant. On the table was a glass of red wine, and to this The Ringer pointed.

"Drink," he said curtly.

The man turned an agonized face to him.

"Is it poisoned?" he whimpered.

"No, but I will tell you very frankly it is drugged. I'm not going to kill you—I promise you."

Julian gulped down the draught.

"Who are you?" he asked, hollowly.

"People call me The Ringer," said Henry Arthur Milton.

It was the last word Julian Graddle remembered.

That night The Ringer had a long consultation with Captain Oring.

"He is the man all right, so we need not distress your daughter by bringing her up to identify him. Where is your ship lying?"

"She's lying at Keeney's Wharf, Rotherhithe," said Captain Oring, pondering the problem before him. "If I thought this was the man—"

"He is the man; but you're to do nothing drastic. He is to be kept alive and in good health. You will arrive at El Sass on the 23rd as I reckon the time—a day or two more or less doesn't matter, because you will be expected. You will arrange to hand him over at night to a crew of Arabs who will come out in a boat for him. Here is the money for his passage—two hundred and sixty-five pounds. His mother is paying the fare."

His two sons were with Captain Oring, and one of them spoke.

"If this is the man, Mr. Oppenton, we don't want any payment. I'd like to take the swine and beat his head off, but if you say no—well, your word goes."

In the middle of the night, the "boys" and Captain Oring went down to the little garage at the end of the garden, where Mr. Julian Graddle was sleeping soundly, and bundled him into an old car. He was taken to Keeney's Wharf when the night watchman was dozing, and laid in a bumpy berth in a very uncomfortable little cabin. . . .

To Ibn el Masjik The Ringer wrote a letter, and sent it overland by air mail. It began:

From his friend Arthur, to Ibn el Masjik, the servant of God, on whom be peace!

I have thought much over the trouble which you confided to me, and of Certain Ones in your house who desire to follow the Western custom, making their hair short like men. Also, that you can find none in your city who may do this service for you.

Now, El Masjik, I am sending to you a man very skillful in such things: a slave who has no protection of the law, and you shall keep him in your house all the days of his life, and I ask only that he be a servant to women, such an one as they may beat with their slippers.

On the fourteenth day of the Month of the Pilgrimage a little steamer shall come to the port of El Sass and you shall send . . .

He gave the most minute instructions for the disposal of Mr. Julian Graddle—instructions that he knew would be obeyed to the letter.

A fortnight later he saw an advertisement in the agony columns of three daily newspapers:

Will Julian Graddle, who disappeared from London, please communicate with his anxious and sorrowing mother?

And when he read this The Ringer laughed. He had read such appeals before, addressed by parents who sought daughters. And where those daughters had gone, and why they did not answer, the angelic Mrs. Graddle knew best.

SOME JOBS
ARE SIMPLE

CHET WILLIAMSON

It took me a long time to find you," she said, looking across the beer-wet table at him. She was a hassled-looking woman, he thought as he looked back and sipped his drink. Young, but not so young that she could hide those bags under her eyes with makeup.

"You sure I'm who you're looking for?"

"If your name's Joe, you are."

He nodded. "Joe."

"I need a . . . something done."

"A job."

"Yes. A job."

"Who told you about me?"

"An acquaintance. He owns . . . owned a fur-storage place."

"Uh-huh." Abrams, he thought. He'd torched the building six months before.

"Not him really. His wife."

"What's the job?"

She looked around nervously. "Can we talk here?"

"See any cops?"

She started to answer before she realized he was joking.

"Don't be so nervous," he said with a thin smile. "You, uh . . ." He glanced down, then up. "You want me to *do* somebody for you?"

"No!" Her eyelids flew up. "Oh no, nothing like that."

"What then?"

"A burglary." She had trouble with the word. It seemed to stick in her throat. He gestured to the half pitcher of beer, but she shook her head. "I want you to burglarize my house. Steal some jewelry of mine."

"Steal your own jewelry. That means insurance."

"Yes. I need money."

"And I give you back the jewels afterwards."

"Well, yes."

"And you pay me."

"Yes."

"You pay me a thousand dollars."

"A . . . that's more than I had thought."

"I'm taking a risk. You see? Any less and it's not worth it."

"A thousand dollars."

"I generally ask for more. Things are slow right now."

"You'd want cash."

He chuckled softly. "Yes indeed."

"Oh!" She looked embarrassed. "Yes. Yes, of course."

"Where do you live?"

"Marion Court. 1636 Marion Court."

He licked the beer from his lip. Marion Court was an upper-class section on the city's outskirts. The houses were widely spaced. "Who else lives there?"

"Just my husband."

"He in on this?"

"He . . . no, he's not. I don't want him to know about it."

"He'll know when the jewels are gone."

"I mean about my meeting you."

"Why not?"

"I need the money for something I don't want him to know about."

"Uh-huh."

"And that's all I want to say about it."

He poured himself more beer and took a swallow. "Once I steal the jewels, how do you know I'll give them back?"

"I would have to trust you."

"I'm a thief."

"If you kept them," she frowned, "I could tell the police you took them."

"Then I'd tell that you hired me to take them."

"You couldn't prove that."

"Then how else would you know that I took them?" A cloud passed over her face, and she moved back, as if trying to decide whether or not to rise from the table. "Don't worry," he said. "You'll get them back. I didn't get my reputation by double-crossing clients. I just want you to know that if you change your mind and get religion, I can take you with me, okay?"

"I won't change my mind."

"Good. When do you want this done?"

"Tomorrow night?"

"That's pretty soon." She didn't respond. "Okay. What time?"

"Two A.M.? You can come in through the kitchen door. I'll have it unlocked. I'll put the jewelry on the desk in the den. It's just off the kitchen."

"Won't your husband think that's odd?"

"He never goes into the den after dinner. When you leave, break the window in the kitchen door."

"Why?"

She beamed as if she were proud of her idea. "That way it won't look as though it was unlocked to begin with."

"Clever. Won't your husband hear it?"

"He's a sound sleeper, and our bedroom's upstairs on the other side of the house."

"Does he have a gun?"

"A gun? Yes. Why?"

"There's always a chance he'll wake up. A chance he'll hear me. Which means I've got to bring a gun."

"No! You won't need it—he'll never hear you, and if he does I'll keep him in the bedroom."

"I'm sorry, but . . ."

"Please, I promise you, you won't need a gun. I'll . . . I'll unload his."

"Bringing it doesn't mean I have to use it."

"I . . ."

"Insurance, that's all. If you know I've got a gun, you'll be doubly sure I won't be bothered."

She sat for a moment, looking worried. "All right. But please, no shooting."

"No shooting. Any pets?"

"No. How can I reach you afterward?"

He scribbled a number on a corner of the paper place mat, tore it off, and handed it to her. "Call this number. If I'm not there, there'll be someone who'll tell you how to reach me. Memorize it and throw it away."

She nodded and stuck the note in her purse. "1636 Marion Court. Two A.M. You won't forget?"

"I won't forget."

The following night he parked his car, a dark blue midsized sedan, four blocks from 1636 Marion and walked to the house. He was relieved to see that it was a good fifty yards between houses and relieved to hear no bayings of dogs as he walked up the driveway and around to the kitchen door. He slipped on his gloves and tried the knob. It was unlocked, as she'd promised, and opened smoothly and quietly. He listened, but the house was still. Closing the door behind him, he took a penlight from his pocket and flashed it low around the room, quickly spotting the entrance to the den. The door was open, and on the desk was a brown leather box. He opened the lid and smiled as the jewelry danced in the light. It was always tempting, but he'd never yet succumbed. With this batch, though, it would be hard, very hard.

His head shot up as he heard the noise, a low squeak, as of a settling floorboard. But he knew the difference between a settling sound and one made by someone's foot. He flicked off the penlight and reached for the .38 Special in his armpit.

"Hello?" The voice was a whisper, high and near. "Is that you . . . Joe?" She said the name as though she knew it was false.

He held the light out at his side and turned it on. She was standing empty-handed in the doorway, a cranberry-colored robe wrapped around her. She blinked as the light hit her eyes. "Jesus," he said. "What are you doing here?"

"I was nervous. I couldn't stay in bed. I wanted to make sure you got in all right."

"Of course I did. I thought you were going to stay with your husband."

"Oh, he's sleeping, don't worry." She pointed to the box. "Those are the jewels."

"I figured."

"And there was another piece I wore today that I forgot to put in the box . . ." Her hand went into the pocket of her robe and came out with a small pistol that fired twice, throwing bullets sharply into his chest so that he staggered back and hit the wall of bookcases, dropping his own pistol he'd been loosely, confidently holding. He slumped to the floor, books plopping on either side of him like giant raindrops. He didn't have to see the blood to know he was dying.

With the same surprising speed with which she'd drawn the gun, she crossed to him from the doorway, knelt, and picked up his .38. He tried to make a grab for it, but only his fingers would move, and those too slowly. "Why?" he asked, tasting blood.

"You'll see. You deserve that much." She crossed to the doorway, turned on the room light, and shouted. "Tom!" There was silence. "Tom!" She wrapped a handkerchief around the hand that held the gun.

A muffled cry answered her from somewhere in the house.

"Come here! I'm in the den!"

"What is it? For crissake, it's after two. . . ."

"Just come in here! Something's not right. . . ." She walked over to where he'd been standing when she'd shot him and looked at him. "Now you get it?"

A few seconds later Tom walked through the doorway, and she shot him in the forehead with the .38. Then she wiped the other pistol and put it in her husband's dead hand. "You'll get yours back in a minute," she said to the man dying against the bookcase. "I've got a couple of things to do first."

He listened to her call the police on the kitchen phone, thinking how frenzied and horrified she seemed. The last sound he heard was the sharp clatter of glass as she broke the window in the kitchen door. From the outside, of course.

STRICTLY ACCIDENTAL

MORGAN TALBOT

On practically every fence there was a sign that said in big black letters, NO HUNTING OR TRESPASSING—THIS MEANS YOU! Dolliver looked at the signs and then his two pink chins shook with laughter in the collar of his flossy red hunting jacket. "You suppose that really means us, Benny?"

He was pretty well oiled. There had been a quart of Vat 69 in the side-pocket of the car when we left Seattle that morning, and there was just one good-sized drink left by the time we reached pheasant territory. Dolliver downed that one, too. I wasn't anybody to share liquor with—I was just the guy that drove his car, and carried his gun, and told him when and where to shoot.

I looked at the NO HUNTING signs and then I looked down at a big mud-puddle on this side of the fence. I said, "Hell, Mr. Dolliver, they don't mean us. They must mean two fellows from Syracuse."

He laughed and laughed, his little round nose twinkling like a traffic light in the frosty morning air. "Then let us negotiate yon fence, my good man. Let us tackle the grackle and make the pheasant quail. Ha! Get it, Benny?"

I'm not kidding. That was the way he always talked when he was drunk, and he was drunk at least nine-tenths of the time. We didn't even take a bird-dog along on these hunting expeditions any more, because Dolliver had shot the last two by accident and then had bawled around like a heart-broken kid. Some guy. Maybe you can understand why his wife wasn't in love with him, even though he did wrap her up in Flato necklaces and Russian sables.

I put down the shotgun and held the strands of barb-wire apart so Dolliver could squirm through. He made heavy weather of it, snagging the seat of his pants on the wire and chuckling away as if that were just about the funniest joke in the world. I had the shotgun ready for him by the time he got untangled. I gave the muddy barrels a once-over lightly with the end of my woollen scarf and then I eased through the fence behind Dolliver.

The spot was a three-acre cornfield hemmed in by ash trees, and it was a hell of a good place for Dolliver to die. I guess the other hunters had taken those signs seriously, because there wasn't a single gun popping. Dolliver had fun. He began to scoot from corn-shock to corn-shock, pretending they were Indian teepees and saying loudly, "Hist, Deerslayer! My scattergun, pard!"

Money or no money, could any woman learn to love a guy like that?

A couple of fat Hungarian pheasants slipped out from behind a corn-shock just ahead, hustling along very close to the ground and gathering speed for a quick take-off. I shoved the shotgun into Dolliver's hooks and yelled, "It's a cinch! Let 'em have both barrels!"

Then I turned around and hurried off through the stubble, running the same way the pheasants had run—very fast, very close to the ground. I'd run about the length of a night-club dance floor when I heard the blast, and the instant I heard it my feet quit moving. I stood there like John Farmer's scarecrow and felt my heart chunking away at my ribs and the skin gathering in tight little pleats on the back of my neck. Even when it's something you've been expecting and hoping for, a thing like that puts the fear of the Lord into you.

The blast had sounded like a howitzer shell tearing through a cast-iron roof, and then I heard the whir of pheasant wings just over my head, and then there was silence thick enough to chop up and sell by the pound to public libraries. Dolliver wasn't laughing any more. He wasn't having fun.

He wasn't saying boo.

I turned around and went back and looked down at him, liking him a little better now that he was worth a couple of million dollars to me.

I'd caught detective story writers in a lot of whoppers—one being the old wheeze about how nobody ever gets away with murder —and I'd often wondered if you really *could* kill a man by putting bamboo splinters in his chow mein, or sulphur in his gasoline tank, or good rich mud in the barrels of his shotgun. Well, I knew one thing for certain now: that shotgun gag was the pure quill. Dolliver knew it too, though he wasn't likely to lodge complaints about it.

The blast had thrown him backward into the side of a corn-shock, and he was sitting there with his legs spread out and his face turned up to the sky and his fingers locked on what was left of the scattergun. There wasn't much of it left. The explosion had ripped it apart just above the breech, twisting the barrels into a choice piece of scrap-iron. Dolliver's face had taken most of the punishment.

I began to think about Vee Dolliver, who was a widow now and a rich one at that. A beautiful one, too. . . . And I thought about the dead-end cell at double Walla, and how a lot of guys had found themselves rooming there simply because they'd insisted on doing things the hard way. They'd had everything worked out in the blue-prints—they'd had their split-second timing and their tricky alibis and their million-dollar tongues—but they wound up on Gooseneck Avenue just the same.

And why? Because when something looks like murder, the blues are going to find a topsy in spite of hell. When it looks like an accident, they're glad enough to let it go at that. Well, this looked like an accident, and nobody in God's world could prove it wasn't.

I thought about all this and I began to feel pretty good again. I wiped the mud off my scarf and then I doubled back and smeared up my footprints so that they didn't tell any kind of story at all. A pint-sized farmer in a gallon-sized mackinaw came loping through the ash trees just as I knelt down beside the late millionaire's corpse.

"You city guys think you own the world, don't you?" he raved. "Posted land don't mean a thing to you, does it? You come down

here and you shoot our cows and you— Get that drunk off my land!
Get him out, damn you!"

I said, "He isn't drunk. He's dead. You got a telephone?"

He had a telephone, all right, but it was at least three minutes
before he could say so.

They held a coroner's inquest down there in the bird country. I
was the star witness, of course, and I spoke my piece just the way I'd
rehearsed it.

"Mr. Dolliver looked at those NO HUNTING signs and then he sent
me into the field ahead of him to see if the farmer was hiding
around anywhere," I said. "I left the shotgun with him, and I guess
he must have leaned it up against a fence post with the barrels
sticking in that mud puddle. The average hunter would know better
than that, but Mr. Dolliver was—well, he'd been drinking all morning and he was always pretty careless with guns, anyhow. I tried to
watch him, but a man can't be everywhere and see everything at
once. It wasn't until he followed me through the fence and blazed
away at those two pheasants that I had any idea what had happened."

Things went my way from beginning to end. Two of Dolliver's
country-club pals had come over from the Coast with Vee, and they
testified that Dolliver had been dangerous company on a hunting
trip because of his eccentric ways with firearms. Vee herself was the
only other witness.

She didn't look at me. She didn't look at anybody or anything—
just sat there twisting her gloved hands together and staring into
space as if she saw something nobody else could see. Her little
heart-shaped face was whiter than a Kodiak Christmas, and there
were soft blue shadows under her dark blue eyes, and her lips trembled so that she could hardly get the words through them. Can you
tie it? Anybody would almost have thought that Dolliver had been
the shining light of her life.

She told about his accidentally shooting the two bird dogs. And
about him feeling so bad afterwards that he cried like a kid. "You
see," she said, "he—he was *kind*. He trusted everybody and everything, and that's why he was always so reckless with guns. He just
couldn't believe that—that anything was going to hurt him. Or
anybody else. He—well, he had *faith* in things. . . ."

The coroner's jury decided that a double-barreled shotgun was a
poor thing to have faith in, and that was that. I wasn't surprised at
the verdict. Not even Vee had suspected the truth, though Vee

knew that I wasn't likely to spill many tears on Dolliver's cedar nightgown. The cops were satisfied, and I was satisfied, and I guess everybody was satisfied except Dolliver.

So you can't get away with murder, huh? It is to laugh. The next time some weisenheimer pulls that one on you, tell him for me that I got away with it clean as soap. And all because there's a right way and a wrong way of doing things.

They planted Dolliver in Seattle. I drove Vee to the funeral, but she was sandwiched between a couple of Dolliver's nephews and so I didn't have a chance to talk things over with her. Not that that bothered me very much. I was pretty sure of my ground, and I could wait.

There had been those long, lazy drives through the suburbs of Seattle. There had been the little roadside inn east of Vancouver, and there had been Vee's soft, shaky voice telling me all the things I'd been waiting to hear. "I love you, Ben. I'm in love with my husband's chauffeur . . . just like—like somebody in a cheap novel. Oh, darling, darling, what are we going to do?"

"You can't stay married to that clown," I told her. "Ask him for a divorce and a good-sized cash settlement."

"Ben! Please don't talk that way about him, dear. He—he isn't a clown. He's kind, and sweet, and sort of helpless, and—Ben, I couldn't hurt him. I just couldn't. It would be like hurting a baby."

So this had been the only way to do it. It had been the best way, too, from everybody's point of view except maybe Dolliver's. There'd be a bigger block of cash, for one thing.

After the funeral, I sat around in my headquarters above the garage and thought about all this and waited day after day for a word from Vee. She never seemed to go out any more, and I didn't even catch a glimpse of her in all that time. The waiting began to sandpaper my nerves before long. It was a whole lot too early to send out the wedding invitations, of course; but still and all, a guy likes to keep his fences in good repair.

After a couple more weeks of this, I made up my mind I was going to have another squint at my hole-card. The big trouble was, old Aiken seemed to have made up *his* mind that I wasn't. He met me at the service entrance the first time I tried to crash through, and his thin, stiff face was about as inviting as the business side of a straight-edge razor.

Aiken stared at me out of his moss-agate eyes and said coldly, "I don't believe you were summoned, Daly. The madam is not making any appointments at present, and I'm sure she has no intention of using the car today."

I thought, *Have your fun while you can, Stoneface. It'll be just too bad for you when I'm doing the hiring and the firing around here.* "The name is Mr. Daly, Aiken," I told him out loud, "and I have reasons for wanting to see Mrs. Dolliver."

You could have split kindling with his face. "The madam is not seeing anybody," he said, "and I'm sure she would resent any such intrusion. If you will state your business—"

"The Packard needs a couple new rear tires," I ad-libbed, "but I don't want to order them without her say-so. It'll just take a minute to—"

Aiken turned stiffly and plodded away. He came back looking like a cagy old tomcat full of goldfish. "The madam says you may use your own judgment, Daly. She does not care to discuss inconsequential matters at such a time."

I didn't like that.

I waited another couple of days and then I tried it again. If the Cord was in need of an overhaul job, Aiken told me, I was to go ahead and give it an overhaul job without bothering the madam about it. Then he sharpened his face at me and said starchily, "I have no idea why you are annoying her with these trivialities, but if you persist in it I shall most certainly recommend your early discharge."

I didn't like that, either. The more I thought about this whole situation, the less I liked it. I'd got away with murder, sure—Dolliver was pushing grass-roots and the case was closed—but the stake I had banked on was beginning to look a little too much like *if* money. I couldn't chew that. Aiken or no Aiken, I was going to compare notes with Vee Dolliver.

I waited two more days, and then I got my chance.

Aiken was out of the way. I'd been using my upstairs window for a sort of conning tower, and I saw him open his rusty old umbrella and head north along the tree-lined street just beyond the house. He probably wasn't going any farther than the nearest grocery store, but that would give me time for a few chummy words with Vee. It was as good a break as any beggar could choose.

I did a One-Eye Connolly through the service entrance and began to case the house. It took me a good five minutes to find Vee. She was busy writing letters in the upstairs study, and she didn't even know I was around until I said softly, "Vee."

She turned from the writing desk. Her chin jerked up and her face went pale and she looked at me as if I were Lon Chaney. "Daly! What—"

"I didn't mean to scare you, Vee. I had to see you, and this was the only way I could do it. I—I guess it's a little early to be talking about—well, about the future, but I want you to know that I still—"

Vee said, "I can't talk to you, Daly. I haven't been seeing anybody since—since Richard's death, and I gave Aiken orders not to admit you."

I didn't like that. I liked it so little that I could feel the blood heating my cheeks and the muscles tightening along my jawbones. "So it's Daly now, huh?" I said. "It was Benny darling less than a month ago."

Her fingers began to play nervously with a long bronze letter-opener. She dropped her eyes and said in half a voice, "I—I know. I guess I haven't been very fair to you . . . Ben. I guess I should have had enough courage to see you at once and tell you that—that—"

I said, "Well?"

"Oh, Ben, don't make this hard for me! Please! Can't you see that Richard's death has—has changed everything?"

"Hell," I said, "of course it's changed everything. You don't have to worry about hurting him now, Vee. We can—"

She shook her head.

"So it's the brush-off, is it?" I said through my teeth. "It's the old runaround."

Vee began to inch away from me. "Don't, Ben—*please!* Try to understand. After Richard died, I just felt . . . different. I thought of his kindness, and his gentleness, and—and everything, and I realized then that it was Richard I'd loved all the time. I was infatuated with you, Ben, but that was all. We—we've got to forget it ever happened. I wasn't faithful to him in life, but I can—can at least be faithful to him now. . . ."

I said, "I love you. I'm not giving you up. Get that? You think I'm the kind of guy a woman can turn on and off like—"

"Ben!"

I kept on moving toward her. Her fingers curled tight around the handle of the letter-opener, but I don't think she even knew it was there. "Ben!" she whispered in a dry-leaf voice. "Your—your face. . . ."

I tried to hang onto myself. But I couldn't do it. The blood was making high, thin music in my ears, and I could feel my lips pulling back from my teeth and freezing that way. "Damn you," I said, "what's the matter with my face? You liked it well enough a month ago!"

Vee stared at me out of eyes that were like pooled ink. Her voice lifted and went thin. "It's the face of a man who would—who'd commit—" She quit talking then, and her lips turned gray, and I could see the idea building in those wide blue eyes. She screamed, "You killed him! You killed him! You murdered Richard because you thought I'd—"

That scared the sense back into my head. "Stop it, Vee! You don't know what you're saying."

She spun toward the door. "Don't come near me! You murdered Richard, and now you're planning to murder me!"

I said, "Vee! For God's sake!"

She bolted out into the hallway, her fingers still clenched on the letter-knife. I threw the door open and went after her, but I wasn't going to do any arguing about that two million dollars now. The only thing in God's world I wanted was to get her quieted down before Aiken or somebody else barged in. "Vee. . . ."

She reached the mouth of the stairwell. Her face whipped back toward me, whiter than white. *"Don't kill me!"* she screamed. *"Oh, God, don't kill me!"*

That was when the thing happened.

Vee's foot missed the top step of the stairs. She made one frantic effort to catch the bannister, and then I could hear the quick *thud-thud* of her body as it toppled down the carpeted steps. There was one last *thud*, heavier than any of the others, and after that the hush came down.

I found her lying in a motionless huddle at the bottom of the stairs, her hair spread out and her face hidden in the carpet. "Vee!" I said, and then I turned her over and stopped thinking for a minute or two.

That sharp bronze letter-knife had been in her right hand when she went down, but it wasn't there now. It was in her left breast.

I pulled it out and tried to dam the flow of blood with my fingers. "Vee!" I said again. "Vee. . . ."

And that was when Aiken got back from the grocery store.

Can you tie it? I mean, can you? Aiken told about seeing me there with the letter-opener in my fist, and the cops found my fingerprints on the handle, and a neighbor woman testified that she heard Vee screaming, "Don't kill me! Oh, God, don't kill me!" The state prosecutor called me a "fiendish harpy who tried to take advantage of a helpless woman in the hour of her darkest sorrow." Then he put his face close to mine and roared, "You killed her, didn't you? When she scorned your advances, you murdered her like the black-hearted beast you are!"

But nobody even so much as suggested that I'd had anything to do with Dolliver's death. So cops are smart, are they? It is to laugh.

I got away with it, didn't I?

I got away clean as soap with the murder that looked like an accident, and you couldn't really call it my fault that they're going to stretch my neck for the accident that looked like a murder!

SUDDEN VIOLENCE

ROBERT PETYO

Myron didn't know who she was. The blonde hair that glistened in the lights as she left the Riverfront Restaurant was all that mattered to him. She was young, maybe twenty-five, and was the kind of woman Myron used to fantasize about. Soft. Full of life. The kind of woman he might fall in love with and marry, so they could move into a nice country house with a big yard, and play with their children.

But Myron had given up those fantasies long ago.

He followed the woman as she circled behind the restaurant toward the parking lot, and in the murkiness between the street-lights along the riverbank and the glowing lamps of the parking lot, he pounced. When he slammed the butcher's knife into her belly she uttered a soft gasp, more of surprise than of horror or pain, and she doubled over as she tried to hold her guts in place. Myron slipped behind her and wrapped his left arm around her shoulders.

He drove his knee into the small of her back and pulled her upright. With the blade he sliced open her throat.

As she crumpled he leapt back, waving his arms to shake off the blood. He hid the knife under his sweatshirt and strode into the darkness beyond the parking lot.

Now, alone on the twisted city streets, Myron was scared. He had lived on these streets for fifteen years ever since he ended a childhood of orphanages and foster homes by running away from the alcoholic couple who tried to save their marriage by focusing their rage on him. He dropped out of life, drank cheap whiskey like water, and tried to survive on the streets. Those streets now terrified him. He wanted to escape the uncertainty of where his next meal would come from, the taunts from hateful people, the hardship of a steam grate as his only warmth on a bitter night, and the danger of sudden violence lurking around the next dark corner.

While he had stalked his victim his mind had been occupied, but now fear quickened his breath and poked his skin. The streets were not safe.

Soon, though, he would escape. There would be no more uncertainties, no more taunts, no more hardships, no more danger.

He had to get rid of the bloody clothes. He had thought there would be a lot of blood, so he had worn a sweatsuit he had found in a garbage can on 82nd Street. The pants were shredded and the sweatshirt stank, but they were enough to shield his regular clothes underneath. However, to be seen in the bloody sweatsuit was too risky. He had to reach his friends at the 13th Precinct, the only people he trusted. Anyone else who might stop him would be an unknown quantity. Anything might happen. There were too many crazy people in this world. Even on the police force. He had heard about what happened to old Mr. Crane, badly beaten by some thugs who found him sleeping under Fulton's Bridge. And one of those thugs had been an off-duty policeman.

Myron shuddered. No, he would not end up like old Mr. Crane.

He put the knife on the ground and tore off the sweatsuit, revealing grubby slacks and a long-sleeved wool sweater with holes in the elbows. He threw the suit into a dumpster behind the Fish House on Morris Avenue. He retrieved the knife and stuck the handle in the band of his pants then pulled his sweater up and over the blade. When he hunched forward as he usually did it was unnoticeable. He hurried to the 13th Precinct.

"Hiya, Myron." The desk sergeant didn't look up from the papers he scribbled on. "What's shakin' tonight?"

"I'm the one you're looking for." Myron's scratchy voice had been scarred by too many cigarettes, and often people made him repeat himself. "The Blade. The one in the papers. The one who's been killing all those women."

He leaned over his papers and peered out from under craggy eyebrows.

"I am," Myron insisted proudly.

Shrugging, he leaned back. "Why don't you sit down?" He gestured toward a row of chairs against the wall. "I'll get one of the detectives to come out to talk to you." Shaking his head he bent to an intercom.

"Thank you," Myron said as he sat and crossed his legs. The 13th Precinct was like home. He liked the soft yellow lights that left the corners shadowy. He liked the thick scent of the deodorizer that never completely covered the stale men's room smell. Though they rarely let him stay long, they were nice to him here. And once in a while he got to spend the night in "The Tank."

"Hi, Myron."

He smiled as he stood. It was Tom Peterson. The knot of his tie hung to his chest and his shirt was wet and wrinkled. "C'mon back. I'll get you a coffee. But you can only stay a little bit." He trudged away.

Ten desks were cramped in the small windowless squadroom. A bulletin board blanketed with papers held on by red pushpins filled one wall. Myron smiled at each detective they passed. Some nodded, some ignored him. Beyond Peterson's desk was the holding cell, "The Tank."

"We're really busy," Peterson said as he collapsed into a chair that groaned under his bulk. "We're working overtime on this Blade thing. The papers are hitting the mayor, the mayor's hitting the captain, and the captain's hitting us."

"That's why I'm here. I want to help you."

Fatigue melted from his face as he straightened. "You saw something?"

"I'm the one you want."

"What?"

"I'm the Blade."

"Oh, Jesus, Myron!"

"I am. I just killed another one tonight."

"This isn't funny, Myron."

"I'm not funny. I killed her behind the Riverfront Restaurant. Less than a hour ago. Somebody musta found the body by now."

He rocked back on the chair. "Who was she?"

"I don't know. A woman with blonde hair."

"And why are you killing blondes, Myron?"

"I don't know. I can't help myself. You have to stop me. You have to lock me away before I kill anyone else."

"Sit down, Myron!"

He stumbled to the side and clambered into the chair beside the metal desk.

"Why are you doing this?"

"I'm trying to help."

"Do you know that I've had four confessions in the last twenty-four hours?"

"You have?"

"Whenever there's a gruesome murder, or worse, a series of murders, everybody and his sister comes out of the woodwork to confess. It's this twisted society of ours. Crazy. We know they're loonies, but we gotta go through the motions. We gotta quiz 'em. I hate it. We gotta waste time with those sickos while the real sicko's still out there. But why you, Myron? Why would a guy who we never picked up for anything worse than vagrancy or drunkenness try to pull a stunt like this? We know you got problems, but are you a real sicko like the rest of the nuts I been talking to?"

"Don't be mad. I didn't—"

"Get outta here!" he shouted. Heads swivelled.

"I'm sorry, Tom. I just want to help." He struggled out of the chair and straightened. "I'm not nuts. The doctors would keep me locked up if I was nuts."

"They do lock you up. But budget cuts put you back on the streets."

"I like the hospital," he whispered.

"Get outta here before I throw you out. I got no time for this."

"No. Please. You gotta lock me up. For the rest of my life."

Peterson cocked his head to one side and rocked in the chair. "Is that what this is about? You want to go to prison?"

"I have to."

"Why?"

Trembling hands found the back of his chair. "I'm tired. And I'm scared. I been living on the streets a long time. It's not safe."

"You think prison's any better?"

"A bed each night. Food. You know what kind of people hang out in the shelters in this city. It's not safe. Phil got mugged the other night. Almost died. Right there in the shelter. At least prisons have guards."

"It doesn't work that way, Myron."

"I can't go on like this. I gotta do something."

"I don't believe this." Peterson wiped the heels of his palms down his face.

"I thought you guys would understand. That's why I came here."

He shook his head. "You're nuts."

Head hanging, he turned to leave.

Then he stopped. He had almost forgot.

"Listen," Peterson sighed, his features softening. "How about if we put you in 'The Tank' for the night?"

"Look." Myron struggled to get his sweater up over the blade.

"What are you doing?" Peterson stood. "Jesus!" He jumped a step back, knocking his chair back to the wall. "What is that?"

Myron took the blade by the handle and yanked it from his pants.

All the fatigue of endless hours of drudging spadework hooded Peterson's eyes as he focused on the knife. Slowly he looked at Myron and twisted his lips as if sucking on a sour fruit. "Drop it!" he suddenly shouted.

"What? I—" Myron heard scrambling noises of other detectives moving toward him.

"Drop it, Myron!"

He opened his fist and the blade jumped to the floor, clattering once on the hard linoleum and slapping to its side. Peterson, Myron, and three detectives who had surrounded him stared at the blood-encrusted blade like it was a wounded creature that might lash out at any moment.

"Jesus, Myron! Is that blood?" Peterson was leaning over the desk, his fists digging into the battered blotter as he studied the blade. "Where did you find that knife?"

"I told you. I told you. I killed her."

He looked up at Myron. "You did see something, didn't you?" The eyes widened with anger. "You saw the guy!"

"I told you, I—"

"You shouldn't've touched it." Peterson circled around the desk. "You got your prints—"

"No! No!" Myron screamed.

Peterson reeled back.

Suddenly Myron dropped to a crouch and snatched the blade. As he did, one of the detectives lunged for it but ended up sprawled on the floor.

Myron scrambled back until he banged into another desk. "Stay back!"

"Don't do this, Myron."

The blade swivelled in a semicircle as Myron looked at the tense faces hemming him in. "I already did it." His voice shook with tears. "I killed her. It's what I've been trying to tell you."

"Put the knife down, Myron."

He turned and saw that one of the detectives had drawn his gun.

"I'm not going to hurt you guys," Myron said. "You guys are my friends. That's why I'm here. I'm helping you with your big case. You arrest me and put me in prison."

"Stop it," Peterson said. "You're not a killer."

"Yes, I am. *I'm the Blade!*" His arms spread out like wings.

There was a commotion to the front of the squadroom and Myron turned. "We got another dead blonde," he heard someone shout from the doorway.

He started to turn back toward Peterson when someone crashed into him from the side. There was shouting and screeching as a jumble of limbs and torsos hit the floor. Myron tried to stand, but he was hurt. His head ached where he had crashed into the desk. And his left hand was burning like a hot wire had been slashed across the palm. He tried to look at it but was contorted on the floor. Someone was holding him down. Someone was on top of him, hurting him. For an instant he saw old Mr. Crane's gnarled face, and he tried to break free.

But he wasn't strong enough. . . .

The blade. He still had the blade.

He twisted, trying to slash free.

"Hold him!"

Another weight crashed onto him, forcing him down. He tried to turn. Someone had his wrist. He saw the blade flash in front of his eyes. There was a sudden pain in his arm as his body was twisted again. A fiery volcano seared his gut. His face squished into the cold metal desk. He couldn't breathe.

"I got it!" The blade clattered across the floor. "Shit! Where'd it go?"

"Look at that blood."

"What's going on here?"

"It's all right. We got it under control."

"Then let's hit the streets. We got another dead blonde."

"Where?"

"The parking lot at the Riverfront Restaurant."

Yes! Myron tried to shout but he was out of breath. He struggled to all fours, but his left arm collapsed when he put pressure on his hand, and he hit the floor. Then somebody helped him up.

"Myron, what did you see at the Riverfront?"

"Are you going to lock me up now?" Myron bobbed his head to the side and saw that the squadroom was almost empty. "No. They're out looking for the Blade," he whispered sadly. "I tried to help you guys." He looked at his left hand and saw blood seeping from a gash just under the knuckles. "Lock me up. I'll be safe." The volcano in his gut erupted again and he gasped. He looked down and saw that his sweater was soaked with blood.

"I got an emergency here!" Peterson shouted as he saw the gaping wound. He helped Myron to a chair. "I need a paramedic. I . . . ."

But Myron no longer heard him.

SWITCH

GERALD TOLLESFRUD

Nikki looked like a hooker. And she was. It had been one of the first things she told me, saying, "Sure, Mr. Danzer, that's what I do. I ball guys for money, fifty dollars for either way or seventy-five for both." Then she uncrossed her legs, stood, and moved forward to bend over my desk, her tawny hair cascading from her shoulders to cradle her breasts. "But I'm a person, I have feelings, real ones. And friends. And Angie is my friend." She had reached into her purse and produced cash and a folded newspaper clipping and dropped them on my desk.

I leaned forward and picked up the clipping, my eyes on hers. "And I'm a P.I. and I do a pretty good job. I like honest people, people who can hurt like you hurt. And I don't care if you're a hooker or a saint." Then I added, "And it's Joe."

She had smiled grimly, hopefully, and returned to her chair while I read what she had given me. Woman murdered in her own bedroom. Beaten, then strangled with a pair of pantyhose while in other parts of the city people were sleeping or working night jobs or taking in a late movie or making love. No sexual assault. Still wearing a bathrobe over a nightgown. Money and jewels missing. A pried window in the middle-class, brick ranch in a nice neighborhood until the night before last, now changed forever, the house where something terrible had happened.

Nikki described how her roommate Angie, also in the play-for-pay business, had accepted an all-night "date," describing the house, the man; it would be safe because she had played night games there before.

Then she hadn't returned in the morning.

"And you think . . . what?"

She stared at an invisible point in the air, chewing her full lips for a moment. "I don't know, Joe. I only know she didn't come back from there. We take care of each other. Maybe . . . maybe she got caught there by the dude's wife. Maybe there was a fight and he went freako. She . . . I don't know!" I didn't usually take cases like this one. I preferred cleaner stuff. Insurance fraud, missing persons who usually wanted to stay missing, company security consulting. But sometimes the boredom made me restless. Besides, one of my best friends had been an out-call lady before quitting the life and moving west to a clean world.

Don Ching, guy I had carried a badge with at the Mid-North station before I switched to a private ticket, told me there were no promising leads. The husband of the murdered woman, owner of a chemical-processing plant in the burbs west of Chicago, was the first to be scrutinized. Standard procedure. Look at the spouse first. Love or money, the motives in most crimes. But the trifecta—means, motive, opportunity—didn't wash; he had been in St. Louis as one of the speakers at a seminar and had an alibi as solid as the vault at Citibank. He had driven back immediately and, in semi-shock, tears streaming, had identified the brutalized body of his wife.

The hooker's concern for her roommate had brought me here, at a spot down the street from the death house in my car with its heavily tinted windows, a cup of luke-warm coffee in my hand. There had been no activity at the house except for the removal of the yellow crime-scene tape by two blues in a patrol car. Until now.

The garage door moved upward and a white, middle-aged Buick

rolled down the drive, paused in the street while the man inside twisted about to scope all directions, then sped toward Palatine Road. I moved into traffic three cars behind in my plain-vanilla Chevy Beretta. We traveled eastward through Arlington Heights, then hung a left through Northbrook and as far as Deerfield. The Buick swung into a small shopping-center parking lot, slowly followed its edge to the far corner, and pulled close alongside a black car with government plates, drivers' windows aligned. An arm extended with an envelope. The arm from the Buick stretched across minutes later with a thicker package. Deal. Arrangement.

As the cars parted I noted the black car's plate number and kept my tail on the Buick. Less than four blocks away it pulled into a Motel Six and nosed in to room 110 on the ground floor. The man must have some Strange stashed; wife's body barely cold. Interesting. After one knock the drapes shifted slightly and the door opened about a foot as the bereaved husband glanced about quickly, then slipped inside. Minutes later he left. There went my first theory; minutes would hardly be enough.

Four hours. Time enough for the brightness of day to fade into early-evening half-light, the sky turning from red to dull purple in the west. Time enough to slip across the street for a greasy hamburger and an urgently needed kidney drain; the jar in my car was already full of used coffee. Finally, as the legs making up half of my six-four threatened terminal cramping, a slender brunette woman in an orange raincoat and sunglasses not needed in the dimming light emerged and walked quickly to the corner. Fifteen minutes later she left the Yen Ching restaurant with a large, white carry-out sack and squirreled herself back in the room. I'd had plenty of time to place myself outside the restaurant and get a good look at her. Dark hair under a scarf. Slightly long nose. No hose. Dirty Nikes on her feet. Bandage on her left hand. When the bluish, flickering light from the room's TV gave way to darkness I called it a night. I needed to talk to Ching.

The stocky Korean leaned back in his chair, lidded eyes focused on mine. "Joe, you maybe got something, maybe not. Working girl come to you, tell you story. You follow man, go places might be okay, might not." He clasped his hands together, hands rock-hard and calloused from his martial arts work, and turned to look through the dirty blinds of his office at the clouds battling for space in the bright morning sky.

"We check man's business. Not doing so good. Goes downhill like sushi bar in Harlem. Many debts. But man had half million insurance on wife, we find out. Now wife dead." Ching's shoulders rippled and bunched under his immaculate white suit as he leaned forward again, scowling. "Motive but no opportunity. Husband in St. Louis when wife strangled. Maybe buy hit on wife but all is guessing. Then you see deal going down and see other woman. What it mean, Joe? You got something or you write script for Sunday Night Movie?"

"Let's try my scam, Don," I replied slowly, starting to pace the worn carpeting. "And get a man checking cabs to or from the dead woman's address, or close by, that the missing hooker could've used. Keep an eye on the brunette's room. Let's see what happens."

"We get back to lab today, see what's under fingernails of victim. Skin cream, blood, whatever. Also check out black car from plate through DMV. Things shape up we call you, put your party together. Must have solid for assholes at D.A. office. Okay, Joe?"

I nodded and smiled, turned in my visitor's badge at the duty desk downstairs, and went back to Danzer Security to get some work done. Melissa, my partner, was nursing her sick mother back to health and wouldn't return for three more days. The office seemed empty without her and paperwork was stacking up while I danced around the city with whores and dead bodies and sneaky husbands.

Ching called just before five. "Car man met used by coroner office. Coroner on vacation in Canada, not back for another week. Can't find clerk who check out car yesterday. Look like he did a rabbit, clothes gone, medicine cabinet empty. Live with girl who keep him happy, she gone too."

"And the woman in 110?"

"She still there, not go out. Pizza Hut stop by hour ago. Also techs find blood under victim nails type B negative, make me wonder about lady in 110 blood type. Maybe donate blood from hand where bandage is. Maybe she hooker, maybe old friend man's wife not know about. Or . . ."

"Yeah, Don. Maybes. Let's try my little party. Shake him up. Tip his hand if he's dirty. Just keep a net on the motel lady. You know the place we talked about?"

"Oriental mind like steel trap, Joe. Make bullshit call."

I faked my way past the guy's secretary at his plant, lying like a thief to get through. He came on the line hesitantly, guardedly.

"My friend," I began, "we have some business to transact. It involves your late wife and ten large in used twenties and fifties for me for silence. I think we ought to meet."

There was a long silence on the other end of the wire. Heavy breathing. Then, in a low whisper, "Who the hell are you, asshole?"

"I'm the guy with the comfort of anonymity, pal. Also, bills to pay that your contribution will cover. One contribution only for traveling money. I'm leaving town." If I had the scenario wrong my plan would sink into a deep latrine here. "Nassau is nice this time of the year. Was going with my friend Angie, catch some Blackjack and sunshine, but . . . what the hell, there's bimbos there, too. You reading me, amigo?"

More silence, more breathing, then, "Why do you think I need to pay you anything, you sleazy son-of-a-bitch?"

"Because it buys my one-way ticket. Keeps your pal at the coroner's office from rolling over to save his own ass. So you can skate. Keeps the brunettes sorted out, like the one watching soaps at the motel who looks like your dear departed. You follow or am I going too fast for you?"

A long pause. Time for the hard-sell close. "It's cash or twenty to life in the laundry and exercise yard all day and punking on your knees all night. Your choice." The puke bought it. We'd meet at eleven that night at the shelter house of a nearby park. Very dark. Well treed and shrubbed.

I got there early. In case he got there early. I wore the same Kevlar vest that had saved Ching's life several months earlier on the shore of a small lake up north in the black pit of a night when I'd also almost bought the farm. The sounds of a night bird and a chirping chorus of crickets veiled the distant hum of the city while I waited. He came through the trees, not from the blacktop park road where I had parked. A guilty move. He had a plan. One of his hands held a briefcase, the other was thrust into a dark windbreaker. I stepped out from behind the stone support of the open-walled shelter and spoke his name softly.

"You the guy who called?" His voice didn't waver; it was strong, angry.

"You got him. Bring the money? You bring the money, you win. Without it, you lose." My gun was in my hand, held behind me.

He hesitated, standing stock-still, only his head moving about to survey the night's blackness and the trees around us, seeing no one. Then, after he was convinced I was alone, a blackmailer fearing the risks as he did, the gun came out. It came out fast, faster than I'd thought it would, if he'd be playing that game. The sound split the night air, silencing the other sounds with its thunder, and the muzzle-flash shone brightly as I stepped back behind the protective stone.

In the next few seconds the shouted warnings of Ching and the two other men rang out and the man was spotlighted by their lights from behind the stack of picnic tables and the far half-wall of the open building. As they cuffed him and radioed for their car I walked past and said, "Even with the money you lose."

The rest was easy. The body of his wife was really that of Angie, a surrogate victim. The hooker was well-chosen for her resemblance and her willingness to go to his bedroom where the wife waited. The killer was still in room 110 when they went to take her in. A failing business that half a million in insurance money could save. A coroner's assistant whose signature on the death certificate would earn him a year's pay and who would eventually be found. Nice scam. Rough, desperate scam.

I looked up Nikki. I had to give her the bad news about her friend. And the cops would need her for I.D. downtown.

Helluva business to be in.

THE TELL-TALE HEART

EDGAR ALLAN POE

True!—nervous—very, very dreadfully nervous I had been and am; but why *will* you say that I am mad? The disease had sharpened my senses—not destroyed—not dulled them. Above all was the sense of hearing acute. I heard all things in the heaven and in the earth. I heard many things in hell. How, then, am I mad? Hearken! and observe how healthily—how calmly I can tell you the whole story.

It is impossible to say how first the idea entered my brain; but once conceived, it haunted me day and night. Object there was none. Passion there was none. I loved the old man. He had never wronged me. He had never given me insult. For his gold I had no desire. I think it was his eye! yes, it was this! One of his eyes resembled that of a vulture—a pale blue eye, with a film over it. Whenever it fell upon me, my blood ran cold; and so by degrees— very gradually—I made up my mind to take the life of the old man, and thus rid myself of the eye for ever.

Now this is the point. You fancy me mad. Madmen know nothing. But you should have seen *me*. You should have seen how wisely I proceeded—with what caution—with what foresight—with what dissimulation I went to work! I was never kinder to the old man than during the whole week before I killed him. And every night, about midnight, I turned the latch of his door and opened it—oh, so gently! And then, when I had made an opening sufficient for my head, I put in a dark lantern, all closed, closed, so that no light shone out, and then I thrust in my head. Oh, you would have laughed to see how cunningly I thrust it in! I moved it slowly— very, very slowly, so that I might not disturb the old man's sleep. It took me an hour to place my whole head within the opening so far that I could see him as he lay upon his bed. Ha!—would a madman have been so wise as this? And then, when my head was well in the room, I undid the lantern cautiously—oh, so cautiously—cautiously (for the hinges creaked)—I undid it just so much that a single thin ray fell upon the vulture eye. And this I did for seven long nights— every night just at midnight—but I found the eye always closed; and so it was impossible to do the work; for it was not the old man who vexed me, but his Evil Eye. And every morning, when the day broke, I went boldly into the chamber, and spoke courageously to him, calling him by name in a hearty tone, and inquiring how he had passed the night. So you see he would have been a very profound old man, indeed, to suspect that every night, just at twelve, I looked in upon him while he slept.

Upon the eighth night I was more than usually cautious in opening the door. A watch's minute hand moves more quickly than did mine. Never before that night, had I *felt* the extent of my own powers—of my sagacity. I could scarcely contain my feelings of triumph. To think that there I was, opening the door, little by little, and he not even to dream of my secret deeds or thoughts. I fairly chuckled at the idea; and perhaps he heard me; for he moved on the bed suddenly, as if startled. Now you may think that I drew back— but no. His room was as black as pitch with the thick darkness, (for the shutters were close fastened, through fear of robbers), and so I knew that he could not see the opening of the door, and I kept pushing it on steadily, steadily.

I had my head in, and was about to open the lantern, when my thumb slipped upon the tin fastening, and the old man sprang up in the bed, crying out—"Who's there?"

I kept quite still and said nothing. For a whole hour I did not move a muscle, and in the mean time I did not hear him lie down. He was still sitting up in the bed, listening;—just as I have done, night after night, hearkening to the death watches in the wall.

Presently I heard a slight groan, and I knew it was the groan of mortal terror. It was not a groan of pain or of grief—oh, no!—it was the low stifled sound that arises from the bottom of the soul when overcharged with awe. I knew the sound well. Many a night, just at midnight, when all the world slept, it has welled up from my own bosom, deepening, with its dreadful echo, the terrors that distracted me. I say I knew it well. I knew what the old man felt, and pitied him, although I chuckled at heart. I knew that he had been lying awake ever since the first slight noise, when he had turned in the bed. His fears had been ever since growing upon him. He had been trying to fancy them causeless, but could not. He had been saying to himself—"It is nothing but the wind in the chimney—it is only a mouse crossing the floor," or "it is merely a cricket which has made a single chirp." Yes, he had been trying to comfort himself with these suppositions: but he had found all in vain. *All in vain;* because Death, in approaching him, had stalked with his black shadow before him, and enveloped the victim. And it was the mournful influence of the unperceived shadow that caused him to feel—although he neither saw nor heard—to *feel* the presence of my head within the room.

When I had waited a long time, very patiently, without hearing him lie down, I resolved to open a little—a very, very little crevice in the lantern. So I opened it—you cannot imagine how stealthily, stealthily—until, at length, a single dim ray, like the thread of the spider, shot from out the crevice and fell upon the vulture eye.

It was open—wide, wide open—and I grew furious as I gazed upon it. I saw it with perfect distinctness—all a dull blue, with a hideous veil over it that chilled the very marrow in my bones; but I could see nothing else of the old man's face or person: for I had directed the ray as if by instinct, precisely upon the damned spot.

And now have I not told you that what you mistake for madness is but over acuteness of the senses?—now, I say, there came to my ears a low, dull, quick sound, such as a watch makes when enveloped in cotton. I knew *that* sound well, too. It was the beating of the old man's heart. It increased my fury, as the beating of a drum stimulates the soldier into courage.

But even yet I refrained and kept still. I scarcely breathed. I held the lantern motionless. I tried how steadily I could maintain the ray upon the eye. Meantime the hellish tattoo of the heart increased. It grew quicker and quicker, and louder and louder every instant. The old man's terror *must* have been extreme! It grew louder, I say, louder every moment!—do you mark me well? I have told you that I am nervous: so I am. And now at the dead hour of the night, amid the dreadful silence of that old house, so strange a noise as this excited me to uncontrollable terror. Yet, for some minutes longer I refrained and stood still. But the beating grew louder, louder! I thought the heart must burst. And now a new anxiety seized me— the sound would be heard by a neighbor! The old man's hour had come! With a loud yell, I threw open the lantern and leaped into the room. He shrieked once—once only. In an instant I dragged him to the floor, and pulled the heavy bed over him. I then smiled gaily, to find the deed so far done. But, for many minutes, the heart beat on with a muffled sound. This, however, did not vex me; it would not be heard through the wall. At length it ceased. The old man was dead. I removed the bed and examined the corpse. Yes, he was stone, stone dead. I placed my hand upon the heart and held it there many minutes. There was no pulsation. He was stone dead. His eye would trouble me no more.

If still you think me mad, you will think so no longer when I describe the wise precautions I took for the concealment of the body. The night waned, and I worked hastily, but in silence. First of all I dismembered the corpse. I cut off the head and the arms and the legs.

I then took up three planks from the flooring of the chamber, and deposited all between the scantlings. I then replaced the boards so cleverly, so cunningly, that no human eye—not even *his*—could have detected any thing wrong. There was nothing to wash out— no stain of any kind—no blood-spot whatever. I had been too wary for that. A tub had caught all—ha! ha!

When I had made an end of these labors, it was four o'clock— still dark as midnight. As the bell sounded the hour, there came a knocking at the street door. I went down to open it with a light heart,—for what had I *now* to fear? There entered three men, who introduced themselves, with perfect suavity, as officers of the police. A shriek had been heard by a neighbor during the night; suspicion of foul play had been aroused; information had been lodged at the police office, and they (the officers) had been deputed to search the premises.

I smiled,—for *what* had I to fear? I bade the gentlemen welcome. The shriek, I said, was my own in a dream. The old man, I mentioned, was absent in the country. I took my visiters all over the house. I bade them search—search *well.* I led them, at length, to *his* chamber. I showed them his treasures, secure, undisturbed. In the enthusiasm of my confidence, I brought chairs into the room, and desired them *here* to rest from their fatigues, while I myself, in the wild audacity of my perfect triumph, placed my own seat upon the very spot beneath which reposed the corpse of the victim.

The officers were satisfied. My *manner* had convinced them. I was singularly at ease. They sat, and while I answered cheerily, they chatted of familiar things. But, ere long, I felt myself getting pale and wished them gone. My head ached, and I fancied a ringing in my ears: but still they sat and still chatted. The ringing became more distinct:—it continued and became more distinct: I talked more freely to get rid of the feeling: but it continued and gained definitiveness—until, at length, I found that the noise was *not* within my ears.

No doubt I now grew *very* pale;—but I talked more fluently, and with a heightened voice. Yet the sound increased—and what could I do? It was *a low, dull, quick sound—much such a sound as a watch makes when enveloped in cotton.* I gasped for breath—and yet the officers heard it not. I talked more quickly—more vehemently; but the noise steadily increased. I arose and argued about trifles, in a high key and with violent gesticulations; but the noise steadily increased. Why *would* they not be gone? I paced the floor to and fro with heavy strides, as if excited to fury by the observations of the men—but the noise steadily increased. Oh God! what *could* I do? I foamed—I raved—I swore! I swung the chair upon which I had been sitting, and grated it upon the boards, but the noise arose over all and continually increased. It grew louder—louder—*louder!* And still the men chatted pleasantly, and smiled. Was it possible they heard not? Almighty God!—no, no! They heard!—they suspected!—they *knew!* —they were making a mockery of my horror!—this I thought, and this I think. But anything was better than this agony! Anything was more tolerable than this derision! I could bear those hypocritical

smiles no longer! I felt that I must scream or die!—and now—again!
—hark! louder! louder! louder! *louder!*—

"Villains!" I shrieked, "dissemble no more! I admit the deed!—tear
up the planks!—here, here!—it is the beating of his hideous heart!"

TERROR'S NIGHT

I. R. AUSTIN

Hamilton was just rinsing off his supper dishes when the bell on
the wall jangled sharply. He counted the rings. Two short,
one long; it was his station. In two strides he was across the cabin
and had picked up the receiver.

"Tolmie Peak lookout," he said.

"Longmire calling. That you, Hamilton?"

He laughed. "Now who else'd be up here on this forsaken peak?"

"Thought it might be Farrell. He oughta be there."

"He's not coming tonight, is he?"

"Yeah, with your supplies. He picked them up in Carbon River
and was heading for Pete's to get the horses. We tried to get him at
Pete's. Listen, Hamilton, there's a killer up there—"

"You're telling me," cut in Hamilton. "I've seen him!"

"Tonight?"

"No, but he's roaming these woods since Saturday."

"Who'n the hell—"

"The cat," said Hamilton. "A nice big black mountain cat. I
haven't had my face outside the station after dark since I saw him."

"Not the cat, Hamilton. McCloney's up there."

Hamilton let out a low whistle. "When did he get out?"

"When—or how—we don't know. We just know he turned up in
Carbon River tonight. Somebody called us. Said McCloney's been

there all evening drinking and shooting off his mouth as how he's gunning for Farrell. Then somebody let out that Farrell's over there packing in your supplies tonight, and McCloney lit out faster'n rabbit—carrying a gun."

A cold shiver ran up Hamilton's spine. "What time did Farrell leave?"

"We don't know. Nobody answers at Pete's. Either they're both out loading the horses or maybe Pete's coming up with Farrell."

"McCloney's not the kind to jump two men. One unarmed man is more his game. You think I ought to start down?"

"No, with the cat loose and McCloney skunking around with a rifle, you'd better stick close to the station. We'll try Pete's again."

Hamilton hung the receiver up thoughtfully. He lifted his rifle from the hook where it hung on the wall, propped it carefully against the door. Then he snapped off the light that lit the second story cabin room which served as kitchen and bedroom, and peered out through the glass that completely circled the upper half of the lookout station.

The blackness made him dizzy. He could hardly make out the railing that ran around the outside catwalk. On a bright night he could see a good part of the trail that wound up the rocky climb from Eunice Lake. It was the only trail a horse could take that last mile up, but there were numerous foot trails, dangerous and slippery, but navigable if a man knew the territory. Tonight, when even the stars were hidden behind layers of grey, rolling clouds, a man could cover the whole distance from Eunice on the open switchbacks without the slightest fear of detection until he hit the open space at the top, that two hundred feet of rocky, shale-covered ground. It was on this area that Hamilton concentrated. Dark as it was, he counted on spotting any sign of movement. Ten minutes passed and the night was still quiet.

Hamilton stretched out on his cot. He would have liked to read, but he knew better than to turn the light on. A man outlined in yellow glass would make easy pickings for a rifle. McCloney might be hunting Farrell, but he certainly hadn't forgotten Hamilton's part in his arrest two years ago.

It had been Hamilton who had first stumbled upon the carcass of the buck, shot between the eyes, but it had been Farrell, veteran of the woods and familiar with the mountain terrain, who had been assigned to the job of tracking down the killer. Forty miles of woods and mountains is no place to go looking for a man who shoots between the eyes unless you know every inch of that territory, know where a horse can climb, know which passes are clear of snow, know the destination of each of those winding switchbacks, the tricky mountain streams, know where you'll turn a corner and face a sheer drop, and most important, know the likely haunts of a lone hunter out for illegal game. But it hadn't taken him long to track down McCloney and his cabin, hidden away up almost to the foot of the Edmunds Glacier—the cabin which served as a cache for nearly a hundred skins, dried, tanned and ready to sell in Canada. The three-day trip from the cabin back to Ranger's headquarters must have been tough. No one ever got the whole story. All they knew was that Farrell turned up in Longmire with a bullet still lodged in his right shoulder, grim but still captor.

Hamilton looked at his watch. Nine o'clock. If Farrell had picked up the supplies at the general store, six would have been the latest. Allow an hour to drive to Pete's, a half hour to load. An hour and a half was plenty of time to make the mountain trail of three miles to the lookout. Hamilton was getting fidgety lying there in the dark. Once he thought he heard something. He waited. It was quiet. He thought, *by this time they ought to be at least to Eunice.* He moved across the room and noiselessly slid back the bolt. Cautiously he stepped out onto the catwalk. The night was still.

Suddenly he gripped the railing and listened hard. He heard the echoes. One shot about a mile down, he estimated. It was hard to tell with the echoes still sounding. Why just one shot? Because Farrell wasn't carrying a gun?

It took Hamilton half a second to clear his mind, and another half to spin back into the cabin for his coat, gun, and flashlight. Halfway down the wooden steps he stopped, swung back up and reentered the cabin. He lifted the receiver from its hook and listened. The line was dead. Hamilton's eyes narrowed and his lips were set. McCloney was not only out there shooting down a man in the dark, but he had made sure no help would get through to Longmire by phone. This time Hamilton took the steps three at a time. Rob was itching nervously around in his stall. Hamilton swung his saddle on the big horse and backed him out.

Rob knew the trail down even in pitch darkness. He picked his way warily, stepping over the loose stones and feeling his way close to the inside. Hamilton held his rifle in position with one hand, and with the other hand the flashlight, ready to break the darkness. He knew the horse would sense the cat before he was dangerously near. The light might keep the cat away if it surprised him. The woods were ominously still, as if all the gentler animals had cleared the stage for the black killer. It was only the cat that Hamilton was worried about. McCloney would probably beat it back to Carbon River and head for Canada.

There was a dankness about the woods. It smelled of decaying leaves and dirty snow. Even in late June there were still patches here and there dotting the mountainside with its dingy white. Hamilton sat stiffly, not daring to relax his watch for even a moment. Somewhere along the path or halfway down the side lay a dark, inert figure. He had to spot it. It might be anyplace between here and Eunice Lake.

The cat would smell blood. A wounded man made easy prey. Hamilton shivered at the picture in his mind. He had to find Farrell soon.

Suddenly Rob stopped. He shied to the right, dangerously near space. Hamilton could see nothing. He turned the light on and flashed it into the woods. There was the frightened whinny of another horse, and Rob answered. Then the fast, muffled beats of hoofs on leaves and a horse appeared from the woods. Hamilton recognized the black mare. It was one of Pete's. Not a pack horse, but one of his best riders. She was breathing hard, but came to a stand when he grabbed her reins. Whatever had frightened her wasn't close now, or she wouldn't have stopped running. Probably the shot had set her off. He whipped the reins around in back and they started on.

Half a mile later the mare began to pull. They slowed, and Hamilton swung the light down to the right. It was a sheer drop. The path ahead was clear, and the woods revealed nothing but a hopeless tangle of underbrush. The mare was pulling hard on the reins, so he let her go and swung off Rob. There was something in the woods, but the mare went no farther than the edge. She whinnied softly as Hamilton waded into the brush. Not far in, he saw a flattened piece of ground where something had lain. A trail of broken branches led farther into the woods. Hamilton was jumpy. The forest seemed to be closing in. There was a crashing behind him. He whirled, and the flashlight shattered against a tree.

"Damn mare," he muttered. "This is a hell of a place to be without a light." There was no use looking farther. He turned and began to feel his way back. He hadn't come in far, he estimated; a hundred yards maybe.

He was close to the horses when it happened. His foot came down on something soft. It rolled as he stepped harder. For a moment he stopped breathing and thinking, then he forced himself to reach down. He felt sick as he ran his hand over the body. It seemed to be one piece. The hand was warm.

"Farrell?"

The man moaned.

"Farrell, it's me, Hamilton. Can you talk?" He heard Farrell catch a breath. "Can I lift you? Where did he get you?"

The figure moaned again. The speech was thick.

"I can't hear you, Farrell. Where are you bleeding? I lost my light."

The wounded man was trying to say something. "Bro—broken," he whispered.

Hamilton quickly felt the leg. It seemed all right, but the body was bent at a strange angle from the hip.

"I heard a shot," said Hamilton.

"Ca—cat," the whisper died out and the form was again limp.

"The cat!" breathed Hamilton. Then it hadn't been McCloney shooting. The mare must have thrown Farrell a good thirty yards. *The shot?* he asked himself. *Farrell must have shot at the cat before the mare bolted.*

He had to get him out of there. But how, with a broken hip, he asked himself. What a tumble! It's a wonder his neck wasn't broken. He only hoped the shot had scared the cat to a safe distance. There was certainly no danger in the near vicinity now, or the mare wouldn't have come barging in after him. But Hamilton hadn't forgotten McCloney. He whistled for Rob. The big horse came sidling up and stood still while Hamilton lifted the limp figure onto the saddle.

There was no question of which way to go. Pete's was over two miles as compared to less than a mile back to the lookout, but there was nothing at the station to cope with a broken hip. Pete at least had a car. They had to go on.

Hamilton was nervous on the mare. He didn't like the way she skittered. She was a rider, not a mountain horse, and not used to the smell of wild animal or the tricky trails of the switchbacks. Rob was setting an easy pace, jogging along easily in the dark, his limp cargo rising and falling with the gait. Rob was as surefooted as a mountain goat, but still he took it slow. Minutes seemed like hours. It was only five minutes to Eunice, but to Hamilton it seemed endless till they rounded the last bend and came upon the little lake. It looked like a smooth, flat table in the dark. They skirted only a corner of the open section, but Hamilton didn't breathe until they were again into the woods. With only the cat to worry about, the woods seemed evil, but with the threat of McCloney again, their enfolding darkness seemed like a protecting cloak.

Just exactly when Hamilton became aware of the uneasiness of the horses, he wasn't sure. It was gradual. But now even Rob was acting strangely. Once he stopped and turned his black nose in towards the woods. He sniffed, then as if to warn Hamilton, he turned his head back and whinnied. There was no doubt in Hamilton's mind. The cat was near.

Hamilton raised his rifle, his finger locked over the trigger. The horses were moving, but they snorted noisily. Hamilton kept his eyes glued to the shadowy wall of trees—waiting. His arm was steady, but the blood pounded in his throat.

It happened in a split second. A long form hurtling through the air ahead. Hamilton shot just as Rob screamed and reared. The cat fell back and Rob regained his footing. At first Hamilton thought he'd hit the horse. The cat was crouching now, ready to spring again. Hamilton fired once more. The mare bolted and he grabbed the pommel of the saddle and hung on.

They covered a mile in what seemed a few short minutes. Rob was no longer in sight. *He must be hurt*, thought Hamilton, or he'd never travel at that speed. The mare began to slow after another mile, because the pine needles had turned to rocks and leaves as the path neared the bottom. The great form of Rob was again visible picking his way over the logs on the marshy end of Mowich Lake. The light was on in Pete's cabin, and Hamilton breathed a prayer of relief.

The door swung open as they came into the clearing. Pete stood outlined in the light, squinting at the arrivals. Hamilton tried to call their usual "Hallo," but his throat was too dry. He swung off the mare and came into the arc of light.

"What the hell happened, Hamilton?" asked Pete.

"It's Farrell," he answered. "Help me get him off."

"Farrell! You're out of your mind! Farrell's inside sleeping. We've spent the evening looking for this damn mare and my best saddle." Pete stepped off the porch and grabbed the reins of the big horse, swinging him around into the light. "Your line's dead. Been trying to call all—It's McCloney! Hamilton, you've got McCloney here!"

Hamilton sat down on the steps. He wanted to laugh, but no sound came forth.

THAXTON'S CALL

JACK DOLPHIN

Moore jammed his foot down on the accelerator and glanced over at Thaxton studying the map. Thaxton's face remained impassive. Moore wondered what it would take to break through this annoying front. Here they were in a stolen Crown Vicky with the remains of one "Jocko" Menna stashed in the trunk, and Thaxton sat there so cool it was making Moore shiver.

And the way he'd done Menna, with the *garotte*, like a real old-timer. Spooky shit, man.

Moore much preferred the impersonal two in the back of the head, but the idea had been to keep it clean, leave no sign of what had happened. Mr. Costa had been very clear on that point. Jocko was to simply disappear.

And Thaxton never broke a sweat, even when they hauled Menna's 300-pound carcass out to the car and folded it up in the trunk.

"Left at the light," Thaxton said.

Moore took the turn a shade too fast, but Thaxton seemed not to notice.

"Look, we gotta get rid of this car," Moore reminded him.

"No rush," Thaxton replied. "Be a couple hours at least before it hits the hot sheet. Gives us plenty time."

Since his look of exasperation was ignored, Moore turned back to face the road just in time to notice the backed up traffic from a red light. He stood on the brake and the big Ford skidded to a halt, inches from the back of a delivery van. Moore craned his neck, trying to look past the van.

"Damn things shouldn't be allowed on the road," he muttered. "Can't see shit past 'em."

"Relax," said Thaxton without looking up.

The van lumbered forward, then its left blinker flashed. Moore swung the wheel right, tromped on the gas and shot a triumphant grin in Thaxton's direction.

Thaxton glanced up at the road ahead and spoke sharply.

"Watch it!"

Moore returned his attention to the road and hit the brake again. This time he barely avoided a front-end crawl up the kiester of a dawdling Pontiac.

"C'mon, c'mon," he chanted softly. The Pontiac started to gather speed, then abruptly the brake lights flashed. The woman at the wheel looked around, as if searching for an address. Moore's hand darted for the horn button, but Thaxton grabbed his wrist in mid-move.

"Kid, either you cool out or I take the wheel."

"Yeah, well, we wouldn't be doing any driving at all if you'd listened to me in the first place," Moore complained, pulling his hand free. "It'd be done and we'd be back at Rudy's right now, throwin' back cool frosties like big dogs."

"Why would you want to go someplace where a dozen guys, who know you but maybe don't like you, can make up their own version of when you got there and how long you stayed?" Thaxton asked. "Be better to go someplace where nobody knows you and people have better things to do than pay attention to you."

"What are you saying? You don't think the guys at Rudy's would stand up?"

Thaxton looked back at the map. "Bear left here and then up onto the highway."

Moore moved the big car over a lane and shook his head back and forth like he was trying to break free of a depressing thought.

"Look, I don't get it," Moore said. "I say stop, you say go. I say black, you say white. You difficult by nature or what?"

Thaxton glanced at Moore, then began folding the map.

Moore went on. "You still haven't told me why my idea is no good. How come? That's what I keep asking myself. Why don't he make with a reason, I say, and my gut's telling me that it's cause you got no reason, what you got is an attitude."

With that, Moore sat back a little and stretched his arms out in an exaggerated driving posture. He felt good now he'd told the legendary Thaxton to stick it in his ear. This was the guy they whispered about, the goddamn ice king, harder and colder and sharper and meaner than anybody else. Supposedly. And Moore had actually looked forward to working with the guy, figuring he'd learn something. So, he'd volunteered. Volun-fucking-teered! All the other guys in the crew ducking their heads and wishing they were in Hawaii or even in stir or some of them actually wishing they were at home with the wives they hadn't had a civil word with in years. Because Thaxton was supposed to be a very scary cat. But Moore wasn't scared. He was psyched. So, he raised his hand and for what? To end up driving around all day with some relic from the old school with an overdeveloped sense of importance. If there was one thing that really pushed Moore's buttons, it was being shoved off like some dumb kid.

"We're supposed to be working together." Moore snarled. "It ain't like I'm some geek citizen. I been involved in my share of jobs, y'know. I done some stuff'd curl your teeth. *And* I been inside."

Thaxton's turn to shake his head. He was going to have to explain it to the kid. Pain in the ass, but apparently that was the only way they were ever gonna get past this crap. Thaxton wondered whatever happened to the days when guys did what they were told and kept their mouths shut. Now, everybody wanted to know everything. Like in the movies—what's my motivation?

So, Thaxton spoke. "You've been *inside*? Am I supposed to be impressed? Why is it that people constantly confuse failures with experience?"

Moore started to say something, but Thaxton just kept talking, calmly, quietly.

"All that tells me is your judgment isn't sound. You don't think like a pro, you don't act like a pro. You seem to think you're dangerous cause you're tough, but that's not the case. If you are dangerous, it's cause you're stupid."

The kid's shoulders hunched.

Time to lighten up, thought Thaxton. Snap him back then play him out. Thaxton had been doing it so long, it was second nature.

"See, you toss Jocko off the San Pedro docks, two things are gonna happen. First, you're gonna be seen. Too many people down there. And second, old Jocko may go out with the morning fleet, so to speak, but what if he comes floating back at sundown? Not to mention the play it'd get in the papers if he comes back in some fisherman's net—dumped out on the dock with the day's catch."

Moore saw it in his mind and had to stifle a laugh.

"This way's much better. We give him the heave off one of the mountain roads, he rolls down an arroyo—by the time anybody finds him, the coyotes and buzzards have chewed on him so long, they'll bury what's left in a Baggie."

Moore thought about it.

"Okay, but what if somebody sees us out here?"

"So what? They see a couple guys in three-piece suits in a big car, they figure us for big shots headin' to Vegas. Beats gettin' spotted wandering around the waterfront with a rolled up blanket."

Moore wasn't completely convinced but he didn't say so. Instead he peered through the window at a slow-moving Volvo that was taking forever to pass the eighteen-wheeler in the slow lane.

"What the hell are you doing?" he growled in the Volvo's direction. "Looking for a place to pitch a tent?"

Then after a moment he turned to Thaxton. "But outta the state? That just gets us in deeper shit. Interstate transport of a stiff or some damn thing. That's federal."

Thaxton played his ace. "Exactly! Now you got two police forces involved, along with a government agency. So nothing gets done cause they spend all their time withholding evidence from one another and beefing over who gets their picture in the paper. Meanwhile, we're up in Tahoe at one of the last truly great whorehouses in America getting our bellropes pulled. We wait a few weeks, soak up some rays, head back to La-La land and collect on some long green."

Moore's scowl faded and a lazy grin spread across his face. He eased up on the gas a bit and settled back into his king-of-the-road pose again.

"Yeah?"

"Yeah!" Thaxton opened the map again. "This exit then a right."

"Sure." Moore thought about things for a minute. Maybe the old guy had something after all. Then, he said, "What if somebody makes the car?"

"Big deal. Between where we drop Jocko and where we go after, there's a guy in a little garage that's already expecting this Ford. He'll have it wearing a new color and new numbers inside of a couple hours. Meanwhile we head north in a mace that we ditch in any Tahoe parking lot we want. Then we hit a Caddy dealer and grab a new Eldorado, like we just won big at the tables."

Moore was impressed. So, the old guy was actually gonna live up to his rep.

Thaxton glanced at the kid from the corner of his eyes. Too much mouth and that made Thaxton nervous, but maybe he wasn't a total moron. At least he realized the plan was sound once he heard it. Costa had asked him to check the kid out and up till now he hadn't been too impressed. He had, in fact, been toying with the idea of chucking the kid down the same canyon he was gonna use for Menna. Costa knew this was a possibility. It was part of what he used Thaxton for, checking out up-and-coming talent. If you made it past Thaxton, you had the goods. If you didn't, well, there were plenty of guys waiting for an opening in Costa's crew. Either way, it was Thaxton's call.

But Thaxton saw something in the kid that he liked. He definitely had balls; Thaxton couldn't remember the last time anybody's talked to him like this kid had. Still, he had a lot to learn.

"I'll tell you something, kid, you learn to keep a lid on your lip, you could do alright," Thaxton said.

"Well, it's just I like to know what's what, that's all."

"Sure. But what you have to learn is that guys who ask questions make other people nervous. People like a guy who keeps quiet, watches carefully, and learns from what he sees. Tell you what, you stick with me, I'll show you some stuff. Okay?"

Moore struggled to keep the excitement off his face. He could see it now. Thaxton's pal. Thaxton's right arm. This was even better than he'd hoped. People would treat him different, now.

"Okay, Mr. Thaxton. You got it."

"Fine. Now let's change the subject. You a baseball fan?"

He sat back and closed his eyes as the kid started rambling about the Dodgers' chances in the coming season. What the hell, thought Thaxton, I'll see if I can teach him some stuff. And if he really does turn out to be a joker, well, we gotta drive back this way to get home anyhow.

THEY TELL NO TALES

FRANCIS CHASE, JR.

The wind, bringing light flurries of snow, whistled down through the scrub pines and whined past taut guy-wires of the windmill that turned the battery-charging gadget George Anderson had rigged up for the storage batteries of his radio transmitter.

Outside the cabin door, George paused with an armload of firewood, staring down the mountain trail to where he thought he had seen a movement, but he knew that his eyes must be playing him tricks. This was only Monday and no one ever came up the steep Summit Peak trail except on Fridays when young Jeff Clapham brought his mail and his week's supplies. All that he could see below him in the dusk was the scraping of the trees on the mountain side under the wind and a faint light or two in the village of Coulee, ten miles away.

He sniffed at the wind. "Snow's a-comin'," he said out loud. In the long, lonely years he had spent in the mountains, he had learned to talk to himself until now all his thinking was done aloud. Then he pushed the door open and dumped the wood into the box back of the big iron stove. He didn't mind the cold himself, but it wouldn't do to have the batteries freeze up. "Got time for another load before I talk to Barrow."

Radio was a miracle the old man would never cease wondering at and, like all his other possessions, he used his amateur operator's license sparingly. "Use a good thing too much," he'd say, "and it ain't good for long."

He lived now for that moment each evening when he turned on the power switch and talked with his radio friend, Steve Barrow in Colon, away down in Panama. He'd tell Barrow all about the ore he'd worked that day, the signs he'd struck up in the headwaters of the creek which looked even better than his big strike. And Barrow would tell him about the ships loaded with diamond shell cocoanuts and alligator hunting deep in green jungles where white orchids

515

grew and tall palms waved in the sun-drenched breeze. It was like living two lives—his own and Barrow's, too.

He dropped the last load of firewood into the box and snapped on the switch. When the tubes were warm and humming and the mike gave back a resonant sound to his whistle, he said: "W2X calling Barrow in Colon, W2X calling Barrow in Colon . . ."

Two miles down the trail, Phil Anderson trotted around in a circle and swung his arms in great arcs to keep his blood circulating. The young man wasn't dressed for the cold, and the sharp wind stabbed through his city clothes like ten thousand pinpoints pricking him at once. Nor did it help his temper to know that his uncle, in the cabin above, was probably roasting his shins next to the roaring blaze. The more he thought about this and the colder his hands and feet and ears got, the blacker became the fury in his heart.

"The old goat's got plenty of dough to spend on radios and tubes and such foolishness," he thought bitterly, "but when his own skin —his only living flesh and blood—gets into a scrape where he needs a few dollars to help him out, he turns him down. And him with money a-rotting away in the bank at Coulee!" He shook his fist up at the cabin. The old miser would get his!

In coming from Denver, Phil had cut west at Leadville, avoiding Coulee so that he wouldn't run into anyone who knew him. Then he had doubled back around the foot of Summit Peak and taken the trail four miles out of town. During the afternoon, he had cut a stout cudgel from the branch of a fallen pine tree. When it was dark, he would sneak into the cabin, strike down the old man with a single, telling blow and then disappear without touching a thing— not even the money he knew the old man kept on hand to pay for supplies.

When Jeff Clapham came on Friday with the groceries, he would find the old man dead. They'd figure he'd just fallen over dead, him being so old, and maybe struck his head on the table or floor in falling. Afterwards, they'd call him in Denver and tell him about his uncle and that all his uncle's money was rightfully his, him being the only kin and the old man not being the type to make a will.

It was dark when he crept up to the cabin. Through the window he could see the old man talking and laughing into his mike like a crazy man. He estimated the distance between the door and where the old man sat and noticed that the old man's back was directly towards the door. Phil hefted the club experimentally. Then, he pushed the door open, leaped across the narrow floor and brought the cudgel down on the old man's head with a sickening thud.

George Anderson sat upright in his chair for a long moment. Then he slid lifelessly to the floor and it didn't take a second look for Phil to know that he was now the sole and undisputed heir to the old man's fortune.

He didn't touch a thing. He moved over by the stove and warmed his hands near its redhot surface. As soon as he was thawed out, he would start back to Denver. His eyes fell longingly on the old man's sheepskin coat, but he didn't dare take it. The wind howled gloomily about the cabin, driving the sleet in heavy gusts against the window-panes and over the slanting roof. It was a regular blizzard and the warm crackling of the fire was an invitation to drowse. After all, he had four days. This was only Monday and Clapham didn't come till Friday. . . .

He lay down on the bunk and coolly went over the whole business. Now that he was warm, it was easy to think and he knew it was silly—downright dangerous—to start out in the dead of night in a blizzard. No one ever came up the Summit Peak trail in good weather and it was a cinch no one would come up on a night like this. He'd get a good night's sleep and start out at daybreak. He could hardly keep his eyes open. He mustn't forget to throw the cudgel on the fire before he left in the morning. Then he was dreaming of the horses running at Hialeah Park and himself, standing there at the rail. . . .

Ernie Beale, the marshal of Coulee, snapped his radio onto the shortwave band, lighted his pipe and settled back in bed to listen to the late war news from Europe. He caught the end of the English news broadcast from DJD in Berlin, and when they started talking in German, he twisted the dial, looking for London. That was when the amateur caught his ear.

> ". . . Listeners in Coulee, Colorado. Please send a doctor to Summit Peak to see George Anderson. When I talked with him a few minutes ago, he suddenly stopped talking. All I heard was a dull thud and then sounds too faint to distinguish. He is an old man and lives alone. Please rush a doctor. This is Steve Barrow in Colon calling listeners in or near Coulee. . . ."

The marshal called Dr. Jordan on the phone and then Jeff Clapham, because Jeff knew the trail like a book. Fifteen minutes later, the trio was pushing its way up the trail with the sleet and the wind driving in their faces.

Phil Anderson was having the strangest dream. He had put all his money on a sure thing in the seventh race at Hialeah and the horse had come in. But as he pushed his tickets across the pari-mutuel window to be cashed, the clerk snapped a pair of handcuffs on his wrists. He was trying to free himself when he awoke covered with perspiration. Still half asleep, he recognized the marshal and Dr. Jordan and Jeff. He knew he was still dreaming because Jeff wasn't due until Friday and the marshal and Dr. Jordan weren't due at all. But the handcuffs were very real, and struggle as he did, he couldn't shake them off.

TILL DEATH DO US PART

DANA MCGUIRE

The gang at the Chesapeake Boat Club thought I was nuts when I said I was going to take Nancy sailing in the bay. The storm was heading our way fast. They said we were crazy to venture out in it.

Crazy I was, all right! Like a fox!

I laughed at the poor dopes. There wasn't a one of the crowd who could handle a sailboat as well as I; and I had my own reasons for taking Nancy on that little trip.

I said to them, "So, all right! Let it blow! My wife and I go sailing every Sunday, don't we?"

I can see Hal Wallis now, camera in hand—he must sleep with

the damn thing—standing on the pier, his face red from arguing with me to change my mind.

"Look, Jim," he was saying. "There's going to be a bad blow."

Hal was a club member on Sundays and a photographer on the *Times* the other seven days of the week. He would have married Nancy himself, three years ago, if I hadn't happened along and swept her off her feet.

I was fresh out of M. I. Tech, easy on the eyes, and big, like I am now. But, Hal—he'll always be a skinny punk with a camera. Sounds as if I don't like him? Well I don't—I never did! If it weren't for Hal Wallis. . . .

But Hal wasn't the reason I took Nancy sailing that Sunday. Not that shutter hound. Nancy's luscious sister, Helen, was the real reason.

Helen was modeling in New York. She was only twenty, but she was a sweet dream. Dress Lana Turner in a shoulder length bob of soft, red-gold hair, poke a dimple in the left side of her face, and there you have a rough draft of Helen Miller. Of course, Nancy didn't know how I felt toward Helen. But then, neither did Helen, for that matter. It was just one of those things.

But Hal was still sounding off about the storm. I said, "So what?" and helped Nancy into the boat. "We aren't going to let a little wind spoil our afternoon, are we, Nancy?"

Nancy laughed and shook her blonde head, which was partly covered by a brightly colored scarf she'd tied under her chin.

"Mama goes where papa goes," she said.

Hal got real pleading. "Look here, Nancy," he said. "Can't you do something with this dope?" Meaning me. "Feel how chilly the air is getting."

"And see how black the clouds are." I laughed, pointing, and jumped into the boat. "Goin' to be a Nor'easter, boy."

But still Hal wasn't satisfied. "Be sensible, Nancy!" he argued.

Nancy laughed and called up to him, "If Jim has his heart set on going, I'd better go along, too. Jim's a big sissy, you know. He's never learned to swim. I might have to rescue him!"

"Okay, you hard headed lugs," Hal gave in, "If you gotta go, you gotta go. But I want a picture for posterity!" He raised his camera and pointed it at Nancy.

"This ought to make headlines," he said loudly.

Nancy laughed and made a face. "Make it a good one, Hal. I want to look pretty on the front page."

"That's right," I added with a show of enthusiasm, and cast off the line. "Wave good-bye to the gang."

Hal caught Nancy just as she waved gaily and said something to me. So I waved and smiled and said something to her. Then I ran up the sail, which caught the wind and billowed out with a flutter, and the boat headed out into the bay.

"Poor Hal," Nancy said loudly from the bow, because the wind was blowing so hard. "He seemed so upset."

"Yeah," I said, seeing a mental picture of the punk and his camera in front of me. "Hal's been upset for three years, now."

Nancy lifted an eyebrow and said, "You've never liked him, have you?"

"Sure I like him," I lied. "Hal's all right. He's a good photographer."

Nancy tilted her head to one side, like she always did when she wanted to be coy and said with a silly giggle, "Why . . . Jim! I do believe you're jealous!"

"Don't be idiotic," I said. She made me so mad with that crack, I wanted to knock her overboard right then and there.

Next thing, she was hollering at me to turn back. I shouted at her to come in to the midship and lend some weight to port. It was raining hard as the devil and the bay was washing in over the gunwales.

I got her to brace her feet to starboard and press down with both elbows on the port gunwale. The wind had ripped the scarf from around her head and her wet hair lay flat and sticky looking across her face. She was scared plenty—and so was I.

Nancy kept begging me to turn back, and finally she cried out, "If it's Hal you're thinking of . . ."

I burst out laughing. "Don't pat yourself on the back." I lit in to her. "It isn't Hal—it's Helen!"

She threw a hand up to her face and cried, "My *sister!*"

I said, "Don't act so dramatic. Didn't you know?" I knew she didn't know, but I wanted to make it sound as if I'd been open about it, all along. It hurt her plenty. Her face took on a hang-dog expression and when she spoke, it was as if she had to drag the words out of her mouth.

"How long has it been going on?"

I said, "Ever since Helen visited us last month."

She asked if Helen loved me, and I said she would—in time.

"She's only a child," Nancy said. She was on her knees, then, holding on to both sides of the rail.

"But how she is growing!" I said, and let the sheet start to slip through my fingers.

Nancy started to spring at me, screaming at me to let Helen alone.

"I'll let her alone!" I shouted, and let go the sheet. The boom swung around and struck her, knocking her into the water. She screamed once, when she fell, and quickly disappeared. I watched aft for her to come up—but she didn't. The boom had knocked her unconscious.

Well, the first act was over, and beautifully done.

Now for Act Two. . . .

Hal Wallis, swinging his camera and looking scared to death, was the first person I saw when I brought the boat in and made her fast alongside the landing.

Hal kept shouting, "Where's Nancy? Where's Nancy?" I thought he was going to jump off the pier into the water.

I put on a blank expression and acted like I was all broken up. I wanted it to look good. I wanted all the blame for Nancy's disappearance.

Somebody in the crowd—I don't remember who—helped me out of the boat. Everybody was talking at once. I started to totter, pretending I was too weak to stand alone. Somebody saw me and put his arm around my waist.

Hal was standing there. I caught a glimpse of his face. It was white as a sheet and he was good and mad. Hal charged at me like a wild bull, shaking me by the shoulders and shouting, "What happened? Where's Nancy?"

I shook my head and said she was gone, surprised as hell at the emotion in my voice.

"I tried to save her," I said, bowing my head and letting my knees buckle, like I was going to collapse.

Somebody caught hold of me and said I was all in and they'd better get me to the club house. I closed my eyes and doubled up and they carried me into the club and laid me out on a lounge. Somebody threw a blanket over me and everybody crowded around. I nearly suffocated. But everything was turning out just the way I wanted it to.

I heard Hal shouting at them to stand back and give me air, so I cracked my eyes open a little and saw him coming through with a glass of brandy in his hand. Hal knelt down beside me and raised my head a bit, touching the glass to my lips.

"Here, drink this," he said.

I groaned and opened my eyes. Time to start my act. Besides, I needed that drink.

I got the brandy down without any trouble at all—naturally. Then I guessed it was about time for me to start explaining things. I'd gotten them all pretty well teed up, by then—especially Hal.

I caught hold of his arm very dramatically with both hands, and sobbed, "Why didn't I listen to you?" The old voice sounded like I was really having a time of it.

I thought Hal was going to cry. "How did it happen?" he asked. I believe he really pitied me.

"The storm struck us broadside," I began, taking my time, because I wanted to keep up the shocked appearance I had managed to display so far. I even panted a little. "Nancy was sitting in the bow. I shouted at her to take over the tiller while I hauled in the sail, and we'd ride out the storm. As she started aft, the wind shifted suddenly. The boom swung around and struck her. She went over the side. I couldn't go after her, I couldn't help her, because I can't swim—you all know that! I threw over the life ring, but it didn't reach her. She was carried away. I saw her disappear." I let the word "disappear" trail off into a broken sob.

After that recital, I relaxed and waited for somebody to say something. There was plenty of talking going on, all right, but I couldn't make out what was being said. So I cracked my eyes open just wide enough to catch their reactions. What a sight!

Everybody had turned away and voices were humming all at once. Hal was on his knees beside me, the empty glass in his hand, staring across the room at something that wasn't there.

I was feeling good. I had committed the perfect crime. Nancy was gone and I was shouldering all of the blame—openly. Even Hal was sympathetic. I gave myself a mental pat on the back.

Then all of a sudden a terrible thought struck me, almost rolling me off the lounge. In my eagerness to let them know how much of a hero I'd been, I had forgotten to get rid of the life ring! The thought of the thing still in the boat, almost paralyzed me. I'd have to get back there and get it, somehow, later on. In the meantime, I prayed that no one had noticed it.

After awhile, Hal drove me home and helped me into bed. He acted pretty decently about it, too. But this time, it was I who was sitting on pins and needles. It had gotten dark outside, and I wanted Hal to leave so I could get back to the boat. Hal made a cup of hot tea and brought it in and set it down on the bed table beside me.

"Anything else you want?" he asked. "Anything I can get you?"

I said no, and thanked him. The only thing he could do for me was leave. I turned my head. Hal was looking at a picture of Nancy, smiling up at him from behind a glass frame on the bed table.

"You know," he said, turning to me suddenly. "I feel damned sorry for you—for her sake."

I smiled like a bosom friend. "Thanks, Hal," I said. "You've been swell."

Hal said, "See you later," turned and walked away.

I allowed Hal plenty of time to get out of the neighborhood, before I got up and started to dress. I'd have to get down to the boat landing—fast. If anyone had seen the life ring in the boat, after my having said I'd thrown it to Nancy while she was struggling in the water, my goose was cooked. It was a fifty-fifty chance, and I had to take it. I told myself that maybe in all the excitement no one had paid any attention to what was in the boat.

The next thing was to get out of the house without being seen. I had to take a chance on that, too; and on the telephone ringing while I was gone, or somebody coming to the door. My car was in front of the house, where Hal had left it, so I decided to go out the back door, come up the driveway, and make a dash for the car. There was no one on the street, and if the neighbors heard me drive off—well, I just had to risk it and think up some sort of an alibi, if they did.

About a quarter of a mile from the club, I slowed the car down and turned off the highway onto an unused side road through the woods. The road came to a dead end facing the bay. At the end of the road, I turned the car around so that I would be all set to scoot out of there after I got back. Then I climbed out and started walking up the beach.

I could hear conversation coming from the club and I guessed the gang was eating, so I wasn't expecting to run across anybody on the landing. On the other hand, the storm that afternoon had turned the air chilly, and the water was still a bit rough.

Keeping well in the shadows, I crept along the beach until I reached the landing. Then I laid down on the sand and listened. I didn't hear anything but the water splashing against the piling, and the pier looked empty. I guessed the coast was clear, so I got up and ducked down to the water's edge.

Taking off my shoes and socks, I started to wade out between the piling under the pier. The boat was bobbing up and down in the water, right where I'd left her. At sight of the little craft, a wave of excitement swept over me. I thought of Nancy, out there in the bay —or, worse still. Suppose she had washed up and was there under the landing with me? My teeth began chattering like a clacker box.

I caught hold of the rail to steady the boat, and waded aft to the tiller. I stretched out my hand and felt the life ring on the after thwart. My fingers trembled like mad as I unfastened it. Then I started to make my way back, stumbling, to the beach. I didn't stop to put on my shoes and socks, but grabbed them up in one hand, while I held on to the ring with the other, and made a beeline back to the car.

Reaching home, I stopped in front of the house, put on my shoes and socks and scooted up the driveway to the back door. I didn't stop until I was safely in the bedroom, where I flopped, panting, into a chair, shaking like a leaf and wet through. But I had the life ring, and no one had seen me.

In a couple of days, I would throw it back into the bay. That would be just the right amount of time it would ordinarily have remained in the water before being washed ashore—from where we were.

I hid the thing inside the mattress on the studio couch in my den, then went to bed.

The next couple of days I spent running to the telephone and answering the door. Friends of Nancy's and mine. Some called; some came around and wept a little; others just sat. They all said the same thing—"You poor guy!" "Tough, Jim!" "If there's anything I can do. . . ." And so on.

Everyone seemed more concerned over me then they were over Nancy—just how I wanted them to feel. But I wished they'd get out of there and leave me alone. I was jumpy as the devil. Of course, everybody attributed that to a natural state of affairs. But the truth was, I was scared—scared plenty. I had killed my wife.

Everywhere I went in the house, I could feel that Nancy was somewhere near. Whenever the floors creaked, or the curtains blew. Whenever there was music, whenever the wind was sighing in the trees.

That afternoon Hal dropped around for a few minutes with a friend of his, Ed Fenton of the homicide squad. But there was nothing unusual in that. Fenton had often been a guest in my house before. Hal and Ed were good friends and often worked together. I went over the whole thing again, for Ed's benefit. But I didn't mind. I guess I'd told the story about that Sunday afternoon a hundred times—since it happened. I knew it by heart now.

We talked about the newspaper's account of Nancy's disappearance. Made the front page, all right, just like Hal said it would—picture and all. I guess my face must have flushed, because Hal called me a poor man and Ed patted me on the back sympathetically trying to cheer me up.

We had a drink and they left. Then I went into the den and took the life ring out of the mattress on the studio couch. After it got dark, I was going to carry it up the beach, a mile or so from the club, and heave it over into the bay. The tide would do the rest, and that would cinch it. Nancy's body would wash ashore, too, I guessed. But I hoped I had gone far enough in the bay for the undertow to carry her body out to sea.

At seven o'clock, the door bell rang. It was Hal. I invited him in, surprised at his sudden return.

"Later," he excused himself. "Get your hat. We're going to the morgue."

The morgue! "Nancy?" I asked in a low, tense voice.

Hal nodded. "Yeah. She washed up late this afternoon. You've got to come down and identify her."

My mouth dried up and I swallowed hard, but I managed to say okay, and went for my hat.

We didn't talk much on the way. But when we reached the morgue and got out of the car, my knees were shaking.

"In here," Hal said.

I had never been inside a morgue before. Everything was white and still as death. Still as death. That was a good one!

Hal led me down a passageway between rows of slabs holding bodies covered in white. I remember the clacking sound our heels made on the bare floor, and how damp and chilly the room was. I remember seeing Ed Fenton and another man I recognized as Doctor Quigley, the city coroner, standing beside one of the slabs at the far end of the room. I knew what was under that white cover. And I wasn't going to like seeing it.

Hal introduced me to Doctor Quigley; and when I turned to speak to Fenton, I was trembling all over. Ed was holding a brown envelope in his hand. Doctor Quigley drew back the cover.

"Is this your wife, Mr. Casslin?"

I swallowed hard. "Yes," I said, and turned away. Nancy wasn't . . . pretty anymore.

Quigley covered her over. I looked at Hal. Ed was handing him the brown envelope. Quigley coughed and began putting on his coat. Hal opened the envelope and took out a couple of pictures, holding one up in front of me so that I could see it.

"Recognize it?" he asked. It was the one he had taken that Sunday afternoon on the landing, just before Nancy and I shoved off. She was waving and smiling.

I swallowed hard, stalling for time. "Yeah," I said, slowly. I'd have to be cagey and not commit myself. "Yeah, I've seen it before. That's the one in the papers."

Hal said, "Good!" and stepped up close to me. He was mad. "Now maybe you'll tell me what you've done with the life ring!"

That was like a slap in the face. "The life ring?" I stammered, trying to pull the words out of my mouth. "I . . . I don't know, Hal," I said weakly.

"You must have gone back to the pier Sunday night and gotten it," Hal said. "It was gone when I got there."

I shook my head. Hal looked like he was going to strike me.

"Jim, you've lied about this all the way through." His voice sounded all chopped up. "You killed her! I don't know why, but you did. I've known it from the beginning, but I've had to wait for . . . this!" He pointed to the bulky thing under the cover.

Doctor Quigley coughed again. You could hear it echo around the room.

"When did you find out?" I asked Hal. I had to know. It was all over, anyway, and in a way, I was glad.

"In the club," Hal said. "When you slipped up about throwing Nancy the life ring." He held the second picture up in front of me.

"This one you won't recognize," he said grimly.

I looked at it. They were helping me out of the boat. My head was bowed.

"See the ring there, on the back seat?" Hal touched the spot with the tip of his index finger.

"Yeah," I said after a time, feeling like all the blood had rushed out of my head. "I see it."

Ed Fenton said, "You'd better come along with me, Casslin."

I nodded. Hal was putting the pictures back into the envelope.

He said, "When are you guys going to get smart and stop making mistakes?"

I must have laughed. Anyhow, I wasn't trembling anymore.

"Never, I guess. It's guys like me that keep people like you in jobs!"

THE TIME IS NOW!

DOROTHY DUNN

It was an ordinary cocktail lounge in an ordinary hotel. There was a penthouse, I discovered later, and an odd woman that I discovered right away.

I was sitting at a table near the bar, waiting for Gary Winstock, and anyone who waits for Gary can build up quite an edge. But his lateness was never his fault. You knew that and kept waiting; Gary was worth it. And he always arrived eventually. There was never the feeling that he was going to forget or skip a date. So I could look around and relax, with the sure knowledge that he'd come.

I noticed Sally Porter immediately and my interest was held. I have a bad habit of watching people I've never seen before and trying to place them in a category. It's amazing how much can be learned about strangers just by imagination, observation and plain rude listening.

She came in shortly after I did and made straight for the bar, settling herself on one of the uncomfortable high stools. The bartender knew her as did the waiters and a portly gentleman on the next stool with black, shiny hair. She lived here, I decided.

I checked her clothes, as women do who are curious about each other. Expensive, but rumpled. The grey suit nipped the waist like nothing under a hundred dollars, but it was certainly ready for the cleaner. Not that it matters, I thought. The dark man, or any other man, wouldn't notice the wrinkles. She had a figure that would have glamorized an old flour sack.

After a few minutes, though, I knew she wasn't making any effort to be glamorous. She had something on her mind under that beautiful crown of auburn hair. I gave the hair a flash thought and checked the color off as natural. Then I went back to picking up the shreds of conversation that I could hear when she turned her head to one side toward the dark man she called Benny.

"Honestly, Benny, you've got to fire that piano player. What he does to my song styling is a sin. Surely you know he's doing it on purpose!"

Benny's broad hand dropped to her back and moved in a motion that was more like a massage than a caress.

"Take it easy, kid. I hate to see you like this."

She jerked one shoulder and reached for her highball, draining the glass. Then she sagged a few inches toward the dark man who had kind eyes and a therapeutic hand.

"I wish you'd fire him, Benny. After all, I'm your drawing card. The people come to hear Sally Porter sing. They do come just to hear Sally, don't they?"

"Sure, baby, they used to. And we'll get you back there one of these days."

"But last night! Did you hear what he did to my song last night? I just won't have it!"

Benny drained his glass and signaled for more. He looked tired as he faced her.

"Last night, kid? *You haven't sung for three weeks.* But we'll get you back."

She gave her head an impatient flounce and attacked the new glass with dangerous gusto. That one's going to hit you, Sally, I thought. You're not giving them time—you're trying to drown your anger with fire instead of water.

She and Benny had their heads turned away from me now. They were listening to a story the bartender was telling, and I couldn't hear enough to keep interested.

I ordered my second martini and snuggled down to a few cozy thoughts of my own about Gary Winstock. I wished he would show up soon. The poor dear so often had his plans interrupted. One never knew what the next demand was going to be on the time of Dr. Winstock. But it didn't matter. There was always the moment ahead when he'd come in, flushed and bright-eyed, eager to begin enjoying himself.

When I looked back at the bar, Sally Porter wasn't there. Her coat was draped over the high-backed stool and her red-tipped cigarette was smoldering on the edge of the ashtray. Another highball—the third or fourth—was waiting for her.

Benny ran his hand through his thick, dark hair. He seemed troubled. I wondered if he were married to Sally and worried about her excessive drinking. Probably not. He must be a band leader, interested in her professionally. Sally hadn't sung for three weeks, but, in her alcoholic haze, she thought she had sung just last night. There was something eerie about that.

The bartender was leaning on the bar and I could see his lips, now that Sally wasn't there.

"It's a shame, Benny. A cryin' shame she has to be that nuts about the guy. Goofiest thing I ever heard of!"

"She may come out of it," Benny said.

So that was it. Emotional upheaval, drinking to forget, and another singer left at the starting gate.

She came back then, not weaving, but walking very, very straight. I noticed her eyes and they looked sad, pitifully tortured. Then I remembered something Gary once had told me about marijuana smokers. They lose their sense of time. The few minutes it takes to walk across a room can seem like hours. I wondered if the drug could keep a person from projecting forward into time. Poor Sally seemed to have lost three weeks somewhere.

She was restless, a roaming drinker. She emptied her glass, asked Benny for a nickel and walked over to the phone booth. She came back with the nickel still in her hand. "Not there," she said, and Benny patted her arm solicitously.

The waiter brought me a message from Gary with the next martini. He'd be along in thirty minutes.

That called for a new face. I headed for the powder room on the other side of the lobby. If I didn't get to be a doctor's wife so I could spend the rest of my days waiting for him, it wouldn't be my fault.

She was sitting at the dressing table when I came out of the other room after washing my hands. Sally Porter, whom I knew so much about. She said, "This is a crummy place, isn't it?"

I nodded and straightened the seams of my hose, a little ashamed of having eavesdropped, of having tried to strip away the film and find out what was beneath the surface of a perfect stranger. Even your friends are entitled to their private lives. We were alone in the room. I knew too much about Sally Porter and she knew nothing about me. It wasn't fair.

She fumbled through her purse, then asked me if I had a match. That cut off an easy exit.

Close up, in the light, her face looked ravaged. The planes of beauty were there, and her hair *was* natural, but mental strain had pulled at the skin until it looked patchy. Dark mantles of sleepless nights lay under her miserable eyes. But her lips still smiled and her voice still held spirit. With an easy mind, she'd have been a bundle of fire, unpredictable, and as quick as lightning.

"I'm going to kill that man!" she said, blowing out a hiss of smoke and tossing her shoulders.

I gave a little laugh. Girls in the powder room are often going to "kill that man."

"Don't be too hard on him," I said, gathering up my purse. I turned to leave.

She caught my arm and I felt suddenly trapped. This wasn't going to be nice.

"I mean it. I'm not kidding. I'm going to smoke this cigarette and then I'm going to take the elevator up to the penthouse and kill my husband. I've been planning it all evening. If Rand Porter thinks he can leave me for that blonde witch, he's crazy. I'd kill him before I'd let him go! It's awful to love a man so much! He makes me furious!"

She sank down in the desk chair again and began to cry. She'd had much too much to drink, and I loathed this maudlin stage. I wanted to get out fast, back to my martini and thoughts of Gary.

But she was swaying on the chair and the lighted end of the cigarette was resting on the skirt of the rumpled grey suit. I took it out of her hand and crushed it in the ashtray.

"Rand is leaving me tomorrow," she said in a jerky voice, looking up through tear-soaked lashes. "He left me a note last night saying: 'Forgive me, but this is the only way.' Then he went off and slept somewhere else. I called him this morning at his office and he's coming back tonight to talk to me for the last time. I'm trying to get myself ready to go up."

It served me right, I thought. I'd read lips and strained my ears to find out what made other people tick. Now I was getting the whole sordid mess dumped into my lap by a jealous woman in her cups.

"How about a dash of cold water?" I suggested. "It'll make you feel better."

"It doesn't matter. I know I look terrible, but that doesn't matter, either. I'm going to kill him when I go up! His note said: 'Forgive me, but this is the only way.' I'd rather have him die! Going off with her isn't the only way. I can't forgive him a thing like that. I just can't!"

The look in her eyes, the purpose in her clenched hands, scared the heart out of me. Tragedies happen this way.

"I'll push him," she muttered to the wall. "Just a little push and he'll never leave me. He didn't even have the courage to tell me. He had to write that silly note. It spoiled my singing last night completely."

Last night? I thought. Honey, you haven't sung in three weeks! Out loud, I said, "You've got to get hold of yourself. Things may look a lot better tomorrow."

She stiffened. "There'll never be a tomorrow!"

Then she walked into the inner room and I could hear water running in the basin, and the splash of it on her face. I shuddered, realizing that she had revealed her plan without knowing she had. I've never drawn an alcoholic blank myself, but I know it can happen. She must have started drinking long before I started counting her highballs downstairs.

I left her. It's dangerous to meddle with the problems of strangers. She had friends here. She'd probably go right back to Benny and have another drink. He'd take care of her.

But halfway down the stairs I remembered her eyes. She was getting herself steeled to go up to the penthouse and push her faithless husband off the top of the building. So she had said. The little fool might really do it! I pictured a man leaning on a low balustrade above the city. Smoking and waiting. Hating the last interview with his volatile and jealous wife. I could see her pushing him, without giving any warning.

It was a hideous picture. She might clutch at him as he lost his balance, and go hurtling down with him. Or she might kill herself afterward. She'd said, "There'll never be a tomorrow!"

I couldn't stand it. There were people on the sidewalk to consider. Chances were, Sally was just talking nonsense. But she had put me in the horrible position of knowing too much. If I didn't do anything to prevent a possible tragedy, I'd feel somehow responsible if it happened.

A phone call would let me out. I could do that much and my conscience would be clear. I could tell Mr. Porter that his wife was coming up in a state bordering on frenzy.

I walked over to the desk, to the smiling clerk. I didn't know the room number and hated to do it this way. But I could make it seem casual and still give the alarm.

"Will you ring Rand Porter for me, please."

The smile dropped away from the clerk's lips, leaving them rounded in astonishment.

"I'm sorry if you're a friend of his and don't know about it, madam. But Mr. Porter is dead. He jumped from the top floor of this building just three weeks ago."

TO THE POINT

HUGH B. CAVE

It was the maid, Miss Myrtle, who found the body.

Whenever she served salt fish and akee, her two aged employers insisted upon having wild susumber with it. And the only place on the property where susumber grew was the deep gully behind the house.

Miss Myrtle could not understand why the two old men were so fond of what she would have called gully beans. Or for that matter even akee, which was the fruit of a tree and tasted like scrambled eggs. Most Jamaicans liked both, of course, but Mr. Duncan Macdonald was a Scot and Mr. Henry Lawson an American. They had worked together for years, however, on the same big sugar estate. Now they were widowers, retired, who had bought this old mountain house in which to spend their remaining years together.

On discovering the body in the gully, Miss Myrtle ran back with the awful news and found Mr. Lawson idly tossing darts on the veranda. He was a great one for darts. When the two men played skittles they took turns trouncing each other, but no other man in the parish threw a straighter dart than Mr. Lawson.

When she babbled the news, Mr. Lawson sank into a chair and

stared at her as though in a state of shock. "Are you *certain?*" he finally whispered.

Miss Myrtle began to cry.

Henry Lawson pushed himself to his feet and went slowly down the veranda steps, followed by his little black mongrel, Soot. He went to the gully and looked at the body of his friend. Then he trudged the mile and a quarter to the village police station and returned with Corporal Roberts and Constable Quint in their Land Rover. Roberts and Quint examined the body with care.

"Whoever killed Macdonald must have been a very strong person," the corporal said. "It isn't easy to break a man's neck with one's hands. Not even an old man's neck. Are you sure the motive was robbery, Mr. Lawson?"

"He always carried his wallet in his hip pocket," Henry said. "It's not there now, as you can see. He must have come here to pick susumber, thinking Miss Myrtle might forget or wouldn't have the time."

"And someone came along—someone who lives around here and was passing through," the corporal said. "Someone with strong hands. Well, Mr. Lawson, we'll do our best to find him, but it won't be easy. As you can see, he hasn't left a clue."

The corporal and constable carried Duncan Macdonald to the house and departed with a statement, leaving Henry Lawson to sit alone on the veranda. While he thought, his fingers mechanically plucked pigeon-fat seeds from his trouser legs. The wild grass known as pigeon-fat was especially abundant in the gully, and with the autumn rains the plump, sticky seeds clung to anything that brushed against them.

While Henry worked on one leg, his little black dog nibbled at the other, curling her upper lip back as she gently tugged the seeds loose with her teeth. This was not an attempt to be helpful. Like most bush dogs, she liked the taste of them.

When the nibbling at his leg caught Henry's attention, he stopped his own seed-picking to frown at the dog. Thoughtfully, then, he stood up and called to Miss Myrtle that he was going to the village.

It was a Saturday, with enough moonlight to brighten the dirt road and make a flashlight unnecessary. With the black dog at his heels, Henry went straight to the only village shop that had a bar. On Saturday evenings the bar was always crowded with peasant farmers.

The place fell silent as Henry entered. By now the whole village knew of the murder, of course, and the men in the bar must have thought he had come from his house of death to drown his sorrow in Red Stripe or Appleton.

If so, they were mistaken. After a single drink of rum, which he sipped slowly to make it last, Henry spoke to his dog and went through to the skittles room at the rear. There another dozen men stood or sat about, watching a game.

Henry looked on in silence while the jukebox hammered out a Jamaican reggae tune and the little black dog explored the room.

After a while, in deference to Henry's grief, someone turned the jukebox down to a whisper and the talk dribbled to silence.

So unnatural was this kind of quiet on a Saturday night that when the black dog crawled under a stool to nibble at a man's trouser leg, and the man lurched to his feet, the crash of the stool was a thunderclap.

The game stopped.

Every eye in the room turned to the man, the dog, and the overturned stool.

He was a huge man. His name was Belford, and he lived alone because no woman would put up with his brute strength and violent temper. He made his living, it was said, by stealing and selling what honest farmers planted. No man called him friend, and when he savagely kicked the dog away from his leg there were mutterings.

The dog, unhurt, picked herself up and darted to Henry, who had risen from his stool and was gazing without expression at Belford's twisted face.

"Come, Soot," said Henry quietly. "We can go home now."

Henry walked homeward without stopping at the police station. He knew what he knew but was aware, too, that the police would insist on hard evidence. A dog was not evidence. Nor was the lingering smell of pigeon-fat seeds on a man's trouser legs.

Alone on the road, Henry walked slowly and listened for footsteps behind him, but was fairly certain there would be none so soon. After kicking the dog, Belford would not be stupid enough to follow him from the shop and kill him on the road.

It was nine o'clock when Henry reached home, and ten—very late for her—when Miss Myrtle finished serving his evening meal and departed.

Henry sent the black dog with her. The moon had disappeared behind a mass of clouds, and the night was dark as pitch.

Henry blew out the lamps. With the house in total darkness, he went to the far end of the veranda and sat.

It was almost midnight before he heard a sound of heavy breathing in the deep gloom at the foot of the veranda steps.

Henry moved his right hand slightly, then leaned forward a little on his chair and became motionless again.

The old wooden steps creaked. A man-shaped lump of darkness materialized at the end of the veranda, where only night had been before.

In Henry's left hand a flashlight clicked softly. A beam of light fastened on Belford's face.

"So you've come to kill me, too," Henry said. "Because you know I know."

The big man raised a hand, and there was another soft click. Like a snake's tongue, a knife blade flashed out from his enormous fist. No doubt he had expected to find an old man asleep in bed, but the sneer on his face said he liked this even better. As he moved forward on his huge bare feet, his left arm shot out to block any attempt Henry might make to get past him and escape.

Henry stood up. Except for a half dozen darts arrayed on the table beside him, he was unarmed. But he was an accomplished man with darts.

So expert was he, in fact, that when he had thrown only four of the six, he was able to march his whimpering captive to the police station, simply by threatening to use the remaining two darts if he had to.

TURNABOUT

COLBY QUINN

The filling station was only a hundred feet ahead when she felt headlights blooming on the road behind her, turned and saw the car slow down. He might be slowing for the filling station, but maybe not just for that. And she wanted a ride badly.

It would be hell to be stuck on a swamp road at night. Paved highway, but the shoulders were mucky and soft, and from three feet on either side of the road began the swamps, with their slimy water, their thickly sprouting trees dripping with moss, that harsh, incessant croaking of bullfrogs. Ugh!

"Want a ride, sister?"

She looked the gray V-eight sedan over carefully and looked intently at the man's face, which was about all she could see as he leaned over toward the window on her side. He was young, honest-looking; handsome even. He looked all right.

He laughed. "I don't blame you for being careful, getting picked up by a man at night. But you can trust me."

She smiled. "Thanks. I'll take a chance."

He opened the door for her. She settled down beside him, pulling her skirt neatly over her knees.

"We need gas." He pulled in at the filling station. She glanced at the gas gauge, which showed almost empty. But that meant, she knew, still a little gas in the tank. Probably enough for a few miles.

Her companion got out, ordered the single attendant on duty to fill the tank, and departed toward the wash room.

Lois leaned out, glancing nervously around. She asked softly of the gas man: "Are there any cops around here handy?"

The fellow grinned familiarly. "Nope, lady, not a one in miles. Don't worry, the law against hitch-hikers doesn't work this time of night. I saw you thumb the ride, but don't worry about me."

"Well . . ." Lois sat back, her heart pounding. "Thanks."

Two hours later they were still traveling together. She could have got away from him before now, if she'd really wanted to. They'd stopped at one more filling station, but he hadn't left the car, and she didn't either. A painful sort of fascination kept her.

He hadn't asked her much. "Where you going, sister?"

"Atlanta." Carefully looking him over as she answered. He didn't seem to be paying much attention to her.

"Long ways off. Well, here's part of your trip." He didn't say how much. She didn't ask.

"Live in Atlanta."

She hesitated. "N-not exactly. My husband just got a job there, and I'm going to join him. He doesn't know I'm on my way."

Instantly she regretted having said that her husband wasn't expecting her. Why, she wasn't sure. If she was in any danger, that wouldn't make any difference. She examined this man again, furtively. You read so much about attacks and murders committed either by hitch-hikers or their benefactors. And certainly she didn't trust this man, despite his looks.

Once she stared intently at a passing motorcycle and he watched her curiously. He said understandingly:

"You don't have to tell me any more than you want to. But I can assure you there aren't any cops along this road tonight."

"I—I was just wondering," she said weakly.

Neither made any more mention of cops, and after another hour, he said matter-of-factly, "I can't drive all night. And there's a place about three miles from here, according to the map, with good tourist cabins. Cheaper than hotels; anyway we don't hit any towns soon, and if we did there wouldn't be a hotel, the size they make towns here. I'll get you a cabin if you want. What do you say?"

Lois drew a deep breath, considering. She was afraid of this man, yet she wanted to stick with him. They'd go on in the morning.

"All right. Thanks."

The young man reported to her, after consulting the proprietor of the cabins:

"They've only one left, but it has two rooms, if that's okay by you."

"All right." Her heart jumped. He'd be right in the next room. A man she'd only met tonight. But she had to take a chance now. She couldn't back out.

Inside her room, Lois set the little suede zipper bag on the one chair and opened it. She drew out closely folded pajamas and then peeled out of her dress. She sat on the edge of the bed and took off her shoes, her stockings, apprehensively watching the curtained doorway. For there was no door between the rooms. Slowly she reached for one shoulder strap of her slip, let it slide down her arm.

It was then that the curtain rustled and her companion stepped casually into the room.

"Pardon me," he said, but his eyes were bright on her thinly clad form, from bare feet to shoulders.

"What do you want?" she asked tensely, one hand going instinctively to her breast.

"Just to say good night." He was still fully dressed. He must have been waiting for her. . . . "And to tell you I'm only going to Mobile. But I'd like to help you get on to where you're going."

Gradually he advanced into the room toward her. Lois stood up and retreated almost to the wall.

"You would?" Her heart was pounding heavily again. And what

surprised her, almost frightened her, was that it wasn't entirely from fear. She was thinking with a hard cool thought that the best thing she could do was stick with this man. Lead him along, until . . .

She had to get along with him now.

She knew he wasn't just big-hearted. And neither was she. Her eyes narrowed as he approached her. "You'd better stay there," she whispered.

He smiled, his eyes still stabbing brightly at her. "I said I wanted to help you."

"You don't need to come any closer to do that."

"I like you, baby. That's why I'm willing to help you." He took another step.

When he took hold of her arm, Lois didn't scream. She couldn't do that . . . but he'd pay for this!

"Let me alone!" she whispered fiercely. But she didn't twist away from him. His arms enclosed her stiff, unyielding figure and pressed her while he kissed her mouth, her face, her throat. Shivers crawled over her skin, and abruptly she began pushing at his chest and face, trying to get away. She knew now she couldn't go through with it, no matter for what advantage.

But she'd let him go too far. He held her, one arm low around her waist. With the other hand he finally captured her two wrists and held them while he kissed her again. He worked her arms down between their bodies and locked them there quickly as he held her tight with both arms.

She moaned, suffering the roughness of his mouth, bruising her lips, parting them. Soft, tender curves were forced savagely against his chest until she could hardly move. When she tried to thresh her legs, he held her back to the wall. . . .

Lois was crying presently, her face in her hands, and he was bending over her, urging:

"Listen, baby, don't take it that way. I like you, see? And I'll help you along."

Fury and humiliation almost choked her, but she managed to lift her face to his and smile. She kissed him, tasting it bitterly. "Thanks." Her eyes still didn't meet his.

He seemed relieved. "That's the way to act. I thought you would."

"Good night."

"Okay, baby. I'll get out."

He did.

538

As he disappeared through the doorway, she called, "Oh!"

When he reappeared, she was standing close beside the doorway with the water pitcher from the table, poised.

She brought it down with an awkward cross-arm swing that took him across the temple. He stumbled, sank to his knees, clawing blindly with his arms and groaning, and she hit him again, this time squarely on top of the head. He folded with his face against the floor.

"Damn you!" she cursed him in a whisper, bending over him. She felt his pulse. It still beat strongly, so she was not a murderer.

She searched his pockets, found the car keys in a license folder; looked at the license briefly and got to her feet.

Lois smiled as she completed dressing and packed the zipper bag.

Outside, she got into the car, found the handbag in the glove compartment, and made up her face practically in the dark. A minute later she was speeding down the road.

With daylight, she stopped at the first place she could find a phone, called the police in the last large town she had stopped.

"I want to speak to Lieutenant Moore. He's not—Well, I'd like to leave a message. This is Lois Wharton. I reported my car stolen last night, and I want to report I've recovered it. I started out hitchhiking for Atlanta, and I must have got a head start on the thief, because he came along and gave me a ride! What? Oh . . . I was scared of him, and I couldn't get to a phone or find a policeman. So I stayed along with him and finally hit him over the head. If he's still there, you'll find him in a tourist cabin at . . ."

TWO MUST DIE!

RIC HASSE

Apparently Sergeant Jaeger was handling this case. Jaeger is Lieutenant Beauchamp's right hand, especially on burglary cases. You see, I know all about the cops in this town. I make it my business to know.

Beauchamp has charge of all the burglary and armed robbery cases, but he's usually too lazy to get out of that nice padded leather chair he has down at headquarters. He gets the homicide cases, too, but there aren't many killings in this town. A nice, clean town, this. I like it. A nice clean town with dumb cops.

Each case is just like every other one to these cops, and they handle them all with exactly the same worthless routine.

Take these four I was riding with. Sergeant Jaeger was a big man, fat and untidy, and right now he was giving me the silent treatment. He came up to my room with his crew and got me out of bed. He told me they wanted me down at headquarters, and said nothing more. I'd washed, brushed my teeth, and put on my dark brown suit that I wear to work. I didn't want to get my new sharkskin mussed up, in case Jaeger got rough on the way downtown.

They took me down to a squad car, and still none of them made a sound. I didn't say anything either, but inside I was laughing. These guys! Thinking they could get anywhere with these corny tactics.

I glanced at Jaeger's sagging, weather-beaten face. He was looking disinterestedly out of the squad car window, and his only motion was when his fat lips shifted the position of the sodden cigar stub he held between his teeth.

I turned my head to the detective on the other side of me on the back seat. His name was Niblack, and he was slouched down, with his head thrown back and his eyes closed. He looked asleep, but I knew he wasn't.

The driver was just a driver, in a police uniform, but the young

540

man beside me was a new one on me. He was wearing a neat blue suit, and from the alert way he carried his head and the way he stared around him, his eyes bright with interest, I figured him for one of the new rookies recently added to the force.

Bright, ambitious youngsters, these rookies. The police Department gives them six weeks of schooling, as if these cops could teach anyone, then circulates them around through the different squads.

I decided to have a little fun, so I asked, "Why don't you guys find someone else to play games with? I wasn't near the Elite Loan Company last night."

I knew what Sergeant Jaeger would say before he opened his mouth. "How'd you know we wanted you for the Elite Loan job?" he would ask.

Jaeger turned his head toward me and looked as though he were surprised that I was still there. He took the cigar stub out of his mouth and said, "What makes you think we want you for the Elite Loan job?" I was fairly close, anyway.

The rookie saved the day. He twisted his alert head around and snapped, quickly, "How did you know the Elite Loan safe was cracked?" Ah, he had me trapped!

I chuckled. "I saw it in the morning paper."

"How, Sanford?" the rookie demanded.

"My landlady always puts the paper on the chair inside my door." I chuckled again. "I saw it on my way to the bathroom."

The rookie opened his mouth to say something else, but Sergeant Jaeger said, "There was a morning paper in his room, Holt. You should learn to keep your eyes open." The rookie's shoulders drooped.

The squad car pulled into the curb, and Jaeger leaned forward. I looked out. We were in front of a third-rate hotel.

"Look, Jaeger," I demanded. "What is this? What are you trying to pull here? You've no right to take me anywhere but police headquarters."

"Tell it to your lawyer," Jaeger said.

He pushed me out, and the detective, Niblack, took my elbow and guided me into the hotel lobby, with Jaeger and the rookie following behind.

The clerk at the desk looked like he was ready to duck as we paraded across the murky little lobby, past the red cigarette machine and up the dimly lighted stairway. We went up two flights and three doors down a dirty, disinfectant-smelling hallway. A wizened little character carrying a black leather case was coming out of the room.

Lieutenant Beauchamp was standing with his back to the room, his hands clasped behind him.

Jaeger said, "Here he is, Lieutenant," and walked over to a chair and sat down. The rookie closed the door and stood stiffly in front of it. Detective Niblack walked into the bathroom, and I could hear him running himself a drink of water from the faucet. Beauchamp just stood there.

"You can't get away with this kind of stuff, Beauchamp," I said finally. "If anyone in town so much as opens a can of beans that don't belong to him, you guys blame it on me."

Lieutenant Beauchamp turned around slowly. He was thin and hard, a granite slab of a man with deep-set eyes that told you nothing. "That's what you get, Sanford, for being the best cracksman in this part of the country," he said.

"Who, me?" I tried to sound confident, but I was beginning to get nervous. "Why I can't open a jammed window by myself."

Beauchamp made no comment. He walked over to the bed, and I noticed for the first time the long, sheet-covered lump lying on it. Beauchamp said, "Come over here, Sanford."

I wiped a shaking hand across my mouth and went over. I stood on the other side of the bed, and I couldn't take my eyes off that sheet. Beauchamp grabbed a corner of the white cloth and threw it back.

The man was big and young, with coal-black hair. His head was thrown back unnaturally, his mouth hung open, and his bulging eyes stared unseeingly at the ceiling. His shirtfront was a bloody mess.

Beauchamp flipped the sheet back over the body, and said, "Know him, Sanford?"

I shook my head, and Beauchamp nodded a signal to Niblack. The detective went to the door, opened it, and motioned to someone in the hall outside.

A fat little guy in a white shirt, with a black tie, came in. He looked scared.

Beauchamp said, "This the man?" and the little guy in the bow tie looked at me and said, "Yes, sir. That's him."

I recognized him. He was the bartender in a joint a couple of blocks down the street. I had been in the place last night.

"Well, Sanford?" Beauchamp said. "What were you fighting with Hammond about?"

"Who is Hammond?" I asked. I was trying desperately to figure this thing out.

"The guy on the bed, that you don't know," Beauchamp said sarcastically. "This bartender says you were in his joint with Hammond last night."

"Yeah," I said. "Yeah, that's right. I met the guy in there, but I didn't know what his name was. I just called him Nick."

Beauchamp turned to the bartender and asked, "Did he meet Hammond in your bar?"

The fat little man put a hand up to his bow tie and tugged at it nervously. "I wouldn't want to swear to it, sir," he said. "But I think they came in together. At least, the first time I noticed them, they were together."

Beauchamp turned his deep, piercing eyes back to me. "What was the fight about?"

"I don't know what you mean," I struggled. "I didn't fight with the guy."

"Tell it again," Beauchamp told the bartender.

"These two guys were back in the corner booth," the bartender said. "It was maybe a half hour before closing. I heard them scuffling back there, and looked back. They went out of the booth and this guy here was swinging at the Hammond guy. Hammond swung back, and this guy went down on the floor. I grabbed my club from back of the bar and went back there and told them it was closing time and they'd have to leave. They didn't argue with me. They just went on out together. That's all I know, sir."

Beauchamp looked at me with the question written plainly on his face.

I remembered last night all right. I'd been in the back booth and this young fellow sat down across from me and started talking. We were drinking the same brand of beer; I think that's how he picked me to jaw to.

I had a half hour to kill before I went out on this job, so I didn't mind a little company. I discussed the qualities of the different brands of beer with this big black-haired joker, then we switched to baseball, and from that to boxing.

Then this guy, who said his name was Nick, laughed and said, "Boxing! Brother, a man who uses his fists don't stand a chance against anyone who really knows how to fight. Here, look at this."

He pulled a scabbarded knife from under his coat and handed it across the table to me. It was a pretty fancy weapon, fairly short, with a shiny black handle.

"I took this away from a Storm Troop officer," Nick boasted. "I broke his arm when he tried to knife me. Here, let me show you how I did it."

He insisted that I get out of the booth so he could demonstrate, so I did. I made a half-hearted pass at him with the knife, its blade still in the scabbard, and—bam! Nick hit my wrist with the back of one hand, caught my elbow with the other, hooked a heel behind my ankles, and I was sprawling on the floor.

By the time I'd regained my feet, this little fat bartender had puffed his way back, and told us we'd have to get out.

I told it to Beauchamp like that; just the way it happened. One side of Beauchamp's thin lips lifted into a half smile. From Beauchamp, that's the same as having someone else laugh in your face. He walked over to the dresser and fumbled through some papers and cards, then walked back and held a little bit of worn pasteboard up in front of my eyes.

There was a date on it, 3/5/42, and there was a name, NICHOLAS HAMMOND, and the notation, 4-F.

"If you'd just met Hammond," he returned to me, in a tired, matter-of-fact voice, "Why did you come up here with him last night?"

"I didn't come up here," I protested. "I couldn't get rid of the guy, so I walked to the hotel with him. I told him good-night in the lobby, and that's as far as I came."

Beauchamp nodded to Niblack again, and this time the detective brought back a bald-headed man with sleepy eyes.

"Tell it again," Beauchamp told him, and the bald-headed man said, "I've already told it to you twice."

"Just one more time," Lieutenant Beauchamp said patiently.

"Okay," the bald-headed man said. "I'm on the desk downstairs last night. Hammond comes in with this guy here," he nodded in my direction. "They walk across to the stairway, and Hammond starts up first. Then this guy here says, 'What the hell you got to be sore about?'"

Beauchamp prompted, "Then what?"

"Then the switchboard buzzes, and I turn around to answer it. Behind me I hear a noise that sounds to me like somebody gettin' smacked on the kisser. When I look around again, they've both gone on upstairs."

"I didn't go upstairs," I said in a voice that sounded too loud, even to me. "I walked across to the stairway with him, because the cigarette machine is there, and I needed some butts."

Beauchamp just looked at me.

"I said good-night to Nick, and he said, 'Nuts to you,' so I said that about getting sore—just kidding him. The noise the desk clerk heard was me pulling the lever on the cigarette machine. Here, look."

I don't know what I expected it to prove, but I dug into my coat pocket and came out with a pack of the mentholated cigarettes I always smoke. Then, too late, I remembered that this wasn't the pack I'd gotten from the machine. I'd taken these from the glove compartment of my car.

The sleepy night clerk looked at the cigarettes in my hand, then raised his eyes to my face. "Mister," he said, "that cigarette machine in the lobby don't carry that brand, and never did."

"Thanks," Beauchamp said softly. "You can go on to bed now."

The night clerk went out, and Beauchamp turned to study my face. "That the same suit you were wearing last night?" he asked, and I nodded dumbly. He was staring at my cuffs, and I looked down at them. There were three brown buttons on the left sleeve, but only two on the right.

Lieutenant Beauchamp shook something from a little manila envelope into the palm of his hand. It was a button.

"Where did you get that," I choked, desperately.

Beauchamp didn't answer me, but from behind me, Sergeant Jaeger's voice said, "It was clenched in Hammond's fist."

"He—he must have pulled it off when he was playing around in the bar."

"Yeah," Jaeger said in a monotone. "And then carried it around in his fist for two hours. He was probably a button collector."

Beauchamp picked up a knife from the dresser, dangling it from a tag tied around the haft. It was a fancy knife, with a round disk at the hilt and a swastika carved on it. Its blade was stained now, and the black, shiny handle was dusty with a fine white powder that made the fingerprints on it stand out clear, even across the room.

"This the knife you were talking about?" Beauchamp asked. "The one you saw outside of this room, but no one else did?"

I didn't say anything. I wanted to scream, but my voice was glued in my throat, strangling me.

"The fingerprints aren't Hammond's," Beauchamp said. "We haven't checked it with yours yet. You want to make any bets?"

I couldn't say anything, so Beauchamp kept talking.

"You fought with him in the bar at eleven-thirty," he said. "And you fought with him on the stairway at midnight. Now, all we want to know, Sanford, is what you did up here between twelve and two-thirty. The coroner says he was alive at twelve-thirty, and probably knocked off somewhere between then and two-thirty. Why don't you be a good boy and tell us all about it."

"At one o'clock I was thirty blocks from here," I blurted desperately. "I was just cutting through the floor to the Elite Loan office. It took me until three-thirty to bypass the alarm system and crack the box there."

Beauchamp smiled his laugh-in-the-face smile again. "You, Sanford? You couldn't open a jammed window without help. Remember? No, Sanford, after all those safe jobs you've been getting away with, we're glad to pin you, all right. But it's not going to be any little five or ten year trip for you. You're going all the way; all the way to the end of the line!"

"I tell you, I pulled the Elite Loan job," I screamed it at him.

Behind me, Sergeant Jaeger said, "We've got the guy who pulled that job, Sanford. A pete man from Chicago. We picked him up a couple of blocks from the Elite Loan. His tools on him and everything. He hasn't admitted it yet, but the boys have him down in the basement at headquarters. He'll confess to it all right."

"I'm the one that pulled that job," I insisted. The blood was pounding in my ears, and I had to make them believe me. "I mailed the stuff I got from the safe. I mailed the gloves I wore, and all my tools. I always have packages all addressed and stamped and ready to mail, before I go on a job. That's why you never get anything on me. I dropped the packages in the mail collection box at Illinois and Thirty-fourth Streets, just four blocks from the Elite Loan.

"They're addressed to J. Fordham at General Delivery, Chicago. I was going to drive to Chicago, pick up the money and mail my tools back to General Delivery here. The packages will prove that I'm the one that pulled that job! I couldn't have killed Hammond!"

I stopped babbling, and stared at them. They were all grouped in front of me now, and they were all grinning. Sergeant Jaeger, Niblack, the rookie, even Lieutenant Beauchamp—all of them grinning at me.

"That'll prove it, all right, Sanford," Beauchamp said.

From behind me, a familiar voice said, "Hey, Lieutenant. I gotta sneeze. Is it all right if I come up for air now?"

I turned around slowly. The body had moved. It was sitting up in the middle of the bed, and there was a big grin under the black hair.

"Hi, Sanford," he said. "You and I will have to have another beer together sometime. Say, about ten years from now. I should be at least a detective sergeant by then, shouldn't I, Lieutenant?"

Lieutenant Beauchamp looked at him and said, "Maybe, rookie, maybe. If you use your head."

UNTIMELY VISITOR

JOHN BENDER

Twice, while he sat there waiting in the richly appointed cabin, the phone rang, but neither time was it Lona calling.

The first inquiry came from the Naysons, the rich, young Hollywood couple down at the other end of the court: could the major make it for cocktails? Which he could not, of course, considering the possibility of Lona's arrival or call. He didn't dare chance going over for the drink, however much he could have used a bracer or two right then.

The second time the telephone summoned him out of the wing chair by the window, he listened to the chilly voice of the resident manager: would the major be good enough to stop over at the office cabin sometime during the following morning?—the matter of the rent. Probably slipped the major's mind, what?

"Quite," the major said, "quite," more worried now than bored with the wasted evening.

He went back to the wing chair and smoked two cigarettes and, for keeping him waiting, cursed Lona Mainwaring in his recently adopted accent. He stumbled slightly on some of the word formations, particularly when the dropped g of current English fashion interfered with the more prevalent Anglo-Saxon terms he employed. But on the whole it was a satisfactory performance for a man who had been no closer to the land of his purported birth than his imagination took him.

Why hadn't she called, at least?

Usually, she was punctual. Like most women who engage in infidelity, the major knew, she had learned she damned well better be if she expected to enjoy the privileges of one life and the favors of another.

But more important to the major, Lona Mainwaring was wealthy. And he had counted on the money.

It was not much, he thought, and this annoyed him further. For a woman of Lona's means, his month's rent of three hundred dollars was nothing. She had told him last week—quite airily, he recalled —not to worry about it, and he had proceeded not to, after a suitable, admirably managed suggestion that he would repay the— ah—loan, you know, directly his next bank draft reached him. He did not, of course, intimate that he had not the least idea of which draft or what bank. Instead, he had dismissed finances from his mind and from Lona's with another admirably managed but by no means reserved suggestion. . . .

The major rose, crushed a cigarette in the tray and paced the luxuriously carpeted cabin. He was a tall man, not thin but finely made, and his attraction to women—of which he was not the least bit unaware—lay in the smoothly silken movements of his well-tended body, the excellent head and shoulder carriage. He could well have been the former English officer he claimed.

Perhaps he had been too careful, too glib in his technique. Perhaps she thought he did not really need the money, though she had advanced him enough. No, he had dropped the hint too often. Lona was not stupid. She was a bored and lovely young matron, but she was not stupid.

It was impossible for him to think that her interest in him had ceased. In that respect, *he* was not stupid.

Her husband? Had that unfortunate lost interest in his money-making long enough to assume the stature of a husband and exert a closer scrutiny on Lona's time and interest? The major hardly thought so. He and Lona had been more than discreet. Their first meeting in the cocktail lounge in town, where Lona waited while George Mainwaring busied himself at a board meeting of his bank, had been the only public association. From that first time, Lona had come here, to the cabin court which she had herself suggested the major take, and both would swear that not a soul knew of their clandestine meetings.

Damn, the major thought, why doesn't she call?

He poked at the logs burning in the fireplace, consoling himself with the thought that she was on her way over here even now, that she had decided to come after all. He imagined the brushing, finger-tip tap on the door, his quickly opening up and her sweeping entrance, the gown a silver flame caressing her lovely body, her dark eyes radiant with excitement. Beneath the mink cloak, her shoulders would be bare, her throat a velvet-smooth column for that exquisite head; and her lips would caress his name briefly before he found them with his own. . . .

He felt warmer, for which he thanked not the fire but his own imagination, and for a little while the glow persisted. But, finally, the room remaining still and empty, his annoyance reimposed itself. He stood above the phone, coiling and uncoiling the wire about his fine hands.

Abruptly he decided; he dialed and waited.

"Mainwaring residence," a woman said.

His keen ear detected the unnatural voice. "Mrs. Mainwaring, please," he told the maid.

"I'm sorry, sir, but she is not receiving any calls. Whom shall I say called?"

"Never mind, thank you."

So she *was* home!

Something was wrong. He felt it with the instinctiveness that had kept him alive professionally for these many years in a career where intuition counted for more than daring. Carefully he put down the phone, his face tight, his head canted to one side. He considered Lona Mainwaring for some moments. She had been a more than pleasant interlude. Fire, cruelty, selfish strength—a girl to stir a man's blood. A companion he might wish to meet under other circumstances. But the circumstances were not that flexible. They were what he had planned them to be, and his critical mind told him that the sooner he got on with this business the better.

With just the faintest trace of regret, he said aloud, "Good-bye, my dear. Good-bye."

He had them in his pocket when he mounted the long flight of stone steps that led to the stately, baronial estate on the city's edge. Going through the formal garden, past the pool, the major tapped the pinseal wallet that bulged his jacket slightly and hoped it did not mar the appearance of an otherwise impeccable cut. He did not carry letters; the collection of papers in his wallet were scrawled notes mostly, and of sufficient legibility to prove their authorship.

Lona Mainwaring, he had observed, was not stupid, and it had taken quite a variety of ingenious suggestions on the major's part to get her to write them. Several notes to tradespeople—directions to leave milk or eggs or butter, instructions to have the major's shirts starched so, his coat sleeves pressed without creases. Lona had suspected nothing when he had asked her to write these notes for him, at one time or another, and probably did not even now suspect their exceptional suggestiveness.

As a blackmailer the major had no affection for letters, with their sometimes incoherent text—though he had one charmingly naive gift note which he had not solicited in the least; it had come with the gold ring Lona had given him and which he wore now. The type of notes he carried, he had learned, effectively suggested not a mere dalliance to a suddenly enlightened husband but a more thorough relationship. A tender love-nest in which the errant lady had concerned herself with the most minute details. . . .

He had no qualms about revealing Lona's other life, nor about the price which would buy his evidence and silence. Five thousand seemed a fair enough sum, to keep the notes out of the hands of several unscrupulous gossip columnists who could do a masterful job of persuasion with this kind of evidence.

Yes, the major thought, pushing the doorbell, five thousand would not bother George Mainwaring too greatly.

"Yes," said the man who opened the door.

The major blinked. "Mr. Mainwaring?" he asked with some surprise. He had expected the maid, or possibly a footman.

"I've dismissed the servants," George Mainwaring said, sensing the hesitancy. He was a tall man in a faded smoking jacket, and old, much older than the major had imagined. The vitality of the man had been sapped beyond belief; his face was gray, lined and weary. He looked almost ill. No wonder Lona had gambled in other fields!

"I've come to see you about your wife."

"Yes, of course." The door swung wide, admitting him. "Come in, sir."

They went through the long hall, past the winding staircase to a main living room, where the older man indicated a chair. From a massive, carved sideboard he produced a decanter of brandy, measured drinks for them both, offered the glass.

"Now," Mainwaring said, his face showing the effect of the liquor. "Now, sir!" He nodded at an open door off to one side which led apparently to a library or den. "Lona is in the other room. Shall I—"

"There's no need to call her." The major smiled. "My—ah— business is with you. Perhaps I should acquaint you with myself," he began, warming to his introductory speech. "I am Major—" He broke off at the look in the other's eyes, the sudden leaping life in them.

"The major!" Mainwaring said. He raised his voice. "Lona, Lona, darling! The major's here! He's come to see you!"

Clutching the major's sleeve he said, "This is a surprise, sir! A most welcome surprise! Come, we must join Lona, by all means!"

Not quite persuaded by this sudden welcome, the major none- theless allowed himself to be led into the smaller room. He looked for Lona, but did not see her—not at first, at any rate. Not until after a startled moment, when he looked down—

"My Lord!"

She was lying on the rug, her hands claw-like, already con- stricted, an ugly stain below her chest . . .

"A surprise indeed, sir!" Mainwaring croaked. "I thought you were the police, in answer to my call. But you're not, are you? You're the major. Her major!"

And he brought up the gun. "Good-bye, sir!"

A Valentine from Teacher

Jim Knapp

It was late January and the city was frozen solid. Christmas was long forgotten but spring was still a million miles away. The Rock River lay still and snow-covered as I stared sourly at it from my office window. The distant winter sun diffused by shapeless clouds left the stark downtown landscape dreary and shadowless.

Darlene Anderson came into my office carrying two styrofoam cups of coffee. She handed one to me and sipped from the other as she propped one plump cheek of her bottom on the corner of my desk and said, "Irma's here. She's waiting in my office."

I grunted.

Dangling her high-heeled shoe from her toes Darlene said, "There's no use being a poop about this, you know. You already agreed to talk to her."

"Only as a favor to you," I argued. "It was a weak moment. This just isn't the kind of thing I get involved in. You shouldn't have asked me."

"Fine," she snapped. "Don't see her! Don't put yourself out. Don't do me any favors. I'll tell her to leave." She stood up and silently slammed the cup down on my desk, sloshing coffee across the polished wood.

I grinned and nodded at her crumpled cup. "Woulda been better if that was a ceramic mug. Styrofoam just isn't much good for slamming."

It was her turn to grunt.

Darlene manages the insurance agency for me. She's good at it, and in the five years she's been with me she has never asked a favor nor has she made any unreasonable demands. I began to feel guilty.

"Darlene, I'm sorry. You don't deserve this crap. Brief me again and then bring her in."

Irma Traplin was Darlene's former teacher and a current friend.

She was having some kind of problem with her seventy-nine-year-old father.

"Look, Lee, I'm not asking you to make any commitments. Just listen to what she has to say. If you can help her, fine. If you can't, you can't. But at this point she's just . . . lost."

Christ! What was I getting into. Ineffectual old-maid school teacher that couldn't handle a senile old man. I have little patience with people who are unwilling to tackle their own problems. I know —it's a shortcoming. I should be more tolerant. Lee Skinner, hard-ass.

She was about what I expected. Teacherish. Thick horn-rimmed bifocals magnified myopic brown eyes. A gray wool suit hid the shape of her body, but she appeared trim and she was tall—five eight or nine. Her dark brown hair was piled unfashionably on top of her head. She had to be in her mid- to late forties, but her skin was smooth and tight and the lines in her face served to accent handsome features. She moved with youthful ease, almost athletically. When she spoke she looked straight at me and her voice was husky. "I'm so sorry to trouble you, Mr. Skinner, but Darlene insisted that I talk to you."

"Mrs. Traplin, let me clear the air. Darlene has told me a little about your problem. I'll be more than happy to hear you out, but in all probability I won't be able to help you. You need to understand that I'm not an attorney and I'm not a shrink and I'm not a private detective."

She looked at me, disappointed, beseeching. "Darlene said that you . . . sometimes . . . took shortcuts . . . if you felt an injustice was being done to someone. True?"

"Yeah. True, I guess."

"Why?"

Teachers. The good ones will force you to think and to justify the things you do. Irma Traplin was, no doubt, a good one. I can be a hothead. Sometimes my anger flares like a roman candle. But I don't go off half-cocked. I don't jump into things without knowing where I'll land. At least, not often. So, her question didn't catch me flat-footed. I had pondered the "why" of it many times.

"From time to time, Irma, I see something so outrageously unfair that it incenses me to the point of taking some action to set it right. I'm not looking for money or recognition. Life's been good to me. I try to pay back a little. Besides, I'm intolerant. To me it's like fixing a squeak. I wish I was different."

After she finished telling her story it took a while to sort out, but it boiled down to this: her father was giving away his money—to his cleaning lady.

Her father, George Kincade, had run a very successful restaurant and bar. Kincade's Steak House had been an institution in Rockford for more than thirty years. A place where you got full value for your dollar. Steaks guaranteed tender and drinks with a generous shot of alcohol served in an atmosphere of old wood and brass and leather. It was a rare occasion if George Kincade himself failed to stop at your table and ask about the food and service. When George was ready to retire neither Irma nor her brother, Rolland, were interested in taking over the business. They had seen too much of long hours, frustrations with employees, problems with difficult customers.

George Kincade had been a hard-nosed businessman and a good money manager. With his savings and the money from the sale of the restaurant he retired with more than half a million dollars. He had lived the good life with Goldie, his wife of nearly forty years until she passed away six months ago.

After Goldie died George changed. He would have nothing to do with Irma or her brother or any of his three grandchildren.

"He became infatuated—almost obsessed—with the cleaning lady. He talks of nothing else. I think he wants to marry her. For crying out loud, she's younger than me," Irma said, her voice rising. "I hate it because she's such a loser. She's had three failed marriages. Her kids are obnoxious . . . probably on dope. That's not fair. I don't know that. But she can't even clean well. The house is filthy. And he thinks she's *wonderful*. Mother would die. She'd just die."

I could understand her frustration, but hell, he was, after all, a grown man. "How is his mind? Is he still with it?"

"That's what's so infuriating," she said. "He's just like he's always been but he just can't see this woman for what she is. She's obviously after his money. Mr. Skinner, I love my father, even though he's not a very lovable man. He's usually overbearing and disagreeable. Except for the family, not many people even like him, except for his customers. Why would a forty-year-old woman spend all her time with an odious, seventy-nine-year-old man if she wasn't after his money?" I could think of no reason.

She told me how she had tried to reason with her father to no avail. She had asked George's own friends to talk to him. He paid no attention to what they said. She had talked to his attorney. Unless George could be declared incompetent, there was nothing anyone could do. Being stupid and being incompetent are not the same thing.

"I'm sorry, Irma, but it *is* his life and his money. Shouldn't he be able to spend both the way he wants?"

"I sound like a selfish money grubber don't I? Believe me, I don't really care about the money, Lee. I just don't want her to get it. I would rather it go to the church or the homeless. I keep thinking about Mother. What would she think? After all those years. He's giving Mother's personal things to that woman. Oh, what's the use. I'm sorry I took up your time. It was kind of you to listen."

Lonely old men and their cleaning ladies. It's not all that unusual. A guy's wife dies and for the first time in forty years the horny old fart is free to get back in the game. Only problem is, the field is pretty narrow . . . except for the women with dollar signs in their eyes. The desperate. The lonely. It was disgusting and it was sad and it was nothing I wanted to get involved in.

As much as I didn't want to be involved, there was a pain in her eyes that I couldn't ignore. "Irma, I sympathize with your situation. I really do. But I don't know what you expect me to do about it. You don't expect me to beat up or bump off the cleaning lady, do you?"

"Of course not!" she said, obviously shocked. "I don't know what I expected. Maybe I'm wrong about the woman. I can't bring myself to talk to her and Rolland refuses. Oh, I don't know, I shouldn't have come here."

I wanted to tell her that I was sorry that I couldn't help. In fact I was preparing to do just that when I caught sight of Darleen's hopeful face peering through the open door from her office. I heard myself say instead, "Maybe I can poke around a little. See what happens."

Irma told me that Lilly Stivitch worked mornings at Perrine's Diner and had a few cleaning jobs in the afternoons. It was a place to start.

Perrine's was just off Main Street on the south edge of town, only a few blocks from George Kincade's home of thirty years. The area had deteriorated over the years, but George had stubbornly refused to let his home fall to the level of its neighbors.

It was almost one-thirty the next day when I parked my Cherokee in the snow-packed lot next to the diner. A beefy woman of about sixty was behind the counter. There were a dozen stools along the counter. A narrow aisle separated the stools from a row of booths along the front looking out on the street.

A grizzled guy, somewhere between fifty and five hundred, wearing a red-checked flannel shirt and bib overalls, sat at the counter. He looked settled in. His coat was folded on the stool next to him. On the counter in front of him was coffee, cigarettes, lighter, and an ashtray overflowing with at least a half-pack of butts. I picked a stool two slots away from him.

"Sign says breakfast anytime," I said. "What's good?"

"Everything's good, handsome," said the hefty woman.

"Hey, not often anybody calls me that," I said with my most winning smile, hoping to set her up for some talk.

"Yeah. Well, don't let it go to your head. All my paying customers are handsome to me. Even old Leo there." She nodded at Bib Overalls. "You can see my standards aren't all that high." She wiped the counter in front of me and asked, "What'll it be?"

"Ham and eggs. Eggs up and runny. Black coffee."

While she was working the grill I said to her back, "I was hoping to catch Lilly Stivitch. Understand she works here?"

"Yeah."

"She around?"

"Works mornings."

I knew that, but it's all just part of "poking around."

Then old Leo dealt himself in. "Gertie here, she don't talk much about her help. Real close-mouthed, Gertie is."

"Don't need to talk much with you around Leo. You talk enough for about four people. Just never say nuthin'."

Turned out she was right about that. "Why are you looking for Lilly?" Leo asked, lighting a fresh Marlboro from the butt of his last one. "You lookin' for a crumby waitress or a crumby cleaning woman?" He started laughing at his own joke but the laughter deteriorated into a coughing spasm. He stared accusingly at the cancer stick in his yellowed fingers, then shrugged.

"Actually, I *was* looking for a cleaning lady," I improvised. "Mine quit and I heard about Lilly and thought I would look her up."

Leo had stopped hacking and said, "Well, you're in luck. She ain't here. I hear she's a terrible housekeeper. A real loser, she is."

Gertie put my order in front of me and said, "Look who's talking."

" 'Sides," Leo continued as if she hadn't spoken, "Lilly says she ain't gonna be cleaning nothing much longer. She's got some dumb old shit on the line and she's gonna marry a half a million bucks, she is. She says she don't care how disgustin' it is to have him grabbin' at her; it still ain't as bad as scrubbin' toilets."

"You talk too much," Gertie muttered at him.

"Maybe so," Leo said, "but I always tell the truth, me and ol' honest Abe share that. We even have the same birthday, we do. Did you know that, Gertie?"

Gertie grunted but didn't look up.

The breakfast was good. Gertie had made gravy from ham or bacon drippings and served it over a mound of crispy fried potatoes along with the ham and eggs. Heart attack on a plate.

As I was mopping up the last of the yoke with a piece of toast I said to Gertie, "You're a great cook. You interested in a job?" Since I wasn't actually looking for a cleaning lady I don't know what I would have done if she said yes.

"Hell, the truth be told, I'm not interested in working at all. But the last thing I want to do is clean somebody else's house."

If I was looking for the honest intentions and feelings of Lilly Stivitch I had found what I was looking for. She was a gold digger and the old man was a fool. It wasn't what Irma Traplin wanted to hear but that was the bald truth of it. Unfortunately, there will always be fools and there will always be gold diggers and there wasn't a hell of a lot I could do about either. I crunched back across the hard-packed snow in the parking lot following puffs of my breath and headed back to the office.

I had nearly forgotten the whole incident when a few weeks later on an icy Saturday afternoon the phone rang. It was Valentine's Day. I had a fire going in the fireplace and a kettle of hunters' stew simmered over the open flames. A bottle of Gallo Hearty Burgundy waited on the counter next to a loaf of sourdough bread and I was set to settle in for the evening with the latest Clancy novel and a very mellow blues tape. Clancy writes good books, but he's a poor substitute for a cuddly valentine of your own. One makes do the best one can.

The phone call interrupted my daily workout. I was in the middle of the third set of bench presses in a bedroom converted to an exercise gym. Sweat was flowing freely and I was looking forward to guilt-free eating and drinking.

It was Darleen. "Irma Traplin has been arrested and charged with murder. Somebody killed Lilly Stivitch and they think it was Irma."

"Was it?" I asked.

"Not funny. She needs your help."

Darleen was waiting in the lobby of the Public Safety Building when I pushed through the door. Irma was being held without bond, and the police wouldn't let us talk to her, but we learned why she had been arrested. Sometime between seven and nine P.M. on

Friday evening someone had entered Lilly Stivitch's apartment and fired three bullets into her chest. There was a rather amateurish attempt of trashing the apartment to make it look like a robbery. However, since there were no signs of forced entry nor of a struggle, the police said it was likely that Lilly had known the killer and admitted him or her to the apartment. The only other possibility was that party or parties unknown had knocked on the door and forced their way in at gun point with the motive of robbery. But, since Lilly was a part-time waitress, part-time cleaning lady, it was unlikely that she would be a target for armed robbery. She lived in a modest, if not downright dingy, apartment in a deteriorating building in an unsafe and undesirable part of the city. Not a prime candidate for money or anything fencible.

George Kincade, distraught over Lilly's death, learned that Irma had been talking to his friends, and his attorney, and anyone else who would listen, trying to stop the old man from marrying Lilly. The police interviewed everyone involved and were able to put together a pretty good circumstantial case. They even managed to find someone that swore Irma had tearfully said, after consuming a couple of glasses of wine, that she wished Lilly Stivitch was dead. Irma remembered the conversation and claimed that she had said she wished Lilly had never been born. Unfortunately, Irma's only alibi at the time of death was her sworn statement that she was at home grading papers.

It was almost ten o'clock when I got home, too late to reheat the refrigerated stew. The coals in the fireplace were red-edged ashes. I carried a can of Coors to the patio doors and drank it as I looked into the winter night. City lights cut through the darkness. The wind blew dusty swirls of snow across the frozen surface of the river. I pitched the empty beer can into the wastebasket and went to bed.

Because of Darleen's faith in her former teacher, I wished that there was something I could do to help. But what could I do? Round up fifteen or twenty witnesses to swear that they hadn't seen Irma in Lilly's decaying neighborhood? They could even testify under oath that they didn't see Irma murder Lilly Stivitch. How do you prove something didn't happen?

They held Irma for three days and ended up releasing her for lack of evidence. The murder weapon could not be found. There were no unidentified fingerprints anywhere in the apartment. Not one witness could be found that had seen Irma or anyone else in the neighborhood that night.

Though there wasn't enough evidence to bring Irma to trial, there was enough supposition to drive away many of her friends. Her father, convinced of Irma's guilt, would have absolutely nothing to do with her. There were even rumors that her teaching contract would not be renewed the next year. Irma's reputation was worth about as much as monkey bars at an old-folks home. The case stayed on the books as "unsolved," though little effort was made to solve it since the police were convinced of Irma's guilt.

The old man had found a new cleaning woman that "could clean *and* was one hell of a cook" and it appeared his obsession was taking a new direction. Irma was considering moving to California. To escape. Forget.

That's the way it would have ended, I guess, if I hadn't got a hankering for ham and eggs and some of Gertie's special gravy over fried potatoes. It had warmed up and the snow in the gravel parking lot had turned to mush. I pushed my way into the old diner and claimed my same stool. Leo was not, however, in the same spot. He was behind the counter frying eggs. A cigarette dangled from his lips. Looking at Leo killed my appetite. "Where's Gertie?" I asked.

He turned and studied me for a moment before recognition struck. "Ham and eggs. Eggs up and runny. Right?" The grin in his weatherbeaten face revealed crooked yellow teeth. "I never forget a face, I don't."

"Right. But today, just coffee." As he filled my cup I asked, "Where's Gertie? Thought she might have found a cleaning woman for me."

"You're lookin' at the new proprietor," Leo said, waving a spatula in one hand and a Marlboro in the other. Ashes dropped onto the grill and melted into the grease. A new twist on Cajun blackened? "Bought out ol' Gertie, I did."

"Congratulations," I said, wondering how long he could keep the place going.

"Yep. Paid one dollar for the joint, lock, stock, and barrel. Kind of a birthday present, it was. Ol' Gertie walks right up to me on my birthday and says she wants to get out of the business. Has another deal workin' and before long she'll be in tall clover. One damn dollar! Opportunity only knocks once, you know, and I for damn sure had figured it missed me altogether until this happened."

In spite of his dirty overalls and craggy, grizzled face and disgusting teeth, I had to like the guy. But I didn't have to eat his food. I left.

I was almost asleep, somewhere in that drifting, no-man's land between sleep and consciousness, thinking about missed meals of hunters' stew and fried potatoes and gravy, when it hit me. Suddenly I knew who had killed Lilly Stivitch. And why. And it wasn't Irma Traplin.

Lilly Stivitch had been murdered on February thirteenth, the day before Valentine's Day. The day before that, Leo's and Abraham Lincoln's birthday, February twelfth, Gertie had signed the diner over to Leo. Like maybe she wouldn't need it anymore. Like maybe she knew Lilly Stivitch was going to die and Lilly's cleaning job with the pot of gold at the end would be available. If Gertie wasn't George Kincade's new cleaning woman I would eat one of Leo's personally cooked breakfasts.

The next day was cold and clear. Some snow had melted, revealing patches of ice on the river's surface. Irma confirmed that her father's new cleaning woman was named Gertrude. Gertie was apparently upgrading her image.

But, what good was this knowledge? There were no witnesses to testify that they saw Gertie, or anyone else, in the neighborhood that night. There was still no physical evidence. It would be no easier to prove that Gertie killed Lilly than it would to prove that Irma hadn't. If I told the police of my suspicions it was doubtful that they would do anything. I had seen nothing. I knew nothing. I was merely speculating, and it didn't make much difference how sure I was of my theory, the police had to have hard evidence to make an arrest, or even obtain a search warrant for that matter.

One thing worked in my favor, however. I wasn't restricted by the law like the police were. I didn't have to say "Captain May I?" before making a move like the police did. I didn't have to give the criminal more rights than the victim. If I could find a way to expose her, legal or illegal, I would do it.

I considered the possibilities. The only thing that would definitely tie her to the murder was the gun that killed Lilly. If she still had the gun. And if I could find it. And if I could figure a way to point the police in the right direction. A bagful of ifs.

If she still had the gun I knew I could figure out some way to make sure the police would find it and do a ballistics match against the bullet that killed Lilly Stivitch. If she didn't still have it there were other possibilities.

When there are too many variables the process of logic calls for you to make an assumption and then proceed to eliminate the possibilities. Best to assume she still had the gun. If that failed, go to plan two.

I checked my watch. Twelve thirty-five A.M. No time like the present to get started. I pulled on jeans, a navy pea coat, navy watch cap, and waterproof Timberline leather boots. I stuck a cellular phone in the coat pocket and a small crow bar in my belt and drove to Gertie's neighborhood and parked several blocks from her home.

Standing next to a large pine in her front yard I punched her number into the phone. I was close enough to the house to hear it ringing inside. After a half dozen rings a light came on. Then a groggy voice said, "Hello." The message of that one word was more like "This damn well better be good."

"I don't want to alarm you," I said, "but this is your neighbor from across the street and I thought I saw a prowler in your yard." Leaving the line open so she couldn't call out I stuck the phone back in my pocket and went to the rear of the house and started prying on a window with the crow bar, making as much noise as I could and hoping I wouldn't really wake up a neighbor.

The light in that room came on and I ducked below the window just as a bullet exploded through the glass, showering me with fragments. I retreated to a tree twenty feet from the house and dialed 911. "Somebody's firing shots from a home at 505 Federal Street. When you check it out, I suggest you do a ballistics comparison with the bullet that killed Lilly Stivitch." I broke the connection and just to keep the excitement high I threw a hard-packed snowball through the next-door neighbor's window. As I ran back to my car the icy wind cut through my clothing, reminding me how good it felt to be alive.

The winter moon bathed the bedroom in silvery light. I slept like a baby. A happy, peaceful baby.

It was Saturday again, a few days after Gertie was arrested for the murder of Lilly Stivitch, and it was still cold. I had put away a pot of coffee and finished reading the newspaper and the only thing on my agenda for the day was a hard workout and a long run. Since I wasn't expecting company the doorbell startled me.

It took a few ticks to figure out who it was. Her hair was down and flowed below her shoulders. The glasses were gone and the face that had been so serious before was now smiling. She looked anything but "teacherish." She had on a long cloth coat but shapely purple spandex legs showed below its hem.

"I don't know how you did it," she said, huskily, as she shrugged out of the coat and set a shopping bag on the kitchen table, "and I don't even want to know. All I care about is that it's over. Dad is speaking to me and while he isn't admitting anything it's pretty obvious he feels a little foolish about his recent behavior." She laughed. "The news stories finally made him face the truth. I'm trying not to scream 'I told you so,' but it's hard."

Her perfect body looked like it had been sculpted from purple marble. "I'm here to thank you," she said, pulling a bottle of dark red wine, a chunk of cheese, and a loaf of French bread from the shopping bag. "Darleen told me you wouldn't take any money." She moved close and wrapped firm purple arms around my neck. "I thought maybe we could think of some other way for me to repay you."

I didn't get in my long run that day. But that was okay. The workout I got was harder than the one I had planned. Later that evening I took the stew out of the freezer and heated it in the fireplace. Valentine's Day came in March that year and I never even thought about Tom Clancy.

THE WHITE SQUARE

EVERETT M. WEBBER

It was a raw, cloudy day—coming dark, and Dirk expected to find his uncle cooking supper, or eating it. But the little windows of the house showed no light as he stopped the buckboard. Then Dirk saw his Uncle Mac down below the corral working on the earthen dam of his pond. He had evidently heard the buckboard for he straightened slowly, one hand at the small of his back, the other still holding the shovel.

Dirk's heart beat a little fast with a mixture of apprehension, excitement and something a little like fear. There was also a tinge of shame mingled with his feeling at being here begging again. But none of that must show.

He waved at the old man, clambered down and swiftly unhooked the horse. Easing the collar a bit and roughing the wet hair under it, he tied the animal to the porch post. And then, seeing that his uncle wasn't coming up to greet him, he walked down toward the pond, careful to close the gates behind him. Bluffly, above the croaking of frogs and the blatting of sheep, he exclaimed, "Hello, there, Uncle Mac! You look younger every time I see you!"

And, as he clambered the grassed-over dam and shook hands with the old man, he saw that his uncle knew he was here again for money.

Sweating, old Mac said, "Well, I don't feel any younger, lad. . . . Guess I've done about enough here. Just fixing the dam a little against the rain. We'll go to the house. Throw your horse in the corral and feed 'im an' we'll eat supper. You're in money trouble again?"

The words graveled Dirk, but they gave him a sort of relief, too, at having the reason for his trip brought up. "Well, not exactly trouble," he said, "but I am needing another loan."

Old Mac grunted dourly, squinting at the heavens as the wind became suddenly dank. And then, before they reached the house, a fine drizzle set in.

"You'll bear in mind," he stated as Dirk presently untied the horse to lead him to the corral, "you haven't paid the other four loans. And like I've told you over and over, I can't let you have any more till I'm paid. But you're welcome to stay the night, or longer."

It was only gradually, after supper, that Dirk brought the matter up again. It was sprinkling rather steadily, now, and as old Mac opened the door to let the extra heat from the fire go outside, the buckboard glistened in the lamp light, and the bare earth of the yard shined wetly. A night hawk zipped past the door and away.

"The fact is," Dirk said as casually as he could, "I've had tough luck at cards, and I promised to pay up in a hurry. Five hundred would hold them off."

Old Mac turned from the doorway and stared at Dirk who still sat at the table, and Dirk saw that his little eyes were troubled as he shook his grizzling head.

Dirk swallowed the black anger that rose within him, and then the entire story was tumbling from his lips and he couldn't hold it back: How he had had to beg like a dog to get a few days' grace to drive the sixty miles over here, across wild prairie, to try to raise a little cash. How, if he didn't get it, he wouldn't dare go back for fear of his very life, and how the men he owed would hog up his land, the well he had dug, and the few cows he still had left.

But still his uncle shook his head. "I can't do it, Dirk. I'm an old man. I can't work forever."

"You could live with me. You could sell out and get away from this God-forsaken place."

"And come to a place where someone else is owner, a place you'll gamble away any day? And this isn't so God-forsaken. It's only four miles from town. I've got friends. It's not that I want to hurt your feelings, nor—"

"But like you say," Dirk reasoned desperately, "all you've got will be mine some day."

"I couldn't live in another man's house, and that's what'll happen if I keep giving—"

With a sudden angry oath, Dirk came out of his chair, jerking at the revolver in the waistband under his coat. The old man stood paralyzed a second, there by the door, and in that second Dirk was upon him, firing almost in his face. Old Mac tottered to a chair, collapsed across the back of it, and then sprawled to the floor with it half upon him. He didn't move after that, but a few drops of blood trickled down onto the wide, clean boards.

Dirk stood there, staring down at him, his heart thundering furiously. And then, half aloud, he panted, "The pennypinching old varmint—it serves him right."

He put the gun back into his waistband and stood listening, lest there might have been someone who heard, or saw, the shooting. When there seemed to be no one, he quickly closed the door. The shades were already drawn. At the fireplace, he worked out the right hand corner stone of the hearth and thrust his hand into the hole.

A short, sharp cry burst from his lips. It was empty. Frantically he leaned low to peer into it, and then he brought up a slip of paper. The red printing at the top said, "Bank of Boiling Springs." And under that: "Deposit Receipt." Dirk stared with blurring eyes at the firm, pale writing under that: "Silver, $670. Currency, $15,665. Gold, $1,445." It added up to $17,780.

Dirk licked his dry lips. The slip was dated a scant two weeks before. He put it back into the hole and replaced the stone and rose.

"The dirty old varmint!" he growled. His heart was slowing now, and he forced himself to steadiness as he rose. "Banking it—now I can't touch a dime." The anger somehow restored him.

But it was his. He was old Mac's only kin. It was all his. And this little ranch, which he could sell for good cash. He wouldn't go back home. Let them take his few cattle and his shack. Why, with cash like this, what couldn't he do! He would go to some city—maybe Denver or San Francisco. Liquor—women in fine clothes—new cars—good horses. . . . Set himself up in a nice saloon in a good part of town. Buy railroad stock and run his money up. . . .

His enthusiasm suddenly cooled. First, he must get the money. And he must avoid getting himself into trouble for what he had done. Maybe it would be best to get on back home and wait to be advised that old Mac had tossed in his chips. On the other hand, it was known there that he had come here—and, besides, that infernal buckboard would leave tracks clear across the country the way it was sprinkling.

Dirk began sweating as he stood in the middle of the floor, racking his brains for a notion of what to do. First off, he guessed he should get rid of the gun. And after that, drive to town and report that he had come to see his Uncle Mac, and found him murdered. Maybe they would suspect him, but what could they prove? Nothing. All they could do, after the funeral, was to hand him the money.

He reached for his dusty old hat and jumper and put them on. The drilled well, six inches in diameter and two hundred feet deep, would be a fine place for the pistol, and in the pitch blackness of the yard Dirk found the little well shed. He raised the cover and dropped the gun in and heard it scrape and bang the casing several times before it struck the water.

The rain was coming harder, now, already soaking him through at knee and shoulder as he headed for the corral. Stooping low, he could faintly see his hammerheaded old horse against the skyline. His eyes were getting used to the dark. He caught the animal by the mane and led him up by the barn and brought the harness out and threw it on. The leather was wet and slick as he fastened the buckles.

It was as he reached under for the belly band that he heard the pound of hoofs and then the rattle of a buggy, and for an instant he leaned there, paralyzed. Whoever it was would be coming here, for no one else lived down this way. Suddenly he grabbed the belly-band and buckled it and caught the bit ring. Let them come. Give him three more minutes, and let them come—

He led the horse out of the corral and flung himself upon its back and rode him swiftly to the yard and slid down. In a second, he had backed him into the shafts and was fastening them. He hooked a tug, then, with the sound of the horse and buggy coming closer, and ran around to hook the other, and as he undid the lines from the hame he could see the moving blackness of the rig coming at him. Swiftly he clambered to the seat.

The rig pulled up. A man said, "Hello, there. That ain't you, is it, Mac?"

Dirk knew the voice. Old man Vanderwet. Then some other man said, "Mac?"

Dirk got a good grip on his voice. "It's me," he said. "Dirk Callen. Uncle—Uncle Mac—has been killed—"

Vanderwet exclaimed, "I told you! I told you something was wrong!" And as the two men piled out of the rig, he added, "Every Friday night for twenty years we've played checkers, and when he didn't show up tonight—I—I knew something must be wrong, so I brought the doctor—"

Startled, Dirk kept quiet as he stepped from hub to porch. He had forgotten it was Friday. Maybe, in the excitement of their talk, his uncle had forgotten it, too.

The rain beat down with sudden fury as he shoved the door open and let the yellow light flood out. That was fine. It would smooth out the tracks he had made, getting the horse up here from the barn. He led the way in and stood silently as Vanderwet moved ponderously behind him. Vanderwet looked at the body for a long time, face shaken and pale and his grey mustaches trembling a little now and then. The doctor, a little man in baggy clothes whom Dirk did not know, knelt by old Mac and took his wrist.

And, in surprise, he exclaimed, "Why, he's only just been shot!"

Dirk tensed. "He—he's dead, isn't he?"

"There's no doubt of it."

"I heard the shot," Dirk explained. "I drove up just before you got here. I wasn't quite to the gate when I thought I heard a gun, and when I came inside, this is what I saw."

The doctor said, "Somebody evidently ate supper with Mac."

"They must have taken out the back way," Dirk declared, "when they heard me."

"But why?" Vanderwet exclaimed. "Why would anybody—"

566

*   *   *

He fixed a long, searching look on Dirk, his little grey eyes peering out above bustles of grey flesh, his brows glistening a little with drops of mist. Dirk forced himself to keep a steady countenance.

"You weren't by any chance the one who ate here?" the old man asked, and his look moved to Dirk's shirt front and back up to his eyes.

In spite of himself, Dirk glanced down and saw the streak of egg yoke down his belly. He felt sweat break upon his body. "I . . . I didn't mean to mention it," he said, "but—well, I was starved when I came in. Uncle Mac was dead. Past help. They had left a little stuff, he and whoever ate with him, and, being hungry, I bolted it down, and started for you."

Vanderwet nodded. "Then you—you must have got here, say, ten minutes ago? Fifteen, maybe?"

"Maybe fifteen."

Vanderwet said, "How long has Mac been dead, Doc?"

The doctor shrugged. "Who can say? Five minutes—ten minutes —maybe a quarter of an hour. Not longer."

"I told you I heard the shot!" Dirk exclaimed. With an effort he toned his voice down. "I heard it."

Vanderwet sighed heavily and picked up the lamp. "I'll hold the light for you to turn around, Doc. Have John and them bring out the very best coffin—that all right, Dirk?"

"Sure." Dirk was getting a little dizzy with relief. "Sure. The best."

"We'll lay him out an' shave him while you're gone," Vanderwet added. He led the way onto the porch and stood there a second and then he whirled on Dirk, drawing a gun from his armpit. He cocked it, holding it unwaveringly on Dirk's middle.

"I would enjoy shooting you," he said, as Dirk backed toward the table in the room. "I hope you move one more step." He came in with the lamp, squinting his left eye against it. "Find his pistol, Doc, and tie his hands behind him . . . and don't get between me and him."

Dirk tried to speak as the doctor moved behind him and felt over his body for a gun, but no words would come. He calculated his chances for a break. They were nil. Then it came to him that he must brazen it out. Old Vanderwet was merely suspicious and trying to stampede him into talking.

"All right. Find my gun," he said. "Since I never owned one of the things, I'd like to see it."

The doctor's hands moved quickly and expertly over him a second time, and finally the man grunted, "Well, there's no gun, that's sure."

"Tie him!" Vanderwet exclaimed. "Out of his own mouth, gun or not, he stands convicted. There's a rawhide lace on the nail behind you, Doc. Put your hands behind you, Callan."

Dirk obeyed before the cold, hungry mouth of the pistol. His sweat had dried. "But—you see I have no gun—" he croaked, his mouth growing dry.

"I'll see something else before snow flies. A hanging."

Dirk felt the rawhide bite into his wrists, and the doctor's warm breath blowing upon his hands.

Then Vanderwet backed onto the porch again, the lamp throwing heavy angles of shadow into the room. "Come out!" he ordered. "Doc, pick up that poker and if he tries anything, brain him."

Something in the man's manner, in his voice, struck an icier terror into Dirk than he had ever felt before. His knees wobbled as he moved out onto the porch, and it was hard for him to breathe. But he would think of something yet. He would admit nothing to them.

"You've been here fifteen minutes, you say, and it's been raining upwards of an hour. The ground is muddy, the road full of puddles." Vanderwet took a deep breath, pointing. "And yet—"

At first, Dirk thought he was pointing at the buckboard, and he stared at it, dripping and shining, but he could see nothing wrong. And the horse, standing dejectedly, looked all right.

"Look under it," Vanderwet grunted, and the doctor gave a sudden cry of understanding. "Take a look under the buckboard, Callan."

Dirk looked. The ground there hadn't been rained on. It was dry and white. A white square of it, in the lamp light, the size of a gallows floor.

WHITEMAIL

JOYCE KILMER

Spike Ritchie and I worked together on the *Daily News* from 1904 to 1907, and I always liked him. He was bright, hard-working, companionable and—I thought—perfectly straight. The other day he told me about a pretty crooked deal he was mixed up in. In fact, he told me that he was an unrepentant blackmailer and traitor. And I like him more than I ever did before.

When I got back to New York last week I looked over the pictures I had bought in Turkey and decided that I had the material for some Sunday stories. So I went around to the *News* office. The elevator man didn't know me—he had been on the job only two years—but he knew Spike.

"Mr. Ritchie is assistant Sunday editor now," he said. "But I don't think you'll find him in his office. Today's Thursday, so I guess he's in the composing room."

I made him let me off at the composing room and went in. There was Spike, telling the foreman that Matty had a glass arm, and making up the fashion page. He had grown much balder, but otherwise he had changed very little since I saw him six years before. He was the same little stoop-shouldered fellow, with the same rat-tail mustache, and apparently the same cigar butt fixed in the corner of his mouth. Also, I discovered in a few minutes, he had the same alcoholic breath.

"Hello, John!" he said. "Wait till I fix this up and I'll go out with you."

Soon we were comfortably seated at a table in Jimmy's bar. Jimmy, I was absurdly pleased to notice, remembered me and put a few drops of syrup in my Irish as if I were still a daily visitor. Spike looked at my pictures and told me to go ahead with the stories. Then—of course—we both grew reminiscent, and after the third drink and a little lunch came his confession. That is, if you'd call it a confession. . . . "You're not the only globe trotter," he said, lighting for the fourth time his amorphous cigar butt. "I went abroad two summers ago."

I expressed interest—without much enthusiasm, for I wanted to talk about Turkey.

"Yes," he said, "I had a little money saved up—I wasn't married then—and I was feeling pretty rotten, so I decided to knock off for a while. I traveled around the Continent for a few weeks and then I went to London. I wanted to see something of the country, so I bought a knapsack and made a leisurely walking tour of the Midland counties. The result of that walking tour was a mighty queer experience. And, in spite of the fact that you are bursting with the desire to tell me how you matched pennies with the Sultan and chucked the harem under its chin, I am now going to take up some minutes of the *News's* time in telling you about that experience. It has never been used as a news story, and it never will. But the villain —unless you call me the villain—is dead now, and I guess it wouldn't do any harm if you fixed it up with different names and made a fiction story out of it. Then if you sell it you can split with me fifty-fifty."

"Go ahead," I said.

"Well [began Spike], I struck a little bit of a market town called Ashbourne that I liked pretty well. So I got a room at an inn entertainingly called *The Green Man and Black's Head* and settled down for a week's stay. There were very few other guests, so the proprietor and I got rather friendly. Of course, like all Englishmen, he was surprised that I didn't know his cousin who was on a ranch in Texas and his nephew who was manager of a grocery store in Milwaukee.

" 'There's one of your fellow countrymen I can't say that I care for,' he said one evening. 'There was a Mr. James Rodney who came here from New York City, and we all wish we'd never seen him, sir. Perhaps you know him—he's a tall, thin gentleman with a sort of a mole over his right eye. He told us that he owned a big flour mill, but I don't know as he told the truth. Do you know a man of that name?'

"I told him that I had never before heard of James Rodney, and by asking a few questions I heard a story that was unpleasant though not particularly strange. Two summers before, an American calling himself James Rodney had come to Ashbourne and stopped with Mrs. Clarke, the widow of the old vicar. She had very little money, and made a living by taking lodgers. He was on his way up north, and he had a two hours' wait between trains in Ashbourne. He took a walk through the town, stopped to get a drink of water at Mrs. Clarke's house, found that she took lodgers, and by that night he had given up all idea of going north. He said that he liked

Ashbourne and the Clarke cottage but, said the innkeeper, 'what really attracted him was Mary Clarke. She was an amazingly pretty girl in those days, sir; in fact, she is still, though she's had a hard time.'

"It did not take Rodney long to make Mrs. Clarke and Mary believe that he was a person of some importance in New York. He seemed to have plenty of money, his manners were those of a gentleman, and he became popular in local society. In fact, everyone was pleased when, after a tempestuous courtship, Mary and he were married in the beautiful old parish church.

"Mary thought that her husband would take her to America at once, but he said that he would prefer to see a little more of Europe. So they went to Switzerland for a couple of weeks and then returned to Mrs. Clarke's cottage. Rodney had received a cable from New York, he said. He must go back to his mill for a little while. It was an urgent matter—he must get the boat sailing from Liverpool on the very next day. He would send a letter by every mail and within a month he would come back for his wife and her mother.

"Of course you have guessed what happened. James Rodney, or whatever his real name was, never came back. He did not write and, what is more important, he did not send any money. Letters sent to James Rodney, the Rodney Flour and Grain Company, 13 West 98th Street, New York City, U.S.A., were returned. His name did not appear on the passenger list of the steamer on which he said he intended to sail. For a while Mrs. Clarke and Mary thought that he had met with some fatal accident, but after a friend of theirs, visiting America, had found that no such concern as the Rodney Flour and Grain Company had ever existed and that there were no mills on 98th Street, they knew that they had been cruelly deceived. In the course of time Mary had a baby, a very nice baby. It was a little boy, as pretty as Mary herself and resembling her strikingly. In only one respect he resembled his father—there was a small but unmistakable mole over his right eye.

"This story interested me very much, and I took the liberty of calling on Mrs. Clarke the next day, on the pretense of looking for lodgings. Indeed, it became more than a pretext, for Mrs. Clarke was such a charming old gentlewoman and the cottage and Mary—it was hard for me to call her Mrs. Rodney—so attractive that I took a room and stayed for three weeks.

"Of course I got from them all that they knew about the mysterious James Rodney, and that was little more than the innkeeper had told me. But just before I left Mrs. Rodney gave me a little kodak picture of her husband and herself, taken by her mother on the porch of the cottage.

"I went back to America with a fixed determination to find this Rodney person, smash his face, and make him send every cent that he possessed back to Ashbourne. You see, I knew the suffering that his little game had inflicted on Mary and her mother and I was pretty angry about it. I confess I didn't have much hope of finding the fellow, but I was going to make a good try at it, anyway. Well, I didn't have to try very hard. I never was much good at this suspense business, so I'll spring my sensation on you right away. James Rodney was Andrew Judd. Yes—don't spill your whisky—Andrew Judd, president of the Judd Iron Works, philanthropist and reformer.

"Two days after I got back, Boss Ridder sent me out to interview Judd for the Sunday edition. Judd had just invented a very fancy sort of model tenement with a gymnasium and swimming tank on every floor. In order to understand just what improvements were needed in the housing of the poor he had spent two days in a tenement house on the lower East Side, and was very eager to talk about it. As soon as I saw him I recognized him, and you can readily understand that my first desire was for a large encouraging draught of the beverage known as whisky. And, by the way, ring that bell, will you? Jimmy, two more of the same.

"Well, of course I thought right away just what you thought—here is one scoop of a story! In spite of the fact that we were running this page interview in the Sunday, the *News* had no particular friendship for Judd. In fact, we were going to oppose him in the Fall, when he was going to run for Mayor.

"I had all the facts and there was plenty of time to get the story in next morning's paper. All I had to do was to flash that little kodak picture (which I always carried with me) on Judd, tell him what I knew of his little European jaunt and let him throw me out of the office. Then back to the *News*, to grab all the space I wanted for the biggest sensation that the paper ever had. Think what a story like that would mean to me, an absolutely exclusive story with a picture to prove it! I saw myself getting a whopping bonus and a regular job to boot. Then, too, you know that I'm not talking sentiment when I say that I was—have always been—loyal to the *News*. You were long enough in the game to find out what a newspaperman's loyalty is—how his first idea when anything big happens is always to hammer it out on his machine and get it in before the first edition goes to press.

"But I had sense enough to hold on to myself for a while. I shook hands with Judd—I guess I stared pretty hard at that mole over his right eye—and I went ahead with the interview as had been arranged. Judd was feeling expansive that day, and he really knew how to talk. He gave me a great little story, full of human interest, and with a lot of new stuff in it, but all the while I was listening to him I was thinking harder than I ever thought before. There were three different plans in my mind—I couldn't, to save my life, think just what I ought to do. After a while Judd felt that he'd given me all I needed and he stopped talking.

" 'Mr. Judd,' I said, almost involuntarily, 'when were you married?'

" 'Why, my dear boy, I don't see what that has to do with what we've been talking about; but I was married five years ago. In St. Marmaduke's Church, of which I am junior warden, if you wish the full particulars. My wife was Miss Emily Lindsay, and here is a picture of her.'

"He took from his desk a framed photograph of a very lovely woman with a little girl on her lap.

" 'I see,' I said vaguely. 'And when was it that you went abroad?'

" 'Well, I really don't think that the public will be interested in matters like this,' he said, 'but I have been abroad several times. Two years ago I spent the summer in England, and then made a somewhat extensive tour of Germany. But I think that I must ask you to excuse me now. I've given you all you need, have I not? Oh, yes!' he added. 'I suppose you will want a picture of me. I think I have some in my desk drawer. I'll look and see.'

" 'No,' I said, in a voice which seemed strange to me. 'I've got a picture already.'

"His back was turned to me, and he was rummaging in his desk. 'But I'm afraid that's been used before. I think I can find some new ones for you.'

" 'This picture has never been used before,' I said. 'It was taken two years ago in Ashbourne.'

"At the word 'Ashbourne' he turned suddenly and looked at the little square of gray cardboard in my hands. Then he grew very white and stood perfectly still.

"For a minute neither of us spoke.

"Then, with a self-control for which I could not help admiring him, he pushed his chair to the desk, sat down, turned his back to me and wrote.

"I heard the rip of torn paper. He whirled his chair and stretched out his hands to me. In his left hand was an oblong of green paper

573

with his name written in the lower right-hand corner. His right hand was empty.

" 'Here is a blank check, which I have signed,' he said. 'Give me the photograph, please.'

"I admit I hesitated for a moment. I am not so devoted to my job that I would hate an independent fortune. But I didn't hesitate long.

"It was a ridiculously theatrical thing to do, but I took the check, tore it into four pieces, and dropped them on the blotter on his desk.

" 'To hell with your check!' I said, in a quiet conversational tone of voice. 'You'll need that money when you start defending yourself against the charge of bigamy.'

"Judd deliberately lit a cigar and sat looking at me.

" 'So, you've got an interesting item for tomorrow's paper, have you?' he said. 'But what's the idea? Just what do you gain by attacking me? That little picture is interesting, but it proves absolutely nothing.'

"I rose to go. 'In the first place,' I said, with my hand on the doorknob, 'I know the girl whom you illegally married two years ago, and the *News* will bring her over here—with her child. We will gain two things—we will be purveyors of a very interesting story and we will bring punishment on a damned hypocrite.'

"He was perfectly calm. 'I see your first point,' he answered reflectively. 'You can publish a very sensational story—there is no doubt of that. But I doubt very much your ability to substantiate your charge, and I fail to see why you are so bitterly enraged at me. There must be some motive. . . . I think I see. Yes, I think I see. But what earthly good will it do the young woman to drag her name into this scandal? You cannot carry out your amiable design of ruining me without also ruining two women.'

" 'All right,' I said, 'I'll tell you what I'll do. You've got to square yourself, and I'll keep quiet about this business.'

" 'Just what do you mean by "square myself"?' he said.

" 'James Rodney must die.'

" 'My God!' he exclaimed. 'Do you want me to kill myself?'

" 'You must kill James Rodney,' I said. 'See here, Mary Clarke has never heard of Andrew Judd. What you've got to do is write her a letter signing your own name, saying that James Rodney was Tom Smith, or John Jones, or anything you like. Anyway, you must say that he was a friend of yours and that he is dead. Say that he confessed to you on his deathbed that he had married and deserted a girl named Mary Clarke in Ashbourne, England, and that he asked you to notify her of his death and to send her all his money.'

" 'I'll do it,' he said. 'I'll do it this afternoon. I'll send her ten thousand dollars—fifty thousand dollars—all the money you say.'

" 'You certainly will do it today,' I said, 'for I'm going to stick around and watch you do it. You will write the letter at my dictation and I will mail it myself. But as to the money that you are sending, you've got the wrong idea. You will send Miss Clarke enough money to buy that little cottage so that they won't have to earn the rent by taking lodgers and enough to pay for a trip abroad for her and her mother. They need a little holiday after the trouble you got them into. Then you must add enough to send your son through school and through the university. I guess we'll put it at twenty thousand dollars—that's letting you off pretty cheap, and I don't want to burden them with a lot of your dirty money.'

" 'I suppose you know,' Mr. Judd said to me, 'that what you are doing is blackmail.'

" 'Today,' I answered, 'I am, in suppressing this story, breaking the commandment of the newspaper business—violating a code of ethics which you could not possibly understand. I am a traitor to the *News* and to my profession. And after that I don't mind a little blackmail.' "

Jimmy had taken away our empty glasses and was ostentatiously wiping the table with a gray napkin. Spike looked at his watch and got up to go. As we walked down the street I turned to him and said: "But didn't Mary What-you-may-call-her ever get wise? When Judd died last year she must have seen his picture in some English paper and known that he was the fellow that fooled her. I should think she'd sue his estate and get good money."

"Sure she got wise," said Spike. "But she wouldn't start anything now. She's perfectly comfortable, I guess."

"What is she doing?" I asked.

"Why," said Spike, lighting his cigar butt for the ninth time, "she's married to the assistant Sunday editor of the *Daily News*."

WHOSE TURN IS IT?

C. J. HENDERSON

Paul stared at the window, watching the snow and the night crowd up against the glass. His fingers dug into the sheet under his palms, tearing to grip the mattress as if a firm hold in his hand might give him one on his situation. Sweat slid down the back of his neck, across his forehead, down his sides, freely from any pore with water left to give.

"Jeez o'man," he thought to himself, the cords beginning to chaff, "How could she do it? How did she even know? I thought for sure —there was no way. No way. No Way."

Paul's mind went back to earlier in the evening. It had been one of their perfect dates. One of the few things New York can be good for is supplying breath-taking backdrops for romance. Paul and Sally had just walked—from Times Square, where they'd arranged to meet after work, over to the waterfront up to Lincoln Center—it had been the nicest evening they had spent together in a long time —none of the usual tension hanging between them.

Of course, it wasn't as if they fought all the time—Paul was always quick to point out that he and Sally rarely had shouting matches, or guilt bickers—to most of their friends they were "that perfect couple." But none of that explained what had happened in the park.

They had eaten at that little Jamaican cafe on Broadway—the one with the bizarrely colored rattan chairs—the one they'd always wanted to stop at but never had. His mind raced through the steps they'd taken after that. Which of them, he tried to remember, suggested the walk in the park. Which one? Was it him or her? Did she suggest Central Park? Did she?

"Are you all right, dear?" Her voice came from the bathroom, a hint of sarcasm in her lilt. "Are you . . . comfy?"

He winced, the terror creeping through his brain making him nearly frantic. Quietly, for the first time ever fearing to let her hear him move, he strained against his bonds, making sure he really was tied too tightly to move.

"Sweetheart," her voice laughed, "I can't wait to see your face when you see the surprise I have for you."

He shut his eyes involuntarily in a shudder of anticipation.

"I'll bet you can't guess what it is."

Black images of dangerous objects, some blunt, some sharp, all in Sally's hands, swam in his brain. If the wad of silken underwear tied in his mouth wasn't perfectly positioned to strangle all sound, his screams would have shattered the windows.

Grasping at his nerve, Paul chased back his fears, trying to somehow get his thoughts ordered. He got himself back to the restaurant and then struggled over their conversation to try and find who had suggested the park. He could see their meals come again, could smell her scampi, taste the pepper in his cream sauce—the wine finished, dessert tray in view, picked over, coffees lingered over, drained, brown rings drying, bill discreetly slipped between them in the chic Manhattan nonassumption of recipient. Laughing, standing, up and walking, out the door, down the street, turning the corner . . .

"Let's walk through the park; it's not too late."

Him! He had said it.

"Oh, and it's snowing. That would be so nice."

And she had agreed. But he had done it. He had said the park. Not her. Him. Damn. Damn. Damndamndamndamndamndamn. Maybe it . . .

No.

She'd steered their route. He remembered now. When they'd stepped out of the restaurant. She pointed them toward the east, toward the park. It had been her! Oh, god—it had been her.

It all started falling into place. Yes, he'd set up a date, but she had picked ending up at Lincoln Center, right across from Central Park. He'd suggested the restaurant, but she had put them in the direction of the park when they'd left. Then, he'd seen the tops of the snowbound trees and been maneuvered into his line.

"Let's walk through the park; it's not too late."

She knew she could count on him to want to walk through the park. She knew he'd say what he did. She knew. Oh, god . . . what's she going to do to me? Just because of two stinking dates.

Dorrie had started working at the same firm he did only a month previous—a New Yorker for only two weeks. It hadn't taken Paul long to spot her. She was a lot like Sally, physically, same legs, same thick, down-the-back hair, thin, nicely drawn smile, green eyes—but not so clever, so hard, so searching, so smugly in charge.

It had been nice, his date with Dorrie. Like with Sally, only back at the beginning, before they had grown used to each other, before the boredom with each other's jokes and ideas and goals had set in, before the games had started. They had talked for a long time, he hearing about why she had come to the city, she listening to his dreams—plans that sounded big and fresh and reasonable being reflected back at him by her newness and enthusiasm. And then the sex.

Dorrie had proved no stranger to double occupancy. They had taken a room in a midtown hotel to avoid their respective room-mates, to cut themselves off from phones and doorbells, television and the evening mail, to be alone with each other and a bed and hours of darkness—new bodies against each other, old tricks and tired habits suddenly as inventive as if they were high school kids. Sweat had pasted them together, the freshness of their love dragging heights out of them both had forgotten. It had been wonderful.

They met again on the weekend, going to a movie, eating Italian, back to "their place." Their manners were so different that even their second time together seemed exciting. Paul had been trans-formed, made younger, walking straighter, acting happier about most everything.

Even his life with Sally seemed better. He found himself talking to her, feeling good about his little affair, and the way it was help-ing his main relationship. He and Sally had been in a rut for such a long time. They had exhausted each other as things of interest months earlier—maybe a year earlier. Everything between them had become pretty much routine, which is, of course, where the games had come from.

It had been his idea at first; stockings, garters, full costumes, and the restraints of hemp and plastic, nylon, tape, leather, metal. Poles to keep the back straight, to separate legs—cuffs to bind, belts to discomfort, masks to hide faces from each other, to build suspense, terror, anticipation. But Sally had taken to it all easily, especially since she got her turns, too. In fact, it was her inventiveness that had kept them together.

Sally had introduced the reality twists, the moments where safety had seemingly gone out the window. She was a good actress, and she loved proving it to Paul. Not that he hadn't caught on to them quickly, enjoyed planning them as much as she did. Sally had still never equaled the time he'd let her see the metal rods heating on the stove and then masked her—told her it was time she was marked as his—and then touched her repeatedly with ice. She'd truly believed he'd burned her from neck to ankle. But tonight was no act. Things hadn't been set up to terrify him. When they'd gone into the park, found Dorrie, that had been no act.

Dorrie was dead. Face unmarked, only a few drops of blood reaching that high. The work had been abdominal; gutting strokes laying her open—insides spread in every direction. They had stumbled across her by accident—but it hadn't been one—going to the top of the rock outcropping Paul loved so much for its view. There they had found her, eyes frozen in pitiful desperation, birds pulling away bits of her punctured organs, their frozen leakage worming through the new falling snow.

The horror of it had sent them stumbling down the rock face, running away through the darkened park. They agreed they did not want to be involved. Who wanted to be hounded by reporters, grilled by police, possibly be the killer's next victim? Or, as Paul realized, connected to the corpse as a recent lover? No—let's just get out of here, forget all about this. Let's go home—come on, we'll just go home and, get "comfy," okay? Whose turn is it, anyway?

Idiot, he thought. Idiot. Whose turn is it? Whose turn? What a chump. What an asshole. She'd set him up—she knew whose turn it was. She knew everything.

The realization had hit him then.

She *knew!* She knew about Dorrie. She had to. Coincidences like this just don't happen. Oh god, oh god please, pleasepleaseplease—oh Christ, oh shit, oh man—

Paul pulled at his restraints in earnest, praying for the slightest slack to generate hope for escape. How had she gotten Dorrie to the park? She had to have killed her there—the blood, the freshness—god, she must have done it just before their date. The storm would have kept people out of the park, certainly off the mount. . . .

Mounting desperation doubled Paul's strength, the bed's headboard bouncing off the wall behind, banging with repeated fierceness. He no longer cared if she heard; what did it matter? She was going to kill him anyway. Panic knotted his muscles as he strained. He pulled this way then that way, harder, harder, all thought gone, erased by fear and the need for release, knowing that just another ounce of pressure, just another few seconds would do it, would free him, would . . .

"Paul?"

He froze. The clammy stain of sweat soaking the sheets chilled him. She had heard him.

"Paul, are you all right?"

She was coming. This was it. He could feel her moving, feel the air parting around her, knew she was reaching to push the door open.

"Oh, silly me. You can't talk with your mouth full."

He buried his tearing eyes in the pillow.

"A mouth full of panties keeps you pretty quiet, doesn't it?"

She entered the bedroom. Ready.

"Keeps all those lies inside where they belong, not running around free getting you into trouble."

Paul braced himself, steeled himself. He had to look, had to see what was coming. He couldn't die and not even see the stroke—

"I guess you know what comes next, lover."

He opened his eyes, blinking at the unending tears, trying to see. He could turn his head far enough toward the mirror to catch sight of Sally moving toward the bed, toward him—of the look in her eye, knife in her hand. Ashamed, he buried his face again. The pain came quickly, nerves letting him know she'd started slicing.

He screamed into Sally's underwear until he fainted, which really wasn't very long at all.

Sally poured the second cup of coffee, leaving enough room for the milk to come. Placing it on the table in front of Paul, across from hers, she said,

"Here you go, nice and hot."

Paul took the cup without making a response, holding it in both hands as if it were the only warm thing in their apartment. Sally laughed.

"Oh, come on. It's daytime. Playland's closed. Stop sulking."

She put a hand on his shoulder, but he shrugged it away.

"What's the matter, dear? Don't like being the scared one for once?"

"Scared?" He put the cup down awkwardly, slopping coffee out of one side. "Scared? I was more than scared. Goddamned plenty more than scared!"

Sally grinned widely with satisfaction.

"Of who? Little me?"

"Will you stop kidding? Who else do you think I was scared of?"

His voice fell into whisper. "You murdered someone! What the hell are we going to do about that, for god's sake?!"

Sitting down across from Paul, Sally arranged a serious look on her face and told him.

"We're going to do what we've always done. Have fun." Going past the questions welling up in her mate, she continued. "All of this was your idea. I'm not saying I didn't see your point and get involved as deeply as you wanted me to, but you started it—so let me ask a few questions.

"Number one . . . isn't the point of these little games of ours to scare the hell out of each other? Isn't the idea to push each other to the edge so that the sex that follows is the best we've ever had?"

Paul nodded, avoiding her eyes.

"Number two . . . after I untied you, after you saw you weren't cut to shreds, that the blade you'd felt had just been a credit card, the running blood just water from a sponge, was or was not that the best sex we ever had?"

"Yes, yes—but . . ."

"No 'buts,' Paul. We play games or we don't."

"But you killed someone."

"You fucked her, I killed her. I could have killed you."

Sally put her arms around Paul's neck. He grabbed for her involuntarily, pulling her around the edge of the table and onto his lap.

"I didn't, though," she told him. "I just wanted to be yours. So some little slut from Kansas dies. So what? As long as it keeps us together."

Paul agreed. He kissed Sally then, wanting her as much as the first time they'd made love, wanting her as much as life. He knew he would never turn her in to the police. As they slid to the floor, kicking chairs out of their way, they tore each other's clothing away, attacking each other with a passion they had no idea they still possessed.

"We'll always be together," he told her.

And he meant it. The police might put her in jail. Probably only some mental hospital. But Paul, Paul could do better than that. He could think of much better things than that. After all, it was his turn next.

THE WITCH'S WAY

JOSEPH SHALLIT

"Cross yourself," Valentino Loreto said to Antonio Lopez, the chief of police. "Cross yourself, for here comes the witch."

"Better that you should not speak such foolishness," Antonio said. "Only children and fools believe such stories."

"Then I am a fool, for it is too late to call me a child by forty years," Valentino said. "Nevertheless, better that you should cross yourself. It is good protection."

"Be still and do not frighten the old man," Antonio said.

Into the doorway, passing beneath the sign reading, Chief of Police, Municipality of Tompon, Leyte, walked Vicente Honorio, leaning on his cane. He wore a brown hempen shirt, blue, cotton American trousers and a brown crust of dirt on his bare feet. He had a large, hooked nose unsuited for his flat face, and a smile that was lost in a jungle of wrinkles.

"I am ashamed that I must trouble you," he said to Antonio.

"It is no trouble, old man," Antonio said. "Sit in this chair."

"I would not come if my rice were not taken," Vicente said, sitting down softly so as not to disturb the chair unduly. "I do not care so much for the fish."

"Tell me what is your trouble," Antonio said.

"My rice," Vicente said. "Three sacks stood on a shelf close to my cooking pots. Late in the night I am sleeping. I hear a noise as of someone walking on the bamboo ladder. 'Who is it?' I say. 'Go to sleep, old man; it is a dream,' a man's voice tells me. Therefore I go to sleep again. When I wake in the morning, I have only two sacks of rice. And of the twelve fish which I myself brought from my fish trap yesterday, I have only two small ones. I do not care so much for the fish, for the sea runs plentiful these days. But two sacks of rice will not last until the next harvest."

* * *

"Why do you weep, old man?" Vallentino Loreto burst out. "Can you not send out your accursed pig to get more rice for you?"

The smile went away from Vicente's face. "It is not an accursed pig," he said meekly. "It is a pig like any other pig."

"Does not your pig run through the roads at night, frightening good people with his golden teeth and causing them to lose their wits?" Valentino demanded.

"It is not true," Vicente said tremblingly. "I know that many people say this of my pig, but it is not true. My pig does not have golden teeth. It is a pig like any other pig, and I keep it in its pen at night."

"And is it not true," said Valentino, half rising from his chair, "that you transform yourself into a large black bird and fly through the night, crying *woc-woc*, bringing trouble to men's homes?"

"It is not true, not true!" Vicente said, almost weeping. He turned a sorrowful face to Antonio. "Ay, all the people say these things of me, but they are not true. My pig is like other pigs. I am a man like other men. But since the time, many years ago, that Tomas Escuadra's little son died of the dysentery as I was walking past his house, people have spoken these evil things of me."

"Do not mind them," Antonio said kindly. "And you, Sergeant Loreto, do not trouble this old man who seeks only to find the rice which has left him."

"Yes," said Vicente. "I do not care so much for the fish, for I believe it stinks already."

"I wish to help you, old man," Antonio said, "but it is very difficult. In every home in Leyte one can find sacks of rice like yours. Is there any one you have a sentiment upon as having taken your rice?"

"Yes," Vicente said promptly. "It is one of my three neighbors: Juanito Repulda, Julio Ontimaro or Salvador Campos."

"You speak quickly, old man," Antonio said. "Why do you name these three only?"

Vicente leaned forward, and his wrinkles twisted as he pondered. "I think about this in the morning," he said. "You know where my hut is, at the end of Juan Luna Street, at the edge of the rice fields. The thief could not go through the fields because they are too wet now. He must go through Juan Luna Street. If one walks from my hut, one passes the huts of my three neighbors, and then one comes to a muddy place. There is rain in the evening yesterday, and it makes the mud smooth. Early this morning I go there to look. There are no foot marks in it."

"You are wise, old man," Antonio said softly. "If you were younger I would make of you a policeman and give you the place of Sergeant Valentino Loreto."

"Very good," said Valentino. "And I shall take the old man's wings and fly at night and cry *woc-woc.*"

"Go, old man," Antonio said. "We shall try to find your rice."

Vicente rose. "You are very kind," he said. "You will receive many blessings for my rice." He followed his cane out through the doorway.

Valentino stood up and gave a snort like a carabao. "That accursed witch! It is some new evil he is trying to make this way. If he wishes to find his rice, he can do it himself. Why does he not make himself into a bird tonight and cry *woc-woc* in the windows of his neighbors? They would give up their rice soon enough for fear of having their wits destroyed."

Antonio took a report form from his desk drawer and began to write.

"Oy!" said Valentino. "You are not going to make serious business of this witch's story?"

"A crime is a crime," Antonio said, "and will be so entered in the monthly report."

"You are too kind to a witch," Valentino said.

"I am not kind," Antonio said. "I think of myself only. Look at this report I must send to the provincial provost marshal this month: Crimes reported—seven. Crimes solved—none. The provost marshal will not like that."

"Oy, but you are making it only worse, for now you will have eight crimes reported."

"Yes, Valentino, but this crime will be solved."

Valentino stared at him. "How will you do that?" he asked respectfully.

"Do you not know that you have already suggested the way?"

That night, at half an hour before midnight, Antonio and Valentino left the police office and walked through the dark streets of Tompon. They went past the hemp warehouse, past the Chinese bakery, past the market shed where the clean-up boys were making music with pans and bottles, past the seamstress' place, past the Liberation Café where a few old men still sat, drinking tuba, past the chapel and into Juan Luna Street.

"Good that there is no moon," Antonio said.

"Yes, for even the moon would laugh to see us doing a witch's business," said Valentino.

The street, of packed dirt and gravel, became softer as they went on, softer and grassier, for few persons came this way. On both sides of the street the low rice fields lay beneath a blanket of water, resting from the harvest.

"Oy!" Valentino exclaimed. "The mud!"

They had come upon the muddy spot Vicente had told them about.

"This is for carabao to walk in, not men," Valentino said.

"Hold your breath and you will not drown," Antonio said, walking after him.

They cleared the muddy spot and continued to walk. And now on their left appeared the nipa-palm hut of Juanito Repulda, standing on bamboo stilts at the side of the road.

"Here we must be very quiet," Antonio whispered. "We must go as a bird goes."

"Then better that a bird were doing this and not I," Valentino said.

They walked to the window. It was covered by a thick bamboo and nipa screen, to keep out the injurious night air.

"Now bend," Antonio whispered, "so that I can put my knees on your shoulders and be lifted to the window."

Valentino looked at Antonio's thick shoulders and thick, round belly. "My wife will have a husband with a broken back tonight," he whispered.

Valentino stooped. Antonio put his hands against the side of the hut and put his knees on Valentino's shoulders. Valentino rose with a quiver and a grunt, and Antonio slid upward against the rustling nipa leaves. He put his mouth to the edge of the screen.

"*Woc-woc,*" Antonio said softly.

"Oy, speak louder and be done with it," Valentino said. "I cannot suffer this burden all night."

"*Woc-woc!*" Antonio cried. He flapped his arms like a bird against the screen.

There was a sudden cry within, and then a voice began to mutter.

"*Woc-woc!*" Antonio cried. "*Woc-woc!*"

The voice became louder. It was saying, "Jesús-Maria-Josip! Jesús-Maria-Josip!"

"*Woc-woc!*" Antonio cried, louder still.

"Jesús-Maria-Josip!" persisted the voice inside. "Jesús-Maria-Josip!"

"Oiga, come down!" Valentino exclaimed. He stooped, and Antonio slid down along the hut to the ground. "It is a terrible sin," Valentino said, "to be speaking a witch's cry against these holy words. A great harm will come."

"Jesús-Maria-Josip!" said the voice inside the hut.

"Oy, let us go quickly," Valentino said. He leaped to the road and ran a few paces.

Antonio came slowly after him. "Do not run, imbecile," he said. "There are no devils here."

Valentino waited for his chief to come beside him, and said, "Oy, it is foolishness for a chief of police to play the witch."

"It is no harm," Antonio said. "Perhaps in this way I can frighten a man into confessing his crime."

"Surely there are other ways to catch a thief."

"If I am dealing with men who believe in witches, I use the witch's way."

"Better that the crime never be solved than to catch a thief in this unholy way."

"I sign the monthly report," Antonio said, "and I shall sign for the sin."

Now they came to the hut of Julio Ontimaro. "Once more give me your back," Antonio said.

"My wife will say to me, 'Go, you are a bent old man,' " Valentino said.

He stooped and raised Antonio to the tightly screened window.

"Woc-woc!" cried Antonio. "Woc-woc!" He pressed his ear against the screen. "Listen, Valentino," he whispered. "Do you hear the noise?"

There was a whirring, grinding sound inside.

"Woc-woc!" Antonio cried. Then he stopped. "I think we have found a thief," he whispered. "He is grinding his stolen rice in the dark. Lower me, Valentino."

Valentino let him down, and they moved quietly to the bamboo ladder leading to the doorway. Antonio went up the ladder. Valentino stooped beneath the hut where he could hear the sound coming through the bamboo lattice floor.

Antonio rattled the door. It was unfastened. He pushed it slightly open. The sound of grinding continued. He took a match box from his pocket and struck a match. He held it inside the door. "Oy!" he said.

"Yes, I know," said Valentino. "It is no rice grinder."

Antonio came slowly down the ladder. "I have never heard such snoring," he said.

"I can smell the tuba from here," Valentino said. "He has drunk so much, a regiment of devils could not wake him."

"If you knew it was not a rice grinder, why did you not tell me?" Antonio demanded.

"I do not interfere in a witch's work," Valentino said with haughtiness.

When they came to the hut of Salvador Campos, Antonio said, "Well, then, this is the last time you must raise me. Perhaps you will cease weeping."

"It is no matter now," Valentino said. "I have become a carabao with a hump. I shall hire myself to farmers and drag the plow."

He stooped and hoisted Antonio to the window. *"Woc-woc!"* Antonio cried. *"Woc-woc!"* He grasped the corner of the overhanging roof, and pressed his mouth to the edge of the screen. *"Woc-woc!"*

"Who is it?" a sleepy voice groaned within.

"Woc-woc!" Antonio cried, striking his shoulder against the screen.

There was a sudden sound of ripping leaves. The corner of the roof moved in Antonio's hand. "Oy!" he cried, his body shifting away from the building. He grabbed for another hold on the edge of the roof. There was a rending and a thrashing, and Antonio came tumbling down, and the corner of the roof crumbled down upon him.

"Thieves! Thieves!" the voice cried inside the hut.

Valentino dragged his chief to his feet. "Run!" he shouted.

"Let us tell him—" Antonio began.

"Thieves! Go or I shall kill you!" the voice cried.

"Oy, let us run!" Valentino shouted. With one leap he was on the road, and his feet went pounding away into the darkness. Antonio tried to think of what to say to the occupants of the house. Then he heard a click as of a rifle bolt.

He heaved his fat body to the road and ran after Valentino.

"Thieves!" the voice cried after him. Then his ears were shattered by a great explosion. He kept running, not knowing whether he still had all his limbs, not knowing whether the wetness that clothed him was sweat or blood. He kept running miraculously until he came to the mud hole. There, in the darkness, he almost stumbled over the body of Valentino.

"Oy, Valentino, you are wounded!" he cried.

"No," said Valentino with a sour voice. "I am resting. And you, old fighting-cock, I see that you also are not hurt."

"Of that I do not know," Antonio said, gasping. "It is too dark to see."

The next day Antonio sat at his desk with all the records for his monthly report spread out before him. The number of policemen on duty. The number of arrests made. The number of crimes reported. The number of crimes solved. The number of illegal firearms confiscated. . . .

"Oy," said Antonio. "Here we shall have something to say. Valentino, we have discovered a case of illegal possession of firearms, have we not? Go to the home of Salvador Campos and confiscate the shotgun."

"Yes, sir," said Valentino. "But I think—" He took a sheaf of papers out of his desk and looked through them one by one. "Yes. Salvador Campos was given a permit to have a shotgun eight months ago."

"Oy!" said Antonio.

A little while later, Valentino exclaimed, "Oy, here comes the witch! But do not cross yourself, for you are his brother."

Vicente Honoria pushed his stooped body into the doorway and tapped the floor with his cane.

"Come, sit in this chair," Antonio said to the old man.

"I am ashamed that I must trouble you again," Vicente said.

"It is nothing," said Antonio.

Vicente sat down by Antonio's desk, and his smile ran away among his wrinkles. "What I must tell you is that I do not wish you to search for my rice because it has been returned to me."

"Oy!" said Antonio. "Valentino, hear what this old man has to tell us. You say that your rice—"

"Has been returned. I am ashamed that I troubled you yesterday."

"It is no trouble, old man. Some thief's heart troubled him and he returned your rice? Is that not so?"

"Oy," said Vicente, "it is a foolish thing. You will laugh at me if I tell it."

"No, no, old man," Antonio said. "Only tell it. Who was the thief?"

"Julio Ontimaro."

"Julio Ontimaro!" Antonio exclaimed.

"The one who slept," said Valentino.

"He heard my call even in his drunken sleep," Antonio said. "But speak, old man. How was it that he returned your rice?"

"It is in this way," Vicente said. "I go to his hut this morning and I say, 'Julio, return to me my sack of rice, or I shall tell the police you are a thief.' Julio becomes angry and he says, 'You are crazy, old man. Why do you say I have stolen your rice?' I take him outside and show him a trail of rice grains going to his door. I say to him, 'There is a hole in the sack of rice you take from my hut. This is the sign of your guilt.' Then Julio begins to weep, and he says, 'Do not tell the police. I shall return your sack of rice and another also.' 'No,' I say. 'Give me only what is mine.' And so he does, carrying the rice to my hut. Now I wish that you do not put him in prison, because he has returned my rice. I do not care about the fish."

Antonio put his hand on his thigh and sat up straight and stared at Vicente. "Old man," he said angrily, "why did you not tell me yesterday about the trail of rice grains?"

Vicente shook his head. "Oy, but it is not there yesterday. I place the rice along the road to Julio's hut in the darkness of this morning."

Valentino began to laugh.

Antonio struck his desk. "Be quiet, you foolish Filipino!" He turned again to Vicente. "You say you placed a trail of rice to Julio's hut? How, then, did you know that he was the thief? Tell me that, old man."

"At that time I do not know," Vicente said. "I place a trail of rice to the hut of Juanito Repulda and Salvador Campos also, and this morning I accuse each one, but Julio is the only one who returns my rice. That is how I know he is the thief."

When Vicente departed, Antonio picked up his pen and dipped it in the ink bottle.

"What are you going to write now?" Valentino said.

"A crime solved is a crime solved," said Antonio, "and will be so entered in the monthly report."